French Tales of the
Yellow Peril

FROM THE SAME PUBLISHER

Jean-Marc & Randy Lofficier. *The French Fantasy Treasury* (3 volumes)
Jean-Marc & Randy Lofficier. *French Tales of Alien Contacts*
Jean-Marc & Randy Lofficier. *French Tales of Cataclysms*
Jean-Marc & Randy Lofficier. *French Tales of Mad Scientists* (3 volumes)
Jean-Marc & Randy Lofficier. *French Tales of the Red Planet* (2 volumes)
Jean-Marc & Randy Lofficier. *French Tales of Vampires* (3 volumes)
Jean-Marc & Randy Lofficier. *Shadowmen: Heroes & Villains of French Pulp Fiction*
Jean-Marc & Randy Lofficier. *Shadowmen 2: Heroes & Villains of French Comics*
Brian Stableford. *Automata: The Imaginative Legacy of Jacques de Vaucanson*
Brian Stableford. *The Plurality of Imaginary Worlds: The Evolution of French* Roman Scientifique
Brian Stableford. *Tales of Enchantment and Disenchantment: A History of Faerie, with an Exemplary Anthology of Tales*
Brian Stableford. *Weird Fiction in France: A Showcase Anthology of its Origins and Development*

French Tales of the Yellow Peril

by
**George Fronval, Jules Lermina,
Camille Mauclair** and **Jean Ray**

translated by
Brian Stableford, Michael Shreve
and **Stuart Gelzer**

A Black Coat Press Book

ISBN 978-1-64932-439-9. First Printing. January 2026. Published by Black Coat Press, an imprint of Hollywood Comics.com, LLC, c/o Greg M. Seigel, 18321 Ventura Blvd. Suite 915, Tarzana, CA 91356.

TABLE OF CONTENTS

Introduction

The global struggle between European imperial powers anxious to acquire a monopoly on the rewards of colonization, and their once-Asian subjects, gave rise to the theme of the "yellow peril" as early as Jules Lermina's *The Battle of Strasbourg* (1891-92) subtitled *The History of the Chinese Invasion of Europe in the Twentieth Century*], included in this volume.

It was soon followed by Captain Danrit's three-volume *L'Invasion jaune* [The Yellow Invasion] (1905-06), both recognized today as significant pioneering works, not so much for their contribution to the myth of the yellow peril, one of the most despicable follies of the imaginative fiction of the period, but for their recognition of the difference that technological advancement and the globalization of politics might well make to twentieth-century warfare.

It is, indeed, the case that the idea of a "Chinese invasion of Europe" did become a significant bugbear on the ragged fringe of future war fiction, luridly developed in the context of English feuilleton fiction by M. P. Shiel in "The Empress of the Earth," serialized in Arthur Pearson's *Short Stories* from 5 February to 18 June 1898 and subsequently reprinted (in abridged form) as *The Yellow Danger*, and the threat of Asian plans for world domination subsequently fueled a very popular series of thrillers by "Sax Rohmer" (Arthur Sarsfield Ward) launched in 1913, whose villain, Fu Manchu, achieved a legendary status.

The subgenre was imported into America, where a variant supplied the basis for one of the earliest successes of the science fiction genre in "Armageddon 2419 A.D." (1928)—which introduced the character of Buck Rogers, who achieved similar legendary status as a hero—and where the experimentation of the pulp magazine genre even produced a brief Rohmeresque yellow peril subgenre in a magazine featuring the dastardly exploits of *The Mysterious Wu Fang* (seven issues, 1935-36), who was then replaced by *Dr. Yen Sin* (three issues, 1936) represented here by Georges Fronval's *Fen-Chu* from 1944.

Brian Stableford

Pao Tcheou is a fictional character from a series of French novels. Referring to himself as "Maître de l'Invisible" [Master of the Invisible], due to his ability to turn himself invisible, Pao is a megalomaniacal Chinese villain, evocative of the Yellow Peril and similar to the famous Fu Manchu; indeed he is supposedly his cousin

Pao Tcheou was created by "Edward Brooker", the nom de plume for a French writer who has never been identified, and the series was continued by the equally pseudonymous "Sam P. Norwood". The first series of novels ran from 1946 to 1947, and the second from 1953 to 1956.

Jules Lermina : *The Battle of Strasbourg*

La Bataille de Strasbourg *by Jules Lermina was initially published as a 43-part feuilleton serial in issues 25-67 of* La Terre Illustrée *between 25 April 1891 and 11 February 1892, where it carried the subtitle* "Histoire de l'invasion chinoise en Europe au XXᵉ siècle" *[The History of the Chinese Invasion of Europe in the Twentieth Century]. It was subsequently reprinted in two volumes in 1895, without the subtitle, by L. Boulanger, the proprietor of the periodical in question. It was reprinted again as a feuilleton in the daily newspaper* Le Matin *between 29 July and 26 September 1900.*

The decision to reprint it was undoubtedly prompted by the so-called Boxer Rebellion, which reached its violent climax while the story was being serialized, the Legation Quarter of Peking having been attacked and besieged in June 1900. The actual siege lasted 55 days, considerably longer than the siege described in the story and slightly longer than the serialization of the novel, but the coincidence did give the reprint a bizarre topicality and lent its early chapters—but not the later ones—a vague implication of prophecy.

Lermina had no idea that any such phenomenon might occur, however, and his novel involves a far more general Oriental uprising, which embraces India and the entire world of Islam as well as the Far East, so his imagined peril is by no means entirely yellow. He certainly cannot be exempted from the charge of lurid xenophobia, in which all fiction of this type participates, but he did have conscience enough to point out in the early chapters of his story that Chinese resentment against Europeans is largely a reaction to blatant white xenophobia and its political consequences.

Jules Hippolyte Lermina was born in 1839 and was still a child when the revolution of 1848 was followed by Louis Napoléon's coup d'état, *which launched in the Second Empire in 1851. He grew up to be a dedicated opponent of that Empire, working from a radical socialist viewpoint. Having married at eighteen, with a baby daughter to support, he tried his hand at various clerical jobs, but either could not settle into them or—perhaps more likely—could not hold on to them because of his political opinions and turned his hand to freelance journalism instead. His radicalism was just as hazardous in that vocation as any other employment, by virtue of the relentless vigilance and oppressive policies of Napoléon III's censors, and he soon attracted their attention. He founded a political periodical of his own,* Le Corsaire, *in 1867, which led to his being imprisoned. He was soon released in response to protest—from Victor Hugo, among others—but promptly repeated his crime, founding a new journal called* Satan, *and was imprisoned again.*

By this time, the Second Empire was on its last legs, and it finally collapsed in 1870 following the disastrous French defeat by the Prussian army in the Battle of Sedan. Lermina was released from prison as soon as the new Government of National Defense took office, and promptly enlisted, either by virtue of a surge of patriotic fervor or because it was a condition of his release. He was only in uniform for a matter of months, but must have had a terrible time. He was far from being a natural soldier—he was short, thin, pale, puny and of a somewhat nervous disposition even when not fresh out of prison—and his regiment, which engaged the enemy on at least two occasions, had no chance whatsoever of stemming the Prussian tide.

Military discipline did not shut Lermina up. He prepared campaign literature with which to stand for elections to the new National Assembly, before the promised elections were cancelled, and wrote an angry open letter of protest to the government when the chief protagonists of Communist agitation were imprisoned. Had he not been busy fighting the Prussians, however, he would almost certainly have taken a hand in the subsequent insurrection, and might well have been transported along with its leaders when the Commune fell. As things were, the whole experience seems to have been rather traumatic, and he took a new direction in life thereafter. One source suggests that he became involved in a project to form the communist colony of Aiglemont in the Ardennes, but if so his participation was brief; he was soon back in Paris, where—perhaps taking some inspiration from the oft-imprisoned activist and prolific feuilletoniste Louis Ulbach—he launched a new phase of his career, concentrating on the writing of popular fiction.

Although Lermina's left-wing views did not change, he seems to have contented himself for the next decade with simply making a living, and his subsequent political journalism was more reflective in kind. He was still writing regularly for Le Radical in the 1890s, though, and his most significant work in that vein, the anarchist L'ABC du Libertaire [The ABC of Libertarianism] did not appear until 1906. His political beliefs are manifest in some of his fiction, including his more extravagant adventure stories—in To-Ho le tueur d'or (1905; tr. as To-Ho the Goldslayer), a noble savage who is one of Tarzan's more significant literary precursors declares war on the symbolic foundation of capitalism—but the great bulk of his fiction consisted of crowd-pleasing entertainment in the great tradition of the French roman feuilleton. He consciously set out to be a loyal disciple of Eugène Sue and Alexandre Dumas; he wrote a Suesque Mystères de New York under the pseudonym William Cobb and produced two sequels to Le Comte de Monte Cristo, as well as many other works in the same vein, almost all of which are nowadays long-forgotten.

Although Lermina had sold stories to the Vernian Journal des Voyages, launched in 1877, he became a much more frequent presence after 1896. Most of his contributions were straightforward adventures stories of a melodramatic stripe, similar to those he had earlier contributed to the less adventurous Terre

Illustrée, *but he also provided such lively and interesting serial scientific romances as* Mystère-Ville *[Mysteryville] (1904) which describes a technologically-advanced breakaway civilization founded in the Far East by French protestant refugees. It was this final phase of his career that eventually produced* L'Effrayante aventure *[Panic in Paris] (1913), which appeared amid a glut of French scientific romances inspired by the example of the British writer H. G. Wells. He would probably have done more in the same vein had he been able to do so, but was then reaching the end of his career and his life; he died in 1915.*

La Bataille de Strasbourg *is one of the first future war stories to exemplify the notion that a worldwide military conflict was not merely feasible, thanks to the development of an embryonic global civilization courtesy of the concerted efforts of colonization and imperialism, but inevitable as a natural repercussion of such efforts.*

In its time, the novel was ground-breaking. It was one of the earliest "immersive fantasies" set in the future—which is to say, a story that adopts a hypothetical future viewpoint without organizing any kind of transitional device, such as a prophetic dream—and it is perhaps the earliest to do so straightforwardly, with no other explanatory exposition than its initial subtitle.

The eventual spoliation should not, in any case, prevent the story from being recognized as a significant pioneering work. Lermina deserves credit for it in spite of the fact that his anticipatory efforts are tentative in some respects and ludicrous in others. Because he was writing before the development of wireless telegraphy and aviation, his images of future communication devices and heavier-than-air flight now seem to hover between the primitive and the bizarre, but his notions are not without a certain speculative flair.

It is equally difficult now to realize how awkward it seemed in 1891 to write novels set in the future which simple adopted a viewpoint further forward in time, without any elaborate explanation and without any apology at all. No one in England or America had yet done that, or would for another decade, and Lermina surely played some part, along with a handful of other pioneers, in enabling that narrative convention to take comfortable root in French fiction some time before it was able to do so in English-language fiction. In this respect, as in the particular technological innovations he envisages, Lermina's work now seems more than a trifle crude, because we have come a very long way in the interim, in terms of both the technological imagination and literary technique, but he was groping optimistically in the dark and can be forgiven a modicum of clumsiness. For all its faults, La Bataille de Strasbourg *is a remarkable work.*

B.S.

PART ONE
THE STANDARD OF THE FIVE HUNDRED GODS

I

On 5 February 19** there was great excitement in Paris. The Societé de Géographie was holding an extraordinary general meeting of its members at midday in the great amphitheater of the Sorbonne, to which all the illustrious individuals representing the new movement of the twentieth century had been invited.

Everyone knows that since the Treaty of Paris had restored the beloved lost provinces to France, and the fall of the German Empire had substituted the Germanic Confederation for the Hohenzollern autocracy, our fatherland, liberated from the burdens and anguish that had forced it to maintain excessive armaments for so long, had been able to devote all of its vital energy to intellectual studies, and merited more than ever the title of the World's Brain.[1]

In all branches of human knowledge, France had resumed its leading role; its literature, freed from the excess of a forgotten naturalism, was the most perfect expression of the ideas of the present and the hopes of the future. With no more internal shocks, Parliament was able to devote itself entirely to the reform of the Law and the great social questions on which universal wellbeing depends. The ordering of financial affairs, the momentum acquired by industrial enterprises and the renovation of our agronomic systems ensured the country a prosperity that nothing seemed able to compromise.

Great interest was, therefore, taken in new discoveries, especially when, as had been recently announced by the entire press, it was a matter of an application of electricity that might be even more marvelous than the telegraph and the telephone.

The invention that had impassioned all curiosity, the experimental demonstration of which was awaited with a quasi-feverish impatience, presented the very particular character that it was due, not to a conventional scientist, a qualified academician or a graduate of the École Polytechnique, but—unbelievably—to a simple poet...my God, yes!

Guy de Norès, who was not yet thirty, had revealed himself to the literary world in a little volume rather disdainfully welcomed at first, *Rêves vrais*, copies of which remained sadly stacked up on the publisher's shelves. Then, one day, a

---

[1] Lermina could not know, of course, that there really would be a Great War prior to the 1920s, when his story is set, which would end in a German defeat, thus terminating the Hohenzollern Empire, and that one of its results would be the return of Alsace and Lorraine to France under the Treaty of Versailles, following a crucial French military takeover of the region that concluded with the occupation of Strasbourg.

critic, the most respected and, to tell the truth, the least benevolent of the era, had devoted a two-column article to it, concluding thus:

Guy de Norès is better than a poet, better than a writer; he is a seer whose genius, engaging the unknown in hand-to-hand combat, has forced it to deliver its secret to us. In these few pages there is more real science than in the heaviest quarto volumes of our official doctors. This little book contains the scientific gospel of the twentieth century.

It was realized then, Panurge's sheep being eternal, that we were in the presence of one of the most original individuals, that the sculptor of rhymes was also a mathematician of the first rank, and that each of his short poems provided a hypothetical but possible solution to one of the great scientific problems.

Indifference had been succeeded by the most passionate infatuation; journalists had seized upon him as on a prey, his life had been searched in the hope of discovering alluring mysteries, but with great disappointment. Guy was a simple individual, working fifteen hours a day, going without pause from his study to his laboratory, simultaneously a chemist and a man of imagination, speaking all known languages, systematically deprived of all diplomas and refusing all distinctions. He was sincerely modest, patient and courageous, and above all, patriotic through and through, dreaming of giving his country the most beautiful of all glories, that which attaches to human conquests of nature.

For three years he had published very little: one semi-philosophical and semi-social novel, based on the influence of wellbeing on civilization and had enjoyed a *succès d'estime*. With the versatility that characterized the great city of Paris then as of old, people had begun to forget him; his friends, or those who claimed to be such, declared in hushed voices that he was finished—burned out, to use a popular nineteenth-century expression—when the announcement suddenly appeared in all the newspapers of the meeting organized by the Societé de Géographie, in which Guy de Norès would demonstrate the possibility of seeing, as clearly as in a mirror, what was happening a hundred, two hundred or a thousand leagues from Paris.

Curiously enough, the sympathy previously inspired by Guy, which had become somewhat dormant, reawakened with more force than ever; it must be said that the renown of the society that was sponsoring him, the indiscretion of reporters and anticipatory descriptions of the discovered methods, albeit vague, contributed to giving the promised experiment the most serious character.

Finally, to reveal all, what had perhaps contributed more than anything else to the universal benevolence was a sentimental story that had spread surreptitiously and which, given feminine sensibility, had in his favor disposed the weaker sex, both ladies and demoiselles alike.

This is it: Guy, having not yet made a fortune, was in love with a young woman whose name was not pronounced but who belonged, apparently, to one of the most highly-placed families in the scientific world. The father, it was said, had placed the condition on his consent that Norès must realize at least one of the items of progress of which he had made himself the apostle—but until then, he must remain separate from the woman he loved...doubly separated, since she was traveling with her father in the Far East.

People take an interest in these tender matters, and everyone wanted the young man to succeed. Generous hearts felt anxious. So, when Admiral Trécourt, who was presiding over the numerous assembly—nearly two thousand strong—that was crowded onto the benches of the Sorbonne's amphitheater, announced that Guy de Norès was about to commence the advertised lecture, a murmur of sympathetic curiosity ran around the hall.

"Mesdames et Messieurs," the Admiral added, "before handing the floor to our young colleague, may I be permitted to say one thing more: what is about to pass before your eyes will appear so strange, and so improbable, that some of you will be tempted to doubt the reality of the phenomena that you will witness. My presence, and that of several of my colleagues in the Académie des Sciences, is a guarantee that these experiments are not based on any subterfuge. We have only authorized these experiments—which I would call marvelous, if you were not all aware that miracles are not of this world—after having acquired the certainty of their astonishing perfection. You can, in total security of conscience, applaud the man that we are happy to call our friend...and, I will say, our master."

One can imagine the effect produced by this little speech, which the Admiral had made in an emotional voice. So, when the man whom the most illustrious were already calling a master advanced to the podium, there was such an explosion of curiosity throughout the auditorium that, within the blink of an eye, everyone was standing on the benches.

Guy de Norès appeared to be about thirty. Tall and very thin, he walked with a slight stoop, as if his head that seemed at first glance to be enormous were too heavy for his shoulders. His thick black hair surmounted a broad forehead of unusual amplitude. His eyes were large and wide open, his gaze escaping like a gleam. His nose was prominent, his mouth wide and his lips as red as those of a child. That ensemble, however, revealed such a vitality, such an exuberance of thought, and such a masculine energy, that a murmur of admiration passed through the room.

He had straightened up now, and after a slight bow, devoid of embarrassment or arrogance, he started speaking with a voice that was slightly muffled at first but gradually became clearer—magnified, so to speak—in a tone that was both sonorous and soft, whose harmony was an additional seduction.

With a few very sober words, in excellent taste, he thanked the admiral for the exceedingly benevolent words that had introduced him and applied the term of master, which he did not accept, judging himself only too glad to be welcome as a pupil of great French scientists.

"Permit me, however," he continued, "not to say any more about that; if you have been kind enough to respond to the appeal of the Society whose hospitality is for me an honor of which I am proud, you are all impatient to know whether it really has been given to me to lift a corner of the veil that nature extends so jealously over her secrets, and I ought not to delay any longer before satisfying your legitimate curiosity."

At the front of the stage was a table covered with a large sheet. At a signal from the speaker, and assistant lifted it up, and an instrument then became plainly visible whose form was strongly reminiscent of a star. The central point was constituted by a large copper ball, and the radii consisted of copper wires fixed to the copper ball at one end while the other was attached to a nickel circle forming an exterior circumference, fitted with as many buttons as there were wires.

"These wires," said Guy, "are in communication with the various telegraphic systems that put Paris in communication with the entire world. By putting pressure on this copper handle, I can open or close at will a current communicating with one of those wires, and, in consequence, with the telegraph wire of which it constitutes the first link."

Then he picked up a mirror, the foot of which he screwed into the copper ball.

"You have before your eyes, Messieurs, my entire apparatus, with the exception of the dry piles producing electricity, which are installed in the basement of the auditorium. Finally, I call you attention to the frame that you see suspended on the wall to the right of the hall, which, I declare to you immediately, is simply fitted with a screen designed to receive, in magnified form, the images that will shortly be produced in the central mirror."

These explanations, clearly given in a distinct voice, aroused increased attention. Not the slightest sound could be heard; everyone was waiting.

"Messieurs," the young scientist continued, "in the book that you might perhaps have forgotten, but which constituted the first phase of my research, I posed this problem. Already, thanks to electricity, human speech passes from one end of the earth to the other, either via the telegraph or the telephone, whose systems radiate throughout the whole world. In a few more years, it will be possible to converse from this very spot with the people of all the nations of Europe, Asia, America and Africa. You know that cables are being laid at present between Australia and the American continent, closing the circle enveloping the entire globe. Electricity has given you light and, thanks to the central beacon of the Hôtel de Ville, the magnificent apparatus that is the finest entitlement to glory of our great Sametel..."

As he pronounced that name, it seemed that the young man's voice suddenly weakened slightly; there was a slight interruption of which people took advantage to applaud the name of the man who had been nicknamed, in memory of the famous American, the French Edison.

Guy continued: "Electricity has given us heat, and, last winter, which was unfortunately too rigorous, the immense heater in Les Halles, suppressed suffering and misery, so to speak.

"Has electricity, then, said its last word, and must we renounce any further demand on that benefactor? Perhaps, if we had to rely solely on its power—but it is possible to provide it with an ally, to combine its energy with energies even more powerful than its own, and we can hope realistically to constrain it to produce new miracles. That is what I have attempted, Messieurs, and I can say without boasting, because the results are to hand, that I have succeeded...

"That idea is, as you have guessed, the magnetic force of the terrestrial globe, the seemingly so mysterious influence to which, for many centuries, the compass has owed its observed, but always unexplained, action.

"I shall content myself with that indication, the technical details of which will be set out in the brochure that will be handed to you at the end of the session.

"Having said that, permit me to draw your attention briefly to a fact whose first revelation was made in the final quarter of the last century, but which was not accorded the attention it merited.

"You are all familiar with selenium, the metalloid of the sulfur family whose electric conductivity, as Willoughby Smith discovered fifty years ago,[2] varies in accordance with the intensity of luminous radiation. That metalloid, which is produced by treating the mineral known as zorgite[3] with hydrochloric acid, could not be obtained in considerable quantities until the recent discovery of zorgite mines in the United States of South America.

"Selenium is modified under the combined action of electricity and light, in proportion to the intensity of the current and the radiation that affect it. In addition, submitted to the action of terrestrial magnetism, which acts in its regard like photographic fixing agents, selenium retains the imprint of images that are communicated to it by the double influence of electricity and light, the former being, in a sense, the vehicle of the latter."

The orator then entered into a few considerations to which the audience listened with the greatest interest, which he summarized as follows:

"So, Messieurs, if you have understood me fully—or, rather, if I have been fortunate enough to explain myself clearly—this is the sequence of events that you are about to witness: at the initial point of the telegraphic lines whose network terminates here beneath my hand, a *camera lucida*, set up at a point where

---

[2] Willoughby Smith published his paper on "The Effect of Light on Selenium during the passage of an Electric Current" in the 20 February 1873 issue of *Nature*, so this statement implies that the story is set in 1923, or perhaps, if "fifty" is assumed to be approximate, a year or two either side of that date. Given that Lermina deliberately plants this indicator and another a few lines thereafter, it is not obvious why asterisks are used in the dates specifically cited at the beginning of this story; I do not know whether the same convention had been used in the serial version.

[3] Copper-lead selenite.

a part of the city is reflected on a screen, with its life and movement, is put in communication with the electric wire, which transports the fluid influenced by the light, in its various degrees of intensity; that fluid strikes the selenium mirror that you see here, fitted to the copper button, which itself contains a magneto-electric apparatus; and on that mirror will be depicted, in all their clarity, the scenes that are passing on to the screen of the *camera lucida* situated fifty or a hundred leagues away…and even further, as you will see shortly…

"These images will be reflected, thanks to an optical apparatus of the greatest simplicity, onto the framed screen that you see fixed to the wall, with the result being that in a moment, while being in Paris, you will see—see in their absolute, positive, living sincerity—the scenes that are unfolding at this moment in the capitals of Europe and…elsewhere."

Guy interrupted himself in order to drink a few sips of water. Everyone took advantage of that moment of silence to manifest their sentiments, and it must be admitted that they were not unanimously favorable to the orator.

"It's incredible!" said some.

"Impossible!" said others.

A peevish professor, who had never invented anything and declared himself incredulous in advance of all progress, even exclaimed: "This is charlatanism!"

Guy de Norès was still smiling, waiting for calm to be restored.

The president rang his hand-bell. "Mesdames et Messieurs," he said, not without irony, "those who speak of impossibility are in error; those who speak of charlatanism are committing an impertinence. But Norès will not take exception, sure as he is of his imminent triumph."

By virtue of one of the habitual mood changes of crowds, there was wild applause.

"Continue, Monsieur de Norès," said the Admiral.

The young man took out his watch. "It is one o'clock, Messieurs. From one end of Europe to the other, the difference in the actual time is more than two hours. In round numbers, it is one o'clock in London and two o'clock in Vienna, two-thirty in Constantinople and three o'clock in St. Petersburg, noon in Madrid and two o'clock in Stockholm and Rome. I'm reminding you of these facts in order that you will be able to explain the differences that you will observe in the atmospheric light of the various countries that will appear before our eyes. If you will permit, we shall commence with our neighbor on the far side of the Channel, whose Parliament finally voted two days ago for the construction of a tunnel that will link the French and English coasts—to London, then!"

He raised his hand and rang a bell; the room was plunged into darkness.

"Keep your eyes fixed on the selenium mirror to begin with," said Guy. "Then look at the screen."

After a few seconds, the surface of the mirror was seen to brighten with a singular blue-tinted light, which gradually turned red, while all beams of light seemed to spring forth from all its parts with such an intense vivacity that the eyes turned away to look at the screen on the wall.

A cry of surprise emerged from all throats.

On the white space, which measured about four square meters, the square of the Stock Exchange appeared, with its stupefying tumult of vehicles and its swarming crowds of people. The production was so bright, so clear and so vivid, the faces, the forms and the movements so perfectly rendered in their activity, that it was the very life of the enormous city that was before their eyes.

There was no more applause, so intense was the attention.

Two Englishmen, in a tangle of vehicles, picked a quarrel and hurled themselves at one another, fists raised; one of them, struck in the face, fell under the wheels of a cab. There was a cry of terror in the hall, but a policeman had leapt forward and had pulled the man away by the arm. The latter, now furious with his savior, belabored him with his fists...

It was not cold and dead photographic projection, but the absolute transportation of life itself.

"Now, Messieurs," said the clear voice of the demonstrator, I am putting the apparatus in communication with the telephone. Listen."

That was something else entirely: over that vast audience, transcending all encumbrances, an immense river of English voices now flowed. The reality of the scene took on fantastic proportions. The flood went on and on, with its own sound, making of a synthesis of all sounds. Sometimes, words stood out, including the cries of coachmen: "Keep left!" and other appeals: "Come here, boy!"

The effect was amazing.

"Now to Saint Petersburg," said Guy.

The English scene disappeared; the selenium mirror seemed to fade out. Then there was the click of a switch, and on the screen, the Nevsky Prospekt extended bleakly, covered with snow, with the occasional sleigh drawn by Ukrainian ponies, and muzjiks disappearing beneath their sheepskins, dragging themselves along, numb with cold.

"Twenty-nine degrees Réaumur,"[4] said Guy. "The Russians are at home around their enormous stoves."

All hands clapped: there was an enthusiasm tending toward delirium. Was it not a true miracle?

No criticism was possible; the solution had been found of the most curious problem that scientists had yet posed—and to what applications might such a discovery lead!

"To Vienna," said de Norès.

---

[4] This must be a mistake; it seems improbable that the author means minus 29°, so it is more likely that he means to indicate the Fahrenheit scale, on which 29 is three degrees below freezing.

And it was the Prater that appeared. Then to Madrid, the Puerta del Sol with its swarm of idlers. An exceedingly pretty Spanish woman, with her head covered by a mantilla and her hair boldly curled, was swinging her hips as she went along, which earned a well-deserved applause. Then there was a silence. But as old Zorrilla,[5] the founder of the Iberian Republic, almost a nonagenarian, was passing in a carriage, the telephone reproduced the cheers that greeted him.

The scene disappeared. Then the lights in the hall were switched on again.

Guy was in his place, only slightly pale.

No man ever received such a vibrant ovation. The Admiral had come down from the stage and, taking the young man in his arms, embraced him effusively. More than ten minutes passed before calm could be reestablished; curious individuals had even leapt over the balustrades in order to examine the apparatus at closer range; it was extremely difficult to get them to resume their seats.

Finally, Guy began speaking again. "Messieurs," he said, "I can't tell you how touched I am by your expressions of sympathy; in my work I have done my duty as a Frenchman, and you are rewarding me beyond my merits..."

"No, no! Bravo! Vive Guy de Norès!"

"I hope to live long enough," he said, smiling, "to do better still. But permit me to show you one more experiment. Thus far, you have not left Europe. I want to take you further: to Peking."

There was an explosion of joyous laughter—not because there was any doubt now, but because the idea seemed particularly amusing to be a few steps from the Luxembourg and yet see what was happening in China, eight thousand kilometers from the towers of Notre-Dame.

A lady leaned toward her neighbor's ear. "His master Sametel is in Peking...and it's Sametel's daughter with whom he's in love...I hope he sees her..."

And as the whisper ran through the feminine ranks, more than one heart began to beat faster, perhaps with a little jealousy. Guy could have placed his affections much closer to home...

Meanwhile, the young man, having ordered darkness again, resumed speaking—although it was observable that his voice was trembling slightly.

"Messieurs," he said, "at this moment it is nine o'clock in the evening in Peking—which is to say that our apparatus is functioning by night. But I know that today, the fifth of February, is when the Chinese are celebrating their festival of the New Year, the first day of the month Li-Chun in their calendar.[6] The Chinese are masters in matters of illumination, and they must have produced a

---

[5] Manuel Ruiz Zorrilla (1833-1895) was twice Spanish prime minister, albeit briefly, in 1871-73, but failed to establish the Republic of which he dreamed; he would have turned 90 in 1923 had he lived.

[6] The movable feast of the Chinese New Year fell on 16 February in 1923, but it fell on 5 February in 1924.

light akin to that of midday, inasmuch as"—he lowered his voice—"the great electrician Sametel will have deployed for the occasion all the resources of electric light. The apparatus is directed at the French Legation, where our compatriots ought to have assembled in order to enjoy the magical sight of the Celestial festival."

He fell silent. The effluvia, blue-tinted and then red and sparkling, emerged from the selenium mirror, and the screen brightened. A general acclamation greeted the scene that unfolded.

On the terrace of a pavilion, bathed in floods of electric light, there was an elegant crowd, very French, of ladies and young women, naval officers and young men in evening dress. In one corner, two young women, next to whom a Russian officer was standing, were chatting animatedly.

"The telephone! The telephone!" cried all the voices.

The young man seemed to hesitate.

The lady who was so well-informed said to her confidante: "You see those two young women. The blonde is Sacha Batowna, the daughter of Prince Batow, and the Russian officer, the military attaché Sandorf Wintscheff, is her fiancé. The other, the brunette, is Marguerite Sametel, the object of our great Norès' adoration..."

At that moment, not daring to resist the general will, Guy put his apparatus in connection with the telephone, and in the midst of the conversations of the guests of our ambassador in Peking, the voice of the Russian officer could be distinctly heard, saying to the young blonde: "I tell you that our dear Guy will succeed, and that I shall be a witness at your wedding..."

All the ladies, who were in the know, applauded.

At the same instant, however, an enormous, monstrous clamor sprang forth from the bright screen, mingled with cries of terror. All the women were fleeing in tumult. Sandorf had placed himself in front of the two young women, as if to defend them...and at the base of the terrace a hideous spectacle appeared: a whirlwind of people, shouting and running, while one of the wretches was carrying at the end of a blood-stained pike, suspended like an infamous trophy, the corpse of an old man, whose wrists were bound to his ankles by cords.

And the multitude of murders shouted: "Death to the foreigners! Death to the devils from overseas!"

Very few people in the auditorium of the Sorbonne understood the words proffered in Chinese, but they all divined the terrible meaning of that scene of horror.

The Chinese crowd rushed to assault the pavilion. Sandorf was seen to fire his revolver at the assailants. Then everything disappeared.

And in the hall, Guy de Norès, haggard, his fists clenched, shouted like a madman: "Help! Help! Marguerite...here I am...!"

And before anyone could stop him, he hurled himself at the wall, as if he wanted to pierce it in order to go to the rescue of the woman he loved.

The impact was so violent that he fell back, unconscious, into the arms of those surrounding him.

The Admiral shouted: "The wire to Peking has been cut. Oh, our poor Frenchmen! It's a massacre!"

Emotion was at its height. As the young man had collapsed into the surrounding arms, two screams had been heard, and two women, standing up abruptly in the first row of the assembly, had run toward him, cleaving through the crowd.

One of them, with a crown of hair as white as snow, dressed in the mourning that widows wear after the death of their husbands, was Norès' mother; the other, an adorable young blonde woman, was his sister.

Fraying a passage, they arrived beside him, and the mother, taking her son's head, set it on her knees, while Marie de Norès placed a bottle of smelling salts beneath his nostrils.

"We need to take him to the library," said a voice. "He needs air."

Vigorous arms grabbed the young man, and a few moments later, he was lying on a sofa, with the two women kneeling beside him, watching for signs of life.

A physician, Dr. Sabirat, who happened to be in the hall, administered his expertise.

In the crowd pressing at the door, comments flew back and forth.

In truth, they were still having difficulty believing that the scene they had just seen unfolding before their eyes belonged to the domain of reality. The effect was nevertheless prodigious, as the individuals evoked on the screen had all the appearances of life. It will be remembered, however, that it was a matter of events happening at that very moment at an enormous distance, beyond the deserts of Asia, beyond the sea, and they were wondering whether they might have been the victims of some astonishing trick.

Admiral Trécourt, however, imposed silence on the incredulous. "Once again, Messieurs, I remind you that I have given you my word—which is that of an honest man and a soldier, which I cannot suppose that you can doubt—that you have witnessed scenes that are, alas, only too real. At this very moment, the greatest danger is threatening our compatriots in the Chinese capital. I wish to God that it was only an illusion, but science does not lie..."

"My son is coming round!" cried Madame de Norès. "My child, my love!" she added, embracing him feverishly.

Indeed, Guy opened his eyes.

First of all he looked around haggardly, unable to remember where he was.

"Mother? Sister? What's happening?"

As he fell silent, in the fear of waking up too soon to dolorous memories, he suddenly put his hands over his face. Then he straightened up.

"Marguerite! Help! They're killing her, murdering her! Didn't you see? We have to run, make haste…"

He stopped abruptly. Then, with a burst of heart-rending laughter, he said: "Two thousand leagues away! Oh, accursed science…you've only revealed that catastrophe to me…are you impotent, then, to do anything about it?" He had drawn his mother and his sister toward him. "You, my dears, understand how I'm suffering…"

"Courage, Brother," said Marie.

"Yes, yes, you're right…a man doesn't have the right to despair while strength and life remain to him." He saw the Admiral, and extended his hand to him. "Who would have supposed that my first experiment would bring me such pain? For you saw, as I did—didn't you?—that furious mob rushing toward the French ambassador, threatening the lives of all those we love. You don't doubt it?"

"No, unfortunately," said Trécourt. "Terrible events are occurring out there…but as you say, what can we do to prevent them?"

The young woman leaned in close to her brother's ear and whispered a few words to him.

Guy shook his head. "A very feeble hope," he murmured. "All things considered, though, I don't have the right to abandon it." He turned to the Admiral. "Can I count on your benevolence, Master?"

"Don't you know that I'm entirely at your disposal?"

"Well then, listen." He drew him to one side. "I've succeeded," he said, "in bringing scenes unfolding thousand of leagues from here before our eyes, but the distance is only apparently suppressed. I've attempted more, attacking a problem that's perhaps more astonishing still. Thus far, I haven't succeeded completely, but who can tell whether, at this critical moment, I might be able to find the desired solutions? I'm going to my laboratory; then, in a supreme adjuration, I'll ask the sphinx to yield me its secret. In the meantime, I beg you, send word to the Chinese Legation and the Russian embassy…to enquire…perhaps news has already reached Paris that might enlighten us in regard to this horrible tragedy…and, as quickly as possible, pass on the information that you've gathered to me."

"I'll make enquiries personally," said the Admiral, "and don't worry; I won't leave you without news for long. Go and work coolly. Remember that we have two battalions of marines in Peking, in the embassy itself. They're vigorous soldiers, and—who can tell?—but for that interruption of the telegraph wires, perhaps we'd have seen those wretched hordes driven back and chastised. Have courage, then…and confidence!"

The young man shook his head. In spite of those hopeful words, an atrocious vice was gripping his heart. That was because he loved Marguerite Sametel profoundly, with a love unique in his life. Before she had left for Asia with her father, the great physicist who had set forth to enable modern progress to penetrate the remotest corners of Asia, the two young people had exchanged the kind of vows that bind people together for life.

In truth, Sametel had not erected any serious obstacle to that affection; he professed for Norès the most sincere esteem and amity, and if he had demanded a delay before the two young people could marry, he had done so primarily because it would be too painful for him to be separated from his daughter.

That mission to China, to organize the entire telegraphic and telephonic network in the Middle Kingdom, was the last that he intended to accept. His formal plan was, as soon as he returned, to grant the wishes of the two fiancés and warm up his old age at the hearth of their happy youth.

Why must people always delay their own happiness and that of others?

"It's necessary to avoid the indiscreet crowd," the Admiral said to Norès. "Follow me. I'll get you out, along with your mother and sister, though the back door. That way, you'll be able to get home more rapidly."

"Do you feel better?" Dr. Sabirat asked.

"Oh, you're here, my dear friend," Guy said. "Excuse me for not having noticed you sooner...yes, I do feel better."

"Don't you think, Brother, that it would be best for Monsieur Sabirat to accompany us home?"

The physician and the young woman had exchanged glances. Norès had seen that, and smiled in spite of his anguish.

"Sabirat is always welcome in our house, if he wants to come. Besides which, I might have need of his advice."

A few minutes later the four friends left the building behind in the Admiral's spacious carriage, which he had put at their disposal."

Not a word was pronounced during the journey. Guy was meditating profoundly. Marie had reminded him at the opportune moment of the boldest project of which he had yet dreamed.

For more than two years, he had been studying a motor whose power, adapted to locomotion, would, so to speak, abolish distance, by means of a rapidity of transit that would put railway engines, and even dirigible balloons, in the shade. Its employment was on the brink of practicality thanks to discoveries realized at the Institut Aérostatique de Chalais.[7]

Marie, who had a serious mind endowed with remarkable scientific faculties almost equal to her brother's, had followed those endeavors at close range, and his success seemed certain to her.

A hundred leagues an hour!

Such a dream had never been realized.

Guy de Norès' workshop was in a large building behind the École Militaire.

---

[7] The French government-sponsored Military Aeronautical Laboratory was established at Chalais-Meudon near Paris in 1877; it was to play a leading role in the development of both airships and aircraft long into the 20th century

A vast courtyard was attached to be buildings, and it was there that Guy completely recovered his self-mastery half an hour after leaving to Societé de Géographie.

The emotion felt by Madame de Norès, whose health was very delicate, obliged her to retire to her apartment. Norès was left alone with Sabirat and his sister.

The two young men were linked by a sincere amity, having worked together in academia, but to the same extent that Guy was audacious, enthusiastic and impulsive, the young physician was, by contrast, at least apparently, cold and suspicious of himself. He was, however, in the direction of his studies, one of the boldest of innovators in the wake of the likes of Bernheim, Luys and Charcot,[8] whose works had brought about a revolution in therapeutics at the end of the nineteenth century, obtaining results by means suggestion and hypnosis that the ignorant still consider to be miracles, but which were nothing more than the applications of principles now universally recognized.

His sole fault was an excessive timidity, not in his laboratory in his clinic, but in social relationships. Thus, having loved Norès' sister for a long time, he had not yet admitted it overtly. It is true that his secret was so poorly guarded, in spite of his efforts, that neither Norès nor Marie was unaware of it, and Norès was only waiting for an opportunity to urge him to speak.

The affection that bound the three of them together, and their mutual interest in one another's activities, is comprehensible.

The prostration that had briefly afflicted Guy de Norès had now disappeared.

"In the face of danger," he said, "it's necessary to stand up straight; you understand my anguish, but I don't have the right to abandon myself to it. It certainly seems heartless to think of lending assistance those one loves when the peril that threatens them is two thousand leagues away, even if the telegraph lines had not been cut, but who knows? So long as communication exists, one can attempt the impossible, but here the problem is quite different; it's almost madness to search for a solution."

He interrupted himself and passed his hand over his face. "And even if I found it, even if I were to risk that supreme experiment, I'd need...how long?— twenty-five, thirty, perhaps forty hours to get to China, and death is there, imminent and pressing. And yet, can I despair?

His brow furrowed, his features contracted. It was evident at that moment that he had been gripped again by the demon of invention. He was silent, plunged in meditations so profound that he seemed to have forgotten where he was. The other two respected his silence.

---

[8] Hippolyte Bernheim (1840-1919), Jules Bernard Luys (1828-1897) and Jean-Martin Charcot (1825-1893), three of the significant pioneers of French neuroscience.

"Let's go," he said, eventually. "Whatever the risks, it's necessary."

He headed for a door, beckoning to his companions to follow him.

They went into the aforementioned courtyard, along which there was a lengthy hangar. The courtyard was surrounded by high walls that defied the curiosity of the neighborhood.

Norès took a key from his pocket and opened the large battens forming the entrance to the hangar and stood aside.

"Go in," he said to the doctor and his sister.

It really was a workshop: tools of every sort, of carpentry or the locksmith's art, a forge, chemistry equipment—nothing was lacking to give the room a quasi-fantastic aspect, characterized above all by the semi-darkness due to the enormous blinds carefully lowered over the large windows.

What was most astonishing of all, however, was that in this vast space, which bore no resemblance at all, in its extent or disposition, to a mistress' boudoir, an atmosphere reigned that was saturated with a singular and exquisite odor, whose nature it was impossible to determine, so much did it seem to be compounded out of multiple perfumes synthesized into one alone.

Finally, in the middle, under a tightly-sealed tarpaulin, was an object of considerable size, rounded in form, the nature of which it was impossible to determine.

Guy had carefully closed the door behind him, not without having ordered a domestic to call him as soon as Admiral Trécourt arrived.

It was evident now that the young scientist had all his mental capacities.

"My dear friend," he said to the doctor who was looking around curiously, "no one except my sister has yet been in here, not because I'm afflicted by the stupid suspiciousness that sees every visitor as a potential stealer of secrets, but because, I confess, I devote myself here to research whose result is to bring into action unknown forces whose manipulation might well have caused the death of more than one imprudent individual. Marie is battle-hardened and more prudent: do as she does and, I beg you, don't touch anything, even objects that seem to be quite inoffensive.

"Don't worry; in our physiology laboratories we run similar risks, and employ similar precautions."

"I don't doubt it, but the warning was necessary. In chemistry, the forces are even more hidden, and one can awaken them just when one least expects it. Now, I'll come to the subject that interests me. Do you believe, Sabirat, that it's possible to construct an apparatus that, launched through the air, would have a velocity almost ten times that of our railways?"

"The problem was posed a long time ago," said the physician. "At the end of the last century, one of our greatest scientists declared that the future belongs to heavier-than-air craft, but on the condition a motor compressing the maximum power into the minimum weight and volume could be constructed."[9]

"That's the very principle from which I started," Guy said. "But in your opinion, what sort of motor would that be?"

"Research has so far been directed toward electricity, but they've only partly succeeded. The results are already marvelous, though, since an airship moved by accumulators can be steered, provided that the wind velocity does not surpass a certain limit..."

"Even so, the speed doesn't seem able to exceed thirty leagues an hour—a figure almost obtained by our new locomotives with five-meter wheels. I'm talking about a minimum, you understand, of a hundred leagues an hour: a speed that can be indefinitely increased, provided that the resistance of the human organism can stand up to such lightning-fast transport."

Sabirat simply said: "Everything seems possible to me, especially after the experiments of which you gave us a demonstration a little while ago."

"That was mere child's play," said Norès, shrugging his shoulders. "From the moment when one has at one's disposal a conductive wire, the transportation of all physical effects is possible: after movement, sound; after sound, force; after force, light. In that I only had to follow in the tracks of my forebears...but this...!"

He stopped, as if frightened by his own thoughts.

"Brother, Brother," said Marie, "you've often told me that you'd reveal your secret to me when the day came. I know very little about it, but I have confidence."

"Dear Sister!" said Guy. "You don't know, my friend, what a precious collaborator this child has been. She has spent long nights here, preparing blueprints, and copying sheets of calculations and equations before which an astronomer would recoil. She's seen me working, knowing vaguely that every move I made might kill both of us, and never so much as quivered or hazarded an indiscreet question. If she saw me hesitate in discouragement, she re-stimulated my energy. I tell you, Sabirat, that it's to her that I owe the little that I am..."

"Oh, Guy, how can you say...?"

"But Norès is right," exclaimed the doctor. "Who can aid us in our work, encourage and inspire us, if not a good, devoted, faithful companion...?"

Sabirat was getting positively carried away. A little more and there would be a declaration that Marie was awaiting, almost smiling as she was.

Suddenly, however, timidity got the upper hand again, and the rest of the sentence was lost in an almost incomprehensible babble.

---

[9] The reference is probably to Charles Richet, who was a neuroscientist, litterateur and pioneer of parapsychological research as well as an aviation pioneer, whose attempts to adapt steam power to heavier-than-air flight were frustrated by the problem in question.

"Go on," he said to Norès, "and forgive me for having interrupted you."

Norès shook his hand, and said: "You're right. Today I have to be an egotist. I'm in a hurry to say everything, but first, I'll show you my apparatus and its mechanical structure. Help me to remove this tarpaulin. And above all, no abrupt movements."

Taking infinite precautions, the two men slid away the great leather sheath.

A kind of angular box appeared, about the side of the body of a large carriage deprived on wheels, but whose prow was equipped with a kind of steel spur forming a blade, which had to serve for cleaving through water...or air.

To either side of what would have represented the ear of the vehicle, two flat steel wheels were disposed like the sails of a windmill. Finally, above the box, there was a kind of helix placed directly in the center.

The box was hermetically sealed, with the exception of a door on one side, and a window-fame in front fitted with a very thick but immobile pane of glass.

"This is the vehicle," said Norès. "Its appearance is quite simple, and I expect you'd have no difficulty guessing the purpose for which it had been designed. It is, however, in that little box that I might shortly attempt the utopian project of going to China after a journey of twenty-four hours at the most."

In spite of his confidence in his friend's science, Sabirat looked at him with some incredulity. "Where's the motor?" he asked.

"There's the motor," said Guy, opening the door and pointing to an apparatus that resembled one of these machines with a double globe used in making Seltz water.

The doctor uttered a cry of surprise: that definitely surpassed the bounds of the possible, and he wondered whether the emotion suffered by the young man a little while ago might have disturbed his mind somewhat."

Norès smiled, like a man whose demonstrations are all prepared. "Wait," he said.

He went to a corner of the room and came back carrying something in the palm of his hand. It resembled a vaporizer, but had no water in it.

"You see this?" he said. "Well, now roll that cannonball you see on the ground over here."

"But it's enormous; I could scarcely even budge it."

"Try anyway."

Sabirat went to the rounded block and tried to move it, but he braced himself and drew all his muscles taut in vain. The cannonball did not move.

"Don't try anymore," Marie said to him. "It weights more than eight hundred kilos."

"Well, since you spoke, dear Sister, prove to our dear doctor that you're stronger than he is."

"What Mademoiselle! You can..."

"Oh, not with my hands," she said, "but with this."

27

And he indicated the pseudo-vaporizer, which Norès appeared to be adjusting minutely by means of an attached screw.

"Go on, Marie, and confound the skeptic."

She approached the iron block in her turn, and directed at the mass the short tube of that we shall continue to call, for the sake of clarity, the vaporizer…and instantaneously, the enormous boulder rolled rapidly across the entire hangar, so rapidly that it would have knocked a hole in the facing wall if Norès had not shut off the current by throwing an enormous iron lever its path.

"That's extraordinary," said Sabirat. "I'm no longer in doubt. But what is that force?"

"That force," said Norès, "is…perfume!"

At that moment, somebody knocked on the door. It was his domestic, announcing the arrival of the Admiral.

"I have to leave you briefly," Guy said. "In the meantime, Marie, give our friend the explanations that you can."

"Oh! I know so little…"

"I'll complete it—above all, no imprudence."

"Don't worry."

He went out. Sabirat made a movement as if to follow him. That was exactly what he feared the most: not exposing himself to the risk of chemical explosions, any more he would have recoiled in his clinic from the operation most dangerous to his life, but being alone with Marie!

How many others would have blessed that circumstance, which permitted him to talk discreetly and respectfully, but positively, about the sentiment that filled his heart? But that accursed timidity! Guy had scarcely disappeared when he felt himself blushing, going pale…

She was so lovely, with her bright chestnut curls, coifed à la Titus, which put a kind of aureole around her delicate face, with its child-like pink complexion and its gracious and smiling lips…

"So," she said, gently raising her voice, "listen to your professor. Do you know, Monsieur Physician, how a particle of musk, placed in a room, fills the entire space with its odor, instantaneously to begin with, and then for weeks and months, but without the most in-fini-tes-imal—what a word!—balance being able to measure the slightest diminution of its weight? Don't answer. That proves that matter can escape in molecules so refined and so attenuated that it requires billions of them to make up the hundred-millionth part of a gram. Is that clear?"

"You're talking," said Sabirat, who was thinking about something else, "of what we call, after William Crookes, radiation."[10]

---

[10] William Crookes had invented the Crookes tube—an electrical discharge tube producing "cathode rays" in the early 1870s, and many physicists had been experimenting with them ever since, but in 1891 it had not yet been discovered

"Say molecular bombardment—the expression is more exact, if you think about the lightning rapidity with which those molecules spread out through space."

"That's right."

"Good—you'll make a very tolerable pupil. I'll continue."

She held her small finger in the air, like a little girl addressing reproaches to her doll. "That bombardment, whose rapidity is beyond calculation, is, like ordinary movement, a source of force. In its usual state, in fact, perfume displaces, parts or transpierces the constituent parts of the air, which constitutes an effort... Don't look at me like that...listen...and don't think about anything else."

Bah! It was all very well for her to say that he mustn't think of anything but the bombardment of molecules! The truth was that Sabirat heard nothing but a buzz, entirely covered by words that resounded in his brain with the rapidity of cerebral radiation: "She's adorable...I love her, I love her!"

Perhaps, in any case, she was taking a malicious joy in continuing in her professorial tone: "Now, the entire science of force consists of the two operations of compression and channeling. Compress by *ad hoc* means the billion-fold myriad of molecules that irradiate from a grain of musk or any other matter disengaging perfume, channel that formidable flow...and you have in the smallest volume the most colossal force ever imagined."

As she spoke, allowing herself to get carried away by the scientific passion with which she had been impregnated in her contact with her brother, she leaned inside the mysterious vehicle.

"Come," she said. "Do you see that sort of sand-glass, the inferior part of which is made of a metallic amalgam that can resist pressures of thousands of atmospheres? In its interior, under the action of magneto-electric power, the molecular bombardment of odorant atoms is compressed; it is sufficient to place a hand on this lever for such a force to be instantaneously developed that, acting on the system of helices fitted into the case, it raises it up to a prodigious height...and that, by courtesy of that tiller situated behind you, one can steer in the air with a rapidity that challenges the flight of birds...ah!"

She uttered a terrible scream.

This is what had happened.

Sabirat had come into the vehicle behind her and, still hypnotized by the gentility that was inflaming him, still prey to the timidity that made him suddenly mute, seeing the admirable little hand almost at the height of his eyes, he had been seized by a kind of folly...and on that hand his own had posed, as he said: "Oh, Mademoiselle..."

---

that cathode rays were streams of electrons, or that accelerated cathode rays could interact with matter to produce the kind of radiation that, when found in 1895, would be called X-rays.

But the hand he had touched had thus been pushed down on to the lever—and the latent force, suddenly set free, had launched the vehicle into the air with such rapidity that it had passed through the roof without any shock being perceptible...

And it was lost in the blue sky, just at the moment when Guy de Norès came back in, exclaiming: "Truncated telegrams...it's a revolt of the whole of China against the Europ..."

He did not finish. The aerial vehicle had just disappeared before his eyes, carrying away his sister and his friend.

And the unfortunate scientist, conscious of the danger involved, and at the same time as his last hope was escaping, let himself fall to the floor, sobbing, half-mad with grief and fear.

II

Before following our unfortunate involuntary voyagers into the air, let us cross the two thousand leagues that separate us from China and recount the scenes that had caused such dolorous excitement in Paris.

This is what was happening an hour before the selenium mirror had entered into the action.

Two young women were chatting merrily.

"Well, Sacha, are you ready? Oh, the beautiful idler, still getting dressed! Six o'clock has already chimed, and you know that if you're any later, the streets will be so crowded by the Chinese that it will be impossible for us to get through. Listen!"

Throughout the city of Peking, the capital of the Middle Kingdom, a rumor was running, composed of discordant cries, the sound of gongs, trumpet-blasts, and—most of all—an incessant murmur of voices, with various tonalities, whose magnified echo resembled the roar of the sea.

Nonchalantly sitting in a bamboo armchair in front of a nielloed mirror in which she was admiring her admirable blonde hair, whose magnificent tresses a chambermaid was just finishing putting up, Sacha replied without turning her head: "Have a little patience, Marguerite. No matter how crowded the streets are, our servants will be able to open a path for us, even if they have to do it with whips...what are you doing, you clumsy girl?" The last remark was addressed to her maid. "You pricked me with a pin."

The person addressed by the mercurial Russian was a tall, young woman of Manchu origin, with a suntanned complexion and hair that was almost woolly, retained as it was by a red silk headscarf. One could not say that she was ugly, but her physiognomy had a certain quality of cunning and hypocrisy that did not dispose one in her favor. What no one had noticed was that she had shivered at the moment when her mistress had mentioned the word "whips," while her little hooded eyes had flashed. She apologized, but Sacha had already passed on to another topic.

"Is your father here?" she asked the young Frenchwoman who was trying to hurry her along.

"No, I came with my cousin Albert."

"The valiant Albert de Mesnes! Oh! He won't let you venture out alone, even to go from the French Legation to the Russian Embassy?"

"But he isn't constituting my escort alone," Marguerite continued, with a certain impatience, "and the handsome Alexandroff..."

"Oh, he's turned up again!" said Sacha, a trifle disdainfully. "I was beginning to believe that he wouldn't come back from Tien-Tsin. It must be admitted that my fiancé is taking things a little casually."

"Don't be unjust, Sacha; you know very well that in the present situation, European officers, especially the Russian and the French, have grave responsibilities."

"Bah! That's attaching a very great importance to trivial scuffles. What does it have to do with us that the Chinese have substituted the Ming dynasty for that of the...? I forget the names."

"The Tai-Tsing," said Marguerite, softly. "A name that, as you know, signifies *very pure*."[11]

"Which didn't prevent the Celestials from overturning it...but look—I'm ready," the young woman added, rising to her feet.

Elena Batowna—Sacha was only a familiar abbreviation—embodied one of the most admirable types of the pure Russian race, simultaneously delicate, aristocratic and yet energetic, beneath an indolent appearance. Her tawny blonde hair formed a crown, whose gold pins could hardly contain her abundant tresses above her face, which was brightened by two eyes with a steely gleam. Her nose was small, her complexion very pale, and her mouth so small as to make it a marvel, if her lips had not been a trifle thin.

In the supple and rounded figure, however, the well-proportioned corsage and the arms, half-bare under the fur mantle that was wrapped around her, all revealed an uncommon vigor allied to all that female delicacy, and also a pride that was perhaps justified by the position of her father, Prince Batow,[12] who had

---

[11] The dynasty that followed the fall of the Ming dynasty in 1644 is nowadays known as the Qing dynasty—which eventually collapsed in 1912 to be replaced by the Republic of China—but Tai-Tsing was a more familiar designation when Lermina was writing.

[12] Lermina is not consistent in his rendering of Russians surnames, sometimes employing "-ow" and sometimes "-off" where other writers might use "-ov." I have mostly left them as he gives them, except to unify the usage where he accidentally uses both versions in the same name, using the more frequent "Batow" for this character, who occasionally becomes Batoff in the original.

been covering the Chinese Empire for ten years with an almost-completed network of railways, struggling against both nature and the ill will of the Chinese authorities. He was a veritable tamer of men and things, which had won him an enormous reputation throughout the Orient and Europe.

Marguerite Sametel, her friend, presented a perfect contrast with her; several thousand leagues from Paris, she was the typical Parisienne in all her exquisite delicacy. Small, brunette, gracious and as lively as a bird—the classical comparisons remain the best—the daughter of Robert Sametel, the great French physicist, was as mild as her friend Sacha was impulsive, as modest as the Russian was infatuated with her nobility and her father's authority.

The two of them liked one another in spite of those differences of temperament, because they met one another on the same terrain: that of true generosity and firmness of conscience.

Moreover, what Sacha did not admit to herself was that Marguerite, very learned and in possession of a reasonable coolness that did not exclude energy, exercised an influence over her to which she submitted without resistance. The little Frenchwoman, as she called her, had, above all, the imposing quality of common sense, and more than once the beautiful Muscovite's paradoxes had had to show the white flag before the just simplicities of her companion.

They had grown together, having arrived in China in 19 , after the famous Treaty of Nanking, which had given France and Russia the monopoly on great industrial enterprises in the Middle Kingdom. They were both orphaned of their mothers, Princess Batowna having died some time after her arrival in Peking and Marguerite having lost hers while she was still in the cradle.

Between the two fathers the difference was as great as between the two daughters.

Prince Batow was a kind of colossus, who was past fifty but still as lively, as ardent and—let us not mince words—as violent as in the full impetuosity of youth. Reckless to the point of imprudence, he had mastered—his word—the most recalcitrant and broken all the resistances that opposed the realization of his civilizing projects, to which Chinese routine had opposed an evident ill will.

Perhaps he had not always remained within the limits of sufficiently diplomatic action, but his nature, impatient with delay, was exasperated by the slowness of Chinese bureaucracy, and more than one mandarin—even those sporting the most honorific buttons—had felt the weight of the irritable Russian's whip on his shoulders.

Charged with completing the Chinese telegraphic and telephonic networks, Robert Sametel had primarily employed the means of persuasion, and, in reality, he had succeeded, all the more so, as it was to be believed, taking into account Chinese hypocrisy and that he had earned the favor of the highest dignitaries of the empire.

During the events to which Sacha had alluded to a little while before, the Tai-Ping insurrection, the taking of Peking, and the substitution of a dynasty of

Mings for that of Tai-Tsing, Sametel had contributed more than anyone else to safeguarding European influence at a moment when it was seriously threatened.

In the year that Han-Ming had been ruling, under the guardianship of Prince Kong, it seemed that all the difficulties inherent to governmental commotion had been ironed out. The new king had even seemed impatient for the telegraph finally to link the various parts of his empire, and thanks to French capital, which had found large remunerations in those operations, the last line, from the vicinity of the Red River in Canton, had just been inaugurated, at the same time as the Mongolian branch of the railway had finally rendered possible the nineteenth century dream of a direct voyage from Paris to Peking.

The two young women were preparing to go out. That day there was a great festival: on the first day of the month of Li-Chun, the equivalent of our 5 February, the Commencing Spring was celebrated.

Guy de Norès, in Paris, had recalled that circumstance. For a long time, with Sametel's consent, he had maintained a correspondence with the young woman who was to be his wife, and he had chosen the date on which to carry out the supreme experiment that we have witnessed with the complicity of the great physicist.

The whole morning had been spent, as is common practice in China, in visits and polite exchanges between families, but it was in the evening, most of all, that the fête took on its truly popular character: a costumed procession with an ox with gilded horns on a cart was to traverse the entire city from the Bell Tower to the Temple of Heaven.

It was well-known that the immutable Peking consists of three cities enclosed within one another: at the center, the Forbidden City, the abode of the Emperor, a residence inaccessible to anyone, which is only open twice a year—and only for the last thirty years—to the representatives of foreign powers; then the Imperial City, a kind of immense secondary enclosure; and finally the Chinese and Tartar cities, the last two combined into one since the advent of the Mings, by the opening of new gates in the walls that had once separated them.

These few ameliorations had had the effect of isolating the foreign Legations—French, Russian and English—whose grounds now extended over the open Chinese city. The German Legation—which had lost its importance since the war of 189*, the revenge of France, again the mistress of the banks of the Rhine—had been installed far from its peers on the far side of the Tartar city, near the Convent of the Thousand Lamas.

The French minister had kindly offered his drawing rooms and pavilions to the Russians of the Diplomatic Corps and the colony, and it was to take her there that Marguerite, whose father was lodged at the Embassy, had come to fetch Elena Batowna.

When the two young women appeared in the waiting room, Alexandroff Wintscheff and Albert de Mesnes advanced to meet them. Both of them, in the capacity of military attachés to their national Legations, were in uniform: Alexandroff, vigorous and above medium height, superb in sky blue with a gilded semi-breastplate and a spiked golden helmet; Albert, a simple naval officer, with the braid of a lieutenant. Both were young, with honest faces and a pleasing physiognomy.

Mesnes was in love with Marguerite, but, knowing that she was practically engaged, merely served as a courteous and discreet escort.

"Will Mademoiselle Elena deign to accept us as cavaliers?" asked Mesnes.

"Is there any need for such a valiant escort to cross a single street in Peking?"

"One can never be too prudent," Sandorf began—but then, as if changing his mind, he added: "I mean that this crowd is intolerable."

"Bah!" said Sacha, laughing. "A crowd of Chinese is a herd of cattle, dispersible with a prod."

As if moved by a secret thought, Marguerite and the young Russian exchanged glances.

At the same moment, a boy, about twelve years old, emerged from one of the lateral doors and ran to Sacha. "What about me?" he said. "Have you forgotten me?"

He was a handsome child with blond hair and exquisitely delicate features. He had thrown himself into Sacha's arms. She kissed him, and her gaze lit up with a gleam of profound affection.

André was Sacha's brother. After their mother's death, the poor child had redirected all his love to Sacha, who had valiantly accepted the task of protection incumbent upon her, and had found a precious aide in Marguerite, whose natural generosity fitted her for the role of pseudo-aunt.

"Since when have big boys like you wanted to see masquerades?" said Sacha, laughing. "They're only good for little girls, like us."

"Oh! Don't you want me?" said André, ready to burst into tears.

"I'll look after you," said Albert, who never missed an opportunity to find a road to Marguerite's heart.

She smiled, as if to confide it to him.

"Tzu! Let's go," he said, employing the Chinese language, with which he had become familiar.

And the five people went out on to the perron of the pavilion.

In the broad streets, a flood of people was passing by, running, waving flags in the air, holding up cut out images of monsters and dragons on the ends of long poles: a multicolored display that dazzled the eyes.

There was a vast palanquin in the first gravel courtyard, sustained on the shoulders of eight porters.

A cold wind was whistling although the evening was fine, perhaps in great haste to celebrate the spring.

Marguerite and the young Russian sat side by side.

"Well?" she asked, in a low voice. "Do you still have the same anxieties?"

34

"They have only increased," Sandorf replied, in the same tone, "and I'm not alone in fearing some cataclysm. I think that there are thoughts in all these Chinese heads that we can't divine. I can admit to you, who are so cool-headed, that I'm afraid—yes I, Sandorf Wintscheff, am afraid."

"But of what?"

"How do I know? Since the Mings have recovered the throne, a wind of revolt has been blowing here, and a hatred of foreigners. At Tien-Tsin, from which I've come, I thought I could see on the paving stones the blood of the massacres of yore, fresh again."[13]

"Oh, shhh! If Sacha heard you…"

The young Russian passed his hand over his brow. "You're right…today is a festival; let's leave everyone to their insouciance…but tomorrow…"

He did not finish.

Thrown from the crowd, a projectile—a ball of paper—had just fallen into the palanquin and had bounced over Sacha's knees.

She started, pale and shivering. "What insolent…?" she began.

But the ports had accelerated their pace, and they were already approaching the gates of the French Embassy.

Without affectation, Marguerite had picked up the piece of paper and slipped it into her pocket. No one had noticed her action.

The palanquin stopped; they had arrived. The gates of the courtyard closed again on the crowd, from which a kind of snigger rose up. But they did not have time now to reflect on certain strange things observed on the way.

A company of lackeys ran forward, helping the young women to get down. Then they went into the drawing-rooms, marvelously decorated, veritable winter hothouses in which spring had been forced to appear already, with heaps of flowers of dazzling colors, with exquisite scents.

The two fathers had come to meet their children, with Prince Batow cheerful and loud, something of a Cossack with his jovial Tartar face and his long beard, whitened by fatigue. He said to Sametel: "Who would believe that this magnificent creature is the daughter of an ugly brute like me…and look at this masterpiece!" As he added the latter comment, he picked André up in his arms.

"Bonjour, Father," said Marguerite, offering her forehead to Sametel.

"You know that I think you're the prettier one," he whispered in his daughter's ear.

"That's because I resemble you," she said, smiling.

---

[13] Lermina had no way of knowing that Tsientsin would become a key focal point of the Boxer Rebellion of 1900, when a fierce battle was fought there by a multinational force against the insurgents and the Imperial Army, the victory in which created a base from which aid could be sent to the foreign nationals besieged in the Legation Quarter.

35

In fact, she was the very image of her father, whose fine features made a singular contrast with the rude physiognomy of the Muscovite. What brought the two men closer together, however, were a similar energy and a similar devotion to their homelands, as an indissoluble alliance cemented on the battlefield had made the two men into siblings.

Let us say right away that in the last thirty years, profound changes had taken place in Russia's governmental regime, which was now submissive to a constitutional monarch—but we shall have other opportunities to return to such questions.

The French minister did the honors of his palace with traditional urbanity. In recent years the French and Russian colonies in Peking had increased considerably. The French Republic, freed by victory from the charges that had once been imposed upon it and the necessity of formidable armaments, had finally been able to direct all its vital forces to great industrial and commercial questions. The colonies of Tonkin and Annam had acquired an extraordinary impetus, and the civilizing expansion of our homeland had extended usefully into the central provinces of China.

Germany, reconstituted as a confederation and liberated forever from Prussian autocracy, was slowly recovering from the crisis in which the Hohenzollern Empire had perished. Still somewhat peevish, and more especially jealous, she kept to herself, leaving Europe to be penetrated by Latin genius and Slavic vigor.

The drawing rooms of the French Republic, here as everywhere, were the center of civilization and life; the pavilions, put at the disposal of the guests, the balconies of which overlooked the Tartar city and the Chinese city, were crammed with an excited crowd, in which the most celebrated names in French and Russian diplomacy, art, and science were mingling.

Julien Pasteur, a great-nephew of the man who had vanquished cholera in France[14] and one of the most eminent members of the Académie Française, was in Peking at that moment, having gone there to study certain celestial phenomena whose interest had been augmented by the recent discovery of the inhabitants of the planet Mars. The editors of the *Journal Français de Pékin*, who were passing on the latest news from Paris, were surrounded. A fuss was also being made of one of the most original Parisian artists, who had arrived by the first train linking the two capitals, and curious young women were pillaging his albums, already full of interesting sketches.

Night had fallen completely, and our ambassador, offering his arm to the wife of the Russian ambassador, had led his guests into a marvelous room en-

---

[14] Louis Pasteur developed a treatment for chicken cholera, but made less progress with his studies of the human disease; the great man was still alive in 1891, however, and the Pasteur Institute, founded in 1887, was in full swing, so Lermina's anticipation would have seemed perfectly reasonable at the time.

veloped by rare plants, with an immense aviary overhead filled with exotic birds. A table with two hundred places had been set up, streaming with lights, crystal and silverware, a thousand masterpieces of French artistry, which a murmur of admiration had saluted.

The ambassador was alone for the moment, his wife having been obliged to return to the south of France for the sake of her health. It was the wife of the Embassy's First Secretary that was doing the duties of hostess.

The English had decided to celebrate the solemnity in their own Embassy: a somewhat maladroit reserve that was attributed to some jealousy on the issue of the great industrial progress accomplished by France and Russia. In spite of the regrettable attitudes of the English and the Germans, however, the true fraternity that reigned between the ambassador's guests was no less cordial. People felt that they were part of a family; a current of sympathy united all the guests, and as the artist Jean Durtal had been obliged to talk about Paris, everyone listened and applauded.

"I've been in Peking for a fortnight," he said, "which means that it's exactly twenty-one days since I quit the Boulevard de l'Opéra. What changes must already have occurred!"

"What! In such a short time!"

"I'm talking about Paris, Madame. Let's see—let's only go back thirty years. Two million inhabitants then...today, four million! A few miserable electric candlesticks pitifully following the line of the boulevards then...today, the great electric central sun of the Hôtel de Ville lighting the entire city. Paltry stoves whose emaciated flues measured out microscopic degrees of hypothetical heat then...today, the electric heater at Les Halles warms the entire city, where snow has become a myth. Public Assistance organized in such a way that every man is assured his daily loaf of bread...a month ago, the first omnibus balloons of the Renard system—you haven't forgotten the name of the man to whose dirigible balloons we owe the greater number of our victories—began to circulate, and they're about to be obliged to double the service...until they have to triple it. When I think that there were plans for a Métropolitain railway! In the arts, three flourishing Opéras at which one is entertained, which is hardly believable; a literary production reduced to fifty novels a month, augmented by three hundred scientific books; the *Petit Journal* printing three million copies and only fearing, as serious competition, that the *Terre Illustrée*, now daily, will soon appear twice daily with news of the entire world brought by telephone.[15]

"Paris is the kaleidoscope always in movement; it's living progress; it's ceaseless effort; it's..." He interrupted himself, looking in the direction of the

---

[15] By the time the novel was reprinted in *Le Matin*, that newspaper was appearing twice daily and boasting in its masthead that it was receiving news from all over the world by telegraph and telephone.

wife of the Russian ambassador, before concluding: "the pearl of the world of which Moscow is the diamond."

At that moment a lackey brought Sandorf a note sealed in an envelope. He opened it rapidly and as soon as his eyes had scanned it, he went pale.

"What's this?" he murmured. "What does this advice, simultaneously mysterious and frightening, signify?"

No one had noticed the incident, with the exception of Marguerite, whose eyes were fixed upon him.

She saw the young man get up discreetly, in order to go out without being noticed.

What's happening? she thought. *Nothing serious, undoubtedly...and yet, I can't get these dolorous presentiments out of my mind...*

And her hand settled on the note that had been thrown into the palanquin, which she had deciphered a little while ago.

It only contained these words, in the Chinese language: *Kieou Ming. Fan Kouei. Yang komitze.* Get out, foreign devils, demons from beyond the sea.

Was it a threat, or only one of those banal insults that the common people often shouted at foreigners?

"Messieurs," said the ambassador, "I can hear the fête outside becoming animated. The moment has come to offer your arms to the ladies and conduct them to the balconies. Oh, I forgot—I have a visit to announce. Our friend Dr. Li-Sin, the director of the Observatory, the only Chinaman who has adopted European fashions, will be here in half an hour. Permit me to recommend him to your generous welcome, for in recent times it has seemed that a Celestial almost requires courage to cross the threshold of our dwellings."

As he pronounced the final words his voice dropped slightly; it was evident that he was attempting to hide preoccupations that the ever-attentive Marguerite understood.

No one was thinking about anxiety, however; The French wines, especially the great sparkling wines of Algeria—which had dethroned champagne ten years earlier—had disposed all souls to insouciance.

At that moment, Sametel approached his daughter and whispered in her ear: "I'm going up to the Ambassador's electricity station—you know why."

"Oh, Father, how good you are. Success is certain, isn't it?"

"Yes, yes—don't worry. Go on to the terrace. I have an idea that you'll give someone great pleasure..."

This rapid conversation, as will be understood, was alluding to the experiment that Guy de Norès was carrying out in Paris. It was Sametel who had set up the *camera lucida* and the reflectors on the roof of the Embassy, and he knew that far away, in Paris, it would be the Ambassador's visage that would appear to the amazed French audience.

When everyone had gathered on the balconies, a cry of admiration escaped from all throats. The spectacle was marvelous; as if by enchantment, the entire city had been decked out with lanterns suspended from every floor of every edifice. Everywhere, there were clouds of multicolored stars—thousands, perhaps millions. And the effect on the deep blue sky was magical.

There was no gaslight, not a single electric bulb. For that evening, doubtless in honor of the national festival, no appeal was being made to the sciences of the Occident; it was Chinese illumination in all its routine purity, but also with all its Oriental poetry.

In the streets, the crowd had become so dense that the people seemed to be one creature with a thousand feet, like a gigantic glow-worm undulating through the boulevards, losing itself in the side-streets, surging forth on every floor of the houses.

"The procession!" shouted a voice.

Indeed, advancing along the road that passed in front of the three great Occidental legations, a crowd could be seen, in the middle of which there was some agitation.

At the same time, a fiery spray burst forth from the heart of the Forbidden City, at the summit of the promontory known by the name of Coal Mountain, illuminating the entire city.

And from the throats and mouths of all those guests, happy and confident a few moments before, a cry of horror and terror erupted.

Yes, it was indeed a procession that was approaching, in the midst of furious, howling vociferations hideous to hear...but it was not a festival procession, for in the forefront, men were marching who were carrying, suspended from an iron hook lodged in his back, the corpse of an old man, whose silvery beard hung down, a patch of which was white and bloody at the same time.

Someone shouted: "The poor fellow! That's Li-Sin, a friend of the Europeans."

And as if that name were a signal, the crowd responded with a clamor:

"Death! Death to the devils from beyond the sea! Death to the foreigners!"

III

It was a frightful spectacle, that of the still-palpitating cadaver against which a furious crowd, maddened by rage and cruelty, was venting its fury. By virtue of a refinement of torture, his wrists had been bound to his ankles, and that triangle of quivering flesh recalled the most sinister imagination of the painters of Hell.

All around, a mass of people was swarming, brandishing sharp weapons, each trying to rip that blood-stained rag, whose form was gradually disappearing under the thrusts. Lanterns were agitating, casting their red, blue and yellow glare over the multicolored groups, giving that scene of death bizarre and startling glimmers.

The grimacing faces, the lungs exhausting themselves in demonic howls...

39

What had happened, then?

The venerable Li-Sin, one of the scientific glories of China, a man whose influence had contributed a great deal, under the last emperor—prior to the revolution fomented by the Tai-Pings—to dragging the Middle Kingdom into the great current of European civilization, was too absorbed in his research and too confident in the justice of the cause of progress that he was defending to have taken heed of certain symptoms of hatred that were gradually increasing in the people against everything that was affected, intimately or remotely, by the Occident. He had only paid distracted attention to a few pamphlets distributed to the crowds and a few furious sermons preached at crossroads, which the Chinese authorities tolerated, if they did not authorize them.

Li-Sin loved Europe, and France in particular, so he had gladly accepted the invitation sent to him by the Ambassador. At the appointed hour, in his half-national and half-European costume, he had set out on foot for the Legation, preoccupied with his calculations and not paying any attention to what was happening around him.

As he passed before the solid arch of the Gate of Chakaomene,[16] which opens on to the highway leading to the Legations, the stroke of a gong had caused him to shudder. At the same time, the crowd that had been following him for some time without him having noticed had drawn close enough to be almost touching him.

As his way was blocked, he had raised is head and asked, in his calm voice, to be allowed to pass.

A man had touched him on the shoulder and pointed with his hand to a sort of poster hanging next to the frame of red wood from which the gong whose chime had disturbed him was hanging.

"What's that?" he asked.

"Can't you read, O literate scientist?"

Curious but not fearful. Li-Sin had moved closer, for his sight was weakened by old age, and had considered the characters traced on the piece of paper.

Then he took a step back.

"This is bad!" he said. "A curse upon the man who has written these lines!"

What he had read was:

The Fathers have spoken, the Ancestors have ordained.

---

[16] I have retained the spelling from the original here, as I cannot be entirely certain which of the several Gates to the Legation quarter is indicated by the reference. I have followed the same policy with other names, although Lermina is sometimes inconsistent in his orthography, but I have used more familiar versions where practical.

The foreign dogs have insulted our gods and outraged the majesty of the King of Heaven.

Let it be by fire and the sword, in blood, that they are punished.

At that furious appeal to massacre—the suggestion of a cruel fanaticism that was not the first—Li-Sin had experienced a surge of anger.

"This is a crime," he repeated, his hand rose toward the incendiary poster, his head held high, his gaze clear.

"You're nothing but a dog, like the *Fans*!" shouted a voice—*Fans* meaning "foreigners."

"He's insulting the Emperor, outraging the Son of Heaven..."

On looking for a second time, Li-Sin had just noticed something that had escaped him at first: that below those criminal lines, a vermilion streak had been traced.

It was the imperial mark, the seal of the State appended to that act of criminal hostility.

"It's a fake!" he shouted. "The vermilion brush could not have sanctioned such a lie."

"He's saying that the Son of Heaven is a liar!"

"Strike him down! Let him prostrate himself before the Emperor's seal. Put him to death!"

The clamors increased, more audacious and formidable.

With his arms folded under his mantle, he replied softly, without anger. He explained that the foreigners were the friends of the Empire, and that they had brought their industries and scientific progress to the Land of Flowers, but the longer he spoke, the more the vociferations increased.

Armed men were slipping through the crowd now, their faces ferocious, and the circle had tightened to such an extent that Li-Sin could no longer take a single step forwards or backwards.

In the face of the mob, Li-Sin did not weaken. He believed that his age was sufficient to impose respect, as it had been previously. Suddenly, however, a club fell on his head. He dropped to one knee, instinctively raising his arms over his head—but the brutal whirlwind had been unleashed.

A hundred men threw themselves upon him. Weapons pierced him, and clumps of his hair and beard were ripped out.

It was a savage fury, in all its hideousness. The executioners stimulated one another with their clamors, to which howls responded from all directions. Li-Sin disappeared under the feet of the crazed mob.

Suddenly, there was a stir; a butcher was cleaving through the crowd armed with a hook, and with a brutal laugh, he had stuck the sharp point into the unfortunate man's back. Then, with an effort of his wrists, he had lifted him up: a horrible trophy of which the wild animals made a standard.

In his death-throes, he was still struggling; a voice cried: "Tie him up!" And cords tied his hands and feet together.

Then, drunk on cruelty, preceded by that infamous burden, the Chinese ran forward along Hatamen Road, leading to the former Tsing-Kong-Fou palace, which had been occupied by the French Legation for more than half a century.

At the same time, as if in response to a signal from an invisible leader, a frightful racket had burst forth everywhere, compounded by the banging of gongs, trumpet-blasts, drum-rolls and raucous voices. To understand what that extraordinary din was like, it is necessary to imagine a city of two million inhabitants—that was the population of Peking in 19 —suddenly giving voice, crazed with instant rage, as if in a fit of epilepsy.

In all the streets and alleyways, at all the crossroads, at the great southern entrance Tchien-Men, the eight gates of the Tartar city, The Tong-Tche-Men Gate that opens in the Oriental rampart, everywhere that a temple stood, in all the sordid corners of the city and the avenues bordered by palaces, everywhere, an innumerable crowd emerged and spread, torrentially, as if drunk, howling...

The great Hatamen Road, a kind of unpaved boulevard bordered by shops—or rather stalls—surmounted by multicolored parasols, extending for a kilometer, disappeared under the swarm of that moving mass, illuminated by lanterns held on the end of poles, overhanging the hideous trophy of the still-twitching body of the murdered Li-Sin.

Meanwhile, from the heart of the Forbidden City, from the imperial residence into which no one penetrated, fireworks were launched into the sky, the evident signal for some cataclysm ordered by the emperor himself, the chief of the Tai-Pings, effectively declaring war on Europe.

Such was the frightful cortege that the guests of the French Ambassador saw approaching the Legation.

At the same time, fearful lackeys precipitated into the main hall of the pavilion shouting: "The Chinese! They're breaking down the doors!"

Facing the balconies, the crowd was massing, shouting ferocious threats, waving the cadaver like a flag of death.

Stones began to fly, still poorly aimed by reason of the distance separating the pavilion from the exterior walls.

There was a moment of indescribable chaos.

Sandorf had taken a stand in front of Marguerite and Sacha, and had fired his revolver into the crowd.

The women, dressed for a party, insouciant and joyful a few moments earlier, had been gripped by an indescribable terror, and had rushed inside madly, seeking exits through which to flee. Very soon, however, the Ambassador and the Russian and French officers had recovered their composure.

What was the exact extent of the danger? They did not know, but they all knew enough about Chinese treason to understand what was happening; several

of them still had the memory of the massacres of Tien-Tsin, the more recent ri-
ots in Nanking, and the ambush of Tchang-Cha in Hu-Nan.

A single moment of hesitation would be an encouragement given to the
cowardice that was only waiting for a sign of weakness.

The French Ambassador was guarded by a detachment of marine infantry,
hardened seamen and elite warriors. In the blink of an eye, in response to the
voices of their officers, they were under arms.

The telephone linked the French Legation to those of Russia, England and
the United States. By virtue of an unqualifiable imprudence born of latent ma-
levolence, only the German Legation had not permitted that precaution to be installed.

In a matter of minutes, appeals had been addressed to the other legations,
whose good will was not suspect—but how amazed the French were when they
learned that the others had been besieged at the same time as the French Embassy.

The situation had become critical: were they confronted by a popular revolt, a mob born of drunkenness, or had the signal really come from higher up?

"Messieurs," said the Ambassador, "We're going to do our duty. I beg a
certain number of you not to follow me, to stay here to protect the ladies." Smiling, he added: "In any case, the danger is only apparent. We know the Chinese...a great deal of noise for nothing."

His pallor belied his words, however.

Albert de Mesnes had run to him, wanting to be one of the first to brave
peril by his side.

A group of French and Russian officers, on the Ambassador's orders, had
gathered at the door of the pavilion, weapons in hand. A deathly silenced
reigned in the drawing room, where all the women, save for a few, were petri-
fied by fear and half-fainting.

First, a word about the palace of the French Legation, a brief description
being necessary to make the events that are about to unfold comprehensible.

A former imperial abode belonging to the Tsing family, the palace was situated at the corner of two major streets, or highways, the Tai-Ti-Chang to the
right and the Toun-tian-mi-thian in front of the palace. Its external appearance
was monumental. A broad perron gave access to it: a stone stairway surrounded
by boundary-posts linked by iron chains. To either side, on pedestals, were two
enormous lions hewn in solid granite. In front of that perron was a vast courtyard extending to the external gate, formed by the central block and two lateral
wings, occupied by the servants.

The perron gave access to the palace, properly speaking, and the reception
rooms; then, beyond those, there were the various pavilions occupied by the embassy's dignitaries, which were divided into several groups by two spacious
courtyards, one known as the Red Courtyard and the other as the Green Courtyard, denominations borrowed from the color of their architectural ornamenta-

tions. At the extremity were the Ambassador's private apartments, parallel to the strictly-defined palace.

Around these buildings extended vast gardens, enameled pavilions, summer-houses and hothouses. To the right of one of these gardens, known as the Lilac Garden, a gate opened on to a broad avenue where the barracks of the marine fusiliers was situated, along with the stables, the lodgings of Dr. Bivert, an embassy attaché, and a small Catholic chapel.

Finally, the entirety of the grounds was surrounded by thick walls six meters high, equipped several years before with an interior gallery, permitting defense against any assault. It should not be forgotten that the wall in question enclosed an area of more than two hectares.

The Ambassador, surrounded by his own officers and the Russians, had advanced as far as the aforementioned perron. Albert de Mesnes was carrying the French flag. A hundred fusiliers formed a hedge to either side of the entrance.

Then, very calmly, ordering those who were accompanying him to remain a few paces behind him, with the exception of the flag-bearer, who was to march by his side, the ambassador advanced toward the door.

On the other side of it the vociferations increased. Pieces of wood and iron objects could be heard banging on it.

The Ambassador had the bugler sound the flag, and then, resolutely, gave the order to open the door. He advanced toward the mob.

The fusiliers, with bayonets fitted, were ready to go to his aid.

When the door opened, there was formidable pressure, but as the Ambassador took a step forward, the mob instinctively recoiled, jostling one another in brutal disorder.

"Who are you and what do you want with me?" the Ambassador demanded. "This is French territory, guaranteed by treaties and Imperial decree. I demand that you leave."

Audacity produced a sure effect even on the most furious. There was a moment of profound silence.

The Ambassador continued: "France is the friend of China; our governments have exchanged sacred promises; respect them as we respect ourselves."

Perhaps that energetic attitude was about to triumph over that still-inexplicable fury, but from the ranks of the crowd a voice shouted: "Death to the dogs from beyond the sea! Throw the French out of China!"

At the same time, with a kind of ferocious vanity, the wretches carrying the cadaver of Li-Sin, having frayed a passage to the first row of the crowd, held it up, insultingly, a few paces in front of the Ambassador.

Coolly, he marched toward them and placed his hand on the shoulder of one of them.

"In the name of your father," he said, in Chinese—for nowadays, our representatives abroad all speak the languages of the countries in which they reside—"I summon you to set that cadaver down."

Was it the temerity of the order that stupefied the brute? He lowered his arms, and set the body of the unfortunate Li-Sin at the ambassador's feet. The latter, taking hold of the flag, lowered it over him.

"This cadaver is my guest," he said. "I shall defend it to the death. Now, go away, all of you!"

That scene had such a grandeur in its simplicity that the rioters stepped back once again. But the same voice, as monotonous as a knell, shouted once again: "Death to the French! Kill! Kill!"

At the same time, detonations burst forth in the vicinity in all directions: the other Legations were under attack, and were mounting a vigorous defense.

The racket seemed to awaken the assailants from the torpor of the cowardice that had made them hesitate in the accomplishment of their crimes.

An arrow flew through the air and struck the Ambassador full in the chest. Tottering, he leaned on the flagstaff in order not to fall.

"Fire!" shouted Captain Lambert, who launched himself forward to support him.

"No, no!" cried the Ambassador. "No blood!"

But it was too late.

At the sight of the wounded representative of France, everyone had lost patience. The soldiers threw themselves upon the rebels, bayonets extended.

But the ranks opened and a volley coming from outside raked the courtyard of the Legation.

There was a danger of an immediate invasion. They threw themselves at the doors and, in spite of the formidable pressure from outside, succeeded in closing them.

At the same time, however, cries rose up from the rear, and a red light was seen that expanded over the buildings, rising into the profound sky. The wretches had thrown incendiary bombs from outside, on the other side, with such skill that almost all the pavilions had caught fire simultaneously.

In spite of his wound, the Ambassador had drawn himself up to his full height.

"Monsieur," he said to Albert de Mesnes, "above all, take care of the flag I've entrusted to you."

"Don't worry, Monsieur, I'm a soldier and will do my duty."

"And now," the Ambassador went on, making energetic efforts to remain upright, "remember that our honor is at stake here. France expects that we will all die at our posts."

The vociferations redoubled.

A rain of fire fell upon the Legation, while heart-rending screams were heard from the pavilion in which the women had been left.

What was happening there?

IV

It will be remembered that the Ambassador had begged a certain number of Frenchmen to remain with the women in order to protect them.

The cries that the initial surprise and terror had drawn from all throats had been succeeded, at first, by a bleak silence full of anguish.

In the vast drawing-room, the ladies, wrapping themselves up in their evening dresses, had huddled together, heaped up, so to speak, hiding their faces in their hands. The most fearful—and could one consider their emotion criminal?—put their hands over their ears in order not to hear the horrible clamors from outside.

Everywhere, in the Occident as in the Orient, popular furies give rise to sinister echoes, but in those countries so distant from our mores and our civilization, in which the last vestiges of our own made follies subsist, such violence takes on an even more savage character. The wild beast reappears within the man and roars with strange, sonorous and profound voices, like the raucous screech of the tiger.

With that growling—for which there is no better comparison than the echoes that make children hurry past the sheet-metal walls of fairground menageries—was mingled the infernal din of the gongs, trumpets and drums that had burst forth with unprecedented force from one end of the city to the other: a frightful orchestra of sharp and ear-splitting dissonance.

In addition, from one moment to the next, detonations crackled, along with prolonged screams in the distance, all the more terrible for being inexplicable.

Marguerite and Sacha were perhaps the only ones to maintain their composure. In Sametel's daughter there was reasoned, positive courage, a resolution that nothing could bend to confront peril with determination, whatever it might be. In Sacha, there was, above all, the feverish excitement of anger.

The Russian professed the most profound scorn for the yellow race, the hypocritical baseness of which she had observed many times, and the rancor of which she disdained. In spite of her genuine generosity and kindness, there was within her, by virtue of her education as a princess, an inveterate horror of inferior races.

If anyone had asked her, she would have replied in all sincerity that for her, a Chinaman was less than human, scarcely more than an animal. Too often, in chastising her indigenous servants, she had obeyed a regrettable prejudice and had not divined that the desire for vengeance was brooding in all those resentful hearts.

If she was pale at the moment, if her lips were taut, it was primarily because of the irritation caused her by the audacity of those she considered as slaves, and whom, for reasons of pride, she did not want to fear.

Holding her brother André, who was shivering, closely, she had said in a low voice to Marguerite: "Nothing serious to dread...a scuffle, with which the soldiers of our Legations will soon reckon."

But Marguerite had shaken her head without making a reply.

For some time, she had observed symptoms of an ill-concealed hostility toward Europeans on the part of the Chinese.

It is necessary briefly to recall its causes.

Toward the end of the nineteenth century, the Chinese, amassing their numbers in America, had been expelled by force. Mass executions—a kind of Chinese Vespers—had even taken place in the large cities of the United States. A massacre of several thousand Celestials had bloodied the streets of Chicago, and in New Orleans and Florida hatred against the yellow race had revealed itself to be as ardent—we might even say as ferocious—as that once directed against black people.

The veritable cause of that antipathy resided, as is well known, in the astonishing competitions that the Celestials offered to the natives, and in accepting such low wages for their work that they had become derisory. The Chinese could live for a day on the equivalent of two *sous*; an income of half a dollar—two francs fifty—was sufficient for them to accumulate considerable savings. At that rate, however, white men died of starvation, and they had resolved to rid themselves of those dangerous rivals at any price.

Under that general pressure, the Chinese, hunted like animals, had been obliged to flee the continent of North America. They had retreated to Brazil, but the young Republic had too much need of its own resources to abandon any evident fraction to foreigners, and once again a *cordon sanitaire* had been formed against the Chinese invasion.

They had attempted to fall back to Europe, not to mention Algeria and the new States of the Congo, but there had been a complete incompatibility between the black race and their own; the persecutions had recommenced with a character of ferocity against which nothing could prevail. Europe, without heaping ill treatment upon them, had been content to expel and repatriate them.

The resistance that the Chinese had encountered in their desire for expatriation had only served to excite them further; fatality had determined that in recent years, famine had ravaged the Middle Kingdom, while earthquakes had toppled entire cities and devastated immense territories.

Very rapidly, as superstition was added to the mix, the Europeans and their diabolical inventions had been covertly accused of unleashing those horrible scourges upon the Chinese—and in any case, what right did the Europeans have to flood into China when they expelled the Chinese from their own empires?

The Chinese who were expelled from America and Europe described those countries to their contemporaries as veritable paradises; they became the promised land on which all their dreams converged.

Prejudices and instincts of anger and revenge were the sentiments that the Ming conspirators had exploited against the dynasty of the Tai-Tsing; the ancient secret association of the Tai-Pings had spread the word of resurrection from the north of China to the south: *Death to the foreigners!*

Strangely enough, however, with the exception of a very small number, the Europeans had not understood the profound causes and consequences of that movement; they had only attributed the revolution that had suddenly substituted an ancient dynasty for the one occupying the throne to palace intrigues. A grave error! The evil had roots in the very entrails of the people. It was the eternal struggle of races reappearing, in opposition to the spirit of internationalism of which the recent Chinese emperors had given so much proof, and opening the doors of their kingdom wide to the progress of Occidental science.

That was what Marguerite Sametel suspected and, in a way, divined; that is why Sacha's disdainful insouciance made such a painful impression on her. She would have reproached herself, however, for saying anything that would have frightened the young woman. Only with Sandorf—who, for reasons she did not understand, seemed to be well informed about the dark doings of the conspirators—had it been permissible for her to exchange a few words about the complications she feared, without believing them to be imminent—but which had suddenly become manifest.

She looked at the pale face of the young Russian who, looming over the group of men by virtue of his tall stature, seemed to be waiting, pistol in hand, for the sudden appearance of some unknown adversary.

Suddenly, there was a loud cry. Rifle shots had just been heard, fired in the Embassy courtyard. Had the battle already begun, then?

"Messieurs," Marguerite shouted, "we don't have the right to detain you! Think that a few paces away, your friends, you brothers in arms, are being murdered..."

She did not finish.

A sinister noise—a kind of brutal whistle—had just drowned out her voice. At the same time, in a dazzling radiance of red light, a kind of igneous ball flew across the room and, having collided with a wooden corner, exploded with a formidable bang, spreading a blizzard of debris around it along with a stream of flame that suddenly extended over the parquet and transformed into a sheet of fire.

What happened next?

How can that scene of hideous terror be described? The women fled randomly, bumping into walls without finding any exit, the flames licking their skirts, enveloping their corsages, snapping at their bare arms and shoulders.

The blast of the explosion had extinguished the lights, and it was the fire alone that was illuminating those frightful agonies, from which heart-rending screams and desperate appeals for help erupted.

Fortunately—if anything could be reckoned fortunate in that dire catastrophe—a second bomb thrown from outside smashed into a section of wall and rebounded into the courtyard, leaving the way free to an interior terrace, and through that exit the women threw themselves, lamentable specters, in a paroxysm of panic, bumping into one another and jostling one another, as in the corridors of a theater on fire.

Fierce egotism recovered its empire. Everything was forgotten except that death as there, horrible and implacable—and that it was necessary to flee, to flee at any price.

The men—those, at least, who were still standing, for several had been grievously wounded by the shrapnel of the projectile—strove to defend the unfortunate women against their own despair, to bring a little order into that mortal chaos.

But how could they succeed?

Thanks to his height, Sandorf had perceived Sacha, dragged away by the whirlwind, courageously carrying little André in her arms, who seemed to have fainted—but that was all. He had not been able to pierce the compact flood in order to reach her.

Cries of impotent rage escaped him.

Suddenly, someone shouted: "The Chinese!"

It was true.

From outside, the wretches had grabbed onto balconies and climbed over the balustrades. Now they were appearing at the extremity of the external gallery, on the side opposite the one where the women were pressing.

When they perceived the women by the light of the blaze, they uttered a cry of triumph—for, perhaps even more than the men, they hated European women, whose beauty, luxury and charm were, in their view, insulting to the superiority of yellow women. And among the attackers, frightful harpies could be distinguished, as ugly as hags, whose sharpened fingernails were threatening their enemies. Oh, with what joy they would soon be lacerating them!

Sandorf, meanwhile, had been the first to understand the danger. Through the bloody light of the blaze he saw the ever-increasing flood of assailants—and those who had the duty of closing the path to that horde were little more than a handful: twenty at the most.

"Let's go toward death, Messieurs," said Sandorf, "and let's hold them off as long as possible."

The Europeans gathered in a part of the gallery forming a broader balcony, and from there a first volley of revolver shots lashed the crowd of assassins. But if the first ranks might have hesitated, they were pushed from behind with a furious vigor, and the troops raced toward Sandorf and his friends.

The gunfire crackled, Chinamen fell, but the others trampled the wounded and the dead. Armed with long harpoons, they hurled themselves upon the group of Europeans, and it was necessary for all of them to do their utmost to prevent one another from being dragged away.

Their revolvers were empty, and what were the swords in their hands worth against an enemy that was not within reach?

Suddenly, there was a flash in the air; other Chinese were arriving armed with tubes filled with some kind of incendiary matter, and from a distance, they projected a jet of fire at the intrepid defenders, who, horribly burned, nevertheless did not recoil, wanting their cadavers to compose a supreme barrier against the assassins.

Intense smoke prevented anything from being distinguished.

Sandorf was now backed up against the balustrade, arms folded, awaiting death with a fatalistic stoicism—and yet, until now, as if by a miracle, he had escaped danger. He was virtually the only man still standing; Prince Batow lay at his feet, his skull fractured, his body half burned.

Suddenly, he uttered a cry that was almost joyful.

In the glare of the conflagration he had just seen Sacha below him, disheveled but alive, running with André in his arms…but a sob rose into his throat, because he had also seen the Chinese a few paces behind her, who were chasing her.

"I'm here! I'm here!" he shouted—and, leaping over the rail of the balustrade, he launched himself into the air.

A drop of a few feet, and he would be beside her.

But he did not reach the ground. Something—a rope, a lasso—had just coiled around his body. He felt himself being lifted up, and carried away in his turn, while a hand put a kind of hood over his head, which, half-stifling him, prevented him from seeing anything more.

Chinamen carried him off on their shoulders, while a woman, running after them, seemed to be giving them orders.

Meanwhile, the attackers, masters of the terrain, had launched themselves after the group of European women, who, not having found any way out, were massed at the extremity of the terrace, palpitating.

Another instant, and the filthy hands would reach them.

A detonation burst forth.

"*Vive la France!*" cried a voice.

It was the Ambassador's fusiliers who were arriving, under the orders of Albert de Mesnes.

The thunderstruck Chinese recoiled. A further discharge, almost at point-blank range, filled them with terror. It was a matter of every man for himself. The wretches rushed toward the exterior balconies.

"Sacha! Marguerite!" shouted Albert.

Among the voices of the women who replied, however, those of the two young women could not be distinguished.

Sametel leapt over, hanging onto the balcony, and reached the gallery.

"Help!" cried the women.

He was the first to arrive beside them.

"Marguerite! My child!"

Marguerite was not there

At that moment, the battle resumed, fiercer than ever, at all points.

The Legation was invaded from every direction.

The fire was spreading everywhere. Buildings were collapsing with a sinister sound.

It was necessary not to think of defense any longer. Particular interests and intimate colors disappeared before the peril run by the flag.

Sametel came back to Albert de Mesnes.

"If they're dead," he said, in a dull voice, "all that remains for us is the horrible joy of avenging them."

Marguerite Sametel was not dead.

If she had not replied to her father's appeal, it was because, at the moment when the French soldiers appeared at the base of the terrace, the courageous child had just discovered a means of salvation for her companions.

The extremity of the pavilion enclosed a long gallery that served as a library, and she had often shut herself up there with her father, for whom she performed secretarial tasks.

That gallery, she remembered, terminated at the wall that separated the Tartar city from the Chinese city, which had not been demolished when the final work had been done that had isolated the Embassy almost completely. A thought had suddenly occurred to her: she had often visited that wall and knew that there were subterranean corridors within its flanks, able to offer a temporary refuge in case of danger.

Marguerite was courageous; she had no fear of death, but she knew that while the women were not safe, the most valiant men would be paralyzed in their defense.

She thought about her father, who, she was not unaware, would not survive her; it was for him that she wanted to live, and also for the man whose name she pronounced in a whisper, Guy de Norès, whose wife she was before her conscience.

So, fraying a passage through the middle of the fearful women, while encouraging them with her vibrant voice, she had attained the extremity of the gallery and had attentively examined the wooden partition that closed the way to them.

At first she saw nothing.

Set on a pedestal was one of those bizarre monsters, of which the Chinese love to sculpt the forms, more grotesque than frightening. With its huge belly, which was surmounted by a frightfully horned, grimacing head, the vermilion tongue sticking out of a wide-open maw, it was obstructing the passage. The mass was solidly embedded in the wall. It was folly to think of moving it, and yet, thinking that salvation might perhaps lie behind the obstacle, Marguerite clenched her slender fingers on the idol of gold and jade, as if she hoped to tip it over.

Suddenly, her finger slipped and, without the young woman intending it, pressed down on the demonic tongue. She felt it yield under the pressure. She pushed down with all her strength, and suddenly uttered a cry of joy.

The monster rotated on its axis, moved by an invisible mechanism, and the much-desired exit had appeared.

Radiant, Marguerite ran back to the nearest of her companions and shouted to them: "Come on, come with me! We're saved!"

A few launched themselves after her, but the greater number, paralyzed by terror, had not budged.

"Sacha!" Marguerite appealed—and a voice that she took for that of the young Russian having replied to her, she bravely pushed on, convinced that they were all following her.

Ahead of her the darkness was profound; only a slight red glow projected by the fire filtered through the high windows of the library, obstructed by blinds, but Marguerite knew the way well. In the middle of the long room, two sets of shelves formed a kind of alley, at the end of which was a sphere mounted on a bronze foot; it was there, she had not forgotten, that the exit to the wall was located.

She was in haste to reach it, and when she did so, she opened a door.

A gust of cold air lashed her face.

And she found herself outside.

Stopping there, she looked behind her. In the indecisive light that transformed the women who had followed her into shadows, she thought once again that they were all behind her, and, renewing her appeal, she set off along the stone rampart.

"Let the last one through close the door behind her," she added.

She found that she was on a kind of narrow round-path enclosed between high walls, through the crenellations of which the flashes of the blaze were sparkling, but she did not pause, impatient to make sure that her European sisters were safe.

Soon, she felt a declivity underfoot; it was there that the slope led to a subterranean passage. She hastened her pace, and soon arrived at a door formed by a grille, which her father had once opened out of curiosity, and which it was sufficient to push. She did, and reached a staircase. She went down, still hearing behind her the footsteps of those in whom she had been able to inspire confidence and who had abandoned themselves to her direction.

After thirty steps, the terrain leveled out, and after a few minutes more, Marguerite stopped, knowing that she must be in a large chamber.

She rummaged in her pocket and brought out one of those charming jewels that all well-off Chinese carry on their person, and which encloses a lantern in the small central cavity. The young woman's however, fabricated by her father, enclosed a series of minuscule facets that illuminated a microscopic electric bulb.

She switched on the beam, which stood out white and bright on the black wall.

She was not mistaken; she had reached the place with which she was familiar. No noise could any longer be heard; the thick stone structures stifled every echo of the din that was resounding in the city of insurrection. Marguerite's reasoning was sound; this was a refuge into which no one would think of pursuing them.

"Sacha," she said. "Come here to me, with your brother."

But there was no reply.

She directed the beam at the group, and perceived for the first time that only half a dozen women had followed her. She did not see her friend—the one she would perhaps have saved first—among them.

"Sacha! Sacha!" she cried. "Say something...haven't you see her? She must be there, a few paces behind us...and you've left her..."

"No, no!" exclaimed the poor women. "We swear to you, Mademoiselle Batowna didn't come with us."

"That's impossible! My God! But then...she's doomed! And she'll accuse me of having abandoned her, like a coward, to save myself!"

One of them, still shivering with fear, explained to her that Sacha, as if mad with terror, had jumped down to the bottom of the terrace with her brother, and had fled.

"Which way? Speak! I need to know. I beg you..."

Someone affirmed, however, that Sacha had fled in the direction of the main courtyard—which is to say, to the point at which the Embassy's forces were concentrated. Evidently, she was safe.

"Well then!" cried Marguerite, "I need to know, at the risk of my life, and I shall."

As she took a step to retrace the route she had already followed, however, the women threw themselves at her knees, sobbing and pleading.

Could she abandon them? Where were they? Did they even know? She could not have brought them to this sinister place only to leave them there, however. That would be cowardice, a crime...

And they clung to her garments, with pleas that almost resembled threats.

Marguerite reflected.

It was true that she had taken charge of these poor women, and that it was forbidden for her to leave her work incomplete. And then again, what could she do now for Sacha? Either the young Russian had succeeded in putting herself under the protection of her father or the Ambassador, assuming that Sandorf had not already saved her, as was his duty, in which case Marguerite's intervention, even if it were possible, would be unnecessary; or...if she had fled at random...how could she find her? Which way could she go? In what part of the city should she look for her?

Marguerite said all that to herself, and her heart was constricted by a grip so painful that she feared that she might die of it.

But no! It was necessary to stiffen herself against any weakness. She owed it to those who were there, and whom she had promised to save. She owed it to her father, to Guy.

Recovering her composure, she said: "Listen to me. Time's pressing, and we don't have a moment to lose. At the far end of this room a long subterranean tunnel opens, which I've never explored to the end, and from which I don't know the exit. However, I have reason to believe that it must end a long way from here, in open country, outside the city. If we can get that far, there's hope that you'll be out of danger. Perhaps our people will already have put down the revolt"—as she said that she shivered internally, for she did not believe her own words—"and all peril will be over. If not, the city will be in the hands of the insurgents, and it will be necessary to look for other means of salvation. Have no illusions: the eventualities are terrible, but there's an old French saying: *Help yourself, and Heaven will help you.* Are you ready to do as I say...and to be courageous?"

At that moment, a singular phenomenon occurred. The women, convinced a little while before that they were safe, believing that there was no further effort to make, and far from being encouraged by Marguerite's words, found all their anguish revived...and only replied with lamentations.

Only one very young woman, almost a child, came toward her resolutely, and said: "Mademoiselle Sametel, I'll do as you say, and I promise to have courage."

Marguerite looked at her. She was a little brunette with short-cropped hair and keen and intelligent eyes.

"I don't recognize you," Marguerite said to her, softly. "What's your name?"

"Oh, it's the first time I've come out into society," said the young woman. "My father has only been in Peking for six months. He's a photographer. He had an invitation, but he felt ill when it was time to leave, and let me go to the Embassy on my own." Laughing, she added: "I didn't have much luck on my debut, did I?"

"But...your name?"

"Rose. My father's name is Nivet—Nivet, photographer of Batignolles, who came to China to make his fortune. A bad idea. Poor Papa!"

In spite of her anguish, Marguerite could not help smiling. Rose was typical of those pert Parisiennes who sometimes support bad luck better than good.

"Well, my dear Rose," said Marguerite, "I'm appointing you my aide-de-camp."

"Thank you," said the photographer's daughter. "That's quite a promotion. So, with your permission..."

She turned to the others, who were still sobbing. "Come on, girls," she said. "Haven't you finished wailing like that? A little courage, damn it! Since you've been told that we'll get you out of this, stop weeping all the time...you'll make the road wet."

In fact, on hearing that youthful and mocking voice, the others suddenly felt gripped by a kind of shame.

There was a vigorous woman of about forty, Madame Perrotti, whose husband, French although originally from Lombardy, had set up a bank in Peking and was presently very prosperous. There was also the widow of an engineer, in company with her daughter, and finally, an old lady, deaf but still alert, a governess in a highly placed Chinese family.

In less familiar terms, Marguerite repeated her instructions. It was necessary to march, even to march at hazard...but they had no choice.

"Forward march!" said Rose.

And, swinging her hips like a drum-majorette, she went on ahead.

That Parisienne impertinence, which was a trifle suburban, to tell the truth, nevertheless introduced a note of energetic insouciance into the midst of that despair, which did not fail to revive a little courage.

Could they abandon themselves while that child was providing an example of resistance?

It was with a livelier step that the women set out to follow the bends of the subterranean corridor.

"I can't tell which direction we're taking," Marguerite whispered in Rose's ear. "Are we going north or south?"

"Bah! What does it matter? We'll still arrive somewhere."

"Doubtless we're going under the walls, but where will we find an exit?"

"Don't worry about it. When we've been walking for two or three hours, there'll still be time to be disturbed. You know, it reminds me of the catacombs in Paris..."

"You're very cheerful. Aren't you afraid, then?"

"What's the point? It doesn't do any good. You say that, but you have for more courage than me, for when you called out to those you wanted to save, it was just in time. Honestly, I was about to faint—yes, faint, like an aristocratic lady..."

"How old are you?"

"Me? Don't tell anyone, but I'm old, although I don't look it. Nearly sixteen."

"But what do you do here in China?"

"Eh? I help Papa...I take photographs. Poor Papa is on his own—it was when Mama died that he had the idea of going abroad. He wanted to leave me in Batignolles. I know that it's the capital of Paris, which is the capital of the world, but I said to him: 'Not a chance! I only have one father and I'm hanging onto him...so let's get going to the land of the apes.' Tell me, Mademoiselle, is it true that they often roast Europeans?"

In truth, Marguerite admired her. In addition to the fact that she seemed charming with her little turned-up nose and mischievous eyes, the girl's tone was suggestive of an innate generosity and a devotion, proof against anything.

"If we get out of this safe and sound," said Marguerite, taking her by the hand, "would you like us to remain friends?"

"Would I! How could it be otherwise, since I like you and you like me? You've no need to tell me that, you see...you're from Paris, too, near Pantin...that's obvious right away. We aren't going to die this time, take my word for it...and we'll give the Chinese a hard time if they cut up rough."

The thought of two young women fighting against an entire people made Marguerite smile sadly. She did not know that those words were almost prophetic.

Meanwhile, the route seemed interminable. The poor women had protested several times already.

Having come to a party, they were not wearing shoes made for walking. Some had bare feet, and a glacial damp was now falling from the subterranean walls.

While they were complaining, Rose had briskly taken off her skirt, made of a rather thick muslin, and had divided it into four scarves, which she wrapped around their necks. And when the old lady declared that her feet, too cramped in her luxurious shoes, could not carry her any further, Rose had presented her own shoes to her, saying: "These aren't brand new, Lady, but they're all the more supple for it."

In the face of that benevolent good humor, everyone found a little more energy.

"Do you know," Marguerite said to her, "that you have the best heart in the world, and that I'm simply going to adore you."

"At your service, Mam'zelle."

How long had they been on the move?

"Look at your watch," said Rose.

"I'm afraid of exhausting the power of my little lantern." So saying, but also pressed by a perfectly natural curiosity, she switched on the white light. Scarcely had she uttered the exclamation: "It's one o'clock in the morning," then the spark went out, however. She had foreseen what would happen correctly; the battery had not been charged for a long time, and had not been replaced.

"Don't be afraid," Rose said to her, divining her anxiety. "I can cope; I'm a real cellar rat."

"You're quite simply a little providence."

"With two feet and no feathers."

At that moment Marguerite stopped abruptly. "Listen!" she said.

They all held their breath.

A singular noise reached the fugitives. One might have thought it an external slithering that was following them.

"My God—there's an animal there, stalking us."

"A snake!" proclaimed someone else.

In fact, it was impossible to come up with a reasonable hypothesis about the nature of that monotonous, regular sound, with a kind of muted modulation.

"Don't move, as Papa says," sad Rose. "I'll go investigate."

And without waiting for a reply, she ran forward.

The darkness was profound; it seemed that she had eyes like a cat.

Accepting her devotion, so frank and so useful, Marguerite stopped the little troop. She did not know why, but in her turn, she had confidence in the cleverness, and perhaps the luck, of little Rose.

A few minutes went by, during which they could hear their hearts hammering.

Suddenly, a bright light illuminated the tunnel, and Rose appeared, with a torch in her hand.

"This way, quickly!" she shouted. "We're saved!"

And as they all raced in her direction, they saw an open bay in which, by the light of other torches, the silhouettes of European sailors stood out.

Saved! It was true! But where were they?

As Marguerite had understood, the tunnel extended along the wall that surrounds the Tartar city. The city of Peking is surrounded by a canal known as the Tung-Chao, whose eastern branch joins the Pei-Ho.

The tunnel in question ended at the junction of the great canal and the branch.

The sailors were French. They quickly brought the young woman up to date with what had happened.

The decisive battle was taking place at that moment within the walls of Peking. All the Europeans, having recovered from their initial stupor, had grouped together under the leadership of Monsieur Sametel.

Thus, the first name that Marguerite heard was her father's.

They had occupied a part of the city located between the Eastern triumphal arch and Hatamen, based in the Catholic mission and the Yamen,[17] the Chinese Ministry of Foreign Affairs, of which they had taken possession so effectively that they controlled two of the gates of the city, the Chi-ho-Man and Tchien-Men.

Numerous European barges were in the Tung-Chao canal at that moment, and by that route, the Ambassadors had evacuated the women and children who had survived the massacre during the first few hours of the battle.

An officer alerted by the sailors came toward Marguerite Sametel.

"Oh, Mademoiselle," he cried, "your father has made himself a hero."

"Do you think he will succeed?" the young woman asked him.

The officer shook his head. "As the soldier said at Waterloo," he added, "there are too many of them. But don't lose any time, I beg you. Come aboard, you and your companions. A tug is waiting for us at the entrance to the Pei-Ho, and we have to get to the quay at Tsien-Sing-Fu as quickly as possible."

"Take care of my companions first," said Marguerite.

The supreme joys are egotistical. The women and the two girls who had just been saved ran to the barge, almost shoving one another to get there sooner."

"You turn, Mademoiselle," said the officer to Marguerite.

The young woman looked at him and said: "Monsieur, if you knew that your father was risking his life for the defense of the flag and the honor of the fatherland, would you abandon him?"

"Mademoiselle?"

"Go, Monsieur, do your duty. I'll do mine; I'm staying."

"Oh, Mademoiselle, you're a worthy daughter of France."

"I only ask you for one sailor to serve as a guide. Oh, don't worry—I'll send him back to you promptly."

"No need—there's no shortage of brave lads here who are burning with desire to go fire a shot with their compatriots. For you he'll be a guide, and for your father he'll be one soldier more."

"Thank you."

The officer called: "Kroarec!"

"Present, Lieutenant!" said a male voice. And a vigorous sailor came to within arm's reach.

The officer explained the situation.

"Perfect, Lieutenant—and you're doing me a big favor. I've been itching to have a crack at these Chinese apes."

---

[17] The Tsung-li Ya-men had been established in 1861 by the then-regent Prince Kong (Lermina renders it Kong and Koung in different places, but I have unified his references) to serve as a Ministry of Foreign Affairs. Lermina was not to know that it would be abandoned in 1901.

"Don't forget that you need to be prudent, until the moment when you've taken Mademoiselle to her father, Monsieur Sametel."

"Mademoiselle is Monsieur Sametel's daughter! Damn it! Beg your pardon—but if she wants. I'll get myself cut in four for her father."

"That's good. *Adieu, mon brave*—and good luck!" He turned to Marguerite and bowed profoundly. "*Au revoir*, Mademoiselle...see you soon, at Tsieng-Sing."

Marguerite extended her hand to him. "Once again, thank you. I commend these poor women to you."

The young man uttered a cry of surprise. "What about this one!" he exclaimed, taking Rose—who had not budged—by the arm.

"*Au revoir*, my dear Rose, to you, too," said Marguerite. "I'll never forget what you've done for us...for me."

The girl planted her fist on her hip.

"You're sending me away, then, just like that! You're getting rid of me. That's a fine way to carry on!"

"What do you mean? The officer's waiting for you—it's necessary to hurry."

Rose took a step toward the officer, bored with comical reverence. "If you're only waiting for me," she said, "don't delay for so little."

"What do you mean?"

"It means that in there—in that cave where we spent a good while—I swore that I wouldn't quit Mademoiselle; that I'd stay with her. That's understood, isn't it?"

"But think, Rose!" Marguerite exclaimed. "It might be going to your death!"

"Don't know...and I like to learn." Then, very softly, she said to Marguerite: "Let me go with you. My father isn't a great man, like Monsieur Sametel, but he's Papa...and I want to find him."

"Come on then, my good and charming Rose...and let's not waste time."

And they drew away in the direction of the city, under the guidance of the sailor Kroarec.

V

It will not have been forgotten that when Sandorf had jumped down from the gallery, at the risk of breaking his limbs, in order to run to help Sacha, whom he had just seen fleeing with her brother André through the fire and smoke, he had been suddenly seized, tied up and carried away. In that brief shock he had lost any capacity for resistance, and, almost at the same time, any notion of the course of events.

Furthermore, his carriers, excited by the voice of the woman who was running after them, had adopted such a rapid pace that the jolts felt by the Russian officer were certainly of a nature to provoke a very natural loss of consciousness.

Before going any further, however, in order that the story can be better understood, let us give a brief description of the mysterious city that was only known, at the end of the nineteenth century, by virtue of the accounts of a few voyagers, and that, even at the time when the events of the story we have undertaken to relate were unfolding, conserved the greater part of the original characteristics of its ancient isolation.

Peking is situated at a longitude of 114° 7′ and a latitude of 39° 54′.[18] The city is constructed in the middle of a vast plain; one might think that the sentiment guiding its sovereigns was the same one that engaged the Spanish monarchs to place Madrid in the middle of a desert.

The sea, in the gulf of Petchili, is seventy kilometers to the east. The Pei-Ho, which traverses the entire province and has its source in the King-Tan Mountains, traverses Mongolia and then separates into two arms. The Pei-Ho passes 24 kilometers from Peking; the place where it is closest to the city is the location of Fort Tung, the terminus of the Tung-Chao canal, which envelops the entire city outside the walls, thus forming a double circle of water and stone. Water is, moreover, abundant in Peking; lakes and ditches are fed by canals drawn from the pools of Iung-Min-Yen, the ancient Summer Palace once sacked by Anglo-French armies.

The name Peking signifies "northern court," in opposition to Nanking, which signifies "southern court." The latter city was once the residence of the Emperors.

Within the double girdle that encircles it, Peking cannot increase in territory, although its population has increased since the end of the nineteenth century by more than half a million inhabitants.

It is thirty-three kilometers around and covers six thousand hectares.

We have already said that Peking is composed of three cities, two of which, the Tartar city and the Forbidden or Imperial City are enclaves within one another; to the south is the Chinese city, a city of commerce and industry, an cluster of shops of all kinds and merchandise of every provenance.

The topography of the Tartar or Mongol city is very easy to understand, the gates being orientated precisely at the cardinal points: to the north, the gates of Peace (Ngan-Ting-Men) and Victory (Tai-Tchang-Men); to the west, the gates

---

[18] The former figure does not correspond to English citations because it is based on the Paris meridian rather than the Greenwich meridian. The data cited by Lermina are derived from *La Nouvelle Géographie universelle* by Élisée Reclus, which was still incomplete in 1891 although the Asian sections had been in print since the late 1870s. Reclus was the most famous of all France's pioneering Anarchists, and compiled the book while in exile. He served a brief term as editor of *La Science Illustrée*.

of the West (Tsi-Tche-Men) and Submission (Pin-Tse-Men); to the east, the gates of the East (Tong-Tche-Men) and the People (Rchi-Koua-Men); and finally, to the south, the gate of the Aurora (Tien-Men), plus Hai-Lai-Men and Tchuen-Tche-Men, which take their names from ancient emperors.

The southern gates communicate with the Chinese city, and it was near one of them, it will be remembered, that the unfortunate Li-Sin was massacred.

Long before American cities, Peking had understood the utility of straight lines for circulation, and from all the gates, broad roads had been traced, intersecting at right angles, and dividing the city into great squares, themselves subdivided by small straight roads into smaller squares, the former analogous to the avenues of New York and the latter to the streets.

One singular detail, however, which can in itself explain the distance that has always separated the Chinese lords and literate individuals from the population, is that on the great avenues or boulevards there is not a single edifice or rich house. On both sides, there are low constructions, shops, or walls allowing nothing to be seen but the parks and gardens belonging to elegant houses hidden in the side streets.

In the center of the Manchu city is the Yellow City—in China, that color is attributed to the Emperor, and honor it shares with vermilion. Thus, in the middle of Yellow City, reserved for high functionaries, is the Red City or Imperial Palace, Huang-Chan-Ti-Kong.

In the Yellow City, remarkable for its roofs, which, under the sun's rays—or, at the time when the revolt broke out, under the reflections of the fire—seem to be covered by a golden dome, the most magnificent edifices include the Pagoda of the Literate, the Pei-Thasse, a monument elevated to the memory of the last king of the Mings, the new dynasty of which recovered the heritage after two centuries.

The revenge of the Mings had given rise to a bizarre ceremony of an almost fantastic character.

In the imperial garden, the tree could still be found from which the unfortunate Ming monarch had hanged himself when the Tartars took possession of the capital. His Manchu conqueror, unable vent his anger on the man he had wanted to keep in his power, but who had escaped him via death, had covered the culpable tree that had robbed him of his prisoner with chains, and since 1644, the date of the event, the withered trunk of the tree had borne the yoke of infamy.

Scarcely a year before, the new Emperor, who belonged to the Ming dynasty, had broken the chains of the old tree in a solemn ceremony, and then had it clad in gold armor, surmounting its top with a crown of the same metal. The strange rumor had been spread through the people that, rehabilitated and revivified by the honors that had compensated it for the odious unmerited punishment, the tree, in one last effort and as if to salute the new emperor, had put out a young and fresh branch—only one—which had dipped in order to bow to the Son of Heaven.

Also in the Yellow City, on the edge of the Middle Sea, itself a vast and admirable lake, is Coal Mountain, a steep hill surmounted by a pavilion of marvelous grace and elegance. What gives that hill, which is not very high, its curious character, unique in the city of Peking, is that if you stayed in the capital of the Middle Kingdom for twenty years, you would not find a single blade of green grass in its streets, squares or even the banks of its canals, as the humblest growth is pitilessly stifled by the sand that blows from the Mongol deserts, and yet the hill of the Yellow City is always green: a fresh, bright emerald green, giving the illusion of an eternal spring.

What accounts for this phenomenon? It is claimed that in times long past, an emperor who was fearful that his capital might be besieged had an enormous heap of coal transported to that location, which was to serve as fuel for his engines of war. The siege did not happen. The coal stayed there, and gradually, under the action of the weather, an enormous layer of vegetal earth, of incredible fecundity, formed over the heap. Is it the heat locked in the bosom of the coal that gives the earth that vegetative force? This explanation is not implausible.

Those two marvels, the Pei-Thasse and the Coal Mountain, dominate the city with their pavilions with delicate tapering horns. When the wind blows from that direction, an exquisite perfume born of plants cultivated by the monks spreads over the city, in consoling contrast to the less satisfactory scents that emanate from the rest of the Chinese city.

To the northwest of the Red City, at the corner of the square, rises the Pagoda of the Literate, the temple of examinations, and the point on which all gazes, from every part of the empire, are fixed. It is from there, in consequence of the examinations on which all Chinese civilization is based, that graduates emerge to occupy the highest positions in the administration and the government.

Of the Red City, Europeans, even in the recent years when the conquests of occidental civilizations have penetrated the country, only know the golden roofs looming above the walls.

At the moment when the last dynasty had been overthrown, the Emperor had invited the European ambassadors to the Imperial Hall built on the summit of five superimposed terraces. That was a veritable triumph for French diplomacy, which had finally overturned the last obstacle opposed to progress by age-old prejudice. The audience had not taken place, however, and death had punished the Emperor for his sacrilege. That condescension had been one of the most powerful motives for the revolution that had carried away his throne.

A magnificent bridge, entirely made of finely sculpted marble, traversing the Middle Sea and leading from the Yellow City to the Tartar City, seems to be guarded by the great monastery, with its immense buildings of white marble, its colonnades of black marble, its chapels populated by grim gods, symbolic animals with terrible faces, and the heads of lions that seem to be jealously defending the entrance to the Fu, the palace of high dignitaries.

Above it looms a high tower, an enormous and menacing mass.

South of the Marble Bridge is the Imperial Pagoda—Kwang-Mi-Tien—all white beneath its roofs of lapis tiles, resonant with the sound of a thousand little bells incessantly agitated by the wind, streaming with flags that flutter like the wings of brightly multicolored butterflies. And yet that graceful edifice is empty. Once, the dethroned Emperor had gone there to offer a respectful homage to the gods of Confucius, but the Mings, who had re-entered the Imperial Palace, abandoned it. Bats had taken possession of the pagoda, and when night fell, their wings brushed the little bells and made them vibrate as if at a funeral.

By contrast, another edifice, once abandoned, had been reconstructed and luxuriously ornamented; that was the Temple of the Elephants, in the western corner of the wall that separates the Tartar City from the Chinese City. The Tai-Tsing, the dynasty of the Very Pure, had renounced the Asiatic luxury of which the elephants seemed the monstrous symbols under the Emperor Han-Ming, who had reigned for two years under the regency of Prince Kong. But under the most ardent representative of old Oriental ideas, the Elephants had taken possession of their palace again—and, training for war, they often hurled at night the sinister racket of their long and funereal cries.

At the moment when murder and fire were raging in the Chinese capital, in response to an order issued from the Imperial City, from the same Imperial Hall that the European ambassadors had failed to penetrate, but where Asiatic despotism had established itself again with all its hateful ferocity, the city took on a fantastic appearance.

There were four colossal fires on the four sides of the horizon. It was the Catholic missions that were burning: to the north, the Peh-Tang, within the boundary of Yellow City, whose magnificent woodwork was no more than a immense furnace; to the south, the Nam-Tang, with its cathedral, whose towers, seen through the red smoke resembled the writhing of two arms imploring the aid of Heaven; to the east and north, the schools, large constructions whose walls were crashing down.

An uninterrupted spray of fire rose from the Coal Mountain, not that of a blaze but a signal of death, incessantly maintained.

On all sides there were explosions, and the dull sounds of collapses. The city seemed to have been shaken by a demonic fury. Gunfire mingled its distressing echoes with the coppery resonance of gongs, and incessantly struck at the doors of monasteries, while the Chinese horde ran through the streets, the swarm of assassins, sacking the European shops, dragging the unfortunates into the streets, over the paving stones, through the mud, until the moment when, weary of torturing them, they finished them off with thrusts of swords or spears.

Never had the folly of human brutality, unleashed in all its savagery, affirmed itself so hideously. Women fled, pursued by troupes drunk on blood, and from the bridge of Pin-Tse, children were hurled into the ditches. On the western side, the Tung-Chao Canal flowed red.

It was as if there were whirlwinds of bestial fury in the air: howls added sinister punctuation to the great clamor audible throughout the city. Sometimes, a strident scream burst forth, like that of a slaughtered animal, or there was a slow, interrupted wail like that of an animal being made to suffer. This time, however, it was the human beast that was in agony.

Vaguely, under the oppression of the gag that was half-choking him, Sandorf perceived these atrocious realities. He was unable to understand, to reason, but it seemed that he was being carried away in the vertiginous whirl of a nightmare.

It went on; the porters had gone past the English Legation, which was now surrounded and invaded, at a run, going around the coal warehouse, and had headed obliquely into the Yellow City, following along the walls of temples where the hammers of gongs were launching deep and ferocious roars; then, following the southern shore of the Middle Sea through the grounds of the Imperial Pagoda, without pausing for a second, they had reached the Si-Hua Gate, and from there had threaded a path through the narrow streets of the Tartar City.

They had passed under the western triumphal arches, made of bamboo with triple openings, decked with steamers that were bright in the gleam of the conflagration, like tongues of fire. There, the crowd had stopped briefly, because the popular furor was overwhelming and hectic.

An Englishman, one of the most important commissioners in the city, had been tied to a stake and was plunged into by sword-thrusts, playing the horrible game of death by a thousand cuts, which consists of slicing a victim into shreds.

One does not disturb executioners at work. But the woman guiding the escort had moved forward.

She was a creature of tall stature, quite beautiful in spite of her Mongol type. She had the simultaneously harsh and intoxicating beauty of Oriental almas, with something akin to the hieratical character of a priestess in the sculptural regularity of her features.

Her gestures had a solemn grandeur. She approached the group of torturers, and with her hand raised and holding two fingers straight while the others we folded over her palm, she pronounced a strange word in a loud voice, composed of two sounds that melted together in a kind of soft and prolonged growl: "Aum!"[19]

---

[19] This mantra is normally rendered Om in English. Lermina renders it Aoum in this passage, but subsequently substitutes Aum when it takes on a key role in his *deus ex machina*; I have unified his references. In Hinduism it is the Word that began creation, and thus symbolizes the manifestation of God.

The torturers were so preoccupied that they did not seem to hear it the first time. Then her hand came down on the shoulder of one of them, as he was drawing breath, weary of slaughter.

"Aum!"

This time the man shuddered, his eyes looked up, and he saw the hand, still raised in a gesture of incantation.

Then he shivered, and, looking at the woman, he recoiled in a kind of superstitious terror. He shoved aside those who were with him, repeating the mysterious syllable.

This time, the effect was immediate; the ranks opened, and while the majority, ceasing to strike, put two fingers to their foreheads and bowed, the band resumed its course. Behind them, the murderers compensated themselves for having been interrupted.

Finally, they came into the long avenue of Chuen-Che; then, heading northwards, they ran for several minutes through a maze of uninhabited streets.

There was a wall, black and mute. Suddenly, the woman uttered a slight whistle and the men stopped dead.

There was a door in the wall.

The woman approached it and knocked, spacing her raps in a particular fashion. The door opened.

There was an abrupt change of scene. They were in a garden of tall, bushy trees, the tops of which were reddened by the reflections of the conflagration, while their bases were lost in obscurity, only pierced by the indecisive glimmer of a few almost-opaque paper lanterns held by men clad in long tunics and armed with naked curved sabers.

The woman went in first.

The fateful syllable "Aum!" was murmured between her and the men who were there. They bowed to her, and then two of the strange guardians detached themselves, preceding her, while the porters followed her meekly with their burden.

They walked through alleyways, narrow to begin with, but which gradually broadened and eventually ended at a stone stairway.

She climbed the steps slowly—seven of them—to arrive on a first platform, from which a second stairway of fourteen steps rose up. On the second landing, a third flight of twenty-one steps commenced.

"From seven, which is shadow, to fourteen, which is dawn—which is to say, light," the woman murmured, punctuating each of her phrases with the sacred word "Aum!"

At the top, a vast pavilion loomed up, superb in its colors and decorations, illuminated in the light of two vast fires that were burning in bronze basins, where an alcoholic liquid was boiling, as odorant as sandalwood, with an additional penetrating acidic flavor.

A vast door the color of emerald sealed the pavilion. Beside it, a gong was suspended, the sculpted copper of which displayed the head of a fantastic chimerical animal.

She seized the hammer and struck it, gently and mutedly, in a rhythmic numerical pattern, akin to a language.

No one came in response, but the door swung on its hinges silently, as if moved by an invisible force.

She turned and invited the porters to go forward, which they did—and the door closed silently behind them.

They had entered into a large room, almost dark. At the back, however, a gleam was visible that was gradually accentuated, and it became evident that light was filtering faintly from the next room through some kind of metallic curtain, which doubtless permitted sight without being seen.

She pointed with her hand toward a kind of sofa set along the wall and ordered that the prisoner should be set upon it. Then she made a sign, and the porters disappeared.

She was alone with Sandorf.

She went to him, gliding over the paving stones without awakening the slightest echo.

Having arrived close to him she leaned over and gently removed the hood that was covering his face. Then she crouched down beside him and placed her hand on his heart.

Her features contracted under the influence of a profound anguish.

Finally, the young man uttered a sigh, and she had difficulty repressing a cry of joy. He was alive.

An intense delight lit up the face of the mysterious woman, who, bending over, kissed him on the forehead.

Then she stood up.

"Mine," she murmured. "Mine forever, in life as in death."

She went to a small sideboard, took out a jade pitcher and a cup; then, having filled the cup with a liquid as colorless as water, she returned to Sandorf and put the cup in his hand.

Mechanically, in the first awakening that makes the throat dry, he raised the cup to his lips and swallowed the liquid in a single draught.

She made a triumphant gesture—and as the young man became agitated, trying to stand up, she withdrew to a darker part of the room, put her fingers to her lips and, having blown him a kiss, opened a little door and disappeared.

VI

Meanwhile, the young Russian gradually came round. Since he had drunk the liquid, it seemed to him that fire was running through his veins, but it was not painful—far from it.

On the contrary, it was life that was circulating in him, active, warm and comforting, while his mind was illuminated by a bright light.

He raised himself up with his wrists, his eyes still closed, unconscious of his own existence, in the singular state that follows lethargy.

At that moment, a singular chant began, strange, monotonous and soothing, which seemed to be coming from a long way away, softened and, in a manner of speaking, filtered by distance.

It acted upon his nerves like an intoxicating song. It seemed that he felt a soft breath passing over his forehead.

Slowly, he stood up and then opened his eyes.

At first he closed them again, as if surprised, not understanding and not remembering. Where was he? A great laziness dulled his curiosity.

The chant was becoming louder, as if getting closer, vibrating in his ears with a penetrating charm.

Meanwhile, there was a sudden relaxation in his nerves, and he found himself upright.

We have rapidly sketched a portrait of the young man: tall, very vigorous, broad shouldered, features imprinted with a character of violent energy. Sandorf bore no resemblance to the Russians of high society who, having strayed onto Parisian soil, seemed to be searching, in mad prodigality and facile amours, for a means of escaping an eternal ennui.

Alexandroff Wintscheff, in terms of his ancestry, belonged to the Kirghiz[20] race—which is to say that he had, in spite of the refinement of a sojourn in the north, the southern characteristics of the Caucasus; but it was not only physically that something of that still semi-savage race subsisted in him. Sandorf—as he was normally called, by way of abbreviation—had in his soul a singular mixture of brutality and naiveté.

Although, in the elevated milieu in which he lived, he had gradually acquired the delicate and slightly feline manners of the aristocratic society of St. Petersburg and Moscow. Though sometimes, as soon as he was delivered once again to his personal instincts, either in the distant provinces of the Empire or in the army, the instincts of violence, impetuous anger, and unreflective enthusiasm that were dormant within him reappeared.

---

[20] The Kirghiz are mentioned in early Chinese documents as northern neighbors, whose territory embraced a part of the ancient trade route known as the Silk Road; after a war with the Uighurs in the ninth century A.D., they occupied the Mongolian steppe, but by the time they were absorbed into the Russian empire in the nineteenth century, they had become indistinguishable from the Kazakhs. The modern Kirghizstan has China to the east and southeast, Kazakhstan to the north, Uzbekistan to the east and Tajikistan to the southwest—nowhere near the Caucasus, although the so-called Kirghiz steppe extends in that direction.

Thus, his passions were ardent, and more than once, already, he had almost compromised himself in adventures of a gallantry that were more than soldierly, and which would have compromised his future markedly if his family and friends had not been able to attenuate the scandal.

As it was important to prevent the recurrence of those eventualities, however, the decision had been made to marry him off, and negotiations had begun between his noble parents and Prince Batow.

Without arguing, perhaps understanding himself that the time of the follies of youth had finally to run out, he had allowed himself to be engaged to Elena Batowna, whose beauty had, in any case, made a deep impression on him. To employ a familiar expression, Sandorf had found himself something of a small boy before that creature, proud of her race as she was and whose attitude contrasted with that of the women of whom he had made facile conquests. She sometimes indulged in disconcerting mockery, playing with him like a cat with a mouse...and if, by chance, he showed signs of rebellion, a glance or a word quickly sufficed to master the turbulent cavalier.

A long posting had been imposed upon him, and the marriage was not due to take place until Prince Batow's return from China to Europe. Sandorf had not accommodated himself very well to that delay, inasmuch as constancy had never been his dominant quality. He felt that he was still an independent bachelor, and the yoke of betrothal often seemed difficult to bear.

One day when he had been prowling the streets of Peking, having nothing else to do, wondering how long he was going to remain imprisoned by the wall of China, he had seen, in a strange cortege that was passing by, in the midst of Buddhist monks, a woman dressed like an idol, her forehead hidden beneath a kind of tiara, draped in a white cloak constellated with strange signs. The eyes of that strange woman had met his own, and within an instant, a kind of bond was established between those two beings who had never met, which was to tighten into a decisive intimacy. How that had happened, and how such a vivacious, dominating passion had been established in Sandorf's heart, the ardor of which invaded him more every day, only the profound mystery surrounding new loves can explain.

The woman had passed by, and while looking at him, had raised to her lips a lotus flower, a golden jewel that she had detached from her cloak. Then, an hour after she had disappeared, Sandorf received a mysterious note: would he like to see the woman who had appeared to him in that rapid vision again?

Was it one of the banal strokes of luck that the handsome Sandorf had so often encountered in his life? What did it matter, after all? The unknown woman had seemed beautiful to him, with a strange and captivating allure. A man has curiosities against which reason cannot prevail.

Sandorf had gone to the location indicated in the note.

Too courageous to hesitate, he had plunged by night into the labyrinth of the old Chinese city, the bizarre quarter surrounding the Passage of the Bimbelotiers,[21] a vast and long avenue entirely populated during the day by ambulatory merchants and sellers of Chinese antiquities.

Did the unknown woman belong to the scorned class of those petty people? Once again, Sandorf did not bother to ask himself such questions; he was carried away; he was not reasoning.

Then, a new life had commenced for him. The unknown woman had taken possession of him, had enveloped him instantaneously with seductions all the more powerful because they were complicated with quasi-marvelous peculiarities by which Sandorf's imagination, poorly educated in sum, and still imbued by old Oriental legends, had been troubled.

And that woman, who had the passionate energies and also the intoxicating languor of the Asiatic, revealed to his eyes a kind of strange, apparently magical power. Sometimes she appeared at the moment when he was least expecting her; sometimes, by contrast, when he found himself beside her, it seemed as if she suddenly disappeared, like a nocturnal vision.

Their rendezvous had always taken place in singular, unexpected locations, and everywhere, even in the quarters from which luxury seemed to have been banished forever, he saw Sithreva—that was the name under which she revealed herself to him—surrounded by a dazzling luxury.

Sometimes, in the street, he shivered, perceiving her in the garments of a pauper, lost in a crowd of beggars; then, a few hours later, he found her again in some sumptuous dwelling, served by slaves who treated her like a queen, sparkling with gems.

When he interrogated her, she smiled with her sphinx-like lips...and made no reply.

Gradually, however, as her empire over her lover had become established more despotically, she had begun to speak to him in less enigmatic terms of an immense power of which she was the recipient. And with an astonishment that was soon transformed into admiration, Sandorf heard her talk as if in a dream about the conquest of the world.

Was she betraying herself, or voluntarily letting escape those semi-confessions relating to a plan pursued for a long time? Sandorf, in the grip of a kind of intoxication, which almost robbed him of any notion of the present and the future, did not even try to find out.

Sithreva's voice and eyes, her simultaneously hieratic and regal attitudes, all contributed to maddening him further...and yet, sometimes, when he was calmer, he remembered certain words he had heard, perceived as if in a dream, which frightened him.

---

[21] The word bimbelotier is occasionally imported into English because it has no ready translation. A *bimbelotier* is a manufacturer and trader in *bibelots*: trinkets, "knick-knacks" or imitation antiques.

Sithreva did not belong to the Chinese race; she had been born in Tibet, in a country almost unknown to Europeans, where, it was said, the secrets of ancient times were hidden in monasteries perched above the region of snows, on the summits of the Himalaya.[22]

"Who is your father?" he had asked her once.

In an indefinable tone she had replied: "I'm the daughter of the Master of Masters, the one who, ten thousand years ago, was called Ram..."

Ram! What did that name mean?[23] And what did that mystical affiliation signify?

But there was one undeniable fact. Sithreva had, anchored in her most profound depths, a hatred of Europeans. As a Hindu, she hated the English, the masters of her homeland, and with them all the peoples who claimed to be civilized, who, she said, came from thousands of leagues away to despoil the Orient, to consume its flesh and its blood.

"But I'm European, and you love me!" he exclaimed.

Then she looked him full in the face, and replied: "I want you to take Europe, to give it to the Orient."

At other times, in the night, she led him through the city, into the wretched quarters where the population swarms are driven by hunger by the thousands toward the Occident, and which the Occident has rejected. And she told him about the curses launched against the whites, against the egotistical and greedy race extending beyond the Urals, all the way to the confines of the Atlantic.

In vain Sandorf tried to combat the nightmare of sorts that was oppressing his brain. Without confessing to Marguerite the source from which his information came, he had drawn her attention to the alarming symptoms that had been manifested to him.

Often, he told himself that he was playing a singular role in all of that. How, as a European, could he tolerate the woman he loved spreading maledictions against the great family to which he was proud to belong? Could he deny, in the profoundest depths of his conscience, that Sithreva was accomplishing,

---

[22] Lermina's eldest daughter was married to Henri Chacornac, a bookseller and publisher specializing in the occult, to whose operations the author provided useful capital, and via whom he became closely, albeit skeptically, involved in the French occult revival. Lermina was therefore familiar with the mythology of the Tibetan Shambhala, which was later to inspire James Hilton's Shangri-La. Like many popular writers of the day, however (lent encouragement by such syncretic occult theorists as Madame Blavatsky), Lermina makes no distinction between Hinduism and Buddhism, and also includes Islam in the same "Oriental" grab-bag.

[23] In this instance, it refers more closely to Madame Blavatsky's theosophist pseudo-history than to the Rama of the Hindu epic *Ramayana*.

before his eyes, almost with his complicity, a nefarious endeavor that threatened his European brethren?

But soon, passion resumed its empire; he felt himself borne away as if by a whirlwind that he could not resist.

It was also the case that Sithreva repeated to him that he would be the greatest of the great, that she dreamed of elevating him to a throne so highly placed that before him, the kings of the world would be lower than slaves...

He listened, stunned and hallucinated...and the savage within him got the upper hand again, and he surprised himself by dreaming about those Asiatic empires of which the leader was almost a god. His memory recalled legends of the Caucasus, in which the Sars, whose citadels of Van were an impregnable refuge,[24] had overlooked the steppes from outside and above the world, according to the songs of the ancient Caucasians.

Pride is an alcohol, as is ambition, and in response to the inflamed speech of Sithreva, all the ancient rancor amassed by the vanquished against the conquerors of the people of the Urals and the Caspian region had risen into Sandorf's mind, and he listened ardently to the enchantress as she was pouring those hateful aphrodisiacs into him.

Such as the man who, on that disastrous day, had been transported to the strange place in which he had now wakened under the influence of the liquor that had been poured for him: a kind of ferment that recalled in its composition the Soma of the ancient Aryans.

He looked around. No lamp illuminated the place where he was, and yet it was filled with a soft light, with which the vague and mysterious chanting that seemed to be emerging from the depths of the earth harmonized.

He started walking back and forth, listening.

Strangely enough, in those distant, seemingly muffled harmonies, filtered after a fashion by distance, he recognized a melody. Where had he heard it before?

Yes, he remembered: he had been nursed by a woman who had come from the Lesghian lands,[25] and it was from her lips, when she had cradled him while

---

[24] The Citadel of Van is a stone fortress build some 800 years before the modern era in what is nowadays eastern Turkey; it still stands, although somewhat dilapidated. The "Sars" to whom Lermina refers are an invention of one of Lermina's acquaintances in the occult revival, Joséphin Péladan, who liked to style himself Sâr Péladan, claiming that the title was descended from ancient Babylonia.

[25] The Lesghians were one of the major groups of Caucasian tribes identified by 19th century ethnologists, along with the Circassians and the Chechens. The notion that they might be descended from the Kirghiz, although based on Mongoloid features resulting from the empire-building ventures of Genghiz Khan and Timur, is fanciful.

giving him her breast that he had heard that song, with its monotonous chorus, the words of which said:

"The Kirghiz is the master of the desert; to him belongs the extent, to him, from top to bottom, the domination. His horse bounds over the steppe, further on, ever further; he leaps over the highest mountains, ever higher, and he gallops forever and ever, launching himself higher, until, with his bit in his teeth, he touches the stars."

That was the song, conserved by his ancestors, which spoke of heroic epochs closed forever.

But why? In millions of years, can the sons of the Caucasus not recover their liberty? Russians, no! Conquered but not submissive, the Kirghiz, Caucasians and Kurds might, on the day they wished, re-conquer the empire of which the Caspian is the great sea.

More than ever—was it the effect of the beverage he had drunk?—those ideas of hectic battle against the Muscovite colossus took on substance in his mind. He felt himself carried away, as if destiny had placed a hand on his shoulder, crying out to him: "Forward!"

But at that moment, the simultaneously intelligent and aristocratic face of Sacha passed before his eyes. There was a kind of oscillation in his consciousness.

He remembered exquisite evenings in St. Petersburg, when luxury deployed all its seductions...the mountains, the steppes are certainly grandiose and limited horizons...but silk curtains illuminated by the gleam of electric flowers, the divine music of the great masters vibrating in that frame of silk and lace...white shoulders beneath the scintillation of diamonds...was there not an all-powerful magic in civilization?

At that moment, a bright light struck Sandorf's eyes.

He turned abruptly in the direction in which the source suddenly seemed to have been illuminated, and uttered an exclamation of surprise and admiration.

One might have thought that the wall had suddenly opened in front of him; in a vast bay solely closed by a kind of silvery gauze that allowed everything to be seen as clearly as through a sheet of rock crystal, Sandorf witnessed the deployment of a marvelous spectacle.

It was a temple, sustained by colonnades that were lost in a vault strewn with luminous tars, at the back of which was a golden altar, to which steps of marble or onyx led up, surmounted by flowers in sparkling colors, in the midst which stood a tall statue of an unknown substance which projected a radiance: a splendid idol in which all the seductions of the Orient were personified, an image of a woman raising her arms in a gesture of benediction, with slender hands articulating the sacred sign of the Hindus, with the middle and index fingers raised while the other three were folded over the palm.

The statue—was it really a statue?—seemed to be palpitating like living flesh, and one might have thought that a breath was emerging from its parted lips, murmuring the fateful syllable.

Songs burst forth, triumphantly, in a vocal purity that penetrated to the depths of the soul, causing the most intimate fibers of the organism to vibrate.

At the foot of the altar, men were standing in two rows—perhaps priests…or rather warriors, for they were all wearing golden helmets and breast-plates, their hands grasping swords whose points were directed upwards toward the idol.

And further back, under the pillars, in a profundity that was lost in limitless shadow, was a crowd clad in white, hands extended toward the altar.

On every step columns rose up, supporting exquisitely wrought cassolettes, veritable marvels of patient Hindu art, which exhaled delicious perfumes and vapors rising in spirals all the way to the vault of the temple.

Sandorf leaned forward, stupefied, but filled with a profound, almost su-perstitious emotion. He was unmoving, though, as if hypnotized, his will en-chained as if in a dream.

Suddenly, the chanting stopped. There was no longer anything but a soft murmur, like a susurrus, on closed lips.

The ranks parted; the tips of the swords, pointed toward the altar, came to-gether, forming a golden vault. And over the brightly-colored carpet, gliding ra-ther than walking, with her forehead circled in gold with a carbuncle in the cen-ter and her figure hidden beneath a long mantle of red and white linen, Sithreva appeared, admirably beautiful, with her marble pallor, her large eyes wide open and fixed upon the idol, her lips smiling as if in ecstasy, and her right hand part-ly raised with a freshly-blossomed lotus flower in her fingers.

She went straight toward the idol, and when she was no more than a meter away, she bowed, throwing the flower onto the steps of the altar.

She remained there for a few moments, motionless; then she slowly turned around and, facing the faithful, raised her arms and pronounced the fateful invo-cation:

Buddham saranam gacchami
Dhammam saranam gacchaml
Sangham saranam gacchami.

Which signifies, in the Pali language: "With Buddha as my guide I go; with the law as my guide I go; with the brotherhood as my guide I go."

They all repeated the lines, one by one, and when she had finished, the clouds of perfume rose more densely into the temple, enveloping her from head to toe and placing a kind of aureole around her head.

Sandorf, dazzled, nailed to the spot, did not take his eyes off her; the daughter of Tibet had never seemed more beautiful to him, and the mad love that he had conceived for her had never imposed itself more victoriously upon him.

She was speaking now; she did not employ the Chinese language, but a kind of Tamil, used in Ceylon, which almost all Orientals understand. Sandorf could speak that language, and he did not miss a single one of the words she pronounced in her vibrant and inspired voice, every echo of which penetrated into the utmost depths of his soul.

This is what she said:

"Orient, Orient, it is from you that everything comes; you are the source, you are the fountain of truth and light...

"In you, and from you the sunlight emerges, to spread over the world. Orient, you are life...and you are justice!

"It is in the bosom of your children, throughout eternity, that the fire has been lit that created science and conscience.

"Sons of the Tien-Ti, have you forgotten? Sons of the Wu-Wei-Keaon, sons of the Ko-Lao, have you abdicated?"

What did those strange names and those mysterious appeals mean? Before going any further, we ought to explain briefly.

For hundreds of years, secret societies have existed in China that bear the names Tien-Ti (Heaven and Earth), Wu-Wei-Keaon (White Lily) and Ko-Lao (Beloved Brother). These societies, whose origins are even more ancient than that of which Freemasonry is proud, in communication with all the mysterious associations of Hindustan, Tibet and the Caspian, count their affiliates in the thousands, perhaps—who can tell?—in the millions.

The crowd knows nothing about them; they are not known to one another; submissive to the authority of the group-leaders, they only know this: that a day will come when all the oppressions of Europe upon Asia will be broken.

The society of the Tien-Ti was the richest of them all; it is affirmed that one member of its council possesses fifty million francs.

In the Philippines, in Burma, in San Francisco and in Melbourne, in spite of the expulsion of the Chinese; in Hindustan, in spite of the persecutions on which the English have attempted, since the recent revolts, to base their tottering power; in Turkestan, where the leaven of revolt increasingly ferments since the trans-Caucasian and trans-Siberian railways have, in a sense, drawn a circle around old Asia; everywhere, the phrase circulated: "The Orient for the Orientals; death to the Europeans!"

Sometimes, a movement erupted at some point in immense Asia, Europeans were massacred, blood was shed, the murderers were ungraspable, and the reprisals fell upon the innocent; the Europeans thought they had stifled the sedition. On the contrary; their vengeance had only served to alienate new enemies. And thus the hatred of the races brooded everywhere, more ardent and cruel, until the day when they would burst forth in a cataclysm of such proportions that no one would have dared to imagine it.

The Tien-Ti had been founded—or, rather re-organized—in China in the middle of the seventeenth century, in the following circumstances.

In 1644 the Tartar Manchus had expelled the indigenous dynasty. Twenty years later, the Tartar Eleuths invaded China and conquered a large fraction of it. The Emperor made a desperate appeal to his subjects, and a Buddhist monk— Kuu-Tat or Hok-Kien, those two names being identical in Chinese and Pali, and signifying "Profound Root"—set himself at the head of his sectarians and drove out the invaders. But a traitor denounced Kuu-Tat as an aspirant to supreme power, and the ingrate Emperor put him to death; his monastery was burned and most of his closest associates perished, but five of them escaped and took refuge in a temple.

As they were walking along the bank of the river Sampo, they saw, floating in the water, and incense-burner which bore a sculpted inscription which they deciphered, and read: *Expel the Chang; restore the Ming.* The Buddhists then organized a vast conspiracy, and the battle was engaged. The society of the Tien-Ti had ramifications throughout the kingdom and the entire world; Hindus as well as the Chinese spread the word that the re-establishment of the Ming would be the signal for Asiatic domination of the entire world.

For two centuries, history registered Tai-Ping revolts, marked by horrible massacres and even more terrible reprisals. But that perseverance of more than two hundred and fifty years was finally about to attain the desired goal...

We have said that the Ming had resumed their place on the throne of the Middle Kingdom. Where the Europeans, always ignorant of the true instincts of the people they scorned, had only seen a change of dynasty, a palace revolution that was only of mediocre concern to their interests, the entire Oriental world had shuddered. It was the epoch fixed by destiny, by prophecy. It was the hour of Oriental revenge that was sounding.

All fanaticisms were ready to be unleashed at the first signal.

And that was what Sithreva, the inspired oracle of hatred and wrath, was saying to those men who had come from all parts of Asia to hear the fateful word that was about to unleash the old world of monsters and chimeras upon civilized and scientific Europe.

"Out of China, the Europeans!" cried Sithreva. "Out of India, the English! Out of Java, the Dutch, and out of Sumatra, Tonkin and Cambodia, the French! Out of the Caucasus and the Caspian lands, the Russians, Muscovites and Poles!

"Rise up, the Orient! From Peking to Baghdad, from Edo to Samarkand, from Aden to Tobolsk, from the Himalaya to the Ural, from the Pei-Ho to the Volga, let the immense flood rush, let the formidable inundation flow and engulf! In millions upon millions, let the sons of the Aurora drive the terrified Occidentals before them, like vile flocks, and precipitate them into the Atlantic, which was their cradle and shall be their tomb...and let the victorious standard of the five hundred gods extend over the fearful world, as black as night, as white as light, as yellow as gold, and as red as blood!"

At the moment that she named the four banners, men brandished them, fluttering, above Sithreva's head. In her exaltation, sublime with fury and a sort of religious rage, she seemed magnified and to be floating above the fanatics that her words were intoxicating.

Then she addressed each of the chiefs individually.

"King of the white Nenuphar," she cried, "are you ready?"

And an ascetic with emaciated features and sparkling eyes cried: "Death to the Occidentals!"

"And you, king of the Mendicants...you, the pariah who, as a tzigane, Bohemian, gypsy or zingari, has dragged you suffering through the cities and the fields of our enemies, are you ready?"

And the king of the Bohemians, the same one who had been seen only six months before in the heart of Paris, followed and acclaimed by the idlers, stood up and said: "I have sworn death!"

And all of them replied in the same fashion: the Lama of Homuch, the Fakir of Madras, the Buddhist monks, the Magi, the Brahmins, the Marabouts, the Great Dervish of Mecca and the Master of Fire, the Great Parsee of the Guebres, all, with a unanimous impulse, swore with their hands extended, brandishing swords.

With a gesture, Sithreva imposed silence upon them, and then, slowly, with an infinite softness in her voice, which had musical incantations, she said: "And who, then, will bring us the word of the Great Mountains, the oath of the Summits? Is the Caucasus alone cowardly? Lesghians, Kirghiz, Moguls, Kalmuks, Chenchens—is there no one who will reclaim the position as your head of the great Shamyl?[26] From the fortress of Ghunid, is there no longer a voice that will cry to the slaves of Russia their shame and their infamy?"

She had come down the steps of the altar, and solemnly headed toward the silvery veil that separated the hypnotized, maddened Sandorf from the temple.

When she got there, she lifted the veil and extended her hand to him.

In order to understand the strange and deadly process that was taking place in Sandorf's mind, it is necessary to remember that, as soon as he had been deposited on the sofa by his kidnappers, Sithreva had poured him a cup of liquor that he had raised to his lips and swallowed in a single draught.

---

[26] The Chechen Imam named Shamyl, Shamil or Schamyl (1797-1871), who led the resistance in the Northern Caucasus against the invading forces of the Russian Empire during the long Caucasian War, which resulted in a conclusive conquest in 1864, is also extensively celebrated in Hippolyte Mettais' *L'An 5865* (1865; tr, as *The Year 1865*, Black Coat Press, ISBN 9781612271002), a pioneering immersive fantasy in whose future history his descendants are credited with the liberation of the Caucasus from Russian rule and the founding of a successful nation.

It was the Aryan Soma, the liquor of the priests of Agni, which burns the breast and exalts thought, with multiplies energy tenfold and, like hashish, multiplies the passions a hundredfold.

And as Sithreva spoke, it seemed to the descendant of the Kirghiz that he heard voices resonating in his ears—better than that, in the utmost depths of his being—that had pieced him before: the songs of the woman who had nursed him, ancestral tales heard while he was still a child in the mountains.

It was true, however, that it was cowardice on his part and that of his brethren to have submitted and accepted Russian domination. Would they never shrug off that shameful yoke? Were they no longer free children of the glaciers, accustomed to roaming the precincts of the enormous Caucasus without masters?

Then a name had vibrated in his ear like a clarion call: Shamyl.

Was it, then, so distant, that memory of patriotism and heroism?

No—not even a century. It was in 1824 that the valiant Shamyl, imam and sultan of the mountain folk of the Caucasus, had engaged with his ally, the Mullah Kasi, a war to the death against the Russians. At Gimry, when the old fortress had fallen amid fire and blood, only the imam had escaped slavery, and had reached the steppes on his horse. Did no one any longer remember the victories of 1842, when Shamyl had invaded the land of the Avars, and Woronzoff had been obliged to retreat, and the Kabarda and Gerghebil fell into the power of the Caucasians? And still, although the Russians had crushed their enemy, he had escaped them, ungraspable, protected as if by a magical power...and then reappeared more ardent, more vigorous and more determined to fight.

In 1859, had Shamyl not entered into Tiflis as a victor? But treason lay in wait for him, and a year later, in the fortress of Ghunid, Shamyl, sold to his adversaries, launched this supreme imprecation: "The Russian Ogre will consume the world!"

And it was both the succession and the revenge of Shamyl that was being offered to Wintscheff—and in what conditions! With the aid of thousands of allies...

What did Europe matter to him? He was, he felt himself to be, a son of the Orient. He hated the civilized people who had corrupted and bastardized his soul...and his ears were ringing with the fanfares of battle.

The Kirghiz is the master of the desert; to him, from top to bottom, domination.

"Friend," Sithreva said to him, "are you ready? Do you want to give liberation to our superb hordes? Would you like to seize the scepter along with the sword? Would you like to be great, to be noble, to be a king?"

And Sandorf Wintscheff bent his knee before Sithreva and said to her: "Through life and through death I am yours...I love you."

And with a cry of triumph, she drew him into the temple.[27]

Let us return to the battle sustained inside the city by the Europeans. The attack, as we know, had been mounted simultaneously on the various Legations, which, in total, had no more than eight hundred men to defend them.

At the English Embassy, the battle had been fierce, but as the English maintain mostly naval forces, they had only kept a very limited number of soldiers in Peking—a hundred at the most—whom the populace had soon dispatched. The Ambassador had not wanted to abandon his post and as he too had invited guests to his palace to celebrate the first day of spring, a horrible massacre had taken place.

Men and women had been surrounded by fire and had perished in the flames. Lord Gordon had been seen, mounted on the highest terrace, brandishing the flag of his nation, before a sudden collapse had precipitated the nobleman and his unfortunate companions into the very heart of the fire.

Several ladies belonging to the highest aristocracy of the United Kingdom had found death in that catastrophe, which it seemed no one had escaped.

The German Legation, which, as we have said, affected only to entertain very frosty relations with the representatives of other countries, although warned of the revolt before it had reached the part of the city where it was located, had not taken any precaution of resist an attack that everything must have caused it to anticipate.

The *chargé d'affaires*, General Otto von Schuld, one of those defeated in the last French campaign, had remained an irreconcilable enemy of the French and Russians who had conquered his homeland. Respectable as patriotism might be, even among enemies, it can sometimes, in its excesses, lead to grave complications.

Von Schuld, informed that the French and Russian Legations had been attacked simultaneously, had forgotten the solidarity that ought to unite all Europeans in Oriental countries. The roads were open before him; he had more than a hundred and fifty men. It would have been natural for him to go to the aid of the embassies in danger, and perhaps, by attacking the Chinese from the rear, he would have greatly facilitated their defense. But his narrow and rancorous mind did not show him his duty in that light.

Let them defend themselves! he said to himself.

---

[27] Sithreva is by no means the first Oriental *femme fatale* featured in French popular fiction, but it is worth noting that similar characters became a staple of melodramas of this stripe; Sax Rohmer's Fu Manchu had a seductive daughter, and Ward supplemented the Fu Manchu series of books with another featuring the exotic *femme fatale* Sumuru.

78

And who knows whether, with the conviction that it was only them to whom the Chinese were enemies, he might have experienced a kind of malevolent joy in knowing that they were in peril.

However, when he saw the red light of the conflagration sparkle in the sky and envelop he city like a frightful shroud, when the formidable howls and jeers of the crowd, already gorged on blood, resounded at the gates of his Legation, he understood that he had emitted a grave imprudence with regard to his own interests.

In vain he tried to negotiate, declaring that whatever the grievances of the Chinese were, his nation at least was not involved in a conflict whose causes he did not even know. It was only when he heard the cry: "Death to the foreigners!" that he appreciated the full extent of the danger.

Perhaps he regretted his egotism then, but it was too late, and nothing any longer remained but to sell his life dearly.

At any rate, he put up a valiant defense; the buildings of the Legation, which had once been a Jesuit convent, were constructed in solid stone and did not lend themselves, like the others, to rapid destruction by fire.

The siege lasted five hours; the Germans were masterful in courage and tenacity, but what can valor do against numbers, against a crowd fanaticized by hatred and by successes already achieved?

The assault was mounted from all sides at once. Rather than surrender—and what would have been the point of a capitulation that the enemy would only have accepted in order to make it a means of treason?—Von Schuld set fire to the powder stored in the cellars of the Legation. There was a frightful explosion that made the old Chinese city shudder all the way to its foundations and killed several hundred Chinese along with the Germans who had survived the battle.

Strangely enough, by a sort of miracle, the Minister, who had remained at his post of honor, was the only one spared by the frightful blast, and it was certainly a bizarre scene to behold him standing, alone, on a section of wall whose collapse had bypassed him, still alive.

Either out of respect for his courage or by virtue of a kind of superstitious sentiment that showed him to them as an invulnerable being or one saved by the gods, the fanatics did not butcher him. He was captured, taken prisoner and disappeared, dragged away by the crowd to the gates of the Yellow City.

Scenes of atrocious savagery unfolded all over the city. All the houses occupied by Europeans had been identified long before and marked in advance for Chinese vengeance.

At the first signal, from the center to the most distant extremities of the Chinese city, all the way to Chiang-Tsu-Men and the Hai-Tien road, the unfortunate Europeans had been attacked unexpectedly, and for the most part, had not even had time to put up any defense. Some had been massacred in their beds, while others had been dragged onto the public highway and murdered with the most ignoble savagery.

Execution Square, in the Chinese city at the exit of the Tshun-Chih Gate, merited its terrible name that night; a hateful crowd filled it, seething and howling; at every moment its ranks opened before some unfortunate who was driven forward with blows of bamboo rods or dragged by the hair. Then the circle closed around him again and for several minutes, sometimes for a long quarter of an hour, madness and the application of torture were pushed to the point of frenzy.

Occasionally, a voice rose up, dominating the crowd, uttering a name: someone forgotten who was being identified to the fury of the wild beasts. Some of them broke away and ran to the designated place; entry was forced into the European's house, his wife and children were seized, half-naked and thrown as fodder to the untiring assassins.

By going along a narrow and obscure side-street that opens onto the right-hand side of the Passage of Bimbelotiers, one arrives at a little crossroads of about forty square meters, a kind of open courtyard, at the back of which, during the day, a shop is perceptible that would have seemed very ordinary to us, but which was genuinely exotic in the Middle Kingdom.

It is necessary to know that Chinese shops, like those which garnish both sides of the major roads, are wooden stalls similar to the temporary buildings that are established in fairgrounds, striped with red, green and yellow, ornamented with dragons or chimeras in carved wood, with streamers of a doubtful cleanliness and indescribable hue at the corners of the roofs. They are, in brief, establishments that the meanest tenant of the spiced-bread fair would not want.

The shop to which we are referring was brown in color, with gold threads heightened with red, but delicately drawn with a brush that was simultaneously skillful and distinguished. Two panes of glass framed a door, similarly glazed, on which the following inscription stood out in gold letters:

Eustache Nivet, Professor, Qualified Chemist and Photographer.

Chinese characters translated the marvelous inscription for the benefit of the profane, uninitiated into the finesse of the French language, and we can affirm that in the Chinese language, the photographer had emphasized his titles no less warmly.

Higher up, on a panel that extended across the entire width of the shop, a picture was displayed, a work of art due to some house-painter of the great city of Batignolles, which represented the following:

The sun, wearing a short jacket and coiffed in a bowler hat, arriving from one side, valise in hand, like a traveler getting off a train, while running from the opposite direction was a person wearing a pointed hat and a long beard: a typical art student of the 1830s, whose mouth, wide open, was allowing words to escape enveloped in a black ellipse: "Come on, then, my collaborator; we're only waiting for you."

This mystical painting, which, following the example of the hieroglyphs dear to occultists, presented a meaning that was simultaneously mysterious and practical, caused amazement to the worthy Chinese, who, holding the sun in great esteem, revered it all the more in the scarcely ordinary form of a belated commercial traveler.

Eustache Nivet, who had tired of Batignolles, had abandoned everything, including friends and fatherland, but he would have cut off his hand rather than not take with him that superb work, of which he had been the inspiration, and was for him a talisman.

To begin with, Eustache Nivet adapted very well to the Chinese climate and had no complaints about business. He had devised a system of double exposure that surrounded the photograph of a Chinese person with little angels—an innovation that, no one knew why, had had the greatest success and brought a clientele of amorous individuals to his door.

What, after all, did he want? To amass a dowry for Rose, whom he loved with all his heart, and, if possible, to reserve a few years of leisure during which he could pursue in depth certain researches in chemistry, of which he was very fond, and which were fairly closely related to the eternal quest for the philosopher's stone.

If he had employed the pretext of an indisposition to send his daughter to the Embassy on her own, it was with the sole aim of devoting himself, alone in his laboratory, to certain manipulations from which he expected marvels.

It would be necessary never to have been possessed by the demon of invention not to understand that, if a cannon had been fired close at hand, Nivet would not have paid the slightest attention to that circumstance, absolutely secondary as it would be for a mortal who is scrutinizing the arcane of nature.

Now, Nivet was scrutinizing; that much is undeniable. He had closed and bolted the shutter of his shop-front solidly, and had installed himself in a large room garnished with materials that would have made an alchemist's mouth water: retorts, alembics, furnaces, conical and round-bottomed flasks filled with various liquids; nothing was missing.

Nivet was a man of forty-some years, tall and commendably bald, his head being like a knee to which a narrow crown of hair served as a garter. He had a long nose, a broad mouth and overlapping teeth, plus two other physical characteristics—not to mention his moral qualities, the number of which surpassed his faculties of calculation—of which he was particularly proud.

First of all, he had a booming voice, something extra-human, tubal and trumpet-like. He flattered himself that he could crack a windowpane with a single burst of his throat—a talent useful to glazers but sometimes inconvenient in family life.

Then, the masterpiece, the marvel of marvels, was a long beard: one meter ten centimeters, not mentioning the millimeters, and so artistically shaped that it formed a point tapering almost as far as his knees, and so beautifully black!

When he was working, he threw it over his shoulder.

Such was the man—a worthy fellow, in sum, a trifle self-important, vain at times—who dreamed of transforming the world by means of marvelous inventions that he could not define very well to himself, but which he declared to be stupefying.

Having only received a very limited education, he had already succeeded in "inventing" things that had been known since Pythagoras, but that was of little importance to him; each discovery was only a step on the limitless road that he was following.

That night, the was on the point of making a compound that was nothing other than bicarbonate of soda, of which housewives have been making use for more than a hundred years, and he had not heard anything—neither the furious clamors of the assassins nor the sounds of explosions and beaten gongs.

He was tranquil; his daughter—the dear child—was having fun at the Embassy. He was quite alone, quite tranquil.

In Execution Square, however, a Chinese illuminator, to whom photography provided a disastrous competition, decided to cut it short by reminding the executioners that somewhere in the vicinity there was a Frenchman by the name of Nai-Vao, that being a Chinese onomatopoeia of the bourgeois name off Nivet.

A cry of joyful rage saluted this communication, and twenty of the bandits, armed with pikes, axes and other malevolent devices, had raced away, howling, to the little square of which we have spoken.

The Chinese, being only twenty against one, were prudent, all the more so because Nivet by virtue of his amicable liaison with the sun—and also his beard, which gave him the appearance of a lama—had contrived to inspire a kind of superstitious esteem in the brigands.

They believed him to be something of a magician—which did not alter the fact that he had to be killed, like all the rest; on the contrary.

Except that, after having consulted one another momentarily, the assailants decided to act with a certain precaution.

It was decided that the man would be drawn out of his home by friendly words; that would be safer than penetrating lightly into his lair, where a demon might come to his aid.

One of the Chinese, therefore—a big fellow who had served with European sailors and spoke a kind of Oriental pidgin, comprehensible even to a child of Batignolles, would go to the door and knock gently to begin with.

There was no reply; Nivet was supervising the cooking of some ingredient, an operation too close to his heart for him to pay any attention to trivial noises from outside.

He knocked louder, but as the silence persisted, it was decided to emphasize the blows, which became violent enough, as the saying has it, to wake the dead.

Nivet was very much alive. This time, he heard, and listened.

Who was that? He was not a physician to be woken up at such an hour. As for Rose, it had been agreed that she would stay the night with a friend, a French shopkeeper, who had been charged with taking her to the Embassy. It could not be her. Who was it, then?

The blows increased their force, and the bandits, in spite of their intentions, increasingly carried away by their wrath, became less effective in dissimulating their intentions.

Nivet had moved away from his furnace, and he leaned toward the door, listening.

The Chinese believed that they were talking in whispers, but in fact, a kind of furious growling escaped from their furious throats, which was not at all reassuring.

The Batignollais had only a very limited confidence in Chinese gentility; he too, for some time, had been noticing symptoms that had caused him some anxiety—to the extent that he had had a presentiment that, one day or another, there would be some kind of squabble.

One of the assailants, more imprudent that the others, launched a very explicit insult; another growled a threat.

"Well," murmured Nivet, "these people don't seem very friendly to me."

He went up a small staircase to an upper floor, where there was a kind of grain-loft.

At that moment, through one of the skylights that opened in the direction of the Tartar city, he perceived the reflection of the conflagration, and heard the rumor of the infuriated city.

With a gesture that was habitual to him when the situation took on a grave character, he tucked his beard under his arm. Then, resolutely, he advanced toward the other skylight overlooking the narrow square, which the twenty assassins filled almost entirely.

He leaned out.

"Who's there?" he asked, "And what do you want with me?"

He spoke Chinese with a suburban Parisian accent, of distinctly bizarre effect.

"Come down," shouted a voice, "We have to talk to you."

"Talk to me about what? I can hear you very well, tell me what you want. You know that I don't take photos at this hour."

"Are you coming down, swine?" howled one of them.

That made things much clearer—all the more so as Nivet, now entirely awakened from his transcendental meditations, could hear the frightful howls of the torturers who were killing people in Execution Square, and the victims that they were torturing.

Doubt was no longer possible; even though he could not take exact account of what was happening, they could only be abnormal and terrible events.

In a matter of seconds, Nivet, who was no fool, had made his plan.

Very mildly, he negotiated for a little while longer, explaining that he would like nothing better than to open the door to his good friends the Chinese, but that they would have to give him time to get dressed…five minutes…three minutes…a few more seconds…

The others, not very intelligent, were delighted with the success of their ruse. In a moment, Nivet/Nai-Vao would open the door, and just as he was stepping outside, they would grab him…and three minutes later, in Execution Square…

But the Batignollais photographer, who understood very well what was at stake, and was very fond of his life—which, according to him, was one of the most precious in the world—had not remained inactive.

He had gone to the back of the grain loft in quest of a kind of pump, similar to those that were used in the nineteenth century to water gardens, a copper cylinder equipped with a piston and a nozzle—except that the nozzle was rather long, about fifty centimeters, and terminated in a copper plate pierced with holes, the purpose of which was obviously to spread the water jet out into a fan over a perimeter of more than two meters.

While preparing the object, Nivet said in a loud voice: "My friends, my excellent friends, don't be impatient…here I am…I'm coming down…there…I'm ready."

The others extended their claws toward the door in order to grab him before he could put up a semblance of resistance.

He picked up a flask, filled a bucket with a colorless but singularly odorous liquid, and then let slip the remark, addressed to no one but himself: "Let's go, my Greek fire!"

The inventor reappeared under the photographer.

Suddenly, the Chinese felt themselves inundated by a liquid that rained down on their heads and shoulders.

They uttered cries of rage. Water! The imbecile had the pretention of driving them away with a cold shower! It was too stupid, in truth.

Deciding to finish it immediately, they hurled themselves at the door.

In order to proceed more rapidly, Nivet picked up the bucket and emptied it over his assailants in one go.

"Death to the Frenchman!" The cry trailed off into frightful lamentations.

This is what had happened:

Nivet had taken a little box out of his pocket, had taken out a dozen matches, had struck them—with a very Parisian gesture—on the back of his trousers, and then had dropped them on the assembled group.

Eustache Nivet's Greek fire was purely and simply the volatile liquid long known as mineral essence, luciline or other more or less elegant names,[28] en-

---

[28] In this context, "luciline" refers to a petroleum extract marketed by Alfred Guérard, who called his petrol refinery La Luciline because it manufactured

dowed with rapid inflammatory qualities. Right when one of the matches touched one of the points where the liquid had fallen, flames instantaneously sprang forth everywhere: on the garments, on the head, in the hair, on the skin…and so bitter, so mordant, eating away the flesh with such rapidity that the wretches, enveloped by flames, were writhing, throwing themselves on the ground, and rolling over, without being able to extinguish the terrible conflagration.

In the narrow space where they were confined, they collided with walls, crushing one another and jostling one another, falling and rebounding: a veritable demonic dance.

Very proud of the result of his chemical combinations and comparing himself secretly to the priests of Dodona who, as everyone knows, defended themselves against the Gauls with thunderbolts,[29] Nivet did not hang around to enjoy his triumph, for a terrible thought had just surged forth in his mind, suddenly illuminated by a poignant anxiety.

Rose! His dear Rose! If the order these wretches were following was "Death to the French!" there was no doubt that the first effects of their rage would have been exercised on the French Embassy.

A good patriot and an excellent father, Nivet did not hesitate. He ran to the far side of the grain loft and, opening the skylight, he looked down.

Behind the house there was a little garden adjacent to waste ground that extended as far as the Hai-Tai Gate. If he could escape, he would have reached the ancient rampart in less than a quarter of an hour, and the Legation would only be a short distance away.

"Come on, Latude!" cried Nivet.

He called by that name, famous for nearly a century and a half,[30] an engine of his invention that bore an unmistakable resemblance to a knotted rope, but the knots of which there were many, appeared to be tightened in an entirely new fashion that would have amazed the most cunning of our mariners. In addition, it was equipped with a hook—another new and very ingenious invention—that permitted it to be suspended from the windowsill. While, on the other side of the

---

lamp oil. It was not sufficiently refined to contain a single organic compound—hence such vague terms as "mineral essence"—but consisted mostly of ethanes like the butane used in modern cigarette lighters.

[29] Dodona was the site of a famous oracle in Greece, originally devoted to a mother goddess who was supplanted by Zeus (hence the defensive thunderbolts). How the Gauls got into the story in Nivet's version is anyone's guess.

[30] Jean-Henri Latude (1725-1805) was imprisoned in the Bastille after stupidly offending Madame de Pompadour, and became famous for his escapes from that prison and others; after the Revolution the Convention ordered that he be paid compensation for his tribulations by his persecutor's family, and he was able to die rich as well as legendary.

house, the wretched Chinese were howling, writhing and fleeing, Nivet let himself slide into the void.

In a few seconds he had reached the ground, and without further reflection, he launched himself across the empty space and reached the gate. Fortunately, the crowd was busy elsewhere, and the few people who were there gave no thought to stopping the man who went past them with the rapidity of an arrow.

As he turned the corner of the old wall, he saw, a few paces away, an old monk who was in a hurry, doubtless going to spread the word of death far and wide. He had a long beard that gave Nivet an idea, and he was wearing a long kaftan that enveloped him entirely, with a sort of miter on his head.

The place was deserted—and he had little choice in the matter of means.

Nivet recalled the good old days when he had played as a boy in the Place de Clichy and engaged in friendly wrestling matches with his comrades. He still remembered a certain kind of throw that, with his usual industriousness, he had perfected. He hurled himself upon the servant of Kong-Fu-Tseu—otherwise known as Confucius—and administered a blow of the fist to the back of the neck at the same time as he took the legs from under his adversary with a skillful thrust of his foot, which laid the monk out flat.

Stripping off the cloak and hat took but a moment, and without apologizing, while the monk, completely stunned, was wondering what devil had just fallen on his skull, Nivet fled.

It was as well that he had thought of effecting that transformation; without it, he would not have gotten ten paces further. Scarcely had he found himself on the main road leading to the French Legation when he was caught up in the turbulent flux of assailants running in all directions. Fortunately, his costume and his beard, which were entirely appropriate to the situation, granted him free passage everywhere.

He drew nearer to the Legation, and now the poor man was prey to inexpressible anguish. Everything was ablaze, everywhere there were cries of agony and despair.

Suddenly, there was an enormous surge.

The gate of the main courtyard had just opened, and all the soldiers that had not yet succumbed, with Albert de Mesnes at their head and the injured ambassador, laid on a stretcher, in the middle, along with a few women who were being carried, ran out, launching vigorous gunfire into the road that had just opened up.

The Chinese rushed them, but our soldiers were armed with repeating rifles. The Chinese fell, and it was necessary to advance by marching over their cadavers.

It was, however, also necessary to fear that the ammunition would run out, or that the ever-increasing crowd might succeed by the sheer weight of numbers in overwhelming a handful of valiant men already exhausted by long efforts, for whom discouragement would almost have been permissible.

Fortunately, at the moment when the situation of the French was about to become critical, and when Nivet was regretting not being able to play in Chinese the priestly role of an appeaser of discords, he suddenly heard a volley of bullets whistle past his ears, while vibrant trumpets resounded with an ear-splitting blast.

It was the Russians, running to join up with the French—and Nivet's tall stature was serving them as a target at which to aim.

He scarcely had time to throw himself flat, face down—a position that presented serious inconveniences for a few moments, because the surprised Chinese were seized, for the most part, by an indescribable panic, and started fleeing, treading on his body as they went.

The French, roused by Albert de Mesnes' cries of "Forward," took advantage of the unexpected respite to contrive a gap, and succeeded in joining up with the Russians.

The leaders of the two troops exchanged a few rapid words. It was obvious that resistance was impossible in the Legations, as they were poorly constructed to resist a siege. It was necessary, as soon as possible, to identify and reach a point where they could regroup and take the decisive measures that the situation demanded.

Suddenly, Nivet, who had slid forward on all fours, stood up between the two leaders.

"Swine!" cried the Russian, raising his saber.

"I'm French—don't be stupid! It's me, Nivet, the inventor, the successor of Archimedes!!"

That name was known throughout the French colony, somewhat as an item of ridicule—but it was not a moment for equivocation.

"What are you doing here?"

"I've come to give you an idea of genius. The Yamen—the Chinese Ministry of Foreign Affairs—is a short distance away. There are never any troops there. Take possession of it; it's a veritable fortress."

"The man's right and the advice is sound," said Albert.

The Russian immediately acquiesced, and the order was given to head for the Yamen.

In good order, holding off the attackers, who were gradually recovering from their terror and reforming more menacingly, the two small Russian and French contingents beat a retreat in the required direction.

The crowd did not understand the movement; they thought that the foreigners were heading for the canal in order to embark, and rushed in that direction in order to cut them off. That error was, at least for the moment, the salvation of the Europeans. They reached the Yamen, which was only protected by an insignificant guard-post. In a matter of seconds the doors were forced and the French and Russians found themselves sheltered in a vast stone building, which did, indeed, constitute a veritable fortress, and which possessed the further advantage of being adjacent to the Catholic Mission, another monumental and solid building.

It was a temporary respite, of which they took advantage to fortify the position.

The engineer Sametel, who had death in his heart because he did not know what had become of his daughter, and had every reason to think that she had been massacred, nevertheless did not fail in his duty for an instant.

Curiously enough, the Chinese, as imprudent as all Orientals, had evacuated the Yamen completely, and the a few subaltern employees that remained were put in a safe place. The Minister was with the Emperor, in the Council where the massacres had been decreed.

The Yamen was indeed a fortified location, equipped with cannon, and also with an electrical network, which, although international communications had been severed, was at least functioning internally and could be usefully employed for the artillery.

Nivet, asking in vain for news of his daughter, had begun sobbing when he learned what everyone believed to be the absolute truth—which is to say, the death of the majority of the women, young and old, who had been in the Embassy. On hearing the scientist Sametel giving orders and disposing of electric detonators, he suddenly felt gripped once again by the demon of invention. As timidity had never been one of his faults, he approached Sametel deliberately, and demanded to talk to him.

It must be admitted that the moment was ill-chosen, especially when one thinks of the almost comical reputation that the photographer had acquired by his vainglorious pretentions, so Sametel initially told him, rather harshly, to go away—but Nivet was tenacious, and by force of importunity, he succeeded in dragging the engineer into a corner and whispering a few words in his ear.

At first, the engineer shrugged his shoulders, but then suddenly became still, listening. He had suffered often enough from the intolerance of others realizing that there is sometimes something useful to be found even in the ideas of a lunatic. And it appeared that Nivet's communications were not without interest.

Suddenly, Sametel seized his arm.

"Your idea is insane," he said abruptly, "but we don't have any choice. Do you know how deep the network you're talking about is located?"

"I confess that in matters of detail," Nivet stammered, who, like all semi-scientists, was ignorant of most of the elements of the question that he pretended to know in depth, "I'm not fully informed."

"It doesn't matter—we'll have to try. I'll give you ten men who'll dig a trench at the point I'll indicate to you. But I have to ask for your word of honor to follow my orders."

The worthy Nivet, who still had a very heavy heart in thinking about Rosette, said, gravely: "Monsieur, I know that, compared to you, I'm ignorant. Give your orders, and I'll carry them out."

"Good. I order you, them, to press the workmen, and encourage them…but don't do anything else. Don't attempt an imprudent and premature application of an idea that might, after all, bring grave dangers in its wake."

Nivet felt rather proud of the responsibility that was about to weigh upon him. "I'll obey," he said, in a tone full of dignity.

While he drew away with the soldiers who were to serve as ditch-diggers, Sametel went back to Albert de Mesnes, and the two of them went to the French Ambassador, still lying on his stretcher, whose features were agonized.

The surgeon had attempted everything indicated by his science, in vain. The representative of France was mortally wounded, but as the two men advanced toward him, he made a vigorous effort, and succeeded in propping himself up.

"Above all, no recklessness!" exclaimed the surgeon.

"Yes, yes, I know," said the Ambassador. "Well, Messieurs—or rather, my dear friends—I've been waiting for you impatiently."

"I've been obliged," said Sametel, "in association with Monsieur de Mesnes, to take all the measures suggested by the horrible danger we're in."

"And you've done well. It's to you, and you alone, that I leave the frightful mission that death will prevent me from accomplishing."

"Death is not yet here."

"What's the point of trying to deceive me?" said the Ambassador, shaking his head. "You know as well as I do that I'm finished, and that my life is only a question of hours, perhaps minutes." As they all tried to protest, he stopped them with a gesture. "Who do you think you're talking to? Here, I represent France, and no mission has ever given me the right to be prouder, but I also know the duty that is imposed on me. Here, a thousand leagues from the fatherland, I am and must be a soldier: not a man who fights with a weapon in hand, but a man who must carry out his obligations with an impassive heart, until death. Well, Messieurs, in your amity, you'll become accomplice to a fault if, by virtue of a fault common—alas!—to many dying men, I gave any credence to your words of consolation. I know that I'm dying; I repeat it to you because it's the truth, and a worthy man does not lie. Dare you contradict me, Doctor?"

The surgeon looked away.

"Thank you," said the Ambassador. "That's the gesture I expected, which dictates my supreme duty to me."

"At least don't exhaust yourself—conserve your remaining strength."

"Oh, I also know that I still have some vigor at my service; I'll prove that to you shortly. And to obey you, to conserve the energy I need for as long as possible, I'm going to talk to you in a low voice. Come closer."

The three men obeyed. In truth, they were paler than the moribund.

"Help me to sit up…that's it! Now listen to me, and remember that what you're about to hear are the supreme orders of the man who speaks in the name of France—and that, no matter what, you must obey me."

"Count on us, Monsieur. We'll obey."

"I am counting on it. So, it's to you, Monsieur Sametel, and you, Monsieur de Mesnes, that I delegate all my powers. It's a matter to taking the gravest resolutions, without hesitation; in order to save the French—the Europeans, for France is the fatherland of all fatherlands—there is no sacrifice before which you ought to recoil. I'm not talking about your lives; I know you won't bargain with them, but it might be that you'll have to risk even more. Some eventuality might be produced that will oblige you to forget all personal sentiment, all pity for yourselves or those dear to you. Accept the sacrifice, whatever it might be, and for the salvation of others, if it's necessary for you to surrender a shred of your flesh, or, which will be more horrible, the flesh of someone else, someone you love..."

Sametel interrupted him. "We understand. Yes, you're right; at this moment, there are those among us to whose patriotic anguish is added the torture of intimate despair...don't worry. If you have to die, go in peace; not one of us will fail in his task."

"I don't doubt you, my friends...and in the dolor in which I'm quitting the combat post, it's a consolation to me to leave in my place men like you. So, everything for France and for humankind...let that be your motto. But that's not all. Come closer I beg you."

It did indeed seem that his voice was weakening—but his eyes were shining with a metallic gleam.

"Monsieur Sametel, how long do you think the Yamen can be defended?"

"Even against the hordes of wretches who are going to come at us, I'm counting on five or six hours."

"Oh, that's more than enough. Now, Messieurs, understand that this is an order: "I want to go to the Imperial Palace."

A triple explanation responded to that statement, so strange that, in truth, they were wondering whether the man who had proffered it was still in his right mind.

As they looked at him I amazement, he relayed: "I'm not mad. I want to go to where my place is. Am I not the Ambassador, the man who has the right, in the name of his country, to talk to sovereigns face to face, who has the duty to remind assassins, even if they are crowned, that crime is all the greater when one has the power to oppose it? Yes, yes, I want to go to that man. I want to tell him, in the presence of his ministers and his slaves, that no potentate, despot or Son of Heaven can violate with impunity the sacred rules of justice, and if I have to fall down dead in front of that man, at least I want my dying breath to be one last protest in the name of France and humankind."

"But you know full well," exclaimed the surgeon, "that to make such an effort is to break the last link attaching you to life."

The Ambassador held out his hand.

"Remember, Messieurs, that you have sworn an oath. Is it having pity on humankind to have pity on one man? You don't understand, then, that I might—who knows?—be able to stop the massacre. The voice of France can be heard. Come on, Messieurs—to hesitate to obey me would be to deny your word of honor."

The three men looked at one another. Evidently, it was madness to attempt the impossible...and it would further abridge that life already condemned...but the Ambassador was right. A representative of France could not recoil before anything, before any consideration; when duty speaks, France has the right to heroic madness.

"But how do you expect to get as far as the palace?" asked Sametel.

"You can't even stand up," the doctor added.

"I'll be carried. I need to get as far as the threshold of the room where the chief of the torturers is sitting." In a firmer voice, he said: "Monsieur de Mesnes, you have the command of your troops here. Monsieur Sametel, you're in charge of the technical aspects of the resistance. Your places are here, and I order you to remain here."

"But what about you?"

"Me!" said the Ambassador, in a voice that was still strong. "You'll place me in the middle of forty of our marine soldiers, with the flag at the head, and they'll have orders to open a way in order to obtain passage for my stretcher."

At that moment, Nivet appeared, red-faced, his features convulsed. He was oblivious to any orders.

"What do you want?" shouted Sametel, angrily. "Get out!"

"Wait!" cried the photographer. "Listen to what I have to say. I've found the subterranean passage that I'd heard about."

"And where does it go?"

"To the Imperial Palace!"

The Ambassador uttered a cry: "You see!"

"But once again," said Sametel, still angry, "how does he know what he's saying?"

"I got it from an employee of the Yamen whose tongue I loosened with my boot. You know what I told you, Monsieur Sametel—that I'd noticed that when the electric beacon on the Yamen was switched on, a beam of light immediately emerged from the summit of the Imperial Palace...so a communication had to exist. And it occurred to me that perhaps we might even be able to blow up the Imperial Palace from here. But it's much better than an electric wire...there's a vast network of subterranean tunnels."

"Well, Messieurs," said the Ambassador. "You were asking how you were going to get me to the palace. This brave man has resolved the problem. Now, don't waste time—I'm in a hurry to do my duty." And he added, in a whisper: "And to have the right to die."

There was no reason to hesitate—and after all, was it not a chance of salvation? Who could tell whether that magnanimous temerity might not change the face of things? Perhaps the Emperor of China was human.

Sametel hastened to give orders. Four men would carry the stretcher, while marine fusiliers accompanied them, ready to open a path by force.

In truth, it was going to certain death, but no one thought about that.

In a few minutes, everything was ready.

The functionary who had given the information to Nivet—whose methods of persuasion had made a particular impact on him—was instructed to place himself at the head of the little cortege, between the soldiers, to whom the order was given loudly to shoot him at the first suspicion of treason.

The photographer insisted on serving as one of the stretcher-bearers—a favor that, in truth, could not be refused to him.

Sametel thought it his duty, however, to remind him that he was a father.

"Don't I know it!" cried the poor man. "Haven't those wretches killed my beloved Rosette?"

Sametel turned his head away, for he too had a tortuous anguish in the depths of his heart.

The route that the Ambassador had to follow passed under the Tartar city and ought to come out somewhere in the imperial gardens. A surprise was, however, possible.

"If any misfortune occurs," said Albert de Mesnes, "how can we be notified in order to send help?"

"See these telegraphic wires?" said Nivet, pointing to the black cables that ran along the wall, illuminated by the torches. "I'll find a way."

"All right," said Sametel. "In any case, our task is commencing here."

Indeed, furious destinations were audible above, as the attack recommenced, more ferociously than ever.

The Ambassador, propped up on his pillows, said: "Remember, Messieurs—and adieu!"

"We'll see one another again."

"Who knows?"

And the cortege moved off into the tunnel, while Sametel and Albert ran to help the Europeans under attack.

The Russians and the French were a single company, acting with admirable unison.

Thanks to the cannons abandoned by the Chinese, they succeeded in keeping the horde at bay, and had succeeded in saving a number of Europeans who had run to the Yamen in search of refuge.

The Russians were commanded by an old Cossack general with a fearsome moustache, courageous to the point of folly. His name was General Butowieff.

As he knew the city well, having lived there for many years, he was the one who had succeeded in rapidly establishing communication with the canal;

the gardens of the Yamen almost extended as far as the wall, and it had been possible to take possession of the gate almost without firing a shot. That ensured a retreat for the women, children and anyone not in a fit condition to bear arms. Fortunately, barges with decks had been numerous, and hundreds of Europeans, belonging to all the nationalities represented in Peking, had already found refuge aboard the ironclad *Suffren*, moored at the opening to the Pei-Ho.

But was that salvation?

VIII

Meanwhile, the two young women, Marguerite Sametel and Rose Nivet, guided by the sailor Kroarec, were hastening through the vast gardens of the Yamen, unfortunately designed as a labyrinth, in accordance with the Chinese mania, so effectively that in order to cover a distance of perhaps two kilometers, the walkers, having been obliged to retrace their steps ten times, had traveled nearly two leagues, and a considerable time had elapsed when they reached the buildings.

And what anguish did Marguerite and Rose not suffer when they heard the clatter of the artillery and the clamors of the assailants!

By then the glare of the conflagration had become so intense, and lit up the sky so broadly, that it was veritably as clear as daylight. Fugitives were flocking through the grounds, running at top speed in a desperate attempt to reach the canal, where there was at least a hope of finding shelter. Kroarec had difficulty opening a passage, because the unfortunates, recognizing him as a French sailor, hurled themselves upon him, surrounding him, seizing his garments, imploring him as if he could save them simply by a act of will.

It was necessary for Marguerite Sametel to name herself in order to protect him and free him—and it is even fair to say that as soon as she pronounced her name, the ranks parted in front of her.

Was her father still alive, at least? No one could give her an answer. At that moment, General Butowieff was in command. No one knew anything more, except that the battle was becoming impossible, as more than fifty thousand Chinese were storming the Yamen, in which a handful of men could not hold out much longer.

"My God!" Marguerite sobbed, dragging her companion along more rapidly. "Has my poor father been killed?"

Finally, she uttered a cry of joy: she had just perceived Albert de Mesnes, bareheaded, his clothes covered in blood, sword in hand, urging the soldiers forward yet again.

She ran to him.

"My father?" she cried.

"Ah! There you are, Mademoiselle!" exclaimed the young man. "Safe and sound. What a joy for your father…come, quickly."

And, seizing her by the hand, he drew her inside the palace.

"My father's alive!" Marguerite cried, joyfully. "But my happiness mustn't make me selfish. Rose, come with me."

"Who's the girl?" demanded Albert.

"The daughter of a French photographer..."

"Nivet?"

"You know Papa?" said the girl, charmingly.

"A brave patriot who's already rendered us a great service."

"He must have invented something—but where is he?"

"He left with the Ambassador for the Imperial Palace."

At first sight, that explanation did not present any terrifying character, and Rose dared not ask for further elaboration.

Kroarec, leaning toward her ear, said to her quietly: "Don't worry, Mademoiselle—I'll get the details." She addressed one of her finest smiles to him—which appeared to give the brave fellow a sense of appreciation.

Sametel was in the midst of the officers, giving orders. Suddenly, he perceived his daughter, and there was a sudden explosion of joy in his fatherly heart. He ran to her and threw his arms around her.

"You! You, my child! Oh, if you knew what terrors I've endured!"

"Me, too, Father. Fortunately, here we are, together—and this time not to be parted again, whatever fate awaits us."

Sametel shook his head.

"The resistance is reaching its end," he said. "What will become of us?" He turned to the French and Russia officers. "So, Messieurs—your conclusions?"

"The same opinion as General Butowieff. Within half an hour, the Yamen will be invaded. We're running out of ammunition, and more than a third of our men are dead or wounded."

"And yet," said Sametel, "we can't surrender the location until we know what's happened to the Ambassador. It's already more than an hour since he left. Has he even been able to get as far as the Emperor? Those wretches are capable of any treason."

"At that moment, a flourish burst forth outside so sonorous and so shrill that it even drowned out the din of the artillery.

"What's that?" demanded Sametel.

At the same moment, General Butowieff came in. "Monsieur," he said to Sametel, in a tone pierced by a strange embarrassment, "Negotiators have presented themselves at the doors of the Yamen."

"How many are there?"

"As negotiators, only three...and one of them..." He did not finish, as if the words he had been about to pronounce cost him too dearly. But he added: "Behind them is a crowd of several thousand men, who'll flood into the Yamen as soon as the doors are open.

"In that case, it's necessary to talk to them from the height of the gallery surrounding the Yamen. Don't you agree?"

"It's the only prudent course to adopt."

"Let's go, then, Messieurs. Monsieur de Mesnes, it's to you that the representative of France had confided the flag. Come on—and whatever fate is reserved for us, let everyone know, at least, that the Russians and the French, united once again, can look it in the face."

Immediately, they headed for the ramparts.

Marguerite and Rose hid behind the row of anxious officers.

In the large square that extended in front of the Yamen, the spectacle was magical. A multicolored crowd, noisy to the extent of howling, was huddled beneath the red light of the sky, which detached silhouettes and illuminated the bright hues of their garments. But more than that: the crowd had suddenly opened up, and through the middle of it a cortege of monks and warriors had advanced, sparkling with steel and dazzling tints.

A phrase ran over all lips, pronounced with a double emphasis of dread and veneration: "The Tien-Ti."

For a long time, the people had known about that secret association, the power of which, multiplied a hundred times by the mystery surrounding it, assumed colossal proportions.

They were all there: all the men we saw a short while ago in the Temple, swearing an oath of hatred and extermination against Europe.

And in the first row there were three individuals:

A man dressed in a long white tunic, coiffed with the Persian tiara of the Magi, servants of Zoroaster.

To his right side, Sithreva, impassive in her hieratic rigidity as a priestess, rendered more beautiful still by the fiery reflection that illuminated the antique regularity of her features.

On his other side...there was another man, of tall stature, dressed in the steel armor of the Circassians, a helmet on his head and a chainmail gorget falling over his shoulders, his face almost hidden by his visor, the three holes of which allowed his crazed eyes to be seen.

That was the one that General Butowieff had not wanted to recognize or name: Alexandroff Wintscheff, traitor and renegade.

Meanwhile, Robert Sametel, with Albert de Mesnes on one side, carrying the French flag, and the Russian general on the other, next to whom an officer was deploying the Muscovite flag, had advanced onto the rampart. On his order, the French bugles had replied to the Chinese trumpets that had launched the appeal for negotiations into the air, and repeated three times.

Robert Sametel spoke fluent Chinese.

"Who are you and what do you want?" he demanded. "Having attacked us in cowardly fashion, have you come to offer your repentance and bring us the first reparations to which we have a right?"

The monk raised his hand.

A deathly silence descended upon the square.

"Foreigners," he said, in a deep voice, so vibrant that it could be heard in every corner of the vast square, "to what treason do you refer? Who, then, has come to invade our country, to wrench us out of the profound peace that has been ours for centuries, to insult our mores, our customs, and our gods? Who, then, has brought the accursed sciences that are nothing but sources of pride and ruination? You and you alone.

"If, on the contrary, we, the Sons of Heaven, the subjects of the only and true master of the world, have wanted to take our place in the lands that our emperors have condescended to yield to you as a privilege, you have expelled us, pursued us, tortured us. You are the enemies, you are the accursed...

"And after having worn away magnanimity to the ultimate limits, we have come to tell you: the time of forbearance is past. The Sons of Heaven refuse to tolerate your insolent vanities and ruinous fantasies any longer. Out of China, Occidentals, out of our territory, barbarians! And listen to that which has been written by the one who is the Light of Worlds..."

All these words had been pronounced in a strong voice, in a rhythmic cadence, in a bizarre and gripping chant. He had unrolled a long strip of yellow silk, one with characters traced in bright vermilion.

"The Son of Heaven," he read, "whose all-powerful hand has fallen upon the culpable, says: To the barbarians, one sole path is still open to salvation, and that is the path of submission. Thus, on the reading of this inscription, marked by our seal, which is the word of Heaven, the barbarians, belonging to the nations of Europe, will place themselves in our hands as prisoners in order, on their knees, to implore our magnanimous pity; they will immediately surrender all their arms, their flags, and their archives.

"At this price alone, the mercy of their lives will be granted.

"If not, the veil of death will be extended over them, and the great Emperor, Han Ming, will go to their capitals to impose his will, which no human power can alter or deflect.

"Thus said by us, Sons of Heaven, representing the Great Dragon and Master of Worlds. Let everyone bow down!"

And at the moment the voice of the monk died away, the thousands of Chinese who were there bowed down, almost touching the ground with their foreheads.

Then the shrill commotion resounded once again.

Sametel had listened with his arms folded and his head held high. When the blasts of the brass instruments had subsided, he spoke, in a voice in which tones of profound indignation resounded.

"Man," he said, "is it true that your master has sent you to bear such insolent words as those you have uttered? By the most cowardly of crimes, the subjects of the Son of Heaven have massacred the Europeans, thus covering themselves with a shame whose memory will never be extinguished. And when you still have the blood of so many innocent victims on our hands, you dare to come to dictate conditions to us that would be odious if they were not insane.

"To surrender ourselves, to lay down our arms, dishonor our flags, which no shame has ever soiled! That is what you dare to demand? Man, go tell your master that, though your miserable torturers tear our bodies into shreds, not one of us will bow down before him. From this day forward, he is at odds with civilized nations; he is the barbarian that will be scorned and chastised. We might all die, but let him remember that beyond the deserts that form a wall for him, there are nations that are able to avenge murders, and inflict a punishment on him so terrible that all trace of him will be effaced from the earth.

"Man, have you nothing more to say to us? In the name of humanity, in the name of human rights, in the name of the eternal principles of Justice, I beseech you to return to the one who sent you and report my words to him...and let him know that every drop of blood shed will be paid for a hundred times over..."

"Is that your final word, Foreigner?"

"That is my final word."

"Well, to your insolence, this is the response of the Son of Heaven."

The monk made a gesture. A man clad in red advanced, holding a severed head by the hair, and threw it against the wall of the Yamen.

A cry of horror and anguish escaped all the European throats. The head was that of the French Ambassador.

"Fire! Fire on these wretches!" cried Sametel.

And from all parts of the rampart, a fusillade burst forth, cutting through the filthy crowd of torturers and assassins who no longer had the right to call themselves human.

At the same moment, Sithreva, drawing herself up to her full height, uttered a cry of war and hatred, and all the bandits rushed the walls, hooking their fingernails and grinding their teeth: a veritably demonic attack.

"At least," shouted General Butowieff, "the traitor will be punished first!"

And with a prodigious bound, the old Cossack launched himself to the foot of the wall, and sword held high, ran at Sandorf, who had not pronounced a single word during the long scene, or even motioned a gesture.

Before the brave Russian could reach Wintschcff, however, the crowd closed round him. He could still be seen for a few moments, towering over his assailants by virtue of his colossal height, striking and killing, but then he fell, and the wretches tore him apart with savage cries.

As for Sandorf, Sithreva had taken him by the arm—and the negotiators had disappeared as if the ground had swallowed them up.

The work of slaughter recommenced...but this time, without hope.

"Russians and Frenchmen," cried Sametel, "Are you ready to die rather than surrender?"

"Yes! Yes!" cried all voices.

"Well then, use every last cartridge and charge! Then I shall be able to do my duty."

Marguerite had also recognized Sandorf. At first she had thought he was a prisoner, but she had quickly observed the more-than-strange attitude of the Russian officer; with her feminine intuition she had divined that he was under the absolute control of the exceedingly beautiful woman whose fanaticism had a character that was both grandiose and terrifying.

But Sacha? What had become of Sacha?

She asked the question, but no one was able to give her an answer. She had fled with her brother André, and no one had seen her thereafter. She was doubtless dead.

And Rose, sobbing, said to her: "As my father is dead. My poor father, so good..."

"Not yet," said a voice behind her.

She turned around swiftly. Nivet was there, laughing and weeping at the same time...taking her in his arms...kissing her with eager lips.

An innate temperament immediately regained the upper hand: "One doesn't kill a Nivet as easily as that," he said. "When I saw that it had gone bad, I made myself scarce, without being noticed...and here I am. But that's not all. I've brought my invention. Where's Monsieur Sametel?"

"Here I am, my friend," said the engineer, whose face was horribly pale—for he understood that the minutes were counted, and that he was about to be required to put his own hand to the powder-keg that would save the honor of the flag, burying all its defenders in its folds—and with them, his daughter. "Tell me what happened."

The story was brief. They had gotten into the palace and reached the room where the Council was sitting, under the presidency of the Emperor. Immediately, however, all the men had been seized and dragged before the Son of Heaven, who had demanded that the French Ambassador offer his submission, in the name of his country.

What Sametel had replied a little while before were the same words that the representative of France had pronounced. He too, in the name of justice and civilization, had reproached the crowned executioner for his crimes—who, mad with rage, had struck him with his own scimitar. The others—the great dignitaries and Ministers—had finished the work, falling upon the injured man, who was soon a cadaver.

It was at the moment when their rage was at its paroxysm that Nivet had been able to slip away.

"But Monsieur Sametel, I've brought you a means, if not of saving everyone, at least of creating a diversion of which we can take advantage."

"Speak, quickly."

There are people over whom the comical never loses its rights. Nivet struck a dramatic pose in order to speak, rounding out his punctuation to the point that Sametel, seething with impatience, spoke a little rudely to him.

And yet, it was true that he had brought an idea of genius.

While traveling through the tunnel that led from the Yamen to the Imperial Palace, he had come across vast bunkers full of powder, dynamite and explosive engines. The idea had occurred to him to detach two of the electric wires that communicated with the Yamen and wind them together, and then he had put them in contact with a powder barrel.

"You understand, Monsieur Sametel. Connect them here to a powerful battery...and the powder will catch fire, and the dynamite will explode, and the Imperial Palace will blow up...and during the confusion..."

"Yes, yes!" cried Sametel. "Nivet, you're a brave man, and I thank you in the name of France. To work! To work!"

In an instant, the piles were ready.

"Hold hard!" shouted Sametel to Albert de Mesnes, who was running back and forth, facing up to the enemy on all sides. Fortunately, not one of the assailants had yet been able to force an entrance into the Yamen.

And Sametel, aided by Nivet, brought the electric batteries into play.

A frightful detonation ripped through the air. At the same time, a column of fire rose up. In the crowd, there was a formidable clamor.

The ground shook, as if in an earthquake.

The Imperial Palace had just blown up.

At the same time, the walls of the Yamen collapsed,

In that catastrophe, the furious attack gave the Europeans a moment's respite.

Sametel and de Mesnes rallied their men, and the decimated troop, in the midst of which Marguerite and Rose were marching hand in hand, beat a retreat toward the canal.

Honor was saved, and the French flag had not been soiled.

PART TWO

THE BARBARIAN INVASION

I

Let us return to Paris.

You have not forgotten the emotion, the despair, and the terror experienced by Guy de Norès at the moment when, returning to his laboratory after a brief absence motivated by Admiral Trécourt's visit, he had seen the aviation apparatus, the enormous power of which was well known to him, projected through the roof and plunging into the atmospheric depths of the sky, carrying away his sister and Dr. Sabirat.

At first he remained motionless, as if thunderstruck.

That accident—that catastrophe—adding to the one that his experiments at the Sorbonne had revealed to him, and which the admiral had confirmed, troubled the young man's reason momentarily, to the point at which he fled, running, and shouting for help.

His mother had come in response to his cries. At first, she did not understand; she thought that her son, overexerted by incessant work, had fallen prey to a fit of fever.

When he recovered his composure, he explained. To be sure, the poor woman could not understand what the formidable apparatus might be that had been able to carry two living beings into space like that, but she knew her son's genius too well to doubt the reality of a fact whose strangeness did not, in sum, surpass that of the revelation she had witnessed a little while before.

Both of then returned to the laboratory, and the hole in the ceiling left no doubt as to the reality of the accident.

"My God!" cried Madame de Norès. "My poor daughter! She's doomed to an atrocious, terrible death!"

Guy shook his head and made no rely.

How could the catastrophe have happened? No doubt it was possible. It was evident that, having gone into the machine in order to examine the mechanism, they had activated the engine. And although Marie de Norès knew the principle on which the new mode of locomotion was based, Guy was convinced that she did not know how to manipulate the various controls.

"You're not answering me, Guy," said the poor mother. "Do you have any doubt, then, about the result of this frightful accident?"

He was stammering, trying to give her a reassurance that he did not share, when the door opened.

It was the Admiral who came in.

"What's happened?" he exclaimed from the threshold. "My carriage had scarcely traveled a hundred meters when I heard a sort of explosion; at the same time I saw some sort of shell rising into the air, which was lost in the clouds. The idea occurred to me that you had had some kind of accident."

"That's only too true," Norès replied, and related what had happened.

The Admiral uttered a despairing groan. "Poor things!" After a moment's reflection, he added: "Is this the invention that you obliquely mentioned to me, then?"

"Yes, Monsieur. I've been working on it for many years, and I curse the day when I finally found the solution to the problem."

"Science should never be cursed," said the Admiral. "I certainly sympathize with the pain that the catastrophe is causing you, but tell me, on the one hand, are you sure that your sister won't be able to steer the apparatus?"

"How can you ask me that question? If she were able to control it, she'd have come back already."

"That's true—unless astonishment and a momentary but very natural fear have prevented her from acting immediately. On the other hand, do you only have one model of the apparatus?"

"I was going to carry out the decisive experiment in a few days' time," Guy explained. "Only then would I have finished the construction of two machines that are presently in the workshop of the company that financed them."

"Can't you finish them right away?"

"What's the point?"

The Admiral looked at the young man in surprise; he divined a profound depression, quite explicable given that in a matter of hours Norès had had to fear, if not mourn, the death of the two people he loved most in the world: his fiancée and his sister.

The valiant officer felt, however, that he ought not to allow that privileged soul to abandon himself thus, so it was in a most energetic tone that he replied: "What's the point? In truth, is that really you speaking, my dear Norès? What's the point of science, then, except to repair that which seems irreparable? It's necessary to react, to fight. Don't you understand that, thanks to your invention, it will be possible to fly more rapidly to the aid of our compatriots who are struggling at this moment under the blow of barbarians? Also, won't you be able to launch yourself to the rescue of your sister and your friend? Where are they now? Are they lost in limitless space, or have they been transported to some place where it might be possible to find them? There's more than one of our mariners, damn it, who'll agree to pilot your machine. Come on, Norès, lift your head up and get a grip on yourself again. You must, I implore you, in the name of those you love and in the name of the fatherland."

That forceful and vibrant voice extracted the young man from the torpor into which he had sunk. He passed his hand over his brow, and said: "You're right. I no longer knew what I was doing—those two consecutive blows had knocked the stuffing out of me, but I need to get a grip on myself. First of all, where are the unfortunates?"

"Can you determine that?"

"Wait."

Norès' features were suddenly mobile; the pallor of anguish had suddenly been succeeded by the animation of research: he had been seized by a triumphant idea.

He ran to a corner of the workshop.

"Provided, he murmured, "that the apparatus hasn't been destroyed by the explosion!"

The Admiral followed him anxiously. Now he was wondering whether the young scientist was really in his right mind.

What could his last words signify? Was he claiming that he could see into the upper atmosphere? By means of what telescope did he think he could follow the voyagers into space?

No, it was not a matter of some kind of telescope.

With a cry of joy, Norès had discovered, beneath a muslin veil, a small apparatus, singular in form, seeming to be made of thousands of juxtaposed mirrors, each one orientated in a different plane. The whole thing might have weighed two or three kilos at the most.

The Admiral looked at it uncomprehendingly.

Norès said to him: "Would you care to accompany me, Monsieur?"

"Gladly—but what's that?"

"You're going to leave me again!" cried the mother, who had been hiding her face in her handkerchief, weeping, until then.

He went to her. "Mother," he said, "I love you and I live for you—no, I'm not leaving you, but, as Monsieur de Trécourt says, so long as a glimmer of hope remains, a worthy man doesn't have the right to despair. Have no fear, I'll be back momentarily."

"At least swear to me that you aren't going to carry out some dangerous experiment..."

"Oh, this time I can swear it to you, Mother. Come, Monsieur de Trécourt."

They went outside, and once they were in the courtyard, Norès started climbing a small staircase going up to the top of the house. He was carrying his apparatus carefully, and moving slowly.

Naturally, the Admiral was most intrigued, having no idea what the young man planned to do.

They arrived on the roof, and followed a pathway contrived between the gutters.

"Where are we going?" asked the Admiral.

"To the chimneystack that you can see there. We need to get up as high as possible, to a point where we can see the whole of the broken roof of my workshop."

They had arrived. The platform sustaining the chimneypot was large enough for both men to stand on it without danger.

Norès reached it first and extended his hand to his companion, who joined him.

Norès set down his apparatus on the highest point.

It consisted, as we have said, of a kind of a spherical mirror formed of innumerable plates fitted together, which had the approximate appearance of a revolving mirror used to catch skylarks. The color of the mirror was not, however, the one ordinarily given to silvering by mercury or silver; it was grayish, but simultaneously very bright.

Beneath the hemisphere was a kind of very short telescope, about the same size as one branch of a pair of theater opera glasses, the ocular lens of which was outside while the other end disappeared under the reflective surface.

"As long as it's not too late," Norès murmured. "Why didn't I think of it sooner?"

He looked around; the air was remarkably clear.

From the position where the two men were standing, a large periphery of the sky was visible.

"That's good," said Norès.

He had knelt down in front of the instrument, and, peering through the ocular of the lorgnette, he rotated the demi-globe as if he were calibrating it.

A few minutes passed thus, during which the Admiral held his breath, so excited was his curiosity.

"Yes, yes!" Norès suddenly cried. "The apparatus rose up to my right, with an incredible velocity...a hundred, two hundred, four hundred meters...the door was closed and no fall had taken place...then...ah! A cloud! I can no longer see anything...wait...is that possible? I can see it again...it has ceased climbing and has departed eastwards with the rapidity of a shell...still no exterior accident...but... There's the horizon...it's lost, disappeared."

"But how can you see all that?" exclaimed the Admiral, who was increasingly doubtful about the young man's state of mind.

Norès straightened up. "Look for yourself," he said. "Concentrate all the force of your will and vitality in your eye. I'll maneuver the apparatus, which you don't know how to operate for yourself."

Indeed, throughout the time he had been gazing, he had kept one hand free to operate a lever that displaced the axis of the mirror.

The Admiral had taken his place—unconvinced, it must be admitted, that he was going to see anything. But he was a sensible man and he did not reject anything *a priori*.

Suddenly, he uttered a cry of surprise. "That's strange. I can see a kind of vehicle being carried away at dizzying speed, a sealed wagon, above which a propeller is rotating so rapidly that one can't follow its movement. Then everything disappears...to reappear a little further away...as you said, heading eastwards...then nothing more. I don't understand."

"That," said Norès, "is the telescope of the past."

"Of the past?"

"Let's go back down. I know what I wanted to know. My dear sister, although she can't control the apparatus completely—for I don't remember having given her a complete demonstration—has at least understood that the greatest danger on departure was rising up to the limits of the atmospheric layer, where respiration would be impossible, and where the apparatus would, in a sense, be quartered. She's stopped it, to depart horizontally. At least that's one danger avoided. Furthermore, I'm aware that my dear Marie hasn't panicked. Sabirat, who's with her, has a cool, precise intelligence. I still have some hope that they'll succeed in getting out of this dangerous adventure."

While talking, they had come back to Madame de Norès, whom Guy did his best to reassure—which, to tell the truth, was not at all easy, for the good woman did not have a very scientific mind.

Finally, she calmed down, and Guy was able to go out with the Admiral, with the aim of collecting the available information on the subject of events in China, and also of taking all the necessary measures that the situation required.

"Can't you explain to me briefly," while the vehicle escorted them away, "what the strange apparatus is that you showed me—the telescope of the past, as you call it."

"My dear Monsieur de Trécourt," Guy replied, "That might be difficult. The apparatus is based on principles so new I'm afraid that if I explain them to you, I might seem to be mad."

"My dear Guy, I hold your mind in too high esteem not to admit that you know a great many things I don't. I didn't believe in your selenoscope, but when you were kind enough to demonstrate its application to me, I yielded immediately."

"That's true—so I can take the risk of explaining to you what I haven't yet revealed to anyone else. Listen, then."

"With all my attention."

"When one places the objective of a photographic apparatus facing an object, the image of that object is fixed on a sensitive plate, is it not?"

"That's a banal observation."

"But have you ever wondered where the image was between the moment when it is, as it were, disengaged from the object that one is photographing and the moment when it reaches the plate?"

"Eh? I confess..."

"That you don't get it. You're not unaware that, according to the data of science, every illuminated body emits luminous rays, the beam of which comes to blossom, as it were, over the sensitive plate."

"That's right."

"Those rays transport the image through space, so to speak, and only stop at the moment when they strike the plate; but a thousandth of a millimeter from the plate, they don't yet exist in a condensed state, and are continually renewed by the emission of the body whose image is being projected."

Monsieur Trécourt was listening attentively. Norès, when he made such demonstrations, spoke in a soft, slightly muffled voice.

"So," he continued, "if you've understood me, you've already grasped the notion that images of everything there is exist, floating, as it were, in space, invisible to our normal senses, but visible when we stop them, conquering them, if one might put it like that, by some development of the personal faculty."

"In sum," said the Admiral, "the idea is logical...but when the object is moving...?"

"Its image moves with it."

"But what becomes of the image previously projected?"

"It endures for some time; then, gradually, it fades away, becoming increasingly imperceptible. And look, this idea that seems so new and strange to you was nevertheless admitted for thousands of years by millions of people."

"What do you mean?"

"The Hindu religion recognizes the existence of an enveloping fluid penetrating the entire universe, to which it gives the name of Akasha, or astral light. It's in that fluid that the images of everything are condensed, numbering in the billions, mingling and overlapping...and their totality produces the visible world—which is to say, in sum, the illusion, Maya."

"Decidedly, my dear chap, you seem to me to be a little lost in the...astral light. Shall we come back down to earth? I prefer, I confess, your comparison borrowed from photography. I'm a positive man, and in matters of hypotheses I demand that one only accepts the minimum possible number."

"You're right, and I apologize for letting myself get carried away further than I intended. There is in these hypotheses a question of intellectual level, of which it's necessary to take account. So, I told you that the images of everything exist in space before being fixed by photography or some other process, and that they remain durable for a certain interval. Well, at the moment when my aeroperfume—a provisional name, of course—is launched into the air, it projects its captured image into space, and it is found there in the various positions taken by the material object. The problem is to arrive in time to be able to capture it before its dilution and its complete volatilization, so to speak.

"My optical apparatus, then, which is based on the principles of photography and microscopy, permits those images to be seen during the time that they remain perceptible. Do you understand, for example, that in an empty room, one can photograph a person who has just gone out? The clarity of the subsisting image depends on the quantity of light and the timing of the pose. Thus, our observation of a little while ago was favored by the bright light of broad daylight. In the same way that the eye sees much more clearly in daylight, the universal retina of the immensity projects images more clearly. Thus, we were able to follow the image of the aerostatic apparatus through space, as Monsieur Marey was once able to photograph the various phases of the flight of a bird."[31]

"All that seems very strange to me," said the Admiral, after a pause...and yet the fact is there. I've seen it."

---

[31] The scientist and photographer Étienne-Jules Marey published his book *Le Vol des oiseaux* [The Flight of Birds] in 1890, shortly before Lermina began serializing his feuilleton.

"Yes, you've seen it. Oh, Admiral, how the ideas seethe in my brain! They'd make me pass for a madman if there weren't men like you, to understand us—the reckless questioners of infinity. But we're arriving at the Ministry. I feel my anguish gripping me again. Come, Monsieur, and may we learn some reassuring news!"

While Norès and his companion go in search of information, let us try, for our part, to discover what had become of Dr. Sabirat and the young woman. Had the scientist's extraordinary apparatus revealed the truth?

Certainly, Dr. Sabirat was a cool-headed man, and he had given unequivocal proof more than once of the civilian courage that is perhaps more rare than military valor.

When he felt himself carried away into the air, however, by that formidable leap, especially when he had heard the cry of distress uttered by Marie de Norès, and had seen the poor young woman's face convulsed by an anguish all the more terrible for being mute, he had been thunderstruck for a few moments, as if incapable of making any movement.

Fortunately, however, he was one of those men in whom the mental reacts to the physical, and the notion of real danger had promptly imposed itself upon him, along with the necessity of reassuring his companion.

"Don't be afraid, Mademoiselle!" he cried. "I'll answer for everything!"

It was evidently a very hazardous cry, but in those ultra-perilous circumstances anything was preferable to prostration, to self-abandonment. Before even knowing whether a struggle was possible, it was necessary to recover the will to fight. Sabirat understood that so well that, when the first moment of stupefaction had passed, he was no longer thinking about anything but taking action. How, and in what direction? He had absolutely no idea, but the idea that dominated him could be expressed as: *Something has to be done, even so.*

He had scarcely had the opportunity to examine the interior of the compartment in which he found himself, a parallelogram whose two sides were closed but whose two extremities were open to space, fitted with thick panes of glass. Through one of those fixed windows a helical propeller could be seen that was presently immobile; through the other, the immensity was visible and of unusual profundity.

There was no reference point. Where were they? It was impossible to hazard any hypothesis—but it was easy to observe that they were climbing with lightning rapidity. Clouds were passing by; they were passing through them like a shell. Then there was the profound blue, and then, once again, an intense vapor that enveloped the apparatus and plunged the unfortunate couple into a kind of darkness.

Sabirat understood what was happening; they were rising, still rising at a velocity of hundreds of meters per second...so it would not take them long to reach the limits of the respirable air; that was death with brief delay.

"Mademoiselle," he said, "I'm not asking you to forgive me. We're both victims of a fatality that nothing could doubtless have avoided. Now, do you know your brother's apparatus? It's necessary that we cease to rise with this alarming rapidity. There is one way, which is to break one of the sides of the box—that pane of glass, for example—but that would lead to a brutal fall, perhaps death by crushing. It's necessary to act upon the engine, to deflect it. Don't you remember any information given to you by your brother?"

And as the young woman, as if emerging from sleep, opened her eyes and looked at him, as it were, without seeing him, he continued softly: "Come on— we only have a few more minutes. Look, Mademoiselle: this is the lever we pushed down which determined our departure. There are two others forming a triangle with it, of which that one is at the apex. I confess that I hardly dare hazard a hypothesis. I beg you, try to remember."

But Marie, her arms hanging down in an attitude of discouragement, only murmured: "I don't know."

Sabirat shivered; it was obvious that the shock suffered by the young woman had momentarily robbed her of her faculties; the nervous distress had been too powerful for that essentially delicate nature.

What could he do? She seemed to be asleep; her vague eyes had no focus...and yet, the peril was becoming increasingly urgent.

Already, Sabirat could feel the first effects of the increasingly rarefied air.

He could hear an ominous creaking in the walls of the hull. At the same time, it seemed to him that breathing was becoming more difficult. Was that an illusion? But he was experiencing the preliminary symptoms of vertigo.

He was confronted, as we have said, by a system of levers, one of which, occupying the upper apex of the triangle, had been depressed by the involuntary pressure and had determined the ascent.

There were two others, one to the right and one to the left. What did the most elementary logic indicate? Evidently, that the right-hand lever produced an easterly direction, and the left-hand one a westerly thrust. And yet, at the moment of action, Sabirat felt a profound anguish.

There are times when one's arm, during a movement of which can determine the life or death of those one loves, feels heavier than lead.

He stiffened himself, however, against the weakness that was invading him.

It was a life-or-death gamble; he had logic in his favor, but how little human reasoning weighs in such moments.

It seemed to him that he saw Marie going pale, and divined that she was having difficulty drawing breath, that her lips were gasping in vain for the air they lacked. Very gravely, as resolute as a pilot adjusting a tiller, he placed his hand on the right-hand lever and pulled it down with a single thrust.

There was an abrupt shock throughout the carcass of the machine, and then an oscillation.

Sabirat was frantic.

Suddenly, he felt the equilibrium, momentarily disturbed, re-establish it-self—and the helix, which had been immobile thus far, began to turn with enormous rapidity.

The aerostat flew through the air like an arrow, in a horizontal plane.

It was salvation; they were no longer rising. Sabirat uttered a cry of joy and hope.

"We're saved," he pronounced, with a clarity all the more emphatic because he wanted to imprint that as-yet-unjustified certainty in the mind of his companion.

And, indeed, Marie, straightening up slightly, repeated the word: "Saved!"

"Yes, Mademoiselle. Listen to me: recover all your composure. You must have courage; the moment has come to show it. We have obtained a first success; I'm convinced that it only depends on your energy to escape the dangers that threaten us."

As he spoke, with his voice becoming calm again, Marie gradually came round. The young doctor was telling the truth; there was an uncommon energy within her. But in fact, the adventure had been so abrupt, so stunning, that more than one man among the most impassive would have lost his composure.

"I beg your pardon, but to tell the truth, I no longer knew where I was," said Marie, striving to smile.

"Well," replied Sabirat, "we're quite simply fifteen hundred or two thousand meters above the level of Paris."

"But if we're still rising, we'll soon be asphyxiated."

"Have no fear," the young man continued, smiling. "I believe that I've succeeded in avoiding that painful extremity."

"Really...how?"

Sabirat explained to her what he had done and how: by simple intuition, he had succeeded in carrying out a saving maneuver. "But haven't you learned from your brother how the levers work?" he asked.

"No, in truth. He couldn't imagine that I would embark first and alone in this terrible machine. But in your opinion, what should we do now?"

"I'm not too sure. However, on seeing the clouds pass by through that glass, it appears to me that we're traveling horizontally."

"Very rapidly?"

"I can't measure it, but I believe that our speed is very rapid."

"If we could find out where we are..."

Sabirat looked around. In fact, there was a total lack of reference points.

Suddenly, Marie uttered an exclamation.

"What is it?" Sabirat asked, fearing another unforeseen complication.

Here on the floor, this key...that copper handle..."

"Hmm!" said the young man. "I confess that I'm not without suspicion. In touching any of the components of this unknown machine, we'd be risking producing a result that might be injurious to us."

"However," said Marie, who had now recovered her self-control completely, "it's not plausible that my brother has installed some means of destroying his own machine."

"That's true."

"Let's put ourselves in his place and suppose that we were the inventors. We'd have the idea of providing a means of rising up and descending, of hovering, of going forwards or backwards, of steering our flight...so this copper handle might serve to obtain one of those results. We already know how to go up..."

"Alas, yes!" sighed Sabirat, who had not yet forgiven his imprudence.

"Well, there still remains one lever in the console; it must be something other than going up or steering to the right. It can only be to go down, or..."

"Would you like us to try it?" asked Sabirat.

"Why not? It's necessary for us to try everything, until we've found something."

The doctor was not entirely reassured; he divined that the life of the woman he loved more than ever—for it seemed to him that the peril shared put an even stronger bond between them than before—might depend on one false move.

And the excellent young man, instead of replying, instead of acting, lost himself in his reflections, wondering whether he would ever return to earth with the woman he was already calling, in the depths of his consciousness, his fiancée.

"What do you think?" asked Marie, naively. "Doesn't my reasoning seem to you to be unassailable?"

"Yes, yes, in truth...and I'm ready to do as you say. So very ready that I'll risk everything."

And he advanced his hand toward the third lever determinedly.

"Not too quickly!" exclaimed Marie. "A little prudence is always necessary..."

Sabirat had placed his hand on the lever; obedient to Marie's advice, he pressed down gently, and then a little more heavily.

The two young people felt the very clear impression that the aerial vessel turned around, slowly and without any shock.

"We're going the other way!" exclaimed Sabirat. "We're retreating—or, rather, returning to the departure point."

Marie shook her head.

"At the height we're at," she said, "It scarcely matters whether we're going in one direction or another. The best thing would be to find a means of descending. Then, if the movement isn't too rapid, we can do our best to land."

"Descending!" Sabirat replied. "But you've seen that we've made use of the three levers, and none of them had that effect."

"With the result that we'll be condemned to wander perpetually, like souls in torment, between earth and Heaven."

"And as we're not souls, we'll inevitably be doomed to a frightful death...of starvation."

The two young people remained silent momentarily.

They were beginning to despair, although, in fact, each of them was thinking about the other. Marie accused herself of having brought the doctor into the aerostat, while, for his part, Sabirat could not help blushing as he recalled the involuntary movement that had led to such a disastrous catastrophe.

What were they to do? They could not resign themselves to going back and forth eternally in the sky. That was poetic, but dangerous in the long run.

"I've got it," said Sabirat. "There still remains the brass handle in the floor."

"That's true—we forgot that. There's no reason to hesitate, since, having found the means of climbing and going forwards and backwards, it only remains to find that of descending. Except, remember that it's necessary to guard against falling too rapidly, for fear of smashing into the ground."

"Don't worry," said Sabirat. He almost added: "I know what I'm doing."

He knelt down and put his hand on the lever in question.

"It rotates," he said.

In truth, they were holding their breath.

This is what happened:

Gradually, a circular opening was uncovered, which initially adopted a form something like the crescent of the new moon, and then a semi-circle, and then a whole circle about the size of the brim of a hat.

Sabirat uttered two exclamations, one of disappointment, because he understood that it was merely a porthole, and the other of admiration.

"Look, Mademoiselle," he said. "It's marvelous!"

Like a large optical lens, the circle allowed the ground to be seen, but with such magnification that the mountains, valleys and rivers appeared in the clearest fashion. It was like a telescope of unusual power aimed at the earth.

Sabirat had knelt down, peering with all his attention. Marie did likewise, and the two of them, head to head, their hair in contact, examined the miraculous spectacle that was unfolding before them.

They could not make out the details, to be sure, but what they saw was like an immense relief map unfurling in an endless scroll.

They both tried to recognize the places above which they were passing, but it was not easy—almost impossible, in fact—because of the rapidity of their progress.

After a few moments of contemplation, Sabirat stood up again.

"Alas, Mademoiselle," he said, "it's quite beautiful, but what good does it do us? We're observing all the more evidently that we're moving with amazing rapidity. Where are we? We don't know, and if we did know, what use would it be, since we haven't found the means of landing?"

He was right; even supposing that they had recognized France, their city, their house, would it not have been a further torture to fly forever without being able to stop? It was enough to drive them to despair.

Sabirat, who was vigorous by nature, and famished, was beginning to experience strange cramps in his stomach. Two or three times already Marie had stifled significant yawns; it was obvious that hunger was coming—and what means did they have of satisfying it?

A bird flies well too, but not in a hermetically sealed cage; it can settle on a tree to catch some insect by the wings, after which, ballasted, it sets off again for the sublime regions. But here there was an excelsior without a term, without a pause, without the hope of alighting on some hospitable branch.

No, no—it was not impossible that Norès, the inventor and genius, had forgotten that essential part of the mechanism, the descent.

It is true that great architects have built edifices in which they have forgotten the staircase, but those distractions are rare, and when it is a matter of an apparatus that rises up thousands of meters, it would be implausible that, having desired to rise, one would not remember the line from old Corneille: "He aspires to descend..."

Sabirat prowled around the wooden box like a wild beast in a cage. He inspected every corner, placed his hand on the knots in the wood, palpated the slightest patches in the hope of finding some secret button, like those for the mysterious doors in the châteaux of the Middle Ages.

But there was nothing; he always found himself facing the three levers again, repeating the observations already made. By lowering the top lever, they rose, and by touching the levers to the left or the right they went north or south—nothing more.

But in that case it was necessary to renounce all hope; nothing remained but to cover the head and await death: slow, frightfully painful death from starvation.

Oh, if Sabirat had been alone he would have smashed the locomotive apparatus. There would have been a brutal fall through space, then a crash—but at least his bones would be broken on the ground and would not have to circulate eternally in the immensity.

But Marie was there, gently and resigned, not uttering a word of reproach. Poor dear child!

And in a surge of despair, the doctor fell to his knees to beg her pardon.

Marie uttered a small cry of fright; it seemed to her that her companion was suffering a fit of madness.

"What are you doing?" she cried.

"What can I do, except tell you that I'm a wretch, unworthy of pity? Isn't it me who has snatched you away from your mother?"

"Get up, please, I beg you."

She had spoken so curtly that Sabirat, fearing that he had displeased her, stood up abruptly, stepping back slightly. His head bumped into the topmost lever, which had been lowered for the departure, and which rose up again in response to the impact.

It is necessary to understand that in the rest state, the three levers projected horizontally. Thus when the excellent Sabirat had put pressure on the young woman's hand, he had provoked the depression of the lever, while now, his skull, touching the extremity, had raised it above the horizontal.

At the same movement, there was a vibration throughout the apparatus; then there was a moment's pause, as when the brakes are applied to a vehicle, before it resumes its course.

That was exactly what had happened.

Yes, the aerostat had stopped; yes, it had resumed its flight...but...

"We're going down!" cried Marie, pressing herself upon the window that permitted an outside view.

Sabirat could not believe his eyes, and yet, nothing was more real. The superior propeller had changed direction, and it was now drawing the aerial vehicle toward the earth.

Marie experienced a sudden revelation.

"Do you understand?" she cried. "Each lever is susceptible to two contrary movements, according to whether the arm is above or below the horizontal. To go up it's necessary to lower that one...and to raise it in order to descend."

"With the result," Sabirat continued, "that according to the greater or lesser angle that the lever makes with the horizontal, the upward or downward effort varies in violence."

"And we didn't think of that! Oh, what a good thing it was," the young woman added, naively, "that you threw yourself at my knees."

"You're not angry with me?"

"Certainly not. But Monsieur Sabirat, instead of gazing at me with your wide eyes, you'd do better to remember that by descending too rapidly, you're now risking shattering us into a thousand pieces on the ground. Come on, pilot—to the helm! Try to slow down the velocity of the fall, so that we arrive without too much damage."

"I'll do my best...but how can I judge?"

"Look through the porthole in the floor, watch the earth becoming more and more magnified. Judge the speed of our descent for yourself. Keep lowering the lever—but always keeping it above the horizontal, of course. That's right! We're descending more slowly...but in what country are we coming down?"

As Sabirat made a moment to look more closely, she added: "Above all, don't move. I'll tell you everything I can see. Mountains...yes, and in the middle, a sort of amphitheater, a ring, which seems to be divided up like a chess-board. It's no longer very bright; it's evident that dusk is approaching. What do you think, Monsieur Sabirat?"

"In your opinion, is it an inhabited country?"

"Oh, certainly. I can see a sort of city…there are towers…minarets…"

"Then we're in the Orient…in Turkey, perhaps. Should we go down?"

"What do you think? You're a better judge of that than me."

"I think that the Turks are good people," said the doctor. "Hospitable enough. Perhaps it would be better to land among them than more civilized folk."

"For my part, I have no objection…decide for yourself."

"Let's go down," said Sabirat.

In a matter of moments, he felt that he had acquired a mastery of the lever and that it was possible to increase or decrease their movements at will. He was even beginning to put a certain brashness into it, like a pilot confident of the tiller in his hand or a horseman sure of his mount.

"We're getting close," said Marie, kneeling on the floor, "but it's getting darker and darker…I can't make anything out. Oh! Crows…"

"Birds of ill-omen," said the doctor.

"Oh! Do you have such weaknesses, then? Then again, in truth…we have to make a decision…we're still arriving somewhere."

"So be it."

There was a silence. They felt themselves descending further, and the physical impression was rather painful, rather like the first symptoms of sea-sickness.

Then there was a sudden shock.

"Be careful," said Marie. "We must be touching."

With a rapid movement, Sabirat had set the lever horizontally. The vehicle had stopped.

The two voyagers remained motionless for a moment, listening.

No noise reached them.

"As long as we haven't come down in a desert!"

Marie could not repress a shudder.

"I'm going to open the door," said the doctor, "And take a look outside."

"I don't want you to risk yourself on your own. What if you are attacked?"

"Bah! I'm unarmed—that's the best way of not causing umbrage to any-one."

"It doesn't matter. I'm coming with you. Are we not bound together in ill fortune?"

"As in good, I hope," said the doctor—who felt, in truth, that he was taking a risk in that clear declaration.

Marie put her hand in his. "As in good," she repeated.

Sabirat leaned over to kiss her hand.

"Be careful," said Marie, laughing. "You'll cause another accident. Come on, make up your mind—open up and let's go."

Sabirat did not hesitate any longer. He was delighted. It seemed to him that in the last minute he had lived more than in entire years. Had not Marie accepted the frank, honest, durable alliance that he had offered her?

And to think that, without that adventure, he might never have dared to say anything. There are, it appears, people who can only admit their love two thousand meters above sea level.

So it was with a light heart that the young doctor resolutely opened the door of the aerostat, now perfectly immobile.

"I'll go take a look around," he said, turning to Marie.

"And leave me alone? No. The apparatus might be seized by some new caprice and carry me into the air on my own. I confess that such a voyage doesn't tempt me...all the more so as the moonlight is superb. We'll surely find someone who'll offer us hospitality."

"So be it," said Sabirat—and gallantly offered his hand to his companion to cross the threshold.

They took two steps outside.

"But where are we, then?" said the doctor, with a hint of anxiety.

They were walking over dry grass that crackled underfoot and sank beneath their weight.

Facing them, they saw a large sheet of dazzling whiteness, like a circular wall in which they could not see an exit. Then they saw a large step of white stone in front of them. Sabirat climbed it first; it was a foot above the ground. He uttered a cry of surprise. A ditch opened in front of him, in the form of a parallelogram about two meters long and barely a meter wide.

Courageously, Marie came to stand beside him.

"One might think that it's a grave," she said, shuddering slightly.

She took him by the arm and, with a very feminine curiosity, in haste to obtain the solution to the enigma, she drew him to the edge of the ditch. But there was another adjacent to it, and then another: it was like a checkerboard of tombs.

Suddenly, Marie stopped, shivering in terror. "Look!" she said, extending her arm. "There! There!"

Sabirat was an energetic man, but in truth, he could not suppress a shiver that shook him in his entirety.

In one of the graves, directly in front of them, a body lay—or, rather, was curled up and on its back—the face blackened beneath the white hood that partially hid it. The hands were protruding from the shroud and were convulsed in a frightful pose, while the legs, folded up over the body, gave the horrible appearance of a monster like those one sees on Indian pagodas.

The two young people had taken a step backwards, but they stumbled and nearly fell into another ditch, from which a flock of filthy crows escaped, croaking.

"My God, it's horrible!" sobbed Marie. "Let's get out of here, I beg you. I feel that I'm going to die."

In truth, the spectacle was horrible, of a nature to cause the strongest to falter.

What was this atrocious charnel house? Tombs everywhere, to the right and the left, in all directions, from which macabre forms surged, nameless beings, all in poses that the most boldly imaginative of artists would scarcely have dared dream: some with their arms raised toward the sky, seemingly threatening some invisible enemy; others half-kneeling, seemingly at prayer...but the most hideous, without a doubt, were those tipped backwards, lying on their backs, displaying their fleshless heads, their bony masks in which two holes were like eyes devoid of pupils, gazing into infinity.

Habituated to the amphitheater as he was, Sabirat had difficulty resisting the horror that invaded him. He felt Marie pressing against him, unsteadily, on the brink of falling.

And yet, it was necessary to act: an insipid, nauseating odor was rising, throwing disease-ridden miasmas into the air, every one of which contained death.

"I beg you, Marie," he said—he no longer thought of calling her Mademoiselle—"be brave. This is an Oriental cemetery. I remember having heard mention of peoples who bury their dead in this fashion."

She made no reply; the fear had been stronger than her willpower, and she fainted.

Then Sabirat took her in his arms, like a child, and started walking slowly over the edges of the ditches, not finding the direction that would take him out of that horrible labyrinth in which any fall would have been frightful. The carrion birds were flying around him with raucous cries, as if furious at being disturbed in their funereal nocturnal feast.

He went on, without knowing where, stiffening his muscles in order not to weaken, feeling that his soul was burdened.

Finally, by dint of searching, he ended up encountering a wider pathway, along which it was possible to walk without fear of stumbling.

The young woman's head was resting on his shoulder, and he saw by means of the moonlight that she was as white as a corpse.

Finally, he perceived the wall, which was only a few paces away from him, and found the bed of dry grass beneath his feet that evidently surrounded the central checkerboard of graves.

He reached the wall and began to follow it, telling himself that there must be an exit, since people came in here to bring in their dead. But he made a complete circuit twice, in vain. Nothing: there was no trace that indicated any kind of door.

What should he do? Had they, then, escaped one horrible danger only to risk perishing now of an even more frightful death?

The young man felt his arms becoming numb under the weight he was carrying. His muscles were weakening, but he did not want to set Marie's inanimate body down on the ground, which was doubtless impregnated with contagious mists. He stiffened himself against the pain that was gradually invading him.

Suddenly, he shuddered; it seemed that he could hear the sound of footsteps. Where was it coming from? For a moment, he had the crazy idea that it was the dead who were about to rise from their tombs in order to surround him and draw him into a horrible *danse macabre*, as in the lurid legends of the Middle Ages.

He leaned over, cocking his ear.

They were muffled human footfalls, the echo of which reached him as if stifled by an obstacle. Just then, the moon was covered by a cloud, and Sabirat remained motionless in profound obscurity, not knowing which way to look.

Suddenly, the sound of footsteps ceased, and voices became audible. Then, it was as if something scraped against the wall, on the side opposite to where the young doctor was standing. The profound emotion he felt somehow increased the acuity of his senses, and he realized that that there were men a few paces away from him, who had just applied a ladder to the wall.

He was not mistaken, because he could hear the creak of the rungs. Someone was climbing up.

Perhaps they were filthy night-prowlers, grave-robbers who did not recoil before sacrilege and had come to despoil the cadavers. He did not budge; all in all, it was still better to find himself facing human beings, even bandits, than to remain in this sinister solitude.

Black forms appeared on the crest of the wall. The moon, although hidden behind the clouds, illuminated them slightly and gave them a fantastic aspect. What struck the doctor first of all were their tall bonnets, which elongated their heads in fantastic oblong forms.

Two of them sat astride the wall. They were looking outwards, so they did not perceive the young man leaning against the wall, still carrying his cherished burden.

They leaned over, as if drawing a heavy weight toward them, and words were pronounced that seemed, by their intonation, to be orders. A dark mass soon appeared on the stone rim, folded up. It was a human body in a sack.

Sabirat remembered then. Although his memory was incomplete, he was sure that he had read somewhere that, among Oriental peoples, burials took place at night. He was, therefore, really in a cemetery, and these men had just brought a new cadaver, which the crows would soon be tearing apart like the others. They were not bandits, not committing sacrilege, but believers of a singular and exotic religion.

Indeed, behind the cadaver, two more men had climbed up. Then the ladder that was outside was drawn up, and now, with violent efforts, it was being dragged over the top of the wall, where it was soon balanced. Then, the heavier part having been slid over, it was lowered into the cemetery and carefully adjusted. Two men came down, reaching the ground a few paces from the young man, while the others, still on the crest, lowered the sack slowly toward the ground. It was received, and the rope supporting it was untied and the two men walked away, carrying the cadaver, over the boundary of the white checkerboard.

Sabirat followed them with his gaze, wondering how the adventure was going to conclude.

He saw them stop and drop the cadaver into one of the ditches, tipping it out of the sack. Then they raised their arms into the air, uttering guttural exclamations that might have been prayers.

A quarter of an hour went by like that.

Finally, the strange ceremony ended, and the men slowly retraced their steps.

This time, there was no hesitation; it was necessary to take advantage of this unique opportunity to get out of that funereal location. Sabirat marched toward them resolutely.

As he approached, they stopped abruptly, frightened.

Evidently, they took the sudden apparition for a fantastic manifestation—perhaps the soul of a dead man that had re-animated a cadaver, perhaps a vengeful god who wanted to punish them for an unknown sin.

After a second of hesitation, they prostrated themselves onto the ground, their arms folded over the top of their head, uttering stifled moans.

Sabirat knew several Oriental languages; he took the risk of speaking the one that, in his estimation, was understood by the greatest number, Persian.

"Don't be afraid," he said in that language. "I'm not a demon, I'm a man: an unfortunate, who is asking you for help."

There was no response at first. He was about to address them in Arabic when one of them raised his head. Sabirat repeated what he had said. "I beg you," he continued, "in the name of the god of your forefathers, help me."

This time, he had the satisfaction of seeing that he had been understood. The two strangers stood up and came toward him. After taking a few steps, however, they uttered a cry for help. Sabirat, who had not thought of looking behind him, suddenly felt himself seized by his shoulders and pulled to the ground.

"Profane dogs! Sacrilegious wretches" cried furious voices. "To death! To death!"

The situation became increasingly perilous. Marie, still motionless, was lying on the ground. Sabirat, stunned by his fall, could no longer find the words of the language that was being spoken.

But what point was there in arguing? Obviously, these people believed that there had been an odious profaning of the sepulchral location.

Sabirat was lifted up and carried away. The men ran toward the ladder. A rope was looped beneath his armpits. He was lifted up as the cadaver had been a little while before. In a kind of nightmare, he found himself on the crest of the wall.

He wanted to cry out: "Marie! Marie!"

But vertigo gripped him while he was slid down the other side of the wall, where he lost consciousness.

II

When Sabirat came to, it was broad daylight. At first, he did not remember what had happened to him, and he looked around fearfully, blinking in the bright light that was descending from above.

To tell the truth, what he saw could hardly orient him to his present situation.

Immense walls surrounded him, topped, above their crumbling, breached summits, by a large expanse of blue sky, profound and immobile: a tower, in fact, with a ruined summit, but still solid in its enormous blocks of stone, strongly cemented. One might have thought it a vestige of one of those cyclopean structures that were said to have been constructed by giants, ancestors of the pygmy humans of today.

It is true that in the nightmarish state of mind the young man was in, everything took on gigantic and somewhat frightening proportions in his eyes.

He moved and let out an involuntary groan.

His entire body seemed to him to be aching atrociously; he feared that one of his limbs had been broken by a fall or violent blows.

Having shaken himself in order to regain is self-possession, he told himself that the best means of making sure of the state of his bones was to get to his feet, and with a thrust of his hips he tried to stand up—but he fell back with a veritable cry of pain.

It was then that he perceived a large ring sealed around the middle of his body, which was connected to the wall by an iron chain.

He was a prisoner—and in what a prison!

Suddenly, he thought about his companion.

"Marie!" he shouted in an anguished tone.

But no voice replied to his, and the sound came back to him in an almost dismal echo.

118

He could not suppress a shudder, because he now remembered the frightful accident that had launched him through the air with the young woman, and then the frightful descent into that sinister and accused place.

What had become of Marie? Had she only escaped one danger to be delivered into one that was even greater?

A prisoner? Of whom? Of some ferocious and savage people. Collecting his memories, however, Sabirat recalled that the men had appeared to understand Persian.

Among the Orientals, the Persians were, after all, those whose sovereign had the closest relations with Europe; it was said that he had imported the seeds of modern civilization into his Estates.

And yet, this brutal captivity and these exaggerated precautions taken against an unarmed foreigner did not testify to a well-developed spirit of humanity.

What could he do? Wait! But perhaps every minute augmented the perils that Norès' sister was encountering. Sabirat told himself that it was his duty to make any sacrifice for the salvation of the woman he loved.

He twisted in his chains, hoping madly that he might break them, but he became increasingly convinced that it was a vain struggle. With his legs and his torso shackled, his arms could not exert their full leverage. He was weaker than an infant, and, reflecting that Marie might be subject to similarly horrible treatment, which her delicacy certainly would not survive, he was gripped by a rage that soon dissolved into the bleak despair of impotence, and large tears ran down his cheeks.

I addition to the fact that he could not make a single useful movement, he could not see anything around him but worn stones, debris fallen from the top of the tower—not even a fragment of iron that he could seize, with which he might kill himself—for, in truth, in the despair that imposed itself upon him, he thought about ending his life. But he stiffened himself against that cowardly thought. So long as he could suppose that Marie, his beloved Marie—for now he no longer hesitated to admit the love that the young woman had once accepted—was alive, he owed it to her, until his dying breath, to think about the chances that might yet remain of saving her.

Very remote chances, it was necessary to admit.

Hours went by while the unfortunate felt his strength ebb away, and a kind of intoxication, doubtless that of hunger, invaded his brain.

So, it was finished. He would die slowly, horribly, in that *in pace* into which fate had precipitated him. He would not even have the supreme joy of looking his torturers in the eyes, insulting them, spitting his hatred and scorn in their faces.

For a Frenchman, to be able to confront one's murderers is to die less dolorously.

Suddenly, it seemed that he could hear a noise. He raised his head abruptly. A shadow was profiled against the sky, at the crest of the wall.

Breathlessly, he waited, thinking that perhaps one of his torturers was about to appear before him.

But it was an illusory hope. From the summit of the tower a rope unfurled, at the end of which hung a basket. The basked came to rest beside him, within arm's reach, and by means of some ingenious mechanism, the rope was detached from it, which rose up again alone, hissing against the wall.

Already, Sabirat, half-standing, was shouting, appealing, using all the Persian vocabulary he had been able to learn at the Oriental school in Paris, where he had once attended lectures, with no suspicion of the unusual circumstances in which he would be enabled to test his knowledge. But the rope had reached the crest of the wall; the human shadow was once again outlined against the sky, and then suddenly disappeared, without paying any heed to the desperate cries of the unfortunate prisoner.

He had a fit of rage, clenched his fists and howled—but what was the point?

Around him, there was nothing but silence, and he was quite certain that his torturers, if they had heard him, were firmly resolved not to make any response. But if they wanted him dead, why not abandon him completely? Why come to add to the initial cruelty the even more cowardly ferocity of bringing him what he needed to prolong his miserable life?

Well, he would cheat them, frustrate their calculations of cruelty. No human power could force him to touch the food that had been offered to make his agony more prolonged. He would not eat, and thus his torturers would no longer have the hideous satisfaction of hearing his impotent imprecations. In their turn they would be irritated that their victim was escaping them so rapidly.

And the unfortunate, closing his eyes, lay down resolutely on the ground, determined to let death come without making the slightest effort to escape it.

How, an hour later, did he surprise himself by avidly devouring the watermelon and the maize cakes and drinking from the pitcher of water in long draughts? Is any other explanation necessary than the will to survive, to struggle against the final destruction that lies in the obscure depths of every consciousness?

Now, his decision was very different—and also much more reasonable.

While a breath of life remains to a truly energetic man, it is cowardly to confess himself vanquished. He will live, attentive to the slightest circumstance, relentlessly on the lookout for an opportunity of salvation. Once again, as long as he had no proof that Marie was dead, he owed it to himself to fight for life.

And the hours passed...

Then a day, and then another...

Every morning, the shadow appeared at the top of the tower. Then, with the same precision, the basket of provisions descended beside him, within arm's reach.

He shouted, he appealed, but there was the same silence, the same heart-breaking impassivity.

But Sabirat stiffened himself against the despair that sometimes took possession of him. What was most atrocious of all was the immobility to which his shackles condemned him. He could scarcely raise himself up on his knees; he could not stand upright—but what was the good of having studied medicine, especially anatomy, if he could not apply his science to himself? The young doctor exercised his ingenuity in creating a kind of gymnastics for his benefit, which exercised his limbs one by one, so well that, even in that more than critical situation, he had nothing to fear from ankylosis.

But the silence!

To tell the truth, during those interminable days, it was a terrible torture not to hear any sound. Above him, always the same sky, bright and bleak; around him, always the same mute stones.

There, too, his willpower triumphed. Sabirat had the courage to work his mind even so, constraining himself to resume his studies and pose himself problems that had not yet been resolved. Then, when evening came, he hypnotized himself and succeeded in going to sleep.

He counted twelve days like that. He did not know how long he had been unconscious to begin with, and certain clues caused him to suppose that a narcotic had been administered to him...to the extent that, in his estimation, he had been isolated from the rest of the living for an entire fortnight, without having obtained any other result than conserving his strength and his mental faculties.

Then, one evening, when the stars were commencing to sparkle above in the hollow of the tower, as if in the field of a gigantic telescope, Sabirat suddenly heard a burst of resounding commotion, the feeble echo of which reached him amid a cacophony that was both harrowing and terrible.

In the situation he was in, it was not an insignificant event. He listened more attentively and became gradually better able to discern the multiple sounds that were reaching him through the thickness of the walls.

Along with the vibration of the instruments—more or less barbaric trumpets, bugles and buccinas—there were the hoof-beats of thousands of horses, and the increasing murmur of a crowd uttering savage cheers. And all of it was getting closer, concentrating, after a fashion, around the opening of the tower.

What was about to happen? Had the barbaric tribe into whose hands he had fallen suddenly been attacked? Was it the exodus of an entire people expelled from their homes? Was it a battle?—for he had heard the detonation of firearms...but they did not seem to be numerous enough to indicate a battle...

Breathless, stretching his neck, he listened, and waited.

121

Suddenly, there was a noise at the top of the tower; shadows, more compact than those that ordinarily appeared, loomed up on the crest, and the young doctor saw something long and narrow descending into his *in pace.*

A ladder! Then men, balanced on the rungs.

Perhaps they were coming to murder their victim…but what did it matter, after all? It was better to put an end to the uncertainty.

"What do you want?" he shouted. "Do you intend to kill me?"

Without replying, two men came down to him and immediately set about freeing him from his chains. Then, one of them said a single word in Persian:

"Up!"

It was not death, but a semblance of liberty. Sabirat was finally able to stand up—tottering, it is true, for in spite of all his efforts, he had not been able to preserve his limbs from a relative numbness. Summoning up all his energy, however, he straightened up, gripped the ladder, and started climbing vigorously.

He did not reflect; he enjoyed the exquisite pleasure of movement, and if he were to encounter an executioner at the top of the latter who would strike him down, at least he would have experienced an almost joyful sensation in not dying enchained like an animal under a butcher's sledgehammer.

He finally set foot on the top of the tower, but at the same moment, he felt himself dragged forward. The men surrounded him; he was hoisted onto a horse, which departed at a gallop, in the midst of other horsemen, who were racing with a tremendous speed.

The night was profound, although the stars were casting a pale gleam over the landscape that was sufficient to distinguish objects.

Sabirat felt such joy in his relative liberty that, without allowing himself to be dazed by the open air, he succeeded in reacting against the intoxication of sorts that was agitating his brain, and examining attentively what was happening around him.

He was being transported amid a multitude of disparate costumes and brutal physiognomies, whose most evident characteristic was an Oriental appearance. He had, therefore, not been mistaken in his initial rapid observations; he was, if not in Persia, at least in one of the bordering regions

Of the men galloping around him, some were of the very pronounced Kalmuk type, with prominent cheekbones and flattened noses; others, on the contrary, had almost regular features and long, slender noses. One might have thought them a strange mixture of different nationalities, connected by an accidental bond.

Some were dressed in superb costumes, armed with rifles with sculpted butts and sabers in sheaths sparkling with ornaments; others, by contrast, with their shoulders scarcely hidden beneath fur cloaks, were brandishing spears of the most rudimentary form.

Sometimes, however, identical harsh and guttural cries escaped from their throats, like exclamations of anger and hatred. He did not understand their significance.

The ride had something fantastic about it; for as far as he could see, he could only make out the host; even those who doubtless had the mission of ensuring his safety, carried away by their mounts, often left enough free space around him for him to be able to run away. But what would be the point? Not knowing where he was, he understood that it was in his interest to continue following the multitude—which, he observed, did not exhibit the anxiety of a troop of fugitives but, on the contrary, the enthusiasm of an attack force.

Sabirat was not unaware that the tribes occupying the immense territories of Afghanistan and Khorasan are frequently at war with one another, lacking unique leaders whose authority can group and direct their forces; perhaps he was witnessing an armed assault by one village on another. In fact, all reasoning was still impossible; it was necessary to submit to chance and wait for some unforeseeable opportunity to seek information.

The gallop was unrelenting; fortunately, Sabirat was an excellent horseman, and now, completely in control of himself, he boldly followed those whom he considered as guides rather than jailers.

Hours passed without any relaxation of the furious pace—but Sabirat sometimes saw, along the roadside, new groups launching themselves into the midst of the troop, joining with it, and then galloping on in the whirlwind, which extended and elongated—multiplying, visibly.

Already, the first glimmers of daylight were arriving, and, as if they were on a ridge, the doctor saw a vast plain before him, black with horsemen. In the distance were the towers of a city. Evidently, they were nearing their goal. The horses were urged on, while the cries thundered more loudly.

In the distance, a troop was advancing, comprised of men whose armor was sparkling in the light of the rising sun.

It was a marvelous spectacle. One might have thought it a scene from the ancient crusades, when knights advanced ahead of vanquished Muslims.

Here there were evidently neither victors nor vanquished, however, but soldiers proceeding ahead of a leader. That was what Sabirat understood, from a few words overheard by chance.

The group of new arrivals stopped in front of a ruined but admirably imposing mosque, which stood on a small hill in the middle of the arid plain.

Like true cavaliers in a fantasia, all the others launched themselves toward that goal at a rapid gallop, uttering cries of "Inshallah!"—Glory to God—while firing rifles. Then they stopped, forming an enormous circle around the central point of the mosque, in the middle of which the tribal chiefs were standing.

Sabirat, whom no one was any longer thinking of keeping under surveillance, pushed his horse forward and arrived in the first row.

Suddenly, he uttered an exclamation: the man who, in the middle of a troop of warriors, was standing at the foot of the ruined mosque, looming over those surrounding him by virtue of his height, was Alexandroff Wintscheff.

Sabirat thought that he was saved; how could he divine that he was confronting a renegade of civilization?

III

The spectacle that Sabirat had before his eyes was both splendid and frightening. The plain was black with horsemen, and beneath the dazzling sun there was an amazing riot of colors, of sparkling banners and immense flags, on which monsters of every form displayed their grimacing faces.

What struck the imagination above all, however, was the enormity of the swarm, conveying the impression of a multitude of which any calculation seemed to defy human reason.

Sandorf had raised his hand, which bore a standard striped with a hundred colors, but which was cut through by a traversal green bar.

In the other hand, he was brandishing a heavy sword.

As if by enchantment, the cries died down, and Sandorf took a few steps forward, climbing a mound, from which he could overlook the plain.

He was not alone.

Next to him marched a woman clad in the long robe of an Oriental priestess; it was Sithreva, who, her arms folded over her chest, was reminiscent of a statue descended from its pedestal.

When he reached the top of the mound, Sandorf began to speak, in a resounding voice.

"Glory to God!" he cried. "Brothers, the hour of vengeance has sounded. For long enough and too long the false gods of Europe have insulted the grandeur of the prophet. His voice has echoed through your solitudes and has ordered you to gather around his sacred standard, and to come and chastise insolent Europe. You have obeyed; that is good.

"Already, from every corner of the ancient world, from the seas where the sun rises, the peoples have set forth toward the accursed Occident. From north to south there is one army, a hundred innumerable armies, on the march. What is your first enemy? It is Russia, which has stolen your lands from you, which has dared to violate your customs and outrage your beliefs. Death to the Russians!"

And like a clap of thunder, the cry, repeated by a hundred thousand throats, resounded in the air with terrible echoes that seemed to resonate from one end of the earth to the other.

Sabirat listened, stupefied, wondering whether he was asleep or awake. What! Was it really the young man he had met in Paris, who, seeking pleasure above all else, had declared himself a hundred times over to be a friend of Europeans, of France, who was speaking, exciting the savage passions of these fanat-

124

ics, who were responding to his exhortations with clamors of death? And these threats, these cries of hatred addressed to those who had been his hosts, who had given him a new fatherland...

It was impossible.

Sabirat, unable to control his wrath, urged his horse forward with an abrupt surge and found himself alone at the foot of the mound that Sandorf had made into a pedestal.

"Wretch!" he cried. "What crimes are you meditating? Are you mad or infamous?"

He had shouted those words in French, a language that no one around him except Sandorf understood. By his gestures, however, and his exasperated attitude, those surrounding him had divined that he was insulting their leader, and they threw themselves upon him.

But Sithreva had leaned over the ear of her lover and whispered a few words into it. He raised his hand and ordered that the infidel be brought to him. His orders had an omnipotent effect. The raised arms fell back, and Sabirat was dragged toward Sandorf. Although he was solidly held, Sabirat, fully determined, struggled with the courage of despair.

Sandorf said to him: "Who are you, and what do you want with me?"

"You don't recognize me?" Sabirat said. "Is that because the bandits you command have detained me in a cruel jail for weeks? I'll tell you my name. I'm Dr. Sabirat, Sametel's friend, Prince Batow's friend, the friend of all those you have betrayed."

At the names of Sametel and Prince Batow, Sithreva had stiffened, in a movement of anger. The name of Batow, which was Sacha's, was no longer ever pronounced. "Is it here, Sandorf," she said, "that you ought to listen to this miscreant?"

"You're right, Sithreva. Let him be taken to Bukhara...and I'll make my will known later."

To Bukhara![32] So Sabirat was separated from his homeland by the Caspian deserts! But this land belonged to the Russians, who had extended their empire from Khiva to Samarkand!

He tried to protest, but as Sandorf, having given his orders, had turned away, Turkmen threw themselves upon him and, with a furious brutality, dragged him toward the designated city, the Rome of Islam, as Vambery[33] called it.

---

[32] Bukhara is now the capital of Uzbekistan, on the old Silk Road. It is separated from Persia (i.e., Iran) by Turkmenistan to the south. Kazakhstan lies to the north, including the "Kirghiz steppe," which extends a long way to the northwest of Kirghizstan.

[33] The Hungarian writer Arminius Vambery (1832-1913), who published a memoir of his extensive travels in Central Asia in 1865.

But to the question he had asked himself, a prompt response was given.

Alongside the road by which he was taken, he saw groups of wretched men in chains, some of them bloodied and mutilated. They were Russian soldiers. Then, further on, heaps of corpses were strewn by the roadside, still wearing European uniforms.

There was no doubt about it; it was the crusade of the Orient against the Occident; the first battles of the invasion preached by Sandorf had been fought. And by means of a kind of sudden intuition, Sabirat connected these facts with the Chinese mob whose first eruption he had seen at the session in which Norès had shown what was happening in Peking.

Bukhara was full of soldiers, if one could give that name to the terrible hordes that had invaded it: Uzbeks, Tajiks, Kalmuks, Kipchaks, even Multanis and Hindus! There were Tartars from Yaksu, Yarkend and Kashgar, Khalks from Shandur, Ersari, Kara, Teke and Yomut.

Vagabond troops that saw a European pass by hurled furious obscenities at him. Fortunately, his guards, fanatical servants of Sandorf, the Pir—the Chief—as they called him, intended to carry out his orders to the letter. Twenty times it was necessary for them to respond with force to those who wanted to take their prisoner from them in order to tear him apart. They carved a passage with sword-thrusts, and more than one person paid for his resistance with his life.

Finally, they reached the center of the city, and Sabirat was thrown into one of the cells of the Teke, the great seminary of Islam, today transformed into a citadel occupied by thousands of Turkmen.

So these peoples, fiercely independent, true brigands who lived by plunder and pillage, who hated one another to the point of setting the most perfidious ambushes in the desert, had suddenly been united by this criminal mission preached to them by a fanatic…madman, rather…for Sabirat, alone now in the dark damp cell where they had locked him up, wondered if he had really understood, if it could be true that a man who had appreciated the benefits of civilization, who had enjoyed them, who had left sympathies and affections in European society, had really come to profess such hatred against that which he had seemed to love.

Scarcely an hour had gone by when they came to fetch Sabirat on the Chief's behalf.

He was taken through subterranean passages, perhaps to protect him from the fury of the wretches whose formidable clamors he could hear outside.

Introduced into a room with a high ceiling and a floor covered in rugs, he saw before him Sandorf Wintscheff, standing up, waiting for him.

The Kirghiz—whom Sandorf had believed to be of pure Russian blood—was pale. "Monsieur," he said, in a voice that he strove to render firm, "give thanks to our former friendship, which persuaded me to save your life—but remember that I'm not disposed to listen to insulting words. I am the master here, and your life is in my hands. I am also your judge, and I order you to reply to me."

Sabirat had completely recovered his composure. He considered Wintscheff attentively, and in spite of the calmness the other affected, dissimulating his agitation beneath the rudeness of his language, the doctor understood that his conscience was far from restful.

"Monsieur," the doctor replied, "I don't know who says that you're the master, nor by what right you constitute yourself the judge of a man who has no crime for which to reproach himself, but enlightenment might spring forth from this interrogation of which I have need, so I consent to submit to it. Speak then, and I shall see whether it pleases me to respond."

Wintscheff made a gesture of anger; he thought that he had inspired fear, but he saw that he was dealing with an adversary who was difficult to intimidate.

"How do you come to be in this country?" the Kirghiz demanded, brusquely.

"That first question," Sabirat replied, "appears to me to be singularly ironic. Does one normally demand of a prisoner why he is in his dungeon?"

Wintscheff drew closer to him.

"Prisoner! What does that mean?"

Sabirat had not lost sight of the slightest play of the physiognomy of the Kirghiz, and he remarked that he seemed sincerely surprised as he asked the question.

"Prisoner, I said," Sabirat confirmed, "and I'm astonished that a gallant man should feign ignorance, when he finds himself facing a man whom a single word could doom."

"Monsieur!"

"Do you not know—or are you pretending not to know—that I've been held captive by your followers for more than two weeks?"

"You! On my honor, I had no idea."

Coldly, Sabirat went on: "I heard you just now proffering words of hatred against Europeans, against the Russians…which proves to me, Monsieur, that perhaps you and I do not attach the same meaning to the word *honor*."

Wintscheff became livid. He plugged his hand inside his jacket, and his fingernails dug into his breast.

There is a banal phrase, which alone can explain the sentiments seething in his brain: *God, how annoying it is to be wrong and to know it.*

To be sure, he only had to make a sign to impose silence on the little physician who permitted himself to cast doubt on his word, but the fashion in which Sabirat had pronounced the word "honor" had been, if one might put it thus, essentially French. Wintscheff had understood the nuance in all its finesse, and he sensed that the honor that was being invoked was not that of his interlocutor.

He contained himself and continued: "Monsieur, I urge you, in our own interest, not to try to push me too far. You're right; we're not of the same race. We have neither the same beliefs, nor the same aspirations."

"You have had them."

"I deny them!" asserted Wintscheff. "Oh, you thought, Messieurs of the Occident, that you would pose as eternal masters of the Orient; you thought that with your great words, civilization and progress, you would forever be the exploiters of those millions of people who have their faith, their past, their strength. Those times are past, Monsieur. Yes, I, Alexandroff Wintscheff, deny the Europe that has enslaved my fatherland, which has debased us to the point that we have even forgotten the names that our forefathers left us. No, I'm not Russian; I'm not European; my name is not Wintscheff—a barbaric name with the ring of slavery. Curbed for too long, I have stood straight. Today my name is Tamir the Kirghiz, the descendant of Timur,[34] who was the master of the world. I am the revolt that raises its head, the slave who breaks his yoke. And tomorrow, the master will avenge himself on those who have had the imprudence to declare themselves his masters."

Sabirat considered him attentively. On that overexcited face he had seen the flame of fanaticism gradually ignite. An entire atavism of savagery became visible through those pupils, as ardent as those of wild beasts.

For the young doctor, that was a revelation; he understood what the alliance of enemy peoples, united by that bond, signified: the hatred of the Occidental. A revolt rose within him, but he succeeded in conserving his composure.

"All right," he said. "I won't argue with you. Let's go back to our point of departure—which is to say, the cowardly act that was carried out against me and a defenseless child."

"What do you mean?" exclaimed Wintscheff, whom we shall permit to retain his European name. "Do you believe that Occidentals have the privilege of generosity?"

"I don't know about that," Sabirat replied, "but I don't suppose that when you came to Paris, for example, with…a woman, anyone separated you violently from your companion and threw you into a dungeon."

"Explain yourself clearly!" exclaimed the Kirghiz.

"Gladly." And Sabirat recounted what had happened to him. He passed over in silence, of course, the fashion—eccentric, to say the least—in which he had arrived in the Turkmen region. It was merely a matter, he said, of a scien-

---

[34] Timur (1336-1405), often known in the West as Tamerlane (i.e., Timur the Lame) was a Turko-Mongol conqueror who attempted to restore the Mongol empire of Genghiz Khan, terming himself the Sword of Islam for political reasons. He conquered most of Central Asia and much of northern India, but did not succeed in conquering Ming China or the Ottoman Empire.

tific exploration, something analogous to the mission once undertaken by Madame Dieulafoy and her husband.[35]

"But you weren't alone?" Wintscheff objected. "You had an escort?"

"I beg our pardon. Our men had remained some distance away. We could not have appeared dangerous, and the brutality of your...Orientals...did not seem in the least justifiable."

"Who is the woman accompanying you?"

"I could, Parisian as I am, reply that it's none of your business, but since you seem curious, I'll satisfy you." He took a step toward the Kirghiz and looked him straight in the eyes. "The young woman who accompanied me," he said, was an intimate friend of Nathalie Batowna, Mademoiselle de Norès."

At the name of Nathalie—of which Sacha, it is well-known,[36] is only an abbreviation—Wintscheff took a step back. In the young man's tone, he had understood everything that the name in question suddenly evoked: the sense of reproach, not to say scorn.

A hundred times, Wintscheff had declared himself to be the fiancé of the young Russian woman.

"Now," said Sabirat. "I demand that you tell me what has become of Mademoiselle de Norès...whether you have had her murdered."

"Monsieur!" exclaimed Wintscheff, again, in a tone of outrage. He made a move as if to throw himself at the young man, but the latter had folded his arms disdainfully and was looking him in the face.

The Kirghiz passed his hand over his face. "In truth," he said, in a voice that anger caused to tremble, "you're wrong to challenge me, as I am the stronger of us, but in spite of my...Oriental savagery"—he emphasized the phrase ironically—"I'll remain calm. Listen to me carefully: I know nothing about your arrest and detention. I only learned two days ago that a European had been detained by a Turkmen tribe. I gave orders that he be set free and brought to me. I therefore do not know what has happened."

"*A* European, you say? But what about Mademoiselle de Norès?"

"I was only told that a man had been arrested."

"Which is to say that the wretches have killed her! That would be the most cowardly and infamous of crimes."

---

[35] The ardent feminist Jane Dieulafoy (1851-1916) adopted masculine dress in order to travel with her husband Marcel in Europe, Egypt, Morocco and Persia, keeping an elaborate diary and engaging in studies of a broad archaeological and theological scope. The Dieulafoys obtained permission to lead an official archaeological mission to Persia in 1884; she published the first of her several novels in 1890.

[36] In fact, Sacha or Sasha is usually a contraction of Alexandra, and Lermina seems to have forgotten that he has previously given Sacha's forename as Elena.

"And the most futile," murmured Wintscheff. He added: "Monsieur Sabi-rat, we shall know the truth."

He went to the window. In front of him, a vast square extended, covered with horsemen, who, while waiting for the signal to depart, were engaging in one of those strange fantasias in which riders and horses seem to form a single entity, bounding, turning, and wheeling like a cloud of fantastic animals.

Wintscheff was spotted, and formidable cries burst forth, saluting the lead-er who was about to lead those furious hordes in the pillage of Europe. For all of them, those lands of the Occident were a mysterious region where gold flowed in streams, where always-gilded crops covered immense areas, where the cities contained immense riches stolen from their forefathers—for it was revenge, above all, that these bands wanted to take; their imams, lamas, and monks had repeated a thousand times over that their miseries were due to the Europeans who had robbed them. It was the patrimony of the Orient that it was a matter of recovering; it was their sufferings of old, their famines and even their plagues, that it was necessary to avenge. All the scourges that had fallen upon them were due to the spells and crimes of the Occidentals: those magicians who adored the demon Shaitan, the enemy of Allah, Buddha, and Fo; it was their gods, too, that they were going to defend.

And Wintscheff, absorbed in his dream of power, told himself that he was the master of all those men, who were only waiting for his signal to rush upon the enemy and constitute for him—for him—the vastest empire that had ever been united under the hand of a single man.

Impatiently, Sabirat waited.

"Well, Monsieur," he said, finally, "have you forgotten once again what you have promised?"

Wintscheff shivered, as if suddenly awakened. Then, without answering, he opened the window and made a sign.

The acclamations had redoubled. With a gesture, he gave thanks.

Then he summoned a servant and gave him an order. Sabirat did not under-stand it.

The silence between the two men was heavy now.

Although Wintscheff took pleasure in proclaiming himself a savage, hating the civilization he had enjoyed for such a long time, there nevertheless subsisted within him more than one vestige of the delicacies that the policed life put into the conscience of a man. He was irritated that, at the very outset of his career, hazard had put him in the presence of one of the people he had known before—and in what circumstances! When he had loved to proclaim himself a Parisian *par excellence*, when he had thrown money out of the window to provoke the admiration of those of whom he now declared himself to be the implacable en-emy!

Then again, what did all that matter now? But he had met the doctor at Norès' house in Paris, when he had been the assiduous cavalier of Nathalie Batowna, whom he had loved and had abandoned, treacherously, in the midst of horrible circumstances in Peking.

What had become of her? Had she perished in the torment? In vain, Wintscheff tried to drive those thoughts out of his mind, which now haunted him again, and he dared not turn to look at Sabirat—who, with his eyes fixed upon him, seemed to be reading the utmost depths of his soul.

Suddenly, the door opened.

The two men shivered involuntarily, snatched from their meditations, and a double exclamation escaped their lips.

Sithreva had just come in.

Wintscheff's cry was merely one of surprise; it was not her that he had expected to see. But on the part of the young doctor it was an exclamation of astonishment, admiration, and a vague dread that he could not yet explain.

Now, the young Hindu with the velvet eyes and the warm complexion, with features of an admirable perfection, was no longer the priestess that we once saw fanaticizing the Orientals arranged under the banner of the five hundred gods. She had abandoned the long tunic and the hieratic coiffure that gave her the appearance of a sphinx descended from a granite pedestal.

The woman had become a warrior. A breastplate of metallic mesh, so fine that it seemed to be woven like silk, molded her vigorous bosom, while on her head, a kind of helmet surmounted by a chimera with deployed wings increased her height almost to superhuman dimensions. A darker fire shone in her eyes, and her hand rested on the hilt of a naked sword, attached to her side by a red sash.

She was the very image of War, and more: the goddess of Vengeance, a messenger of death, ignorant of pity.

"You, here, Sithreva!" exclaimed the Kirghiz. "I had ordered that Ko-Hor, the Turkmen chief, should be sent to me."

"But it's me who has come."

"Why?"

"Because I know what questions you desire to address to Ko-Hor, and it's me who will answer you."

Sabirat's eyes went from one to the other, and in an instant, the young man had understood the drama that he was witnessing. He had divined that the man, so proud, so ambitious for an empire, was the slave of the woman, whose fanaticism doubled her superb beauty.

"All right," said Wintscheff, suppressing a gesture of impatience. "The prisoner tells me that he was not alone when he was arrested."

"That is true," said Sithreva.

"A woman was seized at the same time."

"That is true," the Hindu repeated.

"We don't make war on women," said Wintscheff. "The woman is a European, it's true, but she's harmless, and it would be particularly agreeable to me..."

"If she were set free," said Sithreva, smiling ironically.

"Yes...yes...I've interrogated the doctor"—he pointed at Sabirat—"And he's given me very clear explanations. We have no interest in keeping him captive."

Sithreva was looking at him intently, and Wintscheff, stammering in spite of himself, seemed to be pleading rather than giving an order.

"Madame," said Sabirat, intervening, "I don't know what your authority is here, or whether your consent is necessary for a simple act of justice to be done, but I can assure you that we did not come here as enemies..."

Sithreva interrupted him, turning to Wintscheff. "Do you know the name of this young woman?"

"Yes; it's Mademoiselle de Norès, I believe."

"Which is to say," said Sithreva, "the sister of the man whose name is on everyone's lips today—who, it appears, is preparing engines of destruction against us that will frighten the world."

"Monsieur de Norès," said Sabirat, "is valiantly defending his homeland."

Sithreva did not reply to him; it was still Wintscheff that she was addressing. "This Norès, if I'm not mistaken, is the fiancé of Mademoiselle Marguerite Sametel?"

Wintscheff blushed: to mention Marguerite was to make allusion to his previous engagement to Sacha.

"Sametel!" the Hindu continued. "Another name that it is necessary for us not to forget, for it is that of one of our most ardent adversaries—the Sametel who was the most active agent of the invaders who had sworn to enslave the Orient."

"But this young woman is not their accomplice."

"You think so?" said Sithreva, shrugging her shoulders. "You have for these people, our most dangerous enemies—for they belong to the accursed nation of France, which claims to be at the head of the civilizing movement—a very singular indulgence of which I don't seek to know the cause. But it's of no importance; people, as you like to tell me, are only responsible for their own actions. So be it! And it's for their actions alone that you ought to demand that this man and woman account."

"Our actions?" exclaimed Sabirat. "Are you claiming that we've committed some crime?"

"How do you treat spies in your country?"

"They're put to death."

"Well," said Sithreva, extending her arm toward Wintscheff, "to you, who have accepted the supreme command and who answers for the security of our soldiers, I denounce this man and I denounce Mademoiselle de Norès as spies and traitors."

"Infamy!" cried Sabirat. "Ah! Since it's a woman who proffers that insult, it's from you, felon and true traitor, that I demand account for it!"

And the young doctor, carried away by anger, threw himself at Wintscheff, arm raised.

Before it could come down, however, men had appeared who threw themselves upon him and knocked him down.

"Yes, spies," Sithreva continued, "And more than that. Wintscheff, occupied with military organization and the thousand cares of command, you cannot watch over everything—but have no fear; I am here...and I know how to defend you."

She went to Sabirat, whose guards were now holding him firmly.

"Frenchman, friend of Norès," she said to him, in a wrathful voice that hissed between her teeth, "what is the diabolical machine you have transported into the cemetery of Yeni-Khosroul?"

Sabirat started in surprise. What did she mean?

"Oh! You're feigning ignorance," Sithreva continued. "These Occidentals are audacious in their hypocrisy." To the guards, she said: "Take this man to that window." She went on: "Look now, and tell me if you understand me better."

The window to which Sabirat was taken overlooked an interior courtyard, and there, on a cart drawn by yaks, the doctor recognized Norès' aerostatic apparatus.

Was that, then, what the Hindu called a diabolical machine?

He could not help smiling. He now divined the errors inspired in these ignorant people by the sight of an apparatus with which they were not familiar and of which they could not deduce the marvelous usage.

"What's that?" cried Wintscheff—who, better versed in Occidental sciences, was nevertheless unable to imagine the purpose of the curious machine. "Is it true that you've transported that into this country?"

It would be more accurate to ask, Sabirat thought, *how the machine transported us. In any case, I have no intention of replying.*

"You remain silent!" exclaimed Sithreva. "Your silence is a confession in itself. In any case, do you think that we have not recognized one of those engines of death, formidable destroyers, that your Norès and your Sametels devise for the ruination of their adversaries? It is veritable audacity to have transported such an instrument of murder to this almost unknown region, but the more difficult the action is to comprehend the more we suspect some infamy and monstrous invention. It has fallen into our hands; it belongs to us."

"And what can you do with it?" Sabirat could not help crying. "I defy you to discover its secret."

Scarcely had he spoken than a smile of triumph brightened Sithreva's face. "So," she said, "you admit that there is a secret?"

Sabirat shut up, understanding that he had said too much.

"Oh, you won't keep silent forever," she said, in a singular tone, in which Sabirat detected a threat. "You're not forgetting that you're a prisoner, and I don't suppose that our chief will insist now that you are set free."

"With the consequence," Sabirat replied, "that because you're ignorant, I'm condemned to perpetual imprisonment."

"Ignorant? At last we're asking to be educated. Explain the usage of that machine to us, and you're free."

"So it's a treason that you're asking of me?"

"If the secret of that machine is inoffensive, if it doesn't conceal some means of warfare and destruction, why refuse to speak? And why would you be a traitor, if it's not a weapon of war?"

Sithreva, sure of herself, was speaking with a calmness that was no longer deceptive. And, indeed, the logic of her words was unassailable.

Strictly speaking, Guy de Norès' machine was not a weapon of war, but Sabirat was not a man to make use of sophistry in order to avoid what he knew to be his duty. Whatever it was, the secret did not belong to him, and he did not have the right to reveal it.

"Do with me what you wish," he said, in a firm voice. "I won't speak."

"We'll soon be able to vanquish your resistance!" cried the Hindu.

"Which is to say that you'll appeal to your torturers and you'll tear me limb from limb. Do it. I swear to you that you won't extract a word from my lips."

"But you're not the only one who possesses the secret," retorted Sithreva, after a pause.

"What do you mean?" exclaimed Sabirat. "Do you dare to talk about Mademoiselle de Norès? Would you have the infamy to employ means unworthy of civilized beings on her?"

"You know full well that we are not civilized."

"Wretches!"

Sabirat writhed, attempting to escape the grip of his guards. Sithreva's last words had filled him with fear and horror. Certainly, he knew Marie too well to admit for a moment that she would yield to threats, but if these bandits were to torture her…!

Sithreva had approached Wintscheff and whispered something into his ear.

The Kirghiz had nodded his head in assent, without saying a word.

Sabirat understood that it was his fate and Marie's that was being decided at this tragic moment, so he summoned up all his strength to recover his composure and to be ready to support all the physical or mental ordeals that it might please these bandits to inflict upon him.

But would the young woman have the same strength?

At the thought of what these torturers might make her suffer, he experienced a horrible anguish.

Meanwhile, Sithreva had made a sign, and Sabirat's guards, dirty Turkmen, mere contact with whom disgusted him, took hold of him more tightly and dragged him toward the door.

He turned his head. Neither Sithreva nor Wintscheff was following him. Where were they taking him?

He was obliged to go down long staircases, and then to follow long, narrow, and damp corridors, of which his eyes could scarcely make out the eroded walls, over which water was streaming. Evidently, he was being taken underground to some dungeon, in which he was about to be locked.

Eventually, however, he felt the ground underfoot rising again. A door suddenly opened wide in front of him…and the sun was so ardent, the passage from darkness to light so abrupt, that he was constrained to close his eyes momentarily.

When he opened them again, he saw before him a vast courtyard, closed on three sides by buildings, but open on the fourth to an arid and bare plain.

Around the courtyard, soldiers with ferocious faces were massed, armed with rifles and sabers.

A company, in response to an order, came to surround him, and his guards then ceased to hold him. It was like a deliverance.

But in that movement, the troop that now guarded him had revealed a corner of the courtyard, where Sabirat recognized Norès' aerostat, on the cart as he had already seen, with its shiny propeller, reminiscent of the wing of some fantastic bird.

It was very difficult to divine what was happening now.

The soldiers had drawn their swords and were putting the points to his breast.

As he raised his head, in a movement of pride and disdain, as a true Frenchman, who does not fear death, he saw Sithreva on a balcony, leaning on Wintscheff's shoulder, watching.

He smiled scornfully and folded his arms, taking pleasure in defying the renegade and his fanatical accomplice.

"Frenchman," said Sithreva's voice, full and sonorous, which reached him distinctly, "are you ready to surrender de Norès' secret to us?"

"No," he replied, resolutely.

"Well then, look."

Then the group of soldiers that had their backs to the palace, opposite the side open to the plain, stepped aside, in order to reveal…

Sabirat uttered a fury and desperate cry.

This is what he saw:

There was a cannon—a bronze monster—and in front of it mouth, attached to it, was Marie de Norès, pale but equally impassive, holding her head high.

A prisoner since the moment when Sabirat had been separated from her, Marie had borne the miseries of her captivity courageously, but what dangers

135

she had run in the midst of those brutes with human faces! Fortunately, from the first day, a kind of dervish had been attached to her heels...

He had been the first to divine that the machine, whose purpose he could not determine, constituted an invention for whose secret the Chief would pay dear. Far from employing violence, he had attempted by means of hypocritical kindness to capture the young woman's confidence. She had divined the trap, but, taking advantage of the dispositions of the man who had constituted himself as her benevolent jailer, she had not given him a formal refusal. By means of procrastination and promises, she had succeeded in gaining time, hoping that an unexpected circumstance might furnish an opportunity to escape.

She knew that Sabirat was alive. The night before her departure, she had even convinced the dervish that before speaking she had to confer with the prisoner, who was the only one, she said, who knew the entire secret—and in the fever of his curiosity, the Oriental had consented to attempt to establish communication between them.

Unfortunately, the order to join the main body of the army had arrived abruptly, and the plan had been aborted. And Sithreva, informed of the young woman's captivity and irritated by the hazard that put her in the presence of someone she still considered as a rival, had demanded that she be handed over to her. She had come to interrogate her and had demanded treason, as she had of Sabirat.

Marie had only replied to the infamous proposal with scorn. And the Hindu had sworn to exact a pitiless vengeance.

A little while before, Marie had been taken from her prison and now she was here, attached to that engine of death, which they had had the cruelty to load in front of her. One gesture would provoke its explosion.

She was resigned, fortified by her patriotism and her honor.

Suddenly, she too had perceived Sabirat, surrounded by soldiers, threatened by death, and had allowed a cry of fear and sadness to escape.

The young doctor had raised his furious fist toward the balcony.

"Wretched woman," he shouted, "and you, even more cowardly man, I wish I were near enough to you to spit all my hatred in your face!"

Wintscheff made a movement of rage. Sithreva restrained him.

At the same time, she made a sign, and a man emerged from the ranks of soldiers: a kind of priest with a long white beard, enveloped in a green kaftan, indicating that he had made the pilgrimage to Mecca. He was a Hadji from Chinese Tartary, as evidenced by his white turban.

He had undoubtedly received preliminary instructions, because, without asking what the mute order meant, he advanced slowly toward the young woman, and, when he was a few paces away from her, said in French, in a deep and guttural voice: "You know what Nasib"—Destiny—"has decided for you? Death is touching you. If you have any power over this man here, hasten to use it, for pity is ready to remove you. Let him reveal to the Pir the secret of the mysterious machine, and both of you will be free. If he refuses, you will die first. Then, for a second time, he will be summoned to obey, and if he does not submit, the Angel of Death will take him. Do you understand?"

For all the spectators of the sinister scene, Marie de Norès, very pale, offered the image of proud resignation and nothing more—but a Parisian who had observed her at close range would have noticed something at the corner of her lips resembling a smile of mockery and bravado.

When the Hadji had finished, she replied: "First of all, what influence do you think my voice can have on the Frenchman, my companion, at this distance? He could scarcely hear me, and there is, I believe, a Turkmen proverb that says: *Persuasion murmurs, but does not shout.*"

Thus, while her torturers thought they had crushed her strength by means of terror, she had not lost her composure for an instant, had not weakened for a minute. Since the moment when she had been separated from the man whom she now considered to be her fiancé, as her husband, she had not lost the hope of finding him again and of escaping with him. Even when she had been attached to the mouth of the cannon, the bronze of which was bruising her, her indomitable hope had not abdicated.

She was on the lookout for an opportunity, ready to profit from the slightest circumstance, and, to tell the truth, had a kind of intimate conviction, irrational but instinctive, that she had nothing to fear, and that Sabirat would be saved along with her.

How? By what miracle? She had no idea; she only knew that it was so—and that certainty, which had no basis but was unshakable within her, gave her intelligence and incredible acuity.

The Hadji had remained still momentarily, his clenched hands on his breast. He too had expected tears and supplications, but the young woman he believed to be broken by fear was replying to him clearly, with the most perfect logic.

And furthermore, she was quite right.

They hoped, in order to extract a secret, to abuse the affection that they assumed to exist between the two people; was it on terror alone that it was appropriate to speculate? Would the supplications of the lover not be more powerful?

The Hadji had understood, and in Marie de Norès' tone he thought he had detected the intention to obtain the desired sacrifice from Sabirat.

In truth, the lives of the two strangers were of no importance; one interest overrode all others: the knowledge of the machine, which the Oriental imagination had endowed with fantastic virtues—which was perhaps the case, although not in the sense that they supposed.

"What did she say?" demanded Sithreva, who had not heard.

The Hadji replied in a loud voice, but in Chinese. "She says that if she is allowed to speak to her lover, she has the power to persuade him."

The Hadji was embroidering slightly, but who would not have done so in his situation?

"All right," said Sithreva. "I'll give them five minutes. Let them be detached and brought together."

Sithreva had spoken in French in order to be understood by Marie; there was still a certain vanity among the foreigners in proving to the French that they could speak their language.

Marie shivered with joy.

Was she really thinking of betraying her brother's secret? The death that was confronting her was one of the most horrible the imagination can conceive. Was it not possible that her feminine nerves might be unable to resist that agonizing anguish?

The order had been given, however, to reunite briefly the two young people. Untied, Sabirat had run to Marie, and, my God, forgetting completely what propriety would have demanded in a Parisian drawing room, had taken her in his arms and clasped her ardently to his heart, so forcefully that, greatly troubled, she struggled like a captive bird and freed herself, blushing deeply—but not sorry.

"Before all these people, Monsieur Sabirat!" she murmured.

"That's true—I beg your pardon, but what do you expect; it was stronger than me. I beg you to forgive me."

"Oh, I don't hold it against you—but let's talk and talk quickly, for these people don't seem to me to have a great deal of benevolence toward us. It's understood, isn't it, that you have no more intention than I have of telling these miscreants what my brother's invention can do?"

"Certainly not; it would be a betrayal, which would horrify me."

"On the other hand," Marie continued, "it's very evident that if we don't give them satisfaction, we're doomed."

"Obviously. For myself, I'm not unduly concerned; a Frenchman is a soldier of his country, and owes his life to the fatherland...but you..."

"I'm a Frenchwoman; know that I love my country with all my heart, and am ready to die for those I love."

She had said that so valiantly, with a gaze so frank and expressive, addressed to Sabirat, that he had to restrain himself very firmly in order not to repeat his indiscretion of a few moments before.

"We have no hope, then!" he exclaimed, suddenly.

"Who can tell?"

"Didn't you hear what that woman said?"

"Of course: either we surrender our secret, or we die."

"And what a death! When I saw you at the mouth of that cannon just now..."

"I assure you that it wasn't as uncomfortable as all that."

"You have the courage to joke?"

"It's necessary to have every courage."

"Except that of seeing those one loves suffer. Do you think I'm afraid to die? That's what I want to shout at them...let them take my life...but let you go."

"Do you think that I could live without you?" said Marie, holding out her hand to him. "Perhaps it's not very correct, but I'm sure that Maman won't blame me for getting engaged without consulting her. They're already getting impatient. Will you do as I say?"

"What do you mean?"

"I want you to obey me in everything...as if you were already my husband."

"Can you doubt it? What could I do that would be sweeter for me than obeying you?"

"Well then, step back two paces. There, that's good! Now, pay attention, and above all, look very emotional."

The recommendation was superfluous, for Sabirat was utterly amazed when he saw the young woman throw herself at his feet, while she cried: "I beg you, I implore you...tell them what you know...I don't want them to kill me...mercy, my friend, mercy!"

And she threw her arms around him, whispering: "Push me away and shout: *no, no!*"

He had no clear idea where the comedy was going, but he did as he was told, making grand gestures and trying to free himself.

"So," Marie continued, in a tone of high drama, "you were lying when you told me that you loved me?" Between sobs, she murmured: "Weaken. Begin to be shaken. Say: *But what about the Fatherland.*"

"But what about the Fatherland?" repeated Sabirat, bewildered. "The Fatherland!"

"What does the Fatherland matter? You should only think about me...about me, who loves you." In a low voice, she added: "That's me compromised!"

In sum, the scene had been well enough played for Sithreva to be following it breathlessly, leaning over the balcony with profound attention.

She had a ferocious idea, which, she did not realize, completed the effect that Marie was attempting to produce.

"We need to finish this," she shouted. "Soldiers, seize that woman and carry out my orders!"

The soldiers advanced toward Marie in order to grab her—but the young woman had had time to whisper to the doctor: "Consent now...don't worry, I'll answer for everything!"

And Sabirat, who had begun to glimpse the objective at which Marie was aiming, shouted: "No, no! Stop! I consent...I consent!"

Sithreva uttered a cry of triumph. She had, therefore, crushed the pride of the damned Occidentals, so proud of their patriotism! She could hold them in scorn!

"Bring them here," she ordered.

And a few moments later, Sabirat and Marie appeared before Wintscheff and the Hindu again.

In the long dark corridor through which they had passed, Marie had explained everything to Sabirat.

"I knew full well," said Sithreva, sniggering, "that fear would weaken with your resistance. So much for the courage of the French in the face of death."

Sabirat opened his mouth to reply, but Marie squeezed his hand and threw herself at the Hindu's feet. "He consents, Madame, he consents to everything, but I beg you, don't make him pay too dear for the sacrifice he's making for the woman he loves! You're a woman, don't you understand what he's suffering? Are you not loved—you, so beautiful—sufficiently to admire love in others?"

"Let's not discuss ridiculous sentimentalities!" cried Wintscheff, who could not help feeling ill at ease before the young woman that Sithreva was torturing. Monsieur, have you decided, yes or no, to demonstrate the use of the machine to us?"

Sabirat felt a strong desire to leap at his throat, but he had strength to contain himself. "I'm ready," he said.

"First tell me what the machine's purpose is."

"It's an instrument of war."

"I knew it!" cried Sithreva. "And how did you bring it here?"

"By means of a dirigible balloon," Sabirat replied, earnestly.

"What!" cried Wintscheff. "The trials I witnessed have succeeded already?"

"Almost completely," said the doctor. "And the proof is the presence of the machine in a place where no one saw it arrive."

"But I repeat, what does it do?"

"It's a military televox." While pronouncing that barbaric term, Sabirat maintained a perfectly serious tone.

"Tele…?" queried the Kirghiz

"Televox," Sabirat completed. "Compounded from two words, one Greek: *tele*, rapid; and the other Latin: *vox*, voice."

"But we already have the telephone."

"Oh, it's not at all the same thing. The telephone transmits the voice of the person who speaks into it…"

"Indeed…and the televox?"

"Transmits, by contrast, the voice of another. Which is to say that at ten, twenty, fifty or a thousand meters, once can hear the voice of someone speaking as if one were beside them. It's surprising…and you understand that on campaign, being able to overhear the secrets of the enemy…"

140

It was not very clear, and Sabirat was becoming slightly confused. Marie had told him to invent some kind of apparatus and implant the desire to have a demonstration right away, but that it must not be an apparatus of locomotion or a weapon. The specification was not one of the easiest to fulfill, especially when one only had five minutes to come up with a good plan—but human vanity has incredible resources to come to the aid of brave individuals.

In his capacity as a semi-European, Wintscheff wanted to appear before Sithreva to be well up in matters of modern science, and although he did not really understand, he said: "I get it. It's a kind of loudhailer."

"In reverse," Marie put in. She added: "It's my brother's latest and most marvelous invention, and it's very simple. Now that we've decided to save our life at any price, we can tell you everything. Thanks to that machine, we can hear from here what's being said in St. Petersburg."

"That's impossible."

"It's the case," Marie repeated, boldly. "You don't know then, what electricity can do in the hands of a genius like my brother. Inside the machine there's what we call an orientator. One places the needle on the city to which one wishes to be instantaneously connected, in terms of sound, and it's extraordinary: one can hear the noise of the streets. Then one steers toward the houses where something of interest is being said, and one eavesdrops on the conversations, so to speak. Would you like us to prove it to you?"

"Of course I would," said Sithreva.

"If you'd care to accompany us to the machine, the demonstration will soon be made."

"I'll come with you. Come on, Wintscheff.

The Kirghiz—we could easily say the ex-Russian—torn between his ambition and his memories of being a civilized man, uttered a sigh of relief. To be sure, he was under the absolute empire of Sithreva, but the Hindu's fanaticism sometimes frightened him, and he felt himself being drawn down a slippery slope at the bottom of which he glimpsed an abyss of blood and terror. If Sithreva had given the signal condemning Sabirat and Marie de Norès to death, he would not have raised a hand to halt the executioners, but it was a veritable joy for him not to be forced to ratify a action that he would have considered, in the depths of his soul, to be brutal, cruel, and unworthy of the man he had been.

Thus he hastened in response to the Hindu's summons, and the group now returned to the vast courtyard where, in the midst of the soldiers, the cart carrying the machine was. Solid ropes secured it to the vehicle.

Marie was able to exchange a few words with Sabirat, who had nodded his head as a sign of acquiescence.

"Monsieur," said the doctor to the Kirghiz, "it's necessary, for the demonstration to be useful, for the machine to be taken down from the cart and placed on joists that hold it off the ground.

"All right."

Orders were given and groups of men set to work. Sabirat supervised the operation carefully, making sure above all that none of the external mechanisms were damaged in the process. Sithreva and all the Orientals followed the operation with the profoundest attention. Marie kept very close to Sabirat, and, in truth, the two now gave the appearance of two professors about to make a demonstration of their own accord to docile and attentive pupils.

The most curious of all was the Hadji who had kept Marie prisoner, and who was biting his fists in rage at not having constrained her by force to surrender the secret to him. So, thanks to his holy garment, he had gradually slid into the first row, and was almost touching the machine, wanting to grasp more rapidly than anyone else the key to the enigma that might have made him rich had the known it before anyone else. Even if one has made the pilgrimage to Mecca, one is nonetheless a man, and the worthy dervish would not have disdained a few significant rewards.

Hazard served him marvelously. He found himself placed in such a way that he was half-hidden behind the shell of the machine and could speak to Marie without being seen.

"Frenchwoman," he said to her, "you don't suspect treason. When you've spoken, you and your companion will be killed. I alone can save you by saying that your life has been placed under the protection of Allah. Only give part of the secret to the Pir and reserve the complete knowledge of it for me, and I'll save you. If not, I'll let the executioners do their work."

It was a commission of a new kind that the worthy man was demanding, and it would not have taken much for Marie, on hearing his petty conditions, to give way to involuntary hilarity. She replied in the same tone: "Agreed, but you have to swear to take us under your protection."

"I swear."

"By the beard of the prophet?"

"By the beard of Mohammed."

That was a binding contract, and the Hadji, joyfully, moved even closer to the machine, placing his hands on the doorway that Sabirat had just opened, and plunging his gaze inside. At a glance, the latter had observed that, by an incredible hazard, no damage had been done; the Turkmen, fearful of an explosion, had handled the object with the utmost care, and everything was intact.

Sithreva advanced and, leaning on Wintscheff, asked what experiment they were going to carry out first.

Singularly enough, at that moment, the violence she possessed, with all her Oriental finesse, caused her to abandon all suspicion. She knew—or, rather believed—that she was the absolute mistress of the life of the two fiancés, and that was sufficient for all anxiety to have disappeared. In addition, the scorn and hatred that the Europeans inspired in her caused her to find it perfectly natural that they would purchase their survival with treason.

142

"The best thing to do," said Sabirat, "is to offer you a preliminary proof of the ability of the machine. Say something into Wintscheff's ear that only he can hear, and we'll listen to it from inside the machine and repeat it to you."

That did, indeed, seem impossible, in spite of the short distance separating the two groups.

"Do it, then," said Sithreva.

"But for that," Sabirat added, "we need to close the door of the box."

"Obviously," said Wintscheff, very interested in the experiment, and wanting to be sure that the words could not be heard by ears alone.

Sabirat and Marie de Norès found themselves inside once again.

"Marie," said the young man, "you're not unaware that we're going to risk a terrible death again?"

"I know—but anything rather than remain in the power of these barbarians."

In the meantime Sithreva put her lips close to Wintscheff's ear.

"Are you ready?" shouted the doctor's voice from the interior.

"Yes," replied Sithreva, and added, in a very low voice, in the Kirghiz' ear: "I love you."

But the response to her was a furious cry of rage from Wintscheff, complicated by furious clamors from the crowd, and a horrible howl of terror.

For this is what had happened:

"God's will be done!" Sabirat had said, pressing Marie's head to his bosom—and resolutely, he had pulled down the lever, trembling lest the anticipated effect might not be produced, by virtue of some unknown accident.

As in de Norès' workshop, however, the apparatus, after oscillating for a hundredth of a second, had shot up vertically into the air more than two hundred meters.

Wintscheff had shoved Sithreva away so violently that he had almost knocked her down. Then, raising his arm, he cried in a thunderous voice: "Fire! Fire at the wretches!"

A few detonations burst forth, but at the same instant, the marabouts, hadjis, and other holy mendicants threw themselves toward the soldiers, imploring them not to shoot.

Out of generosity? Hardly.

In consciousness of the futility of that fusillade? Not that either.

For the strangest and most inexplicable of reasons.

It will not have been forgotten that the Hadji who had proposed a subtreasonous treaty to Marie de Norès had positioned himself in such a way that he was in the best place to divine the secret of which the young woman, he believed, was only going to reveal in part to Wintscheff and the Hindu. As it was a matter, however, of striking a sufficiently indifferent pose not to be suspected of espionage, the worthy Hadji, whose name was Ben-Borouk, had perched himself on the external edge of the hull and, in order not to slide off, had grasped one of the blades of the external propeller.

In that fashion, his head was adjacent to the wall, and he would hear what was being said and done inside.

It was well planned—but then, without any warning, the machine had risen into the air with an incomparable velocity.

Ben-Borouk howling—and surely no one would be sufficiently unjust to think it a crime—wanted to hold on, but to what? To the ground, which was fleeing beneath his feet with dizzying rapidity. Illusion! In brief, he let go, and would have fallen headfirst if, by a freak of chance, his camelhair tunic had not been caught up in the propeller, as if by an iron claw.

Have you ever seen a horse being loaded onto a ship? A large strap is passed under its belly, and attached to a crane. Hoist away! And the animal is suspended, its feet in the air, rotating above the quay, looking stupidly bewildered, as old Corneille put it.

The case of the unfortunate Ben-Borouk was absolutely identical.

He was suspended by his back, his arms and legs hanging down...a uniquely delicate situation, not to say uniquely ridiculous, and exceedingly dangerous, for however solid a camelhair garment might be, its resistance has its limits, like everything human.

And the servant of Mohammed howled more and more loudly.

It is now explicable why Ben-Borouk's colleague had stopped the soldiers who were about to fire. Hadjis do not eat one another.

When Sabirat and Marie de Norès had felt the machine leave the ground, and when, through the pothole, they had seen clouds envelop them, they had—forgive them, Lord!—thrown themselves into one another's arms as if they had been married with all the civil and religious sacraments.

It was deliverance; it was escape...and from what a horrible death! They remained motionless momentarily, enjoying that return to life, to hope.

And through the opening, rays of splendid sunlight enveloped them like an halo. It was marvelous, and the children can be forgiven for having lost sight momentarily of the clarity of the situation, inasmuch as Sabirat, who could feel Marie's hair against his breast, was not in the least disposed to philosophy. It was sufficient for him to be alive, and he wanted the moment to last forever.

Women being more reasonable than men, however—that is an axiom we must accept, whether we like it or not—Marie was the first to remember the danger they had run before, when the aerial vessel had previously transported them into space.

"Friend," she said, disengaging herself from his arms, "where are we? Don't you remember?—first, it's necessary to level off."

"That's true," said Sabirat, stifling a sigh. "I forgot everything—forgive me."

"Oh, I forgive you," Marie said.

After a moment's reflection, Sabirat gently raised the lever again, in accordance with the lesson of past experience, and he felt the movement of elevation fade away.

"Fly horizontally," breathed Marie. "Now we need to get our bearings."

And as Sabirat obeyed, she knelt down and uncovered the orifice in the floor.

"The ground can no longer be seen distinctly," she said. "We're out of range, but it's necessary not to remain over this accursed country. You know the two levers that permit eastward and westward direction."

"And also north and south, for now I understand the principle of the movement of the levers above and below the horizontal. Each of them produces two directions, which correspond to the four cardinal points. If we at least had a compass! Which direction should one choose when one doesn't know where one is?"

"Bah!" said Marie, with a small gesture of obstinacy. "Let's go first, and see later. I'm confident."

The fact is that, having escaped Sithreva's clutches, they had a perfect right to rely on Providence.

"Westwards, then," said Sabirat, resolutely. "We're in the Orient, and logic dictates that we should try to get back to our homeland if we can."

"So be it—westwards."

Sabirat collected himself quickly, studied the levers like a pianist before his keyboard, and lifted the one on the right.

There was a formidable purr outside, accompanied by a howl so savage and so strident that Marie went frightfully pale.

"What's that?" she exclaimed. "One might take it for a human scream!"

"I'll find out," said Sabirat, and moved to open the door.

"Be careful!" cried Marie. "If you stumbled..."

"No, no, I'm sure of myself."

Resolutely, Sabirat opened the door and peered out.

What he saw surpassed all description.

It will be remembered that the Hadji had been in the situation of a sack of wheat hanging from a hook—a stable position, although paralyzing—and in the panic caused by the very elevated placement, far above sea level, he had no longer been able to utter the slightest sound, abandoning himself to the will of the prophet, who, as everyone knows, keeps an accurate record of future events: what is written is written. He remained motionless by instinct, moreover, understanding that the slightest agitation might provoke the tearing of the camelhair, his only hope and his only safeguard. Oh, if the goods were shoddy...[37]

---

[37] There is an untranslatable pun here by virtue of the accidental relationship between *camelote* [shoddy goods] and camel. Lermina was not to know that *camelote* would also become, in due course, a slang term for cocaine.

Thus, it was still supportable…until the moment when Sabirat had, so to speak, set a westward course. Because the tiller was linked to the propeller to which the holy man was so unfortunately attached, the propeller had begun rotating.

A sickening rotation! A desolating gyration, for it carried the unfortunate Ben-Borouk with it in its whirl, and he was now spinning like one of those artificial fireworks that are the joy of idlers.

And that as what Sabirat saw: a rotating mass in which he could only distinguish something long that was in circular movement, like the sails of a windmill under the pressure of a strong wind.

Marie had leaned out behind him, also looking with a curiosity mingled with terror.

Suddenly, she recalled the scream she had heard, and launched herself toward the lever.

"We have to stop!" she cried. "It's a man!"

"Not too abruptly!" Sabirat had time to shout.

Indeed, he had understood that the object, whatever it was, would fly off at a tangent, like a stone from a sling, if the interruption were too abrupt.

Marie had heard, and lowered the lever gently to the horizontal.

Now Sabirat could see the Hadji, who was rotating more slowly.

The propeller finally came to a stop, while the aerial vehicle hovered.

Sabirat, who had leaned out, hanging onto an external handle with one hand, succeeded in seizing hold of the wretch, who was hanging inertly, stunned and hypnotized by the rapidity of the gyration.

Fortunately, the young doctor was exceptionally vigorous; otherwise it would have been impossible to carry out the audacious and difficult maneuver by means of which he succeeded in bringing the suspended man over the platform that formed a step outside the door, and finally rolling him inside.

The Hadji collapsed like a bag of damp rags.

"Let's head westwards again," Sabirat said to Marie de Norès. "I'll try to get this excellent savage back on his feet."

And while the propeller, freed from its burden, throbbed with a formidable roar, Sabirat knelt down next to the unfortunate Turkmen and massaged him vigorously.

Success soon crowned his efforts, and he had the satisfaction of hearing the holy personage sneeze vigorously—which is always a good sign.

Ben-Borouk opened his eyes very wide, only to close them again more rapidly. Perhaps the worthy Hadji thought that he had crossed the bridge that takes pious Mohammedans to Paradise, and had experienced a disagreeable shock on seeing, instead of the expected houri, the bearded face of Sabirat—who, moreover, in a voice that had nothing feminine about it, said to him: "Come on, stir yourself—show a little energy."

The holy man was literally bewildered; anyone would have been. Fortunately, Sabirat spotted in his belt something that had all the appearance of a water bottle, doubtless filled from some sacred spring.

He detached it and, before putting it to the Hadji's lips, took a sniff. He could not suppress a burst of laughter; it was barley liquor, something like prime quality raki. Admittedly, its effect would be all the more sure and even more immediate.

The holy man took a long draught—so long that Sabirat had to wrench the bottleneck from between his teeth.

The panacea quickly took effect, and the Hadji, widening his eyes, demanded in a surly voice that proved the complete reestablishment of his lungs: "Where am I?"

"My dear Monsieur," said Sabirat, "It would be impossible for me to inform you very precisely. All that I can say for sure is that you're between one thousand and two thousand meters above sea level.

"What!" said the Hadji, bounding to his feet.

"It's the simple truth, and since you seem to me to be quite well, if you'd care to take a look out of this porthole, you'll soon be convinced that I'm telling the truth."

He had opened the lower viewport, and the Hadji leaned over, shivering in every limb. He invoked Allah an appropriate number of times—after which Sabirat thought it useful to give him a few explanations.

Ben-Borouk had some difficulty understanding what had happened, in so far as his knowledge of aeronautics was somewhat limited, but he was obliged to yield to the evidence. It was not by courtesy of the Prophet that he was suspended in a box hundreds of feet above the mountains. Admittedly, as soon as the notion had entered his head, he was gripped by an intense terror, and, while shivering from head to toe, he begged Sabirat to descend to the ground.

"It's easy for you to say that," said the young man, laughing, "but it would displease us greatly to become involved in an adventure similar to the one from which we've just extracted ourselves so fortunately. Tell us where we are, and I promise to take your request into careful consideration."

Marie intervened. "We must have traveled a long way," she said. "We can't know any more as long as we remain at this height. Don't you think, my friend, that it would be prudent to move closer to the ground and try to get our bearings?"

"Right," said Sabirat. "This time, it's broad daylight, and there's no danger of descending into a place as sinister as the first time."

"But how can you go down?" exclaimed the Hadji.

"You'll see that nothing is simpler," Sabirat replied, who was not reluctant to put on a demonstration of an experiment so dearly acquired. "This is what we do."

He put his hand on the descent lever. There was a slight shock, as when one applies a brake, and the voyagers felt themselves descending.

"All's well," said Sabirat. "Let's moderate the movement in order to remain at a range from which we can inform ourselves precisely."

He knelt down in his turn and gazed attentively through the downward viewport.

"It's bizarre," he said. "It seems that I can see little white clouds rising up in the direction of our vehicle and then suddenly separating and dispersing in the air. What can it be? At the very bottom, I can see a very large white cloud, with jets of smoke at its extremities..."

Suddenly, a crackling sound became audible.

The aerial vessel was going downwards with disorienting rapidity.

Other abrupt noises, similar to explosions, ripped through the air.

"Go back up!" he cried to Marie. "I understand everything—we're being bombarded."

Indeed, as Marie, still a novice in the operation of the apparatus, did not return the lever rapidly enough to the vertical position, shells of enormous dimension began to burst around the airship.

Sabirat had stood up in order to accelerate the maneuver.

Either because the movement was too abrupt, or because some component of the apparatus had suddenly broken down, he sensed that the vessel was no longer obedient.

"My God!" cried Marie. "One might think that we were out of control!"

It was true; a moment ago, the aerial vessel had started spinning, like a wounded bird. It rose up, descended, and headed north, only to veer southwards a moment later. Sabirat tried in vain to regain control, bringing all the levers into play one by one, with infinite precaution, but the expected effects were not produced.

Suddenly, Marie cried: "Look, my friend, at that enormous mass heading toward us!"

He leapt to the lateral porthole and saw, a hundred meters away, a quasi-fantastic form: that of a gigantic fish swimming in the air, which seemed to be heading straight for them.

At the same time, with a shrill whistling, long, thin projectiles cleaved through the air, not hitting the apparatus but flying past it and bursting some distance away with formidable bangs.

"Aerial torpedoes," said Sabirat. "We're doomed if we can't get away. I understand now: we've been spotted by the observers of an army, by some captive balloon, perhaps a dirigible cruiser. We're being pursued, and as we have no means of defending ourselves..."

An enormous voice shouted through the air: "Surrender!"

That was easy enough to say. What could they do to obey? In truth, any thought of flight was insane. Sabirat was beginning to realize that the apparatus, already charged for a long time, was exhausted. Norès' ship was fluttering its wings like a wounded bird, and the moment was doubtless close at hand when it would no longer have the force to sustain itself in the atmosphere. Then there would be a horrible, hectic, crashing fall.

But then—the call had been issued in French!

All these reflections had passed through Sabirat's mind with lightning rapidity.

Marie, very pale and ready for anything, even death, looked at him, wondering what decision the man she had made the master of her life was about to make.

The Hadji, mad with terror, had fallen flat on this face and was imploring Allah, who could not do anything.

Resolutely, Sabirat opened the door of the apparatus and leaned out, waving his handkerchief, the white color of which seemed to him likely to be deemed peaceful. "Don't shoot!" he shouted. "We surrender!"

There was a great silence. The dirigible balloon was drawing closer by the second, circling like a vulture about to fall on its prey.

The detonations had ceased.

Suddenly, an enormous shadow enveloped the voyagers, and coming to a halt, the balloon drew alongside them.

The nacelle—or, rather, the armored suspended chamber that served that purpose—was occupied by three officers.

"Russians!" Sabirat shouted. "We're saved."

"Russians!" howled Ben-Borouk. "I'm doomed."

"Who are you?" demanded a Russian officer, while grappling irons settled on the airship.

"We're French," replied Sabirat. At the same time he uttered a cry; he had just perceived that the hull of the apparatus had been pierced by a fragment of a shell—damage that had almost reduced it to incapacity.

"Save my companion first," Sabirat shouted, seizing Marie in his arms and imploring the aid of the officers.

In a matter of seconds the young woman was transported to the nacelle.

"Your turn, Monsieur," said the officer who seemed to be in command.

"But I'm not alone; there's an injured man here.

"Can't you embark him too?"

"I can't get him to move."

In fact, the Hadji, who regarded the Russians with a horror increased by a terror carefully maintained by the fanatics, had such a fear of falling into their hands that he was clinging onto the levers, from which Sabirat could not succeed in detaching his hands.

By virtue of that action, however, he brought one of the mechanisms into play, and the airship suddenly started to fall vertically.

149

Sabirat scarcely had time to throw himself backwards. He leapt with all the might of his legs toward the nacelle, and succeeded in grabbing hold of it.

The officer, perceiving the danger, cut the grapples still retaining the airship, whose fall would have dragged them down.

They saw it disappear with alarming rapidity.

"Poor fellow!" exclaimed Sabirat. "He'll break all his limbs on the ground."

Suddenly, Marie uttered an exclamation. "Look, Monsieur Sabirat, at the name inscribed on the balloon!"

Sabirat obeyed and uttered an exclamation in his turn: "The *Norès!*"

"So what?" asked the officer.

"But I'm Guy de Norès' sister!" said Marie.

The officer bowed. "In that case, Mademoiselle, I'm very glad that our encounter didn't have fatal consequences for you. In an hour, you'll be with your brother."

"Where are we, then?"

"At Borovichi, on the road to St. Petersburg."[38]

"But this dirigible balloon you're manning..."

"Is one of the scouts tracking the movements of the enemy army?"

"What army?"

"What! Don't you know? All Asia is hurling itself upon Europe. It's a struggle to the death." The officer added, sadly: "And who can tell who'll emerge victorious?"

"You're scaring me. Give me the details."

"This is where we're landing. Behind that hillock you'll find the advance guard of one of the corps that's defending Russia. Monsieur de Norès is there with the Council of War."

While he was speaking the balloon descended to the ground.

As soon as they were solidly moored, the officer helped Mademoiselle de Norès and her companion down.

At that moment Russian officers appeared some distance away. At a sign addressed to them from the balloon, they hastened their approach. The commandant of the balloon entrusted the doctor and the young woman to them. When he pronounced Marie's name, the officers made a military salute.

---

[38] Borovichi is in the north of the Valdai Hills, not far southeast of St. Petersburg. It is not only an extremely long way from Bukhara, but it is very difficult to imagine how the airship could have gotten there by following a westward course, which would have taken it over the Caspian Sea and Turkey, Greece and Italy, more than twenty-five degrees of latitude to the south of Borovichi. On the other hand, it is equally difficult to imagine how the airship got to Uzbekistan, if one considers the manipulations of the controls described in the course of the outward journey.

"The sister of Guy de Norès is most welcome. If you'd care to follow us, we'll take you to your brother."

IV

In a tent before which Russian officers were standing sentinel, naked swords in hand, three men were chatting around a table on which a map was spread.

One of them, clad in a white tunic whose breast as embroidered with a two-headed gold eagle, was named Louis-Alexandroff Romanoff; he was the Tsar of All the Russias, to whom his people had awarded the title of the Great Protector.

Some years before, the internal situation of Russia had been completely modified. On his deathbed, the father of the present Tsar[39] had ordered his son to give his government a new direction. For pure autocracy, which tended simultaneously to tyranny and theocracy, he had been enjoined to substitute a constitutional regime appropriate to Russian mores and habits.

It is well known that under the despotic regime of the old Romanoffs, liberty had been entirely resident in the organization of the commune, the Mir, a sort of fraternal municipal group in which the citizens considered themselves to be bound by an absolute solidarity. Thus far, however, that solidarity had only prevailed as a defense against the demands and the prevarications of the central authority, avid and brutal tyrants who exploited the people and stifled their complaints with the knout, or by depopulating the Mirs and sending the most intelligent and active of those whose determination might cause trouble for them to Siberia.

One phrase always ran through the people like a cry of protest and hope, however: "If the Tsar only knew!"

And Louis-Alexandroff, faithful to his father's wishes, had wanted to know. He had ordered an investigation in every part of his immense empire, entrusted to reliable men chosen from among the most active representatives of the liberal party, those who had until then posed an unrelenting challenge to autocracy. That investigation had been carried out secretly. Two year later, the Tsar had said, smiling: "For two years I was the chief conspirator against my own empire."

And the Tsar had known. Suddenly, between him and his people, there was something like the opening of a great door, through which the light penetrated as

---

[39] When Lermina serialized his story, Alexander III was still the Tsar; he was to be succeeded in 1894 by Nicholas II. Neither had a son named Louis, but Nicholas' actual heir apparent, Alexei, was not born until 1904, so there was plenty of time, from Lermina's viewpoint, for him to have other sons.

far as the throne, previously enveloped by egotistical advisers, shadow, and ignorance.

The Tsar had known…and he had understood that he had a duty to fulfill valiantly his role as a pastor of humans, and that power was not and ought not to be an egotistical satisfaction, but that a man who placed himself above others assumed superior duties in consequence. And Louis-Alexandroff had resolutely undertaken the endeavor of the liberation, regeneration, and education of his people.

How many obstacles he had encountered at first!

All the satisfied, all the exploiters, the entire gilded whirl of courtiers, functionaries, devourers of the budget, from first to last, had risen up, frightened, divining that they were threatened by catastrophe, that the time of enriched idleness, satisfied hatreds, and conquering injustices was about to elapse.

From one end of the immense Muscovite empire to the other, there was a formidable raising of shields against the prince who wanted to be a human being. Bitter struggles were engaged; a permanent conspiracy, all the more powerful because it was supported by means sanctioned by age-old routine, had covered the empire with an inextricable network. Some of its members had even succeeded in recruiting ignorant peasants suspicious of all innovation to the cause of the past.

The Tsar had not weakened. Escaping assassination attempts as if miraculously—it was the so-called nihilists who had then constituted themselves as his voluntary defenders—he had fooled them by courses he had mapped out. He had marched with a firm and sure tread, without deviating by an inch, and a day had dawned when an entire series of ukases had established the new order: municipal liberty definitively founded, federation established between all the communes, represented in great municipal councils to defend their interests, then delegating to the national council men carefully chosen to discuss and settle major questions in the interest of the security of the entire empire.

Above the whole, the Tsar, a kind of pontiff of humanity, took charge of carrying out the decisions, appointing the men to whom executive power had evolved, respectful to all, a veritable father of a still-youthful people, simultaneously a sovereign and a philosopher.

We cannot go into detail about the innumerable reforms with which the sovereign's initiative had endowed his people. Europe, astonished at first, habituated as it was to the immutability of Tsarism, had been enthused by the young emperor who was the first to provide an example of disinterest for the love of justice. It was like a continuation of the great French Revolution, completing the regeneration of Europe, and that thought was further affirmed when universal suffrage, functioning from the Urals to the shores of the Baltic, had been seen to give Louis-Alexandroff something akin to a new and solemn investiture in conferring the title of Great Protector upon him. From that day on, the union between France and Russia had been better than a political treaty; it had been, so to speak, a pact of fraternity, and with all its voices, France had saluted Russia with the name of Big Sister.

Such was the man who, at the moment when we resume our story, was in his tent, studying a map of the Oriental countries.

He was tall in stature, a trifle stooped, as if the weight of his thoughts had curved him into a meditative attitude. He had the vigorous features of the Romanoff family with, in addition, something luminous, vivid, and human that gave a strange and superb gleam to his Russian eyes.

"Ivanoff," he said, to the man who was standing next to him, whose father had once perished on the scaffold of the nihilists, "you've heard Monsieur de Norès; it's your turn to speak."

Indeed, the third person was Guy, the Frenchman, who was looking at the Tsar with an inspired gaze, with his hand on his chin.

Ivanoff placed his finger on the map. "Let's sum up," he said. "It's agreed that Monsieur de Norès knows exactly what our situation is, what we can do and what we hope to do. We're men speaking as one man; there must be no misunderstandings or reticence between us."

The Tsar nodded in assent. "Speak in all frankness."

"So," Ivanoff went on, "we've been surprised by the most frightful cataclysm that has ever fallen upon the civilized world. Suddenly, without any forewarning, by reason of an organization that has been going on for a long time, which we have not detected, the entire Orient has risen up; in a single day it has risen up against us, with colossal forces at its disposal—poorly balanced, it's true, but terrible by virtue of its mass, which might be sufficient in itself to crush us."

He moved his finger over the map. "Here," he said, indicating with broad gestures the reference points of his demonstration," from the polar circle to Ceylon, and entire world is rising against us; from the mountains of Verkhoyansk, the Stanovoy mountains and the Yablonovy mountains, hordes of Ostyaks and Kamchatkites have descended: Yakutsk and Kirensk burned, then Yeniseik; Tomsk sacked, Omsk taken, Berezov set ablaze. The whole of Manchuria is vomiting its hordes on Ourga. China, the colossal volcano, is vomiting its lava from Peking to Canton, from Hang-Tcheo to the Karakorum mountains, from the frontiers of Burma to Lake Baikal the yellow avalanche is rolling its floods of mud and blood. Is that all?

"Here, in the Sea of Japan, the European fleets have been burned by means of the most infamous of treasons. Oh, we were trusting, and we had taken aboard Chinese pilots and sailors. They made us pay dearly for our stupidity. But then, is there not a heroic folly in this fanaticism? These men, these brutes, in order to obey the orders of secret societies, burned themselves along with our ships. From Formosa to Sakhalin a sheet of fire has extended, closing the way to European vessels. From Japan to Luzon Island, dynamite has blown up the sea-bed, displaced the reefs, and caused unknown banks to emerge, reducing all our geographical science to redundancy. Borneo and Sumatra close the circle.

"We're proud of our science! What are we, though, compared to these malignant wills, which, by destruction, summoning all the most redoubtable forces of nature, not to mention the lives sacrificed, the cities destroyed, the continents dislocated, the islands sunk, have been able, in a single day, at the same hour, to declare a war to the death against the old world Europe, terrified of its own impotence. Let's not mince words: we're afraid!"

Ivanoff stopped, breathless. That sinister invocation had made him pale, although he was not a coward.

Immobile, the Tsar, his hand on his forehead, was staring into space at some vision of blood and death.

Only Guy de Norès seemed to have conserved all of his composure. There was only a slight flush in his cheeks. "Go on, Ivanoff," he said, simply.

The latter ran his hands through his hair, and then passed them over his face, as if to recall himself to reality.

"We're afraid," he said, in a dull voice, "because we doubt ourselves, our strength, and even our energy. On what can we count? In a few days, with the admirable organization of mobilization that we've borrowed from France, we've dispatched three hundred thousand men to the Oriental invasion. Where are they? Swept away, vanished. And yet, haven't we had nature for an accomplice? Have you forgotten the Gobi cataclysm?"

The event to which Ivanoff was alluding was one of the strangest and most terrible of which humanity ought to conserve the memory.

It was the day after the battle that we have witnessed in the streets of Peking.

As Ivanoff had said, the conspiracy of which Sithreva had been the organizer, and which had been preparing for years in the shadows the decisive explosion of which Europe was to be the victim, had burst forth at a single moment from north to south and east to west.

Revealed at that time, in all its terrible grandeur, was the organization of Chinese secret societies about which we said a few words at the beginning of this story, and to which me must return momentarily.

Let us recall certain facts that had been forgotten for a long time in the era in which the facts we are recounting occurred.

In 1876, terror reigned in Hang-Chow, from Nanking to Shanghai; an implacable and mysterious fatality seemed to be weighing over the black tresses that are the most beautiful ornament of the Celestial Empire.[40] The mandarin,

---

[40] The "pigtail panic" in Hang-Chow was reported in the *North China Herald* in May 1876. At the same time, legislators in California were attempting to pass laws compelling Chinese workers to cut off their pigtails as a means of trying to force them to leave.

who had been asleep in an dream colored by the enchantments of opium, observed fearfully, on waking up, that the pigtail of which he was so proud had disappeared; the merchant at his counter, the passer-by on the public highway, and the artisan in his workshop suddenly perceived that they had just lost the most precious appendage of their toilette; no social condition escaped the scourge, and the crystal button of the literate was no more spared than the black skullcap of the street-porter. The invisible hand that exercised its ravages indiscriminately over the most humble and the noblest heads did not even respect wigs.

The authorities issued proclamations; solemn prayers were said in the pagodas; the good Spirits received fervent invocations from all directions and the evil Spirits saw themselves heaped with presents designed to deflect their wrath. All the manifestos of the public powers, the ceremonies celebrated in accordance with the rights prescribed by the decrees of Li-Pu,[41] and the supplications and the offerings were futile; the evil continued to make further progress every day. Sometimes the pigtails vanished as if they had been carried away into the air by a diabolical breath, and sometimes they fell gently of their own accord, as a ripe fruit drops from an overladen branch.

Finally, by chance, two men were caught *in flagrante delicto* at the moment when they were cutting the tress off a literate man who was engaged in a lively controversy with a group of passers-by outside the door of his house. They were armed with a pair of scissors so small that they could be hidden in the palm of the hand. The blades of those minuscule instruments were as sharp as razors. While accomplices were charged with deflecting the attention of the victim, the malefactors approached the pigtail quietly and, in accordance with the opportunity, sliced it off with a single sweep and contented themselves with an incomplete amputation that left intact an extremely thin wisp of hair destined to break in a short while under a weight it could not sustain.

The Chinese police oscillated between unbridled curiosity and extraordinary discretion. Let us add quickly that the mandarins charged with watching over the security of the Celestial Empire do not have a monopoly on abrupt changes of pace; there are delicate affairs in which the same vacillations are produced among their colleagues in the Occident. When the authorities in Shanghai and Nanking learned, from the confessions of malefactors fallen into their grasp, that they were in the presence of a secret society, they did not take their research any further, stopped dead as they were by the terror that was excited by the mere name of the White Lily.

What, then, was the White Lily? Originally, a religious sect, at least in appearance, but before anything else a society of hatred against progress and against the Occident. As means of propaganda it employed magic and stirred up

---

[41] Presumably the 9th century Tang emperor of that name.

fanaticism. Here are a few details that we found in a periodical, *Harper's Magazine*:[42]

In 1810, an insurrection directed by the leader of the redoubtable organization almost overturned the emperor Kin-King and the Manchu Tartar dynasty of the Tsings.

Fang-Yung-Tcheng, the grandmaster of the Order, when he was vanquished in a decisive battle, the imperial troops took such a large number of prisoners that, for perhaps the first time in history, highly-placed Chinese mandarins were seen having recourse to clemency.

The viceroy of Nanking, who knew the secret statutes of the White Lily, offered to spare the lives of all the rebels who would consent to eat meat. It was an ingenious means of putting to the proof the members of a sect whose rules ordered its faithful only to nourish themselves on vegetables. A fairly large number of captives did not resist the temptation, but they only escaped the rigors of the official government to be judged, condemned, and executed by the authorities of the occult society, whose vigilance could not allow an oath to be violated with impunity.

Persecuted unrelentingly by the decrees of the Son of Heaven, the White Lily changed its name; it is now known as No Hypocrisy, but it remains just as formidable.

Popular imagination attributes to the members of the society the power to work miracles. They only have to blow on a paper bird to give it life. Educated and enlightened, Chinese have gravely affirmed to an Englishman, Monsieur Balfour, that they had witnessed these marvels.

Those are the simple affiliates; the dignitaries of the congregation can do magic tricks that are even more fabulous. They are masters of holding their breath for hours, entire days if necessary. Their faces turn black, their limbs take on a cadaverous rigidity, and during that period of apparent death, the soul leaves the body and draws away to collect information that it is charged with bringing back. As soon as it has fulfilled its mission, its master recalls it and it resumes its customary place.

One day, it happened that, having neglected to bring back his soul at an opportune moment, one of the highest dignitaries of the Order did not wake up again. That accident, which was potentially capable of compromising the prestige of the sect, caused a suspicious emotion among the initiates. But what did an accident matter that was soon transformed into a miracle? For the people

---

[42] Frederick Boyle's article on "Chinese Secret Societies" appeared in the September 1891 issue of *Harper*'s, not long before this episode was penned. Lermina's decision to import its substance into his story, further breaking the back of Ivanoff's already-interrupted narrative, appears to have been made on a sudden whim.

were convinced that the dead man had been resuscitated and that it was now his spirit that would remain eternally the head of the Conspiracy.

The Society took the name of Tien-Tai. The war of the Chinese pigtails recommenced with a new ardor.

The pigtail worn by the subjects of the Son of Heaven is the emblem of the subjection of the Chinese by the Tartars. To cut off with scissors that mark of servitude was to protest against foreign domination and to reveal the national sentiment deep in the heart of the true children of Han. In the same way that the Muscovite awaited with impatience the advent of the bearded Tsar who was to deliver him from the razors brought by German civilization, China would only become free again on the day when its sons ceased to braid their hair.

The Society took on an increasingly considerable development. The forms of initiation took on a progressively solemn and mysterious character.

According to an English author, when a neophyte wants to be admitted to the Tien-Tai—which is to say, "the Society of Heaven, Earth, and Human Being"—also known by the names of the Triad and the Universal League, he must go to the camp of the faithful and present himself at the Eastern Gate. It is there that the executor of noble works resides, whose naked blade is ever ready to fall upon the head of any profane individual audacious enough to introduce himself into the sacred enclosure without authorization.

The newcomer is clad in white; in principle, he ought to wear a new robe, but if he is too poor, the Society spares him that expense on the sole condition that he has his ordinary costume cleaned with the greatest care. His right shoulder and his knees are bare; instead of braiding his hair, he allows it to hang down freely over his nape, in order to demonstrate that he protests against Tartar domination.

Before crossing the threshold of the sacrosanct Gate, the neophyte pays his subscription, which is the equivalent of 17 francs 50. Once that indispensable formality has been accomplished, eight members of the League cause him to pass beneath an arch of overlapping blades. By a curious coincidence, one of the French paintings that has had the greatest recent success represents the aldermen of Paris crossing their swords over the head of Louis XVI to render him extraordinary honors on his arrival at the Hôtel de Ville.[43] Are the Occidentals, then, so proud of their civilization, merely plagiarists of the Chinese?

Let us return to our fanatic, who is advancing tremulously into the mysterious enclosure. Here he is arriving at the Pavilion of Red Flowers, where the faithful purify their souls in waters drawn from the river Sam-Ho, on the banks

---

[43] A painting by Jean-Paul Laurens depicting the reception of Louis XVI at the Hôtel de Ville in 1789 was exhibited in Paris in 1891. The alleged crossed swords are not obvious in the rather poor reproductions currently available online.

of which the "Five Ancestors" persecuted by the ingratitude of the Emperor and the intrigues of his unworthy favorite Tan-Sing took refuge.

The neophyte then proceeds to the Circle of Heaven and Earth and traverses the bridge of two planks guarded by the Red Young Man armed with a spear destined to pierce any profane individuals who have escaped the vigilant eye of the guardian of the Eastern Gate. On the far side of that fearsome passage is the Market of Universal Peace, the Temple of Happiness, the City of Willows, and the Garden of Fishermen; this is the seat of the Grandmaster.

At the moment when the ceremony begins, the spectacle become even more imposing. The arch of swords is formed again over the neophyte's head. He kneels down, swears an oath of thirty-six articles and declares that all his relatives are dead. In the language of the initiates, that formula signifies that a member of the League no longer recognizes any earthly ties.

After having made that declaration, the fanatic prostrates himself at the foot of the Grandmaster's throne, and the eight swords that were interlaced above his head are placed on his bare shoulder.

He is presented with a cup of arrack; he mixes with that beverage a few drops of blood that he causes to run from his arm, on which a slight cut has just been inflicted; then he drinks it all in a single draught, and the Tien-Tai count one faithful follower more.

And that was the association that had sworn the fall of the Tsing dynasty, which had brought to the throne the descendant of the Mings, previously expelled by the revolution of 1644.

That descendant, who lived unknown to anyone, was designated by the mysterious name of Elder Brother. Government officials denied his existence, as they also mocked the secret society whose ramifications nevertheless enfolded them in stifling fashion.

One day, the Elder Brother had suddenly reappeared and had entered the palace of his ancestors under the name of Han-Ming.

On the same day, throughout the Oriental world, prophets had emerged among the Muslims, the fire-worshipers, and the Mazdaists. Everywhere, whatever the particular confessions were, all hatreds had been suddenly forgotten, to melt into a common, unique, and furious hatred against the Occidentals. And thus, on every part of the globe, at a signal whose point of departure no one could determine, but which had traveled to the four corners of the Asiatic world, innumerable masses of men had launched themselves forward.

The immense Chinese territory, from the Yellow Sea to Hindustan and Russia, had vomited forth millions of soldiers, and that multitude, whose force resided primarily in numbers, had spread like a monstrous flood through Mongolia and Tibet, incessantly augmented by new recruits who seemed to spring from the earth.

It was a frightful human avalanche, devoid of discipline, devoid of cohesion, but linked together by the fury of fanaticism, the worst of all follies. From all breasts the same cry of hatred rose up, so formidable that the echoes reverberated all the way to the extremities of Asia and caused Europe to shiver with an unexplained anguish.

It was not fear; the military engines at its disposal, the presumed cowardice of the adversaries, the consciousness of a strength that had multiplied tenfold in the last fifty years, all contributed to reassuring the most pessimistic.

And yet the Orient had conserved a mysterious, almost fantastic quality that troubled Occidental consciousness.

Meanwhile, at the first news of the massacres in China and the invasion that had followed it, Russia had not faltered in its duty. Was it not the advance sentinel of Europe? Was not its mission, ethnological in a way—the first—to halt the torrent that was threatening Europe with a formidable submersion?

For a long time, in any case, the Tsar had dreamed of exporting civilized ideas into those barbaric lands, and all his cares had been directed toward the means of transportation penetrating all the way to the extreme frontiers of his immense empire. The engineering works of the Transhimalaya were in the process of being carried out, and the principal tunnel of the Devalagiri was due to be pierced within two years.

The mobilization of Russian troops had thus been relatively easy, and a hundred thousand men had been hurled at the Asiatic hordes.

Never had the comparison of a bar of lead melting in a furnace been more apt.

In a matter of days, those hundred thousand men had disappeared, as if swallowed up, devoured by the tide that continued to surge and did not stop.

A cry of pain had emerged from all throats, and for the first time, people in Europe had become conscious that something frightful and inevitable was happening, like an earthquake, or a flood destroying all dykes.

When the news arrived in St. Petersburg, the Tsar did not want to believe in such a disaster, but doubt quickly became impossible. The catastrophe was complete and irremediable.

At the same time, other news no less terrible reached Europe.

The French and the English had combined forces in an operation to go by sea to attack Peking itself and avenge the massacre of the Europeans. All the ships stationed in the seas of China and Japan had received orders to rally and attack the coast of Petchili. But there a further disaster awaited the Europeans.

What had happened? The reality of the event was scarcely believable, but as soon as our ships had approached the Chinese coast, the sea had caught fire around them, and they had been devoured by the conflagration.

The Chinese had found a means of setting fire to the sea. What means? There was mention of blocks of potassium anhydride that had been precipitated into the waves. The force of projection due to the immediate dehydration had been such that the particles of potassium had been distributed over several

159

leagues, transforming the sea into an immense furnace. Water on fire! Is there any dream more terrifying and more sinister?

At any rate, France and England had lost their most formidable ironclads in a matter of hours. The submarine boats had not reappeared. It was a veritable maritime cataclysm.

France, with her usual energy, had told Russia that she would join forces with her.

But then an incident had occurred that had compromised the situation further. At the news of the disaster of Petchili, Germany, in response to the voices of a few agitators who formed a previously-incoherent party around Adalbert von Bismarck, the grandson of the famous Iron Chancellor, had broken the federal ties uniting the various parts of Germany and had given its support once again one of the Hohenzollerns; it was a brutal *coup d'état* that threatened to change the entire face of Europe. It was Prussia crushing Germany once again under its iron heel, and the first act of the new government, directly inspired by the emperors of old, had been a proclamation repeating the ancient pretentions of Germany over Alsace, Lorraine and the Vosges.

It was not yet a declaration of war on France, but it was evident that the ambitious Wilhelm could only enjoy the fruits of his usurpation by flattering the basest instincts of his people, and France thus found herself under imminent threat.

The French parliament had, in consequence, put a stop to the immense effort that it was preparing to direct toward Asia. It was necessary to ward off the more immediate danger and to be ready to respond to the insolent provocations being launched on a daily basis by the reptiles of Berlin.

Russia had been the first to engage France to leave all the weight of the Asiatic war to her. The colossal forces of the Muscovite empire ought to be sufficient for the task. Perhaps the danger from that direction might even be warded off in time for Russia to aid France, if necessary, in chastising the Teutonic insolence.

The invasion, however, was making further progress every day. It was like a puddle of oil growing ever larger.

The Oriental hordes, which the Hindus, Buddhists and Mohammedans were beginning to join, having massacred the English in Delhi, Calcutta and other great centers, and now moving toward Afghanistan to join up with Chinese forces still held up by the Gobi desert.

In spite of the explorations of new voyagers, that part of Asia was still little known; it was still almost deserted. From Yarkand and Khatan to the frontiers of Manchuria, at the intersection of the three great mountain chains of the Altai, the Kuen-Lun and the Himalaya, the Gobi desert—which some people believe to have been the site of the ancient Atlantis destroyed in prehistoric times—occupies a vast plateau made firm by the first two of those chains. Over an area of fifteen hundred thousand square kilometers, it extends from northeast to southwest over a distance of two thousand kilometers. The Tian-Shan or Celestial Mountains divided it into two parts. It is an immense plateau of moving sand, which the winds agitate into gigantic undulations.

Crossing the Wall of China at all points, the Tartars and the Mongols had gradually filled that immense area, and the crowds were compressed at the foot of the snowy mountains, akin to the advance citadels of Europe.

The Elder Brother had just arrived and had deployed before the hordes the standard of the Five Hundred Gods, causing a monstrous chorus of hatred and fury to rise up, avid for blood and plunder.

A kind of proclamation had been hurled in the face of Europe, which was a monument of savagery: "No quarter! Death, nothing but death!"

But then, suddenly, beneath the feet of that multitude, the earth had trembled. It was the entire desert that had risen up, under the effect of subterranean fires that had been believed to be extinct for hundreds of centuries; abysms had opened, launching jets of sulfur and bitumen.

Thousands upon thousands of men had perished in that convulsion of nature, which had only lasted a few seconds.

For a moment, Europe thought that it had been saved. A vain hope! From the depths of inexhaustible China, other hordes had emerged, replacing the dead, filling in the gaps, and after a sort of oscillation in the mass, which seemed to form only a single body, the forward march had recommenced.

That was the catastrophe Ivanoff recalled in the conference in which he was discussing the matter with the emperor Louis-Alexandroff Romanoff and Guy de Norès.

Ivanoff continued:

"It would be criminal to entertain illusions. This very day we've learned that masses of men coming from the depths of Asia Minor are heading for Constantinople. Will Hungary be forced, as in the days of the Hunyadis, to repel the Asiatics? Where is Sobieski? It's up to us to strike a great blow. Can we do it? Today we have at our disposal fifteen hundred thousand well-armed men, who are defending the route to St. Petersburg. But how do we know that, while we are fighting desperately here, the wave will not outflank us?

"All the peoples of Europe are and ought to sense that they are as one against the terrible peril that is menacing them, and yet, look: indolent Austria hardly seems to be stirring; Germany is taking advantage of the turbulence to think egotistically about her particular ambitions, claims condemned twenty times over...and her ill will is paralyzing France. Can Italy come to our aid? Enclosed in her peninsula, she thinks herself unassailable—as if the barbarians of old had not found a way to reach Rome, which is her heart! Fearful England is only thinking about Hindustan, which she is losing, and is directing her energies solely in that direction...and she is still under the influence of the terror caused by the burning of her ships. The picture is grim. I ask you: am I exaggerating?"

"Not at all," said the Tsar. "All that is true."

"So," said Ivanoff, "it's a fight to the death, and Russia will not fail in her mission. Now the human avalanche is heading toward St. Petersburg; our advance troops have been driven back, and if we had not ordered them to retreat, for the sake of prudence, a hundred thousand men would already have been drowned by that monstrous wave. The decisive hour has sounded. Five hundred thousand Russians are gathered under your orders, and tomorrow, or this evening, the battle will begin. We shall say: *For civilization and for the Tsar*...but what does the future have in store for us?"

"Ivanoff," said the Tsar, severely, "I no longer recognize you. Are you really the man that I've seen confronting the most terrible perils without failing? Don't shake your head like that. I've told you: like you, I can take account of the immensity of the task that's incumbent upon us, but I shall be able to rise to the height of my mission. We have to combat numbers in proportions never seen before, even in the most terrible wars of which history makes mention. But you're forgetting what we call Force: no longer the brutal, irrational force that operates at hazard, but scientific, calculated force. Thanks to our dirigible aerostats, thanks to our machine-cannon that can launch five hundred melinite shells over a perimeter of five hundred square meters, thanks to the electric detonators that numb and topple, we shall reckon with this fanatical turbulence. Isn't that your opinion, Monsieur de Norès?"

The young Frenchman raised his head.

"It's necessary to submit to the inevitable," he said, in a grave voice. "You've done me the honor of asking the French government for my collaboration. Without having any more illusions about my own value than are appropriate, I nevertheless observed to Your Majesty that my place was, above all, in France, which, as you know, is threatened by grave perils. Even so, I have come, not only to render myself respectfully to the formal request, but also because it was necessary for me to obtain an exact account of the means of combating these wretches.

"Just now, Your Majesty enumerated the frightful engines of which modern warfare comprises. Let us not forget that they have been invented for struggles between civilized peoples, and that until now, that progress in the art of killing has been the principal factor maintaining peace. It requires all the mad arrogance of a Hohenzollern to think of setting two European nations at odds, when it is certain that the deaths will be counted in the hundreds of thousands! But still, it is a matter of men whose character and temperament we know; in certain conditions we can count on panic, and also on discouragement, on desperation in confrontation with the frightful hecatomb...I will even say that a Head of State, unless he is a monster, could not go to a battlefield, even after a victory, without shivering to the profoundest marrow of his bones.

"Here, though, we are dealing with individuals whose veritable character, whose consciousness is virtually unknown to us. We know that in China, in India, and in Africa, fanatics, in a sort of cerebral intoxication, endure tortures before which Europeans who are no less courageous would recoil..."

Ivanoff interrupted: "I've seen Hindu fakirs smile and sing while the bones of their feet were disarticulated one by one..."

"For those men, pain is just a word, death is not a terror. Their leaders, in appealing to their most profound hatreds, have made them all into as many fakirs, ready to endure anything. What effect will be produced in the ranks of those madmen by melinite, the most powerful explosives, or even the long electric sparks that resemble lightning? In ancient times, to be sure, the priests of Delphi defended their temple in that fashion against an attack by barbarians who fled in terror, but will it be the same today? I'd like to hope so, but allow me to doubt it. To sum up briefly, I don't believe that fear has any effect on these men; I only believe in real, effective, positive, destruction."

"We'll destroy them!" cried the Tsar.

"How many are they?" asked Norès. "Ten thousand, a hundred thousand or two hundred thousand men can be killed, but can you kill a million, two million or three million? For it is in those numbers that it is necessary to count these Asiatics, accumulated over the centuries in excessively narrow limits. It's necessary to take account of the formidable pressure that is driving them forward. In brief, I can say nothing, offer no opinion, before having seen them. There is a psychology of war. That is what provides the elements of resistance and victory."

"But when you've seen?" said Ivanoff.

"Either I will be much mistaken," said de Norès, "or—I say this without false modesty—I'll be able to discover the monster's weak spot...and then, Your Majesty, I, who believed that I would never work other than in the cause of peace, swear to you that for the great cause of civilization, of European life, I will force the sphinx of Science to yield its secret to me."

"And I'm convinced of that too," said the Tsar. "How are you going to observe the battle?"

"In the dirigible balloon, undoubtedly," said Ivanoff.

Norès made an angry gesture. "Oh, why did I have to see the apparatus that would have rendered me master of the air disappear! When I think that that discovery, in which I invested all the hope and all the joy of my life, cost the lives of my sister and my best friend!"

The Tsar knew the details of that painful adventure. "Who can tell?" he said. "Perhaps your sister isn't dead."

"All appearances...I hadn't taught her the use of the controls..."

At that moment the door of the tent was lifted up and an office appeared on the threshold. As he remained immobile without saying a single word, Louis-Alexandroff understood that he wanted to talk to him alone. Without affectation he got up and went out of the tent.

A few minutes went by, during which Norès and Ivanoff exchanged their anxieties. In spite of their valor, they shivered as they thought about the next day's battle.

The Tsar came back in. "Monsieur de Norès," he said, "do you believe in miracles?"

"Outside of pure mathematics, as Arago said, the word impossible does not exist."

Norès had replied with a smile, but at that moment the sovereign lifted the flap of the tent and Norès saw his sister advancing toward him, holding out her hands.

The young man uttered a great cry, and became so pale that he seemed veritably to be on the point of fainting—but already, his sister had thrown her arms around him, saying "Brother, Brother, it's me, it's really me! Oh, how happy I am!"

"And not to displease you, there are two of us!" exclaimed a joyful voice.

And Sabirat came in, his face radiant.

"Alive!" repeated Norès. "What, it's not an illusion?" To the Tsar he said: "Oh, Sire, forgive me this emotion."

"But am I not a man, like you? I can certainly understand, and I tell you that this joy is a good omen."

Norès covered his sister with kisses; he had been so desperate that it had required an almost superhuman effort for him not to renounce the world forever.

Suddenly, the passion of the scientist regained the upper hand. "But what about the airship!" he cried.

"Wounded, but saved," said the young woman.

"What! You mean that it's in my apparatus…?"

"That we arrived here? Certainly—and I can affirm that the airship is a first-rate vehicle."

Norès looked at her in amazement. He seemed unable to understand what he was hearing. "But the controls…," he stammered.

"Do you think that I'd worked by your side for so long without assimilating a few of your ideas. I didn't know very much, it's true, but with the aid of…of Monsieur Sabirat, we got out of trouble well enough."

"And the apparatus is nearby?"

"Half a verst away," said an officer. "It fell with such force that it hollowed out a hole in the ground, where it's embedded like a ship that has run aground…"

He did not finish. Norès had already run outside, making rapid apologies to the Tsar—who, in any case, followed him immediately, propelled by curiosity.

"Oh, these wretched scientists," said Marie, dragging Sabirat away. "He cares less about us than his perfumery box."

That fashion of describing the airship was a trifle irreverent, but Norès paid no attention to it; he ran with the Tsar to the indicated spot, and set about examining the aerial vessel attentively, the entire lower section of which was embedded in the ground.

At the same time, he gave the Russian sovereign summary explanations.

"The damage isn't great," Norès said. "If Your Majesty would be kind enough to supply a jack, the ship can be refloated within the hour."

The sovereign hastened to give the orders, and while Norès directed the operation, he asked his sister and Sabirat to tell him all about their strange voyage.

What interested him most of all was the fashion in which the aerial vehicle had behaved under the action of the various controls, and whether it had not extended its atoms of perfume. All the information they gave him was concordant with his hopes.

"Who can tell?" he murmured. "Perhaps it's the involuntary experiment from which salvation will come."

Meanwhile, under the action of a powerful electric locomotive, the airship was gradually lifted up.

"Gently!" cried Norès.

This was the decisive moment for him. Would the apparatus have resisted the impact of the fall? Would it be possible to repair it and take to the air again, as one says of a ship that is seaworthy?

Slowly, the airship emerged from the hole in which it was buried, and the breathless Norès observed, joyfully, that it had maintained its shape: there were the lateral propellers, whose open gyrations had hollowed out a kind of mold without their steel blades having been broken or twisted; there was the door in place, and the floor...

But Norès uttered a cry of chagrin; he had just discovered the wound inflicted in the airship's flank by a shell fragment. That was the real peril.

It required even more precautions to complete the work. Norès supervised the action of the lifting-tackle himself. He was leaning down to the ground, waiting for the final propeller, which served as a kind of pivot, to emerge from the ground. It was gradually rising up when Norès cried: "What's that? There's a shapeless package caught up in the blades!"

As the machine was now a few feet above ground, they could see something hanging down limply, with rods of some sort flailing the air, and from it, a voice emerged crying: "Allah! Allah!"

"The Hadji!" exclaimed Sabirat. "How has that one survived?"

It was indeed the servant of Mohammed, who had as many lives as a cat—for, when they hastened to detach him from the propeller and lay him down, they observed that he was in full possession of his vital force—certainly not undamaged, but breathing and talking.

His body had been flattened beneath the enormous weight of the airship, stretched, so to speak, to the point of presenting a minimal thickness, and the slight gap that hazard had hollowed out between the propeller and the bottom of the ditch had sufficed for him not to be crushed.

He was so much alive, in fact, that, on perceiving the Russian uniforms with his wide open eyes, he was gripped by a further fit of terror, and howled: "Don't kill me! I'll tell you everything!"

Then, as if he had only expected to be returned to life in order to lose the notion of it, he shivered, threw his arms into the air and fainted.

"Who's this clown?" asked the Tsar.

Sabirat explained briefly.

"What did he mean by his promise to confess?"

"I'd like to clarify that," said Norès. "With your permission, I'll have this individual taken to my tent, and when he's recovered his senses, I'll see what profit can be obtained from his good will."

"As you wish," said the Tsar. "Now, Monsieur de Norès, would you care to explain the purpose of this strange machine to me?"

Now that the apparatus was above ground, Norès examined it anxiously. The damage it had suffered inspired serious anxieties. The entrance door had been badly twisted, and it was with infinite precaution that he succeeded in climbing into the airship. He emerged again after a few moments.

"Fortunately," he said, "the important components haven't been destroyed. I can fix the apparatus in a matter of hours. The shrapnel hasn't reached any of the vital organs. If the Messieurs of the artillery will grant me a corner of their workshop, I'll repair the damage as fast as I can."

That was done. Thanks to the benevolence of the Tsar, Marie de Norès was escorted to the care of a lady of the court who had accompanied her husband, a senior officer, while Sabirat was welcomed by the army surgeons with the extreme sympathy that was never lacking for the French.

The Tsar resumed walking back to the camp, accompanied by Ivanoff, whose pessimism was increasing by the hour.

The approach of the enemy army had been signaled, if it really could be called an army. Scouts were arriving one after another, announcing the appearances of new hordes at every point of the perimeter whose center was occupied by the Russian army.

An hour went by; the Tsar held a final Council of War.

"Messieurs," he said to his generals, "remember that today, it is no longer only for Russia and the Tsar that you are going to fight, but for the cause of civilization in its entirety. We have the responsibility for the great cause of old Europe, which is under threat. No weakness, and forward!"

His vibrant speech armed all hearts; the generals brandished their sabers, enthusiastically proffering the oath to vanquish or die.

The officers of the general staff launched themselves in all directions at the gallop, bearing decisive orders; then, at a signal, the frightful rumble of the first detonations of the artillery was heard. It was like a release of thunder, and on hearing that explosion, which caused the ground to shake, the Tsar said to Ivanoff: "Friend, if I die in this battle, at least I know that I didn't provoke it."

At the same moment, Norès' airship rose into the air, and, alone in his flying machine, of which he had become the master again, he set forth, as he had told the Russian sovereign that he would, to seek a key to the enigma that would permit him to combat the Chinese invasion.

V

This is what the French scientist saw.

The horrible hecatomb that bears in history the name of the Gunstloff catastrophe—the name of a small village, previously ignored, that was the center of the action—cannot be compared to any of the battles recorded in the annals of humankind.

From the height of his aerial observatory, Norès saw the Russian army extended over twenty leagues, magnificent in its attitude: the infantry massed in groups and conserving all its liberty of movement, with captive balloons above indicating the enemy maneuvers; then the cavalry, superb and marvelously mounted, from the Cossacks with horses as rapid as the wind, to the Poles, now the faithful allies of their former persecutors, proud of having become a nation again and burning with desire to show themselves worthy of their recovered fatherland, whose Lithuanian horses could sustain the fatigue of an uninterrupted march for fifty hours.

Then there were the northern contingents, from Archangel, Olonets and Vologda, and from Greater Russia, from Novogorod, Smolensk, Moscow, Nijni-Novogorod, Tula and Kursk...

The Baltic had sent its most glorious children, from St. Petersburg, Reval, Riga and Mittau.

The Finlanders were gathered in large numbers, sons of the Finno-Ugric races who were the first inhabitants of Europe, and to whom ethnic science will perhaps restore the title of ancestors of the present human race: the Estonians, the Livonians, the Lapps, the Zyrians, the Vogults, the Permiaks, the Tchermisses, the Samoyeds, the Teptiares: all those strange tribes which hate Oriental brutality and had come in response to the sovereign's voice.

Among the Tartars there had been many defections; all those that Mohammedanism had touched had sided against Europe; only the Bukhirs and the Yakuts had remained faithful. By contrast, the Caucasian nations—the Armenians, the Georgians, the Lesghians—who had the terrible memory of Asiatic domination, had risen up to halt the flood of their ancient torturers. The Teutonics and the Scandinavians had formed well-equipped corps.

Of Siberia, nothing remained. In the first disaster, the Buryats and Kalmuks had been decimated.

Norès calculated mentally that the Russian army amounted to almost half a million men. What particularly attracted his attention as an engineer and scientist was the formidable artillery, comprising nearly two thousand fiery mouths, with all the improvements of modern artistry, from electric machine-guns to colossal mortars launching asphyxiating shells: all progress in the art of killing was accumulated in that relatively narrow space in which the forces of the two worlds were about to collide. The range of the weapons was such that, with the exception of a few groups of scouts who were distributed at intervals, the adversaries could not suspect their presence.

The balloons, in these circumstances, were doing marvelous service; by means of appropriate and clear signals, they were indicating to the Russian artillery the direction in which to aim the guns, and rectifying the force in accordance with the movements of the enemy.

And, indeed, at the commencement of the action, Norès saw two Asiatic corps, which had launched forward impetuously, annihilated without even having arrived within the range of their own weapons.

In truth, the young Frenchman felt full of hope. He was certain that the Oriental armaments were not comparable to those of the Europeans; of all the tribes that had emerged from the heart of the Iberian steppes or the depths of Mongolia and China, the greater part were only armed with obsolete rifles or even bows and arrows.

To equip that multitude, all the arsenals had been pillaged, but, in those backward countries, they are more like museums in which specimens of outmoded engines are conserved. Cannons could still be seen there whose models went back to the French Second Empire, and Norès observed that their servants lacked appropriate ammunition, and were loading those rifled guns in the same fashion as the bombards of the seventeenth century.

In those conditions, it seemed that the inferiority of the Orientals was such that the European victory could not be in doubt for a moment.

But Norès suddenly understood this:

With a depth so distant that, even from his aerial observatory, he could not perceive its limits, the young scientist saw a black stain, swarming and compact, like an uninterrupted mass, like a single animal with millions of limbs, feet, and tentacles, moving incessantly forward without pausing for a second.

The Russians, encouraged by the signals coming from the balloons, had hastened their aggressive movement, for they had noticed that no enemy projectile had yet fallen on the European ranks, while their own artillery was continually hollowing out gaps in the profound Oriental legions.

But what Norès now observed, with a momentary shiver that was like an involuntary sensation of terror, was something of which only an analogy can give a clear idea.

The dykes have broken; an enormous flood has rushed through and spread out, an immense sheet; then, suddenly, it finds a new slope that directs it toward

168

the plains, toward the villages, toward human habitations. The slope is gentle, the river flows slowly, slowly, but under that mute and incessant flow it seems that everything disappears, everything dissolves. The edifice whose roofs rose up proudly a little while before suddenly seems to disintegrate and collapse.

Before that black advance, which nothing can stop, villages are alive; the flood passes, and they are dead, everything effaced, no longer anything but a memory.

Let humans, in a fit of desperate folly, with the aid of colossal engines, launch entire rocks against that liquid mass; let them precipitate monoliths the size of mountains in order to create an obstacle: the thing arrives, makes a hole, and then the sheet closes up again, and without any change, without the surface even being rippled, the water marches on and on.

Thus was the Asian torrent.

It was a sea in a perpetual rising tide, which never ebbed, a monstrous swell always moving always flowing.

The enormous shells, the masses of iron, the electrical discharges that hurtled into the midst of that human ocean smashed, twisted and tore; a hole was created—and then the flood continued its flow; the wound seemed to scar over instantly, and further on, always further on, without haste, with the heavy monotony of destiny, the horde advanced.

Norès saw that, and understood, perhaps for the first time, the horrible and terrifying force of numbers.

Those men, those brutes, were not doing battle, not furiously charging their enemies, ignorant and careless of danger—and what did a few scarcely-divined hecatombs matter to such masses?—they were flowing forward incessantly, without hesitation, a formidable inundation, an unstoppable creep.

And the moment came when those waves, whose limit could not be seen, which extended to all the depths of the horizon, a swarm such as the imagination did not dare conceive, reached the European corps.

There was an unprecedented spectacle of heroism and despair.

Infantry, cavalry and artillery were all unleashed against that living, moving wall.

Was there any hope? Of what? One, two, twenty gaps are pierced, but when the onslaught is continuous; when, behind every man killed, one finds a hundred more, a thousand more; when, to the right and the left, in front and behind, innumerable enemies are still standing…what charge or flanking movement can be attempted?

One recalls Victor Hugo describing, in his magical style, the furnace in which the regiments of Waterloo "melted like wax in the breath of a forge…"

This was worse; it was the sinister and relentless engulfment of thousands upon thousands of men, horses, and canons.

A magnificent regiment of white cuirassiers charged recklessly, musicians in the lead playing the Russia national anthem at full blast. Norès saw them reach the hideous host, penetrate into it like a red-hot iron…and then the music was extinguished, and the silver plumes disappeared, and the sparkling breast-plates…and nothing at all remained: nothing but the Asiatic multitude passing over the cadavers of men and horses, without its march being halted for a second.

For four hours—four hours of unspeakable agony—the Russian regiments hastened themselves with stoic valor into that ever-growing tide, which swallowed them up.

The Tsar, mad with despair, had wanted to throw himself out of the aerostat that was carrying him, in order that he too might drown in that whirlpool that possessed the darkness of the abyss. His officers had great difficulty holding him back, and it had required the friendly voice of Ivanoff to bring the sovereign out of that paroxysm of madness.

"Louis-Alexandroff Romanoff," he had cried, "Russians are dying but Russia is alive! There's no more valor to deploy here. One can't contend with the impossible. It's necessary to give the signal to retreat."

"But that's dishonor! And besides, the torrent won't stop…it will continue advancing, and the engulfment will continue."

Suddenly, a voice shouted from the air: "Order the retreat, Sire, and I'll save the rest of your army!"

"Who's speaking?" shouted the Tsar.

"Me, Norès!"

And the airship drew alongside the captive balloon that was carrying the sovereign.

"You can do something?" cried Ivanoff. "But by what means?"

"Don't interrogate me—time's pressing. Let your troops fall back at once. I've seen your enemies; they're not pursuing them. They're walking, not running. It's vital that within half an hour, there's a space of a kilometer between the two armies…"

"So be it," said the Tsar. "What else can be done, anyway, except trust your offer?"

A signal flare went up from the balloon. Until then, not a single Russian had recoiled, but the signal was repeated three times, visible to the entire army, and in the conventional language translated by the rockets, it was an imperative order for a precipitate retreat, as prompt as possible.

Obediently, with the precision of regiments maneuvering on the drill field, the Russian troops commenced the backward movement. There was no cowardice in the flight—and yet, how did panic not take possession of all those unfortunates, who had seen half their companions perish?

The withdrawal, since it had been ordered, was now enacted with immediate haste. Fortunately, everything had been so well calculated in advance by the military engineers that the way of retreat was free, and the directions of redeployment had been strictly designated in advance.

Of the two thousand artillery pieces that had been engaged, about five hundred still remained at the front, and they blasted the first ranks of the Orientals, who, as Norès had understood, were not launching themselves in pursuit of their vanquished enemies. They scarcely oscillated under that frightful machine gun fire; they continued advancing, with the same monotony of pressure, with the same fatalistic indifference that nothing could disturb.

Norès airship was still alongside the imperial balloon.

"Well," said Romanoff, whose voice was hoarse, by virtue of the humiliation that gripped his throat, "your orders have been carried out, Monsieur de Norès. In your turn, is there anything you can do?"

"Perhaps," said the young man, "if it pleases science." He added: "If I die, I commend my sister to you."

"You have my word."

At that moment the two armies had broken off all contact. The Russians were more than a kilometer away from the most advanced Asiatic lines.

"*Au revoir*," said Norès—and the aircraft headed for the ground.

It landed on a small bluff.

To understand what follows it is necessary to remember what happened previously in the young scientist's workshop, when Norès, before Sabirat's eyes, had displaced a ball of iron weighing approximately two quintals with a kind of vaporizer. You will also recall the theory provided by the engineer: it was a matter of the incredible force of expansion that is contained in perfumes, one atom of which is sufficient to fill a considerable space in a second. It was by submitting that expansive force to a formidable pressure that Norès had succeeded in constructing a motor of hitherto unknown power.

Now, one of the important properties of perfume is that its faculty of dissociation does not stop; so long as the odorant material exists, the molecules continue to spill from it with equal rapidity, in quantities so infinitesimal that one can only observe a depreciation in weight after a very long time.

Thus, as soon as the apparatus was closed and, in consequence, the external projection was no longer happening, the dissociation continued in the sealed generator and was subjected to a pressure of several thousand atmospheres.

That was what Norès had observed on retaking possession of the apparatus. The generator had exits into several storage tanks, and Marie and Sabirat had only made use of the provisions accumulated in one of them.

It was now almost a month since they had left Paris, and one can imagine the formidable quantity of molecules that had accumulated in the primary generator. Norès had doubted at first that the material of which it was constructed could resist such pressure, but experiments had reassured him, and just now he had had the joy of observing that the force of expansion at his disposal was equivalent to that of the most violent cyclone—which is to say, a wind-speed of about forty meters a second, producing a pressure of more than 160 kilograms per square meter.

According to his calculations, taking account of the quantities of radiant matter contained in the generator, that colossal effort could be sustained for several minutes.

It was then that the idea had occurred to him of attempting to save the Russian army from complete annihilation.

Now, the moment had come to act.

The airship, as we have said, was perched on a slight ridge, a black dot of such scant importance that the Asiatics had scarcely noticed it. Undoubtedly, they thought it was some abandoned artillery battery. They were still advancing, with the same movement of an unstoppable flood.

They were five hundred meters from Norès; it was the decisive moment. He, too, was not about to be engulfed by that sea to which no human force seemed able to say: "You shall go no further!"

Pale, with his eyes glued to one of the interior portholes and his hand on the handle of the great generator—a control that the aerial voyagers had fortunately not discovered, for a false maneuver would undoubtedly have cost them their lives—Norès directed a tapered tube at the line formed by the Asiatics, which he had fitted to the orifice, and which emerged from the apparatus through a kind of peephole disposed for that purpose.

The direction that he gave it relative to the line was an angle of about thirty degrees—which is to say that he was not aiming at them head-on, but obliquely.

"Let's go," said Norès, "and may the justice of our cause aid its success."

He pulled the handle.

A strident whistle-blast resounded, tearing through the air. That was the gas—we shall employ that word in order to be better understood, although the matter projected was infinitely more dilute than the most subtle known gas—escaping from the generator with extreme violence.

In ten seconds, it reached the Orientals, and Norès, whose tight chest was breathless, saw something surprising.

The mass of the assailants was now oscillating like a field of ripe wheat; the men were falling onto one another, forming an obstacle to those following behind, constraining them to turn back. The pressure was so strong that, as in a pool over which a violent wind passes, it formed a vertiginous gyratory eddy, and by virtue of a sort of mutual attraction it seemed that even those who were not touched by the wind were drawn into it. The first ranks, to a depth of more than a hundred men, were knocked down, broken, scythed like wisps of straw by a southwest wind...but the others, experiencing an unexpected, incomprehensible resistance, unconsciously changed direction.

Sir John Lubbock recounts[44] that, having once seen a field menaced by a column of ants composed of an infinite number of individuals, the passage of which had left nothing behind it but ruins, the idea had occurred to him of de-

---

[44] In his pioneering study of social insects, *Ants, Bees and Wasps* (1884)

flecting the direction of the head of the column by a mere two or three degrees. The entire horde of tiny creatures had followed, and the field was saved.

Under the pressure of the hurricane unleashed by Norès, the angle of the Asiatics' direction had changed by more than a quarter of a circle, and now the young scientist saw the black stain heading southwards, having lost the notion of a straight line—and heading southwards with the same implacable slowness.

He could scarcely believe his eyes. Once again, therefore, intelligence had triumphed over brute force—an ephemeral triumph, to be sure, for the leaders would doubtless return the column to its original direction; but it was an assured respite...and perhaps salvation.

The Asiatics disappeared over the horizon.

Suddenly, Norès heard a voice calling to him. He emerged precipitately. It was the Tsar, who seized him in his arms and hugged him delightedly.

"Monsieur de Norès, you're more worthy than I am to command peoples. Tell me, what would you like as a reward? Whatever your desire is, I give you my word that it will be granted..."

"I desire," Norès said "to return to France as soon as possible."

"To leave me!"

"In saving you," said Norès, gravely, "who can tell whether it might not be my own country on to which I've unlashed the danger?"

"At least," said the Tsar, "you'll do me the honor of dining at my table, as I've just been notified of the arrival of European prisoners of the Orientals, who, thanks to the disturbance you produced in the ranks of their torturers, have succeeded in escaping."

"Europeans!" said Norès, going pale. "Are there, then, some who escaped the massacre?"

"Come," said the Tsar—and they hastened toward the camp.

VI

It was in an old dacha a few versts from St. Petersburg that the staff officers who had escaped the massacre were waiting for their sovereign.

To those valiant fighting men who had braved death a hundred times in the most terrible circumstances, it seemed that they had emerged from a frightful nightmare. This was no longer war, alas; it was the folly of Xerxes wanting to fight against the sea.[45] They had seen their battalions disappear like sand in a

---

[45] According to Herodotus, when the first attempt made by Xerxes the Great to invade Greece in the 5th century B.C. was thwarted, after his improvised bridges across the Hellespont were destroyed by a storm, Xerxes held the Hellespont responsible and sentenced it to three hundred lashes. Given that his second attempt to cross it was successful, it is not entirely obvious that the chastisement did not have the desired effect.

crucible—and they remained, not frightened but exhausted, as if annihilated, with the sensation that that they had encountered something superior to any human force.

How had the torrent that was about to engulf them suddenly been turned aside? How had they been brought back to the rear safe and sound? How did they find themselves here, out of immediate and sinister danger? None of them could say. As they had obeyed the discipline that had launched them forward, so they had obeyed the signal to retreat…and that was all. They no longer had the strength to reason, or even to think.

Was that horrible catastrophe to be imputed to a crime? They did not know, but even if the most terrible punishment were to fall upon them, not one of them thought of seeking to avoid it. They felt guilty, since they were alive, and the fatherland had been defeated.

The emperor came in. All heads were bared.

Louis-Alexandroff went to the first ranks, his hands extended, open. With a few words, he comforted the despairing men. No, he certainly had no reproach to address to anyone. On the contrary, he rendered them full and entire justice. They had done their duty, more than their duty, for not one had faltered, and if death had been refused to them, it was not because they had not offered themselves to it.

"But my lieutenants," he said, in a vibrant voice, "it is necessary before anything else that you know the name of the man who has saved us—yes, saved us from definitive and irremediable disaster. His name is Guy de Norès; he's a Frenchman, and once more, the pact of amity and gratitude that has so long affirmed their fraternity has been sealed between the two nations." He turned to the young Frenchman, and added: "Monsieur de Norès, the entirety of Russia thanks you via my voice. I shall offer you neither dignities nor decorations; the service you have rendered to us is not one of those that can be repaid—but I, the Tsar, offer you my hand loyally and I say to you: Your name is henceforth sacred among us."

Norès stepped back modestly, but in a few vibrant words, the Tsar recounted the extraordinary adventure, giving form to the massacre, and all the officers, for whom the new science still retained a whiff of magic, bowed to him with a kind of fearful respect.

"Sire," said Norès, "I'm profoundly touched by a gratitude that I would like to have deserved more completely. But at this moment, if you will permit me to make a request…"

"Say what you want and orders will be given."

"Well, mention was made just now of Europeans who have been brought here…"

"In truth, I forgot!" exclaimed the Tsar. "Where are they? Let them be brought here immediately."

Officers went out to carry out the sovereign's orders. A few minutes went by, during which the Tsar conversed with his generals.

Suddenly, the door opened, and an exclamation escaped all throats.

Over the threshold advanced a group of men and women so wretched and haggard in their appearance that everyone felt gripped by an inexpressible anguish.

Were these diminished, trembling unfortunates, barely clad in rags, tottering forward as if their limbs were unable to carry them really human beings?

Suddenly, a louder, more heart-rending clamor burst forth. Norès launched himself toward those who were in the first rank, astounded, unable to believe his eyes.

He had just recognized the French engineer Robert Sametel, his bloodied eyes closed, and in the woman he was clutching by the hand he had seen...who? Marguerite Sametel, his beloved, the fiancée of his heart.

And as he pronounced the same of Sametel with an accent of ineffable gravity, the blind man said: "Who's calling me?"

"Me! Me! Norès, your son!"

"Guy de Norès!" cried Marguerite, raising her head. "No, it's impossible!"

"It's me, it's really me...but please, for pity's sake, tell me that I'm dreaming, that I'm mad...Robert Sametel, my father..."

"I fell into the power of those demons," said the engineer. "Then, to avenge themselves, they burned my eyes."

"Infamy!"

"Oh, if you knew," Marguerite continued, "to what frightful tortures they've subjected us[46]...why we're not dead, in truth, is a miracle that I still can't explain. My father blinded, me thrown into a dungeon where I was up to my waist in fetid water for a week... Well, no! We're French, and we didn't want to die...then they dragged us in the wake of their hordes through the deserts of Mongolia. I felt almost glad, for they hadn't divined that for me, the worst torture would have been to be separated from my father...and there remained to us I don't know what mad hope of escaping."

"What she isn't telling you," Sametel interjected, "is with what energy, what admirable and unwavering patience, she maintained our courage...by her dignity, by I don't know what quasi-magical influence, she was able to impose a sort of respect on those brutes..."

---

[46] Lermina must surely have intended when he began the serial to relate this part of the story in detail. Did the Sametels and the Nivets, after leaving the Yamen, manage to reach the *Suffren* before being captured? At what point, and how, were they separated from Albert de Mesnes? Did they encounter the German Ambassador, who was also taken prisoner? Who brought them with the Asiatic horde, why, and in what circumstances? We really should have been told.

175

"Let me finish, Father," said the young woman, squeezing his hand to cut short eulogies that were troubling her. When the collision with the Russian army occurred, we thought we were doomed. We knew from experience, alas, that all resistance was impossible, we had the impression of that heavy, crushing, indefatigable force against which no courage could prevail...and we had decided, rather than witness impassively the catastrophe in which the Europeans would succumb, to throw ourselves forward, into the heart of the battle, to perish there, even under the thrusts of our own forces: it seemed to us that death would be less miserable thus.

"How, after hours of anguish, at the moment when we abandoned ourselves to despair, were the Asiatic hordes suddenly struck and disorganized, as if by a miracle? From the point where we found ourselves, behind a compact mass that closed every exit to us, we couldn't see anything, we couldn't understand anything...suddenly, we heard something like the whistling of a hurricane. We saw rows of men knocked down, lifted from the ground, thrown round like wisps of straw by the north wind...and a path opened up before us. I took my father by the hand, and we ran straight ahead, without knowing where we were going. We stumbled through the midst of cadavers...finally, we recognized the Russian colors. We shouted for help...and we were saved."

"Sire," said Norès, turning to the Tsar, just now you asked me what reward I wanted for the service that I rendered your army. Let me tell you that I've been abundantly rewarded, for the man you see here, mutilated by those swine, is Sametel, the man to whom I owe the little I know...and this young woman is my fiancée...my wife!"

Sametel and his daughter were not the only Europeans to have escaped the massacre. Rose Nivet, the courageous gamine, and her father, the genial photographer, had not abandoned them for an instant—but Nivet had also suffered his martyrdom; they had cut off his beard.[47]

"But what became of Sacha Bernstorff?"[48] asked Norès, anxiously. "Was she not the fiancée of the miserable renegade Wintscheff, who has sworn the death of all those who welcomed him like a brother?"

"I can't inform you completely as to Sacha's fate," said Marguerite, "but I believe that she was saved, along with her brother, by Albert de Mesnes. I've

---

[47] The Nivets were obviously intended to play a greater role in the story when they were introduced—and perhaps they have. Why would we have been told about Nivet's thunderous voice if it were not to play some significant part in the plot?

[48] Lermina has now forgotten Sacha's surname (Batowna) as well as her forename, but her story too should also have been recounted in detail, especially as we are subsequently told that she learned an important item of information in the course of her tribulations, although we never find out what it is.

been told that they found a means of embarking for Europe. If we ever see them again, they'll be in France."

"France," said Norès, "is now where we should be. Courage, Robert Sametel…the misfortune that has struck you is certainly horrible, but your genius will survive your martyrdom. Henceforth, I sense—I know—that it's against France that the effort of these horrible hordes will be directed. It's from the Alps to the Vosges and the Rhine that our fatherland must erect an uncrossable barrier to the invaders. All the living force of our nation must stand up, to save civilization, to save the world!"

"And I shall help you do it!" cried the Tsar. "I'll answer for Wilhelm of Prussia. You won't be troubled in our heroic attempt. Count on me. Return to Paris, Guy de Norès, and tell those who are directing the destiny of your great Republic that a Romanoff has given you his hand as a sign of alliance, and that, even if it costs me my last soldier, no German will dare to attack you."

"I receive your promise, Sire. Once more the alliance will be sealed that will render us invincible. And now, there's not an hour to lose. To Paris…"

And the unfortunates who had thought themselves condemned to the most terrible of deaths a little while before, suddenly galvanized by that vibrant voice, repeated:

"To Paris! To Paris!"

EPILOGUE
THE WORLD IS SAVED!

A month has passed since the sinister events that we have just recounted.

That short period had been rich in further disasters and catastrophes.

As Norès had anticipated, the Asiatic hordes, deflected from a straight line, had at first oscillated like a ship without a rudder. They had then spread like a sheet over White Russia to the shores of the Sea of Azof, swollen by all the torrents that were incessantly descending from Tartary and Turkestan and rising up from India and Persia.

The flood had enveloped the Black Sea, swallowing up Constantinople, and had been halted momentarily at the Danube by the valiant efforts of the Rumanians and Hungarians—but there again, numbers overwhelmed courage, and once the barrier had been crossed, Budapest and Vienna had disappeared under the frightful tide.

On their way, the Orientals were beginning to pause occasionally in centers where the pillage went on for a longer period. The brutes plunged into frightful orgies illuminated by the blaze of fires; they were hideous intoxications spiced with unspeakable ferocities.

The main body of the army, however, which had been estimated at some twelve hundred thousand men, was still pressing forward. Its supreme leader was known: it was Wintscheff, whose fury seemed to increase with every success. Before his name that of the legendary Attila paled; it was said that he marched preceded by the standard of the Five Hundred Gods, steeped in blood.

Revolting executions marked the stages of his march; everyone who attempted to resist was subjected to the most atrocious tortures; a Hungarian leader had been cut into quarters, which had been sent as a sign of menace to the great cities of Austria. The cruel theories that the Prussians had once put into action during the war against the French in 1870 were implemented once again by those barbarians from the depths of Asia. No one, including women, children, and old men, found any mercy in the hands of the monsters, whom terror preceded.

A woman, it was said, presided over these atrocities: Sithreva, the Hindu, the furious priestess of Death, drunk on blood and mad with hatred.

Suddenly, however, there was a pause in the ever-rising tide. The course of the Asiatics then turned northwards toward Dresden and Berlin. Berlin was invaded on the day the emperor had declared war on France. He fled, and came to seek asylum in France; ever generous, our fatherland welcomed him, but the terror he had suffered had disturbed his reason; he was mad.

At the center, the Orientals occupied Stuttgart and Munich. To the south, they extended from Innsbruck to Milan and Turin. It was a semicircle that was tightening around France and Switzerland; nothing any longer remained but the barrier of the Alps, the Jura, and the Vosges. Behind those immense bulwarks, France waited, breathlessly.

At present, she was the refuge of all the defeated of Europe, the shelter of all the desperate. To fugitives of all nations she had opened her doors wide; cities and villages had been improvised over the whole extent of the territory, and in hundreds of thousands, Russians, Germans, Hungarians, Austrians and Italians—even Italy contracted a new debt of gratitude toward us, which she would disclaim at a later date—camped in the rural regions, nourished by our peasants, cared for by our nurses.

In those days of peril, Paris presented a striking physiognomy. The great Council of Defense had summoned Guy de Norès to its presidency; day after day, the people were kept apprised of the situation, without any dissimulation. All the men who were able to bear arms had been called up and recruited to the active army and the reserves. The Territorial Army occupied the strongest positions.

The Parisians, calling a truce in their eternal agitations, provided an example of calm and discipline. On the boulevards, in the squares, there was not a single cry, not a single demonstration. The city was like an immense barracks of volunteers, in which no one was thinking of anything except doing his duty.

People grouped around posters put up by order of the government, serious and grave, communicating their apprehensions in low voices, with no fuss and no fear, ready to do anything for the salvation of the nation.

The style of the proclamations was sober, with none of those resounding phrases that can excite the imagination momentarily but which cannot give hearts any real confidence.

France is preparing, said the latest of these posters, *to repel the most terrible invasion that has ever fallen upon a civilized nation. All the living forces of the nation are ready for the resistance; the shock will be frightful, but the French must not lose confidence in the justice of their cause, which is that of the entire humanity. Three armies of three hundred thousand men are facing the assailants, but it is, above all, on the progress of Science that we must count. In this morning's session, Monsieur de Norès has communicated to the Council plans and projects that it would be premature to deliver to the public, but from now on, the Council affirms on its honor that victory is possible. Let the people remain calm, let the press continue its work of discretion and public encouragement. France will not abandon herself! Vive la France!*

A few imprudent individuals, moved by personal ambition, had attempted to provoke an unhealthy agitation in the name of an adventurous general once punished by his seniors for indiscipline. Attempts had been made to present him to the people as a savior whose panache would be sufficient to put the enemy to flight. He had run around the boulevards followed by a band of blowhards escaped from the capital's underworld, but a squadron of police had sufficed to dissipate the rabble; the general had been brought before a police court, where he had been sentenced to two months in prison for misappropriation of funds.[49]

People had confidence in Guy de Norès, who spent his days locked in his laboratory, not showing himself in public. It was said that the young Russian, Sacha Bernstorff, who had miraculously escaped the massacres and had been brought back to France by Albert de Mesnes, who himself was promoted to the command of an army corps in the Alps, had brought him precious information. As legend never loses its rights, much comment was made about the presence close to him of an old Muslim, who was only known by the name of the Hadji, and who, it seems, had furnished him with the most interesting revelations.

A catastrophe almost momentarily troubled the patient tranquility of the great city. Norès' electricity workshops were located on the Buttes-Chaumont, which had been closed to the public. One night, Paris was woken up by a formidable explosion; the ground shook throughout the perimeter of the fortifications.

People ran to the site of the disaster and observed that the summits of the Buttes had completed disappeared into an enormous excavation that had sudden-

---

[49] This sly insertion satirically reflects the career of General Boulanger. Its inclusion is entirely gratuitous, and perhaps odd, given that the author is in such a tearing hurry to wind up his devastated plot. Perhaps he had a hidden agenda.

ly opened up at their base. However, no one had been killed. It was thought at first to have been an earthquake, and it was no mediocre anxiety to see nature aiding the invaders in their work of destruction, but within an hour, a note issuing from the war administration explained to Parisians that the explosion had not been entirely accidental. It had been an experiment carried out by Guy de Norès that had succeeded beyond his expectations, and above all, sooner than he had expected. It was connected with the plan for resistance and gave a near-certainty of success.

The same day, a meeting took place that excited the curiosity of Paris very keenly: the members of Swiss Federal Council had a long discussion with the French government. Although secrecy was strictly guarded, it was known that the discussion had been long and difficult. One singular phrase was widely quoted: one of the Swiss had cried: "We can't sacrifice a part of our territory!"

It seemed, however, that a definitive understanding had been produced, and the official note announced to the public that the meeting had taken place terminated with these mysterious words:

Europe cannot be too grateful to the noble Swiss Republic for the sacrifices that she has consented to make for the salvation of civilization.

The days passed. It was known that the Asiatic hordes, after being interrupted momentarily by the slopes of the Alps, as if astonished in the face of those colossi, had resumed their forward march. In fact, had they not already crossed the Himalaya, the Urals, and the Carpathians? That final obstacle could not halt them for long.

The Parisians were not at the end of their surprises.

It is well known that for the exposition of 19**, an engineer had conceived the veritably eccentric idea of constructing three more Eiffel Towers similar to the first, and then had linked together their summits—and on that platform he had built a further tower rising to a height of 450 meters, which constituted a formidable edifice of 750 meters in height. It was a whim of the constructor, whose utility was far from having been demonstrated, and the public, after having satisfied their curiosity by going up to the top of the tower, had gradually become disinterested in the spectacle, weary of its monotony.

The Espagnet Tower, as it was called, after its constructor—who, desolate at his lack of success, had killed himself by throwing himself off the top—had thus been relegated to the rank of a useless curiosity, of which no one, including foreigners and provincials, any longer took notice.

Then, all of a sudden, it was learned that Norès had had an optical apparatus of exceptional power installed on the topmost platform. In any other circumstances people would have smiled, assuming that the great engineer had the pretention of watching over the frontiers of France—but one day, a notice from the National Defense informed Parisians that they ought not to be alarmed if the sky took on an unusual appearance.

You can imagine how everyone's interest was stimulated. Was it a matter of a meteorological phenomenon, or some kind of bolide of frightening appearance? Some people talked about an eclipse, and the less brave recalled historical legends that attributed to celestial phenomena the announcement of terrestrial cataclysms.

On the night that followed the advice given by the government, all of Paris spread out into the streets, anxious and attentive.

When the darkness was at its deepest, a jet of light, of such great power that the entire city was suddenly illuminated, emerged from the summit of the Espagnet Tower. It resembled a colossal electric beam. Then, instantaneously, in the depths of the sky—and, it seemed, at a distance equal to that of the farthest stars—bizarre characters appeared: three symbols very clear and sharp, whose significance hardly anyone comprehended, stood out as if they had been traced by a brush of fire.

The news quickly spread, through that city in which everything is known, that the three characters belonged to the Sanskrit alphabet and that they formed the word AUM, a sacred formula of the Hindus, from which our occidental religions have borrowed the mysterious Amen.

What could that strange invention signify? The most singular thing was that the inscription remained immovable in the sky, as if it constituted a signal.

It can easily be imagined that imaginations were hard at work, compounded by the fact that, the morning after the curious incident, Norès quit Paris, accompanied by the Hadji. This time, the government abstained from any explanation, or any communication. One might have thought that a profound silence had suddenly fallen over the city; a sentiment of expectation and subconscious anguish gripped the population.

Something was about to happen. Was it salvation, or was it, on the contrary, the final catastrophe?

Two days later, posters with large print were plastered on the walls. They bore the following words:

Mont Blanc has blown up. Norès.

Flooding through Europe, gorging themselves on the spoils of the people, wading through rivers of blood, the Asiatic hordes had continued their fatal march, which no obstacle interrupted. Like a torrent whose dykes have been broken, the human tide was precipitated onwards, noisily.

If any sign of lassitude appeared, if the Oriental brutes, full of conquest, seemed to want to enjoy their victory for longer, the voice of Sithreva rose up, and, reawakening passions that were ready to fall asleep, rendered a new ardor to the exasperated bands.

Sithreva was personified in a terrible incarnation of the hatred of the Orient for the Occident. In her hands, Wintscheff was only an instrument. Maddened by his passion, forgetting everything else—his past and his honor—the wretch lived in a bloody nightmare. Cleverly, the Hindu maintained him in an unhealthy intoxication that no longer left him the free disposition of his faculties; he went before her, enveloped by an atmosphere of crimes, as if hypnotized, unconscious, and numbed.

Sometimes, however, in moments of calm, he had a vague notion of the infamous work that he was accomplishing. As he passed through cities once flourishing with civilization, superb with vitality and intelligence, now bleak and desolate, quivering like mutilated cadavers, a somber melancholy took possession of him; specters haunted his sleep and, like a new Richard II,[50] he saw the phantoms of his victims surrounding him, harassing him, threatening him with their maledictions. He was afraid.

Between the furious excitations of battle and the fits of remorse, madness gradually crept in, setting its iron claw upon his enfevered brain. He had reactions of horror. But the pitiless Sithreva watched him; in moments of weakness she gripped him again.

Sometimes, however, he cried: "When will it stop?"

And, singularly enough, those words, which he pronounced incessantly, by some mysterious means, had an echo in the profound masses of those who were following him.

Stop! It seemed that the syllable suddenly became for them a kind of revelation, a latent and inexplicable desire.

Yes, they still marched even so, with the ineluctable will to crush, but the brute will in question was that of the mass. The leaders dreamed of something else. Like an ogre in a fairy tale, they had scented fresh flesh—which is to say, the joys of civilization: the music, the femininity, the perfumes, everything that forms the galvanoplastic envelope of our Occidental world. Everything was gold; everything was love. And among those brutes the appetite developed, and wanted to be slaked. The frightful pillages of treasures and women had given them a taste for them.

Now, the objective was France, was Paris: France, with its delicacies; Paris, with its exquisite elegance.

Realizing that, the monks, marabouts, hadjis and gurus—all the exploiters of that stupid humanity—were afraid. What if civilization, by virtue of a sort of osmosis, were to penetrate those wretches; if, in drinking of the Fountain of Youth that is France, they were suddenly regenerated; if revolutionary Paris, the perturber of consciousness and illuminator of reason were to take possession of those hallucinated minds, transforming and civilizing them?

It was necessary that they did not stay. The dream of the guides, the Brahmins, was to appease them to the point that, weary, having lain down drunk on

---

[50] Lermina seems to be confusing Richard II, who is not confronted with any phantoms, though has a Shakespeare play titled for him, with Richard III, who is, and also does.

vanquished civilization, they demanded to return home, to the ignorant and submissive world of the Orient.

The danger was real. One does not come into contact with our civilization with impunity. There are contagions of conscience. Already, revolt was stirring in the hordes; some individuals were talking about their rights; some, fatigued by being dogs launched forward, had remembered that they were human.

Then Sithreva, in concert with all the religious leaders, whatever name they adopted, had announced by proclamation that "the Orient must march forward, ever forward, until the sacred sign of Buddha, AUM, appears in the heavens."

Ben-Borouk, the Hadji, knew that—and that was the secret he had offered to surrender in order to save his life.

Now, one night, when the Orientals were hesitant to march forward, at the foot of the Alps, suddenly, in the sky, in the profoundest depths of the zones of the infinite, the fateful symbols had been designed!

A stupefying miracle!

Sithreva, Wintscheff, and all the liars and exploiters who had dragged the Asiatics along, who knew that the prediction was, in fact, a lie, were amazed. Aum, the sacred word of Krishna and Gautama, the alpha and omega of all knowledge, the key to ecstasy, the stairway of Devachan: that was what had appeared, really and materially, in the sky.

Lie! Magic! They did not believe it, since they had reserved for themselves the privilege of raising into the air some new banner bearing the sacred characters, remaining the masters able to halt the innumerable troop whenever they wished.

No, such a prodigy was not possible.

Can you imagine a conjurer who announces an unprecedented trick and sees it take place before him, without his participation being required?

Sithreva and Wintscheff, and the priests of Buddha, Brahma, Siva, Fo, and Mohammed, threw themselves in front of the Asiatics crying: "It's a lie! A lie!"

But they reaped what they had sown. They had exploited ignorance by multiplying it a hundredfold. Ignorance and stupid superstition were stronger than they were. And toward that sign, ablaze in the heavens, all of them—the Chinese and the Hindus, the Tartars and the Samoyeds—raced forward. There, where the sign was displayed, was paradise. It was necessary to reach it, to place themselves directly beneath it, to salute it as the unique and holy banner. In the Five Hundred Gods there was no god; God was the sacred formula.

And crossing the Alps, without fear, paying no heed to abysses and precipices, the Asiatics launched themselves toward the location overhung by the Sign.

It was suspended in the ether directly above Mont Blanc, on the frontier of France.

There was no resistance. Switzerland, that intrepid nation which has the honor of the soil implanted in its conscience, which has the fatherland in its blood, let them pass, leaving the way open, the roads devoid of defenders.

Can you understand now what the members of the Federal Council, representatives of the Helvetic Republic, had conceded to the French Republic? For the good of humanity and civilization, they had alienated their right to die as citizens and as patriots. They allowed those bandits to foul the scared lands, to dishonor the proud summits before which the conquerors had paused.

In the noble Swiss nation there was a terrible tremor, but a promise had been made; their word had been given, and it was kept.

The Asiatic passed without anyone being able to count them. They did not stop. What did the villages matter to them, the huts suspended on the mountainsides, the pastors' chalets, deserted and mute? They passed by, heading for a single goal, toward the mysterious AUM that still lit up the sky from dusk to dawn. There was the triumph; there was the eternal felicity promised by God, by Brahma, by Allah, to whom they were obedient.

And thus they arrived, some at Matigny, others at Morgex and Cormayeur.

There, miraculously, the fateful sign had suddenly stopped, as if fixed in the sky, an inscription retained by the golden nails that were the stars.

In the entire army there was a clamor, like a hymn of deliverance.

It was the goal, the triumph, the repose, and also the satiation of all the contained passions. God spoke, and he said: "Here it is!"

Sithreva and Wintscheff were astonished and irritated. It is the fate of ensnarers of men to collide with the unknown, the incomprehensible. They had allowed the legend of the sacred word to propagate through the crowd in order, on a day chosen by them, to bring an end to the surge and to signal the final victory. They thought themselves masters of the solution: by a kind of conjuring trick, they would impose their will on the credulous...eventually, when their hatred had been slaked.

Now, suddenly, the prodigy that they had invented in its entirety, of which they believed themselves to be the masters, had burst forth regardless, against their will.

In Wintscheff, who still had a savage naiveté, that surprise was complicated by superstitious terror. Were the heavens really taking a hand? Was nature ordering him to stop?

The arrogant Sithreva possessing Oriental science—the science of the past—completely, although ignorant of the science of the present, did not believe in perturbations of the laws of nature. For her, there was no miracle, but some infamous treason for whose authors she sought in vain. Why would she have suspected the Hadji that she had barely glimpsed and who, believing that he would be subjected to the most horrible tortures, had purchased his life by surrendering to Norès the secret that he had discovered.

Sithreva did, however, divine some enormous trap, some formidable peril. She tried to resist; she ran through the camps crying: "It's not true; Brahma has not spoken." But in her turn, she understood that a torrent had been unleashed and that no dyke could stop it.

She ordered, she prayed, she threatened. What did her anger and her pleas matter to those brutes? They marched, their eyes fixed on the heavens. They would have crushed her; it was necessary that she let them go.

And the craziest of all the unthinking was Wintscheff. He too had been gripped by a kind of fury. He wanted to go forward: he was caught up in a kind of monstrous dream of war against the heavens, against destiny.

Sithreva, throwing her arms around him, cried out to him: "Take care! You're going toward the abyss!"

He did not hear her. Haggard, his arm raised toward the snowy summits of Mont Blanc, he said: "It's there…I'm going!"

And the formidably numerous horde followed the same path without hesitation.

From all directions, the march converged on a single point: the mountain above which the sacred word was inscribed.

Through the Col d'Argentières, the Porte de Tiolet, via Scalèfe, Tétatête[51] and Tondu, they encircled the immobile mountain, which seemed to be calling them and waiting for them, always maintaining its fiery crown.

It was an amazing thing to see those black masses invading those white immensities. The glaciers cracked under the weight and abysses opened up that swallowed thousands of men. Were they even aware of it? No solution of continuity divided the innumerable cohort, which seemed to resuscitate and regenerate itself. Under the swarm, everything disappeared: the hamlets of Fratzes and Tuent, the chalets of Herbagères, Annemasse, Bonneville and Balme. At the Pont de la Dioza, which collapsed under the weight, cadavers filled the abyss. The others passed over that viaduct of the dead.

Finally, following the Arve, descending from Brévent and the Aiguilles Rouges, passing by Chapeau and Flégère, the Orientals set foot on the sea of ice.

The AUM was still sparkling in the sky.

The hastiest urged the latecomers on.

At the Géants, the Mauvais-Pas, the Egralets and the Bossons they were densely packed, covering the summits, filling the valleys, so compact that all those individuals seemed to form a single being, like a human carapace armoring the mountains.

Wintscheff was there, at the head, sword in hand. Night was falling; soon the magical sign would burst forth in the heavens, and he wanted to be the first to show it to his soldiers with the point of steel.

---

[51] I have reproduced these names as they appear in Lermina's text, although they seem to have fallen into disuse, if they ever had any significance.

Pale and somber, Sithreva was beside him. She was beginning to doubt everything: her reason, her will power, herself.

Was she really mad? What! That work of destruction to which she had devoted her entire life, and of which she felt herself to be the architect, the prophetess, was suddenly escaping her, taken over...by whom?

For someone who believes herself to be the mistress of destiny, there is no torture more atrocious than finding herself confronted by the inexplicable. She knew full well that there are no miracles, since she was a maker of miracles, since she, with her priests, had mocked the heavens a hundred times over, knowing how to make them her accomplice.

She huddled close to Wintscheff, who, in spite of his strength of mind, was trembling like a child.

The Asiatics were howling joyful hymns.

The scene was monumentally grandiose. The darkness extended. The crowd could no longer be seen, but the innumerable voices of the anthill could still be heard.

Suddenly, although Sithreva still doubted, a luminous dot appeared in the sky, with the splendors of lightning.

Then other dots...then forms that were accentuated...and finally, clear and radiant, the three letters: AUM.

An enormous clamor resounded, furious and enthusiastic at the same time, in echoes repeated thousands of times by the rocks, by the precipices, by the summits, by the valleys...

The sacred sign was there, directly above the highest summit of Mont Blanc.

But that clamor, all hope, salvation and joy, was suddenly transformed into a single scream, or a death rattle...a kind of hiccup, scarcely formulated and quickly stifled...

The earth had shaken; the rocks had collapsed; the summits had been precipitated into the valleys, instantaneously and unexpectedly overturned, as if a hand, emerging from the bowels of the earth, had grabbed those gigantic masses and had turned them over.

It was more than an explosion, more than an earthquake. What was underneath was now on top, and what was on top was underneath: a leveling collapse, a paste of rocks and ice, a mincemeat of humans and things.

Mont Blanc had just blown up.

Norès' genius had triumphed.

How many thousands of men perished in that catastrophe, provoked by the scientist who had utilized terrestrial electricity for the defense of France and civilization, who had brought forth from the abysms of the globe the enormous, immeasurable quantity of force of which the two poles are the piles.

Not all the Orientals had disappeared; some three hundred thousand had escaped the disaster. They fled...but France was alert.

It was at the gates of Strasbourg, the sentinel city, that the crazed Asiatics collided with the French army. There was an atrocious, stupefying battle; there was an insensate heroism on the part of the vanquished; they fought for a week, with a savagery before which the historian recoils...but in the French army, there was not an hour of weakness, not a minute of hesitation.

The Battle of Strasbourg was the greatest work of deliverance of the twentieth century.

France had the burden of it, and the honor.

One interesting detail: Norès did not ask for any reward, and he was held in sufficient honor not to be offered any. He married Marguerite Sametel and was happy, as if he were not a great man.

Camille Mauclair: *The Virgin Orient*

L'Orient vierge, roman épique de l'an 2000, *by Camille Mauclair, here translated as "The Virgin Orient, an Epic Novel of the Year 2000," was originally published by Paul Ollendorf in 1897. It was reprinted in a slightly revised version in 1920, after the conclusion of the Great War, perhaps because the publisher thought that the fact that the novel anticipated a Franco-German war as a prelude to its own Even Greater War might add further interest to it, although the actual Great War had demonstrated clearly that any war fought in the year 2000 would not bear the slightest resemblance to the one featured in Mauclair's novel, which is fought mostly with the technology of the 1890s.*

"Camille Mauclair" was the name used on all his writings by Camille-Laurent-Séverin Faust (1872-1945), who was one of the younger recruits to the Symbolist Movement that was a highly significant feature of the Parisian fin-de-siècle. L'Orient vierge *was his first full-length novel.*

Mauclair went on write several more contemporary novels, and also three volumes of short stories, but the evolution of his fiction clearly illustrated the problems of adapting the techniques and philosophy of Symbolism to the novel, their much readier application being to poetry and to Baudelairean "poems in prose." Mauclair was by no means the only Symbolist whose later novels eventually abandoned all but a gloss of Symbolist theory and technique, and those of his generation who did not die young tended to follow the same trajectory, inclining toward mundanity if never quite consenting to reach it.

Mauclair eventually dedicated himself entirely to non-fiction, much of it reflecting his journalistic career as a critic of art, literature and music, although he also published a number of travel books. His disenchantment with fiction, especially the kind of radical imaginative fiction that he produced in the first phase of his career, undoubtedly reflects the difficulties he had in reconciling his literary ambitions with the prosaic demands of the novel—a struggle all too clearly evident in L'Orient vierge—*but any desire he might have had to persist would have been obliterated in any case by hostile critical response and the increasing reluctance of publishers to repeat experiments of that sort, the prevailing wisdom being that too many readers found work of that kind too difficult to understand.*

Symbolist writers in general were not renowned for the comprehensibility of their work, and Mauclair, as one of the most extreme, must have seemed to some readers to be the most difficult of all. Although L'Orient vierge *is a much more straightforward text in terms of its presentation, and it is deliberately cast as a novel of action, with elaborate descriptions of the key battles in the future war, it is not improbable that many readers sympathized with the stubborn prac-*

ticality of the two villains, who cannot understand what the Idea with which the hero is so utterly obsessed actually is, let alone why it matters.

In fact, the attempt to graft an ideological quest, expressed in Symbolist terms, on to a future war story, creates a bizarre chimera that never comes remotely close to coherency, and the resultant novel one of many works of ambitious imaginative fiction whose reach manifestly far exceeds its grasp—but that is not necessarily a bad thing, however awkward the result, and there is no doubt that L'Orient vierge remains a fascinating hybrid.

Mauclair later tried to reconcile its reflexive racism with the traditional French fascination with "the Orient" as a summation of lush exoticism and a repository of secret wisdom.

The political history that the novel anticipates, in which a new Franco-German war is followed by the advent of a socialist internationalism that brings about a confederation of the European states, is virtually standard for the period, and remained so for some time. As with technological development, however, political development is not something in which the author is actually interested. It is in that sense that the novel is still capable of striking a chord in today's very different historical circumstances, in which the crude and repulsive racism of Mauclair's attitude to the "yellow peril," the confused mysticism of his attitude to "secret India" and the flagrant nonsensicality of his notion of "Aryanism" are all manifestly absurd, and yet the nascent European Confederation that actually exists nevertheless seems vulnerable to the charge leveled by the novel that its domination by commercial and practical interests is both soulless and ultimately self-destructive.

B.S.

He will dream everywhere of the warmth of the breast.
Vigny.[52]

PART ONE
THE FORCES

I. The Solemn Gathering

That evening, toward the darkness accumulated in the high corner of the architraves, with the flames of candelabras, the ardent and devouring voice rose up of the dictator, simply clad in black.

---

[52] The quotation is from Alfred de Vigny's "La Colère de Samson," from Dalila's monologue proudly explaining her role as a *femme fatale*.

189

And above the silent legates, the bellicose words collided and clashed violently, like golden swords.

"...The depositary of a heavy grandeur of centuries on the shores of occidental seas, a strange body vivified by all bloods, a profound soul in which all souls are purified, Europe, Messieurs, seems only to exhaust destinies in order to awaken new ones. A tradition of beauty visits its summits, and that giant and complex being, with its meditative or violent forms, signifies in its very configuration a vivacity and an inexhaustible nativity. Corteges of dreams still surge forth infinitely from that continent, toward which rears up, from the depths of the Pole, the great emblematic lion of Scandinavia; and, over and above the necessities of everyday diplomacy, the whole of politics is adding to those dreams a new subject of amazement for future generations.

"I attest, Messieurs, to the force that wells up from those countries of the Germano-Latin race, finally united, of which your presence here summarizes the mission and the history: the sublimity of politics is to lead States through events and indispensable and immediate precautions toward a new legend! It has required enormous periods of time for so-called dreams to become the essential goal of applied intelligences, the final desire of manipulators of ideas; for science, once considering them with enmity, finally to have a sufficiently high intuition of its true role to grasp them, to legitimate them, and to renew them by means of its own conquests, to dissolve them in itself and to dissolve itself within them, to utilize for one unique knowledge the precious and exalting power that is born from the gift of illusion! It required centuries of metaphysics devoid of foundation and positivist science devoid of a general idea, hollow dreams and equally detestable receipts, for humanity to arrive at no longer separating its material efforts from its meditations, and mingling them together in a single logical harmony.

"Previously, people seemed to consider the imagination and dreams as pernicious sensualities; they had recourse to them secretly after having labored, but they would have blushed to mingle them with their labor, they did not admit that one could ever employ oneself in fortifying dreams; and they did not enjoy anything perfectly, their morality being timid and restricted. But when, instead of disavowing their ideal by experience, they supported one by the other, people united science and consciousness, they became great living and perpetual poems, and thus rendered poets—which is to say, the only individuals that intelligence had previously been unable to declare futile by virtue setting before humankind the concentrated and purified effects of its own genius—useful.

"Those august recorders of human effort, those revealers of the true mental world, those embalmers of the soul of crowds in elixirs of imperishable beauty, artists, no longer had a social role on the day when the liberated individual could be his own confessor and poet, and had no need of anyone to show him the promised land, because he had already entered it. On that day, the experimental age of science, psychology and politics gave way to an age of results; on that day, and on that day only, civilization commenced on earth.

"You are the children of those who saw that unusual evolution, and already it seems to you that it is as eternal as the logic of climates and stars, and that everything before was merely murky barbarism, traversed by lightning-flashes of presentiments. The modern genius is the free and total exercise of the faculties; with the feudalism of the mind fell one of the great despairs of souls, and everything was raised up for humankind. That elevation of humans to the envisaging of their own results drew all morality with it.

"Messieurs, it will have been our recent honor, that of people of the year 2000, to have understood and permitted that supremacy of the dream, to have made it no longer the inane abandonment of the soul in the vague and inexact, but the comforting and lucid sentiment of the unity of all knowledge before the individual mind. We have made the dream the goal of the experimental sciences that once oppressed it: obstinate in despising or hating it, even though the sensed themselves incapable of contenting the heart after the mind, they wandered in the immensity of intellectual realms like blind queens, colliding, impotent and furious, with the impenetrable door behind which imagination was sleeping as peacefully as a baby!

"In the end, the threshold opened, and the extinct and closed eyes were touched by an equal and just light. The science of dream was created, everything was concerted to produce more happiness, and the old threats of the prophets, which predicted with the increase of knowledge a parallel increase in sorrow no longer signified anything and died with primitive errors. We have finally conceived that the labor of all the scientists and the exaltation of all the poets were only made to ornament a constant harmony in the mind of the free individual, no longer to differ but to unite that that result.

"That blossoming, we have seen! Its renaissance is so close to us that I need not remind you of it any further. It is becoming merely history, and it would not be necessary to dig deeply into the soil of our capitals for the deplorable blood that it cost to appear. Those who did not understand opposed it, and disappeared in the surge of the revolution. It was necessary, and it is good.

"The progress of the social creature toward true humanity amid cadavers has led us all, the heirs of the centuries of authoritarianism and lucre, to this great, this unaccustomed political and moral notion of the identification of dream and knowledge, of the fusion of the logical sciences and expansive sensibility. It is on that philosophical idea that our confederation will live; it is therein that the divorce of ideology and analysis of which the age-old actuality presently seems so deformed, so absurd, has been reconciled, to open the new era of the reign of the individual, whose isolated consciousness is the generative image of worlds.

"I can, therefore, no longer astonish, in speaking here about these abstract and simple things, ordered like everything that participates in logic and the abstract, those among you who, whether as legislators or diplomats, study with curiosity the speeches of that abolished period when Parliaments existed, and when 'the eloquence of numbers,' as the people of that poor era cynically put it, was in honor, along with the strange 'sobriety of images,' in which our lyrical vision no longer sees anything but paltriness and platitude.

"I cannot renounce a certain irony in thinking about the scandal my words would cause if eventuality had placed me among them, and if I had stood up to say, as I am saying to you, to those stupid and base assemblies of technicians and speculators: 'Having reflected on the supreme goal of politics, I believe, Messieurs, that with the means at my disposal, I can propose to our State that authentic luxury, *the realization of a dream'!*"

The grandmaster of the Germano-Latin Confederation fell silent momentarily, and leaned over the crowd. The bouquets of immobile flames were radiant; the shadow of the solemn pulpit descended toward the raised faces. A rumor filled the halls, weapons clinked. The scintillation of embroideries undulated and sparkled against the backcloth of scarlet drapes. Groups of Alliance ministers, clad in black, were massed in the embrasures of the colonnades. Hands and faces tensed by expectation emerged from fabrics and bright spots. The rumor of the night over the city was born at the threshold of the vestibules.

Silence fell again; the tall form of the orator straightened, and his prestigious voice rang out again.

"To be sure, those sterile people of a wretched extinct epoch would not have failed to laugh on hearing me pronounce, in their coarsely immediate debates, those words of meditation and dream, of which their skepticism and their abject elegance could not admit anything but the sounds.

"Today, we find it natural to satisfy our consciences with what was neglected by those unfortunate parliamentarians, those bastardized advocates of democracy, who perished without confessing the force of the ideas with which we live! It is a dream that bears us; and if I have come to speak to you this evening, having consulted the generals and the ministers, having spent months revising my project with the collaboration of their technical expertise, it is a dream that I want to expose to you urgently. It is a new legend that I want to propose to you, to feature in future memoirs!

"Messieurs,[53] ancient Europe, I repeat, has not yet accomplished all of her destinies. She has survived the strangest political cataclysms; her fecund earth is robust with bloody sap. After having killed the barbaric world, it was necessary

---

[53] In the 1920 edition this is the second paragraph in the text, all the interim text having been cut. The deleted material is, in fact, inconsistent with the eventual argument of the story, which assumes that the synthesis to which the dictator refers is still far from achievement. Further cuts are made to the remainder of the speech to make it terser and most focused. The occasional deletions in subsequent chapters are much more sparing, usually only removing short phrases.

for her to kill the Roman world. Feudalism died thereafter, and after that it was necessary to kill the kings. And we, after the kings, have killed the bourgeois, who had confiscated revolt to their profit, and soiled life with a putrescence of egalitarianism, mediocrity and stupidity veritably more hateful than everything else! Civilizations have agglomerated and overheated on this extreme continent, art has taken refuge here, and all the sciences of idea. Metaphysics has sanctified the territory where the tyrannical Germany of militant emperors was. The balance of forces has been displaced, the state of armed peace that paralyzed everything has ceased.

"The concert of European efforts was assured, after the last Franco-German conflict, by the socialist alliance of the German and Latin races. Under their combined action, the Anarchistic revolution has triumphed over the parliamentary Republic in France, the Italian royalty in fief to Prussia and Austria; the individualist English constitution was unified with ours after the exile of the last prince. The Russian Empire, installed in Constantinople, having turned almost exclusively toward Asia and becoming semi-Oriental, has ceased to have direct communications with us, and if our evolutions of thought have not influenced its secular authority or suppressed there the ancient error of divine right, at least it has disinterested itself in our transformations in order to occupy itself entirely with its eastward expansion. Those of you who are grouped around me, therefore, represent a rejuvenated and free Europe, occidental guardian of the supreme conquests of the human mind!

"Here we are, Confederates of Central Europe, grandchildren of Carlyle, individualists before the single cult of Superhumanity, aristocratic Anarchists. I, the dictator of the Occident, have just sketchily summarized our recent birth, our spiritual awakening, after the indescribable volcanic convulsion that, from Berlin to London and Paris to Rome, crushed the capitalist assemblies and monarchies in an unprecedented shedding of blood. Well, Messieurs, that destiny, finally edified, the course of events is compromising by the hour. Something formidable is born, which might ruin that which impassions us! In opposition to the unified Occident, the Orient is rising!

"The Orient! It is preparing an obscure and terrible vengeance, and its brutish black peoples are trailing immense and oscillating machineries toward us over their anthills.

"For a long time, the pretended slumber of those enervated races has no longer deceived me. While we were constructing our work and edifying our era, the people out there were slowly stirring as well. But it was an obscure agitation of subterranean beasts, the babbling of embryonic consciousnesses, an indistinct and formless rumor, the stretching of a pug-faced ignorance couched against the topics. We were too absorbed in our own thoughts to pay any heed to those distant symptoms. They have been germinating there for years.

"In its sands and its woods, depressed Tartary began to think; on his reed boat, the Chinaman raised a barely human head; the Indian fisherman ceased to roast in the sun unconsciously; the puny Annamite acquired cunning again. A bizarre birth of who knows what reprisals! The continent of fatalism dreamed of action. Everything changed on the day when, profiting for the revolutions of Europe, the alert Japanese race, having adopted our weapons and tactics, pushed its victorious armies into the depths of the Celestial Empire and commenced the civilization of its stagnant hordes. In their wake came the spirit of precise organization and the classification of forces.

"By means of the omnipotence of method, Japan appropriated Asia with a single surge of its devouring genius, and the danger began to concentrate against us. The successive annexation of all the countries of the Far Eastern littoral, the expulsion of the English hordes from India, the revolts in Burma and Annam, the treaties of the Rajah with the Yellows, and a hundred events of that genre were welcomed here with inattention. They were scarcely mentioned. It was the epoch when the capitals of Europe were burning, when bombs were annihilating in a single agreed night the parliaments of Paris and Berlin, when disarmament threw the rebel hosts out of their barracks, when civil war hurled the provinces against the functionaries, the salaried against the employer, the vagabond against the gendarme, the free man against the magistrate, all the independencies against all the authorities! The Orient was so far away!

"Now, the work is complete. That immense marriage has coagulated.

"Facing us, Messieurs, a unified society is standing up, and it is impossible for us to coexist. An eternal instinct of hatred stiffens against us those masses of men, and suspends above our continent an abominable invasion. The pullulation of those beings is terrible. Superstition, fatalism and somnolence have changed their face; the presentiment of our resources has haunted the Orientals, needs have been born therefrom; they are imminent on our frontiers, and tomorrow, a Timur or a Genghis Khan might arise again and hurl innumerable cavalries upon us. But the scourge will be a thousand times worse! Their armament is already almost ours; the numbers have learned tactics, the locust mentality is no longer sufficient for them.

"No one can imagine what that lugubrious cataract of men with brutal faces upon our provinces and our capitals would be like. The ancient world, fragmented into a hundred nations, no longer admits any but two reigns, two incompatible souls. That cannot last much longer. The Occident in heaped up against the Atlantic, its back braced, its face turned toward the Orient, ready to pounce. One of the two will die.

"You know that the first symptoms have already become manifest. The cables inform us that consuls have been seized and killed in Indo-China and Benares, simultaneously. Every demand for explanation or reparation has been rejected insolently; just now, the latest dispatches have confirmed that those troubles and others are suspected.

"There can be no question of remedying the evil once again within the precise limits of its extent, of limiting ourselves to an envoy of troops, to some partial colonial war that will ignite at a hundred successive points. What is necessary is a simultaneous action; it is to take up arms, before that enormous mass of humans has taken complete cognizance of what it might dare.

"What is necessary, Messieurs, let us say it, is a unanimous rising of Confederated Europe before the yellow peril!

"We can do that. I have thought of it; everything has been anticipated, and it is necessary that it takes place without any delay, that we anticipate the cyclone by cutting the very base of its turbulence with a lightning suddenness. Every hour lost aggravates the concentration of those hordes. The accursed spirit of Asia is agglutinating repulsive masses of armed slaves in camps and on the oriental plateaux. Neither conciliation nor pity can be anticipated. The situation is clear.

"So, this evening my speech must create a decisive resolution in you. The dream that I have come to propose that you render real is the one that pushed Europeans for centuries toward the Far Eastern seas; it is the one that took Napoléon to Egypt; it is the backlash of the civilized against the afflux of Barbarians, the revulsion of the West against the East: something more than a conquest, Messieurs; the affirmation of a law of salvation! But it is necessary for us to go further than Napoléon and all the colonizers; it is necessary for us to depart for a total subjugation, a methodical destruction of every attempt at yellow civilization.

"This is no longer a political war, it is a war of ideas. We can sustain it; everything has been anticipated. America, occupied with its extension and its struggles against the insurrectionists of the South, leaves us every initiative this side of its commercial neutrality. The Russian Empire is reserving for itself an action in Mongolia. Although no veritable sympathy links us to that autocratic empire, its situation makes it the advance guard of the civilized against the barbarian peril; it understands that, and its interests cause it to acquiesce to the will of Central Europe. All diplomatic measures have been taken to assure it the benefits of Asia in exchange for its neutrality in Europe.

"We can therefore act freely, in confederation; and if the Germano-Latin soul, in the presence of the Russian oligarchy, African obscurantism and American indifference, remains alone in condensing and fortifying itself, if it rejects the old threat of the end in order to get a grip on itself, once supreme, if I have come here to tell you that I have prepared everything in order that the immense effort should not be wasted, at least it is necessary for us to succeed in dissociating that which we have allowed to combine, in throwing these recently-armed troops back into a definitive barbarism. Otherwise, the day will come of filthy and ferocious inundations of men!

"It is a matter now of violently turning the face of destiny around: a mission of intellectual enlightenment is incumbent upon us, in the name of the arts, of the philosophical mind, of the plastic or abstract thought that was born here a long time ago. The intellectual nullity of the Orient is the condition of the Occident's existence!"

The dictator fell silent, abruptly. His arms raised, his eyes bright and fixed, he seemed to be raising over the breathless congress the visible image of war. Everyone bristled, but no one budged. The moment seemed vertiginous.

And suddenly, the master's arms fell, and in the clear voice of a logician, he pronounced:

"I, Claude Laigle, man of the people, become by the advent of Anarchism the responsible dictator of the Confederation of Central Europe, propose to the legates, as a glorious, unparalleled and immediate necessity, the declaration of a merciless war against the yellow race!"

The silence broke in a flash. A clamor burst forth; black-clad ministers ran toward the tribune,

"War! War! It's accepted!"

The undulation of the crowd pressed against the walls, beneath the electric chandeliers. The sentiment of a supreme and extraordinary decision seized the throats of hundreds of men.

"War! War!"

The terrible word, with a raucous rip, sprang outside souls like a shiny blade, before a living being, bounded among the colonnades toward the stairways, toward the street, toward the world; pale faces became crimson, mouths remained open in the cry, a convulsion shook the palace, and in the flux of the crowd the grim proclamation went forth.

Near the dictator, descended from the steps and surrounded by generals, feverish gazes shone, adieux and cheers sounded, and suddenly an appeal burst forth:

"Vive l'Aigle! Vive Claude l'Aigle!"

The favorite nickname with which the people, deforming at pleasure a predestined name, saluted the master, ran over the lips like a fanfare.

"Vive l'Aigle!"

Calmly, he saluted with his hand, and slowly went out, svelte in his black garments. The stormy assembly broke up; the doors filled with busy men rushing toward the city; bells rang: ushers hurried; the last members of the audience disappeared, and under the vaults, along the ramps, the decisive word—"War! War!"—resounded over their footsteps and accompanied them to the threshold. It was prolonged for a long time yet in the silence of the great gallery, solemn and deserted.

And then the lights of the chandeliers went out, one by one; the last palpitated and died, and the echo of the murderous word remained, face to face with silence and darkness...

By means of a door opening to the gardens, a man, Claude Laigle went out and headed for the boulevards. The street-lamps were blue-tinted by the mist of a recent shower of rain. It was a little after midnight. Luminous posters poured multicolored joyful gleams into the fog; masses of people were emerging from the dazzling exits of theaters, the terraces were overflowing, flowers were heaped up in peddlers' trays, diamond-clad women were iridescent on silks and furs, the steam of vehicles filled the streets. A great tumult of laughter and confused words rose toward the pale green metallic crowns of aligned trees, where fiery oranges and quivering letters designed their unreal specters.

The dictator allowed himself to be carried along by the human current. He liked annihilating himself thus and seeking solitude in the very din of life, passing unperceived and devoid of prestige, because no one looked at him. He followed the vast avenues, his soul of a logician and an ideologue delighting in feeling itself free and immense in a body protected by its very evidence against any inconvenient curiosity. The sentiment of only being a man of narrow form, a banal and fugitive unit between backs and breasts, in the jostle of a boulevard, delighted him. He bore his soul like an interior fire, which no order of precious stones, no embroidered torsade, no visible sign at all, had any need to symbolize externally.

The cold air touched his forehead deliciously, the formidable odor of life teased his entire being. Within himself, the decision of omnipotence that he had just announced bounded like a magical secret; his lips, previously open to the flow of his great sovereign voice, were now closed upon *the word*, but his mind was growling. "War! War!" it murmured, as he brushed past laughing women and elegant groups, and the sentiment of everything that that single word could do made his heart expand gloriously.

He walked firmly, without anyone paying any heed to him. He glanced mechanically at his hands, and the idea that those two white patches, similar in that night to a hundred thousand other white patches, would set a world in motion tomorrow, penetrated him with obscure thoughts about the nullity of the body before the moral will. He sensed that he was very much a modern man, living only by the brain and renouncing any decorative gesture, any uselessly theatrical custom, the black intercessor of the destinies of a crowd that his gaze alone was sufficient to dazzle.

At one moment, he experienced the need to communicate even more closely with those existences that the force of circumstance confided to him, and, in a corner of the noisiest terrace he could discover, he sat down calmly, and ordered a drink. Without him paying any attention to them, his fingers sketched a map of Asia on the table, and he could not help smiling at that image, studied so many times for months. Those few hasty lineaments were the writing of the entire future. He thought about the new race, about himself, absorbed.

Suddenly, though, an immense rumor caused him to raise his head. Shrill clamors rose up, men brandishing telegrams and newspapers with enormous headlines, still damp, were running along the boulevards. Everyone stood up, jostling one another.

"War against the Orient!"

"Vote of the great Federal Council!"

"The dictator's speech!"

"War!"

"The yellow peril!"

The cries succeeded one another frenetically, from one end of the street to the other the conflagration radiated in outbursts of howls and appeals. Clusters of men climbed on to tables, multicolored pieces of paper flew over heads at the end of griping hands. Women in ball dresses threw themselves into the middle of the crowd in order to find out more, asking questions at the top of their voice in the tumult. The storm of anxieties swirled in the illuminated night.

"War declared!"

"The Council has voted!"

Passengers leapt out of vehicles; the bearers of news struggled in seething groups, songs burst forth, soon broken off by the exasperated clamor of a furious human tide, which disgorged thousand of haggard faces everywhere.

Claude Laigle stood up, threw down a coin at random, slipped into obscurity and reached less populous streets. But the mad and delirious acclamation echoed in his ears: "War! War!"

"Yes, yes, war" he repeated to himself. "It's necessary; they know everything; I've finally unleashed everything."

The flamboyance of pride and resolution invaded his thoughts, which he had wanted to be calm. He turned up the collar of his coat, and lowered his head, fearing that he might be recognized, and marched toward the quais, where a relative solitude reigned. He leaned over the parapets to consider the long trails of blood, lunar steel and gold with which the reflections of streetlights broke the black water—and it appeared to him that everything was ornamented by glory and sumptuousness beneath the enigmatic face of the nocturnal sky.

Behind him, however, the cry was running like a fantastic wild beast, devouring the city: "War! War!"

Tomorrow, the monster would devour convulsed Europe, would raise its glittering cry over the entire world.

"Yes, war," the dictator repeated, pensively. He pronounced the word very quietly, against the placid trees. And, a thin, indistinct silhouette, the little shadows of which vacillated on the ground behind him, he came back along the quais toward the bleak Palais, and rang the bell at a secret door. And the dry click of the batten closing behind the master leapt into his thoughts with the echo of the eternal cry of death.

II. The Faces of the Old World

When Claude Laigle came back he went straight to a simple drawing room where four men were waiting for him. They rose to their feet; a gesture made them sit down again in silence. The dictator remained standing for a few moments in their midst, then, curtly, said: "The Council is open. Let's talk."

After a moment he added: "I wanted to go out to see the crowd, to feel it at close range. It's not good to keep ourselves to our own thoughts. The magnetism of the crowd is salutary; between the public council and our private meeting, that aspiration of fresh air and living souls has fortified me. I've seen the city convulse under the news. I would have liked you to see it, you Ménières, who like the movements of men! The street and the fête bounded.

"It reminded me, Médion, of the evening when we were walking together, waiting for the moment when the Chambre was about to blow up, thanks to you, fifteen years ago. I haven't seen since then an evening so magnificently upset. You remember how attentive we were, and how, all of a sudden, the distant noise of the explosion, the irruption of the crowd, and the clamors of the revolution, made us raise our heads—us, silent passers-by who might have been anyone. It was a moment of extraordinary life, a voluptuous bath of cerebral emotion.

"The cry of war, just now, caused me to vibrate in a similar fashion. To be a man, a thin form, that a carriage might crush in a moment of inattention, to say nothing, to have the appearance of being nothing, and yet to contain that in one's head, to be *the cause*, is quite beautiful and very tasty. Truly, the chiefs of old, with their mania for decorations and exterior signs, were maladroit. It's that anonymity which truly signifies power, which delightfully accentuates a secret."

"Yes," said Médion. "The mentality is everything."

The person who had just responded was a man of forty-five, thin and stiff, with a face framed by a short-cropped back beard, an impassive face striped by hard wrinkles, in which opened two dry bright eyes whose mineral blue was astonishing. The two hands placed flat on the table extended square, tightly-packed fingers; from the thin lips emerged a voice as precise and stiff as the features, and the entire man.

Médion was the foremost sociological intelligence of his era. A physiologist, mathematician and economist, his intransigent hypotheses, equally valiant in general ideas and marked by a gripping intuition of analogies, had frightened the routines of the institutions to which he had one presented his papers, always written with a rigid arrogance whose attitude of abstract conviction alone had displeased. The Anarchist revolution had found in him a terrible and glacial adherent. The silent energy of the scientist was effortlessly transformed into actions like the one that Claude Laigle had just recalled: ideological murder, in his engineer's hands, had become the striking and mysterious fatality of a concluding era.

Sensibility did not count for Médion; he was, according to the expression of his friends, "a living number." Today a Minister of State, he lived on nothing, ignored women, watched over everything, and still found means of innovating in chemistry, in spite of the crushing burden of his responsibility. The sole weakness of that antipathetic and admirable character was perhaps an authoritarian mania of the logician, an abuse of violent and curt formulae on all subjects, emerging with disdain, falling mercilessly in harsh words in which the humanity of the heart never trembled.

Raising a placid face, he repeated: "Mentality is everything. The examination of facts in the brain, the communion of the brain with the facts, the exact exchange: that is the whole of life. You'll come you that, Claude Laigle— you've come to it already. Sensibility is only an error of calculation, a false solution in the permanent mathematics that the mind develops in the presence of phenomena. Just now, in the meeting, I listened to you with interest; you were lyrical, you know how to speak to crowds; but I always have the impression that the eloquence is a means of seducing inferior beings. Your words sound within me without touching me; I only enjoyed the minute in which you squarely proposed war. That's a fact: the rest is but a smokescreen.

"I don't like lyricism any more than stimulants. I believe, definitely, that art and all matters of fantasy, of décor, as means of elegant illusion, are bound to disappear. They were yesterday's forms; we won't keep them for long. We'll go on to something else, to an ideal of mechanical harmony in which humans will no longer amuse themselves by making a god out of each of their faculties. It was very good, your theory of the illusion that leads the energies of State, obviously very good to excite the assembly, but I don't believe in it from the scientific viewpoint. I believe in a cohesion of the machine and individual orders; I believe in the present, and I detest metaphysics."

"Even applied to the science—not the sciences, but *the* science, unified in a single search for knowledge?" said Claude Laigle, slowly. "Even metaphysics linked to the psychology of races and considered as a very broad ethnology?"

"Even that," said Médion. "You've constructed the new society, in spite of everything, on the ruins of the past and faith in the future. Personally I attach myself to the present, and you don't. You all remain ideologues: Girondins or Montagnards, if you like; but you still count on instinct, on the sentiments of exception, on the dream. The dream! Oh, Claude Laigle, I'm astonished that you count on that word: poetry, poetry…in truth, an old song! Personally, I call all my desires a universe of chemistry, as Emerson put it."

"Reactionary!" murmured a voice that was simultaneously slow, sonorous and veiled.

"Reactionary? You say that to me, Ménières?" said Médion, turning round. "Well, if you like, yes: reactionary to your humanitarian ideas, I am. You've founded a society on the union of science and morality: an intelligent concept, but inviable. You've falsified both, and that's all. I intend to put those two incompatible forces back in their place, and elevate science—documentary, physiological, analytical intelligence—above the debauchery of hypotheses and dreams that you're all inclined to allow to grow. That's good for nervous minutes in which we need to draw the masses along; I know, of course, that your eloquence, your continual allusion to abstract verities, are excellent means, and that people only decide on dreams—but afterwards? We can do nothing serious without a scientific mind. We've suppressed religions; let's not replace them with a sociological fatalism—for that's your idea, isn't it, Ménières?

Blond, pale, raising his long musician's hands, Ménières straightened up and relied, serenely.

"Yes, Médion—sociological fatalism, that's a sufficiently accurate formulation. I, you know, am of the race of the unsatisfied, as much by dreams as by actions. I'm there, between you and Claude, without taking sides. I hold that art is a necessary form of cerebral expansion, and that metaphysics, although it was for too long a cloudy construction alongside life, can become a science of generality, a very precious force of synthesis. In that, I'm with Claude, and when he said just now that the essence of politics is the realization of a dream, I approve wholeheartedly.

"I think that you're a reactionary, my dear Médion, because you've retained a utilitarian, not ideological, conception of science, and because your 'universe of chemistry' is still a religion, as inconvenient as those we've swept away. Our attempt at a lyrical and logical State hasn't convinced you. You hold to the present—personally, I have a horror of it. On the other hand, I can't share Claude's opinion when I see him thinking that there is progress in the state we're in, and I readily admit that you doubt it. You know that I don't believe at all in the idea of progress, and you, who appear to limit yourself strictly to facts, have your little corner of intimate idealism even so, in believing that your regimentation of forces will lead to a superior condition.

"Life, as Claude understands it, is one life, and you understand life in another fashion, equivalent if not similar. That he's lyrical and you're exact is your right, both of you, but don't quarrel, and above all don't touch the soul, either to exalt it or to deny it. It doesn't concern you, and only develops covertly, without any preoccupation with progress."

"Don't touch it, except with the conviction that one is acting for its benefit," said someone, loudly.

Ménières looked at the man who had spoken. They considered one another.

Ménières was a childhood friend of Claude Laigle's. A poet and essayist of a delicately profound charm, he enjoyed a desperately amorous and quivering soul; great enthusiastic successes and equally violent chagrins had divided his life. Famous adventures, and striking and desolating amours, had illustrated his name. He had been trailing through the world a luxurious and disenchanted existence, tearful and admirable, when the revolution turned him around, perhaps counting on finding an excitement sufficiently grandiose for his capricious and fatigued genius. The dictator adored him, incessantly kept him close to him, and took his advice, even though Ménières had refused any definite attribution in the new State. For Claude's ardent and feverish soul, there was no more refreshing company than that of the extremely subtle dilettante, ready for anything, intellectual to the point of suffering. Claude's mind was both exact, by virtue of his sociological studies, and innately poetic; Ménières counterbalanced Médion fortunately in that regard, and the three men, linked by an amity fortified by unusual circumstances, loved and esteemed one another while always contradicting one another.

The man who had just interrupted Ménières was Dessort, a thin individual, almost beardless, with a Caesarian profile, singularly feminine eyes, and a wide mouth, creased in a smile that was both ironic and charming. A throaty, slightly guttural voice seemed surprising in that frail person, elegant in the English fashion and sober of silhouette. Before the foundation of the Occidental State, Dessort had been the socialist orator to whom the international congresses listened most readily, the most persuasive of all. He it was who had prepared the mass desertions, had aborted the last Franco-German war by means of a general disarmament, and powerfully aided the establishment of the Anarchist government by bringing it his hosts of indoctrinated workers, when he had understood that socialism could only be an economic movement without a political future.

Dessort was an active force of the State. Claude Laigle did not like him much, but he had a marvelous understanding with Médion. The scientifistic mentality of the one and the communist spirit of the other were associated in a similar version for the rights of sensibility. They regulated public interest perfectly, leaving Claude Laigle to occupy himself with morality and ideology; those were domains in which they never intervened, while nevertheless having a secret desire to intervene in them. Médion desired to unify even souls in a universal mechanics; Dessort thought that a system of ideas might be useful to the crowds, albeit imposed. Both of them believed in Progress, and by force; they imagined that the ingenuity of the mind can aid in the elaboration of the soul of races, and that the elaboration in question is not accomplished freely and mysteriously by laws above human force.

Dessort, stared at by Ménières, stared back. "Yes," he said, "one can touch the soul of others for their benefit."

"What do you call their benefit?" replied Ménières, "and how do you know that a notion, however ingenious it might be, will create benefit in someone? No one is like anyone else. You're forgetting the human factor. The mystery of souls is individual."

"The word *mystery* annoys me, in sum," said Dessort.

"And I find it intolerable," added Médion.

They smiled.

"Regulate hygiene, commerce, material wellbeing and the employment of forces as much as you wish; that's the benefit that it's praiseworthy to augment," replied Ménières, "but leave the rest alone: the interior vibration that your chemistry can't analyze, Médion; the emotion that your economic theories and your satisfaction of stomachs cannot, Dessort, bring to the surface. You really are the democrats of old, with your belief in progress, your wounding pretention to systematize. The spirit of science and the spirit of socialism are, in sum, old sectarian spirits; the union of all that in the spirit of humanity escapes you. Human being is all of that and something else; a human isn't a machine, but that and more! I'm already not happy in demanding of all inventions of genius, in all branches, that they can offer me subjects of meditation, but if I restricted myself to your barracks-State or your laboratory-State , I'd wonder whether we were right to go to so much trouble to shake up Europe, only to leave it there."

Médion and Dessort had stood up abruptly. Ménières, still seated, considered them calmly. There was a silence.

"Enough," said Claude Laigle. "I don't like such divergences of opinion to be manifest in loud voices in the council of fellows. The State is founded on the unification of ideas in one alone, the science of knowledge, both mental and moral. The Occident needs a vision of intellectual verity. Enough systems! I affirmed again, at this evening's meeting, that that entente was the basis of the Confederation; if there's dissent among us, let it only be manifest internally. I don't want our theories to clash here, especially on such a decisive night. I've just seen the eternal conflict in you. We're going to act, let's not argue any more. We're not in Byzantium here; we can do metaphysics when the war is over."

"The Barbarians aren't at the gates," said Médion, smiling. "We're not at the stage where Byzantium was. In any case, I scorn debates, but if someone brings them here, I don't recoil. This is between us, Claude, there's no harm done. Modern humans do everything by cerebration, they're inclined to quibble. Tomorrow, we'll no longer have time; let's amuse ourselves for once before going to face the Barbarians."

"Perhaps it's us who are the Barbarians," said Ménières.

The remark fell heavily between the four men. Ménières' seemingly negligent voice gave him a strange relief. Claude Laigle stiffened, a trifle pale.

"That has no meaning, what you just said, Ménières. Have you even been paying attention?"

"Pooh!" said Ménières, softly. "I don't know. I said it, yes…anyway, I'm the most Byzantine of us all, I have no protest to make. The Orient is a great danger, Claude, you've done well, having charged souls, to raise up one half of the Old Continent against the other. But it's still an invasion, in the eternal fashion…and that can also be called Barbarity.

"It's called Civilization," replied Claude Laigle.

"As you wish," Ménières responded.

"No! Not 'as I wish'!" cried the dictator. "As is correct! As is piously and nobly just! How nervous and bizarre we are this evening!"

He sat down, and then got up again, went to a window and opened it. But he suddenly recoiled; a rumor rising from the nocturnal avenues quivered through the gardens. And like a sinister bird on the wings of a frigid wind, the fateful word entered the room:

"War!"

The four men listened momentarily.

"How they shout!" murmured Dessort.

"Yes, they're shouting almost as if…as if they weren't…"

"What?" said Claude, abruptly.

"Civilized," Ménières completed, with an almost imperceptible irony.

Claude Laigle started violently. "Ah!" he exclaimed. "Is this today or yesterday? We've made the material and moral revolution while holding a few verities to be certain, and now, at the first result of the power we wanted to obtain, the words of doubt come back, as if all that weren't agreed, and firmly agreed. Now you're contesting eloquence and sensibility, Médion; we have, however, made plenty of room for your scientific ideas. Stick to that! You, Dessort, are starting again to advocate intervention is the happiness of others with ready-made principles—but we founded the Occidental State on Anarchistic Individualism, which doesn't admit the intervention of the collectivity in subjective morality. Limit yourself to codes of hygiene and prevention, and don't resuscitate the specter of social religiosity. And you, Ménières, with your undulating, charming and fatal dilettantism, are putting in question, with any airy remark, the very legitimacy of what will be tomorrow the capital effort of the twentieth century!

"So, between you, what do you want me to do? In the epoch of parliamentarianism, oligarchies and constitutional or despotic monarchies, when we were preparing the revolution and, as unknown young men, we were dreaming during nocturnal strolls of the future State that would spring from the bomb—*then* was the time to raise these doubts and debate them. But at present, what are you thinking? The desire to argue is rising again from your heart to your lips. Is doubt, then a recurrent disease? What I affirmed before the legates just now as the very of that State, you no longer think, at the moment when it's necessary, in order to live?

"For myself, I no longer have any hesitation. The superior human of whom I have dreamed, whom I have described, is one who unites science and art in a single intellectual clarity. One who is a character first before being a technician, one who is his own confessor and poet. That human being I can see, I can sense; he exists, even if I'm not him completely, and you refuse to become him. That human being will reign and vanquish, the one that must—must, you hear—be revealed in every individual in the confederation. And if I have decided this war, it's less because of the danger of the Orient's weapons or the peril of its industrial competition than because of that very revelation.

"The unprecedented war that has virtually commenced at this moment is the proof, the purchase of consciousness that I want to give the crowd on the individuality in which I believe. It is in this effort that the still-hesitant consciousness in question will solidify. Oh, that human being, that intellect no longer fixed but living, will not be, if you cannot or dare not. For myself, I know that he exists, I want to draw him from our race, force him to appear, and I shall seek him if he cannot yet be found!"

"He isn't viable," said Médion.. "He's hypothetical; I refuse to believe in him."

"He is viable," said Dessort, "but in dreams."

"He exists," said Ménières. "Claude's right. But..."

"But! Always a *but* in whatever you say!" cried the dictator. "But what?"

"But...perhaps he isn't here," Ménières concluded.

"Where then?"

The four men looked at one another.

"Perhaps among *them*," pronounced Ménières, serenely.

"You mean those we're going to fight?"

"Yes—because you don't know what their soul is, fundamentally. They're ancient; they date from the night; they completed their self-realization in the era when we were still prehistoric. And who knows whether they haven't formed, in the midst of those obscure and seething masses, a being like the one you describe?"

"But the consciousness," Claude interjected, violently, "and the sentiment of moral autonomy, is a notion of ours! It's finished, out there! You know full well that those people have nothing in common with us, nothing but economic theories learned in our schools, weapons, an industrial socialization, a means of practical life and an apparent modernism, that's all! Beneath all that burns a barbaric and voracious soul, bogged down in atavistic fatalisms, heavy with passivity.

"You know full well that the odious Sino-Japanese race has retained the cranium of the beaver or the hamadryad, a terrible cranium with the jaws of a burrower, with polished and finished brows, the cranium of a predator and brute with devouring senses! We're not going to war, we're going hunting, in running against those thousands of militarized anthropomorphs. Do you think that the superior human of whom we've dreamed is there? Nothing, nothing, I tell you, but an animal parodying our usages.

"In sum, Ménières, you're too poetic, if the others aren't poetic enough. The mirage of the name Orient, I don't know what seduction of Bibles and Vedas, has deflected you from the truth. Personally, I envisage it in the real, that Orient, as an ideologue and as a Head of State, and I firmly believe in the intellectual supremacy of the Occident. I see nothing out there but a force of exaction and base enjoyment contained for centuries by obscurantism, awakened by Japan and rushing upon us to rob us, devoid of a goal, dreams and beauty.

"You know what an industrial war we've been fighting against the yellow race for two hundred years; it pours waves of emaciated individuals into our ports, as clever as monkeys, living on nothing, killing the value of European money by their unsustainable competition. Already, the monarchic and parliamentary states were infested by them; already, there were massacres of Chinese workers in various places, fifty years after the opening of the Orient to commerce—and that has multiplied a hundredfold since. If the American State has promised us neutrality in the present war, and the Russian Empire has agreed to join us and operate for its part on the frontiers of northern China—an acceptance of which I obtained a definite assurance this morning—it's because of that economic peril. But I'm acting in the name of higher and more general ideas than those.

"As I said this evening, I'm proposing a dream to the desire of the energy of the Occidental Confederation. I'm proposing to monopolize here, by the crushing of those masses, the intellectuality of the Latin races. We've used the bomb to suppress the governments that were fragmenting us, we've used the cannon to save what the bomb created. And you're now putting those two ideas in doubt? In the name of what? In the name of some pantheism, some benevolent egalitarianism? No, no, I repeat, enough dreams! The intellectual nullity of the Orient is the condition of the Occident. Médion likes formulae, I give him that one; more than any other it's true, urgent and essential! It's the pivot of the future system!

"In sum, I'm weary of these doubts, these reticences, these backward glances, these pities, these hypotheses! Do you know what you represent to me, you three, one with his exaggerated poetic dreams, another with his dreams of exclusive science, and the third with his utopias of the collective education of the race? Well, you represent three synthetic forms of the spirit of yesterday, the spirit that we wanted to kill, and which is trying to be reborn. What are you, this evening, on the eve of the creation of the future? You're dilettantism, intolerance and indoctrination, the faces of the Old World!"

He fell silent, out of breath, his face contracted by anger. For a few minutes, no one spoke. And suddenly, on the long table, stiff and wrinkled hands shifted plans and papers and the dull voice of an old man pronounced:

"If the metaphysics is finished, we're going to work, Messieurs."

They all looked at the man who had not yet said a word. The old generalissimo Luxeilles de Trénan smiled disdainfully, lifting a glabrous and ivory-tinted head from the heap of maps, in which gray moist eyes gleamed, bulging like the eyes of mystics. With his elbows on the arms of his chair, taciturn as ever, he had waited without a muscle of his hard and frozen face having stirred. Only an occasional frisson of impatience had caused him to turn his spectacles over nervously between his fingers.

He was a tall, thin individual, shaven like a priest, with mannerisms that were both unctuous and precise. He was dressed in black, like the others, simple gold torsades at the neck and sleeves signifying, strictly, that the master of arms was there; and one would scarcely have supposed so, on seeing that ecclesiastical face and thin mouth, the aspect of a pastor both troubling and benevolent.

Beneath those glacial and methodical appearances burned the commander-in-chief's great military intelligence. The Marquis Luxeilles de Trénan, retaining without coquetry in the anarchistic state a title that summarized a race, was a tactician without ostentation, less reminiscent of a Maurice de Saxe than a Moltke, implacably exact, speaking little, truly made to lead black armies to whom heroism in the ancient fashion was incomprehensible. He was the logician of death, the tranquil destroyer, the engineer and strategist acting by means of artillery, marches and the commissariat with the surety of a chemist in his laboratory. What Médion had done in the civil war, General de Trénan had done in the last continental wars, his campaigns in Franconia and Bohemia, where the power of imperial Germany had been broken, and thanks to which the social unification of the Germano-Latin race had been able to take place, remained models for the future, perfect mathematical operations systematizing and orientating massacre.

In the superior council, facing Claude Laigle, haunted by lyrical visions of history, Ménières, haunted by dreams, Dessort, preoccupied with fraternary theories, Médion and he were the stiff and violent faces of force, the missionaries of the dynamic modern world over which it seemed that darkness had passed. But in Médion's soul a scientific ideal remained; the soul of General de Trénan was simple. It was a feudal soul, demanding supremacy for itself, exaction for exaction, ignorant of the scruple of attacking a race: a brutal and grandiose soul, savoring war, inaccessible to everything that was not destructive effort.

"I have what will put you in accord here," he said, softly. "These are the estimates of the war. I have reviewed them. They are as exact as your chemistry, Médion. They are, Ménières, rich enough in deployments of energy to surpass your poetic ideal; these stacks of paper, Dessort, contain the wherewithal to put the forces that interest you in motion. And you, Master, will find here a power of certainty that will allow you to avoid rising in anger against doubt. Fortunately, there is one force in the service of the Old World that will give the new one all the time to develop and to modify its morality and hypotheses other than on paper. I bring here the palpable domination of shells. I rely upon that messenger to deliver ideas. Speeches first, that afterwards, to conclude."

"We have spoken," said Ménières slowly, "And you…"

"I, if you wish, will conclude with that," General de Trénan finished.

"It is indeed you who will conclude," said Médion. "The Occident of the future is founded on the shell and it will triumph by the shell."

"The shell is, then, an idea for you, Trénan?" said Claude Laigle, bitterly.

"It's a fashion of pronouncing the word *idea*," affirmed Dessort, sarcastically. "Anyway, you were talking just now about bombs. Means for means, my socialism wouldn't want to choose."

"The bomb was an idea," said Claude Laigle, getting up, his eyes shining. "It was necessary—you hear, Dessort, necessary! Like everyone else, I have my interior cemetery, and I think all that is terrible, when I'm alone. But it was necessary! I don't regret the civil war. But I sense that Trénan likes the shell for its own sake—and oppose that to my fashion of killing if you like. There are various meanings of death. The shell isn't an idea, it doesn't carry anything but our material defense, because our moral defense is in ourselves..."

"Let's say that it's only a guarantee," the commander-in-chief rectified, placidly. "It's already that, and that guarantee, Master, your ideology needs." Smiling, the terrible old man added: "Besides which, I too am an ideologue, since I calculate the energies without occupying myself with the matter. In your rationalizations, you suppress the material being; personally, I too rationalize my art—for it is an art—by suppressing it...once and for all, and seriously, that's all."

"Let us," said the dictator, "allow the principle of death give life to our race, this time as before, in accordance with the eternal decrees. To our new race..."

The end of the sentence expired in silence.

And the five men, three of whom symbolized the three great moral heresies of the modern world, while the fourth was devoid of faith, and the fifth was imploring one, pored over maps, their precise hands touching electric buttons in the calm of the nocturnal council, preparing until the pallor of the imminent dawn the impact of the Civilized against the Barbarians.

III. The March Eastwards

The declaration of war was notified to the ministerial cabinets of Tokyo and Peking and to the Rajahs of Delhi and Hyderabad—which is to say, to the four official delegations of the Asiatic Alliance, early the following morning, The concentration of European forces commenced immediately.

It was already prepared. For months, the active genius of General de Trénan had been coordinating the Confederation armies, getting the arsenals and supply chains ready. The colossal enterprise had germinated in the mind of the dictator as soon as his election to power, and although the first years of his administration had been devoted to organizing the new constitution and erasing the traces of the frightful civil war, Claude Laigle had never escaped his obsession with the Orient. He had been examining it as a logician, analyzing the industrial and military peril, since the conquest of China by the Japanese, and the autonomy of India, reestablished after the expulsion of the English in 1950, had only confirmed him in the sentiment of a terrible future.

That fusion of Hindustan and the Far East had become the obsession of his politics; it was there, at that junction, that it was necessary for Occidental civilization, with a decisive and mathematical stroke, to cut that stormy and barbaric cloud like a lightning bolt, to scatter it into a rain of men permanently disarmed and inoffensive. With the sociological and assimilative genius of the Japanese, a force of cohesion had really been born in those vast stagnant fatalisms; the danger of a Timur leading regiments with equal arms was inevitable; the leader had only to appear.

Claude Laigle evaluated the historical situation with the intuitive clarity that is the prerogative of sentimental individuals, and which as easily makes them diplomats as poets. Claude Laigle was a lyricist and a dialectician; he did not hide from himself that the extraordinary moral and mental effort by means of which anarchism had triumphed had as good as exhausted the active force that overcome the power of reflection of the Occidentals. A crisis of sociological moralism had then occupied, almost exclusively, twenty-five years; philosophies had undulated furiously over the crowds, and energy, in those restricted nations, crushing one against another, had been polarized, in a fashion, toward pure abstraction.

The complication of the modern mind had become extraordinary and, amid all the intellectual research, hardly any attention had been paid to foreign politics. Russia, especially after its occupation of the Bosphorus, had lost interest in the politics of Central Europe. Its autocracy accepted anarchism without welcoming it; there was, between the Occident and Asia, an immense intermediary territory, not at all disposed to encroach upon the West, extending eastwards without meeting any obstacle, And since the Russo-English conflicts in Afghanistan and Kashmir, since England's reversals and the loss of India, Russia was only occupied in a slow advancement in that direction. It hid the view of Asia from Europe.

However, an almost analogous evolution had been accomplished out there, and sooner or later, Russia would have to make a decision between the Occidental Confederation and the Asian Confederation. The egotism of its diplomacy would have to come to an end or become a veritable dementia. Claude Laigle knew full well that the gigantic antagonism, if it was not openly declared, was brooding; and he glimpsed, on the far side of the world, agglomerations of beings of primitive morality, having the enormous superiority of brutality over the intellectuals, and stiffening it with the two or three sentiments that are sufficient to convulse a race: the instinct of eternal westward expansion, hatred against colonial occupation, and the lure of booty conquered from fatigued peoples.

The alternatives had become increasingly precise. The dictator had never ceased to think that it was the capital question of vitality, and that after having, by means of a libertarian explosion, nullified the perils and conflicts of nationalities within its own bosom, Central Europe would only have repose and faith by throwing itself into the most terrible war of all against the obscure and immense yellow peril, increasingly coagulated. The establishment of scientific intellectualism could only ensure quietude after being liberated from the threat of that Barbarism.

He repeated that to himself for years; it was for him an absolute reality that took on the amplitude of a dream. His lyrical vision warned him that everything was bound to end there, that the unification of Europe, coinciding with the unification of Asia, clearly demonstrated the future war, the true and beautiful ethnological war, no longer playing out only in frontier squabbles and annexed provinces, like the paltry conflicts of old, but clashing as much in thought as with swords, setting two irreconcilable worlds against one another.

Asia! Claude Laigle did not only hate it as Head of State. He hated it as a thinker, fond of scientificism, having reforged an idealism above religion and worn-out metaphysics. Asia was the symbolic name of fatalism, of obscurantism, of hereditary hierarchies, of everything that the burning soul of Anarchist philosophy had seen melt in the brazier of the recent revolution, with intoxication. It was the recommencement of feudal dominion, the annulment of three centuries of liberalism. Claude Laigle feared those mental reprisals even more than the material dangers. And as soon as unlooked-for events had clearly delimited the situation, reduced the war to a single motive against the Old World, the ideologue had concentrated in himself and had begun to envision coldly the supreme assault that no nation of fragmented Europe would ever have dared to attempt first.

For long years Claude Laigle had waited for a pretext, and sounded the Occidental soul. It was necessary not to fail. The alternatives of war for diplomatic motives signify little and are reparable, but an ethnological war can only terminate in the extinction of one of the parties, and if it failed, the prestige of the civilized would be ruined, fear would set in, the hope of one day succeeding would vanish, to go foment Oriental ambition. Claude Laigle had let the situation become clearer, so lucidly that there was no longer any hope of a third solution, and the truth appeared evident to everyone. The dream of being the man who would terminate the great struggle haunted him.

Once, as a very young man, before the triumph of Anarchism, he had been, with Médion, one of the first to talk about that problem, and he found himself, going gray, still thinking about it, and having by force of energy, multiplied its importance a hundredfold in the eyes of the crowd. Industrial conflicts, bursting out with increasing frequency, between white and yellow workers, had served him even more than colonial revolts or acts of war.

Claude Laigle knew that nothing excites people more than evidence that results from financial questions, and that in spite of all the individualistic ideas that, in Europe, had penetrated the masses and elevated their moral degree, money remained the great motive of human force. All his genius had been extended to placing at the center of that impulsion, instead of a simple promise of immediate benefit, a profound notion, the very thought of the race: a dream, in truth. That lyrical man conceived a dream, not as a nebulous construction that turns the mind away from ordinary spectacles, but as the highest reality of energy, the intellectual reality *par excellence*.

The most striking mental conquest of the new State had been making everyone admit—for the first time since the beginning of the world—that the reality of subjective beings is as valid and as palpable as that of objective ones, that it is as realistic to meditate as it is to eat, that they are two equivalent actions of life.

And truly, Claude Laigle hoped for everything from all those fatigued races, from the moment that seemingly elementary concession had been obtained.

He had known for so long the bitterness of the intellectual in the midst of capitalists that he had been seized by an immense hope on observing that Anarchism had created the people the notion of the active utility of pure cerebration. Thus, it had appeared to him to be possible to present the war—his war!—in its true sense, and from the day when he had obtained that assurance, he had considered the work as half-done. The material preparation did not seem to him to be insurmountable.

Long and detailed conversations with Médion had planned its economics, and the unexpected good fortune of General de Trénan had brought the dictator a further assurance. During the Franco-German war, two devastating campaigns in Franconia and Silesia, deciding the ruin of the house of Hohenzollern and permitting socialism to impose disarmament, had revealed to the world that a surprising tactician had been born.

The French language and French influence had remained preponderant, the movement of unification had departed from that victory, the international electorate had granted to Claude Laigle the dictatorship of Paris and General de Trénan had become, by virtue of the clear-sighed will of the ideologue, the master of strategy throughout the domain of the Confederation. The two of them, with Médion, had elaborated the campaign, down to the smallest incidents, until the evening when, all measures having been taken, finally decided, the dictator had summoned the legates in order to present to them officially the project of the declaration of war.

The order of mobilization ran electrically from one end of Europe to the other on that very night when the five friends, still vibrant with the decisive acclamation, had stirred the intimacy of their souls, enfevered by general ideas, one final time, and, by virtue of a heroic coquetry, inclined their energy and their certainty before the abstract and eternal doubt of the cherished philosophical dreams that their minds contained.

It was like a supreme adieu, that hour given to pure mental speculation before the action. One final time they had interrogated one another, feeling themselves keenly to be civilized, anxious, modern, free men united in effort but each one privately retaining a different conviction. And when they separated, no trace remained of their secret antagonism. There was nothing more in presence than the organizers of a fact.

The acclamation of crowds broke out all over Europe as the armies passed by. Ancient patriotism was dead, the conflicts of nations no longer existed, but a true ethnological patriotism had risen on the ruins of the other, and no longer had anything absurd about it. The defense of illusory or arbitrary frontiers no longer occupied anyone, but the defense of the civilized soul appeared sacred to everyone. The great eternal cry: "Death to the Barbarians!" traversed the Occidental lands, and there was no one, even among the most rustic, who did not have the sentiment of a sacred necessity.

When Claude Laigle, black,[54] simple and pale, appeared in cities in the middle of a human ocean and raised over the thousands of howling people that proud head whose luminous eyes fascinated to the point of delirium, he seemed more than the dictator and the master; he incarnated the entire race of the Latin Occident, a fugitive vision leaning out of the caleche that carried him toward railway stations, toward army assembly points, toward the unknown and toward hope.

His farewell gesture signified the immense stir, and beside him, leaning on the cushions wearily and thoughtfully, inclining a delicate and pained face beneath gilded hair, Claude's adviser and friend, Ménières, showed him, smiling, on the balustrades of balconies and the arches of avenues, the symbolic black and yellow pennants that the people had suspended to summarize the great struggle. The black people against the yellow people! Black and yellow! The two fateful colors decked windows and edifices everywhere, simplifying thought terribly, opposing the shadow where one meditates to the sun of unconsciousness, the Occident to the Orient, science to fatalism, always and implacably.

Ménières said these things in a low voice while Claude Laigle, lucid, saluted the human floods, his soul convulsed in their enormous cry, feeling himself carried away in the whirlwind of the Adventure...

It was Dessort who, with his supple eloquence and his prodigious instinct of simple sentiments, stirred enthusiasm in the heart of the masses, embedding there the two or three general ideas sufficient to create opinion, suppressing futile complications, illuminating the magnetic blaze, heightening the distinction of the two patriotisms. In the name of the vanity of the old, the orator had preached disarmament once to the international syndicates of which he was the soul; in the name of the intellectual novelty of the new, he preached merciless war.

From city to city Dessort moved, from city to city the dictator sensed his secret influence, his genius for persuasion; at every step the idea, explained and synthesized by the agitator of crowds, appeared to Claude Laigle with a new force. He read on the faces of the spectators who rushed around his vehicle or at the decent from his railway carriage, that the dispatches, the articles and the manifestos of the special press inspired by Dessort had fundamentally insufflat-

---

[54] The symbolic employment of the color black in this passage, which has already been invoked with regard to the clothing worn by the dictator and his associates, but whose significance becomes much more obvious from here on, reflects the fact that the symbolic flag of Anarchism was black, frequently wielded assertively, often in opposition to the red flag of Socialism, in Parisian political demonstrations.

ed the confederated countries with the evidence of the great war and its destiny. All were unified in the same determination.

By night, in the vibrations of the express carrying him across the plains of Germany, Claude rediscovered the rhythmic sensation that intoxicates, which gives a kind of mathematical certainty to effort, and that mastered his insomnia. In the brightness of the narrow saloon, his eyes, after being bathed in the infinite obscurity of landscapes through the windows, returned to the table where, impassive and ignorant of fatigue, General de Trénan was writing, calculating, putting the final touches to every detail of the plan of campaign, his bony head, white and shaven, leaning over his golden collar.

And, absorbing himself in that contemplation, Claude Laigle thought about Médion, who had remained for some time in Paris. He too had a power, but occult; confined in his study or his laboratory, the Minister of the Interior was, behind the ardent flight of the conquest, the methodical and mute calculator of forces of renewal, and also the engineer of forces of murder, unleashing the anonymous powers of chemistry and mechanics against the Yellows, with the coldness that he had once brought to unleashing them in the social revolution.

Claude Laigle sensed that active cerebral reserve behind him, the shudder of the express exalting him to the point of the vision of the hordes of brutes that he would soon see face to face in the land of the sun—and his thoughts bounded with the drunkenness of the hectic course, launched as rigidly as the train into the night, coherent, exact and dense, similarly ensured by couplings, gliding toward destiny with its rectilinear energy constantly multiplied of its own accord, frightfully, with a clouded dream occasionally illuminated by a flash of lightning above their irreversible momentum...

Dawn paled over the landscapes of Saxony and Bohemia. In the rainy capitals, amid the popular acclamation, Claude Laigle verified publicly what he had come to see in secret several times before: the condition of the arsenals and the troops. Everything was ready. Armies were descending to the points of concentration. He turned southwards, traversed Italy in its length, visited the ports of war, crossed the sea and found himself on the soil of Egypt.

Everywhere he found the immense black and uniform crowds of the civilized world, the cavalries, the artilleries and the regiments performing their sinister geometry. The squadrons of the Mediterranean were heading at full steam for the Red Sea; they crossed it by night, with their fixed beacons and their electric fans, stars of a sky of science and death, proposing to consciousness a new and palpable ideal.

The yellow and black oriflamme writhed symbolically at the top of the mizzen-mast of the transport ships. In Syria, Damascus and Baghdad, the accumulation of Europeans troops massed before his eyes in the dazzle of the sun. And in spite of the white costumes of the soldiers ready to depart for torrid climes, Claude saw them still black, abstractly black in the modern color, black and exact, black in accordance with the strange irony of the pirates of old.

Pirates! He smiled at that word, and Ménières smiled too. "Everything is cyclical," the latter said. "We're bringing the spirit of intellectual creation with the hue of death."

In Claude's heart, however, the Idea persisted: he saw it as a svelte and supple statue, which black suited perfectly. "Not the hue of death," he said, "but that of mourning. We're displaying our mourning, Ménières, for the old ideas of the old world. We're wearing mourning for the errors of yore: the Idea will only be dressed in joy later, when all of these things are finished. It's good that everything is reduced to a single hue, like our soul, the hue of exactitude and energy."

Complex dreams visited his heart, and he fell silent.

A vast series of ironclad squadrons attained the Persian Gulf. They were to spread out along the Hindu coasts, land floods of men there, and then go on to the seas of China to gnaw at the east of the immense enemy empire, gripping it in a semicircle of iron and fire, to establish a blockade and, reaching all the way to Shanghai, seize the yellow power from behind.

Great shocks would astonish the naval Orient—but the principal effort had to be directed on the continent. Through Persia and Afghanistan, the European armies would penetrate into northern India, joining up with the divisions disembarked in Bengal. It was there that the tactics of General de Trénan would be concentrated. It was there that his strategic thought would combine with the abstract genius of the dictator. It was in India, revolted, armed and resuscitated with its antique fatalisms, that it was necessary to kill the energy of the old world.

There, truly, the essential danger rose up. That first country, more than China and more than Japan, harbored the devouring soul and the ambitious reprisal of the future. Japan, clinging like an England to Manchuria and Korea, was incessantly pouring through the Celestial Empire its mechanical genius and the dynamic inspiration of its modernism, but India was the advance-guard toward Europe, it was the terrible peninsula where all those inert forces, shaken from the north-east, were coagulating.

Claude's plan was to avoid the immensity of the Chinese plains, to cut Orientalism in India, in the very place from which it might pounce on Europe by awakening Arabia and perhaps the Negroes, to isolate Japan in the distant seas, maintain it there with fleets, ruining its commerce—that was the essential thing. Between an India seized again and vanquished and a Japan blockaded, the immeasurable swamp of yellow men between the Altaï and the Himalaya could become inert and vegetative again for thousands of years. Destruction would have been vain and unrealizable; Claude did not even think of it.

Since the beginning of the world the belly of the Orient had been stuffed with stagnant and pullulating hosts; it was like the humus of humankind; it had only been possible to nibble at its edges; civilized power, attacking it sideways,

214

had been annulled by numbers and extent, like a shell launched into the void. Merely to contain those masses, to plunge them again into barbarity and darkness by suppressing their points of mental revitalization was to decapitate that body, severing the neural connections.

Claude Laigle knew full well that civilization is only born of destruction, that the intellectuality given to those agglomerations of beings was incompatible with that of the Occident, that it was necessary to kill one in order that the other might live. He had chosen.

India and Japan, one giving birth and the other concentrating: Claude Laigle always returned to those two fixed points, around which all his thoughts revolved. Across the Chinese plains, the transfusion of the ideas of the yellow lands operated slowly; ideas of rectitude, the grouping of brute forces, of barbaric socialization, of cohesion with a view to a tidal wave rushing over Europe in future, circulated with difficulty, like overly bitter blood in swollen veins, but they did circulate. In India, they found the support of the old Aryan genius;[55] they became almost similar to those of the peoples of the West; they suddenly contemplated their power over an extremely refined land from which corteges of masterpieces had once emerged, and where a tenacious and admirable magic still burned.

After atrocious struggles, India had once again rejected the English; at present, it belonged to no one, it was dreaming of a reawakening. Newly emerged among its rajahs was a race of cruel and brilliant princes in whom the penetration of modernity had only rendered more precise and more sagacious the ancient ambition of Nana Sahib. It was not for nothing that, seeming to yield, those men had come to Europe with the sons of the Samurai, to bring their assimilative intelligence into the schools, to take from the Occidental world its discoveries, to ripen energies there.

Claude knew that it was high time to stop that interior movement. Japan and India were the brains of Asia; China was merely the reservoir of brute forces, the domestic and armed hosts on which they counted on drawing one day in order to realize their autocratic and ferocious ideal, their hateful feudalism, their eternal dream of dominating migration westwards.

The fleets would contain Japanese power, but in India, it was more than surveillance and diminution that was required; it was a conquest, an absolute

---

[55] When *L'Orient vierge* was written there had been a veritable glut of works in the previous three decades devoted to the scholarly fantasy of the Aryas [Aryan Race], the supposed original speakers of the ancestor of the Indo-European languages,. The most notable French titles included the oft-reprinted *Les Origines indo-européennes ou Les Aryas primitifs* (1859) by Adolphe Pictet and *Origines indo-européennes: Le Berceau des Aryas* (1861), one of several books on the subject by Joseph van den Gheyn. Mauclair's subsequent adoption of the term *Berceau* [Cradle] suggests that he might well have read the latter.

submission, a sterilization of thought, of the terrible Oriental thought incompatible with ours. It was there that the land armies would act. It was at the very foot of the Himalaya, in the Punjab, in Kashmir, in Nepal, in Bengal, at the sources of the Ganges and the Indus, that the real war would be concentrated. The army corps coming from the south via Mysore, Nizam, Gujarat and the lands of the Rajputs, had orders to join up with the troops coming from Persia. The triangle would close in the Deccan, and via Allahabad, Cawnpore and Delhi, over an immense riot of blood and fire, the forces of two worlds would find themselves in a supreme contest. Everything indicated that with a luminous clarity.

The direction of the naval war, Claude Laigle left to the admirals. What impassioned him, what he wanted to see, was the collision in the primitive earth of the ancient Aryans and the new Aryans, turned against their ancestors. It really was a war of races, a family war, of which he dreamed. The action of Russia in Mongolia would drive the Chinese masses back toward that central conflagration. The true war, the war of ideas, would unravel there, in the Himalaya, in the Hindu Kush, near the Pamir, in the eternal places where the germination of the Occident had poured forth at the origin of the worlds,[56] and to which the transformed Occident was about to return in order to confront its enemy brethren, to put in parallel their fateful inertia, their immutable gods, and its own ideal of active and atheistic energy. It was in the very cradle of the race that the great question, which Claude called "the Dream," with his entire faith in the superiority of the new Occident, was about to be settled once and for all.

Behind the walls of Tibet, behind Burma, the yellow masses could sleep. Claude had no fear of them once the enlivening force was removed from them. The immense series of equatorial archipelagoes did not worry him either; what was required there was to kill the consciousness of number, to sever the link between them and the occidental world, prevent contagion via Arabia and Africa.

"The third age will be the age of Negroes," he said. "We are only on the threshold of the age of the Yellows. Later, the civilized will make arrangements. The black continent will sleep too."

In the heart of Africa, no visible ferment had been born. But the sacred land of the old spirit, Hindustan, was seething with fury and convulsed, ready for extraordinary destinies, and behind it, driven by methodical and implacable

---

[56] The idea that the Pamir mountains were the point of origin of land-based life, and hence a kind of focal point of evolutionary radiation, can be traced in France back to Benoît de Maillet's *Telliamed* (1748 in a drastically censored version, third augmented ed. 1755), which proposed an evolutionary theory based on the notion that the Earth had once been entirely covered with water, but had slowly dried out, gradually exposing more of the surface. It gelled conveniently with the theory of the origin of the Aryan Race in the same area, as scholarly fantasies sometimes do, offering esthetic satisfaction and an illusion of logical support.

Japan, the yellow rabble, irresistible in its pullulation, was rising. Claude Laigle could not detach his dreams therefrom. What obscure and passionate dreams tormented his thoughts on joining up with the black armies traversing Iran!

The dispatches arrived one after another, and at each of them his heart leapt in his breast. The envelopment of the fleets was closing around the Asiatic littoral. In the gulf of Bengal, on the coasts of Siam, along the Philippines, the European cruisers were prowling, seeking the enemy. Claude followed them instinctively on the map. They went around the seas of China, leaving to their right the vast and fantastic archipelago with fabulous names: Sumatra, Java, Borneo, Mindanao, Celebes, Luzon; islands crouching in the ocean like clawed monsters, twisting their savage volcanic sequence, vestiges of a catastrophe and an original tearing.

The fleets reached Formosa. Weeks went by without news. Eventually, it was learned that in the first encounter, near the passes of Chusan, five Japanese ships had been sunk. The news was like an electric shock, coming back toward the capitals of Europe. At the same time, the land armies were advancing. It seemed to Claude that he could hear, beyond the deserts and the expanses of water, from rainy Germany to burning Syria, the formidable subterranean sound of one world marching against another. Distances no longer existed; everything was linked.

At Kelat, Claude learned that the disembarkation of the southern divisions had commenced. The squadrons had reached Goa; the troops had been landed after a three-day bombardment. Europe was beginning to bite Asia; the latter's silence was profound. Nothing was known, or almost nothing. It was said that immense forces coming from Annam and Burma had joined up in Nepal and were concentrating there. The Asiatics were waiting on their own ground, fatalistically, perhaps counting on the immanent forces of the primordial divinity.

The dictator followed on the maps the realization of his hypothesis, and General de Trénan, impassively, not paying any heed to his lyrical and uneven speeches, showed him with a smile the mechanical means of his dream. Everything was coming together rapidly, fortune was visibly favoring the Occident. Fleets and armies were unified by the genius of a few tacticians. And suddenly, Claude Laigle, pale and excited, sensed the approach of the supreme impact, sensed that the heart of a race was within him, living in his breast, ramified in him alone; in him, one mere man followed by a little shadow over the sand, millions of souls and blades agitated at his signal.

What a dream! he thought. *There are no more distances: we're going!* He sought the face of the Adversary in the invisible. For him, the continent almost took on a human face.

Toward the end of September, it was known that the Russian forces had descended upon Mongolia, driving south-westwards the disorganized masses of the yellow race, which were falling back to Tibet. Everything would be decided in India. The will to destruction was one.

IV. The Asiatic Heart

Immobile on his horse, Claude Laigle tranquilly removed his cigar from his mouth and gazed at the horizon bathed with light. Smoke was rising up in the distance, tangled with clumps of palm trees.

Suddenly, there was a ripping red flare; the atmosphere was dislocated; at the foot of the mound where the dictator was standing, a shell burst. The battle began.

The day before, the first cadavers had appeared, White, Hindu and Yellow, sparse at first, and then in heaps, amid horses and broken chariots. Over the leagues, the cavalries had filed past the sinister vestiges. Finally, Claude Laigle's escort, launched as an advance guard, had recognized the enemy positions. Near Lahore, after a series of rapid countermarches, the first decisive contact was about to take place.

A sound of horses' hooves and the rolling of wheels caused the master's bright eyes to turn round. Along a sunken road, coming toward him at a rapid trot, through the black pennants, was General de Trénan's caleche. He was ill; his pale and glabrous face, with glacial eyes, emerged from the flank of the vehicle, a gilded arm whose thin hand was clenched, agitated among the officers galloping alongside the vehicle's door.

A second shell fell, in a spray of blood, frightening the animals in harness. Claude Laigle urged his horse forward, leaned over, and shook the fingers of the terrible old man. They smiled. An acclamation grew, abruptly broken by the thunder of a nearby volley, and the air rumbled deafeningly; a few hundred meters away, the European batteries responded to the signal in kind.

"The junction is made!" shouted General de Trénan. "The southern corps has come up the Indus! I have excellent news of the Rajput region! A good day today and we'll be marching on Delhi! You have your war!"

"Yes," said Claude Laigle. "Let's make the dream with blood—it's time. Do you remember the Franconia campaign, Trénan, the dawn when the German emperor, wounded and covered in mud, passed before us between his hussars? That was another family quarrel; the present one will be bigger!"

He laughed, proudly, on his huge horse. The thunder boomed again to the right; the escort moved off at a gallop into the wind. Claude Laigle followed the caleche, shouting words of joy punctuated by the wind of the gallop. The landscape burned his gaze. The black lines of the divisions undulated in accordance with the hillsides, the massed cavalries crowned the crests. A blue river curled in two bends toward a pink plain extended to infinity, drowned in the vibrations of a magical vaporous light. White villages alternated with clumps of trees. Two were ablaze, vertically plumed with thick smoke, striping the azure.

Suddenly, Claude heard a clamor. "Vive l'Aigle!" He saluted.

Mounted batteries crossed his path tumultuously; the escort was obliged to pause; the mass of metal, dense and growling, filed past tumultuously, filling the road. The artillerymen, standing in their stirrups, brought forth a scintillation of sabers, extended toward the master with a joyful gesture. The svelte gray steel cannons stretched out among the rumps and the wheels, jolting in a sinister and exact convoy.

General de Trénan's attentive eyes followed the guns with a strange tenderness. In the din, the dictator tried to orientate himself, to divine the secret destination of the ensemble. The geography of the battle astonished him; the imperceptible vermicular movement of divisions perceived in the distance, almost non-existent in the immense roseate landscape, filed him with a singular sentiment of uncertainty. How little space the effort took up! The living idea animated those black worms crawling over the plain. It became almost theoretical; it seemed to Claude that he was still in the previous night's council, consulting his maps.

Everything was distant, everything was geometrical and devoid of humanity, everything was reduced to those few lines scarcely added to the panorama, quashed into a mutter beneath the sun. And nearly two hundred thousand men were confronting one anther! The swarms on the facing heights quivered and shifted.

And suddenly, the gallop resumed. Claude threw himself to his right, following the banners. A vast semicircle indicated the edge of a wood, and the divisionary lines curved in accordance with it, spreading into the thickets, moving in mathematical harmony with an implacable slowness toward the final engagement with the adverse positions, from which smoke was still rising.

The stridency of a volley of shells passed over the riders' heads. They whistled hideously and heavily. Flies seemed to be dancing at the zenith, blossoming into red bombs, raining down beyond the blue river and disappearing. The interminable batteries assembled. Harnessed vehicles flowed toward them incessantly, swerving sharply, detaching more guns, long and slender. Claude watched servants hastening around them minuscule in the distance. From that uniform series, stretching toward the horizon, no smoke rose. The powder of the civilized was invisible in its volcanic blaze; only wan flashes sparkled. And on the grassy slopes, descending in shelter toward the river, the general staff overtook the artillery.

As the viewpoints shifted, the orientation of the battle appeared more sharply, the cohesion of the forces becoming evident. Near a ruined pagoda, Claude saw regiments rising up that had been lying low since the morning. The acclamation was guttural; they were troops from the States of Central Europe, a division of Austrians whose voices and faces alone revealed them beneath the unification of costume.

Suddenly, Claude Laigle had a singular memory. He had seen those faces in Silesia once, during the Franco-German war. Contingents of Austrians had taken part in it; then he had followed the French army, as a simple officer, anxious about the issue of a conflict on which the sociological future depended; he had seen those men, heard those voices, but in the evenings, in the villages taken during the attack, in the files of prisoners. He was gripped. How things had changed! They were marching with him now.

He had seen Trénan taking the French revenge to them, and he found himself alongside the aged commander-in-chief again, having become the agitator of a world, the ideologue leading crowds, the master of triumphant Anarchism! He looked at the old man, attentive in his caleche. He had scarcely changed, the pale, bony and glabrous face smiling thinly, with the same fixed smile. And he, Claude Laigle, felt solid on his horse. He thought about his own face, the hair scarcely graying, and behind the mask burned a soul just as incendiary, shining in the luminous pupils, as of old. He had the vertigo of the illusion of time; the abstraction of years, places, life and death rose up with a single surge in his devouring mind. The idea appeared to him again over the Oriental landscape, ignited, and undulated in the overheated atmosphere, in the open sky.

Everything is nothing but an idea, even conquest and its real bloodshed, he thought. He smiled; the sentiment of harmony radiated, the expansive law that, with is ace, had driven him from Europe to India, convulsed his nerves and thrust him even further forward.

"Vive l'Aigle!" The cry sprang up as he passed, the impulse of an aide-de-camp saluting him, going past the general's vehicle at a frantic pace, bearing away the dictator's name in a flash. But his name no longer existed, or his form; he felt himself truly the ideologue, cerebral, an abstract force, a number.

How scantly one exists! he said to himself, astonished to find himself thinking lucidly although his body no longer belonged to him.

A number! He thought about Médion, "the living number," glimpsing him across the immense journey, the burning plains, the seas and mountains, still in Paris, the other number, the other god of the world, responding for more than a quarter of the world, creating back there the fatal energy that would decide the material result here. The sensation of the abolition of distance dominated everything.

At that moment, a new corner of the landscape was revealed to the west of the plain. The snaking lines of black men reappeared, swarming in a vermicular movement—and this time, Claude Laigle understood why they no longer existed, why they summarized, in the distance, by their impassive and exact graphic form, from which death emanated without being visible, the mental conception of effort. The idea remained sovereign, matter was abolished.

What beauty! Claude said to himself. *The war of brutes has finished with the old times; modern warfare erases like the stroke of a philosopher's pen. Beautiful warfare without barbaric heroism, without muscles and strangulations, beautiful calculative and synthetic warfare! The intellectual is everything here. The destructive idea remains sovereign, everything is accomplished at a distance, and the hideousness of the human clearance is subsidiary.*

And he thought about the bombing of the Parliaments ten years before, and the sentiment of integral power, infinite in a small volume, overflowed his voluptuous soul. Those black streaks out there, and that crystal ball that a hand could grip, were the same reduction of matter to the minimum, the same silent geometry of Energy...

The cannonade was propagated throughout the extent; over the ten leagues of the plain it burned intensely, for hours. The Yellows held firm, their distant lines did not buckle; the dispatch of shells was regular. The horses of the general staff were leaping over cadavers. They went on and on, going around the hills, traversing the thickets with difficulty, getting bogged down in the sparse marshes, following the curves of the blue river. In front of the entire army, the fortune of the race passed, as the pale and ailing commander-in-chief's caleche filed through the battalions.

The sagacious gaze fell scrupulously on the ranks of men, and next to the leader's vehicle Claude Laigle bounded, black and simple, devoid of weapons his attitude amused and enthusiastic. A cry ran behind them, banners flapped, the flow of cavaliers passed in a swell of manes and flashes.

From time to time, General de Trénan made a sign.

Claude leaned over, and the old man, with his whistling voice, designated a point: "We'll go there...the east is occupied as I wished. It's going to plan. Another two hours of artillery, I think... I'm waiting for news of the Southern corps; the road they've taken is long; there are three large villages to take. It's there, look, over there, that they'll appear, there that they'll seal the final circle..."

His bony hand simulated a strangulation in the void. In an abandoned village, they stopped. It was necessary to change the horses. Everyone drew breath.

"That's good, rest," said the chief of the army, briefly. "Shells from up there will protect us." Ironically, he added: "Under that volley of iron that I unleashed behind us this morning, we'll be sheltered. The people over there will leave us tranquil. The shell has its merits, Master. Do you remember our conversation on the eve of the departure, in Paris? You'll be able to argue again with Médion about metaphysics and sentiment, thanks to my servant. In the meantime let's eat; it's necessary to take advantage of a respite, the day will be hard, and perhaps the night too."

They are, cheerfully, side by side in the carriage. The radiation of the midday sun was terrible, but their nervousness was too great for them to suffer from it. In the host of assembled soldiers, a violent magnetism was active. Near the river, troops of armed men were sitting down, waiting. Ranged behind the batteries, the infantrymen watched the artillerymen work. The volley of death wrote its definitive formulae in the open sky, designing the Idea, geometrical and light, borne upon the parabolas of the shells; frail gyroscopes launched rockets, splashes of fire soared.

Enemy projectiles suddenly fell in the joyous river, and then decreased; the facing cannons, unable to extend their fire any further, drew away, dislodged.

From time to time, General de Trénan, ceasing to eat, stood up in the carriage, leaning on the shoulder of an officer, afflicted by rheumatism but calm, his face almost blissful. The telescope shifted; he was following in thought an invisible equation.

"Look, Master," he said, "here's where we are. The figure is simple; all this is just an abstract problem, fundamentally. There's your war, it's going in accordance with your wishes." He explained with his finger on an improvised map, pronouncing Hindu names tranquilly, and the lucid speech, never embarrassed, of the man of war, enlightened Claude Laigle. The dream took body. Messengers ran up, shouted sentences, corroborated a hypothesis with a word and departed again with the order that would make it real. The immense agency of the battle was becoming clear.

At about two o'clock, Ménières came hurrying from the right, among the generals, and embraced Claude violently. He was unrecognizable, superb, regenerated by the war into which his restless energy had thrust him, reanimated and revivified by a sap of charity and blood.

"Oh, Claude," he shouted, "how beautiful it is! Everything's coming together! All the theories, all the intellectual complications, to arrive here, at this communion! To this law, because it's decidedly a law of the universe! A hundred thousand men with a single heart!"

He straightened up violently. A rumor circulated. The Southern corps was approaching; the direction of the cannonade indicated it, and the retreat of the Yellows moving back to meet it. The Asiatics sensed that they were being cut in two; the hour had come!

In a building of mud and straw, the council agitated. The black men soberly fringed with gold, consulted one another one last time. Heads leaned toward the commander-in-chief. In the middle of the group the dry voice sounded, the white hands ordered.

Claude Laigle went out. Busy soldiers were raising the poles of a field-telegraph, unrolling the wires, briskly disentangling the hollow iron beams and the coils, all the scientific apparatus involved in the intellectual war. Again the fire drew closer, the movement of batteries bringing them forward, and everyone mounted up again, Ménières following Claude Laigle. General de Trénan's vehicle turned and disappeared; the dictator found himself in the middle of the armed host that was racing to cross the river, moving off *en masse*, shouting, toward the invisible conjunction with the Southern corps that had finally arrived.

The black lines modified their position, became concave, now crawling from all points of the plain toward the water, toward the opposite heights. Leafy islets filled up with men, the cavalry descended in a crowd into the turbulent water, breaking cover from twenty different places. The swarm of the civilized interlaced its vermicular network everywhere, under the hurricane of the batteries.

Suddenly, a hallucination seized Claude Laigle. He was at the Asiatic Heart, at the core of the enemy organism, entering into it with Occidental Modernity, with the terrible rectitude of a plunging rapier, and the black lines, sinuous and insistent, were gnawing like mortal worms the rotten flesh of the old world, digging, sterilizing, orchestrating its death-throes.

A frenzy shook the dictator; the gallop accelerated; the magnetic drag of the army condensed in his soul, and, with the torrent of men, he charged, an anonymous black force, a flame in the blood.

Howling up the slope amid the charge of the cavalry, they entered a large burning village. The clutter of carriages halted the surge; there was confusion. Claude Laigle and his escort were dragged toward a partly-demolished temple. The white columns were dislocated, jets of sunlight were falling through the cracks in the roof, piercing the shadow; around a gilded Buddha still standing at the rear, an unusual pile of cadavers appeared, and Claude finally saw the Yellows!

They had been machine-gunned in a group around the effigy, the bronzed or grimacing faces emerging from somber garments like those of the Civilized; the dead flesh was hideous, with a hideousness identical to ours. The dictator looked up at the idol, which a jet of blood and brain-tissue had splashed amid the fade gilt of its cheeks. The enemy Idea became incarnate, springing forth against his cold and sure gaze. The sentiment of triumphant force invaded him.

A hand touched his shoulder; he turned round and saw Ménières.

"Do you remember, Claude, the massacres of Bajazet[57] in the cathedrals, or the monks of Saragossa?"

"Yes!" shouted Claude, feverishly, "But we're doing better—here there's a thought! Matter for matter, this crushing will serve nobler ends. There's a superior meaning in the death!"

A clamor caused them to go out, stepping over the Hindu and Japanese cadavers, the guided chests and faces with hooded eyes and prominent cheekbones.

"Masks, masks, all that!" said Claude

Outside a tumult burst forth, arms extending toward the opposite hills, and clusters of men climbing on to straw roofs in order to see better. Circling the crests, black masses were perceptible, streaming like ants.

"The Southern corps!" The unanimous cry rose up from the army, as the hour sounded in the surge of blood to the hearts of a hundred thousand soldiers. "The Southern corps!"

---

[57] The French version of the name of the Ottoman Sultan Bayezid I (1360-1402), popularized in a play by Racine that had very little relation to actual history.

Finally, they appeared; it was five o'clock. The immense embrace of two armies crushing a third definitively closed its arms of fire.

Huge clouds of smoke flew eastwards; the artillery storm raged behind the mountains; the whistle of shells almost ceased where Claude was. The enemy turned toward the other battle in order to pierce a way through and retreat in the direction of Lahore. Suddenly, anxiously, the mass of the divisions poured torrentially toward the new echo, stumbling in their entirely over the crests of the hills to the far slopes, in order to see.

Below the horizon, a frightful turbulence of vapors hid the collision of the Southern corps with the Indian rout. The Yellow army finally unfurled before Claude's gaze; the zone of the cannonade surpassed, the geometry ceased, the demon of war was within reach. The momentum of the charge of a brigade of hussars passed directly ahead of the general staff's escort, streaming over the slopes and fell into the gulf of fire and smoke. In spite of the distance, the dry and lucid atmosphere of the admirable day allowed the minuscule humans to be seen perfectly.

While troops erupted from a blazing wood in a flock of mantles and manes; the Punjab cavalry collided with the Europeans, a sinister quarrel of iron birds entangled over the foothills of the mountain. Black lines broke up, convulsions ran along them, glow-worms folded up, were tied in knots, unstrung, hideously chopped up, but then reformed; as on the threshold of a voracious ant-hive, and infinite agitation of black or bright dots covered the extreme landscape.

Near Claude Laigle, upright on his horse, a row of gyroscopes was aligned; the deadly rockets leapt into the sky, then fell amid pink and violet fire, and the black dots moved more violently still beneath that strange rain. Voids formed, patches of blue terrain, previously covered with men, became visible again. In the little circle of his telescope, Claude enclosed the massacre, and then lifted it up, aiming higher and further, beyond the deafening inferno.

Beyond the undulations of the ground, a bright city appeared with brilliant domes: Lahore! Beyond that, the unfathomable blue of the firmament mingled with the azure, almost unreal crests of the Himalaya: the sanctuary, the heart! And turning toward the west, Claude's ardent gaze sought Delhi, as if he might discover, beyond the primitive rivers, the odious sacred country, the odious eternal azure...

Suddenly, warning clarions dryly vibrated; toward the slopes rose a confused agglomeration of horses and curved blades; banners fluttered, a fusillade rang out, the petty screech of bullets, like a buzzing of flies, was heard in the hurricane, its special ringing not arriving at the ears but touching, one might have thought, the nerves themselves.

A cry of astonishment went up. A hectic charge of Hindu cavaliers, cut off from their division, was racing toward the general staff, blindly and unwittingly, in a supreme surge of brutality toward inevitable death. Against all probability, they were coming up at the gallop. Hussars hurled themselves in front of them.

Pale and resolute, Claude Laigle drove his horse to join the crowd; standing up in the stirrups he watched the Hindus arrive, sun-bronzed faces with ferocious golden eyes, fists clutching scimitars, a riot of plumes and sashes whirling in the dementia of immolation. And among the admirable wild beasts of the Punjab, little men with flattered viperine heads raised straight sabers: Japanese cavaliers mingled with the others, a disorderly residue of dislocated armies attempting the impossible.

The old absurd heroism rose from Claude Laigle's heart to his lips, in a rush of instinctive blood. "A sword!" he cried.

No one heard him. Horses were bumping into his, the backs of men were interposed. He tried to jostle, to see, but he was trapped in a defensive circle; the savagery of hand-to-hand fighting arrived close at hand like a tornado, and between the heads the flames of revolvers mingled with the flashes of blades. A terrible swell crushed in its undertow a mass of bewildered and furious beings; a severed head leapt bloodily on to the haggard Claude Laigle's saddle; a slain general slid against him, the braided arms grasping at his for a second; and black and bearded faces appeared, crested with plumes and white turbans.

Everything dissolved into a red fracas; he could no longer see, no longer comprehend, and his nervous hands hooked on to the saddle-bow of the stallion, which, mad with fear and fury, was oscillating in the living wave, throwing back its mane into his face.

The moment was abominable. *Am I going to be killed? The idea...* In the depths of his soul, become as barbaric as those of the brutes facing him, the supreme anguish imposed itself with an indescribable rage. And he only understood the amity of destiny when he felt himself being drawn away, while cries of "Vive l'Aigle!" sprang from wide-open mouths.

A bloody head on golden shoulders loomed up before his own, howling: "We're saved, Master! There are no more of them."

And at the same moment, a cluster of plumes, steel and draperies, from which protruded the feet of a horse beating the empty air, fell against the flank of his mount, brushing his leg: the cadaver of an enemy chief, maintained until then by the strangulation of the crowd, collapsing horribly toward him.

He nearly fell, but found himself standing up among lacerated officers brandishing swords. In a flood of blood, a heap of wounded bronzed figures were gasping, fallen in a dense triangular mass, driven like a wedge into the general staff and hacked to pieces.

That was all that remained of the Yellow charge.

Two hours later, as night was falling, Claude Laigle found General de Trénan at the extremity of the battlefield. The circle was closed, the Indo-Japanese army cut into two stumps by the immense scissoring of shells, and one of the two stumps was fleeing toward Delhi while the other was being driven back to Lahore and the northern mountains.

The pale face with the thin lips greeted Claude with the same terrible smile. The exhausted dictator could not say anything; the day of triumph commanded silence; only the eyes were alive. Avidly, they wandered over the army. The first fires were propagating along the slopes, the artillery units were returning, swarms of infantry ere filing the streets and fields. The odor of humanity rose over the landscape along the odors of cannon-fire and conflagration.

In the distance, already obscure, enemy hosts were retreating in fits and starts; detonations persisted, spaced out; the stridencies of machine-guns striped the atmosphere at times. The agitation of the general headquarters brought Claude back to a sentiment of the real; the activity of the war gripped him again; he got back on his horse near the caleche, as in the morning, and passed along the front of the troops. Pools of blood interminable wet the feet of the panting animals; the profusion of cadavers in the red mud was extraordinary, piled up in shell-holes, walls sustaining rows of men shot by rifle-fire, sitting up and grimacing. The horror was nullified by dint of reigning everywhere.

Long escorts of cannons crossed their path, returning from the battle, and behind them Claude Laigle encountered convoys of prisoners. The first torches lighting their impassive faces, the general staff, from the height of saddles, watched them pass between the rifles. They advanced slowly, arranged in a column along the road.

General de Trénan, ever correct, raised himself up and saluted lightly, in accordance with the ancient habit of victors. Claude Laigle and Ménières, pensive, imitated him unconsciously. The captives looked at the embroidered Civilized and the black master without responding. Claude's eyes scrutinized them intently as they passed by Hindu chief, wrapped in colored loincloths dully stained with blood, were rubbing shoulders with semi-naked Nepalese couriers, Rajputs with gilded helmets and faces barred by nasals. Between them were little men in European dress were glimpsed, their centurion in good order, his shoulder-knots retied, strict and elegant, raising flattened heads. They were Japanese officers. One or two Chinese garments surprised by virtue of their yellow silk embroidered with a dragon.

The confrontation of Asia and the old world unfurled thus, interminably, but Claude only paid close attention to the Japanese. He ordered that they be separated for interrogation; hussars pushed them out of the ranks and brought them to the quarters.

They had been part of contingents come via the Ganges from Indo-China and Annam, allied corps that the Ministry in Tokyo and the vice-regent of Formosa had sent to the rajahs. The council questioned them; they stood still, mute and obstinate. Claude Laigle thought he recognized some of them, once seen in Paris, when he frequented the special schools himself, and General de Trénan also murmured, before one of them: "I've seen that man during artillery maneuvers, I don't know where."

The prisoner looked at him strangely, and then smiled. He it was who had, for six hours, directed the batteries on the enemy right wing, the last to hold out, and his method had been that of the commander-in-chief. Claude Laigle might have cried: "Join us!" but the thought of the gilded idol glimpsed in the afternoon, the vision of fatalism, of the hateful revenge of the Orient choosing our weapons for a retrograde design, passed through his mind. The logical war came back to his memory, and he contained himself.

"Messieurs," he said, "the sociological struggle is turning to our advantage. Let us think about Europe released. I raise my mind this evening toward modern science, toward the idea of superior life consecrated by blood and the bomb to Anarchism. The Confederation of the Occident will be saved."

The clear voice rang in the striking silence of the generals. Night had fallen. The innumerable fires designed in the obscurity the vermicular lines of the encampments; they were still eating away the Asiatic heart. Soon they would crawl toward Delhi, toward the sacred summits, toward the sanctuaries; the heart would be emptied of blood, inertia would descend again for centuries in opiate dust over the stagnant masses of the uncultured.

Claude's soul opened beneath the heavens; the conqueror dreamed. A cannon shot expired in the darkness, on the road to Lahore.

V. The Descent from the North

Some time after the battle, important news reached the general staff. The cannoneers coming up the branches of the Indus confirmed it in part. Hyderabad had surrendered after dogged resistance, to the corps disembarked in Gujarat along the chain of the Vindhyas. There was talk of a great unresolved conflict outside Allahabad. Cruisers returned from Surat announced the destruction of two Japanese fleets and the investment of Hong Kong. In Indo-China, grave dissents between the Burman princes and the Japanese generals were paralyzing the Yellow action.

Time passed; the immense installation of military telegraphs was completed. They ended up receiving god news from central India. The other Hyderabad, the antique Golconda crazy for precious stones, was occupied, Nizam invaded. A dissent between Thugs and allies had neutralized the terrible sect of stranglers there. It was thought that in Bengal the route of the Ganges would be open to the Civilized. Nothing essential had been modified in the original plan.

Extraordinary stories were running around. Parsee troops were coming over to the Europeans; their anarchism, in revolt against the autocracy of the rajahs, threw them into the lap of the men of the West. The intrusion of the Japanese also irritated them; between the power of Tokyo and the opposed power, sects that could not choose were agitating dully; popular Hindustan was beginning to seethe of its own accord.

The heritage of its gods and its fatalities could only be stolen by the regulars of one invasion or the other, and the authoritarian advent of the Sino-Japanese in the sacred territory insulted multiple fanaticisms, united in an ambition of autonomy. Placards bearing images circulated; passwords were discovered. The people murmured that it was superfluous to have expelled the English only to see Japanese hordes and European hordes quarreling on the sacred soil. A detestation of uniforms, engines and tactics was excited in the anonymous crowd. But the success of the civilized rallied the instinctive servility of the lower classes.

Dessort, arrived from Europe, stimulated these secret conflagrations with his genius. In a few weeks, he penetrated the mechanism and multiplied its importance tenfold, finding the simple forms that it required to propagate them in India. An association of indigenous couriers took adroit instructions from him, and spread swarms of men into his provinces, bearers of false news and promises. The Japanese armies that were stationed in the region were irritating, by virtue of their exigent arrogance, by their costly presence and the fear of remaining that was visibly established within them, by their European weapons and the cold discipline of their manner. The quarrels in Burma were reported deceptively; the scorn of the Japanese generals for the leaders of the Thugs and the irregulars of Nizam was recounted from one brigade to another.

With a lucid diplomatic subtlety, Dessort propagated the seeds of dissent between Orientals and Yellows, creating racial conflicts in the very bosom of the enemy. The Parsees aided him powerfully; cruel and intelligent, held in suspicion, they were the very soul of oriental cunning, the enemies of castes and rajahs, the mental advance guard of the egalitarianism of the West.

Gradually, the leader of crowds, the perverter of masses, pursued the work of disorganization, continuing under the sky of India his work of psychological decomposition, as he once had against the socialists and powers of Central Europe. Alongside Claude Laigle, ideological strength, and General de Trénan, mechanical strength, Dessort was analytical strength, the terrible solvent of the modern world eating into the ancient one.

The conversations of the three men quickly came into accord on the necessity of simultaneously pursuing the work of death by those three means. With the war of the shells and the war of the incompatibility of ideals, the war of the fermentation of suspicions was juxtaposed. Perhaps for the first time, Claude Laigle glimpsed that his hatred of the Yellows ought not to be uniform, that there were two Orients. The Japanese Orient was, for Europe, the danger of an armed civilization, with similar equipment and methods. The Hindu Orient was the danger of a vast stagnation of anti-progressive and fatalistic ideas in the middle of the world. One danger was active the other inert. And above those two dangerous worlds was the great dormant swamp of brutes, the reserve of unintelligent muscle ready to lend itself: China.

A diplomacy of division could intervene between those two potential initiators of the great barbarian flood. Their ruination might be consummated mutually, their cohesion into one will of hatred against the Occident could not yet have overcome the multiple suspicions between peoples. Claude's ideology was delighted by that idea: the struggle was no longer purely military; it appeared abstract, the hour of the first truly sociological war having sounded in humankind's midst.

In dreaming of the unification of Asia against Europe, the genius of Japanese politicians and the rajahs of India had, as always, imitated the races of the West, accomplishing their unification by the anarchism of the State; but that genius had gambled too soon on ideas, the immense distances had not permitted that, from Punjab to Burma, from Indo-China to Japan and from Tibet to Mongolia, a leverage of intellectual contact could be operated at will. Reciprocal incomprehension would last a long time yet; the method of the cabinets of Tokyo and Peking was superior but too theoretical, and the Europeans had arrived in time to paralyze it.

Claude Laigle understood how indispensable the work of disaggregation pursued by Dessort was; the two methods of the West and the Far East were about to engage logically, over the stake of crowds, in a combat of ideas dominating the artilleries. In spite of everything, matter was decidedly subsidiary, colonial interests were eclipsed by the idea. Only a conflict of consciousness remained, and Claude Laigle, during the vicissitudes of the war, amid the forced slowness of military occupation, began to dream about the duality suddenly revealed in the enemy.

His innate hatred of the people of the sun was no longer unique; two distinct hatreds were intensified. There were times when he could almost have wanted to reach an understanding with the Japanese, so much was their goal worthy of his own, so much did the avid intelligence of their psychology of races force his own to esteem. There really were two spirits of modernism grasping the Asiatic host, from one end of the old world and the other—but the obscurity of the Far Eastern soul threw Claude Laigle back upon the determination to annihilate it. The surprising borrowings of the inventions of Europe served to protect an ungraspable barbaric dream; that brain of the new Asia would refuse the brain of the new Europe; it was necessary to attain it and kill it; there, decidedly, as the real peril.

"What a pity!" That cry filled the dictator's soul. A kind of mental tenderness sometimes took hold of him: the singular tenderness of logicians and those familiar with abstraction for those that they sense to be "strong."

Claude's nervousness was troublesome; he had the sincere ingenuity of the thoughtful man who does not demand to be right as long as reason prevails, and who finds a secret contentment in its triumph even if he has to sacrifice his own argument to it. But those reversions did not last long; the man of action was decidedly predominant in Claude Laigle; the war exasperated that side of his character, effacing the other, and he threw himself back brutally into his cold conception of annihilation.

As for his hatred for India, no intellectual esteem tempered it; there, everything was hateful, especially the conception of an inactive life, the constant determinism—horror itself for Claude Laigle. For the somnolent Chinese masses of the Himalaya and the Altaï, out there, so distant, he only experienced a scornful pity, the disdain of the constructor of refined hypotheses for an embryonic protoplasm.

About those, we'll see later, he said to himself, *whether to imprison them forever or make use them, as we choose. That's fallow material, not even seeded yet. It's necessary to breathe into that colorless paste, as glass-blowers do; the molds are to be found. Or perhaps leave them to their slumber and their abdication, behind the mountains. They existed before...will they still exist, at our whim? We shall see...*

In his soul, the obscure clouds of the north-east sometimes cast vacillating and confused shadows, but disgust for those stupid and sly agglomerations chase away all other thoughts; the nauseating odor of the Chinese repelled him; his overheated imagination sought luminous points, and always came back to the determination of Japan, the obstinacy of India, the resolution of Europe. On those three points, Claude Laigle calculated the ideological circle of the situation.

Insinuation, thanks to Dessort, disorganized India. Significant facts were abruptly learned: desertions were occurring in Nepal. The defeat of a Japanese squadron appeared to be due to the probably-deliberate inaction of a division of cruisers equipped by the rajahs. Mutinies were repeated in Nagpur; a Japanese general was assassinated by the Thugs following an overexcitement of fanatics; the Princes of Mysore made it known that they were disinterested in the struggle.

At the same time, however, it was known that grave checks were slowing down the progress of the Civilized in Bengal. A three-day battle had turned to the advantage of the Yellows. At Midnapour, frightful massacres had given a bloody actuality to the sinister tradition of the well of Cawnpore stuffed with cadavers; a surrounded division, cut off from the rest of the army, had been almost annihilated, and the other corps, led stray by a false strategy, heading for Assam, had been separated from the coast and driven into conflict with superior Asiatic forces.

General de Trénan's anger was extreme, his plan might have to be adjourned for several months.

The alternative endured; there was no good news permitting an advance for a long time. It would have been imprudent to relax the gigantic line linking the European armies, via Kelat, the Indus and Afghanistan, with the infinite series of supply-points set up between the Mediterranean ports and India. At the other end of the chain, Médion, invisibly active, poured a torrential flow of resources. The army remained around Lahore; the distances were immense; the unknown of leagues and crowds was the essential peril. It required cunning, to wait, to commence the war of patience against Oriental tergiversation.

Dismal weeks went by, wearing away the master's feverish activity. The economic establishment, the turmoil of war budgets, the accountancy of the effort, created a painful period. The concentration of forces was pursued with difficulty; results were no longer perceptible; everything was secretly composed without apparent profit. In that phase of the Adventure it was Dessort who took the leading role, his qualities of dissociation priming everything, the annexation of indigenous consents becoming the essential condition of success.

Claude Laigle suffered from that solvent psychology; it was a weapon whose necessity he understood, but because he had not wanted to lead Europe against the hypocrisy of enemy races, his lyrical pride revolted against it, his vision of beauty was diminished; he was no longer anything but the introducer of evil ferments among the evil ferments of the enemy. The perfected Occidental modernism that he had, and which provided the noble goal that he had set himself, carried to barbarity inevitable ruses and perfidies of another order than his own, but the moral level was similar. The sociological war was using base means, like the others; the man of the West, like the man of the Orient, revealed flaws of consciousness.

Claude Laigle sensed something inferior therein; he was gripped by melancholy; each of Dessort's results touched his heart with a vague bitterness; beneath the contentment it persisted, and he disinterested himself in that part of the struggle. He isolated himself with Ménières. Ménières, in his disillusioned soul, retained a keen intuition of its nuances, and pointed them out to Claude. They both appeared to be invalids of heroism gone astray among calculators.

The impassive General de Trénan did not come to them; he was waiting for better news, for the machinations of Dessort to permit the decisive recommencement of the campaign, the re-entrance on to the stage of the artillery. That was definitely all he saw in the conquest: his murderous rigidity shocked the master, conversations that were almost irritated took place.

Claude Laigle rediscovered the impression of the evening in Paris, the sensation of solitude in a dream not accepted by others. For them, the face of the Adversary was different. Dessort was continuing in India his demoralizing experiments previously tried on the socialists of France and Germany; Trénan was killing scientifically in the Deccan as in Franconia ad Bohemia. They were really mechanisms devoid of consciousness and discernment, scientific forces of modernity serving, with the most ingenious methods, the eternal human instinct of domination and blood. The Anarchistic ideal had not touched their active souls; action always crushing the sentiment of a superior morality, it was necessary to choose between that and ideology.

And bitterly, Claude Laigle rediscovered that contradiction in himself; he evoked his speech including the declaration of war with a dolorous irony; he had thought he was formulating at that moment the establishment of a mental progress, but he had only been formulating his desire. Fundamentally, everything remained to be done, the glimmers of the revolution had only illuminated at intervals the supremacy, so ardently desired, of morality over instinct. The solidarity of economic interests had contributed a hundred times more to determine social union than the vision of a world of individual responsibility and mental nobility. Had Claude Laigle's dream put too much hatred into trying to prove itself by action?

But no! said the dictator to himself. *My calculation is accurate, and if it isn't yet, it will be. The conditions of security before all! It's for them that we're here. Later, when the Oriental peril is averted, we'll have to work in Europe, on our return. There will be years of moral education to embark on. It's always necessary to commence with blood: that of Europe flowed to commence the work, that of Asia will flow to fortify it, and afterwards, it will be necessary to perfect.*

Long perspectives of intellectual labor haunted his soul, filled the vision of his old age.

It won't finish with me, he told himself, *but everything is ordered and logical. It's necessary first to make the crowds understand that one can imagine a society with ne consciousness; I've cleared the way for that. Now the crowds have the material means to be themselves, it's necessary to repeat to them that it's accomplished, and they'll end up being obliged to believe it. It's necessary to retouch, to prune, to use cunning, to create methods, develop the sentimental current alongside the scientific current, which serves, but harms if it gets the upper hand. The equilibrium of means and conceptions, that's the formula.*

He dared not confess to himself that his present conception, in spite of everything, surpassed his means. Perhaps he did not perceive it. For long days he came back to it...

They traversed the rainy season thus. The agglomeration of armies had become immense. Journeys took Claude Laigle from one camp to another, through Hindu populations contained by posts or indifferent. It seemed that India was disinteresting itself in the great war between the men in uniforms and its tactics, seeking itself in the infinite extent of its mountains and plains. From the mouths of the Indus to Lahore the Franco-German divisions lined up; they were linked via Gujarat to the sea and the fleets, the filing of transport ships across the Persian Gulf created an incessant flow of supplies, a connection with Europe.

A second army, half-Austrian and half-Italian, was in Nizam, while toward Bengal, creeping obstinately along the Ganges, surpassing Benares and extending all the way to Oude, a third army, mostly English, formed a triangle around the center of Hindustan. All the nations of the Occidental Confederation were there; internationalism reigned, simplified by the adoption of French as the diplomatic and military language. Telegraphic networks submitted almost all those corps to the will of the general staff. It was an encampment of peoples of unified initiative, which was incessantly augmented.

Indigenous defections were numerous. After the neutrality of Mysore, the adhesion of Kashmir was announced. Dessort's campaign succeeded; rivalries between the rajahs and the Japanese became manifest almost everywhere. Finally, the setbacks in the west were repaired; a battle fought near Darjeeling and an unexpectedly successful retreat of the corps gone astray in Assam had changed the face of things.

The fine season was approaching, and the war could resume.

At sea, it was virtually finished. Amazing destructions of fleets had annihilated Japan's naval forces; the squadrons could limit themselves to the blockade of the coasts and the protection of European cargo ships. The last hecatomb of the Gulf of Siam was disastrous; four Japanese battleships ran aground after a pursuit of several days before being destroyed at a distance by torpedoes launched from balloons, which testified to European genius. The skyborne fleet had annihilated the marine fleet; an unexpected magic of war was beginning.

Finally, the new from Kashmir brought the echo of the Russian action. Hundreds of leagues away, the Chinese mass had been dislocated, reduced to inertia, driven impotently back to the high plateaux and the infinite sterility of the desert. The noise of the war was drawing away from its slumber, and it was stagnating.

Again, Claude Laigle's heart was convulsed by joy, and the renaissance of active energy effaced his doubts. He found himself the master once again, and determined.

Then, descending through the Hindu Kush, coming from Asian Russia, there were immense emigrations of strange men. The North, moved by an ethnological magnetism, ceding to an instinctive pressure, came to see the strangulation of fateful India, moved by the obscure, by the planetary rancor of creatures of the snow against creatures of the sun!

The Arctic Circle was displaced toward the Tropic of Cancer; one half of the hemisphere rose up against the other; the ant-hive of races tore itself out of its vegetative existence and the passivity of its destiny to experience and upheaval unprecedented for centuries. Distant peoples appeared in the three camps; unusual faces even astonished the Civilized. The immemorial cold of the steppes had fixed a special soul there. From beyond Lake Balkhash they came, and from the regions of the Yenisei, and further still, from the semi-annual obscurity and pallor of the poles, from places where nothing is known and where dreams themselves expire, for want to warmth and consciousness...

The emigration of the North was frightening. A new crusade was born, but it was also a Children's Crusade, so utterly unknown were those human troops, save for the fact of their descent. It was necessary to suspect them, to give orders to keep them away from the army, to reach an understanding with the military governors of Aral and Irkutsk in order to stem that irrational flow of witnesses running to the division of Asia's flesh.

They arrived, without knowing why, quitting the commerce and the muted existence of the snow-fields, the darkness of Asiatic Russia; they too were barbaric, in fief to a blind cult, to the Northern god who detested the azure swarm. They had returned to the cruel simplicity of primitive humans, to the generative hatred of forces, to the babbling instinct of differing climates creating different souls. An odor of blood was rising from the middle of the world in the overheating of the central light, and humankind steered in that direction.

Pensively, Claude Laigle and Ménières considered those quiverings of races, the eternal magnetism of three or four physiological currents that ordered humanity, beneath the varied modes of mores, beneath the illusory acquisition of the refinements of civilization. The reduction to the simple was striking. There too, as in the fundamental causes of the war, as in the geometry of armies, everything was number, abstraction and polarity; everything happened by virtue of mental reciprocities, everything was scientific evaluation. Dynamism was god.

"In the final analysis," said Claude, joyfully, "is ideology a vain word? All this is the play of ideas—we're philosophizing."

Smiling, Ménières replied. "All this is also poetry. The décor is beautiful."

There was a period of joy for the two men. Among so many beings with various languages and visages, their detestation of old fatherlands and their faith in individual internationalism was reborn.

"I almost believe in progress, in seeing how these people understand one another," Ménières said, one day. "The absurdity of frontier conflicts is decidedly dead; ethnological war at least has an intelligent meaning. These spectators coming from the Urals, and almost from Lapland, have one thought, which pleases me. The men of the cold hate the men of the heat; that's logical, natural and plausible; it's a climatic division that has a reason for being.

"This is the first war that I don't find imbecilic. It's like an instinctive gesture: and what beauty! It's not even a matter of killing to colonize, to install merchant thieves in an exotic land and cheat poor brutes without risk. The governments of old only saw that consequence of their visits to the Asiatics or Negroes; this is better, more noble and saner. The Northerners who are coming to the army have no material interest for coming; it really is a thought that guides them, a mental interest. Your lyrical modernity exists, Claude."

The dictator approved. "Yes, these are symptoms that touch me. The Idea is acting on crowds, the act of killing is beginning to prove worthy. We're going to see more killing, Ménières: blood is the promise of life." And the visage with the luminous eyes contemplated the fatigued and fine visage. "You'll live to see all that, Ménières. Have I've brought you far enough? Is there enough air here

234

for your dreams? How vast our hopes in Paris have become! Here, one acts and thinks together..."

Claude Laigle's enthusiasm infected the army. It expanded everywhere in words of ardent exhortation to energy. Reviews took place, proclamations circulated; adroit guarantees to the population calmed the effervescence produced by the resumption of the campaign. The legations of the Confederated States brought testimonies from Europe of any absolute confidence in the dictatorship. Capitals lit up; the socialist union, from the shipyards of Glasgow to the workshops of Bohemia, voted further credit. Médion's organization was monitoring everything; they could march.

More delays occurred; typhus disrupted the Nizam army for some time; it was necessary to wait and carry out effective translations. But fortune was definitely favoring the Civilized. Victories on the Ganges permitted a rapid march of the third army. Cawnpore, the sinister city, was taken, the queen of Oude capitulated, the rajah of Bundelkund had to yield in his turn.

Everywhere, the Europeans were advancing; the English divisions reappeared on the blood-soaked soil of the ancient Sepoy revolt. The horrors of 1856 were renewed. Terrible things were seen: the burning of Lucknow; six thousand Yellows surrounded in the great pagodas and exterminated by batteries moving through the streets; a broth of humans and horses streaming in the fire under the shells; the terror of the massacre extended for fifty leagues, in the heart of sacred India. General de Trénan's lieutenants pushed their advance-guard all the way to Gwalior. The army of Vindhya came toward them; the triangle tightened around central India; the struggle attained its maximum of atrocity.

The news of the conjunction at Gwalior arrived one evening, brought by Indian couriers in Dessort's service. Those bronzed, semi-naked individuals conferred mysteriously with the chiefs. A frisson passed through the army when the aged commander-in-chief suddenly appeared in the camp. The bony white hand made a sign to the summoning clarions. The generals ran hither and yon, the streets were filled with messengers coming and going, and silence fell.

The old man spoke: "Messieurs," he said, simply, "we're marching on Delhi."

The long-awaited name burst forth. The great war was approaching its end; the supreme effort was about to be attempted; a breeze of relief rose.

In the glare of the fires that sparkled in the night, Claude Laigle saw once again the vermicular snaking of the Civilized, as on the eve of the Battle of Lahore. The Asiatic heart was about to feel the rip of the sword. The sovereign Idea would live! It was exactly fourteen months since the solemn declaration in Paris had awakened its electric resonance had awakened...

An infinite gratitude to destiny, for assuring the triumph of modernity and choosing him to be the leader of that triumph, penetrated Claude's soul. One grandeur was about to annihilate another; he had the intuition of a consent of the part of the world to the supremacy of the North. And, responding to an interior voice, he said:

"I accept. I submit. I shall serve the Idea."

The rumor of the bivouacs approved.

A few weeks later, the investment of Delhi was accomplished. An Indo-Japanese army was surrounded under the walls of the city. Inside, the fortune of Asia, its princes, its gods and its age-old fatalism awaited the end. The times of Nineveh and Carthage were about to reappear in the evolution of worlds.

VI. The Assault on Delhi

From the lines of circumvolution in which the guns of the siege were thundering, the armored cupolas of enemy forts were clearly distinguishable. The reflection of the sunlight from their white paint made them into strange domes of buried temples. They emerged from the soil at regular intervals. A plume of smoke rose up rapidly, and then they were effaced in the undulation of the grassy plain, and the shell arrived.

Delhi was somnolent behind its cupolas, staged on the bank of the Jumna. No sound was born there; it was scarcely visible. Heavy vapors floated in the blue sky; the landscape was desperately serene. The days and nights succeeded one another, with the monotony of an infinite agony, while the batteries thundered. The timetable of death was mathematically regulated by those giant pulsations, which responded to one another in the extent, alternated by the positions of the three armies.

The Yellows riposted with furious cries that were increasingly widely spaced. The aerial exchange of flies of iron and fire spun its turbulent and ferocious network high over the camps and ramparts. The slaughter was invisible; the sonority of the discharges was the only sign of the vast confrontation of men. They were propagated regularly in the direction of the plain, convulsive and intermittent in opposition; the shriveling of the enemy race was detectable.

From time to time, the crackle of machine-guns and the stinging dryness of fusillades, mingling with the throbbing echoes of the cannon, indicated a sortie, a furious impulse of the imprisoned army. Rapid movements carried masses of cavalry and infantry forward; the black ant-hives orientated in the distance an incessantly deformed geometry; the vermicular oscillation of the Civilized designed trapezia, curves, parallelograms, diamonds, broken, remade and dissociated in sudden fractures. The rain of ardent iron fell, and then the clarions sounded the halt, casting everything back into silence. Convoys of wounded moved back; the inertia of the wait imposed itself again.

In the nascent darkness of the night, profound and vague melodies rose up over the odor of blood: the bands of the army corps played symphonies and hymns. The chanting of the Hindu couriers joined in, stridently or languorously, and a strange sensation of intensity took hold.

Above the lines, in the open sky, oblong aerostats floated, their aluminum spurs shining. They drifted, enormous, casting the elongated shadow of their course on the ground, like artificial clouds. They were seen soaring over the city. Their pale lights striped the obscurity, and one might have thought that a squadron was scrutinizing the impalpable waves of a sea of darkness; they sought one another and appealed to one another, the life of the siege continued in the sky; and above the luminous interchange of bombs and the violet light of gyroscopes, their enormous pale stars maneuvered in a phosphorescent rotation, expending the tentacles of blue-tinted squid over the suddenly-illuminated domes of Delhi.

Sulfurous jets leapt up toward the monsters, were extinguished without reaching them, and extraordinary nocturnal combats hallucinated the army. Torpedoes fell from the balloons; their suddenly-stifled crepitation created whirlwinds of stones and flames; vibrations broadened to deafening pitch convulsed the atmosphere. The living stars wandered over those cataclysms, ironically converged their oblique radiations, and then disappeared.

One evening, an unforgettable spectacle caused three hundred thousand men to look up. Two similar balloons rose up from the city and floated; Japanese genius had succeeded in equipping them, and suddenly they too launched torpedoes, at an artillery division. A clamor went up; awakened, the regiments assembled tumultuously, emerging from tents to gaze at the two monsters that were swimming rapidly and casting lights over the camp. The signals sprang into action and a confusion of messengers filled the roads; the anxiety was terrible.

Before an order could be given for the airborne scourge to be driven away, however, other stars converged, coming from the depths of the horizon. The electricians and aerostatic engineers of Europe were alert! A gyration of white rays passed over, the two enemy stars were effaced, atmospheric frictions created an artificial breeze, the supernatural beasts pursued one another, darting dazzling jets in the darkness. The breathless troops sought them at the zenith, a human frisson vibrated from the army to the invested city. And suddenly, in a colorless splash, two of the stars collided, and both were seen to fall, one of them disemboweling the other. They fell on a grove of palm-trees in a horrible collapse, a quarrel of bolides burning over the agony of India, while toward the west a fiery spark fled, pursued by others.

The evolution of the hours seemed a flight of flaming gems; a crown of diamonds sparkled in the night, burst into flames; multicolored rockets rained down from the aerostats, announcing the end of the battle. The two enemy machines had been destroyed.

Long bleak days followed that supernatural drama. It seemed that the soul of the new India, having momentarily raised itself into the sky in order to escape, was dead, and that fatalism was stagnating forever. That effort was the last. The slow strangulation of famine and despair commenced for Delhi. The black belt of the Civilized circled the white city narrowly. The mediocre horror of the artillery battle, assassinating individual heroism, propagated its long-distance devastation methodically. The three camps awaited the moment.

For two days, a frightful battle brought them to their feet; a Japanese army arrived from Bengal, the last that had escaped anterior disasters, tried to force the blockade, attacking the circling forces. The Civilized fought, caught in their turn between the newcomers and a sortie by the besieged. The battle was fierce; one German division was almost annihilated, eight generals were killed—but the third dawn determined the European triumph. The Yellows had nothing to sustain them in the interior of the region; cut in two, they retreated, decimated, and broke up, toward the upper Ganges to rejoin the mountain tribes. The circle reformed around the city; the huge stone beast, after its final death-throes, was no longer shivering...

The division of the flesh could begin.

On the forty-seventh day of the siege, the electric signals, the semaphores and the flags announced the assault.

The enemy forts were mute, their ammunition exhausted; smoke no longer rose up above their cupolas. The debris of the invested army went back into the city; despair descended silently behind the sanctity of the walls. The military bands struck up; the besieging army advanced in five columns.

For hours the cannoneers on the riverbank sent shells into Delhi itself, having forced the passes and the chains of torpedoes established under the water. The invasion was devastating and simultaneous. The infantry crossed the war zone without anything in front of them giving any sign of life. A frightful taciturnity reigned. They passed the extinct, abandoned forts, hardly daring to believe that no surprise would emerge therefrom.

Revolver in hand, colonels went into them. A few luminous bulbs were still shining here and there; the tiled courtyards were empty, the guns dismantled and recumbent, the bunkers collapsed, the armor-plating holed. Broken carts littered the military roads, smashed by the erosion projectiles. A few cadavers were lying in their congealed blood, at the crests of the round walls. Wooden sentry-posts maintained half-burned skeletons upright. Everything was deserted; they advanced in terrifying silence.

Sometimes the general staff halted, almost expecting a distant group to appear, to negotiate; but nothing transpired. Finally, the jagged ramparts of the city appeared, vast extents of glacis, sometimes mingled with old carved masonry, doors with sculpted corbels, vestiges of primitive epochs. And suddenly, as the columns were about to attain it, a furious cannonade burst forth, a blaze of turbulent lightning, volleys of bullets arrived at ground level, breaking the first battalions. The anger of the final day rose up.

Fearfully, Claude Laigle and Ménières were watching the spectacle from a distance. They ran toward it, no longer able to hold still, gripped by the crisis of the irreparable. A swarm of black armies rushed over the crests, twisting into stumps, punctured by red fore. Mines exploded, with clusters of burning men.

The engulfment of the rigid Civilized disemboweled the city with a mad violence, the clarions persisting in the extraordinary tumult of explosions, their curt sonority ripping through the air. The mounted batteries raced, oscillating, trying in vain to install themselves. The cry of the charge finally annulled the monotonous ferocity of the cannons; European nerves were exasperated, and the rush of the white army killed all tactics.

The dictator galloped into the outlying districts of the city. An immense crowd filled them, driving back the artillery vehicles, tipping over the ammunition trucks, the wheels of which dug into the flesh. Dazed clamors shook those human swarms, hurling them into the streets in swarming masses, under fire from houses and terraces.

The assault ran from street to street, house to house, room to room, increasingly specialized in its horror. The confusion was total, gallops of cavalry traversing the accumulation of infantrymen, entire sections of causeway opening up in wells of flame, entire companies falling into them in frightful collapses, and severed heads leaping into the air with bouquets of blood.

In the thick smoke, swirling in enormous spirals, perspectives full of eddying humans and horses and tangles were perceptible, entangled beings with faces convulsed in the wan light. The officers shouted in vain; the order of the assault was dislocated; human force regained its mastery; and unknown magnetism carried the armies away.

Claude Laigle appeared in that tumult without anyone paying any heed to him. Only the odor of blood guided him through that vast city, gripping his throat and his stomach. The five assault columns sought one another, puncturing the mass of stone in every direction. The excitement was as fervent as dementia; there were indescribable scenes.

The dome of one of the great sanctuaries split in an explosion and collapsed on the besiegers; entire colonnades were felled, smashed by batteries, porticos vacillated and fell, in clouds of dust.

Finally, Claude Laigle saw the Yellows again. They were swarming; the city was crammed with them, their variegated bands were surging forth from all directions, the terraces were crowned with semi-naked men. Against the embrasures of galleries, against the angles of courtyards, repulsive crushes launched red spurts; blind alleys were heaped with cadavers, their heaps rising up along the walls. Cannons filed along the avenues, at the end of which seethed floods of human beings. Women fell from balconies, clung on to soldiers, raised daggers above their heads.

The accumulation of flesh was prodigious; the arms of men raising rifles could not find the space to shoulder them; mounted officers were pitching in the human tide along with their horses, howling as they stumbled. Bombs coming from other parts of the city suddenly crashed down from the sky; deadly rockets departed at random; the crepitation of revolvers and the clash of sabers were drowned in the tumult. And from gardens, houses, cisterns, from everywhere, new troops continually surged forth.

Clumps of palm trees were burning, the flaming trunks falling; horses with flaming manes ran madly through the crowd, the impact of their hooves stamping blood-soaked flesh into a hideous pulp. Bands of madmen were murdering one another in corners; naked stranglers leapt at the throats of soldiers, bounded on to the saddles of officers. At one intersection, among clumps of trees, long railings opened up, and tigers released by the slaves of rajahs hurtled into the midst of regiments, mingling their wild cries with the frightful human clamor.

Turbulent agglomerations of men filled the large squares; voids suddenly appeared, filled in by lines of black beings emerging from the streets. The concentric fusillade accumulated amid pyramids of cadavers. In the bazaars and ground-floor rooms, bloody crowds mingled the Civilized and the Yellows; scimitars and bayonets clashed. Murder fumed with splendor.

Hours passed thus.

Livid, the dictator allowed himself to be borne along by the crowd.

Ménières follow him, his eyes dilated, ultimately contenting himself with an unsuspectable dream, a monstrous imagination of his unhealthy genius.

"Carthage!" he shouted to Claude Laigle, in a rare moment when the fracas allowed him to speak audibly.

Claude Laigle remained silent, crouched on his horse, amid the gestures of frightened officers. They moved forward, in spite of everything. House by house, they reached the heart of Delhi, the lines of the battalions reformed in the midst of the burned quarters. The heads of the columns met; one appeared, the other came to intercept it. Cavalry charges freed the streets.

In a vast conquered pagoda, amid the heaps of the dead, the smoke and the red mud, the general staff gathered. General de Trénan arrived. Night was about to fall; in the obscured sky, the flames were beginning to appear formidable and luminous. It was necessary to organize the definitive effort before it was completely dark. The gesticulation of the generals deafened Claude Laigle.

The commander-in-chief seemed as calm as usual. He arrived at the head of the third column, the two others carrying out a massacre on the riverbank; on the far shore the machine-guns could be heard in gusts; they were forcing barricades to the west and south of Delhi. Reserves were entering behind them; the plan of attack was being realized. In the confused atrocity of the carnage, the old tactician saw clearly, orientated himself, rediscovered harmonies. He barked orders, the lieutenants dispersed, the geometry reappeared. From the milieu of swirling smoke the reinforced columns prang in a fan, precipitated by the strident cry of clarions sounding the charge. The terrible old man disappeared with one of them. Claude perceived his gilded arm agitating its white hand amid the rifles.

The assault rushed backwards; already brandished torches were making the horses of the escort snort. The dictator galloped. Around him bounded a black legion; the crowd was dislocated by a volley of bullets; yellow faces leaned over terraces; the clash of blades and the curt cry of revolvers alternated in the chaos. A white horse passed by, carrying a man whose hair was soaked in blood. He almost threw himself upon the mater's horse, but disappeared. Others followed; they fell into the midst of the running infantry. Some were waving cords and strange daggers—stranglers! Thugs! They were killed in short order, though, and they passed on.

An inert general was carried to a street corner, his swollen head vacillating; a cord had seized him by the neck in passing, and Claude Laigle, bending over him, had a sensation of horror even more intense than before blood, in the presence of that green-tinted face from which the blackened tongue was protruding and the eyes were repulsively tumefied.

"Forward!" he cried, madly, and, dropping the cadaver, he ran toward blinding death, crimsoned by fire, chasing from his mind the image of the sly death.

"In beauty, at least!" The key word of all his morality rose incomprehensibly to his lips.

The furnace-like heat created a nightmare. Was it from life or the dream that the pandemonium of flames sprang? The conflagration of the old world was surpassed, and former Anarchist vengeance; it appeared to Claude that a gigantic vertigo was about to roast him like a despicable dust-mote in the convulsively flamboyant heart of India.

Scarcely had he recognized that he was not mad when the immense walls and domes were heaped up to the summit of the sky in a scintillating bouquet of rockets. The sacred pagodas and palaces of the center poured out springs of fire over a square black with people. Cannon fire converged and the porticoes were smashed in the explosions, the galleries of gods shattered. The human tide gesticulated, jostling the batteries, plunging under the vaults with the machine-gun fire; the lines of bayonets undulated; people stumbled in pools of blood.

Breathless, Claude Laigle raced into the first rank, in order that he too could enter, with masculine brutality, with all the males he was leading, into the detested virginity of those parvises. They opened up, ogival and somberly tortuous. The odor of age-old incense sprang abruptly from the holes in walls staved in by shells, the sacrilege of the rape of the old gods leaping with the soul of assassinated India, in blood. Oh, those palaces, those retreats of fatalism, those golden matrices! The rigidity of the European column, stiff and terrible, entered there with a single atrocious thrust, like a black penis, all the way to be depths, in the crushed flesh, in a red dampness, in the tearing of blades and the lust of fire.

Claude Laigle almost fainted as he shouted into Ménières' face, emerging by his side: "What joy! We're in!" He laughed, obscene and sublime in the giant rut. His eyes were hallucinated by the scintillation of vaguely visible Buddhas, rising up into the vaults, licked by gleams. His race was violating virgin India, spattering its soiling there with death!

And suddenly, a pale light rose up from the depths of his being, effacing the gilded specters: the Idea appeared, the unreal metaphysical enchantment that, above the armies of modernism, led the Adventure and his genius. Under the blank gesture, he fell from his horse into the arms of frightened officers, raised his hands, and sank into the unknowable...

A bullet, puncturing his garments without penetrating him, had thrown him down. When he reopened his eyes, the fusillade was drawing away to his right. The great pagoda was conquered; sappers were bringing down the gods with ax-blows, drunk on an instinctive fury, enraged by the terrible war, falling upon the great bronze monsters as if on mute and responsible masters. The eternal surge of the ancient mind armed them; the Idea was crushing the Dream!

"Wonderful!" shouted Claude Laigle. "Smash those dolls for me!"

He forgot the assault, the time, the necessary orders, entirely in the present, gripped once again by lyrical verity, his mind reeling from the collision of worlds.

Ménières' voice shook him. "It's very beautiful, though, Claude. You're scorning the genius of an extinct era. You're killing art!"

Very pale, Ménières stood up, almost revolted. Claude turned round; their blazing eyes met.

"Art! Oh, we don't care about that, in the end, Ménières!" the master cried. "It gets in the way of everything: I hate it, do you hear! It's the artificial, the absurd, one more dirty religion that degrades humans. Their art, in the blood and under the ax, is like them, like everything that comes from them! You can pick up the fragments for our museums, if anything remains and it amuses you. But break those faces of the gods first! Their art, that servility to their fetishes! We'll make one more beautiful when we're rid of theirs: a human art, a true art! Their art! Oh, no pity, no more for the beings as for these forms of error! It's lies and obscurantism that I'm snuffing out here in the presence of sixty centuries. Yes, yes, break!" he cried to the soldiers.

"You're doing as they do!" said Ménières. "Mohammed at Saint Sophia—and to come so far, for that! You're not new, you're imitating. As barbaric as the rest, definitely!"

"Well, yes, let's be Barbarians, as you wish. Barbarians—so be it; you'll understand later, you who were an artist yesterday!" Claude Laigle replied, bursting into nervous laughter. "Art! Are you going to try to stop me with that word? Only the Idea counts here! Obey!"

"I said so," Ménières riposted...

His voice was cut off by the din of an explosion. Side by side they were thrown out of the enclosure in a whirlwind of men, shouting irritated phrases without being able to make themselves heard.

Outside, a flood of cavalry separated them. The confusion was insane, the assault flooding back from the center toward the east of the city, Delhi entire resplendent with terror. The standards of the fifth column were visible in the avenues; the conjunction had taken place, the quintuple star of the European army entangling its branches. The blast of the fusillade arrived from all sides simultaneously.

Claude Laigle, in the midst of the general staff, climbed up on to a terrace, drunk with the unfurling of the battle, which descended all the way to the river. Obscure emplacements indicated a surcease in the combat; from the southern districts luminous signals sprang announcing the victory. The blue lights of aerostats radiant in the black sky, and the direction of the cannonade was clear. There was no more fighting except in the center and the west; the holy city was palpitating in the final spasms of its death throes.

"Vive l'Occident!" cried the crowd.

"Vive l'Anarchie!" replied Claude, dazedly.

Barbarians! He thought, angrily repeating Ménières' word. *Barbarians, to kill barbarity! He doesn't understand any more, and doesn't understand because of art, as the others don't understand because of science! Anyway, we shall see...*

He saw the diaphanous light again, the phantom of the Adventure, smiling in a dawn of linked verities, in the open sky above the world, the mystical obsession floating. He smiled, sensing the indefatigable and devouring genius of a leader of armies, at the divinatory gesture. His soul dilated in extraordinary abstract wellbeing, and he shivered.

To live this is to be! Is it credible?

No man or god had ever been so great, and as the word *die* passed through his mind with the parabola of a bomb flying before his eyes, Claude Laigle straightened up.

I shall not die! he said to himself.

The sentiment of that seemed to him to be insignificant, in any case, his body and his fear annulling it, cerebral intoxication stiffening his nerves above the horror. He searched with his eyes for Ménières, in order to speak to him again, but could no longer see him. It was the glabrous face of General de Trénan that appeared.

The god of shells! thought Claude, and he ran toward the bearer of present Verity to embrace him fervently.

"Yes, yes, it's done—the beast is dead!" said the commander-in-chief. Behind him, a battery escort undulated at the gallop; the pale and blood-stained artillerymen saluting with their sabers, the guns and ammunition-trucks rumbling; and an immense cavalcade was seen racing from along central avenues at the gesture of the pale hand agitated outside the golden sleeve. The man with the ivory head was leading his hordes thundering, with pride, the Angel of Dynamism, with him, toward the old world.

"The assault has succeeded," he said. "You're the master; the living force is neutralized; China will sleep for centuries more beyond the Altaï, metaphysical and mental Europe is yours, Claude Laigle."

The general staff looked at the two men mutely; in spite of their inexorable soul they were trembling with joy; the moment was decisive in the history of human energy, and their eyes expressed an emotion so rare that the generals lowered theirs.

The cannonade over the river ceased. The searchlights of the aerostats indicated that the outlying districts were conquered. In the gardens of the north of the city, the last defenders were being crushed; three of the five columns were returning to the center. Delhi was in the hands of the Civilized.

General de Trénan took the dictator to one side. "I've contained the army," he said. "Mathematical war is admirably passive. It would never have been thus in the past, but the enervation is too great. It's necessary to let the men's nerves relax; these silent troops surpass the human. I ask for my soldiers a feast of blood, the ancient drunkenness of evenings of victory, atrocious and lyric drunkenness, as you say, Master. Those thousands of living beings have been perfect machines; let them live instinctively for one night. You understand my thinking: it's necessary that the animal feeds occasionally."

Claude Laigle acquiesced with a sign. Ménières' recent remark went through his mind: "Barbarians, like the rest!" He smiled bitterly, effaced the ironic memory of a surge of prideful will, and waited...

The light of burning pagodas illuminated the army. Suddenly, the file of artillery became enormous, from the height of the streets all the way to the Ganges. The heat of the fires and the battle excited the delirium of the blood, the age-old soul of triumphs smoldered. The cannons rolled, the compact divisions lining up at a gallop toward the northern encampments, as Claude Laigle sat down, exhausted, on a balcony spared by the bombs, his gaze passing into a dream.

Ammunition trucks filled the streets, brushing the walls, and on them and the gun-carriages, lugubriously illuminated by torches brandished by human hands, naked bodies were tied, tossed about by the jolts of the course. Seized from apartments in houses whose doors had been forced, stolen from the harems and palaces of the old city, howling women were writhing under the cords, their arms twisted above their heads and their legs tied to the gun-carriages, showing their white abdomens, their obscene sexes, their breasts violent amid the floods of hair or shining with jewels. Jets of blood spurted over them when the wheels crushed heaps of corpses, a red mud debasing that white flesh, above which the faces of men sniggered.

The teams of horses were covered with precious cloths piled up and tied; the squadrons were in a hurry, ferrying that lust and that theft, the nostrils of the harassed horses were sneezing fire and drool on the terrified faces of the captives. The infantrymen ranged against the walls, brushed by the rapid wheels, extended their hands toward the women, feeling flesh at hazard while laughing. The interminable gallop of the artillery units drew them into the dark night, the light of the illuminated porticos and domes casting on the steel, the manes, the loins of the women and the bestial faces of the men a terrible alternation of darkness and gold.

That passed like a great dream of horror, and Claude Laigle dreamed dazedly of the sack of Carthage, the burning of Agrigente, the convulsions of ancient capitals, the faces of Scipio's and Titus' legionnaires, the beautiful evenings of Attila and Genseric, the burning of Constantinople, the lusts of the cavaliers of Timur and the Amurats, the frightful magic of Latin, Persian, Tartar or Mohammedan conquests reverberating in the ancient world, from the deserts to the mountains to the oceans, from Syria to Gaul and Rome to Scythia, its tumult splendid with flowers, flesh, metal, thunder and blood.

Claude Laigle had an intuition of the eternal recommencement, of primordial sentiments, of the brutal beauty of instinct suppressing time and details, returning everything to simplicity. The nausea was extinguished within him beneath ideological joy. Matter was nothing, decidedly; forms were always similar; only the Idea...

Yes, he said to himself, *they're like the others, but it's necessary, in making use of them for something else, to make with that human dough another bread of life, that's everything. No need to change them, even if that were possible; only to understand them, and do with them and I wish. And what is it that I wish? That which hasn't yet been tried, to extract even from this beauty...*

Above the sprawling and sobbing women, bare flesh and sabers, the diaphanous specter rose again, floating, the white idea of an unaccustomed heaven hid everything, and the dictator was absorbed in the deafening jolting of the squadrons.

The arriving booty passed, and after it appeared the carts in which strange prey was piled: statues, fabulous or obscure faces, the violation of a population of ruined gods, the ferocious idols of Juggernaut, the figures of man-eaters and devourers of fire, the mysterious deities of fatalism and death; the entire heritage of contemplative Hindustan summoning the great offended shades of Rama and Sita, the singular allegories of fecundity and oblivion, coupled in derisory fashion in the pillage, dragged and knocked down on the bank of the primitive holy river before the rubble of the glory of princes; a long lamentable file of assassinated beliefs passing before the gaze of the new Europe. The distant cannon, at intervals, underlined their desperate march.

And after that came the processions of prisoners, the desolation of wounds, the sumptuous and ragged rajahs, the naked thin stranglers, the sepoys brutalized by rage and fear, pushed toward the stakes of the fusillade, amid the gunfire of platoons heard in the nearby streets. The cavalry were leading them; they ran, hastened by the breasts of the horses, all of them—fakirs, soldiers, insurgents— mocked by the mob of Parsee and Mahrattas adherent to the European cause.

The Yellows followed, a compact host painting in front of Claude Laigle, raising hooded and prominent faces amid the bare cloth. For two hours they passed by. All of Asia seemed to be dying that night!

In the distance, the clamors of the soldiers could be heard, resting in drunkenness and rape, laboring with bare arms in female flesh and the stolen objects, as in the blood and fire before. Suddenly, a rumor spread, wounded Europeans arrived from all directions; the odor of field hospitals gripped Claude to the point of frightening him, the exaltation of victory having faded. A group of cavaliers appeared, in disorder, surrounding a litter, which was pushed into the middle of the general staff. Exclamations sprang forth, heads turned toward the dictator, officers interposed themselves.

Claude Laigle advanced to look.

On muddy straw and carpets, braided cadavers lay: generals. And in the middle of them, Claude Laigle saw a head of golden hair protruding from a roll of cloth.

Ménières!

He had been killed with the others, an hour before, in the east, when an exploding mine had hollowed out the ground beneath an attack column.

The master's hands parted the cloth; the head vacillated and rolled in a sinister fashion; it was no longer securely bound to the body. A mass of burned flesh, filthy, slashed by splinters of stone, bristling with shards of beams, appeared in the dirty serge like a repugnant item of butchery. Blood clots were drying on the shapeless mass. Only the head had not been afflicted; the golden hair surrounded it; the pale lips were closed; the eyes devoid of thought, remained vitreous.

He didn't believe in the work of life, Claude Laigle said to himself, pensively. *He didn't believe. He thought we were barbarians, like the others. Not to have talked to him about that again—what fatality! However, however, he was wrong, he would have understood... He was wrong?*

He raised his head and looked at the impassive face of General de Trénan, the weapons, the fire, the blood—and a strange mist covered his eyes: the white Idea vacillated with a disenchanted smile in his soul, and he was troubled. Doubt in the adventure descended from the sky...

He sensed that his anxiety was visible, anticipated the curious eyes of the commander-in-chief, and shivered.

"I loved him," he said gesturing toward Ménières' cadaver.

He was lying; was not trembling because of that. The certainty of destiny and he beauty of the Forces escaped him, for the first time.

His heart sank.

The army band suddenly burst forth; the triumphant harmonies of *Lohengrin* floated over the blood, and the tottering will of Claude Laigle plunged into the thunder of the orchestra.

PART TWO
THE OBSESSION

VII. The Crisis

For two months, a torpid soul vegetated in Claude Laigle.

Had the white Idea touched him that evening with a bloodstained finger? A kind of paralysis gripped him. Transported by the campaign, he lived almost unconsciously, in the midst of his lieutenants, developing the Adventure. Their multiples cares were employed without him paying any heed to them.

Across the world a confused murmur rose up, the organic stirring of an immense stupor, quivering in the skeleton of mountains, the veins of rivers, the structure of plains and seas. The weapon plunged into the primitive heart of races vibrated from pole to pole; then the torpor stagnated. It seemed that humankind, frightened of itself, no longer dared trouble the silence of the murder.

Delhi bled disastrously in the middle of India, like a beast forced from its lair that the armies had torn apart. The sharing of the flesh had not taken place visibly; calm was almost established.

The great war was over, the final encounters in Nepal and Assam made no noise, and the joy of Europe was too distant. No more was heard about Russian action in northern China; an irremediable silence reigned beyond the Himalaya. The news from the Yellow seas was bleak, confirming the blockade, preventative maneuvers, slow and devoid of beauty, useful but monotonous measures.

The sentiment of a universal weariness floated over armaments and peoples, and above all, an uncertainty appeared. No one yet took account of what had just become the extraordinary and capital fact in the evolution of the Old World. The malaise of relaxation thus extended for a long time before the organization of the conquest was settled. People watched.

Claude's malady coincided with the duration of that indefinable state; not because it was an obstacle to the progress of the Europeans, but it seemed that it symbolized clearly the general alternative. The collapse had been too devastating, and in the same way that the master's brain had almost given way under the pressure of exacerbated will, so the nervous tension of humankind turned abruptly to inertia now that the things had been accomplished. In spite of everything, however, the immense consequences of the stiffening of the West against the East were perceived, one by one.

Asiatic power had been definitively cut in two. The great swamps of yellow beings beyond Altaï and Annam were about to fall back into mental obscurity before having had time to emerge from it. Perhaps for centuries, the vital spark was extinct there; ideas and passwords did not cross the mountains, the empire of somnolence bogged its hordes down in poverty and primitive unconsciousness; that mass of human substance would not take any direction or form.

Japanese supremacy was ruined, two hundred years of brilliantly energetic politics wiped out beneath the crush of Occidental shells. Surrounded by the Confederate fleets, Nippon, exhausted of money and blood, could no longer act or spread out on the yellow continent. India was tightly gripped, the rajahs were dissociated, the junction of their forces with those of Japan no longer existed, and in accordance with General de Trénan's plans. An insurmountable barrier was about to be established in Indo-China and Burma.

The Tokyo cabinet no longer had any armies; the last, which had carried out the campaign in the Deccan, had been obliged to retreat after the taking of Delhi, to break up and fall back to the Ganges. It was learned, when Calcutta was reconquered, that the army in question had been almost completely annihilated, and the European cruisers in the vicinity of Singapore and the isles of Sunda closed the route forever to the debris of the Far-Eastern squadrons. The rivalries of the Burmese princes and the Japanese generals did the rest; the success was unhoped for, the cables and the supply lines brought the acclamations of reassured crowds from Paris, London, Berlin, Vienna and Rome.

The unification of Anarchism was consecrated, the sociological world was free to fortify itself internally; dynamic expansion had found its route. At the same time, the repair began of the coalition's losses.

They were grave. The invasion of one world by the other had not taken place without an atrocious shock; the framework of Europe was cracked; the losses of money and blood were revealed to be enormous. But the disemboweling of the adversary was total and irreparable; it seemed that the colossus of the North, tottering itself, was holding out in its clenched fists the sumptuously dislocated cadaver of Asia and lifting it up painfully before breaking its back definitively and laying it out beneath its impassive sky alongside its mountains and its seas. With one hand it was holding Japan by the throat, surrounded by its ironclad fleets, and with the other it had grabbed the belt of India, and within the span of that frightful embrace, that he magnificent body had finished gasping.

The colossus was able to rest, and needed it. Those twenty epic months had nevertheless extracted for Europe the major part of its vital strength. The conscription of men had been excessive, the displacement of finances had almost overturned the markets; everything had truly been wagered against everything, with nothing held back. International organization had saved everything; no alliance in the diplomatic fashion of old could have sustained a similar effort. The Confederation had shown an admirable cohesion; maintained and indoctrinated by Dessort, the industrial masses had poured toward Suez and the Persian Gulf inexhaustible accumulations of food and weapons, without hesitating over a sacrifice, genuinely stiffened by the evidence of an abstract principle.

Médion, finally arriving, depicted for Claude Laigle the enthusiasms of the North and the Occident. The word of beauty had germinated back there, the peoples had understood the Adventure. Through the Minister's coldly lucid formulae, the convalescent Claude glimpsed intellectual landscapes that reanimated him. How great the return would be: not the trumpeted grandeur of military triumphs and illuminations, but the certainty of an ideological future finally illuminated by the virgin fire of an intellectual responsibility, a modern consciousness simply raised!

The odor of blood faded in the master's soul. He looked at Médion hopefully, completing his dry phrases with an interior lyrical exaltation, interrogating him less about facts than about ideas, scrutinizing him less with his words than with his eyes, searching the mineral irises for the European expression almost forgotten during the twenty months of Asiatic sojourn. That face, as rigid and geometrical as the thought that inhabited it, almost pleased Claude; he rediscovered therein a certainty, an order, after the delirium of sun and carnage in which his great voluptuous soul had been maddened for some time.

Ménières face was erased from his languid memory; he no longer saw it vacillating above the infamous serge putrid with red mud, among the golden hair; he sought in vain to remember is expression of disavowal and anger during their quarrel in the great pagoda. The artist's denial was extinguished beneath the din of victory. "Barbarians like the rest!" Ménières' last words seemed to Claude less violent, distant and incomprehensible.

There was an element of truth in it...yes undoubtedly, an element...but he went astray. What a pity that he died! He died for not having believed...now he'd see, he'd understand...

For slow days, among the gardens and the white minarets, in the unconscious enchantment of the light of Asia, Claude Laigle's fever was calmed by the precise discourse of Médion. He almost liked him, and the terrible logician, as if he had understood the master's crisis, seemed to incline toward him, to invent a kind of affection, a careful persuasion, a concession of his exactitude to the unquiet lyricism of the leader of peoples. By an effort of his dry intellect, did Médion admit that Claude's romanticism was an organic necessity?

Singular currents of the soul were established between the two men; Claude gradually recovered his strength, became anxious about details, interested in the economic and financial labor that would complete the work.

The news received from General de Trénan confirmed that renaissance. The commander-in-chief, departed for the South, indefatigable in perfecting the mission of his artillery, announced the pacification of provinces. It was known that the squadrons were cruising without encountering adversaries; the rumble of cannons was decidedly vanishing from the midst of humanity, the effort was becoming mental.

I'm still here, Claude said to himself. *It's now that it's necessary to stay here, now that it's necessary to create.*

He understood that the essential was now to be accomplished after the necessary, listened internally to the noise of his vitality, and felt strong.

To stay here, to finish everything, and after that and only then, to go home and resume working, he thought. *Manipulate the brute, organic matter here, and then triturate the thinking matter back there. I'm still young; I can do it; I'll only be able to prepare, but now is one of those hours when the main thing is to prepare.*

The vision of a Europe developed on his givens, impulsive with regard o his future action, shivering like a child in the depths of his flesh, the eternal pride of designates raised him up again.

How much there is to do! It's necessary...

His convalescence was thus completed by surges of impatience life. The gardens were opulent in fruit and flowers, everything was weighed down by fecundity and sap; the vital example was universal. In the sunlight, Claude Laigle saw his blue shadow trailing behind him, small and bizarre, and smiling; thus his memory would trail behind over the thinking world, but it would be an immense metal shadow, a true shade, a haunting of consciousness, a visitor of souls. Would that shadow be the diaphanous sister of the white Idea, linking his truths with the open sky of adventure?

He saw it again, dreamed it, slowly, with a sentimental enjoyment, a sweet sentiment of mystical espousal leading his glory and his energy to the eternal altar of human destiny. Thus he was cured, amid the efflorescences of parks, and close to him, without impatience, Médion waited, with his firm and insensible soul.

The descent of the Ganges was delightful for Claude. In the vicinity of Benares, the affirmation of his compromised energy was completed, in sensations of beauty.

The voyage proceeded under triumphant blue skies, between the giant banks ornamented with white temples, sometimes disemboweled; the traces of the war remained. The cries of soldiers, from the top of ruins, saluted Claude Laigle; the dusks were gripping in their majesty, the grandeur barbaric; ancient ostentations were evoked in the landscape and the firmament. Within him the dictator bore modern grandeur, the abstract ostentation of the master spirit: the comparison was pleasing.

He disdained the voluptuous beauty of sites, was scornful of the confines of Hindu empires. Convoys he encountered impassioned him; they were dragging away the debris of the heritage of fatalistic arts—steles, statues, stolen gods—carrying them to European steamships to relate in the museums of the Occident the further collapse of a race, to put their gilt to sleep under the dust of time, next to the dusts of Assyria and Egypt. The white man reigned.

The arrival of Dessort changed everything. He came to take account of the recent organization of the conquest, the task of moral decomposition being complete in all the provinces, due to his cares, and again Claude was gripped by the awkward impression he had experienced after the Battle of Lahore. The socialisator calculated coldly, in accordance with an ensemble of psychological laws, the decline of humanity; his immense and singular endeavor acted from the north to the south, exciting the Indian princes against one another, dissolving the fermentations of the people with the acidity of a politics of hypocrisy and concessions, troubling the crowds, paralyzing communications, flattering sects, creating everywhere a vicious mental respiration that anemiated the soul of the great peninsula.

There was, beneath the military cataclysm burning cities, a slow and progressive fissure through which that soul was escaping into the depths of the earth, and Dessort, an evil workman in the shadows, in the cellars of the magnificent collapsed palaces, was enlarging that insupportable rift. The thought of India was broken under the ground as the skull of a man struck on the head is sometimes fractured beneath the intact skin. Claude sensed that singular swarming, that work of undermining, in the cities through which he passed and he was horrified, although accepting it.

Dessort's face frightened him; clear, with its sharp contours, the caesarian head with the persuasive years appeared immutable; the long, then, feminine smile of the socialisator had not changed. His administrative genius was enunciated in harmoniously simple phrases. While he was explaining his plans, Claude listened to him, almost seduced by the charm, the famous charm that had once coagulated the massed workers of internationalism. It really was the same method, applied to human matter in effervescence, the eloquent insinuation, the speech adapted with admirable hypocrisy to the instinct of crowds. And if Claude Laigle turned to Médion, the impression was similar—and if he thought about the active force of old General de Trénan, if he reread his messages, he found one again the same systematic impassivity.

Those three individuals really were the regulators of a world: a universe of chemistry, socialization and organized murder; their three ideals were very modern, inaccessible to any sentimentalism, noble or puerile. Between the three of them, Claude divined that he was quite alone, sensing that they were strong and strict, strangers to him, excusive and marvelously contrived. For them, there was neither morality or amorality, no sensitive datum existed; everything was nothing but continuities, polarizations, directions, antinomies, balances of forces, energies, currents, associations, amplitudes and categories. Those names replaced the ancient names of the affections of the soul; they were the names of future virtues. Admirable moderns, odious people!

Bitterly, Claude thought about his speech at the declaration of war, his extraordinary flight toward a directive metaphysics of races, and he perceived how unrealizable that prophecy still was. He had been allowed to say it and he understood why. In the eyes of those men, he had only agitated great phantoms before the legates; but those men were too intelligent not to understand how a Head of State, a responsible word-bearer, had to make use of phantoms in order to give a relief to public decisions.

A hundred years before, the scientists had shrugged their shoulders, shown their public scorn for those hollow images; at present, truly developed in their concept of modernism, Dessort, Médion and Trénan, sociologists of the first order, admitted in their "balance of forces" the value of "verbal illusionism," and were content to make it a scientific element, a force auxiliary to their exact ideal. They made use of Claude and his decorative speech; they made use of his prestigious power. He represented in their calculations the love of crowds, an element they needed for the task that they did not disclose.

And Claude Laigle sensed them around him, the ardent constructors of an epoch to come, obedient to obscure ethnic laws, yielding to his will and nevertheless drawing him; as minuscule insects crushed by a great blade of grass move beneath it, dragging it to their lair while seeming to submit to it; those men were working without dreaming, silently edifying around him the terrible constructions that only the obstinacy of subordinates, the anonymous army of men in the background, can lead to a successful conclusion, when the most imperious genius is exhausted therein. In India, as in Europe, they were continuing to be themselves, to apply their systems on a larger scale, to satisfy their respective manias.

Dessort, with a keen comprehension, created clubs everywhere, gave substance to the demands of coolies, tolerated democracy, divided everything into groups, used the sects against one another, enervating everything by clemency and half-measures, talked to populations "for their own good," won them over to a communist ideal while taking account of their heredity.

Médion acted upon the Parsees as on the class of university malcontents in Europe. He assembled around himself those intelligent and wily individuals, graduates of Bombay or Calcutta scorned by the castes and armed against them by modern method and knowledge, and made them into the natural leaders of Anarchism in Hindustan.

And thus everything was about to recommence, on the model of the Occidental Confederation, and that was good; it was only for that reason that Claude had wanted the war, and everything was normal and logical. And yet, deep within him, an indistinct, confused, almost organic distaste was beginning to arise: an infinite and unformulated disavowal of his *double* regarding the intervention in the extraordinary heroism of the Adventure of the obstinate force of banality, of utilitarianism, the planned and the ordinary.

Those systems transported to other climes, that clockwork cerebration, dismantled and reassembled like naval machine-guns and campaign telegraphs, that impassive transposition of methods into the collapse of an age-old fatality, made Clause Laigle feel slightly sick. He was subject to the crisis of the man of war and clamor brought back to a job as a book-keeper; the insipidity of the useful disturbed him.

By acquired habit he occupied himself with details and arrangements, presided over meetings, straightened out the surprising entanglement of the politics of conquest, and muffled the profound and embryonic rumor that was had been born within him, but his soul had been touched; a reaction to the effort was beginning, and he had to admit that to himself regardless.

Am I, then, above all the familiar, the lover of Forces? he asked himself, on certain evenings. *Am I not, as much as I was before the man of the Idea? The Idea is slow to separate out; all that labor, all those categories and formalities veil it; plunging in the sword is seductive and clear, drawing it out again is less interesting, it's true, but nevertheless, nevertheless, the Idea exists. It was to arrive at this gray period that I constructed the whole of the red period passionately; now the intermediaries are here, that's the hardest phase to pass through for people of my kind. But I have faith; it's necessary...*

He evoked the unreal face, the white Adventure reeling off its future promises in the metaphysical sky. In spite of everything he thought of it like those who maintain in amity a woman they have possessed, and claim no longer to love, and tranquilly see someone else cherish her: something very beautiful and untrue intervened, he no longer kissed the diaphanous form on the lips, and shivered to admit it to himself.

The period was difficult, almost terrible. He no longer loved the Adventure as much; it no longer appeared to him entirely in the future, desirable; it was partly realized, he was living it. The sovereign Idea of his existence was already partly detached from him, misted by reality, extracted from his brain and his dreams by time. He was living it, but would he be living it much longer?

The hypothesis, taking on substance, was beginning no longer to belong to him; other men were taking possession of it, burrowing into it like termites. He still loved it, but it was beginning no longer to love him, like a child who, growing up, goes his own way, separately, trying the arms of will that have been given to him—and he sensed that he was going to have to resign himself to no longer loving the Adventure exclusively and jealously, although could not see anything else as yet that he could love, nothing great enough, and in any case, it would not be the same thing. Thus, those who detach themselves from a rare woman cannot imagine that a similar power can ever arise in their life.

And he was alone, the sole passionate individual among the comprehensive individuals who could, even if the Adventure had not existed, employ their energy and their systems to some other construction. For the first time, the crushing majesty of the Oriental sky, instead of being a harmonious decor for Claude's proud will, oppressed him like a mute menace. Was the counsel of fatalism born of those colossal landscapes the revenge of India on the violator of its destiny?

Does this land still conceal sorceries that impress me regardless—or am I growing old, or missing the air of Europe?

In his mind those questions came together, and to all three he responded negatively; there was, however, a element of verity in all three, and he dared not ask himself the fourth question, the real one: is modernism truly unassailable?

He skirted that without formulating it; his animal being sensed that it was deadly; in the depths of his being, the very cells protested darkly against that mortal seed.

He thought he was fatigued, avoided returning to those things. *I'm over-complicating*, he said to himself.

Perhaps, however, he was simply beginning to see.

The crisis developed further. Everything aided it. The aspect of scientific modernity, under that admirable sky and in the hectic lushness of overheated nature, definitely repelled Claude Laigle. The artifice of practical reason revolted his dreams. The establishment of fiscal regimes and confederative modes appeared to him to be derisory in its slowness.

An event! Something...! He could almost have wished for a revolt, the disembarkation of a Japanese army. Risings occurred, but were too easily repressed. There were serious anxieties for a week, because of a retaliatory offensive by the rajahs of Kashmir, threatening to cut off the route to a European division that had imprudently advanced too rapidly. Claude Laigle was regripped by passion for the Idea—but the news of the victory arrived almost at the same time as that of the trouble, and everything fell back into calm.

The forces were decidedly complicit, the repercussion set in, and after having struggled joyfully against events, he had to struggle coldly against the lack of events, against the quotidian, against the trivial...

The identity of methods and formulae depressed Claude, and filled him with remorse against himself.

Do I no longer want the same things, then? What am I complaining about? Everything is in conformity with my aims, and yet I'm discontented. I want something else...what? It's childishness, perhaps fatigue. How terrible it is to pass through neutral periods! I've supported others, though...

This one did not end. Everyone around the dictator seemed to consider it not as neutral but as definitive; they had conquered, they were organizing, incorporating, annexing: a perfectly natural period, the evident corollary to a great effort.

Claude attempted a few insinuations on the subject to Médion and Dessort; they did not even notice them. Médion was absorbed in his doctrines of scientific diffusion, creating faculties and courses, choosing in the Hindu mind the assimilative fractions and groups them together. Dessort was systematizing labor, talking about disciplining the masses "for their own benefit." Their own benefit! The face with the persuasive eyes and then thin and feminine smile was troubling in endlessly repeating that formula, in which Claude sensed an unfathomable irony.

Around those men a legion of lieutenants strove to second them, all intelligences avid to exercise their mechanism, beginning to triturate this new substance like Europeans substance, butchering the immense cadaver, commencing the autopsy after the murder. Everyone was occupied with the Orientals. That led Claude to take an interest too, to see at close range what they might be.

Fundamentally, he had never formed a very serious psychological idea of them, he had only envisaged them collectively as enemy powers. His hatred had denied them any moral existence outside fatalism and contemplation—which is to say, two notions irrespirable in the Europe of his dreams. In repose and inaction, however, he had the time to admit that that analysis, sufficient to lead the war, became absolutely superficial in the period that was now inaugurated.

His lieutenants seemed to have known that far longer than him. What struck him was that they did not appear to detest the Orient, as he did. One might have thought that they glimpsed the possibility of linking themselves to it, of reaching an understanding with the subjugated peoples. Were not crowds and their laws identical in all climes? The hatred had faded away; it had only lasted as long as the war, while the "yellow peril" existed. Now affinities seemed to be born; people were less occupied with sterilizing Oriental military force and preventing its offensive return permanently than with trying to insinuate occidental principles there. By virtue of a singular attraction, the two parts of the old world, violently divided, appeared to be seeking to join up again.

Claude's thoughts were abandoned. Who was in the right, his ministers or him? Was it the attractive baseness of masses that was active in that, or a law of human alliance higher than hatred? He did not know what to think, and doubted.

Certain facts, in the countless reports that were submitted to him, astonished him. Unexpected links definitely attached the Oriental world to his own. Japanese prisoners were affiliated to freemasonry; it was observed with surprise that the field hospitals of the Yellow army belonged to the society of Geneva; armbands with white crosses were found on cadavers.

A hundred facts of that sort accumulated; something that was almost a comedy took form: a cold comedy of Japanese in suits, mandarins using telephones; the comedy of anachronism becoming an ethnological verity. Claude Laigle perceived that they were ready to reach an understanding with his ministers, having been unable to devour Europe: modernism had identified the contraries, industrial leveling was the master, transportable methods had penetrated everywhere, and the conception he had formed of Orientals had, after all been very romantic and behind the times. Metaphysics and his lyricism had made him see falsely in the detail.

He became impatient. *Oh, let the others occupy themselves with the detail; they're excellent for that*, he said to himself. *I'm alone in synthesizing, in dreaming the moral aspect. I'll make use of their fragmentary remarks to construct my abstract edifice.*

He relived the epoch of extreme socialism in which Anarchism had been elaborated in Europe fifteen years before. *It's a malady, the leveling*, he thought. *It's good for the formation of active forces; afterwards, the notion of the superior individual is detached by disgust; it's necessary to endure that confrontation with detail first. It will recommence here as it did back there. Fundamentally, is it always the same thing? But if the modification of souls isn't accentuated, is it worth the trouble of disturbing ourselves so much? It will be necessary, if this turns out like that, for me to intervene. Médion, Dessort and Trénan seem to believe that we've simply warded off a material danger; that's only half the Adventure, and I'm at least as committed to the second half!*

In spite of everything, the Orient attracted him. To have something to do, in order not to return to Europe to occupy himself solely with European affairs, but to leave mental traces after the traces of the war—that new concern gripped him without him being aware of it. Once he had thought that, once the yellow peril was averted, it would not matter to him what the vanquished would think; now that worried him and amused him; conquering avidity caused him to emerge from the frontiers of his race.

Immense and torpid China no longer occupied him; he still thought of it as a repulsive swamp, far in retreat from life; but Japan and the new Hindustan, the Parsees, the curious elements...perhaps there was something to be made of all that. He did not see that his initial conception, brutal and unjust but clear, was beginning to be falsified in the dangerous solicitations of inaction, and that psychological interest was breaking it down.

The pacification decidedly accentuating, Claude Laigle resolved to confront the unexpected question that had come to his mind, and he departed through the provinces. He went northwards from Benares, relived the horror of Cawnpore and it well full of stranglers, reached Lucknow avoided Delhi, went along the frontiers of Rajputan and the deserts, and reached Lahore, studying, interrogating, and making his hypotheses more precise.

In Lahore, Médion, who had gone with him, parted company in order to rejoin the Indus. Claude stayed in the Punjab with an army, determined to fathom the soul of the mysterious region. Weeks went by in the sumptuousness and enchantment of the landscapes.

The extraordinary beauty of India, sank like a fainting woman into the depths of Claude Laigle's heart; in spite of everything the beauty of India gripped him, an irresistible sensuality born of the soil, and Claude finally began to glimpse how that sensuality, that annulment of thought before love, might, in alliance with the spirit of contemplation born of peace, create the fatalistic mysticism that, in Europe, had irritated his energy so madly.

The hatred of the soil united in him with the hatred of the sons it bore, but it was no longer a hatred founded on antipathy and ethical theories; he no longer found that way of life repugnant; he sensed that it was dangerous, but complete and appreciable in itself, no longer inferior to the scientific way of life of occidental modernism but juxtaposed, parallel and, in sum, equally legitimate. He already admitted that the danger had a right to exist. He no longer had within him the sudden start of the civilized man warding off, with a direct strike, the abject offensive of the uncultured, but the rational envisaging of a different race. The struggle became abstract, one mentality against another.

The enemy rose in Claude's esteem. He understood now that the remarkable individuals among the enemy were not, as he had once lightly assumed, those who had adopted methods from Europe, but those who, obscurely and tenaciously, conserved the primitive soul.

Well, so much the better; one can reason with them as equals. If I had believed them equal during the war, I might have weakened; now, it's worth the trouble to think about it. I no longer hate them in the same fashion. They don't disgust me; they impassion me.

He did not admit that they had already conquered him a little, by virtue of the very fact that the desire to conquer them intellectually had taken the place of his original desire to kill them...

Claude Laigle quit Lahore to visit Kashmir, the sources of the Indus and the Hindu Kush. He had decided to go back to the ultimate origins of the white races. Everything was in order; the latest correspondence determined him to devote six months to the ethnological investigation that he wanted to complete before returning to Europe.

Already, for a year, he had heard talk of vast mystical communities that had been established in the far North, toward the plateau of Pamir. Information regarding them was vague, even the indigenes knew almost nothing about them. Semi-legendary rumors circulated on the subject of those citadels of fatalism, buried in gardens in the hollows of the mountains. Prophecies were propagated; only widely-spaced pilgrimages brought news of a life mingled with strange oracles, in the retirement of those sacred convents.

Claude's instinct quivered within him; from those mountains and those cells perhaps descended, like spiritual rivers, the terrible contemplative ferments spread throughout Hindustan. It was there that he had to go; he signified his desire. At the head of the Punjab divisions he headed toward that region. Couriers spread the announcement of the European intrusion, and India experienced a secret frisson.

At Peshawar, the dictator, centralizing the forces, awaited a deputation of communities. The negotiations concluded amiably, as he desired; women appeared, bringing on behalf of the convents the acceptance of the European visit. Their cortege arrived in the camp; the master received them in a little wood. They came accompanied by servants, but without equals. Their vast agglomerations had become autonomous fifty years before; the colleges of fakirs did not meddle therein; and the meditative power of women in coalition radiated a singular mental clarity from the depths of their retreat. Claude Laigle gradually formed an obscure and great idea, sensing there an axiomatic truth, an unknown role.

One woman led all the others, a mystical empress, of abstract and vast power, about whom Claude Laigle knew almost nothing except for her Parsee origin and her entirely European origin. Mrs. Freany Teema had been, for many years the astonishment and admiration of the university of Calcutta, having traveled in Europe and then, in the era of the expulsion of the English, retired into the mountains. An immense occult influence was attributed to her in the organization of Hindu feminism. Silence had apparently fallen over her. It was known that, abandoning all the prerogatives of modernism, as if touched by an indefinable resolution, she had renounced showing herself in the peninsula, cultivated secret studies, and even abdicated her family name, living in the mystical communities under the name of Erodia.

Interested, Claude awaited that enemy priestess.

She was the last to appear. He was astonished, having anticipated something different. Her black robe made her indistinctly Oriental and modern; tall, with an energetic, passionate and weary visage, she opened large moist and bright eyes. The extension of feline pupils and the undulation of her hips signaled exoticism more specifically; a noble secret force emanated from her.

Salome grown old, Claude thought.[58] Her forty years spread a spicy and strict prestige.

They looked at one another, immediately alone among the ceremonials. Claude was not afraid, and was not harsh. The first exchange of glances did not inaugurate anything special. They spoke. She expressed the consent of the communities with hauteur and abandon; he acquiesced. Their two black and sober forms were allied in the radiation of the palms and the azure; they secretly understood one another, and esteemed one another.

"You shall see our sisters," said Erodia. "They have singular thoughts, modes of the soul that you do not know in Europe. Conquest has not shown you everything."

"I sensed that, and that is why I have come to see," said Claude, simply. "I have set down the sword in order to contemplate."

"Yes," Erodia murmured, "yes...an exchange of forces. You have violated the Orient, but as yet, that is not finished. It is necessary that you put down the sword; it will not be of any use to you for what remains to be envisaged..."

"And that is?" Claude replied.

"Oh, I don't know how to put it...exactly. It is...yes...the *virgin Orient*."

Claude eyelids fluttered. He glimpsed, in a flash, the face of Ménières on the evening of the council in Paris, saying: "Perhaps the being you seek is among them." He shivered; she sound of the voice had been identical.

---

[58] This reference emphasizes the analogy between Erodia's adopted name and that of Salome's mother, Herodias, although it seems equally likely that the name's primary significance relates to the same root that produced the English word "erode". Mauclair was fascinated by the character of Salome and her relationship to the myth of the *femme fatale*; one of his several essays on her symbolic figure is reprinted in *Les Clefs d'or*.

Straightening up, he looked Erodia proudly in the face. And the leader of souls suddenly illuminated in her large and luminous pupils a strange landscape of pure fire. Then she lowered the lashes very slowly, a mute promise of the invisible. And with her lashes, Claude's lowered too, and he sensed at that precise moment that, following the curve of their eyelids, he was *redescending* the other slope of the adventure.

VIII. The Cradle

They departed for the sanctuaries of the North.

For a long time they traveled side by side without looking at one another, black and haughty forms meditating dissimilar worlds and enemy beliefs. When they brushed one another the friction of irreconcilable thoughts vibrated between them, and the waited mutely, very calm, savoring the rare voluptuousness of estimating one another as parallel forces. They did not feel, at first, the need to talk.

At the hazard of encampments, Claude Laigle glimpsed Erodia among her women. Her svelte somber silhouette passed back and forth between the tents. In the evenings, she returned to her quarters, beneath the foliage or in the rocks, and no sound arrived from the direction of the Hindu recluses. In the mornings, she appeared on horseback, joined the dictator's escort, and they went on.

The master treated her as an equal; she accepted with a strict and easy simplicity, habituated to living in the European fashion, speaking a very pure French, responding to the salutes of officers with a tranquil elegance. No woman was any more familiar to her than any other, she marched ahead of them all, alone. The caprice of the roads brought her close to Claude Laigle during the marches, or drew them apart; for orders, runners went to one or other of them alternately, the corteges separated out or mingled.

An immense peace descended from the zenith with the heat of the azure. Claude Laigle meditated, and did not know what special thoughts were alive behind the forehead and eyes of Erodia. The soldiers were astonished by her; she galloped in their midst at top speed, with an indifferent flexibility, casting a cold and arrogant stare over the infantry. Litters followed without her reposing thereon; nonchalance was scarcely revealed in the corners of her long eyelids, signed with oriental circles. Claude found her singular and very modern, without saying so to anyone. She was not at all what he had expected, but secretly, he was not surprised; it seemed to him that he had imagined her thus once, obscurely, in indefinable dreams.

They arrived thus is the heart of the mountains, on the extreme slopes of the Himalaya, amid the prodigious accumulation of pink rocks. The exaltation of the natural beauty gripped Claude Laigle. Erodia seemed, as she approached her refuge, to relax her suspicion somewhat and to rediscover her sovereignty. They isolated themselves from the troops, spoke to one another more, and then made definite contact, soul to soul, proudly.

Claude Laigle was impressed by the admirable intellectuality that the tall woman revealed, discovered her logical and lyrical, like himself, perceived treasures of mental refinement, resolved to study the leader of souls before exploring her realm. Since Ibsenian creatures, European women had made a great deal of progress in a hundred years, and Claude Laigle, although having had little contact with them, had glimpsed enough complexity and nobility in them not longer to hold them in systematic and vain scorn. Sociological anarchism had taken very useful root in women and had opened wide the doors of intellectual life to them, while liberating them from their instincts and their unions—but this one surpassed any that Claude had been able to see.

He only perceived the modernism in her; the other face, the Oriental face, was mysterious; Erodia seemed to be reserving it for the terminus of the voyage—but the modern face impassioned Claude Laigle's mind. That intuitive Parsee, sprung from a detested race, fortified in its genius by the reprobation of castes now ruined, truly had surprising gifts, a faculty of scientific comprehension infinitely developed.

She's evidently artificial, like everyone, the dictator said to himself, *but she'd delight Médion! I'll put them at odds when he rejoins us.*

As he was thinking that, smiling, he did not see the long, blue-tinted eyes, the torsions of the indolent and muscular hips in total, the torpid lightning that was Erodia. He saw her beauty poorly, like all those that souls interest first.

He told her about the revolution in Europe, the parliaments blown up in the middle of the capitals in a single night, the defections of armies, the flights of sovereigns, the social masses docile to the information of free consciousness, the intoxication of the triumph of ideas. She had seen some episodes, as an anonymous visitor; she had scented the odor of the new times among the people of the Latin race.

She spoke about her childhood and adolescence of study, her late nights in the laboratories of the University of Calcutta, her theological research in the sacred cities of Hindustan, strange meetings with the fakirs, her revolts of consciousness, her abstract joys taming sensuality, her exile in the hidden country, her initiation into silence and dream. And Claude, in listening to her, found common methods, analogous elaborations of the soul, with a scarcely-dissimulated surprise.

Sometimes, ardent enthusiasms colored the clear voice of the Oriental. *I don't know, after all, whether she would delight Médion*, Claude then objected to himself. *She isn't as dry as he is. Dessort would accept her better*. But immediately, he thought that Dessort's persuasive and ornate eloquence did not have that passionate gravity. The woman decidedly persisted beneath the intellectual, and in a mixture so accurately dosed that the conqueror found an indefinite charm therein.

Erodia was strict, not without languor, but without insistence; she was not seductive, and Claude appreciated that reserve, approaching the mind very closely, without being solicited by the flesh. Otherwise he would have been suspect, as a male. He only savored the charm of pure reason there.

An exchange of forces slowly united them; the esteem grew, they measured one another more deliberately; in the oppressive enormity of the landscape, their humanity increased; the mutual sentiment of active consciousness became more precise before the magnificent inertia of locations. In the evenings, when Erodia went back to the Hindu camp, among her women, Claude Laigle savored, pensively, the magnetism of the nocturnal summer. He scarcely saw the strong face amid the hair with profound reflections, but he heard the grave and musical voice, lent to the lyricism that he loved so much.

That priestess is truly astonishing, he confessed, with a half-smile. And a pleasant disturbance, the joy of finding in those solitudes a soul at the height of his own, froze on his lips the specious and facile reflection by which his irony was about to try to safeguard his superiority as a man. He did not even perceive that that was in play. After the discouraging period of his convalescence, the intellectual voyage delighted him.

I have India by military power, and now I'm visiting my conquest, scrutinizing the living force of the hostile Orient. I'm the master.

That security vivified him; nothing in the landscape disconcerted him any longer. He was about to enter the sanctuaries curiously, but without dread, with an armed mind, ready to experience anything without weakening. The unknown of those populated deserts attracted him without fever; everything was normal.

Reassuring news still reached him from the armies of the Ganges and the Indus. Then they plunged decisively into the escarpments, toward the Hindu Kush, toward Pamir; they were reaching the end of the long journey. Claude and Erodia arrived there almost friends; the leader of souls became more mysteriously serene.

Finally, the first convents appeared. Vast quadrilaterals of white buildings were staged amid palms and fountains, spacious farms and fecund fields announced them. Claude and the army were astonished. The region was reputed to be uncultivated; the maps said nothing about them. Rare explorers had passed through them a long time before; a few had perished there, the sun had drunk their blood and nothing more had been heard of them. Had that blood enabled these white constructions to germinate? It was, rather, the mind of Erodia that had created everything. She seemed to Claude to be suddenly transformed, smiling at an interior certainty.

The Europeans made contact with the luxurious communities. Where they had expected a savage life, masses of huts, and primitive hermitages, stood perfectly grouped edifices in which a spirit of modernity was allied with Orientalism. Series of brightly-illuminated rooms opened on to gardens; outcrops of rock suddenly rounded unmasked others, infinitely. Their organization was logical and simple; the ventilation was good, isolated pavilions served as retreats for the sick, and a comfort inexplicable in these remote regions was revealed. Erodia took the surprised dictator to visit them, anticipating his questions.

"All this is the work of patience," she said, "and the scorned Parsees are rich. Fortunes have accumulated what you see here, by means of immense transports. The work has been slow and secret, the rajahs have had no suspicion of it—they were so uncultivated from that point of view! The precious stones of the heirs and the money of the merchants of our race have aided it, along with the tithes of the poor. For the order that there is here I spent ten years in the laboratories and the hospitals of Calcutta, and I had memories of Europe. We're not so far away from you. I've told you that the Orient was not what you thought—and then again, this is a special Orient." With her eyes half-closed and in a soft voice, she added: "The virgin Orient."

"I thought," Claude said, "that there was nothing here but wilderness."

"There was," she replied, "but fifty years have sufficed, since the English quit India. And there was a long time when everything you see was dreamed, for what you see materially is trivial. Your emigrants to Australia and America have done more astonishing things. But we were not seeking what they were seeking; our goal was dissimilar. It's not what you perceive that is important, but what these installations and locations permit to our dreams. We have stopped in time, my sisters and I, on the road of material progress. In any case, it was necessary."

"Why?" asked Claude. "Was the difficulty too great?"

"No. We could have done more. You can't imagine the tenacity and fidelity of my associates. This land has its unknown routes, its undetectable means. You can imagine, in any case, that it was easy for us to perfect the details of our installation, since we were able to bring it to its present point without being troubled by the rajahs—and the monetary resources could be multiplied tenfold tomorrow, if we desired.

"If it had pleased us to establish ourselves beside the sea, we could have equipped a fleet, surrounded ourselves with torpedoes. I thought about it. It would have been an autonomous and impregnable State. Then I recognized that isolation would defend our white buildings better than cruisers or melinite, and I believe I saw accurately. Do you know that I'm the mistress of more gold than the queen of Oude or the princes of Bundelkund? Not to mention will-power.

"The electrical networks linking your armies to Europe animate crowds less rapidly than the mental magnetism that animates my affiliates. My messages go from here to Travancore or Assam more slowly but more surely than yours. Our cables can't be cut. During all your military operations last summer, I never ceased to receive my information through your sieges, your blockades and your marches. I even had news from Delhi two days before the assault.

"The beings and plants in this land concur with superior wills. With regard to slowness—which, in any case, is relative—it has been sufficient for me to organize my intellectual calculations in a special fashion in order not to be thwarted. Time is only what we imagine it to be, and my curiosities are no more hurried than the mental phenomena that they monitor. What we await is not enclosed in telegrams and cannot be intercepted."

"There is, however, the question of delays that paralyze all action," said Claude.

"All...visible action," Erodia replied. "But there are orders of dynamic acts."

"I understand. Your *influence*. But that's a preparation for action."

"Or a conclusion..."

Astonished, Claude looked at the smiling Erodia.

"That's true," he said. "But given what you've just told me, why did you stop at a certain degree of material progress?"

"Because it's always necessary to stop in what you call the *material*, and limits are indiscernible," replied Erodia, tranquilly. "And as we didn't come here to stop, we have, to a certain degree, quit the form that would have failed us one day or another, and taken a new one."

"A moral form of progress?"

"Mental—because moral form also has its evolutionary limits, and that also is finished for us," said Erodia.

"And you believe that the form of mental progression of your race isn't limited in its turn by natural laws of ethnology?"

"Of our race? What race are you talking about?"

"But...the Hindu race, or even the yellow races fused with yours."

"And what tells you that we're limited to our race?" Erodia pronounced. "Do you take us for recluses concentrating the soul of their native land?"

"Do you claim to be concentrating the soul of other lands?"

They looked at one another.

"But why not? You've come here with your people, and with your European ideas, bringing the soul of the Latin races, meditating a mental conquest. Why shouldn't we go to your homeland?"

Claude, amused and a little proud, said, softly: "For that, you lack certain means of...visible action, especially at present, and we have...traveled a little rapidly for your actions to be truly such."

"I understand you; I've understood what is called irony in Europe, although I haven't wanted to retain it for my own usage. But there's an error in terminology at present. You speak about the *yellow peril*? You have brought that to a conclusion, after having made a very ingenious theory. But a theory comprises several aspects, and several conclusions. In other terms, there are *indefinite* theories, like certain mathematical solutions—and in mentality, all theories are like that."

"What does that mean?"

"But...that you have, by means of your *voyage*, concluded by the assault on Delhi, brought to a conclusion what you envisage as a solution, but that that

263

doesn't forbid us a parallel and dissimilar solution by means of another order of...voyage," said Erodia, placidly. "You spoke of race, of my race? Observe that I haven't told you that our communities are linked to the intellectual development of Hindustan, according to itself. You made allusion to your suppression of the yellow peril? I also have not told you that anyone here is meditating a new phase of the war. I've spoken to you of mentality. What your generals do does not disturb me. Believe me when I tell you that I have seen all that as a spectator. I have a horror of the Japanese, and the Hindustan of the rajahs doesn't interest me. I'm a Parsee, but I haven't even taken pleasure in being avenged by you for the ancient persecutions of my sect. The question is distinct from those nationalizations, for you as for me. I won't even say that you helped me."

"You're not a mystic?" said Claude.

"Not at all, and nor is any of my sisters. There's no trace of religion here. Do you believe, then, what you've been told about our communities? The vulgar think that we're simply recluses guarding the traditions of the Vedas, but I thought you were better informed. The Vedas suffice for the moral current of my women, but we have other concerns."

"Political concerns?"

"Even in the mouth of the leader of Occidental Anarchism, the word 'politics' isn't clear to me," said Elodia.

"In sum, the object of your meditations is a force of expansive mentality?"

"Yes," said Elodia.

"I have an analogous objective—and that's the reason for my presence here," said Claude.

"I knew that."

"Oh? Then you also admit that, next to my first solution, I place another, parallel, like yours?"

"Yes."

"And you're not anxious about that? You don't imagine that it might render your...expansion superfluous?"

"Not at all, for your solution will be mine."

"Do you mean that you accept my views?"

"I didn't say that your solution *is* mine, I said that it *will be*."

"You're speaking obscurely."

"And you a little too quickly."

They fell silent, considering one another gravely, with esteem. Singular sentiments were born in Claude Laigle's soul.

He said: "You're closer to me than I thought, in certain respects. I understand you better here, in your home, than on the road. You seemed to be expecting me. Was I mistaken?"

"No," Erodia replied.

"You mentioned dynamic acts, secret messages, magnetism. I imagine that your expansion requires abstract means. Should I understand occult forces?"

"It's evidently not the force of the shell. The shell is only an idea for me."

"For me too, believe me."

"I do believe you."

Claude shivered, remembering that he had made a similar reflection on the evening of the council in Paris—and the ivory face of General de Trénan appeared in his mind's eye, and like the terrible old man, he rectified his remark: "But the shell is a guarantee."

"I haven't prevented you from adopting it. As I told you, the work of your generals doesn't hinder me; it doesn't help me either."

He became irritated. "In sum, you have a goal? And a goal that you avow to be expansive?"

"Certainly."

"And you think it identical to mine?"

"Yes."

"And what if it isn't? What if you get in my way?"

"I'm astonished," said Erodia, impassively, "that an angry thought should come to the mind of a leader of sociological anarchism when he thinks of sedentary individuals. You only have to displace a soldier and his mentality is free, according to your own principles."

"I was joking," said Claude, surprised. "You're strangely focused."

"Like a woman, like the notion of the present that she incarnates."

"I thought I conceived that you were expecting me in order to be my ally, that you're preparing here—you, a Parsee educated in modern science—a new cerebrality, made to accord with my conquest..."

"After you have obtained your...guarantees against the rajahs and the Yellows? And that I would be a kind of intermediary between Asia and you?"

"Yes." Claude Laigle was struck internally by the clarity with which he had pronounced that word. So, his primitive conception really had been modified! He no longer wanted to sterilize India between Europe and the Japanese power. Decidedly, the country interested him; he no longer hated all the so-called uncultured. How ideas changed! How the action of shells ended in unforeseen hypotheses! He was resolutely dreaming that new dream. And he waited almost with certainty for Erodia's acquiescence.

But she pronounced, with an imperceptibly disdainful mildness: "I told you that our solutions were *parallel*."

"I said *alliance*. You understood an *exchange*?"

"A mental exchange, yes."

"And it can take place, now that the war is materially terminated?"

"Certainly—and only now is it possible, since we finally find ourselves on a level, on the same plane of intellectual dynamism, with the same instruments. At present, you're more than a logician, like me. You know that I'm disinterested in the ancient Orient, that there can be no antagonism of ideas between us there, and that I'm applying abstract methods toward a goal coexistent with yours. Why should there not be an exchange?"

"You're truly disinterested in the ancient Orient?"

"Certainly. It didn't hinder me, but wasn't useful, any more than your armies. I'm thinking of other things."

"You're not an Oriental, then?"

"I believe that we'll soon find, together, a clearer definition of that word, and even of the name Occidental, for it's necessary to understand one another. I'm not a dissident, and I'm not an intermediary between Europe and this land I'm here, and more so than this conversation might lead you to think, but I'm not what you think I am. I repeat that we're acting in concert, but separately. I believe in the Orient, but my faith is not in that to which your hatred is addressed."

"Yes," said Claude Laigle. "I'm beginning to glimpse what you mean. 'The virgin Orient.' You're guarding a rite of which I'm ignorant. Three months ago, I would have thought it irreconcilable with my ideas. Today, I'm waiting. But what are you brining to the exchange?"

"Simply the idea of this," said Erodia, indicating the white constructions.

Dusk was falling. They separated.

In the garden, in the bright halls, in the white rooms, lived a small population of women. They were not veiled; their faces were placid and imprinted with an interior liberty. Many were, like Erodia, former pupils of the Faculties, educated in the European fashion, and had worked in that fashion. In laboratories and clinics their adroit hands had manipulated retorts, leafed through tomes, touched sick people subtly. There was no trace in those communities of religion or of art. The concentration of mentality alone created something holy and harmonious there. Discreet and inoffensive disciplines appeared to regulate the recluses easily; nothing concerned them but the employment of time. Extreme isolation, the natural mildness of the vegetation and the days, simplified the detail of living.

Few men were perceptible—servants circulating. Muscular and handsome young men lived separately, hunting and guarding the enclosures, almost all of them Parsees and whites. At night, the women received them in their homes. Some did not receive them, limiting the satisfaction of amour to reciprocal kisses, and that question was not the object of public reflections. Liberty on that subject was identified with various tastes for one dish or another, a contestation would have appeared anachronistic and negligent. The exaggeration of appetites, matched to the inspiration of the climate, contained by that very fact their accepted legitimacy.

Children were invisible; as soon as they were born they were sent to hidden places, some in the cities of modernized India, others remaining in the mountains. Informed progressively of the conditions of their birth by affiliates

266

disseminated from Kashmir to Bengal and from Kabul to Calcutta, they opted freely for a life to their taste, returning to the communities or serving them at a distance, or, if they wished, disinteresting themselves in them, receiving civil estates permitting them to present themselves to the world with a suitable identity—but they were dead to their mothers. Those defections, in any case, hardly every occurred.

The economy of the material resources of the recluses, their information networks and the surveillance of convoys was regulated by special services via consultation. Nothing apparent distinguished the association of a free convent from a phalanstery of intellectuals cooperating, by mean of their fortune, in an ornate, mutually agreed retreat. Similar societies did not astonish Hindustan or surprise the Europeans, among whom the first form of anarchism had been thus revealed by private initiative. The tradition of mysticism and the retention the sacred principles of India sufficed for the indifferent respect of neighboring rajahs; rumors of discreet debauchery contented superficial opinion and the skeptical curiosity of the vulgar. A fear of sorcerous sciences created the respect of anonymous crowd. The authentic idea of the grouping remained unsuspected. No one talked about it outside, and the messages seized by the complicity of a few faithless couriers in the early years had not revealed anything to the governors of the province—and calm had descended on the subject.

Visiting the various communities, Claude Laigle observed those apparent details, similar everywhere, of a minuscule civilization whose harmony seemed attractive to him, but whose essential reason was not obvious to his mind. The astonishment of finding such an organization of mental forces in this wilderness struck him; the idea of his initial error on the subject of the Orient was increasing fortified, effacing completely his former conception of the enemy race.

What surprised him even more was not finding any trace of fatalism, and the conversations he had with the women convinced him of the absence of that detested sentiment. They lived, thousands of leagues from Occidental Anarchism, with an absolute intuition of its principles, and went further in several respects. Their active intelligences scrutinized sciences and sociologies in silence, and their morality was liberated without being dismembered; the equilibrium of individualism and the strength of association was perfect; that State of women had no faults.

They're truly very superior, and very sympathetic to my ideas, the master said to himself. *Is it because women, unlike men, understand what the present is, and are nascent with the energy of cohesion?*

But he could not understand how that unexpected revelation of a sensitive intellectual Orient could be of use of him. He was far from any hatred against the recluses of the Pamir; they were no hindrance to him and they pleased him, but they seemed to exist apart from the ancient Orient and the new Europe. What exchange had Erodia meant, and of what did that ambition of *expansive* force consist, among these wise beings, who seemed, on the contrary, to constitute an end, to be complete in all respects?

"The virgin Orient" Claude certainly perceived, and he thought about Dessort's astonishment and Médion's suspicion when they came to know in their turn the little concentrated group, proud and white, retrenched in the Hindu crests. But in what way could that "virgin Orient" second him? Behind the first secret, was there another? He could not discover it, and considered Erodia, seeking the enigma in the frown of the clear forehead and the long, circle eyelashes—but she remained impassive, watching him. Since their first veritable encounter, she appeared to be waiting, keeping out of his way with a measured courtesy, as if her consent to explain herself depended on an evolution in her adversary's mind.

That evolution, irritated curiosity, the majestic sensuality of the sky and the landscape, intellectual satisfaction, the odor of an unknown soul, and distance from Europe all activated in Claude Laigle.

Have I before me the last refined Orientals, all that the sumptuous and ferocious imbecility of fatalism has been able to spare in this punished land? Are they the creatures the penetration of the modern mind has been able to awaken some beauty? Are they our intellectual children? Or have I before my eyes the first witnesses of a regenerated Asia, as Erodia seems to understand, beings formed in the depths of the Orient, of its very blood, not forgetting it but mingling it with the acquisitions of the Occident, and meditating an unknown future, pagodas raised to the cerebral god? But that would change the question infinitely! Is it the result of an infiltration of the west into the ancient Orient that I perceive, or a reaction of that Orient awakening to march toward us with our abstract arms? From which side will the exchange commence?

I sense that, although we have the appearance of having arrived as masters, there is something here that is also commencing. And that woman affirms positively that she is heading toward, outside of my control, by parallel ways, to a solution reconcilable with mine! And yet she doesn't solicit an alliance!

What, then, is the virgin Orient? Who has left it virgin—the rajahs of the ruined regime, or my armies? Erodia says that I have not saved it, that Orient, by coming, nor have the rajahs saved it. They did not kill it in the egg, and nor have I. How, then, does it exist between those two contrary forces? Is there an Orient that is neither the ancient one nor the one of whose transformation I dream, which is developing at its own whim?

That's the question to which I always come back. One might think that Erodia is eluding it. Is it because there's nothing there but a void, and she's guarding an imaginary secret? No; that ruse wouldn't lead me astray. It seems to me, rather, that she's waiting for me to find the answer in myself.

These alternatives filled Claude Laigle's mind.

Deep down, he glimpsed more clearly with his sensibility than with his reason a mental empire, concentrated in a few groups of buildings, just sufficient to nourish the bodies of its inhabitants: an abstract empire, a floating manifestation, a college of concentrated beings, summarizing in a simple frame the dynamic accumulation of the world and acting by insinuation in the ideological universe.

It was necessary not to search for the virginity of the Orient in this communist State founded in the distant mountains, nor in the safeguards of that State against the rajahs and the conquering armies. That primary virginity was surprising, made to impassion; but there was a second, and that must be the true one, the essential one. But would it dissolve, that unassailable virginity, in the age-old traditions of the Hindu soil, or a new comprehension of the intellectual future? Did she think it could be saved forever by the inertial resistance of ancient Asia, always prostituted and always intact, or by the admiration of Europe? To what did it tend?

Thus turning, in an attractive series of hypotheses, Claude's reasoning blossomed.

At that moment, Dessort and Médion rejoined him. He observed them increasingly affirmed in their idea of civilizing the conquered country, of creating in India a current sympathetic to Europe, to fashion it into a future obstacle between the Occident and a possible reawakening of Japan and the Yellow masses. They would give prerogatives to the people, develop industry, open wide to all the facilities of obtaining rank, of socializing.

Claude explained the situation to them, his research and his curiosities since the beginning of his travels, expecting anger or scorn. On the contrary, Médion and Dessort seemed delighted by "the virgin Orient." They were interested in it.

"An excellent center for the propagation of Europeanism," said Médion. "You've found a precious force here, Master."

And Dessort added: "This Erodia is one of ours. She's working for us. These intellectuals will help us, even though they'll forbid themselves to do so, and you know what a growing force the intervention of the new woman will have."

They fell into accord on the fashion of considering the mountain communities: a group of intermediate intelligences, renovating the Orient, opening it up to Europe. They immediately attached themselves to that utilitarian formula, easily. Claude Laigle wanted to believe them, and then was almost shocked. How simplistic they were, those men with theories! Erodia's eyes sometimes signified things that truly further complicated the question that the arguments of the two ministers would not admit.

"A few more months, Master," Médion assured him, "And we'll return to Europe with everything set in place. Our agents will only have to continue on our givens."

That tranquility, instead of convincing Claude, left him doubtful, in the malaise of an increasing incomprehension. The aggravation increased of finding

Médion identical, faithful to his "universe of chemistry," and Dessort, with his dreams of organization, his irritating administrative genius! They had not changed; the extraordinary Adventure had passed over their heads without surprising them. A year before, Claude would have seen that as an admirable strength of soul; at present he discovered therein a narrowness of mind.

There are, however, combinations of circumstances that overturn living beings, unless those beings are atonal, having only the appearance of dynamism, are mediocre! he said to himself.

And in a second, he glimpsed as mediocre those he had before him, ordered and sectarian, and Trénan with them, and the entire world left on the road to Europe...that limited technologists! The ideal of the future civilized Orient broke in him the image of the society of engineers in which he had lived.

Useful, yes, certainly, but second-rate all the same! Have I made the conquest with those men, for those men? And he cried: *No!* internally with such force that he was alarmed by it.

The image of Ménières, almost ironic in the council in Paris, almost revolted in the assault on Delhi, passed through his memory, reappearing very visible. How haunted that dilettante had been by strange prescience! Claude sensed that he was less distant from him than the others, and suddenly he had a crazy, absurd idea, a fugitive flash of the radiance of superior truth.

Erodia is Ménières resuscitated!

Implicitly, he loved Erodia. The strong visage with the noble eyes, the pale face surging from the blood and the mud from the infamous serge, the two heads of hair, everything mingled, in a single embracing image, so violently that Claude, dizzy, clasped his hands to his torso, seized by a neuralgia of the heart.

He thought: *If he revived, if he saw her, we'd all three of us understand one another, in opposition to those men!*

He shivered, having spoken aloud without taking account of it, but he was alone.

From then on, his soul let go.

The diaphanous visage of the ancient Idea floated in his dreams, untying his bouquet of verities in the open sky of the Adventure, as before, but so fluid, so frail, that he could only now discern in those brilliant curls the tresses of Erodia and Ménières, confused...

By means of successive short journeys, Erodia drew Claude Laigle into the mountains, to visit all of the communities. During that period their intimacy was accentuated. The leader of souls was smiling, the serenity of the sky remained marvelous and the long-contained lyricism rose once again to Claude's mind, and calmed it. Everything collaborated in that calm: the echo of the immense catastrophe was distanced, quivering now in the confines of the habitable world; European power soared. They were consoling and decisive days. The reversion in the dictator's thoughts attenuated the wait for a new route, perhaps broader, more surprising, and everything depended on Erodia's secret.

She did not seem to be in any hurry to speak, but revealed herself luxurious and gentler, as if soothed by an interior harmony, Claude finally saw her, savored her beauty in the spacious landscapes. She seemed more Oriental, always black and strict, but the surrounds of her elongated eyes beneath her luminous hair were more emphatic.

Salome grown old, Claude had thought at their first encounter. At present he did not see Erodia's forty years, Salome was no longer perverse or a little girl, but the torsion of the hips and the languid gleam of eyes crying youth and triumph.

One evening, she announced the final voyage, to the heart of the Pamir.

"You'll understand all my ideology then, Master," she said.

They left, with Dessort and Médion, who esteemed Erodia, counting in her a future force and support, but keeping their distance from her and Claude, with a secret base design. They reached the great plateau thus. The last buildings were visited.

"But there's the landscape," said Erodia. "It's necessary to come."

They went; she guided the men and the camp, with a sign and a smile, almost like an elegant excursion, became entirely a woman, free and cheerful.

They camped on the plateau of Pamir; Claude Laigle waited.

And there, placidly, the annunciatrix, drew him away and showed him the solitudes. And she said: "Do you know what we call this desert, surrounded by our communities? Our supreme windows open over it. I sometimes come here to consider it. This is what matters, this empty space, circular, hollow and defended..."

"I don't know," said Claude.

She half-closed her eyes, and pronounced, in a very low voice: "We call it the Cradle."

Her voice was strange, changed, as if born from the depths of the Earth. Claude shuddered. Erodia had taken his hand, touching him for the first time.

Very rapidly, she said: "It's here that the first races were born. It's from here that they radiated out over the world, that they descended into India, and toward the Occident. It's here that you were rendered possible, you and yours. There is neither Orient nor Occident here, there is neither right nor left, nor north or south, do you understand? Here, humankind was cradled by the unconscious song that rose up when chaos was finished! When all the white men had departed westwards to solicit destiny, it remained solitary, the curbed and sad plateau, with its arid soil, beneath the sky. But under the clear earth human imprints were still germinating the eternal seed. Why did they all believe that the Cradle was empty? They went away without looking back, out there, far away, beyond the mountains and sea, in millions! They went into exile as if they were going to conquest!"

She stopped, appeared to repress rapid words, and only repeated, softly and sadly: "Why did they all believe that the Cradle was empty?"

"This time I understand, Erodia," said Claude, very pale. "Behind those who departed for the Occident, believing that they were only leaving a desert, the Cradle didn't remain empty. Souls reformed, and if the hosts had gone, that was because it no longer mattered that their temporary mass, anonymous and vain, remained there. A thought sufficed."

"Yes," said Erodia.

"And that thought, you've heard living for centuries under the ground, and you've drawn living beings from it, and you maintain it in silence."

"Yes," she said, again.

"And what the rajahs and my generals haven't been able to attain or fortify, is that thought of the fecund Orient guarded by your recluses. What you come to contemplate from the extreme windows open over this plateau is that thought, dormant in that curved and hollow Cradle of the men of the white race..."

She lowered her head, smiling pensively.

"And now I understand what you mean by the virgin Orient. And I also know what you're waiting for and why you were waiting for me."

"Say it," murmured Erodia.

"When all the white men had gone, without looking back toward the empty Cradle, that which you have thought, firmly hoped for, was what they remembered. What you're waiting for, Erodia, is for them to *come back* to the virgin Orient."

She looked at him proudly. "You have understood, Claude Laigle."

"And I understand why you're women gathered here," he said. "It requires gentle hands to guard the Cradle; you're obeying the immortal instinct of *gardiennes*,[59] and you're cradling the cherished thought, in order that they will find here the uncompromised source of life, saved by your cares while waiting patiently for them to come back."

"Yes," she said.

"*I have come back*, Erodia," said Claude, softly.

She let go of his hand, shivering. They considered one another. The sun was setting obliquely; violet shadows and red enchantments of an infinite splendor filled the curved horizon.

In the mute Cradle, the central point of races and thoughts, Claude Laigle sensed a new man born and palpitating within him. And he attached his eyes to those of Erodia, upright and immobile; he moved very close to her; in those two

---

[59] Because all nouns in French are gendered, many words referring to human roles come in distinct masculine and female forms, only a few of which are reproduced in English. Here, *gardiennes* is employed in a special sense, essentially restricted to women, and it would be misleading to translate it as "guardians."

magnetic pupils millions of lives dwelt, outside of dates and countries, outside ages, purified in the permanence of time.

"Erodia," he said, "now that I've come back, would you like, in order to guard the Cradle and raise the thought-child, for there henceforth to be a man and a woman?"

She acquiesced silently. And he was perhaps about to say something more, but their faces were so close that the kiss came more rapidly than the words.

That evening, in the obscurity of the sleeping camp. Two shadows cautiously leaned out of a tall tent. A glimmer of light colored the curtains. The silence was total. A few paces away, on a carpet, soldiers were asleep. The two shadows suddenly shifted slightly, together.

"The kisses of a woman through a closed door," one of them said, and added, ironically: "The virgin Orient."

"He'll weary of it," said Dessort. "It's dangerous when, having passed through what he's passed through, one starts to occupy oneself with that. But it's something, all the same, isn't it? And then, it might be useful to us. In any case, I think it'll pass..."

"No," said Médion. "He's lost. It's not the woman yet, but...I sense clearly..."

"What?"

"He's made an error of calculation."

They went away without adding anything.

IX. The Visitor

She said:

"You have not come in vain to the calm Orient. The echo of the cannon is dead. Rest. Here, among the high palms and skies as open as young hearts, there is a thought that time will never trouble. I have waited for you patiently beside the Cradle, and now you have come back from the confines of the world, with your artillery, your crowds and your wrath, as I hoped. O son of my race, long distant! Who spoke to you of Orient and Occident? Mingle their names on my lips; I love you with tranquility; our bloods are not dissimilar. Here, among the mildness of instinctive plants, the distinctions of tribes are diminished.

"Those you have brought with you no longer understand you, Master, but the word of truth is valuable in itself. One seed is sufficient to summarize the crop. Your conquest is secret; it is virginal too, as was my silence; now it belongs to you alone; in you it will open and slowly flower, at your whim, unknown to your armies and our ministers, now that you truly dispose of it, you think it, it no longer has anything material; it lives behind your forehead, is transparent in your eyes.

"How I have waited for you! You are almost unchanged; you have the signs of the primordial man, the surprising heir of a long series of masters. You are simple: your unprecedented enterprise is simple too. You thought to conquer, and you came back. Thus, those who raise dreams in dreams only do so to rediscover their veritable being and to recover their wellbeing, and you have only come back to your authentic childhood. Now the second period of your power is accomplished. I am with you in order to dream of the past beauty and to edify the future beauty.

"Alas, Master, do not think, because I am a woman, that I am triumphing over you. I am beside you; our means are different and our thoughts parallel; here, no one is above anyone; the gardiennes are not triumphant women, and this soil has not known, like that from which you come, the idea that woman is evil. You do not believe that, for you are not of that land. You are of this one, which does not belong to anyone, and you know that it is the only fatherland of beings like us. It has remained empty of men and women, and we shall not repopulate it.

"See, even I remain on the threshold; I only contemplate it from the extreme windows of my convents. There must live, alone, the original thought of races; that is what it is necessary to guard. What does it matter to me what the vulgar believe, thinking that I have retired here with my women in order to conserve the Vedic traditions? Here, beyond religions, something holy palpitates that surpasses the secrets of rites, a pure and inviolable evidence.

"You have come back, you have touched it; and you have never forgotten it, in the depths of yourself. You have only forgotten the name; it is of this that you were thinking in standing up against Asia a vast apparatus of war. All forms are good to return to what one guards in the depths of oneself. I have waited for you; I have waited for you ardently and confidently. The echo of your approaching cannons already brought me the voice of the return. I heard therein the joy of solemn salvoes that also saluted peace by the howling of the beasts of death.

"You came here to force the final secret and you thought that I ought to hate you; I am smiling at that now. I have detested the Yellows that the stupid rajahs summoned here to stop you; I have feared for a long time that they might go to your Europe to take you a false and abject idea of the beautiful primitive Orient. Your captains, ignorant as they are of the real nature of things, have seen in my eyes how I rejoice in their work, and they love me without understanding me, as they will love you now.

"You tried in vain to distract yourself from the meaning of the truth. In vain you thought to depart in anger against what you called the yellow peril, the indolent fatalism of Asia. That Asia is not what you imagined her in your mind to be. You were only able to vanquish those who misunderstand her, the Mother. Now the figure of peace is rising up for you, and these desert plateaux disdain the passage of armies. It is thus that you have returned to the first place of the white races, and my kisses, for years, have reached you beyond the mountains and the seas.

"I had glimpsed you during my voyage, out there; but the time was not yet ripe, and I could only speak to you here. I glimpsed you, out there, without you suspecting me, an anonymous passer-by in the rumor of capitals. How necessary it was to contain ardent and rapid dreams! The truth worthy of you did not want to be spoken, and when I found you again in Kashmir, until I brought you here, into the presence of the excellent earth, I clenched my teeth upon the words the cried on this side of my lips!

"Now, love me as I love you, for the long patience of my great desire. I have infinite and multiform souls within me, living souls of blood and aromatics, ripened for the leader of old and grave souls..."

She kissed him, smiling, the strong face with the circled eyed paled by voluptuousness beneath the somber tresses, and they gripped one another ardently.

Claude loved her like a dream finally clothed in visible flesh, beneath the opulent sky of the wild country. The svelte diaphanous Idea, autumnal with her tresses of semi-loosened verities, and her pale promises, the svelte Shadow of the Adventure, thinned in the dusks of Europe, finally descended into his arms, and he found her stronger and prouder, drunk like him on solar savors, nourished by light and calices in all her supple gilded flesh. His fingers likewise modeled the dream of his life; the animate statue was real, he savored her with greed and fervor.

The secret exchange burned in both of them; they enclosed it between their twin lips, and in the middle of the kiss they drank it like an extraordinary fruit. While, joined at the mouth and their hands clutching hips and shoulders, they aspired it in the same convulsive or calm rhythm, Claude penetrated Erodia's elongated pupils with his eyes. Half-closed in the blue-tinted torpor of the great rings, among the reeds of lashes, they unveiled verdant water in which appeared a transparent sky; shadows passed therein like clouds, immemorial shadows; thousands and thousands of voluptuous and pensive faces emanated from the earth and sanctuaries.

The warm odor of breasts rose toward those eyes, a feverish perfume of juices and aromatics, phantoms floating in the pupils hallucinated by them, spinning indistinctly; and suddenly, the blue-tinted curves of the eyelids narrowed, and the moist gleam of the irises was annulled, rolling the specters and the clouds into sudden obscurity—and Claude, alarmed, felt in his shoulders the mute bite of fingernails gripping more tenaciously...

The lips tightened then in their nervous flesh the word ready to spring forth, caressing it, tasting it with the cynical tongue, then strangling it, preventing it from mingling with the breath, driving it back into the depths by the penetrating and voracious advance of kisses between the teeth. The alternating beat of their hearts arrived through the flesh, harmonized with the quivering of the lips, and alone remained alive in the silence and the sweat of the embrace.

The inappreciable time passed, followed by the surge of two breaths; then they yielded, exhausted by the exchange, and Claude's fixed and empty eyes saw, slowly reopening between the unclenched lashes, the stretched and glaucous pupils...

At other times, in the totally sexual play, they suddenly became motionless, savoring the secret contact, the head upstanding and free; they looked at one another, drew apart, only vibrating imperceptible in the centers. The irritating intoxication exasperated by the wait, they did not yield to it, smiling, a smile taut over cold teeth, hands open and swinging, holding back the wild desire to seize one another; and they considered one another with a refined care, he savoring himself alive in her, she savoring the shiver of masculine strength. That double invisible vitality was as if separate from themselves; they allowed it to exist apart; their thoughts, really vaulting above the act of their bodies, floated lightly, happy and hollow, borne between them on the odor of amour.

It was an immaterial and delectable moment.

Then, the enervation of inferior life rose up, attaining them all the way to the hands that sought one another, the eyes that dilated, the mind that was maddened; the woman with the erect breasts undulated first, and they threw themselves upon one another, sighing.

They made love in the remote gardens, in the dusk, waiting for the enormous azure to become very deep, and for forms to become indistinct. Desire made the fingers haunting their waists almost cold; she, pliant, offered the calyx of her mouth while murmuring very softly; an incomprehensible clarity remained scattered around her hair, which suddenly slid, rolling, down to her hips, defining her with a savage and sulfurous contour. He sought the loins of the great feline woman, and his arm was lost in that warm and fugitive fleece. He became irritated, parted it in handfuls, threw it back like a curtain, and burrowing in the heavy waves divided them, uncovering the nape of the neck and the hollow of the powerful shoulders, kissed that odorous flesh in the darkness, relentlessly, until Erodia, half-convulsed, turned, gave her mouth above the shoulder and the hair, with a sharp gaze whose magnetism reached him in spite of the obscurity.

They walked thus, staggering, linked by the center of the visage, mingling their legs brushed by palms. The army bands and the somnolent recitatives of the Hindu couriers reached them through the woods and the rocks, a melancholy softened their hectic souls; and, releasing one another in order to take hold of one another cautiously, they kissed one another on the cheeks and the eyes like children who have been afraid together, and ended up going to sleep in the even warmth of the Oriental night. And the roseate fire of dawn touched their unconscious eyes.

Beneath her grave and passionate head with the profound and weary expression, she displayed a perfect body, whose svelte flight tapered desirably toward the abdomen, and which, suddenly curbed for amour, softened a golden flesh into unctuous folds, elastic and subtly nourished by aromatics, sometimes coppery, sometimes very white, as pulpy as the heart of warm fruit and resistant under the dampness of hands; a full and highly cambered cleavage made the warrior more womanly and more amorous. The torsion of her hips was sovereign.

Claude contemplated that body pensively and discovered there all the Orient of dreams, Judith and Herodias, Balkis, Queen of Sheba, the great Semiramis, and the recluses of the pachaliks, and the unknown dominatrices of the emirs, and the Persian princesses living in the crystal, and those who, in tales, entertained themselves with genies in subterranean caves were their tremulous lamps illuminated bones and treasures, and those whose nudity was heightened by the sun in the bazaars of Basra, in the gardens of Golconda, on the white stairways descending to the Ganges from the heights of the palaces of Benares.

Then he returned to the face, touched by abstract thought, marked by secrecy, sensuality, dolor and dream, with the long reticent and meditative eyes, to the bitter mouth, the round white forehead, the lubricious and tenacious chin, and he rediscovered the Occident, determination crowning passivity, the dualism of worlds conciliated by that head and that body, the one able to be queen in the dusks of Europe, in the nuanced air of intellectual modernism, the other made to be ambered and candied in the sunlight and the languor of roseate countries.

It seemed to Claude that the link between two worlds was clear, signified between that head and that body by the neck, robust in its birth at the bosom and shoulders, and suddenly tapered, bearing like an undulating stem the visage-flower weighed down by the hair; that the great tresses, winding around the noble statue and enveloping it with life, also linked the two strange landscapes of flesh with the hectic wave of its strongly perfumed curls, of which secretly warm memory persisted obscurely in the groin.

The gardienne of the Cradle united the two races, revealing one alone, primordial, the age-old race of the white beings descended from the mountains of the original earth, toward the Occident and toward the South...

Together, Erodia and Claude wandered on the edge of the desert Cradle, and their kisses never had more moral and voluptuous savor than in the presence of those dry rocks and sad sands, to which the sun gave the color of the body.

They loved that primitive flesh, asleep for eternity among the sharp stones. Their limbs were harmonized in amour by the thousand indescribable attachments that, above inclination and sentiment, magnetize one body toward another for life. It appeared to them that that illusory flesh of soft sands was also similar to their own. They were unified with that soil. Their fingers took up the sand and allowed it to filter through; it was a singular caress. Soon, they lay down upon it, naked, their great musculatures of tamers of men imprinting themselves upon it, and they believed themselves to be three in the embraces.

The warm body of the desert bore theirs; they possessed it, inert beneath and between them; the flamboyance of the azure made them delirious; they cried out spasmodically in the middle of that arid wave, and swam in it as if in living water. There were unusual delights for them, a confusion of sensualities and ideas, equally exalted by the sky, the impression that they were rediscovering one another after a voyage of many centuries, as at the awakening from a dream, not having budged since the origin, beyond dates, places, history and death.

The virgin Orient effaced all the simple and naked prestige of its blond sands; they fell asleep there in silence.

Sometimes, in the repose of fine afternoons, they lay somnolently beside one another on the beloved ground, hearing nothing but the quiver of the mysterious Idea that rose within them, which rose through them from the depths of the quivering earth with the oblique sunlight, and which penetrated their bodies and their souls in the vibrations of the heat. And Claude no longer thought about the skies of Europe. The fever took hold of them, and with pleasure they watched the women advance, bearing cold sorbets and precious fruits to their dry lips.

In the morning, amid the cares of councils, in the middle of the troops, in conferences with the ministers and the visits of the communities, Erodia passed by, svelte, clad in black, devoid of jewelry, having become intellectual and strict again, attenuating the sentiment of the immense exile in the heart of the Europeans by means of conversations and modern mannerisms, a free and expert talker at meals or a disdainfully elegant amazons in rides through the camp and excursions. Her savant and incisive speech born of a scarcely indolent voice, she truly became once again the torpid flash that Claude had vaguely suspected at their first encounter. And he considered her with amazement, remembering the night.

Their eyes met without retaining anything of recent hallucinations; she brushed him tranquilly, with neither perversity nor reticence. Only the Oriental body hidden beneath the somber silks revived the luminous head of thought, constrained by the long luxurious tresses, now tightened in narrow torsades. Claude rediscovered the woman born of the Cradle but departed, like him, for the Occident; the duality of the body and the visage was affirmed, and yet, by imperceptible signs, he perceived that Erodia was one.

But, suddenly alone, the kiss rose up from their flesh and seized their heads to join them violently to one another, in the torsion of loins and the collapse of sumptuous hair, the male lover recognized the orgiastic female lover with the seeking hands, and there were rare and equivocal attachments, the intellectual attitudes of the queen of the recluses and the leader of armies yielding abruptly to naked sex, faun and satyress clasped like beasts of prey, with joyful bites...

When they were talking one evening about oriental princesses born of the Cradle and famous among men, she smiled without saying a word, went out and reappeared. A ribbon of precious stones circled her forehead and her cheeks were illuminated, making her ringed pupils darker; straight and slender, she swayed thus, at the summit of a heavy rigid robe, a bouquet of blue jewels, lamps on the floor casting her shadow on the drapes of the tent, and she danced, extending her strong arms, the wrists of which were brilliant. He was silent, astonished by the game.

She did not look at him, gripped by an ancient rite, her gaze fixed, her entire body attentive to the ceremony. All the India of warm seas, forests, pagodas and deserts inspired her silent dance; the implacable claustration of the harems of Asia, conserving voluptuous secrets, seemed to have meditated its most astonishing inventions in that moving statue. Claude, frightened, recognized Salome, the eternal indifferent dancer; the feline odor emitted by that great living calyx, followed by an exact or deformed reflection, awakened desire in him; he felt desperately human, perceived, in a flash, the eternal conqueror subjugated, startled by fear and lust.

But suddenly, tearing off the precious stones and kicking over the lamps, she threw herself on to him in the darkness and he felt tears among the urgent kisses, and she took him in her arms, murmuring:

"That's a game; I detest it; I wanted to show you one of the forms of our soul, one of the forms that you hated once; I wanted to show you, since we were talking about past charmers, that I too knew...

"Forgive me, don't think about it anymore; love me in the present; I'm present; I'm your sister in thought and the flesh, we have no need of extinct grandeurs. That which is dead is hateful, we shall edify something else...

"I was playing, I was playing with the past..."

An overturned lamp threw of a last and more vivid flame; he gripped Erodia's visage between his hands and turned it violently toward the light. And he suddenly perceived the eyes. They were grave in the scintillation of tears, the Oriental lie was no longer revealed there, they opened as pure as Northern lakes. He rediscovered the north, and shook the evil cloud from his soul.

Then, he adored Erodia without reserve.

She visited his mind and his heart with the gentle and admirable psychology of loving gardiennes.

She was not only gentle with him in the physical sense. She approached him with a perspicacious soul expert in sounding wounds. They hugged one another for long intervals. Their thoughts remounted the stream of time, bound to one another by a fraternal lust; it was a spiritual nuptial voyage beneath a perpetually serene metaphysical sky. They drifted together on the canals of the invisible, leaning over cisterns filled with marvelous thoughts, finding in the depths of sensations the salt of strength and the jewels of meditation, and climbing once again, souls laden with discoveries, spacious grottos in which ideality sleeps like a child in a supernatural light. Their mutual grandeurs confronted one another with wisdom in the simplicity of the Cradle. In that central place, it no longer seemed to them that ideas could escape toward the North or the South, like races; they rebound their essential bundle, and they both contemplate them without difficulty.

What lofty hypotheses exalted them during the nights when, insomnia reigning over their flesh liberated of amour, they considered one another, quivering, bewildered to be mastered by one another. Claude, especially, was animated, finally returned to himself after years of political cares, studies, anxieties and actions, thrown back into his native lyricism, bathing therein at his ease. The past and the future no longer haunted him; he became a being of the present; here, only the present had any meaning, like the place, like the woman. He had the sentiment of finally grasping something essential, of no longer waiting, of no longer preparing, but of holding, and whether it was Erodia's mouth, or the intuition of moral plenitude, he *possessed* it.

His conqueror's soul savored those beautiful preys; he was happy.

Pensively, Erodia listened to the indefinable murmur of that happiness within him, studied it, and watched over it. Solely by the sentiment of the tradition of the race, she had acquired the plenitude of the imagination for which all others beings seek in the exceptional of the universe; she had found her central and real point, the very landscape of her certainty, which other individuals only glimpse in dreams, and her joy was fortified in being shared with Claude.

The Occidental returned to the Cradle brought her thoughts transformed, an original bouquet in which she recognized the species, but whose calices had become paler, as of diaphanized by the damp and tender skies of Europe. She mingled slowly therein the odiferous crimson of the flowers of Asia; they rose, nonchalant and heavy, above the astonishing spray, and they both placed those offerings on the edge of the rediscovered Cradle. Erodia continually collected new ones in Claude's soul; she discovered tremulous heroisms there; the leader of races was worthy of surprising destinies.

There was no longer any question of time, nor of customs, nor of ancient or modern details; everything was unified—and slowly, slowly, the visitor allowed herself to elaborate her future projects.

"Do you see," she said, "how admirable the words are, since they have led you here? And do you see how detestable the words are, since they almost caused you to stand up against me with hatred, in return? What do you discern now, Master, between the Oriental and the Occidental? Between brother and brother is there any other distinction than that of their very duality and their double dwelling, and does that lead to irreconcilable anger? Is fratricide inevitable, by virtue of the fact that they are two? They are united in the mother, and you are in the Cradle here. The words right and left, up and down, only have meaning relative to the human being, who is central.

"What are we, you and I? Do you not see that we are central beings, a man and a woman, children of the central place? Oh, Master, Master, between the Orient that you hate and the Occident that feels threatened by that Orient, there was an unknown land, a little desert patch, a seed from which ours grew, and that was the virgin Orient, which belonged to no one.

"There are no directions here; everything is stable and meditates continuously in the present; there is no progress here, Master, there are only dissimilar forms, multiple signs that color the world variously. The mechanical progress of which your armies and your people confederated in their modernism are so proud raises up clever machinery *in relief* over invariable sentiments, over an amour, a beauty, a death and a silence that never changes. That progress is accomplished in parallel here, but *hollowed out*, in the mental domain, among my reclusive gardiennes—and you have discovered that with astonishment, and now you are no longer astonished and you find it natural that I am here, with my dreams and my kisses!

"You have come back, you have come back to the homeland of the men of the white race. I don't know why I said that I detested the yellow peoples and the Hindu princes who summoned them; on reflection, I almost love them. Without their coalition, perhaps you would not have come for many years—and perhaps I would have grown old, you would have found me too late, a white-haired gardienne, her eyes burned by waiting!

"Turned in the direction of the West, my desolate face would have visited your dreams, you would have suspected me vaguely as a specter throughout your life, and we would finally have confronted one another with a flesh deprived of charms, and our elderly kisses would not have been able to reanimate the bright virginal Idea that we can still seize with our warm lips. But our secret god was alert, and here you are, arrived in time.

"The man returns, when he is mature, to primitive pilgrimages. You were in exile, my love; you have returned to obtain the counsel of your ancient birth, and later, you will obtain the counsel of what was before it—for is what we call death before or after life? There are no directions there either; there too, everything reigns in the present."

"The present," said Claude. "That's true... that is all I have really conquered."

"And there was nothing but that to conquer. What will you call progress now, and what meaning will you give to that word, which suffices for the rudimentary ideal of your ministers?"

"None, it's true... their science is foreign to me."

"I have fathomed it too," said Erodia. "It is utilitarian. Admirably ingenious, but utilitarian; it cannot serve us; it is false, no more than a unification of analytical faculties with a view to knowledge. It is not cosmic; it is killed by empiricism; the industrial triumph of applications holds it back; it is local."

"I've tried to take it back to its sources... it was more intellectual in the Middle Ages. I've tried; I thought, since Anarchism, that it would reconnect with metaphysics. That was a dream that they didn't want. Metaphysics, the great insulted! Oh, Erodia, if you knew what hatred that name still awakens back there! Half of the detestation of the world is focused on that name, as if it specified a racial remorse!"

"Remorse? No, Claude, regret—the regret of having quit for damper skies the country of the observers of the stars. You are their leader, you see, but perhaps you're not for them. Here, I am the queen of a small white people nourished on the central thought sand augmented in solitude, but you, you're too elevated for them, or are you dissimilar to them? Alas, my love, the authority of the prophet surpasses all the others, but his renunciation is universal. They want to raise a hand against their mother, and you have led them, but you have recognized and saluted that mother; will they forgive you? You have raised that immense horde of men; will you be strong enough to drive it back to the other side of the mental world?"

"Do you hate those I have led?"

"I don't hate them at all. I'm waiting for them to understand, and I adore them as one adores imminent forces, for they can do what is necessary now. I'm waiting for them to understand, and I hope that they will understand, through you. Their cannons are futile. Science is futile. But they love their cannons and their science. Will they find in themselves, in the obscure memory of origins, a more powerful means than the ones that delight them? Will they conquer the virgin Orient, will they carry away this desert landscape in their souls as the visible image of the promised land?

"Oh, let them remain in India if they wish, or return to Europe, provided that they retain that vision! I hope that the astonishment of having found an unknown State in these reputedly arid mountains will be a sufficient sign for them. With the memory of my white communities the Idea will be enclosed—and you will tell them that, won't you, Claude? You will tell them that? Since the yellow peril is no more, which might have threatened their interests, they won't refuse to admit the idea? They won't create that frightful divorce between themselves and the Cradle, they won't be unjust enough, insane enough, to separate themselves, the white people, from the birthplace of the white race! They'll rally Hindustan, they'll make it the extreme barrier against the hideous swamp of coppery men dormant beyond the Himalaya and the Altaï, won't they, Claude? It's the same thought, in sum, but broader, than the one that guided you here, and of which they approved!"

"Yes," replied Claude Laigle. "I've thought of that, and I believe instinctively that they'll come to it. They've already reached an understanding with the southern provinces. The primitive conception has been modified, but not contradicted."

"Ah!" exclaimed Erodia. "You see clearly! I'll help them; I'll bring them my secret allies! You don't know what I can do in India, what obscure webs I've woven during the years of voluntary reclusion. It really is a question of Vedic fatalism; I've occupied myself with the gods of the Ganges and the sanctuaries of the upper Indus, and all the old Hindu thought that the rajahs retained. A new

India can be born through me, Claude—a modern India, an India of genius, young enough to astonish young Europe.

"Oh, if they wish, your people will see! They'll see what the Idea of the virgin Orient has been able to prepare! The face of that country is weary of dreams, like mine, but its body will surprise you, as mine has surprised you! My body is its body; you have embraced it in embracing me; it will give itself to you as I have given myself! Benares and Hyderabad are its breasts, the Pamir is its pensive head, Gujarat and the Oude swell like its hips; with the tip of its foot it plays with the marvelous Ceylon, and within the complete triangle that it forms, the warm and odiferous triangle, saturated with light and aromatics, you have sensed your male strength quivering, as within me.

"You will retain my body as a symbol; to your people I give the body of this country. I shall render the Cradle to all. Then, perhaps, they will understand that under various climes, the same life palpitates. Tell them that, Claude! Is it for nothing that the highest mountain in the world separates us from the yellow people? Is it for nothing that the extraordinary limit of the Himalaya contains those masses? Dormant Pamir leans against it, like a sleeping head. The wall of the white world is there; there commences the vast series of thoughts unfurling all the way to the Occidental ease. Is it not logical, is it not simple?"

"Perhaps I can explain it to them," said Claude. "Perhaps they'll follow me. But it's an almost total change of direction. I'm frightened myself by the change that has taken place in me. Oh, Erodia, you really are the great gardienne of the Cradle, responsible for our race, and however warm our kisses might be, it's still from the lips of an abstract mistress that I suspend my lips when I touch yours. The diaphanous phantom of Anarchism and conquest has put on flesh. But you are above all a Visitor of Souls.

"I don't know any more whether it's you or what you guard that I love. Will I be alone in talking to my people or will you be with me? I don't know. It seems to me at times that if you went away, the Idea would be sufficient, and yet you summarize it, and to possess you is a repose for me. I touch in you the earth that renders strength. And it also seems to me sometimes, Erodia, that if the Idea were annulled, your presence would retain for me a sufficiently clear reflection to guide me. You are the Visitor of my Soul, and my soul is not different from the one that you have guarded in the Cradle. Thus, indissoluble mixtures are produced in me."

"It will be necessary for you to speak alone, Claude. You are the Master and they don't trust me. I no longer ask to speak; the influence of the woman will live eternally, but it must remain occult. I have deliberately renounced all public life and chosen, in order to act, the mode of solitude and secrecy. And I would no longer be the same in your Europe, my friend, my Master; I would only be the attentive traveler who once perceived you in the crowds, whom you did not suspect. It is thus that, growing old, I will come back to your capitals to consider the completed work. There are only various forms, Claude; I am one form, nothing more. I have told you: although I am a woman, do not believe that I am triumphing over you. I will be the latent form of your actions. Gardienne I was, gardienne I shall remain. Of the two of us, the one whose hands are gentler befits that role, and the Cradle does not want to be alone. From the extreme windows of my convents I shall watch over it as before. Its sunlight will be happier over its sharp rocks, and over its sands, the color of which is that of the body."

"Are we quitting one another, then, Erodia? Can I not act from here?"

"They would not listen to you, Master. I love you, but what does it matter that you see the distant capitals again, now? You have come back in thought, and I have no fear that you will forget that return. Your actions might be produced out there, but I know that you are here, because our reason for being, the reason for our intercourse, remains enclosed here. I will rejoin you when the time comes, when your people know what they need to know, when the Idea has given a goal to their science, a framework to their quest for progress. They would think that I have shackled you; back there, decked in the prestige of the false return that they believe to be true, they will listen to you without suspicion. I have waited for you here; out there it is you who will wait for me, and I will only come when they have forgotten my name, our adventure extinguished in the din of the triumph."

"You're right," said Claude, going pale. "How you live the Idea, Erodia!"

"You are the Idea now, and it's necessary that it goes to the Occidental countries. The two of us have savored it, but no one ought to be deprived of it. If you stayed, we would be inferior; I would be bad for you. Here," she said, sad and smiling, "woman is not bad."

They embraced, drunk with a kind of joy; and in the hasty kisses, speech died, aspired by their breath, stifled in the flesh of their lips.

The next day, in the council, Claude Laigle announced curtly his resolution to depart for the South. Médion and Dessort started in surprise, which made him smile internally.

"The voyage that I wanted to make is finished; I know what I wanted to know," he said, loftily. They inclined, anxiously, and communicated the latest news. General de Trénan was waiting for the dictator and his minister in Delhi, which he was fortifying as a stronghold. The last uprisings in Nepal were extinct. It was known that the blockade of Japan had determined the cabinet in Tokyo to negotiate a peace-treaty. It was the consummation of the enterprise commenced on the evening of the declaration of war in Paris.

The dictator agreed the measures taken. Erodia appeared next to him for the last time, careless of insistent stares. The ceremonies of farewell were exchanged. And while the "boots and saddles" was being sounded the impatient ministers approached Claude Laigle, speaking in low voices.

"These recluses…what plans?"

"Everything remains as it is," he said, coldly.

"Will they help us? It appears that they really can," said Dessort. "I know that from my couriers. A number of them obeyed them before obeying me. You've surely understood, Master, what these women can do, the secret reason for their grouping. Your voyage of convalescence had a goal."

Claude smiled. "Assuredly."

"Is the alliance made?" Dessort asked.

"Will you take coercive measures later?" asked Médion.

"I shall not take any, at least as you can think of them, Messieurs," Claude declared. "The alliance is made...mentally," he added, with an indefinable nuance.

Disconcerted, they said no more. Médion followed him with his eyes for a long time, dubiously, his hard face contracted with concern, but Claude Laigle was already drawing away, saluting Erodia. She and he, observed, stiffened; on the threshold of the white communities, the laboratories and the gardens, the solitary Intellectuals gazed, amid the troops and the horses, at the two svelte black forms of the Masters. Above the palm trees staged on the extreme slopes of the roseate rocks, the plateau of Pamir opened its shallow curved horizons in the even and silent light. The violet shadows moved over the ground. The European clarions sounded.

Toward the occidental South, Claude Laigle, bearing a new soul, descended from the Cradle.

X. The Denial

In Delhi, the dictator, listening to General de Trénan's explanations, was astonished by the fortifications commenced—recent grassy slopes, white circumvolutions bristling with multiple piles—and the geometric impression of modernism gripped him. The hammering of foundries and the screech of saws rose up from construction-yards, alternating with jets of steam; carts cluttered the roads; an army of workers lined up in squads at a gesture from the engineers; flying cranes gyrated on the edge of the Jumna, encumbered by barges and dispatch-boats.

Claude did not recognize anything of the burning city into which he had once hurled himself on horseback, with the diaphanous Idea leading, in the madness of the assault, amid the red smoke, the fulgurant destinies of the Adventure. He had left a place of terror and he came back to factories. He traveled through the city, confusedly evoking the route followed on the eve of the battle. At the crossroads, ruined pagodas and palaces appeared, patched with fresh plaster over the traces of the conflagration, held up by stays and embankments.

The great gardens of the rajahs displayed rowed of charred tree-trunks, mostly lying on the ground, fissured domes open to the sky, colonnettes remaining upright with fragments of entablatures. A dung-heap of rubble and mud, thrown out in heaps, bordered the avenues. On that debris, among the palisades, the huts and mattresses of sepoys were agglomerated, along with improvised shops, all the miserable flora of demolitions. A busy population filed the canteens and the tents, a repulsive life born from death; the cries of merchants were odious. From the top of rattan miradors, European bells rang. Children were swarming obscenely in the harsh sunlight.

Claude Laigle went past the construction-yards, reaching the northern districts; their bleak streets extended clay walls; the rare windows were closed; violet and languid shadows loomed up interminable between the houses, furtive and earthen Hindu faces surging from wretched loincloths on the thresholds. And Claude thought about the communities of the Pamir, spacious and cheerful, with their slender women with bright eyes, under the palm trees next to fountains. Here the ancient Orient was veritably rotting.

The obsequious greetings of people were disagreeable to him; he would have liked to detect hatred in a face, but the listless people, won over by Dessort's concessions, and above all by the idea of cannons, sickened him. And yet, many of the men he saw in these side-streets must have seen him on the night of the assault; nothing apparently remained of all the horror. The soldiers and colonists were circulating among the shops, fraternizing with the Hindus. For the dictator, it was an impression analogous to that of the days after the revolution in Paris, and he saw once again the stalls erected in the debris of the Parliament, the drinking-dens and popular gossip-shops, the curious attitudes of women, the rubbish, the newsvendors, the recommencement that followed the thunderclaps, the eternal people who always ate lunch, as if the sublime and the terrible had not raised their heads: life, in short...

Life...

But here the sky was dissimilar, and there was no longer the strange black anger, the contraction of faces charged with thought, as at the dawn of Anarchism. Here, people were clearing up and tidying up; everything temporary, all the multicolored mediocrity that there was in the word "colonial" was becoming manifest. And it would be necessary, after the thunderbolts of shells and torpedoes, to insinuate the thunderbolt of the virgin Idea into that industrialism...

Claude was troubled, a trifle weary.

Dessort, satisfied, explained the plans: Delhi, reconstructed and fortified, commanding central India, with a retrenched camp, and all the Deccan in fief to the military power of the Europeans as an advance guard, a barrier, against the Yellows., if they ever reformed.

"It's coming along; General de Trénan's organizing everything admirably—see what he's done! This country will serve us."

Claude listened, embarrassed. They reached more formless rubble, and in a vast quadrilateral of blackened walls, the dictator recognized the great pagoda where he had seen Ménières' gilded head alive for the last time, raised up in revolt against the violation, crying his disavowal. He shivered. And the idea of the violation rose up again, the savage sensuality of the bloody penetration, the ogival wombs dilated by the rigid assault columns, engulfed with brutal clamors. He was no longer vibrant, sought the enjoyment in his flesh, was astonished, and suddenly felt reborn, but gentler, more profound, under a distant firmament, among rocks rosy in the sunlight, on sand the color of the body...

Erodia...

And he considered the dislocated arches with a confident sadness. Through them, and beyond the hysterical stiffness of his male loins, he had touched something eternally virginal; the buildings had become kisses, and the kisses had become almost-maternal caresses, up there, toward the curved and flat cradle.

Claude looked away, and closed his eyes. In the vibrations of light persisting beneath his eyelids, a dear head lived, a strong face with golden hair, and that head emerged from muddy and bloody serge. Ménières and Erodia were a single being. Love had spiritualized the death of the one and the life of the other, he perhaps having died in order that she might appear...

A profusion of debris strewed the soil, confused heaps piled up against the walls. Claude wanted to see. Old rusty weapons, scimitars and helmets with nasals, rifles with their twisted metalwork bristling next to stacks of cannonballs, spiked guns, torn coats of mail, cartridge-belts: an entire set of ancient armaments snatched from cadavers and thrown away scornfully. Ragged clothing lay in heaps, sometimes swollen by the semblance of bodies under their heavy dusty folds. Brown patches splattered them, stiffening the cloth, and an atrocious odor of cooled and insipid blood rose from all that wreckage.

Through the breaches, on waste ground, regular undulations of the soil could be seen: symmetrical blisters, revealing the recent excavation of trenches. A word from Dessort explained. They were the vestiges of mass graves dug in haste the day after the assault. A great many had been burned, the Hindus having demanded it. These had been filled with the Japanese, officers and soldiers, pell-mell, decomposition threatening under the torrid sky. They had immediately set to work on that repulsive clearance.

Claude imagined the scenes, like those back there in Europe once, after the bombs: all that meat in linen, the stretcher, the spades, the stink, the entire harvest of war...

He shrugged, drew away, and then smiled. It was necessary. At least it was the wherewithal to make admirable triumphs of ideology, especially now that he knew. It was over bodies, inevitably, that one pursued and caught up with the Idea.

But that cold flesh, carried in armfuls by the soldiers...

He thought about the warm and supple body of the Visitor, weakening under him, against him, experienced a frisson, and abruptly quit the rags, the weapons, the broken Buddha, the lamentable display of the ancient Orient. It was necessary to erase all that, to live in the present.

The present! To attain a certainty, the instant one knows that it must be, that it *is*, not *will be* or *has been*. The exhausting and unique research of the superior human being standing up in the incessant unfurling of the images of life! Claude had just had a certainty, and already it lacked continuity; it was important that it endured. He looked around; people were still preparing, it was still the intermediary of the temporary. When would they finish elaborating? He sensed disorder everywhere, a poorly equilibrated soul, like those palisades, those banks, those heaps of debris, those carts, those gesticulations of carpenters and laborers. And always, however, always that European method, exact, geometrical, applying uniform frames, transporting systems for the mind as for the body, that method served by impassive executives, believers in number and dosage, manipulating, planning, regulating, with closed faces and stiff hands, chemists, electricians, artillerymen, the surprising and icy wires of Modernity and Dynamism!

To them it was necessary to speak. Would they listen, occupied with successive ideals, to elevated words of long range, the synthetic words of effort?

Decidedly, on seeing them again, Claude rediscovered his disappointment, the anxieties of his convalescence a few months before, and the very evening of the declaration in Paris, when he had only tried to insinuate a minimal idea compared with the one that haunted him today. How alone he had felt that evening! But then, nothing ideological can be discussed essentially before one knows the fate of the forces of war, and in the deployment of those forces all controversy had calmed. Since then nothing: universal contentment, the intoxication of the ends of battles, the fever...

One single memory: the prophetic cry of Ménières before his disappearance in the mine blast...

And then, the virgin Orient, the Visitor moving, with a simple finger, all the genius of the leader of the Occident...

And how to make himself understood? How, first of all, fully to understand himself? For the contradiction was resident in the master's soul, and considering himself, he was frightened; regripped involuntarily by the spectacle of his own people, by the thousand attachments of habit, sobered of the intellectual dream of the virgin Cradle and a Statesman once again, he felt keenly that his conception was as yet only mental, and that its practical communication was not ready. Up there, when his gaze had met Erodia's, the essence of the idea had been sufficient for them, but here? The gray and insistent ideas of Médion, the ambiguous pupils of Dessort, the unknown of those men, their suspicion, surely, perhaps their enemy calculations, something finished between them and him, the alliance exalted in the battle and untied with her...

Those companions in murder might not follow him in the idea. They had followed him once, and remained as before. One ought not to change one's soul when one is a leader...

"The authority of the prophet always surpasses the others, but his renunciation is universal." The dear mouth that had said that!

"Prophet?" Claude confessed, smiling bitterly. "Fundamentally, what faith? I don't know anything."

A singular and perilous juncture! Was it necessary to return to Europe, to hope that the credit of the triumph, the magnetism of the soil, would cause his new thought to be accepted? But that was to isolate himself from the parallel action of Erodia. Beyond the seas, the Orient would seem so distant, the Cradle so theoretical. And there would be other projects out there, other constructions, other progress! No, it was on this bloody earth that the word had to be born; everything ought to be consummated here; it was necessary to return with all the work, with the coronation of his thought as with the triumphant sword, to say everything at once to the hosts of Europe, to return with an army won over to India, to change the soldiers into messengers of the good news, instead of meditating alone a project whose delay would be mortal.

I shall speak here, and everything will be decided here, Claude Laigle said to himself, proudly. *It's up to me to find the necessary words. After all, I have been further than all men, and people have followed me. They only understood gradually, but they obeyed first. The annexation of India, the union of the Aryan races, India no longer hated but allied, a sister against the Yellows, that is what will nourish their activity. Erodia will elaborate the conversion of the Hindus; I shall decree it in Europe. It is necessary that people understand that we are not going to kill an admirable force.*

He resolved to explain himself without delay.

The magnetism of the Visitor made him tremble; something holy drove him toward the peril; he rediscovered his lyrical energy; the inertia that had followed the conquest and had extenuated him came to an end. The great mental period of Anarchism, the first of his life, and the great period of the detestation of the yellow races, were about to be followed by a third, and definitive one: a period of love and ardent intellectuality, more beautiful and broader. And what grandeur there would be in the annunciation of the return, if he succeeded! It would no longer be the triumph of the illustrious Killer, the age-old and atrocious triumph; the man with the red hands would bring life! He would rediscover once again the voluptuousness of seizing the present, once again before growing old...

I'm going gray, and there's much to do, but am I strong enough?

Yes, since I believe! Claude avowed. *I see what it is necessary to say, and I alone can say it. In any case, it's simple, like everything abstract. I have detested the Orient, because of the yellow peril, and because of ideas opposed to the European world. The yellow peril is annihilated, and I recognize that my beliefs were ill-founded. I no longer hate India; I want it to be ours. Behind the Orient that I hate I have found another; where I imagined sterility there is life, and perfect life, mental life as developed as our mechanical life. At one end of the land of the white race there is an active force, at the other a meditative force. And the latter is the essential one, for it safeguards the common tradition of both, the Aryan tradition.*

The limit of the modern world, which I placed on the threshold of Hindustan, I shall extend to the Himalaya. I have tamed the land that was opposed to my present conception; now that the Yellows and their allies the rajahs no longer constrain these people, what I want from them is not passive obedience but their comprehension. Erodia will help them to understand. I must help my people to understand that new idea. I left with hatred, and because of her, I'm returning with love. That's clear.

My ministers see nothing here but colonial expansion, annexation, industrial profit and indemnity of war; it's up to me to make them see more nobly, to explain to them the ideological value of the recluses grouped in the Pamir. The Idea of the white races guarded by them, the virgin Orient that cannot die and which is the true one, above that of the Vedas and the revolutionaries of 1856. That is a politics based on a lyricism. Perhaps they'll smile, but we shall see.

He isolated himself for a few days, meditating haunted by the diaphanous Face, strong beneath the luxuriant hair, the face of Erodia, of Ménières, unified into that of the Adventure. Now it relaxed, that svelte figure, in the metaphysical sky of sprays of bright and colored verities, and those verities wanted to flourish in the open azure, between the sapphire of the zenith and he blood of the soil, powerfully...

He was decided.

Everything, in any case, seemed to be soliciting a denouement. Claude Laigle's internal fever left him all the lucidity of observation. He noticed the preoccupied expression of Médion, the subtle and attentive manner of Dessort, their reticence, their questions retained with difficulty, their coldness. They were too intelligent not to sense the transformation of the master's thought, and in spite of the moral hierarchy established in Anarchism and strictly respected, the long sojourn in Hindustan, the immensely extended vice-regency and the enervation of the war and the organization gave them a liberty of appearance greater than in the councils of Europe. They too had developed, affirmed in their theories, they too were forces, adjacent but individual, and the interest of the difficult contest impassioned Claude.

He understood that he had been more the master before the declaration of war, when it was only a project that was in the mind; since those men had contributed greatly to its success, they had appropriated the thought and action of a promoters; the Adventure belonged to them as well as to him. What he was about to present to them was authorized less by a prestige now shared as the mystery of another conception still virginal in his mind. Thus the second stage of the conquest would be elaborated.

After the passionate rise of the departure, until the assault on Delhi, the descent of the Adventure, glimpsed in Erodia's eyes during the first encounter, had plunged into mental regions under the apparent inertia succeeding the war, and then stopped at the Cradle; now it was about to rise again, the Adventure having become ideological, and return with the army to the Occident having touched the unforgettable earth.

Days passed in cautious consultation, in urgent regulation, in diplomatic concerns, as if he adversaries were drawing away before the decisive words. They observed one another in the councils, and as before, the impassive General de Trénan remained silent among them, with his cold and ironic expression, interjecting rare polished and mordant remarks.

The terrible old man was worn away internally, the life was retreating from that ivory face; the long precise hands no longer trembled but were placed flat, as if dead, on the pointed knees. The shaven head with the cruel blue eyes was decidedly that of a priest—the priest of a religion now abandoned. A carriage ferried the old man continually through the artillery batteries, along the rows of cannons; he was almost incapable of getting down, but he leaned out, extending his arms, touching the breeches of the guns as he passed by, handling the rockets and detonators, obsessed with ballistics and explosives, dying of his passion for the shell now that that frightful idea, his idea, no longer sprang from his will toward the horizons.

Claude considered that man with an indefinable pity. And Dessort and Médion had changed too; the socialisator's feminine smile was twisted; his velvety eyes were tarnished, and the face of the engineer had thinned, the temples hollowed out, the forehead striated, the bone-structure of the nose more curtly prominent. Claude felt weary himself, although younger; the neuralgia of the heart recurred from time to time. Only the voices remained the same.

Oh, the aftermath of conflicts in middle age! And Europe was so far away!

They all considered one another with esteem and dread, not daring to commence, to say the thing that would ignite everything. But it was said, however, of its own accord, among the futilities, one evening, as they were regulating an arrangement of colonization, of permissions to set up trading posts and establish manufactories on the cost of Gujarat. Dessort insisted, showing certain economic and industrial advantages and several times already the dictator had replied: "Accepted," in an indifferent tone, his mind absent, when a remark by Médion caused him to raise his head.

"And then, for the posts in the valley of the Indus, the location designated in excellent; it requires an entrenched camp, surveillance is important. The populations are still restless, we're already having enough trouble establishing ourselves in Bombay, which became a Hindu city again a few years after the expulsion of the English. It's necessary that all that ceases once and for all, that the Europeans are the masters; and I'm also thinking about the upper Indus and the Kashmir region. There are germinations of ideas there, in spite of everything, that it's necessary to render impossible. In addition, the profits to be extracted from the mines and restricted salaries..."

"I no longer accept," said Claude, curtly. "Your expressions, Médion, are those of a dominator. My thought is different; I want allies. I only want to take advantage of the restriction of salaries as a measure compatible with the simple life of the indigenes, not as exploitation. We haven't made war uniquely to enrich merchants. And then, we no longer understand one another, I fear, with regard to the 'germination of ideas.' I don't perceive those ideas as you perceive them."

"However," said Médion, "these tribesmen..."

"They aren't 'tribesmen,' Médion. You're neglecting ethnology. They're Aryans, like us, and I desire to treat them as such, with commercial laws analogous to ours, and established rights."

"Your conception of Europeanism had been greatly modified, then?" Médion replied.

"And your conception of anarchistic individualism?" retorted Claude Laigle. "Return to it—you're forgetting it somewhat."

"I've helped enough to render it possible politically..."

"Morally."

"No. Morally...that's your affair, but mine is political...in order not to forget," said Médion, coldly. "But until now, I only considered it applicable to the Confederation of Central Europe, not to it enemies."

"You mean the Orientals?"

"Evidently, since it's to safeguard anarchistic individualism against the enterprises of Oriental fatalism that we've followed you here."

"It was primarily to safeguard the material interests of modernism against a coalition of Yellows that you accepted the war, and it's in those material interests that you've always thought and still think," said Claude.

"So be it—I was talking about your abstract point of view."

"Resume yours, Médion. Mine has changed. I no longer consider the Orientals in the original fashion, and I separate the Hindus clearly from the 'yellow peril,'"

"They marched against us with the Japanese, summoned by their rajahs."

"I'm not talking about the Orient of the rajahs. That's finished, and the fatalism too. I'm talking about a new Orient, with a thinking more appropriate to serve and enrich our colonists. I accept that thinking today, and that's why, far from being frightened of 'germinations of ideas,' I oppose the creation of entrenched camps, especially in the upper Indus."

"I'm beginning to glimpse," Médion said, tranquilly, "that this...thinking and its penetration are doubtless the result of your recent voyage."

"Yes," said Claude, rising to his feet, pale but also tranquil. "I haven't traveled, personally, uniquely to study where camps or factories might be established in the upper Indus."

"I have no intention, however, of establishing any higher up—in the desert regions of the Pamir, for instance. There's no commerce possible there, and it might trouble the communities, whose ideas are agreeable to you, metaphysically speaking."

Médion's voice did not reveal any sarcasm, and yet there was a terrible silence. After a few seconds, Dessort intervened, as a conciliator.

"In any case," he said, "it's a matter of mining exploitations to protect, and there can't be any question of the Pamir. The projects concern lower regions..."

"The mines don't matter to me," Claude Laigle put in, dryly.

"As for entrenched camps," Dessort went on, "it's a matter of emplacement very different, in sum, from the upper Indus, half-way between the coast and Kashmir..."

"Distant or not, I don't see any real utility in them," said the dictator. "The posts distributed from Gujarat to Delhi and to Cawnpore suffice for a military supremacy that the northern provinces aren't disputing with us, having no armies. The sources of the Indus and the Ganges can remain free of surveillance, and as for the surveillance of ideas, since that expression has been pronounced, I've already said that the ideas coming from the Pamir or elsewhere don't appear to me to be contradictory to ours. It's pointless to want to isolate central India from them by a military regime, whether it's installed in the regions themselves or lower down, between them and the Deccan. That constraint, disguised or avowed, doesn't suit me."

"But it's not exactly a matter of a constraint of that sort," Dessort objected. "The project simply concerns the anticipation of offensive returns dangerous to the security of our industries."

"You know full well that those offensive returns can't be produced in the high regions," said Claude Laigle. And I know how that material surveillance, costly and superfluous in itself, could rapidly be combined with another, with your prefects and your theories. Do you think that I don't sense your thinking—yours and Médion's. Do you think that I haven't divined the mental preoccupation that's been haunting you since my voyage, and which reappears in your attention to detail?"

All three of them looked at one another.

"There's certainly one that's been haunting you since the same voyage," said Médion, curtly. "Well, yes, we have something to say to one another: your idea is rubbing against ours too closely, I imagine, for us not to come into confrontation."

"I'm ready for that, although I don't know if you are," said Claude Laigle disdainfully. "I could speak only in Europe, to the legates of the Confederation, but I'll content your curiosity sooner..."

He interrupted himself, considering the two men. They were sitting down, their gazes cold, their attitude defensive and contracted. Something tragic was occurring. Claude shrugged his shoulders,

"Is it your curiosity, or your summons, that I ought to say? You seem to be waiting...do you intend to judge me? I don't know what indefinable expression astonishes me in those eyes that you're raising toward me. I can shut up."

"You ought not to count on the assembly of legates," Médion replied, simply.

"That's true, but I believe I'm speaking here to collaborators, to friends...." Brusquely, Claude Laigle said: "Come on, Médion, Dessort, let's drop this tone between ourselves. My thought is entirely peaceful, and if we're not in sympathy, at least let's esteem one another and let's not talk of accounts to settle. You were much closer to me during the conflict, because our logic was in accord; but now it's a matter of continuing, of accomplishing intellectually, and your support is perhaps more precious to me than ever. Forget the dictator, see the man. Yes, we have something to say to one another. You've thought apart from me and I've thought apart from you. Let's bring our conceptions together, let's bring our legates a unified system, a moral result after the material result. What my voyage has revealed to me, I'll tell you, and afterwards, we'll examine together what the future might be."

He stood up, resolutely, and spoke. He spoke for a long time, with an enthusiastic eloquence, the energy of a lucid conviction, an infinite unfurling of images and thoughts ornamenting one central idea: the idea of the Cradle orientating modernism, taking away its hatred and its dryness, creating, above the cult of mechanical progress, the cult of the Aryan race, giving the war a higher conclusion, am expansion of sensibility and love, a tradition of ethnological simplicity finally sustaining a certainty for all, a return to the primordial laws of evolution. With broad violent and ardent strokes, he depicted the modern ideal, safeguarded by the recluses of the virgin Orient, and without pronouncing Erodia's name, his words, addressed to the beauty of the forces of life, trembled with passion and tenderness as if he were holding, in his empty open hands, the very body of the Visitor, become the immaterial envelope of the Adventure. At any rate, his heart overflowed his mind, one vivifying the other—and he did not feel that the voluptuous expression with which he was ornamenting the logical truth undermined it.

The two ministers, pensively, listened to him less than they considered him, pale and enthusiastic, entirely vibrant with that great interior sonority that rose from the depths of his being, and of which the burning jet came to crystallize on their cold and impenetrable souls. He sometimes had an intuition of that, and, excited in all his combative and fervent nature, wanted to vanquish that mute antipathy to his lyricism with even more lyricism. Suddenly seized by the demon of speech, making an abstraction of himself, of the persuasion undertaken, of the hostility sensed, he yielded to the superior perversity, and said everything, because a prophet ecstasized by beauty in itself, with the exclusivism of the man of dreams who always opens an abyss between the world and his vision.

Asia entire took its revenge in his fatal and admirable intoxication, reappeared alive in that son finally returned, incarnated in him its contemplative centuries, the immensity of its torrid skies, the immortal renaissance of its metaphysics meditated among the palms. And the two moderns, through the master's words, glimpsed her, their enemy, the luxurious queen of the ancient world, rising up once again to face the irreconcilable Occident in the person of that pale man who had led them to the idol and had become her priest, seduced by the ancient world.

An excitement gripped them too, but inversely, the intuition that above the three bodies, the invisible drama was playing out of two essential and contradictory verities. The original antagonism of the act and the dream, which only the abstract laws of the universe can resolve, and which it is not given to human beings to unite. And each of Claude's phrases awoke in them an echo of a dissimilar consciousness, augmenting the irreparable sentiment of an antinomy, separating the two conceptions emerged from the same fact of conquest further and further.

The eloquence of the master operated upon them, but by making them remember the very foundations of their adverse life, and the fracture that had been snaking for months in those three arrogant and silent souls suddenly burst, becoming a gulf. Speech acted above them, simplifying the situation by the divorce of the individual paths. And between the two seated men and the one who, standing, was pronouncing the definitive rupture by invoking union, the sensation of intellectual death rose and floated, inertly, like the great exhausted old man who, his material strength extinct before that conflict of mental forces, listened mutely in his armchair, waiting for the decision to be made for him, the hands falling, the glabrous face with the cold gray eyes leaning over the golden collar...

The dictator fell silent.

For several minutes no one moved. One might have thought that they were all waiting for an invisible being to leave. And Claude, confusedly, sensed that it was the old amity that slowly vanished with the vibrations of the irreparable words.

The faces of the two ministers remained glacial, fixed in attention. Claude's insistent pupils sought theirs in vain. And as the unreal specter dissolved, the eyelids were raised, as if relieved. The eyes finally met; Médion's lips parted, and he said: "Is that all?"

"Yes," said Claude, accepting the terrible doubt.

Dessort raised a hand, swung according to his custom to the rhythm of his nonchalant voice.

"The very considerable conception that is yours, Master, seems to me, whatever luster your eloquence adds to it, to deviate singularly from the very meaning of our initial effort, and is perhaps founded on a...shall I say hasty?...appreciation of the Oriental mind. I don't contradict the utility of the hy-

295

potheses, without going so far as to summarize them in a fact—and it's a matter here of such a considerable modification of ideas that it would lead us almost immediately to facts, privileges conceded to the Hindus, even participation in federative consultations—for in sum, if I've understood you correctly, it wouldn't only be a matter of material rights, but of rights of mentality.

"Now, I confess that the soul of this country, even directed by the occult influence of the communities of the North, does not appear to me, at least for a long time henceforth, sufficiently clearly compatible with the European soul for us to be able to present to the legates, on our return, a guarantee permitting the immediate concession of intellectual rights. I will even add that that eventuality is distant, and that in any case, it is necessary to wait for a more complete assurance, on the part of the communities, of aims identified with ours..."

"Wait...gain time...," said Claude. "No. I wouldn't have spoken if I didn't feel that this matter ought to be settled immediately. There are links, by the very fact of the mother-idea of my project, and the longer we wait, the more difficult those links will be to retire. It's immediately after the ruination of the ancient India that we ought to awaken the sentiment of the new India and quit the enemy attitude in its regard. As for the communities, I can pronounce that I will answer for them. I told you when we quit the Pamir that the alliance is made, mentally. What does Médion think?"

"It's quite simple," said Médion. "I think that there's nothing here but hypotheses and more hypotheses, and that we can't return to Europe, which has been bled white for two years for an idea proposed by all of us, in order to declare that that idea no longer suits us, and propose in exchange a hypothesis."

"I thought I was expressing a verity," retorted Claude Laigle.

"A verity of what order? A factual verity?"

"No, a verity of mentality."

"It doesn't involve, thus far at least, a factual verity; and that kind of verity, I call metaphysical—which is to say, interesting and seductive but worthless. Yes, worthless, and it's clearly evident that it was born here, in this land that can't produce others and which has died because of that, as much and more than because of us."

"It isn't dead, and it's that very new life that I'm bringing you."

"Yes, I know, the virgin Orient...but the experience has been harsh, for centuries. This land propitious to enchantments charges forms easily; the Occidental consciousness will see the ancient monster behind the new face. It will see that your 'mental verity' is the dream of a summer, and that it can only make those kinds of dreams."

"The dream of a summer?" said Claude Laigle proudly. "I hear you. Are you insinuating that I'm bringing the counsels of Erodia here? Go on, dare to say it!"

"I shall not bring into such a grave discussion the consideration of a woman, who is, in any case, intelligent and who, if well-directed and carefully monitored, might be useful to us later."

"Useful to *us*? Who do you mean by *us*?"

"I still mean Europe, you and all of our people."

"But I don't mean that anymore."

"Us...and you—so that makes two, now?"

The simple and terrible assertion fell between the three men. In his corner, General de Trénan shuddered weakly. Médion and Claude measured one another with their gazes, enemies now."

"That's one statement too many, Médion."

"You forced me to pronounce it, Claude Laigle."

"You misunderstand me. I spoke too soon, I believe, just now. As for Erodia, this is the respect in which *we* and *you* make two, as you put it. She will not be *useful* to me as you think she will be *useful* to you. She is outside utilizations, she will not propagandize your idea or mine; she is and will remain free. But it happens that her thoughts and mine are in accord, and will act separately.

"That's fine, with regard to your hypothesis. But as for facts, if the communities and their leader are not the couriers in India of the Occidental modernist spirit, they are indeed of no use, to you any more than to us. They will vegetate. And Europe will find it good that they are monitored—oh, not rigorously, simply to avoid the singular attempts to which inertia can push overly searching consciousness, the possible...materializations that minds overheated by solitary metaphysics might attempt."

"Is it in your name that you speak?"

"I believe I am speaking, this time, in the name of the entire Confederation, of its need for peace, of its fatigue with dreams succeeding dreams and throwing it into adventures when it ought to be fortifying its position."

"Still your refusal of general ideas, then? You haven't advanced since our conversation in Paris on the eve of the war?"

"I've advanced in my direction, and you in yours."

"So, your 'universe of chemistry,' your science, your exclusive Occidentalism, and nothing more?"

"So, one is an ideologue when one is Head of State?" pronounced Médion, dryly.

"Well, so be it. We'll see whether one can be both. It's my very idea that you're refusing?"

"Europe will refuse it too, I assure you. There's no point in going as far as a disavowal. It's Anarchism itself that you're compromising if you persist."

"What is it, however, if not an ideology?"

"It has become a State, and demands facts. The Parliaments have been blown up; that's a fact. We have ruined the yellow peril, in order to be able to work tranquilly at home; that's another fact. Don't excite us to emerge therefrom at the very moment when we're about to go back; that would be a third fact, which would annul the other two. That's what Europe will say, and you can't go against her will; you're the master but you won't be any longer if she refuses to follow you."

"She has had faith in me."

"She won't any longer. I regret having to tell you such things."

"Don't insist, Médion. I sense—I know—what your regret is worth."

"It's sincere, Claude Laigle. But you're taking us too far, and I can only attribute it to the influence of this pernicious sky and this accursed soil, where abstract systems have germinated a cerebral aberration to which a woman is no stranger."

"Ah! You're coming back to that!"

"I repeat that by 'a woman' I mean the detestable Idea that she represents. The rest doesn't concern me."

"But admit, then," cried the dictator, "that you hate the virgin Orient as much and more than the old, because you're afraid of it!"

"Yes, I'm afraid of it, of the ancient monster with multiple faces, since it can deform a man like you. The Occident is irreconcilable with the State you dream of aggrandizing. Whether or not we set out from your Cradle, we won't return there in thought; out there we've made a new life. May it remain desert! And may its reclusive metaphysicians, whose secret correspondence is so zealous, not talk too loudly about the security of their phalanstery! You ask whether I hate it, this poorly killed Orient that is reborn and is absorbing you? Yes, I hate it, like the abstract laws that oppose the active will. And you—am I mistaken?—confess that you now hate the Occident!"

"Médion!" Dessort intervened, alarmed.

But Claude Laigle, startled, cried to the minister who had become a judge: "Well, yes, I hate it, if that's what it is! I hate it, your modernism, your labeled world, prostrate before I don't know what mechanical progress, what ideal of exact science torturing thought, edifying and order and a harmony on silence and blood. After the kings, after the bourgeoisie, after the tyranny of money, now there's the tyranny of Dynamism, and I shouldn't detest it? But it's like the others, it kills egotistically like the others, it has the number for a fetish as the others had the crown, the ballot or the check-book, and what you call progress is putting a hideous plaything in the place of those who have served too much.

"Your science is killing sensibility, and I don't want it, your life fragmented into formulae, I don't want your aluminum cities where firm and inexorable faces go by beneath electric lights—I don't want it! Your Occident, with its regulated barbarity, deprived even of the free instinct that is so beautiful here, I refuse it; you can arrange it as you wish, with your compasses, look in your retorts to see with what oxides you'll transform its rottenness into wellbeing! But if I've had to accept power and all the responsibilities of my life to be the great leader of your mechanisms, the accountant of your derisory equations, I shall go away laughing, so ridiculous, even more than odious, do I find you all, engineers, the bizarre population of geometry that I shall treat as Gulliver did!

"Has it taken you until now to understand that I wanted to do something extraordinary with you? On the evening of the declaration of war, when I said that the sublime of a politics was the realization a dream, you didn't understand, and you threw yourselves immediately into the Adventure in order to give a fine role to your torpedoes, your telephones, your gyroscopes, to all your means, which you made into ends, and also to enrich the merchants, you offer yourselves colonial theft on a grand scale, to carry to other skies the prestige of the modern as you understand it, the strict gentleman with his pince-nez, his notebook and his syphilis!

"And you think, perhaps, that after having led you to ideological war against the Parliaments, I'd compensate you by permitting your avidity this vast gallimaufry, under the pretext of protecting yourselves, permitting you the reflective elaboration of a new consciousness? Get away! You haven't understood anything of what I see, but I'm bringing you forces more elevated than your technical perfections, and you'll understand, or you'll yield; those forces won't be belied; they'll hold sway in spite of you; I shall use the rest of a life, not caring whether it ought to be yours, in crying out to them, in prophesying to them.

"I shall address myself to that which is eternal in humans, the heart, the instinct, and I shall address myself to the baser parts if the mentality has been too poisoned by your dogmatism, but it's necessary that your fetishization of the number, you who speak of mine, goes with the others into the red mud were the obsolete ideals stagnate, the dung-heap beneath humankind!

"Oh, you persist until I speak for myself, you want me finally to say what I've thought for a long time about the fashion in which Europe, at least as you've shaped it, uses the Anarchism that I gave it, and you think that I'm going to accept that everything continues to go on as before, the petty trafficking, the petty formulae, the transportable methods, all your apparatus of progress? Well, now you know what I think.

"We had, in coming here, a stake, India. We'll have another out there, and we'll see which of us, you or me, will raise up that great mass of human beings bogged down in error and throw it back into the current of the river of life. In the meantime, I'm still the master, and I know where I'm going. You'll silence your suspicions, you'll give way until my return to Europe, and you'll obey me!"

He stopped dead, terrible. Médion and Dessort inclined impassively.

And suddenly, a voice that they scarcely recognized rose up behind them, stammering: "The shell...the shell...was a guarantee... It was worth the trouble..."

They turned round. The bloodless face of General de Trénan, leaning over the golden collar, showed vitreous eyes, the pupils half veiled with gray under the narrowing of the eyelids; the thin lips were colorless. The tall, thin old man was weakening after the work done. They drew closer.

"A guarantee..."

His mouth formed a rictus, and remained inert. Outside, a sudden racket burst forth, a dull rumble of mounted batteries passing at the gallop; the ground trembled, and the dangling hands of the cadaver, long waxen hands, stirred slightly with that vibration.

XI. The Ellipse

The veritable funeral of General de Trénan was to take place on the return to Europe; no ceremony, beyond an embalming in the presence of a few mute witnesses, announced officially that the master of the artillery was dead. The hasty building of forts and the multiple cares of administration attenuated the effect of that loss. Already, the idea of the reintegration with the Occident, the conquest terminated, was floating over the army. The soldier stood aside before the civil element, the colonist and the engineer taking up their roles, and the disappearance of the commander-in-chief had less impact on minds. There was no funeral eulogy, except for the orders of the day and an imposed silence.

Claude, self-absorbed, left the expedition of current affairs to the ministers. With the great murmur of material disarray that was agitating everywhere, his determination faltered, sensing a disaggregation brewing. In order to get a grip on himself he shut himself away.

The accumulation of decisive circumstances rose around him, stifling him and keeping him upright at the same time. The demonic Adventure, alive and shrill in itself, demanded its solution, developed to the extreme without concern for interior ravages, and he sensed it stirring in his flesh like a child, or the millions of microbes of a disease ready to burst forth. There was nothing more to defer; everything was imposing; everything was coming to term; the hypotheses had expired; life had simplified things terribly.

The unreal bouquet of verities, unbound by the Idea from the metaphysical sky, had let its flowers fall, their germination had blossomed, insistent and devouring, and it was necessary to die in the torpor of those perfumes or to uproot the spray once again with a masterly fist.

The situation was complex, but so synthetic that Claude's mental system adapted to it with an absolute precision, and he had the sentiment of being confronted, without the hope of escape but also without deception, by a double obstacle, material and intellectual. At least that clarity of the peril stiffened him now, with a clear gaze, to envisage his despair; in the midst of his anguish, the perversity of logic created within him a strange joy, the intoxication of living intensely, exceptionally, a drama of unknown proportions in which he as the essential actor. The cerebration was killing him as it exalted him. He felt driven into a corner, concentrated in himself.

What should he do? In bringing about the irreparable argument between the ministers and himself, had he clarified the situation or sealed it forever? The problem had at least been posed, but had not the negative solution been pronounced at the same time? Was everything finished, or was everything about to begin? It had been necessary to speak, evidently, and Claude did not regret anything, sensing that evasions, unworthy in themselves and repugnant to his nature, would in any case have been futile or even harmful.

The new Idea was one that did not admit petty means, and which had to be presented in its totality or never. It was, therefore, in accordance with his nobility, his logic and his future that Claude had acted in speaking—but he also sensed clearly that the ministers' refusal was decisive, and that the European soul, progressive and modernist, had passed in their response; the quarrel with the ministers was not a difference of reasoning but a formal antagonism of races. Europe would not ratify his position; either it would be necessary to force it to do so, or resign.

Dictator, having served in their interests, resign when it's a matter of explaining to them the mother-idea of so much fatigue? Get away! Claude said to himself, revolted. *I'd be too forgetful of the ancestor Nietzsche and "the aristocracy of masters." I shall fight—like the sovereigns of the old times, but as a true anarchist. Deep down, these people are still socialists. It's the mental habit of the masses that is standing up against me.*

And he avowed that he would anticipate them. The face of Erodia appeared to his mind's eye. "The authority of the prophet surpasses all others, but his renunciation is universal." Well, yes, a prophet, and a modern prophet, choosing between authority and renunciation. He accepted the alternative internally.

What can that do to me? I have nothing left to lose if I lose my conception. They'll understand and give in or I shall...cease.

Life, with its violent forms, as in the time of the bombs, as in the taking of Delhi, raised a pitiless landscape in his soul.

After all, I've struggled alone, or very nearly, against the Parliaments, when I was young; I'll begin again, as an individual leading the collectivities. And will I be without adherents? That remains to be seen.

The revolution of the masters, then, after that of the people?

Well, if they don't understand, regardless...why not? It seems to me that I'm only now recognizing myself as an anarchist. The masters, that was what the bosses once called themselves, but I'm against the material bosses and for the ideological bosses. That's a religion in the fashion of the positivist calendar; it's a trifle silly, but people only find it so when others want to impose it on them, when it's in a silly form...

He smiled, sadly, listening to two contradictory voices, the mass, isolated, the brutes from which everything germinates, and the sterile, who understand and lead the brutes, the antinomy that had rotted all societies since the primal era.

And then what? There'll be blood again, they'll kill the masters; they always kill the masters, and yet it's the instinct of every anonymous individual to be a master. Is it my fault if they led me there? It's not me who's demanding, it's the Idea that wants it, and ideas are more powerful than men, more powerful than them and more powerful than me. Except that it's always necessary to attain them through the flesh, to extirpate them messily, like children, in blood...

Always that red glue, which sticks, and also causes the forces to skid into one another...

It's never tidy, as soon as one acts. But it's that, or submit, with a heap of thoughts in the belly that want to get out and call you a coward...

He sensed that he was not the master of the choice, that within him the Idea was identified with instinct, which could only be stifled along with his respiration.

Too bad, too bad—it will come out. It's up to me to see that it doesn't cost too dearly, that the childbirth isn't too messy. They're expecting, back there, another infant, which I've promised them. Well, one can be mistaken. I'll explain, that's all. Will they disinherit the child because the physician anticipated another? I'm very much afraid that they won't want to hear anything; with their modernism, they imagine that the Orient is antinomic to them...

All that's still a matter of customs. Modernism, to them, is still frock-coats and phonographs; understood like that, how stupid modernism is! To think that I believed in it—me! Yes, I believed in it, in spite of everything; I realize that I was a prisoner of the habits and the décor of Paris. Oh, the décor! But at least I'm liberated from that now; they're still there.

They want to give machines and top hats to the Orientals, and that doesn't worry me, but as for admitting the Orientals as their own, never! They invoke the rights of conquest, the money to be made from colonial trafficking. They'll nobly grant the telephone and the black suit to the Hindus, while making the observation that it's an act of generosity, but it won't be out of the desire to give them something better than they have, but in the spirit of domination, of leveling, of socialism! And they'll believe, because they're dupes themselves that they've brought the Occidental soul here.

Oh, businessmen, accountants! And the foundation of all that is always the old hatred of ideas, always the execration of those secret leaders that inject them, like sperm, into the bourgeois belly, prepare their descendancy, and are always obliged, in the end, to emerge violently, with blood...

All that turns in the same circle. And there isn't any reason for it to finish, that's the grandeur of humanity, it's with that that they want to make things!

He plunged himself into successive projects. To fight head on if Europe was obstinate? Dangerous and impractical. It was necessary, then, to assemble the aristocracy of masters, to found a State within a State? Might as well found it here, then! He glimpsed the whiteness of the communities among the roseate rocks and the palms, the sand of the Pamir with the color of the body, Erodia, an inaccessible realm, conserving the traditions of the white races in their very

Cradle, and felt the desire to let go of everything out there, the land of mechanism, to fade into the dream of happiness—and then started.

Oh, no! If I return to the Cradle, it won't be as a prodigal son, alone and naked; Erodia would ask me what I had done as a son, she'd reject me; that would give the lie to the Idea, the laughter of Europe would arrive here, and if we resisted, the Idea wouldn't resist. Not to mention that the posts of the upper Indus and Médion's plans wouldn't leave you tranquil in decline for long...

More blood, decidedly, whichever way I turn...and then, if I fail, at last Erodia will remain intact. She'll continue, her recluses will choose another, later. Blood for blood, it's better that it's shed back there...

Everything pressed him to return to the Occident. After the real forces that he had led away, the abstract forces that he would take back, the ebb and flow of the same red tide.

His conquest had become exclusively cerebral. From a group of facts, it had become a group of ideas, and all those ideas, born of a desire to bring him back morally to the Orient, united nevertheless to take him away from it materially. There was an inexplicable contradiction there.

I'm really quite disorientated, Claude said to himself, and suddenly burst out laughing. *Disorientated! Oh, words and their justice! Yes, I've 'lost the Orient' in wanting to 'lose North.' Disorientated? Of course, since I'm a man of the Occident! Is Médion right, then? How droll it is!*

He interrogated himself, almost amused.

So, he said to himself, *everything is lined up to take me away from here, and yet I came here and found here my true reason for being; so, what led me here in spite of everything? Was it some absurd law? There are no absurd laws. It wasn't colonial politics, nor the annihilation of the yellow peril; they're apparent and circumstantial reasons, now laws. What is that law? I realize that it isn't my personal will. Oh, yes, Claude the willful, tell yourself that it was you alone! You wouldn't have been sufficient, you'd already be dead if you wanted to offer yourself to that dream of your own accord. It's a law that's amusing itself in leading you and giving you the necessary strength of endurance...but what is it? I can see that it's what's leading me, but where is it taking me? And yet they have to be reclusive! What a singular thing! In the first sense, I can conceive the Adventure very clearly, and in the second I perceive it even better. But between the two slopes, in the present, where I am now, what am I, who is asking the question, going to do?*

The obstinate mutism of destiny confronted Claude like an extraordinary wall.

It's annoying! If I occupied myself with theology it couldn't be more unknowable—and yet these questions have a material basis; it's an ethnological matter, after all, there are methods! Oh yes, methods! They lead to contraries, and the contraries form identity. And to think that moderns of Médion's sort live

*in tranquility dreaming of a universe of methods! What a pity! How petty that is!
Do I believe in God?*

He smiled.

*No... Yes... I don't know any more. It depends. And to think that I'm not
skeptical and that I'm bursting with faith in the midst of all these people...*

He was crazy for days, like a metaphysician constructing a theory. But if a
theory is false, it remains interesting, and it is only a matter of making another
while awaiting a third. That is dilettantism. Whereas, given that the situation
was complicated by too many material interests, and active energy, how was it
permissible to be mistaken? Misfortune was waiting at the door, and he did not
have much time in which to decide. The ministers must be studying their plans
too, and as their theory was much more rudimentary, they would move more
rapidly in the examination of the measures to be taken.

Pensively, Claude walked the streets of the poor quarters, obsessed with
the Idea, gazing around him vaguely, almost as Newton must have been gazing
the instant before the apple's fall.

One evening, at dusk, cries caused him to look up. Children, having taken
possession of a large empty barrel, were climbing on top of it and amusing
themselves by making it roll, maintaining their equilibrium by means of a continual tread. Suddenly, one of them, unable to maintain himself, slipped and fell,
and the heavy barrel passed over him, half stifling him. At the moment when
Claude looked up he saw the little body caught under the curvature of the thick
staves, lying underneath the round mass, which continued to rotate. An image
struck him and he went pale.

Already, the other children were lifting to the weeping and bruised child
and taking him away, amid the remonstrations of the women who had hastened
forward. Claude drew away, almost running, and went back into his apartment,
pushing past the sentries.

*That child is me, and the great round mass that passes over him, that
throws him underneath simply by virtue of the fact that it continue to rotate... is
the earth!*

Slowly, the idea awakened by the analogy rose up symbolically, took form,
became a specter, the specter of the Adventure itself sitting facing the frightened
dictator. A certainty emerged from it by degrees.

But that's it! Imbecile that I was! he suddenly exclaimed. *What have I
come to do, what idea has led me here in spite of all the circumstances that are
now taking me away and casting me down? What did I see descending again
with Erodia's eyelids in our first meeting? But it's quite simple! It's the movement of the earth continuing. It's the hemisphere that rises around the axis and
descends again, and I'm descending again with it! And I'm caught underneath!
In the previous rotation I rose with it toward the Orient, and now it's necessary
that I follow it and pass underneath it, in order to reappear on the other side.
And if I remain still, like that child whom the ground stopped and prevented him*

from making the compete rotation, I'll be crushed, like him! There's no fixed point!

What have I come to do? I can see it clearly now. I've come as Napoléon wanted to do, but he stopped in Egypt, and I've succeeded, I've been as far as India, like Alexander. And how is it that I've succeeded materially where Napoléon failed, where Alexander's attempt had no serious duration, where the domination of the British East India Company was broken in 1856? How is it that I've succeeded materially? I understand the pride of my ministers; that fact consecrates for them the right of the Occident to tame Asia. But what they can't comprehend, the poor fellows, what it will be necessary for me to explain to them, and what they'll never admit, is that my material success is an irony greater than Napoléon's failure, for if the destinies of the Orient have permitted me, against all probability, to come here, it's in order to be caught by this very country. The Occident thought it was sending a conqueror but it has only sent them one follower more, a hostage! I've come here, yes but to change my soul, and it's once again that the Orient is obtaining the upper hand. Once it rejected the men of the West; now it's welcoming them, but modifying them!

The law that has pushed me here is the terrible law of evolution—not the evolution of races, but astronomical evolution. And that's where we'll never understand one another, the Europeans and me! What has brought me is the Ellipse, the fleeing curvature of the Ellipse, which governs the course of terrestrial evolution, and I'm making the tour! I've been brought, I'm being taken away! And I thought I was led by the natural expansion of the Occident! No! That was an illusion. The movement of the world has thrown me into the Orient; that's why I've succeeded where my predecessors failed, and I can't maintain myself any more than the child n the barrel just now!

He stopped, bathed in a cold sweat, a sudden idea opening up.

"Also, it's not natural," he said, in a low voice.

He went on, slowly:

"What's happening is just. My conquest, such as I undertook it, wasn't natural. The failure of my predecessors ought to have shown me that. I thought that modern perfection would enable me to succeed; I was short-sighted, and the immediate political interest hid the abstract consequences of my contact from me. I made an error. The perfection of weapons and the State wasn't in question, they only served to drive me further into an impasse, and instead of succeeding more than Napoléon or the English, I've simply taken failure to its extreme. My conquest is *abnormal*."

The decisive words were born, one by one, from his mind, hesitated on the edge of his lips, and then emerged—and his life went with them.

He said to himself then:

Abnormal, yes. I understand now the unknown disturbance that hasn't ceased to haunt me since the departure from Paris, and which reappeared as soon as the racket of the war eased and let me think. But I couldn't see; it was necessary for me to go to the depths of the error, from me to come here for that. What irony! My conquest is abnormal, because it's contrary to the movement of forces, which is from East to West. Like the child on the barrel I've leapt on to the world at the moment when it was passing in one of the directions of the ellipse, and now, by virtue of the natural force, I'm falling again.

I knew full well that there was something contrary to nature in that success. The movements of conquest are always produced from the Orient toward the Occident, in a quantity infinitely superior to the others; and neither Alexander nor Napoléon, nor the Crusades nor the British, have been able to succeed. They were going against the Ellipse, and the rotation had brought them back. I've made the movement of moving closer to a hearth, and that made me think I'd succeeded; it has taken me much further in the inverse direction, but I've been thrown back all the more rapidly in the true one.

The Europe that is drawing me back might well install itself here materially, but mentally, she can't; it's still the Orient that will come toward her; and she senses that obscurely and hates it. The Oriental descends toward her from the height of the plateaux, and arrives by the conquest the old Aryan genius brings it: the flood of Tartar, Hunnish, Finnish or Mongol hordes created the Franks, or the Russians, or the Slavs, but the contrary current is impossible. The Aryan genius doesn't move back toward its source; that makes no sense.

He interrupted himself, pensively:

"Was Erodia wrong, then?"

No. She isn't asking us to come back. Her idea is greater, and unassailable. She's simply asking that we remember the Cradle, that we don't forget that we're the sons of the virgin Orient. She told me that: our coming is neither a hindrance not a help. She isn't afraid, nor desirous, of a real presence, but she wants a mental presence. There are neither Orientals not Occidentals from her point of view; there are Aryans. It's because of that idea that she also told me that I'd come back. She's right. I came back to the Cradle, but it wasn't with my armies, by way of them or for them that I came back. I was reasoning politically, to prevent the yellow peril and destroy the India of the rajahs, which had also forgotten the Cradle, but I was wrong to give Europe the hatred of the Orient.

I've broken, by my attempt, a cosmogonic law, the immutable law of the Westward evolution of the East. That's why my conquest is absurd and can't last. The more my lieutenants try to consolidate it, the more they'll be obstinate in the error. If they try to annihilate the virgin Orient, it will be them who become the Barbarians, Oh, Ménières told me that in Paris: perhaps we are the Barbarians, and the being we seek, which Médion and Dessort declare to be impossible, is here! It's Erodia who incarnates it.

And even if that were maintained, if I installed the Occident here by force, as my ministers wish, wouldn't the secret counter-direction burst forth one day or another? There would be a latent voice, and it would develop as a direct consequence of its opposition. No, no. Nothing can be founded on an initial error, and this one has already lasted too long. It's something anti-natural. I only oc-cupied myself with the political interest of my conquest, but now that the facts have fallen silent, where's the why of it all? A revulsion toward the moral ori-gins of Europe, yes, but not a material installation. The sociological divorce of the races, yes, but not a mental divorce—and it's exactly the contrary that I wanted, and that Europe, drawn by me, still wants! It's necessary to repair that.

He let his head fall into his hands, overwhelmed.

Repair that! Oh, I've moved a sphere that's too heavy! How superior the women of the virgin Orient are to me! They're in the right; they've understood the eternal movement. They've remained at the Asiatic center, at the Cradle, and in the midst of the incursions of Europe and the despotism of the rajahs, they've safeguarded the idea of races. We believed, stupidly, that behind our exodus we'd left a desert, and that there, where our race was born, everything was fin-ished. As if there were no more fields when the crop has been harvested!

They're taking responsibility, the silent ones, for showing us the contrary. They'll remain behind us, they'll reform, intellectually behind the emigrants we were, they'll use our scientific inventions and our moral and theological libera-tions, but rejecting that which stains them with error. They'll remain, they won't go in the counter-direction, they won't try like us to throw themselves East-wards—to regenerate the Yellows, for instance. Turned toward us, their forgot-ten brethren, they'll remain in conformity with the Ellipse of the world, of which they're one of the focal points, and they'll wait! "I was waiting for you," Erodia said to me.

And now, now that we've come back, as enemy brothers, they remain unas-sailable to fratricide; they've summarized their power in a system that doesn't even need a representative ideological material, and which an army can no more annihilate than, for instance, the idea of weight. The enemy brothers have come back to lose everything , and now they're redescending, changed in me, and with them the mother-idea will redescend, Aryan thought once more af-firmed by those who wanted to kill it. The eternal conquering exodus of the East toward the West, it's my armies that will undertake it, unconsciously. Oh yes, we are the Barbarians, in every fashion! We were Barbarians in the atrocious fash-ion, in coming here to exterminate, and we shall be in the vivifying sense, in re-taking the road of Attila and Timur with a fecund thought!

He raised his head proudly.

I shall lead them! Come on! I'm a man of the Orient myself, a son of the Cradle, an Aryan who remembers! I'm at home here, and I've felt it keenly. Perhaps alone of all European armies, I've been logical in returning, I've been right. But all the rest were wrong to return with ideas of hatred. Fortunately, I haven't been killed by an imbecile bullet before understanding that. Ménières sensed it before dying, and it's necessary that the thought lived on in someone, since Trénan has died of consumption after the cannon was killed that kept him alive, dead like the hatred that I brought from Europe, which he incarnated.

307

I'm a man of the Orient, and I'm only beginning to be a man of action, a conqueror, in returning, with the next rotation of the Ellipse, to the Occident with the idea of the virgin Orient. I ought to have departed alone to seek across the mountains, away from Paris, the central idea of Anarchism, the true new religion of which machinism is just a parody, but if the armies have accompanied me, it's as an ambassadorial escort. There's been nothing here but the simulacrum of a conquest; the veritable one is about to commence.

Oh, I really am an Oriental, yes, since I'm now going to return with my troops against Europe! But I won't return like Attila or Timur, for theft and murder, as my ministers have done here; I shall summon mental Europe in order to give it the faith for which she is searching! A continual exchange takes place; everything that has passed Westwards has passed inversely and exactly here; Europe has sent a Timur in my person, as Asia once dispatched one; Europe had sent a Pierre l'Ermite against Asia; the virgin Orient will render her another, and it will be me! There was a Sepulcher to deliver? There is now a Cradle to recognize!

Everything balances: but why is it necessary that the exchange seems treacherous? The Europeans led by me were traitors and fratricides toward the Orient, and now I know that Médion, Dessort and all the others will judge me a traitor and a fratricide toward Europe! Is the exchange impossible, then, without violence? Always the childbirth in blood, always the Idea attained through the flesh. What fatal misery!

Come on! Have I truly arrived at the bottom of my idea? Let's see, let's see...yes, now, I'm confronting it totally. But have I the strength? It's frightening. I understand, I see, what has to be done, but...but what? What's wrong with me? What's retaining me here, sitting down with my head in my hands?

He was gripped by a contraction of the heart. He stiffened himself, haggard, his hands flat on his breast, immobile.

The pain passed.

Poverty of the body, poverty of the soul! There—that's because I see what has to be one and that I no longer have the desire to do it!

Is it because I'm growing old, because I feel that I'm alone, sick with the neuralgia of the heart that will carry me off one of these days? Is it because I'm afraid of the consequences of my second conquest? Is it rather because, now that I've clearly satisfied the idea, my soul is satisfied and no longer finds it interesting to realize it? Yes, that's it! Intellectual perversity, then, but in reverse! Instead of doing something because everything indicates to me that I shouldn't, I no longer want to do it because everything indicates to me that I must. But that's absurd, absurd, and I sense that the absurdity, born within me, is growing, devouring all the rest. Let's see...I'm tired, I'm going astray...

He listened to himself, livid, and murmured:

"To go against the Ellipse...to force the initial error to its most extreme consequences...make it a verity...maintain oneself in spite of everything until the next rotation of evolution will perhaps put things back in place...to be obstinate in Napoléon's dream...that would be grandiose too! Very grandiose, very extraordinary! And Europe, this time, would consent, while in the contrary case I'll have to take possession of everything again, assuming that I can...

"To go against the Ellipse...to struggle against the ethnological laws, the cosmogonic laws—what a terrible ideal! There it is, the abstract struggle, the intoxication of the geometer and the astronomer applied to the material power..."

His arm described a series of ellipses in the air.

"Yes, there are the focal points, the curvature...to struggle with that sign, face to face, to tame that... That sign, which my arm follows easily, that's my enemy..."

And suddenly, he shivered, and almost shouted: "Oh! But what about the virgin Orient, and Erodia, and my faith, and what I said to the ministers, and everything? I'd be denying all of that for the desire for power! But that's insane, that's inviable, that's false...and yet, why is that what I've thought, after all that I've promised myself? Perversity or fatigue? I know full well that if I go against the Ellipse, it will succeed for a time and end up by failing, while the other conception, almost impossible at the outset, will inevitably grow into verity. Is it, then, that I don't love verity enough? Is that I'm an Occidental all the same? Truly, this is becoming madness; a man can't touch what is simple without going mad..."

And, prostrate, with cold tears trickling between his fingers, stuck to his face, Claude Laigle let himself go. The energy overtaxed for months, for years, finally abdicated, leaving him inert, on a swell of sobs.

I dare not, I dare not, that's all...I'm not sure... Oh, Erodia, how far away you are! But it isn't you who's troubling me and driving me to despair; your Idea is just and calming... It's the Ellipse that frightens me. Ought I to yield—and what labor before the disavowal of odious Europe! Ought I, impiously, violently to remount the course of the movement of races, disavow the eternal order! Do I even have the strength before that abominable, infamous and despotic thought? It's tempting me, Erodia, it's tempting me! It's because I lived for too long out there, before knowing you! If I'd come here younger... No, no, I'm lying. It's out of cowardice that I want to go against the Ellipse, because I wouldn't be alone, because the others would help me, because it's easier... What shame!

In a low voice, he called: "Claude Laigle? Where are you, Claude Laigle?"
He laughed, bitterly.

It's really the Idea you believed to be alive that's killing you, Claude Laigle. You thought you were an ideologue? But you've never been strong except in action, always weak before ideas, fundamentally. You really are a conqueror, an active man, you're only good for that, you see. You're the Timur, the Genseric, the stupid and grim leader of brutes who demolished in order that his people

309

can install their petty systems, devote themselves to their tasks, satisfy their manias and their habits, as if at home.

You've taken a bath in blood here, months ago, and now your soldiers and your engineers are building, arranging, leveling, applying their methods. You can see that you've taken a great deal of trouble to do exactly as the others did. You're good for nothing before the Idea, you can see that you're too small to do anything with it...

At least your rivals couldn't see, and were quite tranquil. You've sought your doom, Claude Laigle. You've pushed the round machine in one direction, like the children you saw, and now it's turning, without paying any heed to you, and you're falling, and it's the entire world that's pushing you to make you fall...

And you're not accelerating the movement because you'd be alone in trying, and you won't go in the reverse direction because your people wouldn't suffer that either...

You're an ordinary man, an episodic, and moreover, you have the misfortune to perceive it, and to perceive that you've run out of strength.

Claude Laigle, Claude Laigle...oh, who can envisage an essential Idea without terror?

The phantom of the Adventure, untying the unreal flowers, got up, threw them away, dead, and left. And Claude, exhausted, watched it draw away through his tears, with an ironic face laughing over its shoulder.

XII. The Supreme Evening

There was no further mention of the violent conversation at the conclusion of which the commander-in-chief had died. Médion and Dessort remained strict in the councils, and outside the regulation of everyday questions, Claude Laigle enclosed himself in an absolute silence.

Some time having gone by, he received a message from Erodia.

Have you spoken already, or are you waiting for the return to Europe? she wrote. *I have been working on my side; the Idea is steadily gaining ground. I have good news of adhesions throughout the valley of the Ganges, attachments in the Oude, an almost complete consent in Mysore and Nepal, which, in any case, have secretly favored you rather than detesting you. Many marched by force, under the orders of the Japanese and the princes. Do your ministers know that? My associations are gaining power and making contacts everywhere; the Aryan Idea will be saved. I need to come as far as Lahore, with a large escort, a party of my women, and a number of affiliates that I shall bring with me. It is useful that we see one another again. Can you leave Delhi and come to meet me?*

He hesitated, and then decided. Delhi was odious to him, doubly so, by virtue of the obsession of blood and the broken idea of the Ellipse that had just attained him there. He announced a plan to inspect the camps in the direction of the Kashmir frontier, and departed for Lahore. The ministers were to accompany him there, and then quit him to travel through the provinces. He acquiesced to that measure of solicitude, in which he divined suspicion, and made the voyage indifferently with them. In any case, they avoided him discreetly when their presence was not indispensable. He isolated himself in the marches, ill, suffering from his heart and of a kind of dull stupefaction only glimpsing confusedly a reawakening of his intelligence by means of the confrontation with the Visitor of Souls.

Perhaps I'll recover at a stroke, on seeing her...

Familiar landscapes struck his eyes. They were following inversely the route they had taken from Lahore after the great victory, toward the investment of Delhi, and he rediscovered impressions, the sentiment of decisive action, the sentiment that had once hastened his gallop alongside the terrible old man's caleche. But a world of dreams had risen up since then, and how dissimilar!

They traversed vast encampments. Everywhere, on the military roads, the dictator observed the preparations for departure, which the ministers had hastened. Divisions crossed their path heading toward the valley of the Indus and transports were moored on the river. Others astonished him that were heading northwards, parallel to his escort. He interrogated Médion; evasive pretexts although quite plausible, were given—except that one morning, Claude no longer saw the troops whose direction seemed menacing. They had disappeared, traveling behind the woods and hills without him being able to suspect their presence.

All around him, in the villages and the forts, the mobilization was stirring for the exodus to the Occident, with a surprising activity. The force was withdrawing too precipitately not to cause Claude Laigle anxiety; it seemed that Médion and Dessort had quickly renounced their ideas of surveillance.

Convoys of artillery cluttered the passages. The Occident was decidedly commencing the reflux of its tide of men; everything revealed the breakage, the slow attraction of the lands quit, drawing the sons of Dynamism away after the completed task.

In the approaches to Lahore the impression was accentuated; the military quarters were no longer empty, but an immense quantity of carts had accumulated there, all overflowing with piled-up baggage. Europe was taking back her own. Claude was struck by that.

To maintain them here, against the movement of Ellipse, in a contradictory effort? he said to himself. But they're the ones who seem no longer able to hold on; they're leaving with urgency. Is the solution I wanted the one that they're ultimately adopting, mechanically? Evidently, Médion and Dessort are stimulating all this, pressing the departure; I can't see their intention clearly; one would think that it's been modified since our conversation.

Yes, but the point isn't to go back as they departed, but to go back with a changed soul, and their soul is the same. Morally, they haven't learned anything

311

or forgotten anything, and it's there that it's necessary for me to intervene. Come on, I shall act! I shall act! I was mad to think of maintaining the effort in the counter-direction; I don't know what moral depression came over me. It really is the other solution that's necessary, the Idea of the virgin Orient remains; I'll no longer be afraid when I've seen Erodia...

He felt reassured, hopeful. As they got closer to the North and the Cradle, the Oriental he was recovered his strength.

He reached Lahore observing and meditating. Nothing suspect had appeared to him, however. When he arrived, there was news of Erodia. A few more days would be necessary yet for her to join him. He decided to wait, quite calm.

In those few days, amid external cares, the encumbrance of the troops and the preparations for the departure, an extreme confidence took hold of him again. He was almost joyful, reanimated, not by the imminent presence of the Visitor, but by the sweetness of the Idea, reappeared in his mind after months of doubt. The spectacle of the reflux of the Occidentals penetrated him with the conviction that it was necessary to act before that reflux carried him away, a more important unit, but dissolved in the mass.

He was ill, but his mind was clarified by the illness itself; he had arrived, beyond the anguish of his logic and his energy, in the relatively calm regions in which one enjoys an idea abstractly for its own sake, without tumult, like the areas of calm reflective water at the center of a maelstrom. The contradictory rotation of forces gripped him and maintained him in a relative equilibrium; he was in the depths of the cyclone but believed that he was floating above it, out of reach. The strange illusion of moribund individuals who talk about voyaging in fresh countries sustained him in an ideological wellbeing. One last start brought him upright, and he believed at the first moment in a rejuvenation of energy. Thus, he waited for the Visitor.

And suddenly, he became anxious. His happiness, as it resumed a tangible form and drew nearer to him in the appearance of an individual, seemed to expose him to a peril that he could not define. Was it the magnetism of amour that warned him in that fashion? He recalled the suspicious and prepared attitude of the ministers, Médion's closed expression, Dessort's taut smile. Perhaps they were meditating some surprise...

Get away! I'm the master, no one here budges without my wishing it!

In spite of everything, he would perhaps prefer it if Erodia were not coming at that moment. He dreamed about her still up there, inaccessible, the enigmatic deity of the virgin Orient, with her recluses ready, when she grew old, to ripen the conserved Idea, if she had not yet enabled it to flower. He almost thought of telling her that, summoned couriers, and then sent them away without a message, revolted by the thought.

What would she say? Decidedly, I'm still weak, to have such scruples. I'm like a mistrustful tyrant; it's ridiculous.

An anxiety remained, which irritated him fully without him succeeding in chasing it away or defining its causes precisely.

The rainy season had returned; stifling storms floated, bursting in warm torrents; the odor of plants and the overheated earth caused malaise, and the electricity in the air exasperated thought. Claude attributed that vertigo of doubt and suspicion to that.

The days passed; Erodia did not appear, delays evidently due to the season held her up on the route. At the same time, Claude Laigle observed singular troop movements in the vicinity of Lahore. Taking advantage of a calm in the rains, he left the city, and recognized with surprise and dread the divisions he had seen following roads parallel to his since Delhi, which had suddenly disappeared on the way. They had not, then, veered eastwards toward the Indus? Why had they come as far as Lahore, openly at first, and then secretly?

A terrible suspicion went through his mind. Médion was playing with him! What was the objective of this convergence of troops? He recalled that those divisions had disappeared one morning, after a question posed by him, and interrogated Médion distractedly, and then the commanders of the corps. The responses were vague...he must have been mistaken about the numbers of the regiments...these troops were partly destined to replace the forces that were about to quit the city and Kashmir. The confusion was quite understandable in the great upheaval of the mobilization. Then again, half the troops that he saw really had quit the other half, which ought now to be descending the Indus toward the transports...

Reasons of management and administration were established, precise in themselves, but tedious, obscured by the multiplicity of details. Claude Laigle renounced seeing clearly, and then turned away, gripped again by the Idea that effaced everything. He remained on his guard, but judged his anxieties excessive. Between and undeniable ill will and a direct assault there was an abyss that no one dared cross. The Dictatorship, in any case, with the terrible discipline of Anarchism, created a right for him, protected him. Médion and Dessort, even if they dared, would not ruin their own cause before the Confederation—and there would be an immediate court martial...

No, it was too improbable. Their hatred would only be free to express itself in Europe, after the decision of the council of legates. Absorbed in the Idea, Claude gathered his strength again for that alone. In any case, Erodia's arrival was announced. One more day, and her free escorts would be camped south-east of Lahore. Claude received the news in Médion's presence, observed his face, but only saw a sullen indifference, the expression of a discontentment on seeing something stupid occurring about which nothing could be done—and he smiled internally.

His rank, and the ceremonial customary before the Hindus, forbade him to go to meet Erodia and her cortege. He waited for them to arrive. The next day, the establishment of the Hindu encampments was known at three o'clock, but a new storm abruptly burst, frightfully; the streets of Lahore and the military quarters were inundated by tumultuous rain; an immense whirlwind developed with unusual violence, and disorder followed. The reception could not take place; it was necessary to wait.

Claude was irritated. At four o'clock the storm attained its greatest intensity. In the dictator's house a crowd of officers and dignitaries had gathered for Erodia's coming, anxious about the weather. Everyone was mingling, leaning out of windows or over the edge of the terraces, talking animatedly.

Suddenly, Claude Laigle, in the din of a thunderclap that shook the house to its foundations, felt his arm gently touched, and looked round. A sepoy officer saluted him ceremoniously. When the man's head was raised again, the eyelids fluttered. Claude shivered, recognizing one of Erodia's servants, seen beside her once in the Pamir.

The man spoke, very rapidly and quietly.

"She has been here since yesterday evening, and it is not the storm that prevents her from coming. She is anxious. There are cordons of European troops south-west of the city; they have replaced the sepoy troops of which I am part, and are ready if you have need of them. Know that orders have been given for that."

He drew away; a new clap of thunder burst, and fell as much upon Claude Laigle's soul as on the city. He tottered, dazzled by rage and terror, and leaned on a balustrade. People hurried around,

"Nothing," he said. "A fleeting pain in the heart. The repercussion of the thunder. It's nothing."

His eyes sought Médion and Dessort, saw them calm and impassive, seemingly bored.

"Messieurs," he said. "the reception is decidedly postponed until tomorrow. You're free to retire at the first calm."

Haughtily, with a brief salute, he disappeared, went back to his apartment, a surge of violent ideas leaping up in his soul as if to break it, and at the same time stiffened by the danger, which finally saved him from his doubts. Anything rather than doubt!

The blood was rushing within him like the seething of a cataract. He dug his fingernails into his palms, and stammered: "Oh, I knew full well... Act! It's necessary to act! So they dare! Well, I like that; we're going to settle this right away!"

Anger convulsed him, and for a second he became the Claude Laigle of Anarchism, the conqueror of Delhi, the Master.

"We're going to see whether I have the army or not, whether subordinates..."

A thousand plans jostled furiously in his mind. He thought about having Médion and Dessort arrested immediately...

But no—they're surely not alone; they have affiliates among the troop commanders. That would alert them; I don't know anything...and then, let's not rush; there must be evidence. An arrest would give the others time to destroy the evidence. Then these orders would be explained slyly...no, that's not the way. First of all, it's necessary to save Erodia, to find a pretext, a ruse, to prevent the troops from...

What luck that this storm prevented the meeting! Everything might have been irreparable by now. I have until tomorrow to think! What a filthy mess! But I'll save her; there's still time. I'll be there; I'll talk; I'll lead the army, even if I have to make use of indigenous regiments to be in with to prevent a skirmish. Would they dare assassinate her, all the same? But what about me, then, who also has the Idea? No, they'll want to use cunning, gain time, simply invent I don't know what delay...

Then again, perhaps they believe that it's me who's meditating some violence against them, and they're being wary...

What alternatives! But first, first, see her! Oh, how that Occident weighs upon me! I've had enough of it! To quit everything, yes, to live up there, at the Cradle, with her, as an inaccessible emperor, and slowly conquer by mans of books the world they're disputing with me in deeds! Yes, but...that would be to retreat, all the same. They're acting, I shall act. Tomorrow, I'll be north-west of the city, with Her, with her women, and her genius, and the sepoy troops, and tomorrow I'll bring that elite of the true civilized down on Europe, on Dynamism! I'll bring them back to Europe with me to direct my crowds and sow the Idea there, and we'll see whether anyone will dare to raise a hand against me! This is a minute that will decide everything; I'm no longer hesitant. They wanted it; it's not longer as equals that I'll bring back the Orientals—it's as masters!

The fury that was strangling him burst out as a terrible joy, with a brutal change of direction, and he stood up, ready.

Two hours later, in a wretched cart hitched to the team of an artillery ammunition-wagon, Claude Laigle rolled through the suburbs of Lahore, heading for Erodia's encampments.

He had got out without any difficulty, the house empty of visitors, the ministers disappeared. Under the torrential rain the streets and courtyards were deserted. No vehicle in harness remained there; he had had to go as far as a neighboring post and requisition horses from an artillery battery; the artillery men had had great difficulty finding a cart with a tarpaulin cover in a hangar, which he had adapted as best he could.

The four horses were galloping among the jolts and the splashing mud. Darkness had fallen; it was almost cold now; the extreme humidity intense. The downpour had relented, but the roads were in a parlous state.

Wrapped up in his martial cloak under the rough, soaked tarpaulin, Claude Laigle, exasperated, expecting the unknown, was no longer thinking, almost unconscious, living a purely physical existence, gazing at the bounding rumps of the horses, where lantern-light vacillated, the dark landscape, the palm trees broken by the storm, and the city's lines of firelight. At the advanced posts he leaned toward the officer of the guard, showed a abruptly-illuminated face, snapped "Secret mission!" and the horses galloped on amid the jolts, under the whip of three drivers whose large cloaks were flapping.

It resembled a flight, that departure toward the triumph of the Idea, and a bitter irony sometimes gripped Claude Laigle's heart. The night, the downpour, the wretched cart: all the sinister and pitiful aspects of the Adventure were thus denounced in mud after being born in blood. But tomorrow, perhaps an unreal Sun would rise!

Images passed vaguely through his mind: Louis XVI on the road to Varennes, an old engraving contemplated in childhood...the boulevards of Paris on the evening of the explosion of the Élysée...the assault on Delhi...Ménières' face over the dirty serge...Erodia, the roseate rocks, the opulent horses, the curved Cradle...Trénan inert, fallen on the arm of his chair...

And the Idea rose up, floating in the improbable sky of metaphysics.

"Are we getting close? I can't see anything. Are we nearly there? Nothing can be heard."

The suburb was deserted, sulfurous gleams trailing on the pools of water. The carriage, bogged down by the mud, swerved on to a round road; distant lights appeared. Claude started. Was that the camp of the recluses and their escort. Yes, that was the direction. The lights became more precise in the curtains of rain, which were become less dense. Erodia! Erodia!

Distant rumbles of thunder rolled over the plain; the storm was resuming, but dryly; the downpour cleared, almost stopped.

Suddenly, a more precise noise mingled with the rumbling thunder, in abrupt spasms—a noise that Claude thought he recognized, but almost indiscernible in the storm. However...

No!

He leaned over the edge of the cart and shouted: "How long before we reach the lights?"

"Another three-quarters of an hour," replied a servant, half turning.

"Hurry, hurry... Are they so far away, those lights? We're almost there..."

"There's no air, but it's some way off. And the road..."

"Can't you hear anything, apart from the storm?"

"No," said the man. "It's making a noise like machine-guns...one might think, but...."

He shouted, in gasps, in the jolts of the cart and the whistling of the wind: "The sound of machine-guns?"

"Well, yes...there's no reason.... But I heard it said in camp today that there was a sepoy mutiny, and that it might get hot. One's never sure with these people. It's already arrived..."

"But the sepoys have been moved; they're not in that direction. If there were trouble, even so far as necessitating cannons, the noise wouldn't be coming from that direction..."

"Perhaps...I don't know..."

Claude threw himself back into the shadow. *And no one's following me! What does that mean? Another three-quarters of an hour! No one's following me! Is it because they believe I won't do anything? They must have seen me leave—I didn't hide. Or is it already too late? Would they dare? Erodia! Erodia!*

Time passed. The artilleryman closest to Claude turned round abruptly. "There are cavalry ahead and to the side, but I don't know what it is..."

"Cavalry?"

"Yes—listen, you can hear..."

In the calm, there was a dull and regular rumble.

"It's not sepoys, at any rate...they aren't mounted. There's no danger..."

"It's a guard unit!" shouted the voice of the driver at the front. "They're ours! No danger!"

Is it them? Claude wondered. *No danger*, he added, bitterly...

The sound of hoofbeats grew. From the depths of the darkness indistinct silhouettes separated into two masses coming to meet them, one head on, the other obliquely.

"Don't stop!"

The team kicked on, enveloped by whiplashes; the carriage rolled furiously, drawing Claude, both frightened and calm. If it's then, everything's finished...

And suddenly, the horsemen seemed very close; he heard distant cries, a "Halt!" The password was ready to leap from his lips, but the others did not should anything, and broke up. The carriage flew. The great shadows wheeled, drew aside to let them pass, and then came alongside at a rapid trot, on both sides of the cart.

Suddenly, in a gust, shouts overlapped:

"Confederates!"

"Who are you?"

"Confederates!"

One, two vivid flashes shone to the right of Claude Laigle, surging from the tarpaulins. A cavalier almost brushing the cart stretched out his arm; two revolver shots rang out, and then three more. A terrible jolt stopped the cart dead in a muddy skid; one of the horses fell, a lantern smashed. The driver nearest to Claude uttered an oath.

"Confederates, you were told! Are you deaf or mad?"

A face leaned over.

"You didn't respond, either!"

"A horse killed! Now we're in a mess! And urgent service!"

317

The horsemen surrounded the vehicle. Claude stood up, resolved. He was about to shout: "Another horse, quickly!" when the words froze on his lips. By the light of the remaining lantern he recognized the man who had fired.

It was Médion.

The latter pronounced, very rapidly: "No need to continue. *We've come back.*"

Claude stammered: "You've dared...!"

"The idea remains to you," said Médion, with a sneer. "You can use it as you wish, alone. As for the people *up there*, they were superfluous. Europe will approve. Anyway, *she* was hit by chance..."

In a mist of blood, Claude heard the thunderous voice of Dessort.

"What an error! After the skirmish just now, that disorder...understandable. We didn't hear you when you shouted. Hitch up another horse. Service of the dictator!"

Claude's hand clutched at his belt, seeking his revolver. Médion saw the movement, threw himself backwards, and Claude, with a single movement, braced himself against the edge of the cart, his arm extended to kill. But suddenly, in the effort, an abominable pain seized his heart, a decisive rupture of life.

His hand shook, the revolver fell, and his body, folding in two, collapsed, spinning, the neck dislocated, the arms outside the cart, in the void.

Médion leaned over.

"The Master has fainted!"

Heads approached. Claude's tongue, between the parted lips, stirred.

Médion shouted, very loudly: "An accident! His neuralgia of the heart afflicted him again this morning. That storm favored it. He wanted to go out all the same..."

"Yes," shouted Dessort, "to see the skirmish with the sepoys. We dissuaded him, but he went out in spite of his condition. And that alert just now...the shock..."

Claude's tongue was no longer moving. Everyone shut up. There was a frightful silence. And suddenly, the cart shifted, the dictator vacillated, and the poor inert head came into the light, displaying the revulsed eyes.

"The Master is dead!"

The soldiers bustled, terrified, a disarray of horses and men clattered, drowning out the ministers' words. They came close together, driven toward the cadaver, gesticulating.

"It's necessary that no one knows," said Médion, in a low voice.

"Assuredly."

"An accident...a sudden and fatal crisis..."

"The consequence of so much fatigue for the cause...he died after the work was done..."

"His work...ours...that of the evening of the declaration of Paris...."

With a cold gaze, they understood one another.

Claude Laigle, his body folded in two, was still hanging over the edge of the cart, his arms outside, dangling.

As the rain continued to stream over the soft face of the cadaver, they tore the silk lining out of a hood, and someone covered it.

Harry Dickson

LE SHERLOCK HOLMES
AMERICAIN

No. 106   Le Chemin des dieux   Prix fr. 1.50

C'est lui! murmure-t-on autour de Dickson, c'est lui, l'épouvantable mandarin!

Jean Ray: *The Path of the Gods*

The original series of pulp magazines which eventually became Harry Dickson *began in Germany in January 1907 under the title of* Detektiv Sherlock Holmes und Seine Weltberühmten Abenteuer *[Sherlock Holmes and His Most Famous Cases]. Published by Verlagshaus für Volksliteratur und Kunst, also responsible for* Texas Jack *(a* Buffalo Bill *imitation, 1906) and, later,* Lord Lister *(a* Raffles *imitation, 1908),* Detektiv Sherlock Holmes *was likely written by Theo von Blankensee and Kurt Matull (the creator of* Lord Lister*) and a team of anonymous scribes. It eventually ran for 230 weekly issues, ending in March 1911.*

The fact that the name of Sherlock Holmes was actually used on the cover created some concern about the wrath of Sir Arthur Conan Doyle's lawyers, and with No. 11, the series was retitled Aus den Ge-heimakten des Weltdetektivs *[The Secret Files of the King of Detectives], even though, inside, the main character was still called Sherlock Holmes. Doctor Watson, however, was soon replaced by a younger and more dynamic man named Harry Taxon. In 1908-09, a number of issues were reprinted under the new title* Harry Taxon un sein Meister *[Harry Taxon and his Boss], giving the limelight to the younger assistant. The covers of the first 125 issues were painted by the renowned, Pomerania-born artist Alfred Roloff, a member of the Berlin Academy.*

Sixteen issues of the original German series were then adapted into French, between October 1907 and March 1908, by publisher Fernand Laven of La Nouvelle Populaire *under the title* Les Dossiers Secrets de Sherlock Holmes *[The Secret Files of Sher-lock Holmes]. That title appeared only on the first issue and was immediately changed to* Les Dossiers Secrets du Roi des Détectives *[The Secret Files of the King of Detectives] with No. 2. Like in Germany, however, the protagonist inside was still identified as Sherlock Holmes, but his assistant was Harry Taxon from the start.*

In December 1927, Dutch-Flemish publisher Roman-Boek-en-Kunsthandel (which also published Buffalo Bill, Lord Lister *and* Nick Carter*) launched a Dutch translation of the original pre-WWI German series, this time entitling it* Harry Dickson, de Amerikaansche Sherlock Holmes *[Harry Dickson, the American Sherlock Holmes]. The Dutch series lasted 180 issues, until May 1938. The Dutch publisher decided to sever all connections to Sherlock Holmes. Their first issue was a translation of No. 49 of the German series. The detective was rechristened "Harry Dickson" (this was the first time that the name actually appeared), and his young assistant Harry Taxon became "Tom Wills."*

Some scholars have speculated that that name "Harry Dickson" was a logically derivation from that of "Harry Taxon."

Others have remarked upon the similarity be-tween "Harry Dickson" and "Allan Dickson," the star of Allan Dickson, le Roi des Détectives Australiens *[Allan Dickson, the King of Australian Detectives], a short-lived but popular French pulp series created in 1906-07 by Arnould Galopin, the author of* Le Docteur Oméga, *under the pseudonym of "Max Dearly."*

Finally, others have noted the existence of a 1913 movie serial by René Plaisetty entitled Les Aventures de Harry Dickson, *in which the eponymous detective hero was played by Edmond Van Daële. However, that serial no longer exists. Some have claimed that, to name his hero, Plaisetty combined the names of two then-popular singers, Henry Dickson and Harry Fragson, not forgetting Harry Taxon, already known to the French public.*

Whatever the origins of the name "Harry Dickson," in 1928, Ghent-based Belgian publisher Hippolyte Janssens decided to translate the Dutch series into French, for publication in both French-speaking Belgium and France.

Janssens' new French-language edition was also entitled Harry Dickson, le Sherlock Holmes Américain *[Harry Dickson, the American Sherlock Holmes]. It began in January 1929 and lasted 178 issues, until April 1938.*

We do not know the identity of the first writers who were hired by Janssens to translate the Dutch magazines into French, who penned the first 19 issues and thus set the style for the rest of the series. (Some have speculated that Gustave Le Rouge might have been amongst them.) We do know, however, that a contract dated 1929 was signed between Jenssens and Belgian writer Raymond De Kremer, who also lived in Ghent, hiring him to translate subsequent issues of the Dutch series into French, starting with No. 20.

Raymond De Kremer (1887-1964), better known today as Jean Ray, was already a prolific writer and journalist who had authored numerous stories for young readers, as well as comic strips, detective and horror stories, in Flemish-language magazines under the nom-de-plume of John Flanders. His tales of the fantastique, written in French under the pseudonym of Jean Ray, have since become horror classics. They include the novels Malpertuis *(1943) and* La Cité de l'Indicible Peur *[The City of Unspeakable Fear] (1943), as well as short story collections such as* Les Contes du Whisky *[Whiskey Tales] (1925),* Les Cercles de l'Epouvante *[The Circles of Terror] (1943) and* Les Derniers Contes de Canterbury *[The Last Tales of Canterbury] (1944).*

Scholar Hervé Louinet claims that Ray edited, translated and/or adapted 148 issues of the French Harry Dickson *series, from No. 65 onward using mostly the titles and the covers by Roloff as starting points for very loose adaptations of the originals. It is no exaggeration to say that Roloff's covers, which had been purchased in bulk by the Dutch from the German publisher, greatly contributed to the success of the series. The very month after Janssens discontinued using them, the French* Harry Dickson *was cancelled.*

The adventures of Harry Dickson *have delighted several generations of French readers. Because most of them were penned by an acknowledged master of the fantastique, they are more fantasy-oriented than the traditional* Sherlock Holmes *canon. The best and most fondly remembered* Harry Dickson *tales are not those where the great detective fights a spy ring or a blackmailer in true Holmesian fashion, but the ones which pit him against some monstrous fallen angel, a mad scientist or some larger-than-life villain, in the true traditions of the pulps. What the intellect lost in logic and deduction, the readers gained in pure entertainment and fantasy.*

This episode was initially published in 1934 under the title "Le Chemin des Dieux".

J.-M.L.

1. The Ridiculous Dinner

They were getting bored. Lord Denverton's receptions were never very entertaining, but this one beat all. Dinner dragged on, and had been mediocre besides: the soup had been served lukewarm, the pasta was half-cooked, the appetizers were dressed in too-sour mayonnaise, the fish wasn't fresh, and the poultry arrived with the wings burned and the meat limp and bloody. They'd been served grocery store wine and drugstore whisky. When the ice cream showed up it was half melted. That was the last the straw: the guests were on the verge of complaining.

Denverton, presiding at table, didn't seem bothered by the dreadful standard of the menu. He did nothing but look off into space, and his guests might well have thought he had something against them, to make them sit for hours in front of dishes of doubtful quality, badly prepared, in an atmosphere reeking of boredom and awkwardness. But Denverton was fabulously wealthy, Denverton was powerful, Denverton could afford to offend cabinet ministers and members of Parliament and other big shots. He declined the dish of gooey ice cream the headwaiter offered him, and absentmindedly peeled a very hard peach, which he left untouched on his plate.

Dinner was reaching its end, and the guests, knowing his lordship wouldn't keep them long past dessert, began to breathe more easily. Coffee and liqueurs were served. Then came a moment of watchful silence. Finally the headwaiter returned carrying a large tray on which lay a pile of yellow envelopes, one for each guest. He slowly made the rounds, each guest avidly taking the envelope meant for him. The headwaiter skipped only one guest, who shook his head. And yet that guest had already gotten a note, right at the beginning of dinner: *Don't eat! Stay here with me this evening!*

He reread the note, which it had cost him no regret or difficulty to obey, so bad had been the food. Then he went back to observing his twenty or so fellow guests seated around the table, all looking much happier now that they'd gotten their envelopes. They were mostly people of modest station: clerks and shopkeepers in the City. Their presence in this setting, the opulent dining room of the Dukes of Denverton, was a genuine shock.

Finally his lordship rose; that was the signal for a general withdrawal. A few of the guests bowed awkwardly to their host, who returned their politesse with the slightest, stiffest bend of his body. Most fled straight to the cloakroom; others tore open their envelopes and counted the banknotes that dropped out: "Fifty pounds! What are the odds!"

In the dining room now remained only the guest who'd received the note from Lord Denverton, and Denverton himself. They stood on opposite sides of the room and watched each other without drawing nearer. The host moved first. "Mr. Dickson," he said carefully, "how does it happen that you were among these guests chosen at random?"

Harry Dickson nodded slightly. "The invitation went to a man I arrested a few days ago for a string of crimes, each worse than the last. He gave it to me, saying, 'Well, friend Harry, go to Lord Denverton's in my place. I think you'll find it a couple of profitable hours.'"

Denverton blushed. "Is that all, Mr. Dickson?"

"Yes... But are you acquainted with the people who just left?"

"Not in the least!" cried Denverton.

A strange reply—and yet it didn't seem to faze the detective. "I thought as much. Let me tell you about them: Samuel Bird, hat maker in Battersea, three times a bankrupt. Lewis Stoneroad, seven convictions for forgery. Morris Lapland... hmm... a few morals charges that made him familiar with Dartmoor. Gustave Parant, one murder on his conscience, though there wasn't enough proof to hang him—but a nasty customer even so. I could go on like that, down to the twentieth man."

Denverton was in agonies. "I don't know whether it's God or the devil who sent you, Mr. Dickson, but allow me to invite you to share my personal dinner, and we can talk..."

Sensing a mystery, Dickson accepted with a simple nod.

They were served in a small room draped in magnificent silk and furnished with uncommon taste and discretion. The menu was exquisite: caviar, cold duck, foie gras, fine fruit. They ate in silence, or close to it, exchanging only small talk.

The detective plucked one perfect golden grape from its bunch. "Was it a wager?" he asked finally.

"No. I'd rather have lost."

"Quite right, I understand."

Silence fell again. A servant quietly brought champagne. Denverton swallowed two full glasses, one after the other. "A clause in my uncle Denverton's will," he said softly.

"Your whole fortune came from him?" asked Dickson casually.

"Yes, I'm the last of the Denvertons."

"How long have you been in possession?"

"Since his death, three years ago."

"So this was the third dinner of that kind you've given?"

"The third, indeed. And it'll go on…"

"Can you show me the clause?"

Denverton once again poured himself a generous glass of champagne. "Of course. It's not long, and I know it by heart:

Every year, on this date, twenty guests you do not know—and whom you must not know—will take their places around the formal dining table of the Denvertons and will be treated to dinner by you, my heir. At the end of the meal, at which you will preside, you will hand each of them the sum of fifty pounds."

"That's it?" asked Dickson in surprise.

"That's it!"

"What penalty did your uncle prescribe in case of noncompliance?"

"None clearly defined. Just this:

Beware not to disobey this order, or calamity will fall on you from all sides, and the fortune of the Denvertons will be lost to you."

"Is it the same guests each time?"

"Not at all! They're different every year. I've researched the process carefully. The invitations are sent out by an intermediary, a notary well respected in the City. He knows no more than I do. He gets the invitations, with my request to distribute them, and he collects a handsome fee for doing it."

Dickson let the champagne fizz and grow still. A hundred questions rose to his lips, but he suppressed them all. The late Stanton Denverton had been neither an eccentric nor a madman; just a man of good common sense whom all England had known as such. Finally he asked simply, "No other clause?"

"Um, not really… I can make no alterations to this old house. I'm especially forbidden to make changes to the formal dining room."

"The room where you receive your annual guests—whom by the way you treat rather shabbily!"

Denverton smiled. "My only revenge!" That moment of levity helped to drive away the atmosphere of gloom.

Dickson reflected aloud. "No one's harmed. No one complains. I came because I was driven by the curiosity that's natural to my trade. In fact, my role here should end now, without ever starting."

Denverton reddened slightly. "And what if I asked you to find out what's behind this whole peculiar business?"

The detective observed the nobleman's glum face for a long while. The man was so miserable, it wasn't surprising that he radiated misery all around him.

"Would you permit me a few questions?"

"Please!"

"Lord Denverton, you had no fortune at the time your uncle's death gave you possession of his title and his wealth?"

"Not only no fortune—I had debts. My name was only Wrenworth. From time to time my uncle had sent me subsidies. He kept his distance from me, and hardly ever left this vast mansion. In his youth he'd traveled a great deal."

"Is the staff here the same as in your late uncle's time?"

"No, there's been a complete turnover. The will set aside suitable bequests for all the old servants at Denverton House."

So now what? Dickson's initial curiosity was fading. He felt boredom rising toward him like a dark tide. Where could this investigation lead? To some senile whim of the deceased, some deep obsession nursed for years by the fantasy of a spoiled old rich man. Bah!

He thought again of the old crook on whom he'd found the letter of invitation, and who'd held it out to him, saying, "Why would a moneybags like that invite a rascal like me? The great Harry Dickson should go find out!"

Though he'd been skillfully questioned, the crook knew nothing about it himself—which had made it all the more enticing to the detective. His interest had held up through the entire ridiculous dinner, but now it was flagging...

An obsession! A folly that a mischievous old man, now dead, wanted to prolong beyond the grave by the simple trick of a clause in a will, perpetuating his senile wishes. With an irritated gesture Dickson cut the tip of the splendid Henry Clay his host had offered him, and slightly broke the leaf. He raised his eyes, looking for an ashtray in which to set the damaged cigar. Then he lowered his head again. He couldn't be sure what he'd just seen: at the far end of the room, some rapid and menacing movement—maybe a hand. He couldn't have said. Something had happened, but what?

Having set down the cigar, Dickson drew back his hand and rested it on the arm of his chair, where it encountered something hard and cold: the jade handle of a small dagger, sunk to the hilt in the club leather, a few inches from his heart. "So," he murmured, "someone was targeting me! Therefore I must be a nuisance to someone in this house. All right! That settles the last of my hesitations!"

He pulled out the little weapon and slipped it into his pocket. Denverton had seen nothing, and was yawning.

"Well, sir," said Dickson, rising, "purely for the entertainment, I'm happy to look into your late uncle's strange intentions. My blood's up, as they say—or it nearly was!"

Denverton shook his head without understanding. For him the important thing was that Dickson not abandon him to his misery, that the detective find a way to put an end to those awful obligatory dinners! "Have a little more whisky, Mr. Dickson, or some brandy."

Dickson declined; he needed to be alone to think. An obsequious butler showed him to the door. The street was foggy, and the newly lit globes of the streetlamps were surrounded by the reddish halo that precedes the famous London fog.

Dickson went a few steps in search of a cruising taxi. Seeing a cab approaching with its flag up, he put out his arm—but another hand held his back.

"What kind of mess are you getting yourself into, friend?" murmured a voice in the fog.

The detective whirled around and found himself face to face with a little man, badly dressed and badly groomed. But Dickson's experienced eye could see through the makeup, and he recognized the voice. "By heavens, it's Bun…"

The other man cut him off. "No names, please! Even more than the walls, the fog has ears! I'll see you at your place in an hour!"

Dickson hailed another cab and had himself driven home to Baker Street. On the way, paying no attention to the dark streets that rolled by, he frowned and murmured, "Bunny Lipton! What kind of a crazy business is he going to drag me into now?"

2. In Which the Path of the Gods
is Mentioned for the First Time

Bunny Lipton, head of the Oriental division of the secret police, and a man well acquainted with the most terrible secrets of China and India, had already been mixed up more than once in the adventures of the famous Harry Dickson. He was a small, clever, capable man. Like Dickson, he had courage, patience, a lawman's intuition, and trust in that mysterious luck of the avenger known as fate. He lacked the great man's genius, and he readily admitted it.

He seemed to be in a very bad mood that evening when he showed up at his famous colleague's house.

"I thought you were off somewhere in the boondocks of China, Bunny," said Dickson after shaking his hand warmly.

"I wish to God I was!" replied the policeman sadly. "I'd happily solve the most Chinese of puzzles in the heart of China—but not here, in London! Cases pick up a different flavor here, they get Europeanized, which is no help to me when I'm trying to solve them… You know, Dickson, on the one hand I'd rather see you a thousand miles away from that wasp's nest tonight—and on the other hand I'm delighted to find you by my side once again."

Dickson burst out laughing. "To tell you the truth, I don't have a clue what's going on. It was just curiosity that led me to Denverton House tonight. I'll tell you everything I know…"

When the detective was done, which didn't take long, Lipton remained silent for a moment. His eyes shone. "That's exactly it, Dickson! The dinner held for twenty good-for-nothings on the same date every year. By the way, did you notice anything particular at the table?"

"Yes: one seat remained unoccupied!"

"The twenty-first place! Right! All's for the best in this, the best of all possible worlds—unless it's the worst one, after all! Lord Denverton didn't attach any importance to that absence; he's not smart enough! But that's the key to the whole thing, Dickson: the no-show guest!"

"I'd be grateful if you'd shed a little more light for me, Bunny."

"Alas! I'm forced to tell you a Chinese story, one that's indeed a genuine chinoiserie! It's twenty years old."

"Reign of terror over Peking! Reign of terror over the European concessions! Communications had been cut. The native population was fleeing, and some of them were trying to take refuge inside the concessions. Fuh-Suh had come down from the mountains and was crossing the plains at the head of an army of pirates, Boxer rebels, and Taiping rebels recruited from all across the enormous land of China. He dreamed of driving the Europeans into the sea and drowning them—unless he could chop them to pieces first.

"He practiced every horror: villages burned and leveled, fields plowed under, inhabitants wiped out. The British flag was his particular target—Anglican missionaries who fell into his hands had suffered the vilest tortures.

"For years, Fuh-Suh had exercised his reign of terror over the distant plains. Now he'd become greedy: he wanted the capital, the Imperial City, the Forbidden City, and above all the European concessions. For days the scales of destiny truly seemed to be tipping his way—and then a terrible epidemic broke out among his troops, decimating them more effectively than the most powerful artillery in the world could have.

"That was when the allied powers hastily landed fresh troops, who went on the attack against the invader. Fuh-Suh's army was cut to pieces, but he himself didn't fall into the avengers' hands. He was believed to be dead—but then skilled informers managed to learn that he was far from it.

"Fuh-Suh continued to kill from the shadows. He'd evolved from a conqueror into an assassin. For lots of Chinese, he'd become God. Years went by. Fuh-Suh's crimes continued unabating. Suddenly there was a let-up. Then it was learned that a secret society had been formed—as if there weren't already enough in China!—a society that hosted an annual dinner for twenty bandits. I know the society's rules; they're not long:

"*Every year, twenty crooks will be summoned to a meal. They will eat, and will be paid for coming. A year will come when the guest who is always absent will show up and take his place at the table. That will be Fuh-Suh, who will return to earth along the Path of the Gods.*

"It might be tempting to see it as just another ritual, like so many others in the Orient; and essentially it's just a symbol of the final resurrection. Fuh-Suh, now dead, will return to take his place among the living—and of course he'll be delighted to find himself, at his first earthly dinner, surrounded by villains and reprobates. We had only a faint interest in it—when suddenly I was called back to London. I got here a week ago, and was taken to meet the Prime Minister's private secretary. For several months now the P.M. himself, Lord Dambridge, has been convalescing from a serious illness at a seaside resort on the Continent.

"'Lipton,' said the secretary, 'I brought you back to reprimand you.'

"'That's a fine way to welcome a fellow, sir,' said I.

"'Are we going to allow Chinese ways to take hold here?'

"'Certainly not, sir, because they can't always be recommended!'

"'Well, then! For months now I've been inundated with anonymous notes, all of them saying, more or less, *Annual Denverton dinner equals annual Fuh-Suh dinner. For solution ask Bunny Lipton.* Fuh-Suh's name brought back too many ugly memories for us to ignore that advice; so I treated myself to the extravagance of summoning you from Peking to London.'"

Here Lipton turned to Dickson. "Well, that damned secretary's no fool, Dickson. Without really knowing why, I felt there really was an odd similarity between those mysterious dinners, taking place so far apart."

"We have no evidence that the mystery is in any way criminal," objected the detective.

"Alas, Dickson, that's not the case. The evening I arrived I received a parcel at my hotel, which contained a freshly severed head—the head of an elderly Chinese man whom I haven't succeeded in identifying. But I'd stake my life that he was the author of those anonymous notes addressed to the Prime Minister or to his secretary; and some unknown master has punished him for high treason!"

"It seems to me that you might investigate why the late Lord Denverton included such a peculiar clause in his will."

"As if I hadn't already done that, Dickson! I've overturned half a dozen notary's offices and questioned half a hundred lawyers in the past few days. Oh, I went to a lot of trouble, but… goose egg!" moaned Lipton.

"As I recall, the late Stanton Denverton was a man of good common sense, a little misanthropic, not a bad fellow. He'd traveled a lot."

"Yes, but not outside Europe. He was satisfied with very long stays at spa towns in France, Germany, Switzerland, Austria… He didn't like England; the climate disagreed with him. That's all I learned about him. As for his heir, he's an utter imbecile, equally incapable of good or evil."

"I share your opinion, Bunny. What do you think about the staff at Denverton House?"

"Unremarkable. Not one of them is worth a moment of our attention in this investigation."

"What do you say to this?" Dickson held out the little jade-handled dagger.

Lipton stared in it in horror. "The key to the Path of the Gods!" he cried.

"If I understand you, the Path of the Gods means the path to death?"

"More or less, but with a nuance. It really means the terrible road traveled by Death's emissaries—or should I say the dead themselves who wish to return among the living. I can't put it more clearly. It's a matter on which I've only ever gotten the vaguest information."

"So why give that strange name to this little dagger?"

"Have you looked at it?"

"Not yet."

"That's a little deadly treasure you're holding there," said Lipton with a smile. "The blade is pure platinum. The jade of the handle is unusual too; it's of a very rare variety. Look at its translucent green: it's called 'corpse cheek,' and it really does suggest an unhappy cadaver. But that doesn't stop collectors from paying enormous sums for it... I assume the clumsy knife thrower who meant that charming dagger for you will make some effort to get it back."

A silence fell between the two men. Dickson set a glass of whisky in front of his friend, who drank from it, his thoughts elsewhere.

"Hell if I know where all this is headed," said Lipton. "Have you ever started down a trail as muddled as this one, Dickson?"

The detective smiled; certainly, it had happened to him more than once. Silence. Lipton took small sips of the warming liquor. Dickson smoked. They could hear Mrs. Crown, the housekeeper, back in the kitchen, moving dishes. The clock on the wall slowly counted off the quiet seconds: one, two, one, two...

With surprise, Lipton followed his friend's eyes to the large clock face. "Are you expecting someone, Dickson?"

"Yes and no... Someone who shouldn't have left."

"Your assistant, Tom Wills? Indeed, I'd have liked to shake his hand."

Dickson pressed a buzzer. "Where did Tom go?" he asked Mrs. Crown when she came in, wiping her hands on a dish towel.

"But... he never left, sir!" cried the good woman. "A little before you came back, Mr. Dickson, I heard him pacing in the library."

"Very good, Mrs. Crown, that'll be all. I believe you didn't hear Tom leave."

"Fine—why not just say I'm going deaf!" grumbled the housekeeper, and she slammed the door.

Dickson went slowly toward the library and put his hand on the doorknob. Why, at that moment, did he and Lipton hesitate equally? Why didn't they immediately open the door to that familiar room? They both felt that something vague and dreadful lurked there.

"Dickson," murmured Lipton with a sad sigh, "I'm not sure why I'm afraid, standing before this door—the door to the room where Tom was heard for the last time! I encountered this kind of thing many times in China. Be careful!"

Already the detective was breaking the spell. With an angry growl he threw the door wide open, reached out, and flipped the wall switch. Bright light filled the room. Dickson and Lipton leaped back, so unexpected was the scene that met their eyes.

A creature of repellent ugliness crouched on a chair; his excessively wide eyes blinked in the bright light. His mouth hung open with incredible pendulous lips; an inhuman grimace distorted his face and gave it a bestial coldness. He uttered a menacing croak as the two men approached.

"Look out!" cried Lipton. "Don't touch him. Right now he's as strong as ten men, and he'd kill you with a sweep of his hand. He doesn't recognize us... I know this foul witchcraft."

"Recognize us..." stammered Dickson, glimpsing an awful truth. And then he noticed the familiar clothes, shredded by fierce claws. "Tom!" he cried.

The creature growled savagely.

"What's happened to him?" the detective cried.

Lipton took his arm to hold him back. "It's Chinese devilry. He must've been injected with yun-yun, a kind of oil that in less than an hour can transform a reasoning person into a monster like that."

"Is it incurable?" cried Dickson.

"Luckily, no. It seems that after a while the effects wear off. There's an antidote—but damned if I know where to find any of it here! Let me think..."

Tom didn't move, but a wild animal's growl emerged from his throat, and drool ran from his lips. He gave every sign of absolute cretinism, though a savage and sometimes murderous light shone in his enlarged eyes.

After pondering, poor Lipton shook his head; he knew of nothing that could help his friend.

Suddenly Dickson opened the door and went behind Tom, and then with an effort he pushed him onto the stairs. With another animal growl, the young man hopped down the stairs and reached the street.

"Quick, Bunny, after him!" called Dickson. "We have to keep him from hurting someone, or from being hurt. I expect the bandits who played this trick on him will try to get near him."

It was a dark night, and the fog still hung in places. After a moment's hesitation, Tom had begun to run. The two detectives had trouble keeping up.

3. On Tom Wills's Trail

Tom moved along erratically; sometimes his hesitant steps looked from a distance like the stumbling of a drunk. He went the length of Goswell Street, turned sharply onto City Road, and began following it toward Old Street.

"My word, Dickson," said Lipton, catching his breath, "he's heading to the house you just left."

"Denverton House? After all..."

331

Dickson didn't finish his thought. His face hardened, and he matched his pace to Tom's. In the distance the young man's silhouette was already receding into the foggy night.

"So much has happened in just a few hours!" murmured Lipton. "Hell if I know what there can be at Denverton House."

"Look out!" cried Dickson. "He's approaching the house. Oh! That's a little much!"

The two detectives had just watched Tom vanish as if the ground had swallowed him.

"Ah," murmured Dickson as they ran forward, "I should've thought of that: the basement! Still, I was shaken for a moment."

Indeed, a basement window opened onto street level, and no doubt led to the cellars of Denverton House.

"Do you understand how he got here?" asked Dickson.

Lipton nodded. "In the state he's in, I'm not surprised. He's being led by the will of another, who's guiding him by some kind of hypnosis. But it mustn't be at full power, I think, because they're drawing him here to complete the job. Well! We're going to shove a stick in their spokes!"

Without a word, Dickson slid through the open window and set foot in the cellar; Lipton followed him. For a moment the two detectives stood still: footsteps fading into the distance proved they were on the right track. In total darkness, Tom was advancing without the help of any light. Dickson and Lipton didn't dare switch on their flashlights; and they were forced to make their way blindly by following the sound of Tom's footsteps. Still, their eyes gradually adapted to the dark, and they were able to proceed without too much stumbling or tripping. Ahead of them they heard a door close, and the sound of footsteps ended.

"He's gone up to the main floor," murmured Dickson.

A few seconds later they bumped into a stone staircase leading up to an open door. A faint light shone at the end of a long corridor. Dickson recognized where they were. At the end of the corridor was a hall, onto which opened the dining-room where the ridiculous dinner had taken place. They could hear the footsteps again, now reverberating in the hall.

"Let's hope no one intercepts him," murmured Lipton. "Can you imagine if they gun him down as a simple burglar?"

"I assume he's been drawn here for quite a different purpose," murmured Dickson.

Still, they hurried to keep up with Tom. They'd reached the hall, which was lit by a single Moorish lantern that threw a prismatic glow around it and left the rest of the room in darkness. The double doors to the dining room were open; that room was lit, not by its great chandelier, but by two standing lamps with pink shades placed in a corner. Tom stood—alone, unmoving—silhouetted in front of one of the lamps.

Then the two detectives started: from some unknown location, a strange voice rose and chanted in a harsh tone and a bizarre language.

"Ancient Chinese!" murmured Lipton.

"Can you understand it?"

"Fairly well... Let me listen."

Lipton pulled his friend behind one of the open double doors, and in a low voice he began to translate what the invisible voice was singing. "O traveler on the Path of the Gods: offering it up as a sacrifice to you, I have taken the soul of this young barbarian, to punish his master, so that he may turn his impious eyes away forever from the sacred road you follow."

Here, a silence fell. Tom remained still, outlined against the pink light of the standing lamp.

The voice went on in a tone of genuine sadness, "You do not answer, O traveler on the Path of the Gods, because the time has not yet come."

"But I'll answer you!" boomed another voice.

It was Dickson—and Lipton came awfully close to crying out in fear. "Fool!" he cringed.

But Dickson went on, "If the soul of this young man is not immediately restored, I, Harry Dickson, will blow up the formal dining room with the grenade I have in my pocket, which has a time delay that I can set to go off whenever I want. Answer me!"

A few seconds passed. Then the voice spoke again—but this time in perfect English: "I accept, Harry Dickson. Withdraw into the small white-draped room where you dined earlier this evening. In ten minutes your assistant will be restored to you, in full possession of his wits."

Lipton broke in, speaking in Chinese. "Do you swear it by the traveler on the Path of the Gods?"

After a few seconds came the low and somber reply, "I swear it. But will your friend return the jade dagger?"

"Yes," said Lipton right away.

"As he withdraws, let him set it down on the little table by the lamp. Now give me your word of honor as well, that you will not return to this room until ten minutes have passed."

"Agreed," said Lipton.

They withdrew into the small side room described before, where nothing had changed since Dickson left it. They switched on a wall sconce and were silent for a while, lost in their own thoughts.

"I wonder how Denverton's mixed up in all this," said Lipton.

"Ask me again tomorrow," said Dickson, "but I'm afraid my answer will still be what it is now—that the present Lord Denverton is nothing more than an utter imbecile."

They kept their eyes on Dickson's pocket watch, which he'd set under the lamp. From the other side of the door they heard not a sound.

"Nine minutes!" said Lipton. "Only one more... I'm afraid..."

Dickson threw him an unhappy look, and began to follow the second hand as it made its way in short pulses around the marked dial. Finally he rose and went to the door. "The ten minutes are up," he called in a loud voice.

No answer.

He threw the door wide open. The dining room was brightly lit by the great chandelier. In an armchair, fast asleep, sat Tom Wills—with his clothes still in shreds but with the familiar smile on his face.

Dickson rushed to him. "Tom, my boy! Wake up!"

The young man stretched, yawned, opened his eyes, and smiled at his employer. A moment later he looked around in surprise at the setting for his awakening—and then in surprise at the unfortunate state of his dress. "My good brown suit! What happened to it?" he wailed.

"We'll talk about that later," answered Dickson, squeezing his hands affectionately.

"I'd be very interested in examining this peacefully slumbering house," said Lipton. "But I feel that for the moment we've agreed on a truce with whoever it was who restored Tom to us. I suggest we don't break it till tomorrow."

"Agreed," said Dickson.

The mysterious voice spoke not a word.

It was very late by the time they got back to Baker Street; still, Tom was invited to tell them what had happened to him. The question seemed to surprise him. "It's rather I who should be questioning you two," he said. "I must've fallen asleep in the library, and I woke up in an unfamiliar house with my good brown suit in rags!"

"Make an effort, Tom," said Lipton. "Tell us if you can remember anything at all that happened before you fell asleep."

Tom frowned and tried to think. "I was the library, looking for a book... I can't remember what book... Yes, I can, a book by Jack London. I couldn't find it right away... I could hear Mrs. Crown rattling pots and pans in the kitchen. I could smell fried fillet of sole, and that made me happy—my God, this is all so banal, so commonplace!"

"Never mind, my boy," said Dickson. "Keep going."

"I remember nothing else, or almost nothing... But something, like a cloth, touched my face. Oh, yes!... Before that, a book fell off the top shelf. Dust flew up..."

"Shush!" said Dickson. "I think I've heard enough: a book that fell, dust, a cloth... from the top shelf... But when we found Tom, everything in the library was in its place, and I automatically locked the door when we left. Come!"

He tiptoed to the library door and flung it open, and quickly raising his revolver he sprayed the top shelves of the bookcase with bullets. A body fell heavily in the darkness.

"Lights," said the detective.

Lipton and Tom stood there, stunned. On the floor writhed a Chinese man in his final agonies.

Lipton came close, and his face expressed his horror. "A Taiping! Let him die, Dickson, and above all don't try to help him. He'd use his last strength for some nasty trick—I know the type!"

The man glared at the three of them with an awful look, burning with hatred. Then his eyes rolled back and he lay still.

"Two bullets in the head," said Lipton admiringly. "Now that's called relying on your lucky star when you shoot! I assume this bandit was instructed to get all three of us; faithful to his orders, he would've waited."

"And in the dining room at Denverton House, they were expecting all three of us—but not quite in the manner in which we showed up," said Dickson. "Now, Bunny, I'll throw back at you the question with which our encounter this evening began: What kind of wasp's nest have we gotten ourselves into?"

4. The Second Chinese

The next day Harry Dickson received a letter from Lord Denverton. It was brief and formal:

Mr. Dickson,

Yesterday, in a moment of whimsy or boredom, I asked you to look into a couple of mysteries, or what I thought were such. I believe I do not have the right to dig into my uncle's past, or to require that he give me some kind of posthumous explanation. Let his wishes remain sacred. I would therefore beg you to drop this matter. An hour after you left, I and all of my staff quit Denverton House, where I've been unhappy, to go to my castle in Yorkshire.

I will not return until a year from now, on the occasion of the next obligatory dinner. I enclose a check for two hundred pounds, which I beg you to accept as your fee.

—Denverton

"Well, my boy, that explains why Denverton House seemed abandoned," said Dickson when he'd looked over the letter, "and proves that the young lord is nothing but a weakling and a fool."

"Maybe someone put the fear in him, Guv," suggested Tom.

"Possibly."

"What do we do? Leave things as they are?"

"I don't believe I will," said the detective. "Still, I'll wait to hear what they tell that excellent Bunny Lipton at the Foreign Office, so we can match our actions to his."

335

Lipton wasn't long in coming; he hadn't breakfasted, and his ill humor showed it. Only the grilled toast, tea, and jam Mrs. Crown served him smoothed away his frown.

After he had read Denverton's letter he set it down crossly. "You're your own boss, Dickson, and you can drop the case if you like, but I've just been given explicit orders: Solve it! Solve what, I wonder? When I think that I'll have to face this chinoiserie—that's the word for it—alone, it doesn't exactly leave me feeling rosy."

"And what if I stick with you?" proposed Dickson.

Lipton gave a joyful yelp. "Rosiness returns! Rosy as the dawn, rosy as a peach, rosy as... all that's good and great!" cried the little man, his eyes shining with delight.

Dickson had trouble suppressing a smile at such enthusiasm, though it touched him deeply. "We'll have to part ways for a while," he said. "I don't believe we've reached the heart of the matter yet. We have some dull research ahead of us. For my part, I'll go spend a few days on the Continent."

"At a spa town?" asked Lipton with a wink.

"Good guess," answered Dickson, shaking his hand.

Lipton stayed in London to keep an eye on Denverton House. Dickson and Tom packed their bags that same day and went to Charing Cross Station. They took the night train to Dover, and the ferry to Ostend. From Ostend the express carried them across peaceful, happy Belgium. They got off at Luxembourg and went to the Hotel Continental at the center of that lovely city.

A late-afternoon sun gilded the grand ducal city; the murmur of moving water rose from the lush, verdant lower town. Everything about the old gabled houses leaning over the river's edge breathed peace and love of life.

"I'd rather nothing here be mixed up in a crime, Guv," murmured Tom as they strolled through a solitary rose garden, where the first buds were opening. He happily watched the people making their way slowly, by switchback paths, toward the upper town.

"I hope we'll find no more than a corollary to a crime here, my boy," said Dickson. "I mean something that was the hidden consequence of the original crime. As I said to Bunny Lipton, old Lord Denverton traveled a great deal on the Continent, and—but let's not anticipate. I believe I've discovered a faint glimmer of light, thanks to a fairly mundane deduction for which I can't claim much glory. I remembered that Denverton didn't die in London, but here in Luxembourg, and his body was taken back to England."

Dickson fell silent, and then Tom heard him murmur, "Schneider... I imagine there must be plenty of people by that name around here!"

"Who was Schneider?" asked Tom.

"Denverton's business agent in certain spa towns. The person who arranged his stays. He received a fairly handsome bequest at the old man's death. He's another element in the mystery of the late Denverton's life."

The street they were following, the walls of whose houses were stuccoed in green and pink, led toward the dismal grand ducal prison, then turned at a right angle down toward the river and more pleasant spots. A large garden opened up before them, with hedges of spindle bush, and green spaces that were half lawn, half vegetable plots. At the rear stood walls of gray stone covered in vines. An old gardener was weeding with the careful wisdom of experience, and he rose stiffly when he saw visitors approaching.

"Monsieur Schneider?" asked Dickson.

"What do you want of him?" asked the old man.

"To see him and speak with him, if possible."

"Hmm. To see him is easy enough; he's not ill-humored. As for speaking with him, that's another matter," chattered the gardener. "Come along anyway…"

With a gesture he invited them to follow him, and went into the large gray house that stood before them. They went down a long flagstone corridor, as cool as a cellar, which opened into a bright room, partly converted into an aviary. A frantic chirping greeted their arrival.

"Well, then, old Balthazar, how are the canaries this morning?" asked the gardener, stopping in front of an armchair that held a shapeless form.

The answer was a grunt. From out of a heap of clothing, a trembling hand emerged and reached feebly toward a side table on which stood a glass of rosé. The glass was lifted and carried to an enormous mouth in the middle of a face as simple-witted as could be imagined.

"Monsieur Schneider," said the gardener, introducing him with a certain irony.

Dickson clenched his fists. A memory no more than a day old came back to him. "I assume he hasn't always been like this?"

"Oh, no!" said the gardener quickly. "He was a perfectly sound man before this happened."

"And when was that?" asked the detective.

"Hmm… At my age, memory isn't what it used to be, you know," said the old man, "but it was a few years ago, anyway… after he stopped traveling. That's when it took him. Some days he's bad-tempered, other days, like today, he's not—or less so."

After giving the gardener a generous tip, Dickson took his leave.

"Time wasted, Guv?" asked Tom, looking at him sidelong.

"Not at all, my boy! Consider that not so many hours ago you looked just like that poor Schneider we've just left!"

"Impossible!" cried Tom, horrified.

"The Chinese poison took effect quite a long time ago. Unfortunately I don't know the antidote, so I can't try it on that living ruin we just saw."

"Would there be some benefit for us?"

"No doubt, but I can get along without it, I suppose," said the detective playfully as they walked up the hill toward the new town.

"If they wanted to keep that man from troubling them, Guv, why didn't the poisoners just kill him outright, rather than putting him into slow motion?" asked Tom.

Dickson stopped and stared at the fine foliage of a distant grove of oaks.

"What do you see, Guv?"

"There? Nothing at all, my boy, but it's you who've allowed me to see something. God's blood! Why was that man put into slow motion rather than killed? Ah, Tom, have you put your finger on the solution to the mystery?"

"I just asked the question, Guv," admitted Tom.

"When the problem is presented correctly, you can envision its solution, my boy," said Dickson sententiously, "I believe that if we can find an answer to your question, part of the mystery of Denverton House will be a mystery no longer. And now, let's eat!"

The Grand Duchy of Luxembourg dines well. Dickson still had fond memories of the bushels of crayfish and exquisite fried trout he'd enjoyed on a previous visit—an adventure to be told another time.

A bus full of happy tourists was going by just then. "Still two seats available, gentlemen!" cried the jovial conductor. "We're headed for Echternach!"

"All right," said Dickson, "with pleasure. We plan to have dinner at Larochette."

"Excellent choice, sir—but the road that direction is under repair, and I'll have to make a slight detour. I'll have to drop you at the Binzel-Schleft, and you'll have two kilometers to do on foot."

"Just enough to give us an appetite, my boy," said Dickson approvingly, as he took his seat on the bus next to Tom.

The glorious landscape rolled by like a movie. The sun was setting, but the tops of the trees in the forest and the crest of the rocky ridges glowed like molten gold. The deep Schluchten valleys, already filling with blue shadows, looked as formidable as chasms. The woods themselves, with their dark depths, were full of adventure and mystery—though on every peak a joyful fire seemed to blaze. A roaring stream thundered by next to the road. The last birds still awake called to each other from the dark underbrush.

"This is the Binzel-Schleft, gentlemen!" said the driver as he stopped the bus. "Follow the road. It's a twenty-minute walk to Larochette, where I'd recommend the Hôtel de la Poste."

In a cloud of dust, the bus disappeared around the next bend in the road, leaving the two detectives alone. On their left yawned the great dark Binzel fissure; steps cut into the rock led up the mountain.

"I'd like an extra fifteen minutes to have a closer look at this rock, Guv," said Tom.

"Granted, my boy," said Dickson, falling into step behind him.

They climbed the granite steps, pulled themselves up between boulders, rising from ridge to ridge and overlooking greater and greater depths, until they finally reached the top of the Binzel-Schleft. In truth it wasn't such a bad climb: the rocky plateau rose over the road by only a couple of hundred feet, and simply gave them an enjoyable view of the area—a rather dark view, because the dusk that was already noticeable on the path up had become almost night in the woods.

"Say, there's a car stopping," said Tom at the sound of brakes rising up from the valley. "The Schleft will have visitors even later than us this evening."

In the darkness they could hear footsteps rising toward them. Dickson and Tom waited, curious, to see the other tourists... but the wait grew long. No one was climbing now, and the Binzel-Schleft fell silent. Tom felt a strange unease; he'd been standing at the very edge, and had been the first to hear—and then not hear—the footsteps. He retreated toward his employer, whom he found searching the darkness with his eyes.

"Heads up, Tom," murmured Dickson. "There's someone behind those trees. He climbed straight up the rock, without using the stairs. Now he's behind us. I can't pinpoint his location; so let's be on our guard, my boy."

Suddenly a voice rang out from the sky over their heads—a voice Dickson recognized as the one he and Lipton had heard at Denverton House. "Drop your revolvers, gentlemen! They'd do you no good, since you can't see me, whereas I could easily kill you in your tracks if I felt like it."

Pop! Pop! They couldn't tell exactly where the sound came from—but a foot from Dickson's face a rock shattered under the impact of a bullet fired from a gun with a silencer.

"You see, gentlemen, I'd only have to aim a little to the right to end your lives. But I won't do it—as long as you obey me. Kindly go back down and get into the car that's waiting at the foot of the stairs."

A Chevrolet sat on the road, with all its lights off and one rear door open; it was a left-hand-drive, and no one was at the wheel.

"Kindly get in, gentlemen," said the voice, now closer than ever.

"No choice, or we'll be on the receiving end of a well-aimed shot," muttered Dickson.

They settled into comfortable seats. Then—without their seeing anyone—the door was slammed shut.

"Tom," said Dickson quickly, "do you have the wax? Fast!"

Both men bent over and rubbed their hands across their faces. That allowed them to stuff small balls of soft wax into their nostrils, and to slip into their mouths a little device that Dickson had invented only a few months earlier. It was a tube four centimeters long, that they were to keep in their mouths, making sure to breathe only through it. It contained one of the most effective poison-gas filters yet devised, designed by a young industrial-arts student in London.

339

They'd barely finished their maneuver when Dickson heard a soft whistling; and in spite of their precautions the two prisoners could smell a thick miasma enveloping them. The detective nudged Tom, and a few seconds later they both sank back onto the seat cushions like men who were fast asleep.

Just then a slim figure leapt out from the side of the road, got behind the wheel, and drove off at high speed. No one had gotten in next to the driver; the prisoners therefore had only him to worry about. By the glow from the headlights Dickson had seen the cruel visage of a Chinese man, and he decided to take steps accordingly.

Shortly before the Mullerthal region, a sharp bend in the road required vehicles to slow down. Little by little Dickson's hand had crept toward his backup revolver, and now he held it aimed at the driver. "The end justifies…" he muttered.

As they reached the sharp bend he went into action—like a thunderclap: two pistol shots hit the driver in the nape of the neck; at the same moment Dickson hurled himself against the glass partition, which shattered into a thousand pieces. Reaching over the fallen body of the Chinese man, he seized the steering wheel—just in time, because the car was veering dangerously off course. But Tom quickly opened the front door, pushed out the driver's body, and stepped on the brakes.

"Whew!" said Dickson, breathing in the fresh night air. "Darkness, the forest, solitude: we have everything we need to settle this business privately."

The Chinese man had been killed instantly. The detectives learned nothing by searching his pockets, and Dickson spent a few silent minutes thinking.

"I'm not going to give up now," he muttered. "Let's see what else we can get out of this, since for the moment we're one step ahead of the enemy. Look out!"

That last was a shout of alarm, because a powerful car was approaching from a distance, and the white beams of its headlights could already be seen under the dark sky.

"Put on the driver's cap, Tom," he called, "and make sure they don't see your face. I'll take care of this fellow!"

Matching his actions to his words, Dickson heaved the body into the back seat, propped it up against him like a man asleep, and assumed the same pose himself. Tom was already accelerating when the other car roared up behind them. In a few minutes it had caught up with the Chevrolet.

"Hey, lemon head!" shouted a voice in German. "The orders are changed! Don't cross the border at Irrel, because there's a night patrol. Orders are, go back to the house!"

And with that, the powerful car pulled past them and vanished into the night, and the sound of its engine soon faded in the distance.

"Guv! Guv!" cried Tom. "Did you recognize him?"

"I was sleeping, my boy, remember?"

"Luckily I wasn't. It was the old gardener from Luxembourg! But, by all the saints, he seemed to be in better shape tonight."

"So, I deduce that the orders are to go back to Schneider's house," said Dickson. "U-turn, my boy. Let's see what's going on in that run-down house."

"And the Chinese fellow?"

"We can't be burdened with him. Throw him into the bushes, which are dense enough to hide him for a while."

Dickson took the wheel, turned around, and headed back toward Luxembourg. When they passed through Larochette it was fast asleep, and only the windows at the Hôtel de la Poste were still lit. Tom bid a silent sad farewell to the crayfish and the trout. But the Chevrolet, with an excellent appetite, ate up the kilometers…

5. A Night of Adventures

A few hundred meters into the grand ducal city, Harry Dickson parked the car in a side alley, where no one would see it. Then he and Tom walked briskly toward the city center, taking care to stick to the back streets of the lower town.

The town was asleep in the peace of the evening, cradled by the great murmuring waters of its river, forever washing the pebbles on its bed as smooth as skulls. That wonderful evening silence of small towns, hardly broken by the silvery leap of a trout, by the whisper of a night bird's wings…

The detectives would've been happy to linger, to forget that in the midst of this tranquil beauty they were on the trail of a crime—but a bend in the road put them right across from Schneider's house. When gilded by afternoon sun it had looked inviting, with its spindle hedge, its planters, and its vegetable plots; now it loomed dreadful and hostile out of the darkness. All the windows were dark; those on the ground floor were protected by heavy oak shutters. Around that silent house the only sound was the wind rustling the trees and the ivy that grew on the walls.

Dickson examined the grounds at length before making a decision. The peacefulness of the house had to be an illusion, a trick.

Behind the house stood outbuildings and a garage. The garage door was wide open, and the detectives approached it. There were oil stains on the concrete floor of the garage, but no car.

"The car driven by the mysterious gardener didn't come straight back," began Tom—but Dickson put his hand over his assistant's mouth to silence him. A car was coming down the steep street, and Tom recognized it: the one that had passed them on the road to Echternach.

The detectives leaped behind the spindle hedge. They'd barely hidden before the car roared into the driveway crossing the garden and entered the garage. From where they were, Dickson and Tom could hear the gardener-chauffeur give a grunt of surprise and say to himself, "Well, well, the little jalopy isn't back yet. But it can make good time when it wants to."

Leaving the garage door open, the chauffeur walked toward the house. He was no longer the stooped old man of that afternoon, but a well-built and much younger man, though his face—covered in wrinkles and marked by senility—would've fooled anyone at first sight. He went inside by the servants' door, and the two detectives could hear him quickly climbing stairs.

Dickson knew it was time to roll the dice. "Tom, we need to part ways for an hour. The chauffeur is probably going to be told to go find the Chevrolet driven by the Chinese man. Run back to where we hid the car; park it on the side of the road like it's broken down. The chauffeur here will get out of his car to see what's wrong. Jump him—and above all take him alive. One shot of the drug we always have with us will do the job, if need be.

"Then drive like mad for the Belgian border; you can get to Arlon in a few minutes. On the Rue de la Montagne in Arlon you'll find the office and home of Anatole Lamy, shipping agent. Wake him up and tell him I sent you. Nothing will surprise him, and you can trust him completely. I don't know what's inside this house. If by dawn I haven't met you at Lamy's, ask him to take action. He'll understand what that means, and he knows his way around action. Now run, and God protect you!"

Dickson remained alone, hidden behind the hedge. The gardener-chauffeur hadn't returned, which pleased him, since he figured that would give Tom enough time to get back to where they'd left the Chevrolet. Finally the servants' door opened and the chauffeur emerged. He looked unhappy and afraid. The detective could hear him swearing under his breath as he started the car and then reversed it down the driveway to the street.

"He's going the right way," Dickson rejoiced as he saw the car head out the main road toward Echternach.

The kitchen door had been left unlocked. The detective crawled carefully toward it, making sure to stay under the cover of the shadows of the spindle hedge. He reached the door without trouble, and a few seconds later he was inside the dark, silent house.

Tom had barely parked the Chevrolet by the side of the road, with its running lights lit, when he heard the powerful engine of the other car. He plunged into the nearest bushes, paying no attention to the brambles and nettles that scratched him.

The Chevrolet looked like a car abandoned by the road while its owners had gone to get help nearby. The vehicle approaching was a big French car that Tom knew well. A few meters from his hiding place the car braked to a stop, and the chauffeur got out and walked calmly over to the Chevrolet.

"Hey, Su-Su!" he called quietly.

At that moment Tom leaped out of the bushes and struck the chauffeur so hard with a bludgeon that he dropped to the ground and lay still.

"Now for the shot," chuckled Tom, holding up a hypodermic, "and then hitting the road for Belgium! And to think that I've got my choice of wheels!" he said, comparing the two cars. "That's all right, I'll stick with that Chevrolet— it's brought me luck!"

He parked the big French car where the Chevrolet had been, up the side alley. Then, with his involuntary passenger fast asleep on the back seat, Tom sped toward the border.

"This sweet little car has certainly seen service as a mobile dormitory tonight!" he laughed to himself. He drove through the sleeping city of Luxembourg, wondering what his employer could be up to, then headed for the border. For the past few years that border had become purely nominal, since the Belgium-Luxembourg customs agreement did away with any border posts between those two friendly nations.

Down the road, a few distant pinpricks of light denoted the railroad signals at the Arlon station. Tom passed it on his left, and entered the small country town. An antique streetlight on one corner dimly lit a sign, and with satisfaction he read, in white letters on a blue background, *Rue de la Montagne*. A little further on, a fine copper nameplate announced to passersby that this was the residence of *Anatole Lamy—Shipping Agent—Customs Agent*.

Lights were still on at the home of this solid Arlon citizen, because Tom could see bright lines between the slats of the sliding shutters. And indeed he didn't have to wait long: at his first ring of the bell, the door opened and a man in shirtsleeves eyed him curiously.

"Monsieur Lamy?"

"Himself, my dear sir. How can I help you?" the man replied cordially.

"I come on behalf of Harry Dickson," murmured Tom.

Lamy didn't bat an eye, and answered in a peculiar way: "Of course, Monsieur Sellier! Delighted to be of service! I'll go open the garage door. Put your car in there, and come join me in the dining room. I'm a night owl, and not easily inconvenienced!" He'd spoken loudly enough for all the neighbors to hear, if by chance they weren't deep in their beauty sleep.

Lamy himself soon opened the double doors of the garage, and then closed them again behind the car. Tom gestured to point out the man asleep in the car, and Lamy replied with a barely perceptible nod.

"Mr. Dickson wants him alive," said Tom quietly. "If all goes well, he'll be here himself at dawn. If he's not, I'm supposed to ask you to accompany me back to Luxembourg, to the house of a Mr. Schneider."

Lamy didn't move, but Tom saw that he had his full attention.

"What shall we do with my prisoner?" asked the young man.

"We'll put him someplace where he can wake up when he wants, and even make as much noise as he wants," said Lamy, opening the car door and taking the man in his arms. Tom was astonished to see Lamy—a little bald man with muttonchops that made him look like a country notary—display such physical strength: he carried the chauffeur like a sleeping child being carried to bed.

But, though Lamy seemed like a man not easily taken by surprise, he exclaimed, "But—it's Arno!"

"You know him?"

"There must be a mistake," murmured Lamy. "There's been a mix-up! Why is Arno a prisoner? He's one of ours!"

Before Tom could answer, there was a knock in a distinctive pattern at the back door.

"Ah!" said Lamy, setting down his burden. "We'll find out right away what happened."

He unlocked a door at the rear and let in several men dressed in European clothes, but whose yellow faces made clear their Asian origins. Tom retreated, with vague fears of a trap. But those fears were soon cleared up: behind the three Orientals appeared a tall, thin figure, and Tom recognized the smiling face of Harry Dickson.

Dickson presented them to his assistant: "Messrs. Matsuko, Saito, and Timotu. Not Chinese, but Japanese, as their names suggest. As it happens, we followed the wrong trail, though these gentlemen will acknowledge that the honors of the day are ours."

"It's true, Mr. Dickson," said Matsuko, a stiff little Japanese with exquisite manners. "It's true! We thought Su-Su was one of ours. In fact, he was an accomplice of the headless Voice, and he proved it by helping him take you both prisoner. By shooting Su-Su on the road to Echternach, gentlemen, you executed a traitor."

Tom stared dumbfounded at his employer.

"I wonder if these gentlemen could explain matters to my assistant," said Dickson.

"Come into the parlor," said Lamy. "I believe there'll be much to say."

Once they were settled in comfortable armchairs, with cigars and hot tea in front of them, Dickson began, "It turns out that these gentlemen, private detectives in the service of His Imperial Majesty the Mikado—and incidentally accredited by all the European powers—have been pursuing the same investigation as I have: the Path of the Gods."

"Ah!" cried Tom. "So we're finally going to find out what that damned Path is?"

The Japanese shook their heads sadly. "That's what we don't know yet. As of now we can assert only that it will lead to unprecedented horrors that will drench China in blood and cause the death of thousands of European and Japanese expatriates."

"The return of Fuh-Suh the Terrible," said Dickson.

The three Japanese nodded as one.

"But what connection does all that have with that tidy little house in the suburbs of Luxembourg—the quietest town in the world?" cried Tom.

"Plenty," replied Matsuko. "Monsieur Lamy will agree: that's the house that always attracts the headless Voice."

"Huh? That's a hell of a name!" exclaimed the young man irreverently—earning him a disapproving glance from his employer.

"Well, you can always hear the voice, but you never see to whom it belongs," said Saito.

Dickson nodded in turn. "I've heard it myself, twice: once in London, once last night, when it almost got me. But for something that's only a voice, it's pretty handy with a revolver."

"Could that be Fuh-Suh?" asked Tom.

They all shook their heads no. "Not at all. Fuh-Suh was a dreadful being, acting with incredible mastery, a leader of men, a genius... The headless Voice must be some kind of familiar, a demon he domesticated. That fits the legends. In any case, for a servant his skills are still formidable."

"But Fuh-Suh disappeared," said Tom.

"He'll come back along the Path of the Gods," said Timotu with a grave face. "I promise you, that's already common knowledge in China."

Matsuko turned to Dickson. "I can't tell you how delighted we are to have you with us on this strange case, sir. Up to now we were unaware of Denverton House—whose role in all this is as unknown to us as it is to you. But we've had our eye on Schneider's house for four years. You found it in three days—that's impressive, you have to admit!"

"How did you learn that Schneider's house might also be involved in all this?" asked Dickson.

"Partly by chance," replied Matsuko. "Mr. Arno, a European detective in the service of His Majesty the Mikado, was vacationing in Europe. One day in the street he noticed Schneider on his doorstep and recognized his symptoms as those of a man under the influence of that mysterious Chinese drug—whose nature and antidote are both unknown to us. He sensed that something suspicious was going on, notified our agency, and was given orders to remain on the spot. Arno got himself hired as a gardener at Schneider's house—the management of which is entrusted to a Belgian notary, thanks to a referral by Monsieur Lamy, who's a friend of Japan as well as of England. Arno had a Chinese servant, Su-Su, whom he wanted to keep with him. He set him up in Luxembourg at a prosperous confectioner's shop. Every evening the boy would go to his master for orders. Did you notice Schneider's fine aviary? Well, that was a clever trick thought up by Arno. He knew that everywhere the headless Voice was heard, whether in China or abroad, birds were caught and eaten alive. Bizarre, isn't it? But it's a fact that we've confirmed, without being able to explain it. From time to time, indeed, birds disappeared from Schneider's aviary, and Arno found

345

nothing but the bloody remains. And he heard the Voice itself, scolding some-one in Chinese and issuing dire threats."

"Poor Arno!" said Tom repentantly.

"Oh, well! You did him a good turn by eliminating Su-Su—a traitor, who was probably getting ready to knock him off, as soon as the headless Voice directed him to."

"And now," asked Lamy, speaking for the first time, "can I arrange for you to get some sleep? I've put Arno to bed. Tomorrow he won't feel any the worse for what Mr. Wills did to him. If you'd like to go to bed yourselves, gentlemen, you know my house is as comfortable as it is roomy."

Dickson shook his head. "I'm afraid, gentlemen, I must inflict a sleepless night on you. Or should I say, at least on me and on my assistant, Tom."

"Allow us to join you," insisted Matsuko.

Dickson shook his head again. "Too many people could hinder my plans. By the way, Dr. Matsuko, those bird disappearances probably happened at night, no?"

"Indeed, Mr. Dickson."

"And the headless Voice, likewise, seemed to prefer to make itself heard at night?"

"Mostly, yes... What do you deduce from that?"

"Nothing for now. But, with a little luck, we should soon be able to tell you more about that extraordinary Voice."

6. The Disembodied Voice

"No, my boy, we won't be getting any sleep tonight! Too bad—we can rest later. We're headed back to Luxembourg, and even beyond: we're going to the Binzel-Schleft!"

"Such happy memories!" said Tom, getting into the car, to Dickson, who was already behind the wheel. "Tell me what happened to you at Schneider's house, Guv."

"Oh, the story won't take more than two minutes to tell, my boy. I'd barely gotten into the house when I heard voices nearby in the parlor. Voices speaking Japanese, not Chinese. In the darkness I could see bright light at a keyhole. I was curious and put my eye to it. I'll admit I was stunned when I recognized those Japanese detectives, with whom I'd already been in touch and whose integrity and trustworthiness were beyond doubt. Instead of being behind enemy lines, I was on friendly soil. Without hesitating, I burst in. Though it isn't easy to startle those good Japanese, I promise you I had a moment to enjoy their stunned faces. It didn't last; we soon explained ourselves, and learned that we'd been following different trails leading to the same mysterious goal."

"Say, Guv," said Tom, "Bunny Lipton must be having quite a time in London right now!"

"Good old Bunny can take it easy: nothing's going to disturb the London peace while the headless Voice is away."

"Sure, Guv, but you don't think it's a widespread conspiracy?"

"Not at all!" said Dickson simply. Then he fell silent and gave his attention to the road. Luxembourg was far away. The road wound through enormous dark woods. No lights shone in the few villages they passed through; barely even a watchdog barked from time to time.

High looming rocks stood silhouetted to the right of the road, and Dickson slowed down.

"Are we at Binzel?" asked Tom.

"No more than a kilometer away, but we'll do the rest on foot. Our best chance for success is not to be heard."

Tom shuddered as he saw his employer draw from his pocket a long dagger whose blade was blackened to avoid nighttime reflections off the steel. "Are you going to need that wicked thing?" he asked uneasily.

"Could be," answered the detective. "From now on, speak only if I say it's all right. Much depends on it."

Without exchanging a word, they walked for a long while, not on the paved road but on the thick moss along the shoulder, which muffled their footsteps as effectively as the best felt soles could have. Finally Dickson motioned to Tom to stop, and pointed to a dark fissure in the granite cliff: the Binzel-Schleft. Now that deep night surrounded it, how menacing and full of dangers seemed that dark opening in the rocks! As he followed on his employer's heels, Tom pictured himself climbing the steep steps of a castle turret some cursed midnight, at the mercy of the worst whims of the Beyond.

At last they reached the rocky plateau, and from there they plunged into the dense woods that covered the Binzel ridges. It was no longer pitch black, because the moon had risen; it was still low behind the trees, but its thin silver arrows already split the sylvan darkness. That feeble light was enough to allow Dickson to move forward without stumbling too much against trees and stumps, and he led Tom along behind him.

A sad, mournful howl rose from the depths of the woods: the cry of the wildcat on the hunt for its nocturnal prey. It came closer, drew away, came closer again, then fell silent among the distant trees.

By the faint moonlight filtering through the trees Tom could see that Dickson was crouching down and stretching out on the moss, with one hand reaching forward. A slight shadow extended beyond that hand—and Tom recognized it as the strange blackened blade that reflected no light.

Other creatures of the night called, shrieked, howled... and then in perfect unison they all fell silent.

Tac... taca... tac. The sound rang out in front of them—the only sound in the night, as if everything held still for it. And yet it was only a soft, crisp snap, like two small pieces of wood struck against each other rhythmically. Tom pic-

347

tured a clumsy, fearful child playing the castanets as quietly as possible, so as not to disturb the sleep of some terrible adult.

Tac... taca... tac. What menace that dull sound conveyed to the young man! His feeling was followed by the proof—when he saw his employer retreating as cautiously as possible into the shadows of the massive oaks that surrounded their hiding place. Tom couldn't stand it any longer, and he crawled back quietly until he joined Dickson.

The sound began to fade as if it were moving away from them, deeper into the forest.

"What was that?" asked Tom in a voice barely above a whisper. "It gave me the creeps."

"A Chinese birdcall," replied Dickson just as quietly.

"What for?" asked Tom in astonishment.

"That's the sound Chinese poachers use to attract game birds at night. It seems to have the power to awaken birds like pheasants and partridges and to make them hurry toward the source of the sound. Silence—it's coming back... Anyway, it might very well do our job for us."

Tac... taca... tac. The sound became clearer, and this time seemed to be headed cautiously, hesitantly, straight toward them. Tom watched his employer tear a few twigs off a nearby shrub, twist them, then raise them to his mouth. They made a staccato sound, followed—to Tom's complete astonishment—by a *tac... taca... tac* almost identical to the sound from the forest.

The answer came immediately, and was repeated feverishly; and then it sounded very close by. Dickson set down his improvised birdcall and stood still, his nerves on edge, his hand stretched out on the grass.

"Look out, my boy," he murmured to his assistant. "Keep your revolver at the ready, but fire only if you see that things are going against me. Silence!"

Tac... taca... tac. Now it was very close, to their left, where the moonlight had begun to shine a little brighter. And then Tom saw it: a squat shape, barely bigger than a ten-year-old child, was advancing slowly from tree to tree—not crawling but upright on stubby, severely bowed legs. The massive torso suggested uncommon strength; the head, sunk between the shoulders, couldn't yet be distinguished.

The creature was now advancing only imperceptibly, while still making that peculiar sound: *tac... taca... tac.* Finally, fully lit by a moonbeam, it stood out against the darker bushes. Tom felt Dickson's hand on his arm, imposing calm and total silence.

It was a terrifying sight: tucked deep between great round shoulders, a revolting head cackled in the moonlight. Its muddy yellow complexion shaded to green around two enormous bulging eyes. It had almost no chin, but the lower half of its nightmare face was split by an immense mouth, out of which stuck two terrible white canines. Its eyes were as fixed and lidless as those of an octopus. In their murky depths could be seen an intelligent, desperate cruelty. The creature had stopped its bird calls; now from time to time it growled quietly in anxious fury.

Sometimes it sniffed the air forcefully, and then it growled even more. Could it smell the presence of danger? Tom was inclined to think so, and he tightened his grip on the revolver in his fist. The monster stood still in a circle of moonlight, and now the detectives could see that it was dressed in a filthy black loincloth that left its legs and arms and hairy torso exposed. The completely bald head only added to its repulsive ugliness.

Tac... taca... tac. Tom almost cried out in fear, because Dickson had begun making his own birdcall again, though the horrible creature was now only ten paces away. But the idea of a trap didn't seem to occur to the monster: it crouched down, then crawled rapidly toward the two detectives' hiding place. They were completely in shadow, with a bush screening them from the advancing figure.

It came straight toward them, and as it left the circle of moonlight they could see only its dark, massive silhouette. That was for the best, because if Tom had seen that terrifying face approaching he wouldn't have been able to resist firing a couple of metal-jacketed bullets into it—whereas his employer had clearly said, "Intervene only if things are going against me."

The monster reached the bush and stretched out a simian paw to part the foliage. At that moment Dickson's hand lunged at the lower half of the creature's torso. Tom heard a muffled "Huh!" and got ready to fire, but the thing stood still, its talons stretched out toward the bush, its hideous face a little thrown back, its bulging eyes reflecting the moonlight. Then, with a long sigh, the creature slid to the ground and moved no more.

And now in turn Dickson sighed deeply. "Help me carry this thing to the car, Tom," he said, pointing to the body.

It was hard work. In spite of its short stature, the monster was very heavy, and Dickson urged his assistant to make no noise. The strange wild-animal smell the thing gave off almost made Tom nauseous.

"Easy, my boy, easy," said Dickson as they took the peculiar cadaver down the steps of the Binzel-Schleft.

"Why, Guv? Isn't the headless Voice dead? What can it do to us now?"

"Dead? I should say not! As for being dangerous, that all depends where it is right now. Remember the shots fired by that gun with a silencer!"

Tom shook his head; once again he'd given up trying to understand, and now wasn't the time for questions.

"Bring the car up, my boy," said Dickson. "Stop when you reach the foot of the Binzel, but don't turn the engine off. The moment I'm in, along with our passenger, take off in high gear. We're returning to Arlon by a back road."

"We're a regular taxi service tonight, Guv!" murmured Tom. "Or more like a hearse service! Fascinating work!"

349

He carried out his employer's instructions to the letter. When the car was once again speeding down the road back, Dickson sighed with relief. "Thank God, IT was deep in the woods. Otherwise that might've cost us dearly."

"IT, Guv? The headless Voice?"

"Indeed, my boy. Did you think, even for a minute, that this horrible sallow brute, that we've just slain like a rampaging beast, could possibly speak in the civilized way the Voice does, or could make such learned use of the fearful poisons of the Middle Kingdom, or could handle a well-aimed revolver with such skill?"

In the back rolled the lifeless body of the strange Oriental, striking the doors and the seats with muffled thuds. The smell of musk and decomposition it gave off was so strong that by the time they reached Arlon both detectives felt truly ill.

The three Japanese and Monsieur Lamy were soon awakened, and they gathered around the awful remains.

"I believe it's an orangutan from Borneo," said Matsuko. "They're mysterious creatures, with a capacity for training and even a certain devotion to their masters. Are they human? Are they apes? I'd lean toward the first option, because they can be taught a few simple words. When they're angry they're terrifying. I know that a few Chinese mandarins keep them."

"But the Voice..." began Saito.

Dickson smiled. "It still lives, but not for long. I promise you: its death warrant is already signed. Monsieur Lamy, please ask the grand ducal government to close the Binzel woods to the public for a week. That's longer than we'll need."

Timotu, who'd been bent over the man of the jungles, stood up and showed them his smudged finger. "My word! This creature must've been wearing makeup and false whiskers!"

"I can easily believe it," said Dickson. "And indeed it's very likely. But now, gentlemen, I beg you to grant me—and my assistant—a few hours' sleep. Here comes the dawn, rising over the beautiful countryside of the Ardennes."

7. The Disembodied Voice (Cont'd)

Harry Dickson spent a day around Arlon, thinking. Lamy had come through handsomely, and the trout and the crayfish arrived by special delivery. The three Japanese did justice to the food as well, and by a sort of truce little was said about the mystery of the Path of the Gods. During the day Dickson had telephoned London and spoken with Bunny Lipton, who was deeply bored on the banks of the Thames.

"I'm sorry, Bunny," said Dickson. "But you'll have to suffer patiently. Denverton House will remain quiet, and I give you permission to spend your time drinking ale and reading the satirical papers."

Two days passed before Dickson suggested to his friends that they return to Luxembourg. They found Schneider's house in perfect order and perfectly quiet. Arno, who'd gone back there, reported that nothing had happened. Schneider himself continued in that vegetative state they'd already observed.

Arno very decently had no hard feelings toward Tom. "Those are the risks of the job," he said. "Maybe some fine day I'll return the favor, my dear boy, but for now let's have a glass of rosé and drink to our reconciliation and lasting friendship."

Dickson and the three Japanese joined heartily in that invitation, and they all spent a charming, cordial hour together.

"And now," said Dickson, "back to the Binzel."

Arno took the wheel of the big French car, while Tom drove his favorite, the Chevrolet. A representative of the grand ducal police joined them for the journey. Two kilometers in each direction from Binzel, a discreet watch had been posted, whose principal job was to keep strangers out of the woods. But since it was still early in the season, there were hardly any tourists to be turned away by the ban.

As they were all climbing the brown rock steps up the fissure, Dickson seemed to have doubts again. "I wonder whether two days will have been enough to overcome the last of his powers of resistance,' he murmured. "But you never know…"

Matsuko started with surprise, and he came close and whispered in Dickson's ear. The detective smiled. "Quite right, doctor!"

"Yes," said Matsuko, "I noticed those small cuts behind the orangutan's ears, but I hadn't thought of THAT. In fact, they say that in the terrible Fuh-Suh's entourage…"

He didn't finish: all of them stopped and stared at each other. From the depths of the forest emerged a harrowing roar that rose and fell with a strange, piercing tone, sounding like a cry of distress but also of despair and incredible anger.

"The headless Voice!" murmured Arno, turning pale. "My God, I've never heard anything so awful."

Dickson stood still, listening, with a serious expression. Matsuko turned to him. "You think that…"

"It's dying," said the detective.

"Dying of what, Guv?" asked Tom.

"Of hunger!" came the strange reply.

Saito spoke up. "I once witnessed the torture of a Chinese bandit, who was condemned to be buried alive in an anthill."

"Good Lord, it's awful," murmured Dickson. "And yet we'd be risking our lives if we went any closer."

"Is it a man, Guv?" asked Tom.

"Barely," said Dickson gruffly. He stood thinking, with his brow furrowed. "But it doesn't matter—I'd rather risk my hide than listen to that agony any longer. Mr. Saito, I hadn't considered fire ants. We have to put an end to the torture."

Clearly the detective's mind was made up: he was already giving them detailed instructions. He'd go on alone. Matsuko would follow him at a distance, so as not to lose sight of him and to able to intervene only in case of dire need.

The Voice was already getting quieter. It was only a moan, growing gradually weaker, broken from time to time by a long howl of rage and agony.

Dickson advanced toward it, slipping from tree to tree, followed at a distance by the Japanese detective. Then Dickson stopped: the Voice had begun again, but now it spoke in words of despair: "The Path of the Gods! Too late!"

Ahead of the detective the trees thinned out, and a small clearing lay in a slight hollow. The Voice arose from its center. When he'd reached the edge of the clearing, Dickson took cover behind a thick tree trunk and looked out intently.

Matsuko—contrary to orders—joined him. "Do you see something, Mr. Dickson?" he murmured.

The detective shook his head. He saw only moss and small thorn bushes, nothing that could conceal a human form. The clearing was empty. And yet only a few seconds earlier the moaning had come from its center.

"Ants!" said the Japanese suddenly.

A patch of red rippled at the center of the clearing, moving around an object that was certainly no more than two feet high and that resembled a shapeless lump of soil. Suddenly that object howled, "The Path of the Gods—finished!"

"Heavens!" cried Matsuko. "That's what it is! How awful!"

Had the shapeless thing heard him? An arm gnawed to the bone rose above the swarming mass. The tip of that raw stump held an automatic revolver with a silencer attached. But two shots had already rung out from the edge of the clearing, and the small arm fell back among the voracious ants.

Dickson plucked up a handful of dry grass, lit it, and stuffed it into the anthill. The innumerable, infinitesimal army stampeded away, and a strange thing came into view: a human head, its flesh already half eaten away by ants. It was attached to a stunted body—indeed just half a torso—with only one tiny arm, the one that held the revolver in a hand no bigger than that of a small monkey.

Matsuko fell back in superstitious fear. "I thought that's what it was! But you figured it out first, Mr. Dickson! A living Buddha! A vampire Buddha! The orangutan was both his means of transport and his food source!"

Drawn by the sound of the shots, the other Japanese, Lamy, Tom, and the grand ducal official stared at the scene, stunned.

"Gentlemen," said Dickson, "the curtain has fallen! The lead actor has left the stage. But the mystery remains unsolved—and the solution lies in London."

"Off we go!" cried the Japanese with an enthusiasm quite incompatible with the composure typical of their nation.

"There's plenty of time, gentlemen," laughed Dickson. "We'll rendezvous at Denverton House in a year. No invitations will go out. We'll be the only guests at Lord Denverton's ridiculous dinner."

8. The Path of the Gods

Indeed, Lord Denverton had rather few guests to entertain. The lawyer who, for four years, had received the invitations to pass on, hadn't had to worry about it this year. Around the table in the formal dining room at Denverton House sat only the great Harry Dickson, the three Japanese detectives— Matsuko, Saito, and Timotu—Bunny Lipton, come back for the occasion, and Tom Wills. The young lord presided over the dinner. It wasn't ridiculous, as the previous years' dinners had been; and the menu had been planned with meticulous care.

"What exactly are we waiting for, Mr. Dickson?" asked Denverton.

The detective shook his head in perplexity. "I don't know myself, my lord. I'm certainly waiting for something, but..." With a look of intense thought, he pushed away his glass of fine Napoleon cognac. "The dinner takes place at a set hour on a set date," he murmured. "And nothing can be altered in the formal dining room. That's all I have as reference points to reach a solution."

He leaned back in his chair and gazed at the ceiling. Then he began to laugh. "It was too easy, after all." He drank down his cognac without tasting it, and his eyes shone. "Everything's set, gentlemen. We just have wait a while."

"A long time?" asked Denverton a little impatiently.

Dickson gazed up at the skylight in the ceiling. "Oh, let's say no more than twenty minutes!"

The three Japanese, as if transfixed in their seats, fastened their black eyes on the detective with a look that was both admiring and slightly envious.

"Ten minutes!" announced Lipton.

Dickson kept his eyes on the skylight. A ray of sunshine came through it and lit the top of the room in gold. The other guests could see that Dickson was breathing heavily and clasping his hands nervously. His eyes never left the ceiling.

Suddenly he leapt up and went to the wall across from him. "A cane, a stick, anything!" he cried. He pulled a sword off a display rack of weapons and hurled himself at the wall. He'd just heard a slight click at a place high up on the molding, where a small spot of sunlight had just appeared. With all his strength he struck the center of the bright disc.

Lord Denverton and his guests began to shout: part of the wall had vanished, revealing a white marble staircase ornamented with designs in gold and jade.

"Gentlemen," said Dickson with feeling, "would you care to follow me along the Path of the Gods?"

"Ah!" murmured Matsuko and Lipton together. "So that's what it was?"

They all climbed the staircase, which was cleverly concealed inside the massive walls of Denverton House. An ebony door encrusted in gold and ivory stood at the top of the stairs, on a tiny landing tiled in jade and onyx. Dickson seized the silver door handle. Bright light immediately flooded the staircase, and now they noticed small, exquisite electric sconces positioned alongside the steps.

After great hesitation, Dickson opened the door. They were struck by a heavy, piercing odor of musk, incense, and myrrh, plus some other indefinable scent. The open door revealed a room of modest size, furnished half in European and half in Oriental style. Out of magnificent Chinese vases grew enormous artificial chrysanthemums—looking entirely alive.

"A man!" cried one of the Japanese detectives.

Someone dressed a dark silk kimono was stretched out in an armchair at a desk covered in papers; he looked asleep.

Dickson bent over a yellow face with narrow eyes, and lightly touched a cold, leathery cheek. "Dead." He thought a moment, then said, as if to himself, "They say certain Chinese drugs can prevent decomposition for many years."

Then Matsuko cried out in fear. "Mr. Lipton! Don't you recognize this dead man?"

"Oh!" murmured Lipton. "This is too much! I only caught sight of him once—but it's him!"

"The mandarin Fuh-Suh! The terror of the world!"

Dickson approached, holding a handkerchief soaked in powerfully scented rubbing alcohol. "Gentlemen, let this remain forever our secret! Or at least let it be shielded from public scandal. Lord Denverton, take a close look at this."

He began to rub the leathery face. Slowly, a thick layer of yellow pigment rubbed off, and wrinkles became visible, and the slanting eyes changed shape.

"Dear God!" cried the young lord, terrified. "Dear God—it's my uncle, Lord Denverton!"

"Known to the rest of the world as Fuh-Suh the Terrible," Dickson added gravely.

When everyone was seated around a table again—not in the formal dining room but in the young lord's private rooms—Dickson addressed them. "According to official records, Lord Denverton traveled to China only once, in the flower of his youth. During that visit he must've decided to embark on one of the most extraordinary adventures ever conceived. Its beginnings are murky, and shouldn't overly preoccupy us: if someday an adventure novelist wants to write the astonishing life of Denverton-Fuh-Suh, it'll be up to him to do the research. At university Denverton had had a friend named Schneider, who resembled him somewhat, and whose only ambition was to live, as splendidly as possible, at the expense of his near-lookalike.

"Denverton took it as a sign from the gods: from now on he could live a double life. For years and years he sent Schneider to stay—under his name—at various Continental spa towns. On the rare occasions when Denverton himself came back to London, Schneider stayed quietly at home in his native Luxembourg. Meanwhile, Fuh-Suh was born: he became a mandarin, a rabble-rouser, and a warrior—the terror of the Middle Kingdom.

"But little by little Denverton grew into the role: he began to believe in his Asiatic mission. Under who knows what religious influence, he became convinced that he was the emissary of the Eastern gods. It matched an ancient legend, that a mandarin warrior named Fuh, after a certain interval of years spent in the kingdom of shadows, would return among the living and resume his role. A sort of Chinese Frederick Barbarossa, if you will. Believing himself to be that legendary mandarin, Denverton acted accordingly. The same legend claimed that the prophesied return, along the Path of the Gods, would take place at a dinner hosted for crooks chosen at random.

"Steeped in that millenarian superstition, Denverton made ready for his return among the living, once death had struck him down. He came back to London, built a special retreat inside his house, and made his will accordingly. Here again the legend contributed a detail: it was said that, at one of those dinners, the sun itself would open the Path of the Gods to the mandarin returning from the dead.

"Denverton gave the gods a little help: he installed a solar lock. When the sun shining through the skylight struck a certain spot high up on the molding, a trigger made from ultra-sensitive metals would release the lock. If that was indeed the moment for the resurrection, the newly awakened mandarin would only have to open the door and rejoin the world of the living. If it wasn't the right time, then the cooling of those same metals would relock the secret door, and everything would quietly wait another year.

"That's why you saw me hasten to strike the spot lit by the sun. You'll observe that the place was chosen so skillfully—I should say, so astronomically— that the sun could only hit it from a position it reached just once a year. Extraordinary calculations in celestial mechanics must've been required to produce that result. So all of this involves a mixture of superstition, fanatical belief, science, and trickery.

"Still, that wasn't enough: he needed servants ready to protect the secret. That job went to a living Buddha, malformed, almost totally paralyzed, but gifted with enormous intelligence. That monster made use of an orangutan to compensate for his own deformity, as we've seen. Denverton had only one other servant, the one we killed in the library at Baker Street. That was a terrible setback for the Buddha, because his own movements were always at risk of discovery. But—by disguising his orangutan as well as possible—he managed to get back to Luxembourg and take refuge in Schneider's house. Once there, he corrupted or won over Arno's Chinese servant, as we know.

"Why, you might ask, didn't he eliminate Schneider? Simple: he too believed in the resurrection of Denverton-Fuh-Suh, and he thought having Schneider around as a double would subsequently become necessary again. So he merely turned him into a vegetable, whose wits he could restore when the master had returned along the Path of the Gods. Oh, there's no doubt—that living Buddha, Fuh-Suh's right-hand man, was prepared to fight for his master's cause."

"Why didn't he kill us, Guv?" asked Tom. "He had plenty of chances."

Dickson turned to Bunny Lipton. "I assume we owe that to the reputation our friend Bunny enjoys in the Orient. Remember that the sinister midget tried to kill me by flinging his platinum dagger at me, when he heard young Lord Denverton asking me to investigate. But he wasn't as handy at knife throwing as he was with an automatic pistol. Then he must've figured that Tom and I would make excellent hostages in case Bunny Lipton solved the mystery of the Path of the Gods. So instead of using murder weapons he turned to the ancient Chinese arsenal of toxicology."

Tom looked around the table. "Can I ask, what's meant by the term 'living Buddhas'?"

"They're strange creatures," answered Lipton, "raised by Buddhist monks for the faithful masses to worship. They're often children. When those Buddhas reach the age of reason they're summoned to the great Buddha—meaning generally that the monks send them on their way using poison. But occasionally some of them have real ability, and then mandarins pay very well to acquire them. That's what happened to the deformed, intelligent creature Denverton made his slave. I have no doubt the monster believed in his terrible master's return as much as he himself did."

"And what about the rascals Lord Denverton invited to dinner?" asked Tom.

"That was a leftover of the Chinese ritual. Of course he had to choose English crooks—who aren't in short supply—to witness the master's awakening. I assume that if by some miracle it had really happened, the lives of those present wouldn't have been worth much. The invitations were sent out by the living Buddha servant."

"The vampire Buddha," murmured Matsuko.

"It's true," said Dickson. "The malformed being lacked normal digestive organs, so he fed on human blood—that of his own coolie, the orangutan. I expected we'd run across a creature of that kind once I heard about birds disappearing at night. When we killed him he was out hunting for sleeping partridges."

Lord Denverton ordered champagne served. It was already foaming in the glasses when one of the Japanese lifted his head and sniffed the air. "It smells a lot like fire."

He'd barely spoken when a burning wave seemed to envelop them. Through the open door they saw a silk wall hanging curl up, engulfed in flames. At that moment the servants cried out, "Fire! Fire!"

"It must be coming from the Path of the Gods!" muttered Dickson, leaping up. He was right: flames were pouring out of the secret door.

"Alas! Three times alas!" cried Lipton. "Fuh-Suh's room was full of documents!"

But they had time only to flee, as the fire gained on them from all sides. When they had reached the street they were impotent witnesses to the total destruction of Denverton House.

"I assume that fire was planned," said Matsuko. "The entry of an intruder into the hidden room would set off some kind of secret clockwork that only initiates would know how to disarm. It's not that surprising. And we were wrong not to have thought of it in the joy of our triumph."

"Oh, well," said Dickson. "This destruction will help preserve the secret surrounding a distinguished name. Fuh-Suh is no more, and that's the main thing, isn't it, Bunny?"

Lipton winked in agreement.

Thus ended the strange case of the Path of the Gods. But there was one addendum: a few days after the fire at Denverton House, poor Schneider fell ill, and his condition quickly worsened. Arno urged Dickson to come. At the gates of death, Schneider gradually seemed to regain his sanity. There was little the detective still needed to know, but even so he tried to question the dying man at the last.

"Didn't Denverton die in Luxembourg, in fact right here in this house? Wasn't his body taken back to London?"

The more Schneider's suffering increased, the more Dickson noticed his extraordinary resemblance to Denverton-Fuh-Suh. Suddenly he motioned for Dickson to approach. As the detective did so, the dying man lifted his hand and struck him right in the heart. But his arm was too weak, and the weapon that would've ended Dickson's life fell to the floor. It was the little platinum dagger with the jade handle.

Dickson stared at the sick man, whose face was now filled with terrible hatred.

"Even so," he howled, "I came back, along the Path of the Gods!" Then he fell back on his pillow and died.

As he traveled back to London, Dickson was troubled by doubts. "Which of them was Fuh-Suh? Schneider or Denverton?"

The express train he was taking seemed to hammer out the two names on the wheels, between the bumpers of the cars, under the steel of the bogies: *Schneider... Denverton... Schneider... Denverton...* and the steam engine puffed out *Fuh... Suh... Fuh... Suh...*

"It doesn't matter," murmured Harry Dickson, letting himself relax and laying his head back against the seat cushions in the first-class compartment. He sensed that some small mystery still hovered around this business, which seemed to be coming to an unsatisfactory end, like a badly told fairy tale. He fell asleep a little weary in spirits, a little less at peace than he usually felt after one of his fierce struggles against human crime.

George Fronval: *The Mysterious Fen-Chu*

George Fronval, whose real name was Jacques Garnier, was born on January 16, 1904, in Paris and died on February 23, 1975, in Fussey, Côte-d'Or. He was a French journalist, cartoonist, and novelist, who used numerous pseudonyms during his prolific career.

A journalist from the age of 18, notably for L'Intransigeant, *he was also the co-founder of* Cinémonde, *and a frequent contributor to* La Vie du Rail *and the comic magazine* Pilote. *Garnier was also a technical advisor on many films, and an occasional actor. A friend of Jean Renoir and Erich von Stroheim, he arranged the meeting that allowed the latter, who had returned penniless from Hollywood, to land the role of the German officer that made him famous in* La Grande Illusion *(1937). He can be seen at the end of the film, playing the German soldier who takes aim at Captain de Boëldieu (Pierre Fresnay).*

Garnier was also known as an avid collector of comics, pulps and film memorabilia. He was renowned for his research and extensive knowledge of the publishing houses founded by the Offenstadt brothers and wrote numerous articles on Jean de La Hire and José Moselli. Passionate about the history of the American West and piracy, he became one of the leading experts on these subjects in France.

As a writer, Garnier penned numerous comic book stories and nearly 800 popular novels, of which L'Enigmatique Fen-Chu, *here translated as* The Mysterious Fen-Chu *is but a sample. It was originally published by S.E.N. in 1944 with a superb cover by René Brantonne. Fen-Chu is yet another Asian mastermind bent on world conquest, in the mold of the notorious Fu Manchu invented by Sax Rohmer in 1912. It is worthy to note that when the novel was reprinted in 1946 under the title* Le Maître des Robots *[The Robot Master], the role of Fen-Chu was then attributed to a European mad scientist.*

A specialist in the history of the American West, Garnier was the only European writer to be a member of the Western Writers of America. A friend of the grandsons of Geronimo and Sitting Bull, a friend of John Ford, Gary Cooper, and John Wayn, he regularly traveled to the United States to gather material for his books.

J.-M.L.

I

This morning, as usual, Robert Marchal, a reporter for *Paris Journal*, arrived at his office at the stroke of six. He had stepped out of the elevator and was heading to the newsroom when an office clerk spotted him and planted himself in his way.

He said, "Good morning, Monsieur Marchal, the editor-in-chief asked me to tell you that he'd like to see you as soon as you're in."

"Thanks, Paul. I'll go see him right away."

The young man hurried down the big corridor, pushed open the glass door to the room reserved for reporters and went straight to his usual place. He glanced at the mail, then at the memos tacked to the central board.

One of his colleagues, hunched over his notes, apparently having serious problems editing his article, looked up and said, "Oh, it's you, good old Marchal. Dumesnil's screaming his head off for you. He's called a bunch of times. It seems he needs to talk to you about a very important matter."

"I know, Paul already warned me."

"It's obviously to give you a sensational story. You're lucky to be one of the lead reporters here. I'll never get that chance. I'm condemned for eternity to the missing cats and run-over dogs. When Dusmesnil calls me into his office, it's usually to rake me over the coals or tell me I don't know what I'm doing. And yet, I've been here for six years."

Robert Marchal wasn't listening to his colleague. Having taken off his hat and coat, he left the room where an eerie silence was looming, which, when the clock had sounded, should have turned into a deafening commotion. The young man went down the glass hallway until he got to a door that capital letters announced, "Editor-in-Chief". He knocked and walked straight in.

Jacques Dumesnil, his direct boss, was sitting at his desk piled high with typed texts and scattered photographs. He was dictating some urgent letters to his secretary. Barely raising his head, he gave a friendly wave to his reporter and motioned to a big, leather armchair across from him.

"Hello, Marchal. Sit down and wait a minute. I have something very serious to talk to you about."

The young man sat and lit a cigarette to kill time. Ten minutes later the secretary left.

Leaning forward on his desk, Dumesnil declared, "Just us now, my friend. You've certainly heard about the mysterious wireless messages received lately."

"Yes. I only know what the wire services are reporting. I don't see what's so interesting. It's sounds to me a lot like some lunatic or else a bad joke."

Far from sharing the skepticism of his colleague, the chief editor looked worried. "Make no mistake, it's a lot more serious than you might think at first and I'm afraid that the author is more dangerous than a simple practical joker. Let's go over the facts."

He turned to the file cabinet on his right, opened a drawer, ran his fingers over the meticulously arranged records, stopped at the letter "F" and pulled out a file with a green cover. Inside this file were maybe ten pages, each with a newspaper article cut and pasted on.

Every attempt at domination by whites over the Asian continent and in the Pacific Islands must stop immediately. I give you 48 hours. If, after this deadline, nothing has been done, I will act. I have spoken. Fen-Chu, Master of the World.

Putting the paper back into the file, the editor of the *Paris Journal*, after a short pause to light a cigarette, went on:

"What do you think, Marchal?"

Shrugging his shoulders, he responded, "It's obviously the work of madman. What normal person would dare to provoke the most powerful nations in the world?"

Jacques Dumesnil was about to read some more when the reporter raised his hand to stop him.

"Let me say something."

"I'm listening."

"Do we know exactly where these messages are coming from?"

"No."

"And yet, I believe there's an easy way to track these clandestine transmissions. Even if I don't know much about wireless technology, I've heard about direction-finding systems. So?"

"The search made along those lines were, I believe, negative. Anyway, later you can ask a specialist who's more competent than I am. But let's get back to Fen-Chu, all right? The next day, Saturday, March 12, Fen-Chu resent his threats and added more of the same. He did this for five days. On March 18 he was silent, likewise the next day. This silence was disturbing, but wasn't really noticed because two very important events monopolized the news. Remember?"

"Of course. On March 18 the British ocean liner, the *Scotland Express* of the Blue Star Line, heading to Singapore, full of passengers, went up in flames off the coast of Sumatra and sank, lock, stock and barrel. Only one man miraculously survived the disaster."

"That's right. And the next day..."

"A horrible fire broke out in Santa Rosario, Mexico, incinerating some big oilfields and half the city."

"Indeed. What do you think of these two disasters? I'm sure you know that it's a mystery how they were started, but what you certainly don't know is that both catastrophes had some things in common. Each of the fires was preceded by a long whistling sound, then a thick, purple cloud appeared in the sky, right above the *Scotland Express* and, the next day, over the oil wells of Peninsula Petroleum. Then an explosion rang out and immediately after, the flames sprang up, coming from who knows where, spreading so fast that it was impossible to stop them."

"Incredible. The whistling, the purple cloud, the explosion... the flames... it could've been..."

"Yes, it was Fen-Chu. Seeing that none of his threats had been taken seriously, he retaliated. And he didn't try to cover it up. The next day, March 20, several times during the day, he sent this message:

"The person who set fire to the Scotland Express and to the oilfields in Santa Rosario, is none other than me. These are the first two proofs of my almighty power. Tomorrow, if the French government has not heeded my demands, I will be forced to come down hard. I have spoken."

Jacques Dumesnil crushed his cigarette in the ashtray, coughed, and went on, solemnly.

"That message came three days ago. Nothing in particular happened until last night."

"Until last night? Did something serious happen?" Marchal asked worriedly.

The editor nodded and answered, "Last night, at 9 pm, a wicked fire destroyed almost the entire small town of Sainte-Marie on the island of La Reunion. Like the last two blazes, there was a whistling, a purple cloud and an explosion before it broke out."

"So, it was another Fen-Chu crime?"

"Yes! His retaliation against our government. The whole thing, which sounds pretty trivial at first, is taking a tragic turn. We can't keep it a secret any longer. This morning, already, most of the foreign papers have long articles about it. The situation is very serious. The prankster we thought we were dealing with might be a madman, but he's certainly a dangerous madman. A formidable man and his threats are not empty. We have to expect all kinds of things from him. Fen-Chu, who has potent and unknown means at his disposal, isn't going to stop showing off his infernal power. The state of anxiety and uncertainty that our country and the entire world is going to suffer is likely to cause some major problems. It's a critical moment. Starting today, in our evening edition, as prudently as possible, we're going to reveal the facts to the readers, asking them to stay calm, no matter what happens.

"Right now, at Place Beauvau, in the Ministry of the Interior, an important conference is taking place. Besides the Prime Minister, the British and American and Mexican ambassadors are there. And even though they're not yet involved in this affair, representatives from several other countries, namely Belgium, Germany, Italy and Hungary, in the spirit of solidarity, insisted on being present at the meeting. What will be the result? Obviously an agreement to fight Fen-Chu. We'll know from Cluzel and Brissard, whom I sent over there, when they get back."

Dumesnil closed the file, crossed his arms and continued:

"Marchal, I want to give this to you. Your trip to South American can wait until later. I'm giving you carte blanche so you can do some sensational reporting worthy of *Paris Journal* and its readers. Do whatever you think best. Starting today you have unlimited resources. What I want is to get a series of absolutely extraordinary articles as soon as possible. Are you up for it?"

"And how!" Robert Marchal answered, jumping out of his seat.

The two men walked together to the door and stopped.

The chief editor asked, "Do you already have a plan in mind?"

"Of course," the young man replied with a cocky grin. "What would you say about finding Fen-Chu's lair and going to pay him a visit? I'll get you an interview."

"Now that'd be great. But be careful, Marchal, this Fen-Chu isn't an ordinary man. You'll be dealing with a formidable adversary."

With a friendly handshake, the young reporter bid his boss farewell and went back to the newsroom where he sat for two hours, lost in deep thought, despite the rampant noise. When he left, his face was brightened by a big smile. He looked more than satisfied. Putting on his hat and coat he declared, "I think I've found the best solution."

He was just about to step out when a telephone rang. One of his colleagues called out, "Hey, Marchal, it's for you. Dumesnil wants to talk to you."

Marchal took the phone and listened to his editor telling him, "There's news in the Fen-Chu affair. Don't worry, it's not another disaster. According to the latest information released after the conference at the ministry, they've located the origin of the mysterious messages. The station that sent them is in Tibet, around the valley of Shekar-Dzong, on the borders of Nepal, China and Manchuria. That's news that should be very useful to you."

Marchal hung up and left. As he went down the monumental staircase he was trying to come up with a detailed action plan.

"The news makes things a lot easier. Before going to see my friend Blanchard, I'll drop in on the explorer Langeville who might be able to give me some good advice since he just came back from spending a few months in the highlands of Tibet. I'll see him this afternoon."

Forgetting about Fen-Chu and all his threats for a short while, Robert Marchal went to eat lunch at a restaurant near the imposing building that harbored the offices of *Paris Journal*.

II

The next day, after the department heads had left the meeting that took place every day in the office of Jacques Dumesnil, the editor-in-chief kept Marchal behind and asked him, "Well, where are you at? Have you got a plan worked out?"

"Of course," the reporter said. "In a case like this one, it's important not to waste a single second. So, yesterday I hit the streets. Thanks to what you told over the phone, knowing now that Fen-Chu's hiding out in Tibet, I've decided to go there as soon as possible. I talked to the explorer Langeville who told me some very interesting things about the country and even offered to accompany me. In the evening I saw my friend Blanchard who also wanted to go with me to Tibet. He's got an airplane that's ready to take off at any time. So, I accepted both their offers. In fact, they're sitting in the next room right now."

The editor-in-chief rang for the office boy and ordered, "Bring in the two men who came with Robert Marchal."

The clerk vanished and a few seconds later the explorer Langeville and the pilot Blanchard entered the office. After Marchal introduced everyone, the two men sat in the comfortable armchairs.

Dumesnil, sitting behind his desk, told them, "Our friend Marchal has told you about the critical events that are happening. I want to thank you for the invaluable help that you're both offering to our paper. You, Monsieur Langeville, will be a knowledgeable guide. Thanks to your plane, Monsieur Blanchard, our friend will be able to reach Fen-Chu's lair. But be careful, you'll be dealing with a determined and dangerous man who seems to have tremendous capabilities at his disposal. The adventure you're about to take will be hard and undoubtedly full of surprises. Believe me, the 'Paris Journal' will never forget your collaboration."

Langeville took the floor, "It seems to me that under the present circumstances it's everyone's duty to do what he can to destroy this mysterious Fen-Chu. Yesterday afternoon, when Marchal came to see me and to tell me about the recent events, I was stunned, couldn't believe my ears. And then hearing the latest information that this so-called 'Master of the World' is living in Tibet around the valley of Shekar-Dzong, I couldn't hold back my surprise. I know the area pretty well after spending six months there. It's arid, a desert, at a high altitude, constantly lashed by the winds coming from the Himalayas. I explored the region extensively because there happens to be traces of a very ancient, Asian civilization, which sent me all over the sandy expanse. So, I'll be a useful guide and advisor to our friend."

"I think so, too," Dumesnil replied. "And I'm sure that thanks to your help the search will be a lot easier." Turning to the pilot, he asked, "And what are your plans?"

Blanchard said, "It's very simple: starting today, I'm at the service of Marchal and *Paris Journal*. I was planning to leave for South America next week, but I can put the trip off until later. The idea of being your collaborator is too enticing. See, I've got an irrepressible taste for danger and adventure. In the present adventure, the dangers we'll be facing don't scare me, they attract me. Right now in my hangar in Villacoublay, I've got a long-distance plane ready to take off and it'll get us to the little explored region, maybe never flown over, without any problems. I'm just waiting for the signal to leave."

Robert Marchal, who had remained silent up to this point, stood up and declared, "We can't waste any more time. Every minute is precious and we have to fight Fen-Chu quickly before he gives more proof of his demonic power. Nowadays we don't have to take months to prepare a distant, laborious exploration. We've got ultra-modern means at hand and we have to use them. We have a plane to get to Tibet in record time. We have a guide who can lead us quickly to our goal. I say we leave immediately."

He turned to Langeville and Blanchard and asked them, "Are you ready to leave Paris tomorrow?"

With the affirmative response of the two men, the young reporter turned to his editor and said, "Well then, the die is cast. We're leaving tomorrow, early in the morning."

Dumesnil walked around his desk, saying, "Thank you, messieurs, for volunteering. I'm sure that the three of you will get the job done. And you, Marchal, with the help of your two friends, I have no doubt that you will deliver not only a sensational story but also a work of justice. The entire world will be grateful to you. As of now, war is declared against Fen-Chu. We'll soon see whether or not he's as invincible as he claims to be. In this war, one side is bound to lose. It will be him, you can be sure."

At that very moment, the ambient silence was disturbed by a strange noise coming from the street. Intrigued, Dumesnil and his visitors went to the window, opened it and looked outside. On the front steps and on the sidewalk the crowd of pedestrians seemed to be unusually agitated. Groups were forming, looking up at the sky, while others were bustling about feverishly. Like a miracle, the ruckus stopped. A heavy silence fell upon the crowd. Little interested in the incident, the four men were about to go back to their conversation when a long, shrill whistle screamed out. In the sky, right over the city, a purple cloud took shape. From that point on, panic struck the Parisians. Informed by the latest editions of the newspapers in the capital, they feared the worst and running hither and thither, they were searching for any kind of refuge. A low buzz ran through the crowd, then loud shouting in which one word rose above the others, laden with fear and menace: *"Fen-Chu"*.

From their observation point, Robert Marchal and his colleagues had watched this weird scene and they, too, wondered what cataclysm was about to hit the city. Without uttering a sound, they stared at the elliptical purple cloud, which was quivering slightly over Paris, and waited for the fatal explosion that would put an end to their pending adventure. But it didn't come. After hanging in the sky for three or four minutes, the purple cloud gradually dissipated until it vanished completely. The sky was clear again and life, momentarily interrupted, went back to normal.

Jacques Dumesnil went back to his desk and lit a cigarette. "What do you know, another show put on by this cursed Fen-Chu. Until today he'd limited his field of action to distant countries: Mexico, La Reunion and the Dutch Indies. There was never any reason for us to fear he'd work his evil deeds on our continent. I guess it's a show of strength. So, there's every reason to believe that we'll soon be lamenting disasters on our own territory."

Marchal and the other two visitors remained silent. While they were lost in deep thought, the "printing" used by the news agency to telegraph the latest information started clacking in its glass cage. Automatically, the young reporter went over and watched the keys striking the roll of paper that was slowly rotating.

All of a sudden he stiffened up. "Ah, come on now, this is unbelievable!"

"What is it?" the others asked.

He tore off the paper and brought it to his editor.

Dumesnil sat up and read the newly printed text aloud:

The Mélan Dam near Annecy in the Haute-Savoie has just been destroyed under mysterious circumstances. This morning, around 11 o'clock, a crack suddenly appeared in the main wall, causing considerable damage. The water held in the upper lakes immediately flooded the surrounding valleys, drowning huge plots of land and resulting in multiple victims. More information will be forwarded when it comes in.

When he stopped reading, Dumesnil looked at his reporter and asked, "What do you think of that?"

Marchal shrugged his shoulders and replied, "I don't know. Maybe we're looking at another Fen-Chu crime."

The explorer Langeville, who was foremost a man of action, said, "We're not going to go accusing Fen-Chu of every tragedy. Maybe it's just a simple coincidence. Why not blame him for the accident of the Paris-Brest train or the fire that ravaged the Galeries Parisiennes last week?"

While the two visitors were sharing their opinions with Robert Marchal, the chief editor picked up the phone to the newsroom and told one of his reporters to investigate the new disaster.

The "printing" started clacking again. All at the same time, the four men jumped over to the machine. Letters appeared, forming words, sentences...

They read:

According to the latest information the accident at the Mélan Dam is to be credited to Fen-Chu. In fact, the chief engineer running the electric plant nearby, in one of the few undamaged areas, stated that a few seconds before the dam broke, he heard a whistling sound and saw a purple cloud in the sky.

This information, which only confirmed their worst fears, filled the four men with dread.

Blanchard muttered, "When is this going to stop? I don't have to tell you that we have to put an end to this evil man. So, it's agreed, we leave tomorrow?"

"Everything's ready for the trip. There's nothing keeping us in Paris. So, yes, we leave tomorrow," Marchal announced.

Jacques Dumesnil, who had just hung up the telephone, told them, "There's a special meeting of at the Interior Ministry this afternoon. We'll let the official circles blabber away and we'll do what we think best. Besides us four, no one knows about our project. The trip should remain a secret because

366

the slightest indiscretion could compromise your mission and prove fatal. To-morrow morning, when you leave Villacoublay, you just have to tell any busy-bodies that you're off on a report about Australia."

Turning to Robert Marchal, he added, "Come back to see me this afternoon and we'll wrap up the preparations for your expedition. We'll set up a secret code so we can communicate while you're away."

Then to the explorer and pilot he concluded, "I'll see you tomorrow morning at Villacoublay, messieurs, before you take off.

III

Blanchard's plane had taken off without a hitch from the Villacoublay air-port. On board were four passengers, namely, the pilot Blanchard, the explorer Langeville, the reporter Marchal and the mechanic Ludovic Bougon, the faithful companion of the pilot, having gone with him on all his previous trips and be-come both a valuable partner and a devoted friend.

Following the usual route of long-distance flights to the Far East, the plane had to make stops in Athens, Castellorizo, Damascus, Baghdad, Jask, Karachi and Jodhpur. From there it had to turn north towards Kabul. From this city it could head directly to Tibet, to the unexplored and mysterious regions.

The first part of the trip went smoothly and Blanchard and his companions were graced with beautiful weather. While the pilot sat at the commands, Langeville stayed next to him, scrutinizing the land they were flying over, mak-ing meticulous notes and checking the map for the different geographical fea-tures he was seeing.

On this day, around noon, he announced, "Be careful! We're around Ske-kar-Dzong and therefore in the danger zone!"

A few moments later, pointing at a rocky bluff that was still tiny in the dis-tance, the ethnographer explained, "That's the Kalahari peak where the foothills of the high plains begins."

Hearing this, the passengers all felt gripped by an uneasy emotion. The mechanic, who was a real rascal from Ménilmontant and had kept them amused with his witty repartee and cheerful mood, had lost his smile and looked unusu-ally grave.

Having drastically reduced speed, the airplane was flying low over a region that looked desolate and completely devoid of human existence. It was, as far as the eye could see, just a vast expanse of sand randomly dotted with tall, black rocks that reinforced the rough and wild look of the place.

All of a sudden, one of the engines could be heard spluttering, then back-firing and stopping. The other quit too. The plane glided in wide circles as it slowly descended.

Marchal looked at the pilot worriedly, "What's wrong?"

Shrugging his shoulders Blanchard answered, "I don't know. A break-down, but I've got no idea why?"

"It's unimaginable," the mechanic said. "Before taking off in Kabul, I checked everything thoroughly and filled up the tanks."

"All right," Blanchard the philosopher remarked, "we'll just land and see what's what."

Guided by an expert hand, the plane headed for a narrow stretch of sand, the entrance to a valley entrenched between two rock walls. The space was small but still big enough for a pilot like Blanchard, who had seen others, especially in the Rio de Oro and the Andes. The aircraft touched down smoothly and rolled 100 feet before stopping.

The pilot got out of the plane, unbuttoned his leather jacket, which was smothering him, took off his helmet, swallowed a few mouthfuls of air and said, "I'm going to check the engine. It's probably something minor and easy to fix."

Ludovic Bougon also stepped out and grabbed his toolbox, ready to help his boss.

Robert Marchal had followed them and while the two aviators were buried in the delicate organs of the aircraft, the reporter walked around smoking a ciga-rette. He thought the breakdown was weird and wondered whether the unex-pected layover was really caused by chance. In spite of himself, he felt a lurking fear creep over him. A gut feeling put him on the defensive. An imminent dan-ger was threatening them. He scrutinized the surroundings. Not a trace of human beings. They were lost in the middle of the Tibetan desert, far from any civilized area and yet close to the spot where Fen-Chu was supposed to have built his lair.

He tried to dispel the anxiety weighing on him by muttering, "It's ridicu-lous for me to be rattling my brains and seeing danger where there isn't any."

Then he turned around and went back to the plane.

"Well?" he questioned the two aviators.

"There's nothing wrong," Blanchard responded. "The engines are in per-fect working order."

"And the gas," the mechanic said, "is clean, there's nothing clogging the hoses."

The three men got back into the plane and closed the door behind them. Blanchard sat behind the controls, pressed a button and the two engines started up normally. The plane was rolling, getting ready to take, when they heard a loud noise, like an explosion. At the same time, one of the propellers burst into pieces. The plane was immobilized.

The four passengers looked at each other's pale faces. Fearing the worst, no one dared to share his thoughts.

A few seconds passed in agonizing silence, soon broken by a second ex-plosion, followed by a loud crack. One of the windows was smashed to smither-eens.

"No doubt about it," Langeville said, "they're shooting at us." Then, pointing at two shapes behind a rock, running towards them, he added, "Look, our mysterious enemies."

Bougon, without wasting a second, had grabbed a Winchester hanging nearby and shouldered it. He was about to pull the trigger when, without warning, he dropped the weapon and cried out in pain. The three others looked at him in surprise.

"What's wrong?" Blanchard asked.

"I don't know. I was going to shoot when I suddenly felt my right hand burning up."

And Bougon looked down. He saw a purple circle on the back of his hand, which hurt a lot. The pain lasted for less than two minutes, then let up as the circle faded away.

This incident had grabbed the attention of the passengers who realized too late that two men were standing in the doorway of the plane, holding them at gunpoint.

They were taller than average, built like titans, with typical Mongolian features, but their faces showed no emotion. Without saying a word, using only hand signals, they made the four men raise their hands and get out of the plane. Holding back their anger, the four passengers followed orders. They were prisoners. Of whom? Of Fen-Chu without a shadow of a doubt.

Silently, in single file, they followed their two bodyguards who led them towards the entrance of a narrow pass. After ten minutes of walking, just as they got there, a sudden detonation made them turn around. Their plane had just exploded and was engulfed in flames. Thus, their last hope was dissolving, they had no more chance for salvation. Except for a miracle, the four of them were condemned to never see the civilized world again.

At the entrance to the pass, the small band was joined by a group of men who looked like the ones who had captured the four travelers. The two guards and their comrades exchanged a few hand signals, interspersed with grunts and growls. Then the prisoners and their guards were back on their way. They ended up in a kind of cul-de-sac where the path stopped at the foot of a steep rock wall. To their great surprise, the captives saw a huge block of rock swing open, revealing the entrance to a tunnel. The file of men resumed their march down a straight, narrow corridor with an arched ceiling that was a barely high enough for them to stand up. The electric lights placed at regular intervals were bright enough for them to move safely and steadily.

Robert Marchal, who was paying close attention to everything around him, figuring that it would come in handy at some point, was counting the number of steps. After one hundred, they came to a spiral staircase that had thirty steps, which led down to a big, round room with a number of corridors much bigger than the last one. All along the wall they saw the horns of loudspeakers, but an eerie silence loomed over the room. The prisoners were anxiously wondering what the future held for them.

Soon the calm was disturbed by a crackling sound as one of the speakers turned on. A voice, sharp and metallic came through. It was just like the one that had, since Monday, March 7, been heard several times, sowing fear and panic around the world.

It declared, "It's my pleasure, messieurs, to welcome you. You'd like to see me, you're looking for me, I believe I can make it easy for you by bringing you directly to me. Now you are prisoners of Fen-Chu, the Master of the World."

A click followed, then silence again. A light at the entrance to one of the corridors flashed three times. At this signal the jailers motioned to the four prisoners to start walking again. Under the supervision of the guards, Marchal and his companions went down the chosen corridor. It was dark but in the distance they could see the exit as a small circle of light. The reporter counted almost three hundred steps this time. The room they came to was narrow and empty. There were three impressively large, metal doors. The middle one slowly swung open without making a sound. One of the Mongols ordered the four Frenchmen to advance, which they did. Almost right away the huge double doors closed behind them. They were without guards in a high-ceilinged, square room that looked like a well and was lit by a dim electric light. Finding themselves alone, the reporter and his friends took a few deep breaths and shared their impressions.

Langeville was the first to speak up. "I'm wondering if this isn't all a dream. It's so strange, so staggering. I would never have believed that an underground installation like this could've existed in such a region. When I explored this area six months ago, I had no clue that I was traveling over a series of tunnels equipped with modern technology."

"Well, we were looking for adventure," Blanchard said, "I guess we've found it. If we get out of this, Marchal, you'll have the greatest story of all the time."

The reporter smiled shyly and replied, "Right, if we get out of this alive... In the meantime, my friends, I'm sorry I dragged you three into this expedition. I'm responsible for any harm that comes to you and if it does, I'll regret it for the rest of life."

"Bah!" the pilot said. "Don't get melodramatic on us. All's not lost and if fortune is smiling on us, we'll pull through without a scratch."

"I think so too," Ludovic Bougon agreed. "I feel good about the future. Besides, a fortune teller told me that I'd die at a hundred years old as the father of a big family. Right now I'm single and I don't think this Fen-Chu is a matchmaker or that he'll let me tie the knot with one of one of his subjects... if there are subjects here. Personally, so far, the adventure hasn't been so bad. It reminds me of one of those cliffhanger films. Anyway, I'm anxious to meet the master of this place, I'd like to get a gander at his mug."

"That's easy enough," announced a voice they recognized immediately. "You just have to turn around."

Astonished and intrigued, the four prisoners turned around and were startled. During the brief announcement, one of the walls had disappeared and in the space, in front of a bright light, a man stood motionless.

This man was none other than Fen-Chu. He looked strange and mysterious. Tall, thin, proud, he had an enigmatic face, an inscrutable mask in which two bright eyes sparkled. He was dressed like an oriental with a loose, black silk kimono buttoned to the collar. He wore thick-soled sandals, which made him even taller, and a black silk cap topped with a coral button.

Fen-Chu, whose face looked sculpted out of an old block of ivory, sported a thin mustache that cascaded over both sides of his pinched, arrogant mouth. In a theatrical stance, he had his arms crossed and his hands hidden inside his wide sleeves.

Fen-Chu snickered sneeringly and pointed his slender index finger with an unbelievably long, sharp nail, which resembled a vulture's claw, at the four men and said, "You have come here to measure my power. Well, messieurs, you will be satisfied. I'm going to show you and tell you everything. And it will be no risk to me since you will be wiped off the face of the earth, in a manner of speaking."

Robert Marchal and his friends remained silent and still. Fen-Chu was snickering again and with a wave of his hand two Mongols, exactly like the ones who had escorted the Frenchmen here, showed up and approached him. The Master of the World made a few weird signs, to which the two henchmen bowed several times.

"Let me introduce you to Koung and Rahang," Fen-Chu said. "From now on they will keep me informed about you. They will be watching over you day and night and keeping me abreast of your every move. And I'm warning you that it's useless to try to outwit them. Besides, they can't understand you because, like everyone who works here under my command, they're deaf and mute."

The demonic creature paused before continuing.

"Now, messieurs, go along with Koung and Rahang who will show you to your rooms. I'll see you later when you've recovered a little from your fatigue and your emotions. We'll be able to get to know each other better and talk more. For the moment, I'll give the world the news about you and tell Jacques Dumesnil, editor-in-chief of the 'Paris Journal' that Robert Marchal and his partners, the explorer Langeville, the pilot Blanchard and his mechanic Bougon have arrived at their destination."

Abruptly, Fen-Chu turned around and marched off, leaving the four prisoners in a state of utter dismay.

"That they stopped us in mid-flight is understandable, given the extraordinary means he seems to have at his disposal," Marchal exclaimed, "but that he already knows our names and our project with Dumesnil is unbelievable."

"And we were the only ones who knew about it. There were no leaks or slip-ups."

"The man is diabolical," Langeville said.

In silence, resigned, the four men followed Koung and Rahang to their rooms, or rather to their prison cells.

IV

With Koung and Rahang as their guides, Marchal and his companions headed to their accommodations. They went down a long, narrow hallway that ended in a round room. Automatically, a grated door opened onto an elevator. With a sign from their guards the prisoners stepped in and the door closed behind them. The elevator started with a quiet hum. It rose for almost a full minute before the car stopped. They got out and stood in a lobby that looked as comfortable as a modern hotel. The floor was covered with a thick carpet that absorbed the sound of their footsteps and the air felt fresh, constantly ventilated by big fans. They walked to a small door with a narrow opening in it, through which they could see what was happening on the other side. Koung and Rahang motioned them to stop. One of the Mongols pushed the door open (apparently it wasn't locked) and entered the room, inviting the others to follow his example. Marchal and his friends did as they were told and their two jailers stepped out, closing the door behind them.

The four prisoners were in a pretty big room with a high ceiling, far from uncomfortable furniture and a few lamps that diffused a soft, pale light. There were four bunks covered with warm furs, the same number of leather armchairs and a big table in the middle of the room. Along one wall were shelves holding a wide range of books and across from this small library the prisoners saw a latest model wireless radio.

"Fen-Chu seems to like to do things right," Blanchard said after a quick glance around the room.

"I would never have believed there was such a comfortable hotel in the middle of Tibet," Langeville declared.

Making an inspection, Marchal looked into the other rooms: a bathroom and showers and a small dining room.

"As pleasant as our captivity might be here, I have no intention of hanging around."

"I feel the same way," Blanchard agreed, "but I'd still prefer this comfortable set-up to a dark cell with a straw mattress."

"It seems we should be enjoying our misfortune," Langeville said. "Fen-Chu had the bright idea not to separate us. If we weren't together, it'd be hard for us to join forces to escape seeing that from this moment on we have to get working on how to slip out of his clutches. The Master of the World made a mistake to our benefit. We have to use it."

Overcome with fatigue, the four men lay down on their bunks and were soon fast asleep. They dozed for several hours. When they woke up they were surprised to find on each armchair a pair of pajamas and outfits of shantung silk. On the table in the middle of the room, a simple but savory meal was waiting: During their sleep a butler had come in to set the table, bringing some roasted lamb and a big plate of rice, accompanied by a basket of exotic fruit and golden biscuits instead of bread. In the porcelain teapot was herbal tea.

"There's no end to surprises here," Robert Marchal remarked. "At least Fen-Chu hasn't sentenced us to bread and water."

Inhaling the pleasant smell of the dishes, Bougon was elated. "All this excitement has given me a hearty appetite. The look of these tasty treats makes me want to sit at the table at once. That lamb reminds me of being in Marrakesh when I was in the 6th colonial infantry."

"Hold your horses a little longer," Blanchard said, understanding his partner's eagerness but with no desire to hear him launch into one of the endless stories he liked to tell about his adventurous life. "We'll eat shortly. First we should take a refreshing bath and change our clothes."

The mechanic frowned and then grimaced when Marchal half-teased, "Why are you in such a hurry? How do you know that all this food isn't poisoned?"

"That's true," Bougon muttered unhappily. "I've just lost my appetite. Now I'm not hungry at all."

The explorer comforted the poor guy, "Listen, we'll enjoy the meal in peace. If Fen-Chu wanted to kill us, he wouldn't have prepared all this for us? From the moment of our ill-fated landing, he's had hundreds of chances to wipe us off the face of the earth. If he's left us alive, it's not out of the kindness of his heart but because it fits his plans. He's counting on using us for some trick of his or else as hostages for an exorbitant ransom."

Without further ado, the four of them took turns in the shower, which washed away their final fatigue in the blink of an eye. Then, bright-eyed and bushy-tailed, comfortable in their new outfits, they sat down at the table and ate heartily.

The meal was excellent and when they were finished, Marchal proposed, "I feel like taking a stroll. An hour of walking would do me good."

"That's pretty far-fetched," the mechanic said, "unless you walk around the room in circles."

"That would be too boring for me," Blanchard remarked. "I'd rather take a nap."

The three others objected, "Oh, no, we've slept enough already."

Bougon searched the pockets of the clothes he'd taken off and shouted in joy, "Messieurs, we're in luck. I've just dug up a pack of *Gauloises* and there are four cigarettes left. One for each of us so no one can be jealous."

The four prisoners smoked with relish, finding real comfort despite their critical situation.

"The next time we see our friend Fen-Chu," the mechanic said, "we have to remember to ask for a deck of cards. There are four of us so we can play hand after hand of belote. And then, by God, since our host seems ready to do things right, we'll ask him to supply us with more tobacco."

"No need," Langeville spoke up. "This Fen-Chu is amazing. He thought of everything, even that."

"What do you mean?"

The three others approached the explorer who had just opened the drawer of the table.

"Look and take your pick. The Master of the World gave us all kinds of French cigarettes and Havana cigars."

"This hotel is definitely first class," Blanchard joked. "If it weren't for the weird-looking manager and his staff, the trip would be well worth the detour."

The mechanic disagreed, "Not for me, you know, I'm not made for palaces. You can have your luxury hotels, I'll take my shack in Pavillons-sous-Bois or my room on Rue des Pyrénées."

While the pilot was fiddling with the radio to the rhythm of a New York orchestra filtering through, Robert Marchal scanned the books on the small bookshelf.

"There are plenty of surprises left for us. Do you know what I've found among the books? The most recent editions from Paris, books that came out barely eight days ago."

"Great, now we just have to ask for a regular delivery of *Paris Journal*," Bougon joked, back to his usual good mood and sharp wit.

The four men killed time. Marchal and the mechanic skimmed through some books while the explorer Langeville and the pilot Blanchard battled through a game of chess, which was found in the second drawer.

At the end of the afternoon the door opened and Rahang placed a big platter with the evening meal on the table. The reporter and his friends did it honor and when the meal was over, they lay down on their beds and soon drifted off to sleep.

The next day, up early, all ready after a breakfast of grapes and grapefruit, the four men heard the voice of Fen-Chu coming through an invisible speaker.

"Messieurs, I will see you in a few moments."

A few minutes later, Koung and his comrade came to bring the prisoners to the Master of the World. The elevator they took a long ride in dropped them off on a landing where two Mongols were waiting. After a brief exchange, Koung and Rahang disappeared. Following their new guards, Marchal and the others went down a long corridor, then down a short staircase and came to a small door that opened without a sound. The four Frenchmen found themselves in a huge, bare room with a high ceiling. In the middle, on a small platform, stood a throne on which Fen-Chu was sitting, dressed in his large, black silk kimono.

"Come closer," he ordered.

Walking side by side, the prisoners did as told and stopped a few feet in front of the odd character. He gestured to the two guards who stepped away for a moment before coming back with four chairs that they placed behind each of the captives. When they were all seated Fen-Chu went on:

"I hope, messieurs, you're not too unhappy with your first day here. I'd like your stay to be satisfying. I'm sure the last twenty-four hours have given you plenty of surprises. I'll warn you that there are more in store for you. I intend to show you everything, to give you a tour of the veritable city I've set up in the middle of the Tibetan desert, in an unexplored region of these rugged mountains. I'm also sure that you're going to ask what purpose I have in mind and what I plan to do with you. I'll satisfy your curiosity at once. I have no intention of forcing you to do my bidding. I feel a certain pleasure and pride in being able to show men like you what I, Fen-Chu, have accomplished. I do it even more willingly when I have no fear of indiscretion on your part. As I said when we first met, you are henceforth stricken from the book of the living. Whoever enters here can leave only when I decide, meaning when they're dead. My domain is a prison nobody gets out of. No escape is possible, unless by a miracle. And here, only I perform miracles."

Fen-Chu turned to Robert Marchal and went on:

"You left Paris planning to write an article on your adventure. The moment has come, Monsieur Journalist, to open your eyes and ears. You want to know who the mysterious Fen-Chu is? I'm going to tell you.

"I come from Mukden in the province of Ching-King in Manchuria. My father was a humble porter and worked all day long to support his big family. From a young age I was teased and taunted by the other kids who were bigger and stronger than me. One day robbers in the region entered the city, ransacked part of it and kidnapped me. They brought me back with them to the mountain and I lived the life of a slave among these nomads. Despite the hard labor I had to do, I loved the adventurous life because I could go from city to city and see a whole different world.

"For six years I'd led a nomad's life when one morning I found myself in a village in Chinese Turkestan. I was separated from my masters and taken away by a Protestant missionary who adopted me and gave me an exceptional European education. With him I first went to North America, then to England. One day, desiring freedom, I left my benefactor to live my own life as I wanted. But everywhere I went, because I was 'yellow', I encountered nothing but mockery and contempt. Suffering the worst insults while suppressing my rage, I traveled across Europe to further my education. That was how I took classes at the universities of Paris and Oxford, Strasbourg and Rome, Prague and Nuremberg. I did everything possible to pierce the most jealously guarded secrets. I used every means in my power to accumulate the knowledge that would serve me in the future. I patiently earned money by submitting to the cruelest bosses and accepting the most arduous work. One day, when I had enough money, I started climbing the social ladder, buying scruples and forcing respectable people to compromise themselves treacherously. That was my first victory. But it wasn't enough. I needed more. My first successes fed my ambition. I decided that I alone would become the most powerful man on Earth. I wanted to be the Master of the World. It took me years of work and patience during which I suffered many hardships, resigning myself to the vanity and disloyalty of the people I was forced to deal with.

"I was in New York, watching a play at the Crystal Theater, when a big fire broke out causing an indescribable panic. Everyone thought only of themselves, shoving others, trying to reach the exit and get to safety. I was pushed around, knocked down, trampled by a human herd. When I managed to crawl free, the man I called out to, (a very prominent public figure), refused to help me and shoved me back into the flames. I almost passed out but I gathered my failing strength and managed to get out of the burning building just moments before it collapsed. My life was saved by a miracle. From that day on, my hatred for men only grew stronger. I tried to forget about this tragic event but I couldn't. Something always revived my memories. Like this."

On saying this Fen-Chu stood up and opened his cape, showing his audience the mutilated left arm that was reduced to a hideous stump. Continuing his confession, the Master of the World declared:

"My patience had been tried. When I figured I'd learned enough to accomplish my plan, I left the so-called civilized country and made a long, hard trip to Asia. At first I went to China and witnessed the terrible tragedies there. Everywhere, even in the face of natural disasters—I saw massive floods and deadly epidemics—human selfishness reared its ugly head. I was crestfallen and dragged myself deeper into the deserted regions until I came to the high plains of the Pamir Mountains where I took true pleasure in the wild and mysterious region.

"One day, I met a Tibetan monk who was coming from Lhasa where he'd gone to elect the living Buddha and was going back to his monastery in Gyantse. For several miles we traveled together and the venerable old man amazed me with his knowledge and wisdom. Just before leaving me he confided certain secrets that would allow me to put my plans into action more easily. I explored this so-called undiscovered region long before you, Monsieur Langeville. Unbeknownst to you, I kept abreast of your work and had a good laugh at your discoveries and your childish enthusiasm. What would you have said if you'd unraveled the same mysteries as I had? Six months ago, while you were camping with your supposedly comfortable means that I considered merely expedient, in the valley of Shekar Dzong, I was finishing my installation. See, using the information of the Buddhist monk, I first came into this region around six years ago. I did the necessary research and surveys to get a good start on the project I'd planned. A short stay in Mongolia got me a team of workers who bent to my will and thanks to whom I was able to complete the forbidding task of the creation not only of an unimaginable underground city, but also of an ultra-modern factory where you will find the biggest power plant in the world and a laboratory equipped with extraordinarily powerful machines of my own invention.

"You've already had a taste of my power. I intend to show you very soon a few other testaments to my mighty force."

The four prisoners listened to their host with a mix of interest, astonishment and skepticism. What was really true in this speech and what was just pompous show? Despite all his claims, Fen-Chu (what was his real name?) seemed more like a dangerous fanatic, a braggart and a madman.

The Master of the World had stopped talking. He came down the stairs of his little platform and said, "If you'd care to follow me, messieurs, I'll give you a tour of my laboratory."

Marching majestically, the odd character headed for a door followed by Marchal and his companions.

Fen-Chu reached out and pointed to the heavy, metal door with his index finger. At the same time, a little red light turned off and on several times, then the door opened. The Master of the World and his guest entered a strange laboratory, a huge room the same size as the previous one, looking like both a chemistry research center and an alchemist's lair. The place was cluttered with complicated machines of all shapes and sizes. As far as the eye could see there were long, metal tubes, glass bulbs of all colors, panels with numerous dials and elaborate gears.

Seeing the surprised look on his visitors' faces, Fen-Chu smirked and said, "You're no doubt wondering what's the point of all this? You must be thinking that at night I shut myself in here and like some Cagliostro or Count de Saint-Germain I search for the Philosopher's Stone. You're wrong. Why would I make gold when I've got an even greater power?"

Pointing to a giant screen covering the wall and at which, a short distance away, was aimed a device that looked like both a film camera and a video recorder, the Master of the World went on:

"Messieurs, you're going to think you're watching a film. The machine you see before you and that I'm turning on is my own invention. Based on the principles of television, it allows me to take quick, wonderful trips without having to leave my laboratory. In mere seconds I can take you anywhere in the world. Where would you like to go? Europe? America? Africa? I know no borders and distance is no obstacle for me. Look at the screen. If you don't mind, I'll take you to Cairo, a place that everyone can recognize even if they've never been there. Or would you like to go farther? South America perhaps? Rio de Janeiro, for example?"

On the screen, the Pyramids were replaced by the famous Guanabara Bay, overlooked by Sugarloaf Mountain.

"But this is just trivial scenery," the enigmatic scientist said, savoring his triumph. "I'll take you to a city that you know well—Paris."

The image on the silver screen faded. The next scene, at first blurry, cleared up and Marchal and his friends saw a familiar site.

"Isn't it marvelous?" Fen-Chu asked. "But I'll do better. Instead of this cheap postcard, you'll see the place where the three of you met a few days ago."

With that said, he turned a few dials and the big picture of Paris on the screen was replaced by the inside of Jacques Dumesnil's office. The Editor-in-Chief of *Paris Journal* was sitting at his desk and having a lively conversation on the telephone.

"Now that's a miracle, wouldn't you say, messieurs? And there's more to come. We're going to hear what your boss is saying over the phone."

At that moment a speaker turned on and the four prisoners clearly heard the chief editor speaking thousands of miles away from them. The young reporter could not hide his astonishment. And he understood right away how Fen-Chu had discovered their secret.

V

Standing off to the side, Fen-Chu was gloating. "As you can see, messieurs, nothing can be hidden from me. Thanks to this machine I can know every move and the best-kept secrets."

On the silver screen the editor of the "Paris Journal" was still talking on the phone and every word was clearly heard by Marchal and his companions.

Dumesnil was saying, "I've taken due note, minister, of the important information you've just given me. I did indeed receive Fen-Chu's message last night, which gave news of our four travelers. Our paper is determined to support by all means possible the strong response the French government is preparing with its allies. What I can't understand is how the guy found out about our plans. You'd think he had spies everywhere and agents even embedded in my departments. The more I think about it, the more stupefied I am. It's not possible, and yet! There were only four of us who knew about Marchal going to Tibet. When they took off from Villacoublay, the few people at the airstrip didn't know the destination of the plane. But then again, who knows if Fen-Chu was telling the truth in his last message. It could be that, after being informed by one of his accomplices who overheard our conversation in my office, the diabolical man is trying to make an audacious bluff. I'll go this afternoon to Place Beauvau, minister, and I thank you again for inviting me to this secret meeting."

As Dumesnil was hanging up the phone, Fen-Chu laughed arrogantly.

378

"It's a formidable invention that took me more than ten years of research and hard work. It uses gamma rays that are a lot stronger than X rays and that I pick up from the sun. In my underground tunnels I've installed giant storage cells inside of which one those buildings you're so proud of would fit. They're filled to the brim with mercury and can store incredible power. This machine works so simply that a child could use it. Just put your eyes up to these two openings to see on the frosted glass the objective. Moving the levers there on the right up and down or side to side, you can change both the distance and the direction. It's like the famous rifle invented by the legendary Baron Munchausen, with the only difference being that my invention really exists. When it's focused, meaning when you see the objective in the frosted glass, you just have to push this button to turn it on. Immediately, at the end of this tube, a spark will appear and create a purple cloud, which will only take seconds to speed off to its goal. Then you wait five minutes maximum and the devastating power of my invention will start working. Nothing can stop it, nothing can block its effects. I alone control it. I just have to push this other button to cut the current and the purple cloud fades away. The other day, when you were meeting in Dusmesnil's office and preparing your trip, I gave you a little demonstration. If I'd waited a minute longer, Paris would've been annihilated and you along with it. But out of the kindness of my heart, I let you take your chances coming here."

The visit was reaching its end. Leaving the room with the curious machine and crossing back through the laboratory, the four prisoners went with Fen-Chu to his office. Koung and Rahang were waiting for them and at a sign from their dreadful boss, they brought them back to their cell. When they were alone, the reporter and his friends, who hadn't said a word on the way, looked at one another in bewilderment.

The rest of the day was spent waiting in vain, in monotonous despair: reading and playing chess were their main activities. In the evening, after a good meal, they gathered around the radio and shared their impressions in hushed voices. Marchal advised them to be extremely careful. Fen-Chu was probably spying on them and listening to their every word. While the radio broadcast a concert from Shanghai, the four of them, like conspirators, discussed the situation.

The mechanic proposed, "I think we should go for broke. Tomorrow morning, when our guard brings breakfast, we'll overpower him and get out scot-free."

"Great idea," Marchal replied, "but scot-free? To go where? No one of us knows this place. We won't get 100 yards down the corridor before running into some nasty Mongols or Fen-Chu himself."

"You're not thinking, Ludovic," Blanchard agreed, patting his partner amiably on the shoulder. "Let's say that by some extraordinary chance we don't run into anybody, how are we going to find the exit to this maze?"

Nodding, the explorer Langeville declared, "Yes, barring a miracle, we're condemned to stay here at the whim of Fen-Chu, who doesn't seem to have any plans to let us go."

Ludovic Bougon, who felt the wily fox of old being reborn in him, promised to stay on his toes and not let any opportunity escape that might change their desperate situation.

The opportunity came the next day. At the end of the afternoon, Rahang had brought their evening meal and left, but he forget (intentionally or by mistake?) to lock the door behind him. While his companions were busy with their usual distractions, the young man, without informing the others of his intentions, slipped silently out of the room. Excitedly he snuck down the long corridor lined with doors, each one alike and each one numbered. The hallway ended in a small rotunda in the middle of which was a spiral staircase. As cautiously as he could, making no noise on the metal steps, Bougon went up the stairs and took another corridor identical to the last. Halfway down, he stopped. A huge bay window looked out upon a vast, brightly lit courtyard. He stepped up to it and glanced outside. What he saw froze him solid. Involuntarily, without even trying, he'd just discovered a new secret of Fen-Chu.

The Master of the World was standing in the middle of a huge worksite cluttered with winches, machine tools and sophisticated equipment. Draped in his black cape, the diabolical inventor was overseeing the work of fifty or so Mongols who were silently, submissively, like slaves, like automatons, toiling away. Working in a line, they were continually repeating the same movement to the rhythm of the different colored flashes from the lamps in front of them, which were blinking on and off.

When he got over his initial surprise, the mechanic decided to take advantage of his situation and, with all the daring he could muster, he approached the mysterious worksite. At the entrance, slipping into a dark corner, he hid behind a big, metal rack and watched the strange activity. At the orders of their boss, they were building an odd machine. Obviously some new invention for the madman to quench his thirst for vengeance and destruction. Presently, a door slid open revealing a kind of storeroom. From his vantage point Bougon could see the machines lined up inside. There were twelve of them—robots, metallic men, of outlandish proportions, squat and stout but terrifying.

The young man had more surprises coming. When the Mongols had finished their work, the robot they were building moved on its own, lumbering mechanically to take its place in the storeroom. To do this, Fen-Chu only had to turn a dial on a small device that sat on a table next to him.

Not wanting to linger too long, Bougon decided to go back to his friends to tell them right away about his fantastic discovery. He got back to the room without incident. When he dropped into an armchair, the others came over and listened to him attentively.

He told them, "Listen, I saw the door was left open and went out into the corridor. Nothing was stopping me so I went exploring. I came across a worksite where our host Fen-Chu was supervising some work. We've already had plenty of proof of his power since we got here. He really is the Master of the World. He's not only got an army of deaf-mute Mongols under his command, but also a bunch of robots who will carry out his every order."

"What! What do you mean?" Marchal was intrigued.

"I'm telling the truth. In a room next to this worksite I saw rows of mechanical men who seemed to be controlled by a wireless device. Imagine men of iron, ten or twelve feet tall, looking like the diving suits used for deep-sea diving, meaning they look like men but also like machines. Fen-Chu has a little, portable device he uses to control them. These iron men must be unbelievably strong. Nothing will stand in their way and whoever tries will be pulverized."

The night was spent in an atmosphere of sadness and melancholy. The four prisoners were starting to question their luck.

VI

A week passed without the slightest change in the life of Marchal and his companions. One morning, one of the Mongols put their lunch on the table and, like before, forgot to lock the door. Bougon, who was always on the lookout, noticed this and told the others.

"We've got to do something. One of you come with me and I'll show you the robot factory. Like that you'll know I wasn't selling you a bridge."

"What are you trying to prove?" Blanchard protested. "We believe you. This is no time for playing jokes and your exploit last week is completely plausible since we're living in a bizarre world."

Langeville said, "If I offer to go with you, it's not to check on what you said but simply because with two we can see more."

"I think so too," Marchal agreed. "This time, you two can check it out. The next time it'll be Blanchard and I. But be careful, don't do anything stupid, don't go too far and get back here as fast as you can."

Afraid the Mongol might come back too soon, the explorer and the mechanic snuck silently into the corridor.

Fifteen minutes later, they were back, shaken and shuddering. The journalist and the pilot ran up to them, worried.

Marchal demanded, "What else did you see there?"

"It's very simple. Bougon and I had barely gone out when we heard a weird noise. There was no time to turn back so we hid in the recessed doorway next door. Staying as flat as we could, holding our breath, not moving, we waited there on pins and needles for a long time. We figured it was gone and we'd run back but then we heard some knocks on the door behind us. It wasn't regular but it sounded like Morse Code. I answered in kind and soon, I was quickly having a conversation with a mysterious person. I don't know who but he's obviously another victim of Fen-Chu. We've got to do everything we can to contact him. Maybe we can work together to find a way out of here."

The mechanic added, "It's simple. We just have to follow the example of Edmond Dantès when he was prisoner in the Chateau d'If and he met the abbé Faria in *The Count of Monte Cristo*. I saw it in the cinema."

"That's not a bad idea. We should do it right away."

Robert Marchal and his friends, with renewed energy and motivation, were transformed. Smiles lit up their faces and hope sparkled in their eyes.

Langeville quickly found the appropriate spot. He pointed to a corner of the wall and said, "That's where we should start."

"Very well, but if there are huge blocks of stone separating us we won't have much of a chance to get through."

"Bah! Nothing ventured, nothing gained."

Moving the radio to act as a screen, the four friends started working. Compensating for their makeshift means with passionate enthusiasm, they attacked the wall. Luckily, it was rather brittle, a kind of limestone, like chalk. The four men took turns. While one of them dug, the three others got rid of the debris in the bathroom and kept watch. At the end of the first afternoon, after grinding away without pause for almost eight hours, they'd managed to dig a deep hole almost four inches wide and six inches high. They put the radio back, cleaned up all traces of their work and sat in the armchairs waiting for the Mongol to bring their evening meal. They ate well. As soon as dinner was over, they went to bed, having agreed to get an early start on their well-begun task.

Five long days passed by, made the most of by the four prisoners who were satisfied with the progress of their work.

"How long is this going to take us?" Blanchard wondered aloud. "We don't know how thick the wall is or if we're digging in the right direction. Our hole is around three feet deep and we still haven't hit anything."

With the metal curtain rod that they'd taken from one of the coat racks and used as a pick, Langeville started rapping against the back of the hole in Morse Code. Then he asked everyone to keep quiet while he listened at the opening. A long moment of anxious expectation passed. Then he thought he heard a muted sound coming from the other side. He repeated his experiment and the same sound came back.

Turning to his companions, the explorer looked triumphantly at them and said, "Buck up, friends, we're in the right direction. We haven't been wasting time."

That night after dinner, ignoring their fatigue, the four prisoners went back to work. Around midnight Blanchard, who was digging at the time, felt the wall give way under his homemade pick. He alerted the others who were guarding the door, except for Bougon. They rushed over.

"What is it?" Marchal asked.

"I think we've reached our goal."

Indeed, from the other side of the wall, the stranger had also started digging and had succeeded in reaching them, guided by sound. Sweeping away the last of the debris, the man cleared the narrow tunnel so that they could see his face in the shadows.

Placing his head in the hole, whispering as softly as he could, Langeville murmured, "Are you a prisoner of Fen-Chu?"

The stranger's weak voice, with a hint of a Nordic accent, answered, "Yes. It's been months and months since the wretch has kept me here. Who are you?"

"Four Frenchmen who dared to hunt down Fen-Chu and unfortunately fell into a trap."

"Count yourselves lucky that he kept you alive because this diabolical man hates people meddling in his affairs."

A long conversation followed. Marchal and his friends learned that their neighbor was Professor Staylon, a Swedish scientist who'd actually been imprisoned for years, along with his daughter, Elfy. Fen-Chu was forcing him to work for him by threatening to punish his daughter if he refused to do as he said. Professor Staylon, who was around sixty years old, had invented and discovered several things that the Master of the World simply stole. In spite of himself, the Swede had helped build the mysterious underground city and expand the Asian's power.

Around one in the morning, not wanting to be careless, the four Frenchmen bid farewell to their new friend and promised to meet the next day. Now they felt less alone, they had an ally who might be useful and with whose help they would try to put their plan into action.

After hiding the hole behind the radio, they had a short discussion together in which they changed their plan.

"Tomorrow we'll talk again with our new Swedish friend and with the information he'll give us we'll get out of this prison and settle accounts with Fen-Chu."

The following day, Professor Staylon answered their call and told them about his own tragic odyssey.

He had met his future executioner in Stockholm, ten years ago, when the Asian was doing some research in the University library there. Chance had it that they were next to each other in reading stalls. After some brief small talk, their conversation turned to more serious matters and Staylon, amazed by the rare intelligence of the man, broached the most complex and arduous of subjects only to find a person who understood him and shared the same points of view. This first meeting led to many others and Fen-Chu, who was calling himself Song-Wa and saying he was the son of a rich Mandarin from Ning-Soo, became a regular guest at the Swedish professor's house. Staylon was a widow and poured all his affection on his only daughter, who was eight at the time, and he had only one passion: his scientific work. To pursue this, he needed a laboratory and substantial financial backing. Unfortunately, his meager stipend from the University of Stockholm was barely enough to meet his everyday needs. The so-called Song-Wa offered to finance his research and lend him money on the premise that it'd be paid off through profits from the business. Although Professor Staylon was a renowned mathematician and a brilliant chemist, he was a poor businessman and without realizing it, he signed documents that were bound to put him in dire straits. Song-Wa knew how to play his hand close to his chest, then one fine day, he lay his cards on the table. Unable to live up his commitments, Staylon had to give in to the adventurer. He'd just made an important discovery that was bound to revolutionize television, but to avoid a scandal he handed the invention over to the man who was playing him.

But the wretch decided not to let his prey off so easily. He had more compromising documents in his possession and used them to blackmail the Swedish scientist, threatening to give them to the press. Staylon then realized what a fool he'd been. He'd signed the documents in good faith with a so-called friend, barely skimming through them, not seeing the trap that was being laid. Ignoring his rights and fearing for his daughter's future, he let himself be manipulated by Song-Wa, who imposed draconian conditions.

From that moment on, Professor Staylon was nothing but a weak and submissive plaything in the hands of the rogue. He followed him on his distant journeys until the day that Song-Wa got back to Shanghai after a long absence and announced his desire to live in the middle of Tibet by building an underground city, a kind of impregnable fortress, an inaccessible lair where Song-Wa, now Fen-Chu, would dictate the law to the entire world.

The Swedish scientist knew then that he was dealing with a madman. He smiled and refused to participate in such an undertaking. But the villain was unrelenting and renewed his threats of blackmail. Not knowing what to do, with nobody to confide in, Professor Staylon once again gave in. He followed Fen-Chu on the long and uncomfortable trip into the deserted regions of Tibet all the way to the valley of Shekar Dzong where he was forced to draw up the blueprints. He designed a gigantic and bizarre underground city that was dreamed up by the man who wanted to become the Master of the World. When all was ready, Fen-Chu suddenly disappeared only to reappear two weeks later. He came back with a huge caravan of Mongols recruited in Karbine and who were all deaf and mute.

The professor would learn later that the lunatic, fearing any betrayal, intentional or not, had subjected them all to this shameful mutilation. Other caravans arrived over the next few days, bringing the materials and machines to carry out the work, which lasted many long months. Then one day, when everything was set up, Fen-Chu revealed himself to the world for the first time. The Swede was appalled, ashamed, and refused to collaborate any longer. But Fen-Chu, who now felt so much more powerful than the modest Song-Wa, bent him to his will by threatening his daughter, who was now a pretty, eighteen-year-old young woman. A prisoner like her father, she was losing hope of ever getting out of this hell. The professor and his daughter were thinking they'd remain forever in the hands of this dangerous criminal when, out of nowhere, a glimmer of hope appeared. Now they were not alone, there were four friends here and by combining their efforts, they all had a chance of escaping.

The escape plan was studied meticulously. For a week the four Frenchmen met their Swedish friend several times during the day and had long talks with him so get a good picture of the layout of the place and also a better understanding of the fearsome power that Fen-Chu had forged.

The Master of the World seemed to have forgotten his prisoners. Since the day they were brought to the laboratories, he had seen them only twice in his office to tell them trivial things and boast about being invincible and all-powerful and able to bring the universe to its knees.

One evening, Rahang brought the platter and put it on the table with a few French newspapers. Fen-Chu was continuing to menace the civilized countries and was still making headlines.

"Once again, Fen-Chu committed a heinous crime. Last night the famous high-speed train, the 'Flying Scotch', which runs between London and Glasgow, was derailed outside the town of Kilmarnock. It was coming fast out of a tunnel, starting onto a long bridge when a thick purple cloud hovered over it. Moments later an explosion was heard and it plummeted into the narrow inlet that crossed under the track. Most of the passengers were killed in the attack that the sinister Fen-Chu was responsible for, causing worldwide condemnation and protests. The latest report states that the number of victims has reached 500. We will give more details of this deplorable catastrophe in the next edition."

Langeville looked alarmed. When questioned by his companions, he responded, "The situation is becoming intolerable. Every day we do nothing is a day of victory for Fen-Chu and a day of dread for the rest of the world. If you want my opinion, we've waited long enough. Starting tomorrow we have to make a move. So, right now we have to figure out how. I propose we consult Professor Staylon. He's probably our best advisor."

"Good plan," Marchal and Blanchard agreed.

The four men went to the wall, moved the radio and tapped out the prearranged signal. While Bougon acted as lookout, Langeville started talking to the professor and telling him their plans.

"It sounds very risky," Staylon said. "Our means are feeble compared to what Fen-Chu has at his disposal. I'd like nothing more than to help you, provided that you promise me that if I don't make it through, you'll take care of my daughter Elfy. Right now I have to go meet Fen-Chu who wants an update on my work. When I get back I'll have some valuable information. All I can say for now is that he's unusually nervous and only this morning he was in such a foul mood that he severely punished four Mongols whom he thought weren't being obedient enough."

With this, Professor Staylon said goodbye to the Frenchmen and promised to alert them when he got back.

VII

When Professor Staylon entered the office, Fen-Chu was at his desk. Without looking up, completely absorbed, he waved to him to come closer. The Swedish scientist did so and sat on a stool, waiting for the Master of the World to say something. He watched and noted again that Fen-Chu was unusually nervous and couldn't hide his vexation.

"So, you're here, Staylon," the strange man burst out as he looked up. "I'm glad to see you because I need your assistance."

Standing up, Fen-Chu started pacing the room, stopping from time to time to grumble and curse.

"I'm not at all happy. It's not working here like I wanted. The output of the workshops is lower than I expected and the production of my robots is making little progress."

The visitor shrank in his chair and shyly uttered, "I'm not responsible for the work of your Mongols."

"I know! I made them pay dearly for their laziness but it's up to you to improve the tools so they can increase and accelerate the productivity. But I called you here for something a lot more serious: the gamma ray machine is working but I wanted to use it today and to my great surprise I got no results."

Professor Staylon shrugged his shoulders and replied, "Before giving you an answer I'll have to look at it myself."

"Right, follow me."

The Master of the World and the Swedish scientist went into the room off the laboratory where the astounding machine was kept. Staylon examined it meticulously while Fen-Chu awaited the verdict.

The Swede said, "The machine has, in fact, been damaged for awhile. It'll take at least a week to fix it."

At this news Fen-Chu reared up, "A week! That's impossible! Do whatever it takes but it has to be in perfect working order within three days. Alert all the workshops, use as many men as you need, but I want this machine working again in three days."

"That's impossible."

"What do you mean? You know very well that I hate that answer. Don't play games with me, Staylon, you know I've got foolproof ways to crush your resistance. Don't make me put you through what happened in Stockholm, New York and Shanghai. Don't forget that the feeblest attempt to cross me will bring immediate retribution against your daughter Elfy."

Hearing this, Staylon turned pale. Suppressing his panic, in a flat voice he said, "If I ask you for more time, it's not for myself but for the work. A part needs replacing, the crystallizer-sensor, and this part has to be made in duroxine, a special alloy that takes a long time to prepare. Asking you for a week is still pushing it for me."

The scientist's argument seemed to calm the madman down a little. Then he suddenly relaxed and said, "So be it, I'll give you a week, but no more. In eight days the machine has to be up and running. Do what you must, you've got carte blanche and I'm going to tell everyone so you'll be fully supported."

The meeting was over so Staylon said goodbye to Fen-Chu who was grumbling again against the annoying setback. Now, for eight days, he was going to be doomed to total inaction. For eight days it was going to be absolutely impossible for him to give to the world more proof of his power. This was intolerable.

The Swedish scientist went back to his room and right away went to the wall separating him from his friends. He gave the signal and the four Frenchmen answered in kind.

"Good news," the professor declared. "For one week Fen-Chu can't do any harm. His transmitter device is broken and I'm in charge of fixing it."

Langeville replied, "So, for eight days the world is going to have a truce."

"We have to use this time to act. Fen-Chu is at a disadvantage," Marchal said. "We've got an edge. Not a big one but it's something."

The four friends had a long conversation, drew up a plan and decided to put it into action the next day.

The following morning, while Staylon was in the lab and starting to work on the gamma ray machine with some Mongols assigned to help him, Robert Marchal and his friends waited impatiently for lunch to come because that was the moment they'd decided to act.

"It's very simple," Bougon said, "we wait for the Mongol to come in with his hands full and then to put the platter of food on the table. You're in the armchairs like always while I'm walking around smoking. I get behind him and with a quick jujitsu chop I knock him out."

"It seems chancy," Langeville said. "First of all, our Mongol might scream and alert someone. Maybe he won't let you get behind him. Don't you think it'd better to let him leave and do like we did the other day?"

The mechanic disagreed, "How do we know he'll forget to lock the door? If he doesn't, we'll have to wait for him to come back, meaning in at least eight hours."

"Nothing ventured, nothing gained," Blanchard exclaimed, "I'm with Bougon. In tight spots, we've got to be ready to lay it on the line. There are four of us so it shouldn't be any problem dealing with the one Mongol, no matter how strong he is. And how's he going to scream when our friend Fen-Chu had the bright idea to cut out his tongue?"

"That's true," Marchal laughed. "I'm with you two. I'm tired of just sitting around, waiting. I want to do something."

The rest of the morning was a long wait. Around 11 am Professor Staylon came back from his lab and was immediately informed by Langeville.

"After we knock out the Mongol, we'll go into the corridor and take our chances."

The Swedish scientist was wavering. He was made for learning, not for action. "Do you really think we can succeed?"

"We'd rather try our luck than stay prisoners of Fen-Chu. Thanks to your input, we can navigate the maze of hallways and get out of this cursed place."

Staylon sighed timidly, "God willing."

As luck would have it, lunch was served late. It wasn't until around 1 pm that Koung showed up with the usual platter. Hearts beating fast, the four Frenchmen watched him come in and when he was at the table, just when he was putting the food down, Bougon, who had slipped silently behind him, lunged, grabbed him around the neck and threw him to the ground. The two men rolled around. It took the surprised Mongol a minute to realize what was happening. By the time he did and tried to react, it was too late: Bougon and Blanchard had tied him up and gagged him. The guard was dragged into a corner and left there. Rolling his frightened eyes, he struggled to get free but in vain. The four prisoners didn't linger in the room. They ran straight into the corridor., which was deserted. The coast looked clear. Langeville went to the next door and knocked hard. Moments later the Swedish scientist joined them. He was accompanied by a young lady, his daughter Elfy.

"This is no time for talking but for action," Marchal ordered. Let's not waste any time. You know the place, so get us out of here at once."

With the Swede in front as guide and his daughter in the middle they walked in single file, staying close to the walls, trying not to make a sound. They went down endless corridors, stopping at every corner, listening for sounds, ready to react to the slightest noise.

For nearly fifteen minutes they followed the Swede who seemed familiar with the layout and led them without hesitation. Then they came to a kind of platform, a real eagle's nest, that overlooked the whole mysterious city. Stopping here a moment, Professor Staylon gave his friends some explanations.

"Everything you see is Fen-Chu's realm. What's hard to believe is that to understand the extent of it, you have to know it thoroughly. It'd be really hard for a stranger to fathom the whole place, partly underground, partly camouflaged in the open, with its rocks and sand dunes, its modern factories, workshops, laboratories and storage facilities. To the right is the private residence of Fen-Chu. We can see from here a few windows that look like deep clefts in the rock wall. To the left, those dots sparkling in the sun are parabolic mirrors that capture the gamma rays, meaning the main energy used by Fen-Chu not only to work the machine that brought you here, but also to provide energy for everything else. Gamma rays are the foundation of his power. Destroy the parabolic mirrors and the giant batteries that store it and Fen-Chu will be rendered help-less. He won't be able to sow death and destruction anymore."

Finishing his exposé, Staylon pointed to the main workshops, the one where the robots were made and the place where the giants were kept.

Marchal said, "That's some very interesting information. Our friend Fen-Chu isn't as invulnerable as he claims. Now we know his Achilles' heel. Let's hope we can strike it when the time comes."

The escapees headed back into the underground maze. Pointing to a long corridor that tunneled through the rock on the right, the Swede said, "That's where the batteries are."

"We have to destroy them before leaving. Too bad we don't have any ex-plosives on hand."

"I know where Fen-Chu keeps his munitions," Staylon offered. "When you're building an underground city, you've got to blow up a lot of rocks with dynamite and cheddite."

"I suggest we take a detour and get enough to demolish everything Fen-Chu built here."

"I second the motion. It'll take us off track but it'll be worth it."

Staylon moved agilely, knowing how to avoid the pitfalls that might hinder their progress. Sneaking around the workshops where the Mongols were slaving away, they came to a small, armored door guarded by a vigilant Asian. They stopped and sized up the situation. Then they decided that the professor would walk up to the guard who would suspect nothing since the scientist was author-ized to go anywhere he wanted. Staylon would keep the guard busy while Bou-gon would do his thing and rendered the poor guard helpless with his wrestling hold.

Once agreed upon, the plan was swiftly executed. A few minutes later, the ambushed Mongol was lying on the ground, passed out. Marchal and the others wasted no time jimmying the lock and opening the heavy door, which pivoted slowly on its hinges. They entered the small, dimly lit room with a low ceiling. The shelves were packed but in one corner were some crates lined up. It was the supply of explosives, enough to blow up the infernal city.

The reporter and his friends stuffed their pockets with sticks of dynamite, planning to use them either to destroy Fen-Chu's property or as weapons in case they were caught. Fully armed, the escapees left the munitions room and headed for the batteries.

Professor Staylon, who had been timid and hesitant so far, was more confi-dent and lively. In the company of Marchal and his friends he had found again his self-assurance and was determined to make Fen-Chu pay for all the insults and abuse he had suffered over the years.

The underground city looked desperately monotonous—nothing but inter-minable corridors ending in rotundas from which other corridors sprang out, as interminable as the former. At one junction, before going any farther, the journalist and his companions stopped to catch their breath and make sure that the coast was clear. Listening carefully, Blanchard, whose vigilance was always keen, thought he heard an unusual noise. The silence was disturbed by a faint rumbling.

"What is that?" he asked worriedly.

"Don't worry," Staylon replied. "What you're hearing is just the sound of the transformers in the room next to the batteries. Another fifty yards and we'll be there."

During this first challenge Elfy Staylon had shown real bravery. Not wanting to be a bother or an obstacle, she had contributed her share so that she was not considered as a young lady but rather as a comrade. At every pause, she kept watch and in the munitions room she had supplied herself plentifully.

No trouble seemed to be on the horizon so Marchal encouraged the others to keep going. They were about to leave when a loud alarm, like a siren, suddenly rang out. The fugitives flattened themselves against the wall, all their senses on alert.

"It's the alarm…" Staylon was as white as a sheet.

"You think…"

"That they found out we escaped? Of course. There's no doubt about it. Fen-Chu's been told and immediately launched his security measures. We're done for. Now all the exits are closed and the guard posts are on high alert."

Hearing these tragic announcements from the Swede, Bougon couldn't help expressing his anger, "Good God, we're caught like rats in a cage!"

"Maybe," Marchal responded, "but Fen-Chu won't catch us. We've got means of defense now. Before he traps us for good, he'll have to answer to us. For my part I'm ready to fight it out to the end. You too?"

The others rallied behind the pilot.

"We're not unarmed. With these sticks of dynamite we can do some serious damage and, who knows, maybe put an end to this wretch Fen-Chu."

The alarm bell, which had been ringing for a good two minutes, suddenly turned off. An anxious and mysterious silence followed. Then, all of a sudden, the lights went out, plunging the corridors into total darkness. Marchal and his friends were in a critical situation, utterly unable to move even a step forward.

One minute passed. Then the lights came back on. At first blinding, it took a moment for the fugitives to adjust their eyes. And they were about to get moving again when they experienced what they thought might be a hallucination: Fen-Chu was standing in front of them.

Still dressed in his black kimono, his hands hidden inside the sleeves, the mysterious man was standing still in a theatrical pose, grinning from ear to ear.

The escapees wished they were dreaming but they had to face reality. Their enemy was there, taunting them, believing he had the upper hand.

"So, messieurs, you thought you were stronger and smarter than me," the Master of the World spoke solemnly. "I warned you. There are no miracles here without my knowing. You leaped blindly into a bold adventure, but it's impossible to leave here if I don't allow it. Even with the help of Professor Staylon, who will pay dearly for his betrayal, you wouldn't be able to pass through the gates of my realm. You're going to go back to your rooms and later, when I feel like it, I'll explain what you want to know."

While the strange villain was giving this speech, Blanchard slipped behind his companions, pulled out some cheddite and was about to throw it at Fen-Chu when the latter directed his focus on the pilot and said, "Please, Monsieur Blanchard, don't be childish. You're being silly. I have great power at my disposal and you'll be sorry for being so reckless."

With this Fen-Chu pointed something that looked like a flashlight at the pilot. A ray shot out and struck Blanchard's wrist. At the same time, the poor guy felt paralyzed. He was hobbled. Fen-Chu was apparently, as he claimed, invincible.

On a sign from the Master of the World, two Mongols appeared out of nowhere and searched the fugitives, confiscating all their explosives. After that, following the orders of their boss, they led the prisoners back to their rooms.

An hour later, Fen-Chu summoned them to his office. He seemed to be in a good mood after the situation had turned to his advantage.

"I could hold you to account, messieurs, for your misconduct," the strange man said, "but after thinking about it, I don't regret the incident. It shows you categorically that I'm not to be trifled with. I was ready to give you special treatment, but considering your hostile attitude, I'm forced to take action against you. From now on you will join my work teams. Like that you won't be idle and you won't have time to cook up new escape plans."

Blanchard, who had listened quietly so far, jumped up and stepped forward to face Fen-Chu, stare him in the eyes and thunder, "I guess you think we're just going to bow to your decrees. You should know that we French are not as passive as your Mongols. We'll refuse to work for you and become your slaves. You can be sure that as long as we're here, as long as one of us is still alive, there will be someone here whose only goal is to defeat you. You take yourself for the master of the world but you're really just an insidious brigand possessed of uncontrollable pride. Or maybe simply a dangerous madman. Watch out, Fen-Chu, your power is not permanent. Even if we fail to stop you, others will come after us and they won't give up until you're utterly destroyed. They'll have powers equal to yours and you'll be squashed like the vermin you are."

Astonished, not believing what he was hearing, Fen-Chu's face turned red, his lips pursed and his eyes grew big when he shouted at the pilot, "Shut up! I am the master here! You have to obey me!"

Unfazed, Blanchard didn't look away. "You can order me to be quiet but that won't change the future. I'm obviously your prisoner, but there's nothing forcing me to do to your evil bidding. You can threaten me with the cruelest punishments, torture me to your heart's content, I will never, you hear me, never work for you. I refuse to be an accomplice of such a contemptible creature, a cowardly, vile, degenerate crook."

"Shut up!" Fen-Chu yelled again, unable to contain his anger, as he raised his scrawny hand above his head.

In front of his friends who were stupefied and speechless, Blanchard, in the heat of the moment, lunged at Fen-Chu, who panicked, backed up to his desk and grabbed a sharp knife that he used as a letter opener but that turned into a defensive weapon.

The pilot was out of control. He didn't stop. He wrapped his two hands around the wretch's throat and tried to strangle him. There was a merciless struggle between the two men. Despite his size and stature, Fen-Chu possessed unexpected strength. He managed to break free of his enemy's grip and slip behind him and stick the knife between his shoulder blades. The pilot collapsed to the ground in a pool of blood.

The scene had unfolded so fast that neither Marchal nor Langeville nor Bougon had time to intervene. Besides, what could they have done with the two armed Mongols on either side, waiting there for a sign from their master to strike. But Fen-Chu was only worried about not getting strangled and didn't think for one instant of calling his guards to help.

Ignoring the body of Blanchard lying on the ground, the villain went back to sit behind his desk. Then he addressed the other prisoners, "Let that serve as a lesson to you. You see that my power is infinite. When I give an order, I expect it to be obeyed without question. No one is allowed to pass judgment on my actions or my character."

Crestfallen and apprehensive, Marchal wasn't listening. He was staring at his poor friend on the ground and wondering anxiously if he was still alive. On a sign from Fen-Chu, one of the Mongols went to examine him. When he stood up he made a gesture that proved without a doubt that all hope was lost. Blanchard's reckless attack had cost him his life.

Controlling his grief, but unable to hold back his anger, Marchal shouted, "You're a monster, Fen-Chu, you're the most abominable person ever to walk the face of the earth. The rest of my life will be devoted to avenging my friend. I, too, refuse to do your bidding. I, too, refuse to work."

Langeville and Bougon straightened up and declared, "We also refuse!"

"That's fine," the sharp, slightly trembling voice of Fen-Chu replied. "Go back to your room and we'll see which of us is the first to give in. I'm sure that in a very short time you will be tame as kittens and do whatever I say."

The three prisoners, escorted by the two Mongols, left the office. In the doorway, the three Frenchmen turned around one last time to wave goodbye to their comrade, whom they had sworn to avenge no matter what the cost.

VIII

When the door of their room was locked behind them, making sure they couldn't escape again, Marchal and his two friends felt hopeless. Blanchard's death had hurt them all but Bougon even more because the pilot had been not only a great boss but also a good and modest friend.

By the time their initial sorrow passed, the reporter had decided to act. Langeville, who could control his feelings, looked unruffled. He hurt just as much as the others but he forced himself not to show his feelings. He said:

"Blanchard, by dying, has given us a new mission—vengeance. From now on we have to try anything and everything to succeed. In my opinion, we should let Fen-Chu believe that we've given in to him and when we see him letting his guard down, we strike."

"We should tell the Swede about what happened," Marchal suggested, walking over to the opening in the wall.

"Good idea."

The reporter made the signal but no response came back. He did it again but still nothing.

"That's weird," he muttered. "Do you think something bad happened to the professor?"

"Very well could be. Fen-Chu would never forgive him for helping us. We all heard him threaten to make him pay dearly."

"What do you think he'll do to our friend and his daughter?"

Langeville just shrugged, imagining the worst, "Let's hope they're still alive. Fen-Chu has no reason to kill either of them. He needs the first to fix his gamma ray machine and to finish his so-called inventions. Fen-Chu's smart enough to know this and that the day Staylon is separated from his daughter will be the day he won't do anything more for him. I think our two friends have simply moved farther away so they can't communicate with us. Still, I'm worried about Elfy's father because the lunatic holding him in his grip will never forgive his rebellion."

A few days passed.

Marchal and his friends were left alone for the first two days. Neither Koung nor Rahang showed up and they were sentenced to fast.

"I guess Fen-Chu means to starve us out," Langeville said.

On the morning of the third day one of the Mongols came in. The prisoners understood they were being taken to his boss. A few minutes later they were standing in the villain's office.

Fen-Chu was in his usual place. After inviting the three men to sit down, he spoke to them. "I've made some important decisions about you. If, as I hope, you agree to work, you'll be sent to different workshops with simple tasks. Your unfriendly attitude towards me has annulled any possible special treatment. If you refuse, I'll be forced to punish you until you give in." Turning to Marchal he asked, "What have you decided?"

The journalist looked at his two friends for a moment, then he answered, "I accept."

Fen-Chu asked the same question of Langeville and Bougon who also accepted.

"Finally, you've seen that this is the best solution," the Master of the World smiled contentedly. "It would've been very unpleasant to continue your fast. This afternoon, after you've enjoyed a good meal, Koung and Rahang will take you to the workshops where you'll be working from now on."

Fen-Chu stood up and walked toward the door, saying, "You'll adapt quickly to your new life. You would've got tired of doing nothing and been bored stiff just sitting in your room for hours on end."

The men said nothing. They were leaving to go back to their jail when Fen-Chu stopped them and said, "I should tell you what happened with your comrade Blanchard. He had a native funeral service that was typical of this region. His body was taken to the highest terrace and exposed to the wind. He became food for the sacred vultures of Tibet. Understand that it's considered fantastic here."

The journalist didn't respond. His blood was boiling as he listened to the creep joke about such a serious matter.

In the afternoon, as soon as soon as lunch was over, the three prisoners were taken by their guards to the workshops. For the first time, Robert Marchal and his friends were separated and they wondered whether they would see each other again after work. Fortunately, around eight at night, after constant toil, the reporter went back to his room and was pleased to be greeted by Langeville and Bougon. They shared their impressions. Exhausted, the three of them, each in a different team under the watch of foremen who allowed them no rest, had to carry heavy, bulky packages..

"I'm dead tired," Marchal sighed.

"Me, too," Langeville said.

Only the mechanic seemed in good shape. He was used to this kind of physical exercise. Smirking, he declared, "I'm not complaining. It loosened up my muscles that were starting to get rusty from stagnation. You realize, right, that intellectual occupations sometimes have their downsides. If, like me, you were used to heavy work, you wouldn't be suffering right now from backaches and sore muscles. But don't worry, after a few days you'll be fit as fiddles and doing your work 'with a smile', as Maurice Chevalier would say."

The explorer and the journalist smiled at their friend's witty retort. Even in tough times he could make them laugh and his ideas, though sometimes ludicrous, offered comfort and distraction.

"We did well to accept Fen-Chu's orders," Marchal said. "Like this we've pacified him and maybe he'll be a little less suspicious of us."

"Plus," Langeville added, "with each of us working separately we can explore different parts of this mysterious underground city and, who knows, we might make some interesting discoveries. While we're working we have to keep our eyes open and become familiar with the layout of this place."

"There's another reason we were right to accept," the mechanic concluded. "You heard Fen-Chu. If we kept refusing he would've starved us. Now, if we're going to escape we'd better be in good shape and stock up on vitamins and calories."

"You're right. When we're in the workshops, the surveillance could be a little lax and we might just find an opportunity when we least expect it."

The explorer, who thought of everything, made the following suggestion, "In case an opportunity does arise, we should agree on a place for all of us to meet up."

"Good point," Marchal agreed, "but hard to do. Let's say you saw a chance to escape from workshop 'F'. How will Bougon in workshop 'C' or me in 'R' know about it? It'd be too risky to make some kind of signal because that would inform our enemies as well."

"True. So, we have to wait until we're together to act, unless some big event happens during the work time. Keep faith in Destiny and then take our chances."

Two days passed. The three men, solving their immediate problem with patience, adapted to their new life, bending to the demands of the strict rules. In the afternoon of the third day, an unexpected event happened, which was bound to have serious consequences in the future. The three prisoners were in their respective workshops, joined to their team of Mongols and transporting, like dock workers, big, heavy crates. The hands of the giant clocks showed 3:28 pm. Nothing seemed any different in this monotonous, methodical existence when all of a sudden a loud explosion was heard. Sirens wailed and the alarm bells rang out. While the Mongols, having stopped working, carried out the orders communicated to them by the multicolored lights, each of the prisoners took advantage of the confusion and left their workshops, hurrying to their meeting point.

Marchal was the last to arrive. "What's going on?"

"I don't know," Langeville replied, "but it seems to be pretty serious."

Bougon said, "Serious trouble, I think. We should take advantage of it and strike hard."

Chance, for once, seemed to be on their side. This was a lucky opportunity to get out of the underground city.

In fact, Fen-Chu's lair was being bombarded from the air. There were squadrons of planes flying overhead at the moment. Arriving from both the south and the east, two groups of fifty planes had soared out from behind the snowy peaks of the Tibetan mountains. One had come from the British airbase in Allahabad, the other from the International Concession in Shanghai.

Using the element of surprise the pilots had managed to reach their target unencumbered and before they got spotted they had dropped the first bombs, which fell haphazardly, doing little damage.

Fen-Chu was at his desk. He jumped up when he heard the first explosions. Running out to the terrace he saw the planes in the sky in perfect battle formation, preparing to launch another attack. The rogue turned deathly pale and for the first time felt vulnerable. The gamma ray machine was barely fixed and might not be effective. So, the Master of the World set off the alarms, thus ordering everyone to go to the posts assigned to them under such circumstances. A fierce battle ensued between the attackers and the villain.

Running into his bedroom, Fen-Chu went to the gamma ray machine, flipped a few switches and turned it on. It rumbled. The demonic man smiled gratefully—the destructive machine was working.

In the sky, turning in wide circles like vultures, the airplanes were dropping their bombs at regular intervals, causing more and more damage. Out of nowhere a purple cloud appeared over two of them while an eerie whistling sound could be heard. Moments later several of the planes plummeted to the ground where they crashed in fiery flames.

Fen-Chu snickered. He would win. His enemies had the gall to track him down to his lair, but he knew how to foil their plans and give them the welcome they deserved.

But the Master of the World was gloating too soon. There were still a lot of planes in the air that were doing their job. A small group swooped down to a low altitude, skirting death, and dropped a string of bombs that exploded in a deafening roar. The room of giant batteries was blown to smithereens. Now Fen-Chu was disarmed. The gamma ray machine was out of commission. There was no stopping the assailants. The coast was clear for them after the purple cloud vanished into thin air. A few squadrons dove down, one after another, and released tons of explosives on Fen-Chu's lair.

The Master of the World saw then that his luck had run out and his enemies had the upper hand. He was scared. Turning around to call to his Mongols for help, he realized that they had disappeared, choosing to take refuge in a safe place rather than stay with their boss in a dangerous spot. This solitude frightened the wretch who, for the first time, didn't know what to do. The explosions were getting closer, causing critical damage. The brigand could think of nothing but saving his own hide. He fled, scurried through a lab and as fast as he could got to the deserted underground.

In the meantime, Robert Marchal and his companions were not idle. Bougon, who had gone to see what was happening, was back with satisfying news.

"Fen-Chu's having a hard time these last fifteen minutes. He's getting bombed to hell right now. Some friends have come in planes to pay him a visit and they're giving him a good thrashing. A lot of damage. Some of the workshops are in ruins and the battery room we wanted to blow up the other day is no longer standing. As far as the Mongols, they panicked and disappeared as if by magic, leaving their boss to fend for himself."

"Our luck today is unbelievable," Marchal said. "We've got to use it to settle accounts once and for all with this damned Fen-Chu."

"What about Staylon? What's happened to him?" Langeville asked. "We can't forget him. We have to try to find him and help him escape with his daughter."

"That's right. Let's go looking for him at once."

The three Frenchmen went blindly into the corridors. Crossing deserted rooms and huge, silent, galleries, they came to the laboratory that they knew was the professor's thanks to some information gathered the day before by Bougon. They went in. Nobody was there. On a table, among all kinds of documents and papers covered with chemical formulas and geometric figures, Marchal found a text written by Staylon with the ink still fresh.

"Our friend can't be far. Look, this proves that he was here just a few minutes ago."

"There are only two doors to the lab, the explorer Langeville remarked. "The one we came through and the other one across the room. I believe we should continue our search through that one. I have the feeling that we'll find the new rooms of the professor and his daughter over there."

"Good idea," the reporter said. "Let's go."

The mechanic added, "You've got the nose of a detective, Langeville. You're going to give Sherlock Holmes, Commissioner Maigret and Inspector Bayard a run for their money."

The three men, encouraged by these first findings, continued their search. The second door, like the first, opened onto an endless corridor with doors lining both sides. Walking slowly, they went looking for any clue that might signal the right door.

At one of them Bougon bent down and examined the floor carefully. Then he cried out, "Hey, I've found something interesting here."

The journalist and the explorer joined him. Standing up, the mechanic showed them a tiny object he was holding in his hand.

"I just said Langeville was a kind of Sherlock Holmes. Well, here I am turning into his inseparable partner, Dr. Watson."

"I see you know your classic detective stories," Marchal replied. "But what do you have there?"

"A hairpin! Don't you get it? A hairpin belonging to a woman. Now, until proven otherwise, there's only one woman here: Elfy. I found it right in front of this door. So, everything leads me to believe that we're in front of the room presently occupied by our friends."

"Excellent deduction. Now all we have to do is verify it."

Thus said, Marchal knocked and then pulled open the wooden door. He stepped into the entryway that led into a big living room. It was deserted.

"We've taken a wrong turn," the reporter sighed. "Poor Ludovic, your deductions were mistaken."

Disappointed, the three fugitives were about to leave when a voice suddenly called out. On hearing it, they jumped for joy because they recognized the Nordic accent of Professor Staylon.

"What luck! My friends, we're together again," the Swede said. "Fate strikes again."

The four men shook hands and hugged one another. But with no time to lose, they drew up a new plan.

"And your daughter?" Marchal asked.

"She's in the next room. I'll go get her right away. But what happened?"

"What? You don't know?"

"No. I was completely absorbed in my work and my lab is so far from everything…"

"Fen-Chu's in a tight spot. Squadrons of bombers are attacking his lair and they've destroyed a bunch of it. The Mongols panicked and abandoned him. The whole underground city is in chaos. It's time to get out of this infernal prison. Fen-Chu is vulnerable so we have to capitalize on it."

"You're absolutely right. I want to make him pay for everything he's put me through."

"All right, we'll settle accounts with him and then leave this bleak place."

Professor Staylon went to fetch his daughter. When they came back, Elfy recognized her new friends and gave them a big, teary-eyed smile.

"Now let's get going!" Marchal ordered.

"It's payback time," Langeville added.

And Bougon, to keep up his reputation, chuckled, "*Mesdames et messieurs*, welcome to the final round. The champion Master of the World, Fen-Chu, is going to be knocked out and stay out for the count."

IX

While Robert Marchal and his companions were looking for Professor Staylon and Elfy, the bombers were keeping up their campaign of destruction. Pouring massive bombs and big missiles onto Fen-Chu's lair, hitting their targets with rare precision, they soon transformed the place into a mass of indescribable ruins and a wasteland of flames.

With their mission accomplished, they soared off to the east and south. They had lost twenty of their own, brought down by the mysterious gamma rays, but they had managed to strike a terrible (if not lethal) blow to Fen-Chu.

Disoriented, pale and crushed, raging mad, he who had called himself the Master of the World was wandering around, alone, in the middle of what were his busy workshops just a few hours ago. He was silent and dejected, with a ghastly grin frozen on his face, looking all around him. In only a few minutes his life's efforts, years of hard work had been wiped out. Of the underground city there were only a few specks, so to speak, left intact. Among them was the emergency lab used by Staylon for his research, the robot workshop and store-room where twenty of his iron men were waiting, and a few unimportant build-ings, like the one housing extra bedrooms. Nothing remained of his own labora-tory or his own bedroom with the gamma ray machine. Gone were the giant bat-teries that stored all his radio-electric energy.

But the madman didn't consider himself defeated. He was determined not to give up the fight. On these ruins he would rebuild a new city, which would take many long months or more. After that, the entire world would hear from Fen-Chu again and would experience the even stronger and deadlier proofs of his power.

Fen-Chu was lost in his thoughts when, all of a sudden, a voice made him turn around. A few feet away, between two half-crumbled walls, Marchal and his friends were walking towards him.

At the head of the small group, the reporter pointed to him and said, "The time has come to pay your dues!"

Finding himself unarmed and absolutely unable to defend himself, the dia-bolical creature figured his only chance of safety was in flight. So, he ran as fast as his weakened state allowed, aimlessly, and then toward one of the few build-ings still standing. It was the robot workshop. He entered laughing and then turned around at the door to face his enemies.

"I'm not finished. Fortunately, I still have powerful weapons that you can do nothing against."

Without waiting for a response Fen-Chu shut the doors to the building.

Marchal and the others stopped. There was now an impassable obstacle be-tween them and their enemy.

"What weapons does the wretch still have?" the reporter wondered.

Professor Staylon stood for a moment, pondering, then suddenly burst out, "I've got it! He's thinking of his robots. They were spared in the bombing and the controller is in the workshop."

"Is there a way to reach him and stop him from using them?"

"Maybe. I know another entrance. With any luck we'll get there first and beat him at his own game."

The Swedish scientist ran like he was twenty years old again. In front of the others he dashed around the building and came to a low door that they had to break down. There were metal stairs that climbed to a narrow platform. They scrambled up and saw at the other end of the space, maybe 100 yards away, Fen-Chu heading for a glass booth.

Staylon pointed at it and said, "That's where the remote control for the ro-bots is. Run over there. On a glass table there's a small leather briefcase that looks like a portable telephone. Hurry up and try to beat Fen-Chu to it."

Marchal launched into a spectacular sprint. But his prowess proved useless. The brigand was faster and closer and got to the booth before him. He grabbed the briefcase, opened it and pressed a few buttons. A faint, steady hum was heard: The robots were ready for action. Coming through the door of the storeroom, lumbering jerkily, one after another, the robots obeyed the commands transmitted to them by Fen-Chu by means of the electromagnetic waves.

Carrying the precious case with him, Fen-Chu ran into a corner of the workshop and on top of a ramp he hunkered down to guide his mechanical men who slowly spread out and encircled the rebels.

The situation was critical for the fugitives. There was no chance of escape as they were surrounded by the stout metal giants that measured over twelve feet-tall, monsters right out of the *Apocalypse*.

From his vantage point, Fen-Chu was savoring his victory, picturing getting rid of his pesky enemies once and for all. But all of a sudden a figure surged out of the shadows and pounced on him, clutching his throat, forcing him to stop his attack. It was Marchal who had spotted him and managed to sneak silently up the ramp in order to risk it all.

A savage fight ensued.

On the narrow walkway that overlooked the room from a height of about thirty feet and that had no guardrail, the journalist and the madman grappled each other. A fierce battle took place, each of them desperately fighting for their life and trying to kill their enemy. Several times they rolled toward the abyss and for a few seconds they were on the very edge, half hanging in the air.

Fuming with rage, knowing that this was do or die, Fen-Chu mustered all his remaining strength for one last ditch effort. Managing to free himself, he stepped back, braced himself against the wall and prepared a violent blow to the neck of his enemy who was tired and trying to catch his breath. In this short pause by his adversary, the brigand rushed forward and was about to hit him with all his might when Bougon yelled to his friend to watch out. Marchal had just enough time to dodge the swing and land a hard uppercut on the jaw of the Master of the World who was dazed by the punch. Wobbling and trying to grab onto anything to steady himself, Fen-Chu lost his balance and fell over the edge. His body dropped like a rock and crashed onto the floor where he lay motionless, as if dead.

The panting journalist leaned over and stared wide-eyed below him. Surely, the enemy was killed by the fall. But to his great surprise as well as the others, the demoniacal character groaned loudly and made an effort to get up. His broken limbs, however, refused to obey.

While this merciless duel was being fought on high, the situation of the other fugitives didn't become any less critical. Continuing to advance, the robots were closing in on the group. Staylon glanced around trying to figure out his chances of survival. They were slim. He decided to try the impossible. Risking it all, inching across the wall, he managed to escape the danger zone. Just in time.

A few seconds later it would've been impossible. The old man ran as fast as he could up the stairs to the glass booth and then up to the journalist. He grabbed the control device, flipped some switches, pressed some buttons to stop the iron men from moving forward. Nothing happened

The robots were only fifteen feet from Bougon and Elfy. A few seconds more and the metal monsters were going to pitilessly crush the two of them flattened against the wall awaiting their fate.

The Swede, sweating bullets, tried again. The remote control seemed to be broken. The robots were plodding within ten feet now. Not knowing what to do, Staylon slammed his hand onto a lever at the bottom and the robots suddenly turned around, changed direction, and continued to march forward.

Elfy and Bougon had just barely escaped a hideous death. Aware of the terrible danger they'd escaped, the two young people stared at each other for a long time. Then, squeezing her hand, Marchal gave her a big smile full of hope.

The iron men, meanwhile, were shuffling their way directly to the body of Fen-Chu. The villain roared like a wounded beast in the jungle, his eyes bulged, his mouth twisted into a hideous grin. He knew that his day of judgment had arrived. In one last jolt of pride, he tried to stand up but failed. He was going to pay his debt to society for all the monstrous crimes he was guilty of. Nothing and nobody were going to shield him from his fate. The first robot poked him, then increased the pressure, throwing all its weight and force onto the inert body. Fen-Chu let out a scream that was abruptly cut short. The robot had crushed him like a wisp of straw.

Fen-Chu was no more. From now on the universe had nothing to fear from the Master of the World. Justice had been served.

X

Robert Marchal and his friends had witnessed, mutely, the punishment of their fearsome enemy. They'd anxiously watched the march of the robots without being able to stop the metal monsters. Elfy couldn't watch. She turned away and buried her face in the reporter's chest.

"What a horrible way to die," she sighed. "The man was a villain, but still..."

Professor Staylon and Bougon stood beside them.

The Swede said, "Fen-Chu was a rogue consumed by boundless pride. He suffered the punishment he deserved. He was beaten by his own weapons."

"There's proof that everyone has to pay for their actions and in the end, no matter what you do, you can't change fate."

Silently they walked away and stopped at the doorway of the workshop to turn around one last time. They saw the robots banging into one another, pushing and shoving, a formless mass of metal burying the mangled body of Fen-Chu, the Master of the World.

Staylon sighed, pulling his daughter Elfy through the door, and said, "Like the old adage says, live by the sword, die by the sword."

Such was the eulogy of the worst villain of all time.

Outside the workshop, as the four friends were recovering from their mix of emotions, Bougon suddenly burst out, "Hey, where's Langeville?"

He had disappeared.

The four of them looked at one another worriedly. Their comrade, they just realized, hadn't entered the workshop with them. Some unforeseen incident had obviously held him up. Without losing a second, they went looking for him, retracing their steps. To make matters worse, the lights suddenly went out. Professor Staylon had a flashlight so they could keep going through the deserted city. After fifteen minutes of searching, they heard a faint groan and headed for the sound. To their great surprise as well as their great joy, they found the explorer lying on the ground, not moving. Marchal tried to wake him up. After a minute or so Langeville moaned and opened his eyes. He looked perplexed at the reporter, then recognized him.

In an almost inaudible voice the explorer murmured, "Oh, it's you. I'm sure glad to see you again. I thought for a moment that I was a goner."

Slowly, he regained consciousness and got hold of himself. He stood up and took a few steps with the help of Marchal and Bougon.

"Thanks, but I think I'm all right now," he said as he stepped away.

"But what happened to you?" Staylon asked.

While the now complete group followed the route that the Swedish scientist pointed out with his flashlight, Langeville summarized his adventure.

When Marchal went running after Fen-Chu, he was a little slow to follow and suddenly found himself attacked by a group of Mongols who managed to get the better of him. The poor explorer was half-conscious and taken away by the men. But they were quickly seized by panic and dropped him where he was. They'd vanished as if by magic.

"What a story!" Staylon said. "What drove the devils to attack you like that and what mysterious reasons suddenly threw them into a panic? More puzzles."

"Yes, but this isn't the time to solve them," Marchal replied. "We'd best not dawdle. We should get out of this godforsaken place as fast as we can."

"And Fen-Chu?" Langeville asked. "What happened to him? Did you take care of him?"

"And how! He's dead. The wretch paid for all his crimes at the hands of his own robots. But before that, I managed to trounce him long enough for Staylon to save us by redirecting the evil robots."

"I think I can find the exit without a problem," the professor said. "The corridors look deserted and now that Fen-Chu is gone, there shouldn't be any danger. I don't think there's anything to stop us."

"Good. You guide us but first of all take us to the munitions room. We shouldn't leave any remains of Fen-Chu's work here. What wasn't destroyed by the planes can't be left intact. With a few time bombs we'll bury the place under a heap of ruins."

After a maze of endless corridors, Marchal and his friends arrived at the door they recognized right away. But this time there was no guard before it. The Mongol, like the others, had left for who knew where.

Langeville got through the lock easily and threw open the heavy, iron door. Inside the room they searched the shelves until Professor Staylon called out to them, "I think I've found what we need."

He was pointing to a row of metal cubes, lined up side by side and each bearing a number.

"They're bombs with easy-to-set timers and really powerful despite their small size and relatively light weight."

Marchal, Langeville and Bougon each took two.

"That's plenty for what we want to do."

Without wasting any more time, the group left and went to all of the buildings still standing, the robot workshop and storeroom, the research lab that had last been used by Staylon and the remaining bedrooms. In each place they strategically placed the bombs and adjusted the hands of the timer to explode in six hours.

When the final explosive had been set Marchal said, "Now, my friends, if we don't want to blow up with the remains of this infernal city, we'd better get out as fast as we can and put some distance between us and this hell."

"Follow me," Staylon ordered.

Hurriedly, guided by the professor who seemed to be very familiar with the way, after half an hour, the chance survivors reached a huge, iron door that looked embedded in the rock. It was controlled by an electric switch.

"Curses!" Langeville shouted. "We might end up stuck here if we can't fix the switch."

"Don't despair," the mechanic ordered. "First, let's see if there's another way. Fen-Chu might've been a scoundrel but he was clever. He most certainly thought of a power failure. I wouldn't be surprised if we found some backup generator. Then we just have to turn it on and off we go."

They all agreed with Bougon and started searching for the generator. It was, in fact, their only hope and the only way to open the monumental door.

For many long minutes, in the small guard shack usually occupied by Mongols who had also, apparently, flew the coop, they looked feverishly in every nook and cranny, their hearts beating nervously.

Another half hour passed in a vain and fruitless search. They were starting to give up hope and they wondered what cruel trick fate was playing on them.

"It'd be really bad luck," Marchal grumbled, "to fail so close to the goal. Freedom is right here, just a few feet away. We have no choice, we have to find the damn key."

Ludovic Bougon, who was scrambling around more than anyone, searching the cracks, suddenly cried out, "Here! I think I've got it!"

The others ran to him.

"Look at this battery. It's hooked up to this cable that's connected to the alarm. Now, it's got to take a certain amount of power to run it. Who knows, maybe the same power can open the door. We can always try."

The mechanic found his old calm and competence as he unhooked the wires and connected them to the door-opening switch. Then the heavy door clicked open and through the crack the fugitives could see the deserted plain that stretched out as far as the eye could see. From now on the coast was clear. No more obstacles seemed to lay in their way.

"Let's not waste any time," Marchal recommended, looking at his watch. "Forty-five minutes have already ticked off since we set the first bomb. We need to get far away from here and fast."

Streaming through the door, they went down a narrow corridor between two steep cliffs until they reached a plain, the one where the four Frenchmen had landed after the mysterious breakdown. The survivors of the fantastic adventure were somber seeing, half-buried in a small sand dune, the remains of the airplane.

Walking single file with the explorer Langeville at the head, the troop marched for hours. Mustering all their strength, they fought against the fatigue that numbed their legs. They events they'd lived through had left them unprepared for such an ordeal.

During the next break, Professor Staylon was asked by the others to tell them what had happened after their failed escape attempt.

"It's very simple," he responded. "Fen-Chu called me into his office right away and exploded in anger, threatening me with the worst punishments. I let him vent and after he had calmed down, I told him that he could no longer count on me. Fuming with rage, his eyes bloodshot, he came at me and was about to grab me but at the last second he held back and called in two Mongols, ordering them to whip me. I was brought to a special room, a kind of torture chamber, where I was stripped bare to the waist. They tied my hands and raised my arms to attach them to a hook in the wall. After that, one of the Mongols, a good disciple of the famous Chinese torturers, took up a whip with a long, leather strap. He gave me a wicked lashing, leaving painful marks on my back and shoulders. I tried not to scream but I could hold out only so long and with one loud wail I passed out while my wounds bled profusely. When I came to, I was lying on a bed. They'd carried me to a new room, the one you found me in by some miracle. Fortunately, my daughter was there too.

"I lay on the bed for two days in terrible pain, then a Mongol came to get me because Fen-Chu wanted to see me. I was in such a state, weak and bruised, that I couldn't move. Another Mongol came in and smeared a strange, smelly ointment on me, especially on my wounds. I felt better immediately and in no time I was back on feet and able to walk without help to see the Master of the World. He asked me if I was ready to obey his every word because he needed me to fix the gamma ray machine as soon as possible. Since I hesitated and I wasn't willing to be his accomplice anymore, the wretch lost his temper again and shouted that the next punishment would be carried out on my daughter Elfy. He ordered his guards to fetch her and bring her back. Moments later, he had her by the wrists, squeezing her against his chest, staring at her with a weird glimmer in his eyes, like a cobra hypnotizing its prey. My daughter was trembling in fear, speechless in agony, begging me with her eyes. Fen-Chu gave me a choice: either Elfy would become his wife or I would submit to his will. As always with him, it was contemptible blackmail. But this time it was straight-forward, insistent, final. I had to give in. I'd put up with any indignity before seeing that wretched creature lay one finger on my child.

"For a few days, working slowly, I tried to fix his broken machine. Fen-Chu was constantly on my back, continually pushing me because he saw I wasn't going fast enough. One day, the machine was working and almost perfectly, I just needed to make a few minor adjustments. That was yesterday and Fen-Chu had decided to try it out today. The surprise attack he suffered without being able to retaliate as fiercely as he wanted had foiled his plans and finally destroyed his formidable weapon for good. While the bombers were flying over his lair, I was in my lab, unaware of the events unfolding around me. Like I already said, it was only after you broke into my room that I learned about the sensational turn of events that would change our lives forever."

After a ten-minute break during which Marchal and the others rested while listening to the Swedish scientist, Langeville stood up and gave the signal to depart.

The group had come to a region of craggy mountains where the path wound between the rocks along a narrow ravine. The reporter kept looking at his watch. He was thinking of the explosions that would demolish the cursed city and he wondered whether, after five hours of hiking, they would be free of the danger zone.

Since the explorer Langeville had noticed his preoccupation, he asked the reporter what was wrong. Marchal answered, "We have to be ten miles away from the mysterious city to be safe. We have no time to lose. If every leg of fifty minutes gets us two miles farther, that's only one mile as the crow flies since we're winding around this path. A little while ago we were trudging through sand. Now we're on a mule path and have to climb over rocks, which slows us down a lot."

"You're right," Langeville agreed. "That's why I'm proposing that we make a serious effort to walk without stopping from now on. We're about to reach the pass we spotted earlier and it'll be easier going on the other side of the mountain. So, we'll be safer and can duck into caves when we hear the explosion."

They all supported this wise decision and left right away. To keep their spirits up, Bougon, who was right behind the explorer, started singing a marching song that was taken up by all of them as a welcome diversion. Half an hour later, they were through the pass and trotting down a narrow path that led to a few huts whose thatched roofs could be seen among the rocks.

Marchal was still checking his watch and at a certain time he alerted his friends, "It shouldn't be long now. Let's stay on our toes. Our six hours are up so watch out."

A few minutes passed and then, all of a sudden, a dull sound echoed in the distance. The first bomb had just gone off. The group ran to a small cave and hunkered down near the wall, figuring they were safe from any falling debris.

The first explosion was followed soon afterward by other, bigger ones as the western sky was blotted out by black smoke.

The fugitives looked at one another, their hearts gripped by an inexpressible emotion—this was a defining moment in all their lives. They had experienced a kind of miracle. They'd escaped safe and sound from a place that no one had ever come back from. They had defeated Fen-Chu and succeeded in destroying his evil work. Their mission was accomplished. All their pain and suffering had paid off.

When they got back on the road, the sun was going down, tinting the distant, snowy peaks of the Himalayas with blood red.

An hour later Marchal and his friends arrived at a humble, native village comprised of meager huts that were home to some rugged highlanders. They gave the newcomers a warm welcome and all the hospitality they could.

The end of the ordeal was near.

XI

The next day, around noon, after spending the morning on final preparations, Robert Marchal and his companions were back on the road, guided by the explorer Langeville. No untoward incidents hampered their progress and at 4 pm the group arrived at a monastery of lamas. They knocked at the door and were welcomed in. After many bows and greetings, the Buddhist monks invited the travelers to rest and wait until the next day to leave. One of them was, in fact, going to Lhasa and could not only offer his service as a guide to the sacred city of Tibet, but also introduce them to the High Lama and get them the mandatory authorization to stay in the city of 20,000 monasteries.

Marchal accepted the offer of Chang Hsue Liang, the all-powerful head of the Kazak monastery. During the evening, after a better meal than they'd had the night before, the visitors were amused to hear, without understanding a word, their friend Langeville tell about their adventure, highlighting every detail with appropriate gestures. The monks who formed the grand council of the monastery and who surrounded Chang Hsue Liang, their superior, listened attentively to the story, continually nodding their heads.

The guests said good night to their hosts rather early and went to the cells that the monks had tried to prepare as comfortably as they could for them.

In the morning, when the first rays of the sun broke, while the monks were blowing the long, brass horns on the terrace, inviting the residents to meditation and prayer, the Europeans were getting ready to leave. Acting as interpreter, Langeville climbed the steps to the small terrace, approached the superior and after bowing low, said that he hoped to thank him by receiving Buddha's blessing for them when he was at Lhasa in the presence of the High Lama, the all-powerful leader of the region.

Everything was ready in the courtyard. The monk who was acting as their guide to the holy city was waiting, already mounted on his small horse. Waving goodbye to everyone the travelers got on their way. It was going to be a long trip: Lhasa was fifteen miles away.

When they got to Lhasa, the small troop mixed with the crowd of faithful and monks who filled the roads, some stopping to prostrate themselves on the ground. Marchal and his friends were a few of the rare Europeans who had managed to enter the Sacred City in our age. And yet nobody seemed to pay them any attention since the pilgrims were so engaged in prayer.

Behind their monk guide, they climbed the monumental staircase that led to the grand lamasery where they were welcomed with the usual ceremony. The priest who opened the iron door handed them white scarves, a sign of welcome, and wished upon them the blessings of the All Powerful. The explorer Langeville, who seemed to know the protocol, replied with a great deal of bowing, saying that he was very touched, he a humble white man, along with his friends, to be allowed to enter the temple that housed the living Buddha.

The voyagers were taken to a kind of dormitory where they could rest. Four hours later a monk knocked on the door and announced that the High Lama was ready to see them.

Langeville and his friends were brought into a spacious reception room with a huge gong at the entrance. On a platform stood a number of dignitaries of the Buddhist religion, dressed in black, surrounding the High Lama, he alone dressed in white.

The supreme chief, the preceptor of the living Buddha, greeted the Europeans kindly and listened to the story of their adventures. When it was done, the white monk, through one of the members of the great council who spoke French very well, announced that he would let the world know about the events of which they were, despite themselves, the heroes. Like that their family and friends would know that they were safe and the world would be relieved to be rid of a terrible menace.

The High Lama kept his word and a few hours later, thanks to the modern means at the disposal of the priests of the great monastery, the news of the death of Fen-Chu and the total destruction of his work was broadcast around the world.

Jacques Dumesnil, the editor-in-chief of *Paris Journal* was surprised and happy to hear about the end of the adventure that he had sent Marchal and his friends on.

Marchal himself and the others were impatient to return to Europe. Trying not to rush the monks who had so kindly and cordially received them, they prepared to leave.

The trip back passed without incident and one fine morning the group arrived in Shanghai. A steamship was scheduled to leave Shanghai two days later. The survivors of the grand adventure found places on board and were, one can imagine, the stars of the crossing.

The heroes of this fantastic adventure have gone back to their lives. Refusing honors and in no way intoxicated by success, they carry on their work as diligently and eagerly as ever.

Professor Staylon lives in Pavillons-sous-Bois where he has access to a modern laboratory. Along with his daughter Elfy he leads a quiet, hard-working life. He can now devote himself to his favorite research without the pressure of an eternal threat. Tireless, he has already made many important discoveries that he gifted to France and that will contribute to the well-being of humanity.

The explorer Langeville, who brought Ludovic Bougon on as a partner, is gone off on new adventures. Right now he's in South America among the Jivaro people, heading a big expedition to find the source of the Amazon.

As for Robert Marchal, defying the adage that journalism leads to everything as long as you get out of it, he is still at *Paris Journal* where he's one of its star reporters. In secret with Jacques Dumesnil he keeps an eye out for important projects and before long he will surely be off on a new adventure.

The day before Langeville left for South America, all of the old team got together and at a certain point in the evening they said a prayer for Blanchard, their comrade, the first man who had dared to defy Fen-Chu.

www.ingramcontent.com/pod-product-compliance
Lightning Source LLC
Chambersburg PA
CBHW020253030726
47499CB00001B/181